ISBN-13: 979-8-9862103-0-8

Cover design by: miblart
Printed in the United States of America

D0145529

This book is dedicated to Ed Davis, Kelly Nee, and Linda Coughlin for their invaluable guidance into the world of Boston Policing. To Dannielle Cabler and Emma Smailes for helping me turn this into something resembling readable. To my wife Regina for listening to me read the story to her night after night during proofreading. And my kids for always believing in me.

CONTENTS

Copyright

Dedication

Forward

1	1
2	11
3	16
4	26
5	37
6	43
7	54
8	59
9	67
10	73
11	82
12	91
13	95
14	103
15	112
16	121
17	126

18	134
19	141
20	151
21	158
22	164
23	169
24	176
25	184
26	195
27	200
28	213
29	217
30	223
31	233
32	237
33	244
34	253
35	260
36	270
37	276
38	282
39	291
40	302
41	310
42	318
43	323
44	337
45	348

46	354
47	359
48	371
49	377
50	382
51	387
52	399
53	407
54	417
Epilogue	425
About The Author	439

FORWARD

What does one say when one achieves something monumental? I don't mean monumental in delivering a great work of art or walking on the moon. I mean monumental to the self. For many years, I dreamed of writing a novel. I started many times with one idea or another, unable in many cases to press forward past a certain point because of one thing or another. This one somehow was different. It was almost as if the universe was pushing me toward this.

Some years earlier, I met Ed Davis, the former Police Commissioner of Boston. Ed and I worked on a few PR events for my employer centered around combating voter fraud. After a few of these, I screwed my courage to the sticking place, as Shakespeare would say, and asked Ed if he would be willing to let me interview him for research on a book I was writing.

Blood Rituals was just a twinkle in my eye at this point. But, Ed agreed and gave me a wealth of information on the structure, history, and inside goop about the Boston PD. It was nothing salacious, simply the facts. But it got me started. A month or so later, Ed referred me to Kelly Nee, former Lieutenant for Boston's Homicide Division, and current Chief of the Boston University Police. He also got me in touch with Linda Coughlin, a Detective out of Lowell, Mass. They were both a treasure trove of knowledge about police procedures, and Kelly gave me tremendous information on how Boston Homicide works. Linda turned out to be a hoot to work with, and I absolutely loved our interactions.

A few weeks later, I turned out three chapters. And that was it. It seemed that Blood Rituals was doomed to languish like so many of my other projects when I met one of the two greatest inspirations in my life, outside of my mother and my wife, of course. Dannielle Cabler, a work acquaintance who took on the tremendous and somewhat fraught responsibility of reading those first few chapters.

I had no idea what she was thinking at the time, unaware that she was praying that what I'd written wouldn't be a "Funny Farm" moment, where she'd be crying because it was so bad, and she'd have to tell this "new friend" not to quit her day job. Fortunately for her and me, what she found were a few rough diamonds amidst the wreck of material I'd given her that made her want to know what was going to happen next. Those were her exact words to me. "What matters is that when I got to the end of what you'd written, I wanted to know what happens next. You should keep going; it's not bad."

Note that she didn't say it was good. She said it wasn't bad. She continued to encourage me, sending me copies of Stephen King's 'On Writing,' and Anne Lamott's 'Bird by Bird' as inspiration. And so, I was inspired and encouraged, and I wrote. Day after day, I bled all over the pages, slapping down 190,000 words of prose into my copy of Scrivener by the time I was done three months later. Dannielle changed my life in ways I scarcely thought possible, reminding me constantly that I was a "precious peanut" and that being a part of the journey "brought her so much joy." Without her standing next to me, I never would have finished. I probably would never have gotten much further than the three chapters I had first given her.

So here I was, with around 600 pages of crap story slapped on paper. The diamonds were still buried, and it took the second inspiration, Emma Smailes, one of the editors for the Cast of Wonders Podcast, to take me to the next step. Emma and I had known each other for a few years by that point. I had no knowledge of her work on Cast of Wonders when I mentioned that I'd written a novel to my gaming group.

A day later, Emma offered to "beta read" it. Though she will thoroughly deny it, she actually meant that she was going to become my development editor. And, as if it were fate once more, for three months, she diligently read every last line and paragraph, offering edits, changes, and character ideas, letting me know what didn't work and what did.

Amazingly enough, as if by magic, my writing improved. Before she was halfway through, she'd so helped me improve my writing that I had given the book a 60,000-word haircut before she'd even read the last page.

And, after almost seven months of what seemed like endless rewrites, here we are. But, I didn't write this for them. I didn't write it for my wife or my friends. I didn't write this for my parents or children. I wrote this for me. And while I hope that anyone who reads 'Blood Rituals' will enjoy it, I know that there will be some for whom it is not their cup of tea. But for those of you who find the joy of escape between its pages, please know that it came from my heart and soul and whether I ever know who you are, I will love you forever because I was able to give you the briefest moment of enjoyment.

1

I wake to the soft chime of my phone—zero six-hundred. I am a light sleeper, always have been. Three AC units wail against the desert heat, delivering a comforting white noise. Although I cannot hear them, the noise plants itself in the back of my mind, something distant and remembered. Slipping soundlessly from under the blanket, I put my feet to the floor and stand. There are three beds: mine, one next to me, and an empty one across the room—Specialist Rutherford's. The empty bunk kindles a vague feeling of loss.

The bed next to mine is occupied. I watch Morgan, Specialist Kennedy, for a long time. Her broad, soft curls are a red wave sliding over her pillow, and I am captivated. A sliver of buttery sunlight shines through a crack in the plywood over the window. Moments later, it strikes her eyelids, and she turns, gracelessly flopping one arm over the edge. I stifle a laugh. It's truly adorable, almost childlike, much like her personality. She is a goddess, tall and lithe and strong with fire in her hair. I sit for a bit, just watching. Somewhere, dimly, I remember this moment. Foggy anxiety begins to creep in. It's ephemeral, like a shadow that flits out of view as you turn to look at it, a ghost of something once terrible, a little tug of nerves that pulls at your stomach and your breath.

I am standing outside watching the Marine sniper team load their gear into the Humvee. My fingernail absentmindedly worries at the chalk-paint letters scraped onto the side of the vehicle. "Betty," they display proudly in iridescent pink, though the B has become thin, looking for all the world like a "P." Sgt. McCall, today's sniper, is carrying a pair of rifles. The first, a .308, is standard; it loads readily into the Humvee. Then McCall hauls the second, an M84A1 Barrett .50 caliber, into the vehicle. The fifty is for light vehicle control and hardened targets. McCall fusses with it for a second but eventually gets it stowed.

I watch Specialist Kennedy while McCall's spotter, Sgt. Holley struggles behind me, hoisting a gear bag into the Humvee. The bag is bulky, probably two hundred pounds, carrying a couple of blast blankets that McCall rigged together. The blankets are steel and Kevlar, and just one of them is heavy as fuck. Holley is struggling with it. I lift the two hundred pound bag into the Humvee with a grunt. Holley raises an eyebrow.

"What?" I ask at his surprised expression. "You know I've been working out. You should try it." I say it flatly, a matter of fact —Kennedy snickers at his embarrassment. Misogyny runs deep around here, and I feel a twinge of anger. This time, though, the feeling swells to rage. Holley's a real piece of shit. There is bad blood between us, the kind I can never forget—or forgive. I sneer at him, but he's facing away, getting in the vehicle.

The morning sun is beating down, but I can't feel it. The grit in my mouth feels real enough, though. I run my tongue against the roof of my mouth to rid it of the muddy, gritty sensation, finally grabbing a plastic water bottle and taking a swig to wash it out. Dust blows to and fro around the camp, seeking any orifice. Opening one's mouth is risky in this place, in Mosul, in Iraq. You will swallow dust and dirt; that's just the way of it. After two tours here, I'm sure my recent stomach problems are less medical and more geologic. Kennedy squeezes behind the driver's seat.

The sniper team is loaded, and it's time to move out. A pair of Humvees with the rest of the patrol lumbers ahead of us. The anxiety is more palpable, squeezing at my chest. I feel like crying, but nothing comes out.

"Specialist Reagan?" Kennedy's voice doesn't register at first.

"Caitlin! You coming?" Kennedy hollers from behind the driver's seat, finally getting my attention. The velvet tenor of her voice, confident and enticing, should thrill me. I don't feel anything positive, though, not really. Instead, it conjures a momentary pang of loss.

"Yeah!" I reply, taking shotgun and pulling the battered door shut. It takes a try or two, but it closes noiselessly. Not how it happened, but it never is.

We roll into our operating area around 1400 local time. At this point, I can feel a burning in my eyes and a squeezing in my chest. I know that I'm dreaming now. I know the dream. I know I'm already crying in my bed. I know how this ends. God, I want to wake up.

McCall and Holley select an abandoned apartment that looks over the most vulnerable point of the patrol group's route. For defensibility, it sucks—too many entrances. But it's the only decent vantage point.

Kennedy is leaning against the Humvee. We're parked a couple of burned-out houses away from the sniper position—I'm talking to her about my ma's Bolognese sauce. I'm standing by the front quarter of the Humvee, passenger side, looking at Kennedy across the hood. Wisps of Kennedy's red hair stick out from under her helmet, blowing in the breeze as she flashes that dazzling smile at me again. But it's not Kennedy. Instead, she looks like me at sixteen with close-cropped hair in jeans and a t-shirt.

"Behind you!" not Kennedy's voice says, echoing in my head, a stranger's alto, though familiar—I'm not sure from where.

I turn and raise my rifle in a single fluid movement. Drawing a bead on the first bad guy, I pull the trigger instinctively. Pop. Pop. Pop. The gunshots of my weapon are a distant muffled thud like something heard through a pillow. I see the man drop and sight in on the next one. Kennedy's M4 is also peppering the air with shots behind me. My leg is hit, burning with a bullet wound I can see but can't feel. There is a blast from the sniper position; Kennedy and I start running, firing at the closing bad guys all the way. Kennedy goes down, right side bleeding from the liver. I think she'll bleed out. I pull her up, and we limp toward the next house over.

We are inside the small abandoned apartment, a block away, with the sniper team. Holley and McCall are in bad shape. McCall looks dead. Holley's left arm is completely fucked up; the .308 is wrecked. Kennedy lies in the corner, bleeding profusely from her wound. I look at the M84 in horror. It squirms like a thing both dead and alive, a corrupter. It is a stealer of innocence. I think I have none left to give. But I do. I will.

I drop down behind the scope, and it's just a weapon again. I peer in. "No, no, no, no," I try to say, words muffled in my mind like trying to scream with your mouth held shut. What comes out is all wrong, the wrong words, the actual words. "One hostile, a juvenile in a suicide vest." I hear my voice screaming now, sobbing somewhere, but not here. I don't want to see it. I don't want to know. I don't want to think about it. It doesn't matter, I'm thinking about it. Now, I'm looking down the scope of the M84 again. "One hostile, a juvenile, suicide vest," I repeat. The kid is running toward my point of view through the scope. He's waving something around, a stick, I think. Somewhere, in a haze, I think the suicide vest doesn't fit him. It shows through the dragging, threadbare caftan. I try to squeeze my eyes shut, but they won't close.

"Shoot, goddammit!" Holley screams at me, the bastard.

Everything slows down. My chest burns with a pain so deep my soul cracks. I can feel the burning in my eyes as the tears stream, though my vision is clear. There is an eerie silence as I squeeze the trigger gently and obliterate the little boy in the suicide vest. The concussion of the monstrous rifle rains dust and plaster from the ruined ceiling of our hide. The sounds are surreal things heard in turns with a banging clarity or muffled softness. Finally, I hear, perfect and distinct, the plunk, plunk of the grenade. I am standing. Not-Kennedy is standing in front of me; her cherubic teenage face is screaming soundlessly now. I fall to my knees. "Please stop, please stop, please stop," I plead. She points. I grab the bag with the blast blankets and throw it and myself onto the grenade.

❋ ❋ ❋

I woke with a heaving gasp of air as if I'd been holding my breath. Each respiration came shallow as I tried desperately to quell a suffocating panic. After a few minutes, the machine-gun drumming of my heart eased, and I dragged my right hand free of the twisted, sweat-soaked sheets. I pawed at my face, furiously wiping away the tears and sweat so I could see the clock. The fading red numbers glared accusingly — 1:08 AM.

"Fuck," I murmured to the black. I hadn't been asleep long, and the early hour gnawed further at my rising sense of despair. Closing my eyes to take a deep, cleansing breath, I hiccuped instead, seeing the explosion that ended a small child imprinted with the mill-dots of a rifle scope. I squeezed my eyes even tighter, trying to banish the vision.

"God," I cursed. "I need to get back to my therapist."

PTSD is insidious. It slowly crawls in behind your eyes then fucks up your entire life. According to my therapist, it was imminently curable if I did the work. But that was the hitch; I had no interest in 'doing the work.' Chasing it down meant facing a morass of guilt and anger that had already consumed me on the inside. It also meant opening a closed door of bad things where I'd stuffed every crappy relationship and shitty experience from my childhood — the door where I'd sealed away Sgt. Holley and his booze-sodden breath filling my nostrils on a latrine floor.

The burgundy jacquard comforter, decorated in gilded French designs, lay in a pile at the end of the bed. It had been unseasonably warm for October. But last night, the heat had finally abated, and the absence of the comforter left me shivering slightly as the sleep sweat began to evaporate. I dragged myself up, flexing my scarred left hand, sniffing and wiping my eyes. The details of the nightmare were starting to fade again, even if the gnawing feeling of grief wasn't. I looked around my bedroom, positively tiny by adult standards, a six-foot by nine-foot prison cell. I'd shoehorned my queen-sized bed and a nightstand in here, but there wasn't any room to spare. The battered AC unit in the window rattled. I'd turned it on before bed and had left it on for hours.

Fuck, I thought. *There goes the electric bill.*

I could scarcely afford my apartment as it was. I should have taken the damn thing out of the window weeks ago since the weather was finally shifting, but I just hadn't had the energy lately.

I pulled the bedclothes together and was just falling back to sleep when a ball of orange fur decided it was time to walk across my head to find a warm spot. "Jesus, Jabba, really?" I griped as he finally got off my forehead and settled in.

Of course, I hadn't named my cat Jabba. He was a rescue, and I had initially just called him 'cat.' But an asshole detective at the department asked why I had a photo of Jabba the Hutt on my desk, and the name stuck. If I was honest, it fit. He was fat, lazy, and pretty much ruled the house from his throne on the couch, missing only Han Solo frozen in carbonite next to his food dish.

I tossed and turned until four AM, when I finally gave up and took half a Benedryl, making the next few hours blissfully dreamless until the doleful vibrations of my cell phone dragged me back to consciousness. I fumbled about for the damn thing, successful only in knocking it off the nightstand.

"Shit," I swore and snatched it off the floor. "Homicide. Detective Reagan."

It was Gabe, my boyfriend. "Hey, gorgeous. How'd you sleep?" He sounded chipper as always.

"Morning, honey. Not too bad," I lied as I stretched in the bed and stifled a yawn. "I woke up for about an hour around one but managed to get back to sleep. You at the office?"

"Yeah. The big boss is in town, so I had to come in early." Gabe worked in drug sales for Kineda Pharmaceuticals, part of one of Japan's largest Keiretsus. He was always up early. "You sound tired, bad dreams?"

I instantly regretted telling him I'd woken up in the night.

Nice, Cait; next time, keep your mouth shut. I closed my eyes and sighed inwardly. "Nope," I lied again, decorating my voice with false cheer. "Just woke up out of nowhere." A chill wind pushed the veranda doors open, making me shiver harder.

"Have you talked to your therapist?" he asked, brushing past the excuse. Gabe harassed me regularly about getting back to therapy. I couldn't make him understand that picking at my wounds would open them wide; I wasn't ready yet. I'd seen other detectives fall apart. I had no desire to be sent to the Peer Support Unit, informally known as the rubber gun squad. It wasn't a way any cop wanted to finish their career.

"Gabe," I warned, feeling the heat of anger flush my cheeks.

"Okay," he said, backing away from the conversation with a shitty tone. "Sorry, I'll put that on the list of taboo topics, along with marriage and moving in together."

"Gabe, look, please don't do this. Let's talk about something else. What's your day looking like?"

"Fine," he said flatly. "The reason I called is that I'm meeting a new client out in Charlestown and, since I'll be passing by, I thought we could have lunch before you head into work. Maybe?" His voice rose as he feigned a childlike tone.

I plastered on a smile. "Sure." At least he was off the topic of my therapy. "How about meeting me at Modern?"

"Modern?" he whined. "That's not a lunch place. It's a pastry shop. You know I can't eat anything there except black coffee or water."

"They have a restaurant downstairs. It's pretty good."

"It's all fried ravioli and pub food. I can't eat that either."

"Next year's marathon," I said, remembering that he had started his training. "I forgot. Okay, how about Pauli's."

"I guess, but there's never any place to sit." He still had a bit of whine in his voice, and it grated on me. I had just woken up, hadn't had any coffee at all, and wasn't up for trying to chase down a place where Gabe would be happy eating.

"Shit, Gabe, you pick a place," I snapped at him. "Just make sure it's in the North End. I'm not driving out of the way for a quick lunch today. I've got too much to do."

"Okay, sorry. We can do Pauli's." He sounded like a whipped dog.

I sighed. "Look, I'm not trying to be a bitch. I'm just tired. But, don't worry, I'm a Boston Cop. I can get us a table."

"I love you," Gabe answered.

"I know; I love you, too," I responded quietly. I hit the end call button, squashed my pillow over my face, and screamed. Gabe was fucking up my Wednesday, and Gabe knew that. Wednesday morning always marked the beginning of my five-day stretch at work. And, every Wednesday, I started it off right with a cannoli and coffee from Modern Pastry, just down the street from my apartment.

It's not that Gabe was a bad guy. He was generally charming. Gabe always opened the door and pulled out my chair. He played the perfect gentleman. But, underneath all of that was a streak of self-indulgence and a mild narcissism. It was typical male behavior, and it rankled me.

I rolled onto my back and blew out a breath. I wanted to go back to sleep for another hour, but that wasn't going to happen. So, I got out of bed and pulled on a hoodie to ward off the morning cold.

The hardwoods were freezing, and I hopped about until my feet got used to them. As I opened the fridge and looked inside for something to eat, one of my numerous refrigerator magnets clattered to the floor. With it dropped the ten-year-old letter from Morgan I'd never opened. I fingered it briefly before putting it back up on the door.

I didn't know why I had kept it. Not long after Iraq, Morgan had gone back to Montana to marry her high school sweetheart, Clint or Clay or whatever the fuck his name was. I remembered feeling like she'd abandoned me when I needed her most. So, best friend or not, I'd ghosted her and moved on.

After a few minutes of rummaging around for something for breakfast, I stopped. "Fuck this," I said to myself. "I'm getting my Cannoli."

Forty minutes and a six-mile run later, I was sitting at a small table inside Modern enjoying the blissful wonder of a Modern Pastry Shop cannoli. Despite being hot, sweaty, and needing water, I sucked on a cup of smooth black coffee —so much better than the burnt brown soup that passes in the squad room. I tried to relax and soothe my fraying nerves about Gabe. I wasn't good at relationships. I knew that. But, Gabe seemed to act like my world was supposed to be subordinate to his. I'd put my foot down on the whole marriage thing at least three times before, but he just kept prodding.

My stomach tightened. I didn't feel it was a good idea for anyone to hitch their wagon to me right now, anyway. I was damaged goods. More honestly, though, I wasn't really in love with him. I couldn't see myself living with him in a cute house with a white picket fence, two-point three kids, and a German shepherd. Hell, I couldn't see myself having kids or a white picket fence. The dog, maybe; I liked dogs. I probably should have broken off my relationship with Gabe months ago. Still, I didn't want to find myself alone—again.

I ran my hand across my face. *Fuck! What is wrong with me?*

The burning of tears pressed behind my eyes at just the thought of yet another failed relationship. I tried to shake it off by taking another bite of my pastry.

Seconds later, mouth full and eyes still tearful, I nearly launched out of my seat as my ass vibrated. Nowhere to wipe it, I sucked the sweet ricotta filling off my finger and tapped my earbud, desperately trying to keep the sticky substance out of my hair.

"Homicide, Reagan," I answered around a mouthful.

"Hey Reagan," The voice belonged to John Dooley, the Homicide Unit's Administrative Sergeant. "The day shift second squad picked up a case at four AM. White male, early to mid-thirties, I need you to take the lead on it."

"Okay, where's the hand-off?"

"At Schroeder, and it's a weird one."

"Fucking great," I griped. "Are we talking wood-chipper

weird or just an odd caliber weird?"

"The first one. The guy was decapitated right in front of the Bunker Hill Monument."

I sighed. "Lovely."

"The crime scene is buttoned up, so Vic will make the hand-off at HQ."

I took a sip of my coffee. "Okay, I need to run home, shower and change. I'll be there in about forty minutes."

"I'll let Vic know, and thanks." He hung up. One thing about Dooley, whenever he assigned you a case, he always said thank you. It was just his way. He appreciated people who cooperated and recognized that managing the team sometimes resulted in shitty assignments. In return, I never bucked an assignment. It was just the job. Besides, it's not like I had a family at home; it was just Gabe and me.

Shit! Gabe. I'd call him when I got to work.

2

Passing through the lobby at One Schroeder Plaza, I waved to Jim Sheldon, today's desk officer. He was arguing with a middle-aged white gentleman about what sounded like a traffic accident report. Jim gave me a half-hearted nod.

"I pay your salary, you know," the man bleated at Jim.

"Really," Jim retorted in his thick Southie accent. "Well then, since you haven't given me a raise in four years, I'd like to complain if you've got a minute."

The man became positively apoplectic. I barked an uncontrolled laugh, then covered my mouth. I knew that Jim would eventually help the man. If it had been me, I'd have sent the guy back to his local district, maybe after an hour of 'looking' for his traffic report.

On the second floor sat an ugly cube farm that served as an 'office' for the homicide unit. As I exited the stairwell, I spotted Vic, the second squad day-shift lead. He was headed toward my desk with a set of case files.

"Wow, you look like hammered dogshit," I told him. His Tom Fords were splashed with a bit of blood, as was the cuff of one pant leg. His hundred fifty dollar shirt was wrinkled and sweat-stained; his coat and tie were absent. Vic looked rough, exhausted and disheveled. He'd had a long night.

"This everything?" I asked, gesturing to the folders.

Vic ran a hand across his copious five o'clock shadow. "Yeah.

I typed up the scene report, but the witness statements are still handwritten. Honestly, it's fucking strange. The guy was not only decapitated, but the perp stabbed him in the heart, too."

"Wow, you always bring me the best cases."

He ignored my sarcasm and continued. "The victim, Jesse Caldwell, thirty-four years of age, is an administrative assistant for Carson Logistics. He was wearing what looked like a ten-thousand-dollar Rolex, and his wallet still had all his credit cards and about four hundred in cash."

"That rules out a robbery," I muttered. I lowered my head and pinched the bridge of my nose, waiting for the rest.

"Carson Logistics has an office in Charlestown, where the victim works. It doubles as the local residence for the CEO, and it's all of, like, two hundred feet from the murder scene. According to the housekeeper, Ninetta D'Angelo, the victim left work after midnight."

"Is she a suspect?"

"You'd have to see her, little slip of a thing. No way she had the strength to do this. She was scary though, like Italian mama scary," Vic replied.

I chuckled at that before turning serious again. "Perp was waiting for him, then?"

"Seems like it." Vic leaned back and closed his eyes for a second. "It certainly doesn't look like it was random."

"Location sucks," I told him, thinking of how exposed it was--that and the fact that the city would have wanted the scene buttoned up quickly. The Bunker Hill Monument is a tourist stop on the Freedom Trail.

"Tell me about it. Patrol spent half the time trying to keep the press from getting an angle on the body. It'll be on the noon news for sure."

Vic flipped the page on his legal pad. "Ms. D'Angelo told us that Ms. Carson is flying back from London tonight. I already called British Airways and confirmed she boarded the plane in London and lands at six forty-five. You'll probably want to talk to her as soon as she gets in."

I looked down at the folders as Vic took a sip of coffee. One contained the scene report, and another had photos. The third one, the one I was most interested in, contained witness statements. I thumbed through the handwritten notes, most of them in Vic's crazy neat handwriting. I could never figure out how he could write so fast yet deliver a print quality rivaling a laser printer.

"What else?" I asked.

"The 9-1-1 call came in at around three fifty-nine AM. The lady who called it in lives on the square and starts her day at three-thirty in the morning. The medical examiner put the time of death just after one. So far, no one actually witnessed the murder, and we haven't found any surveillance.

"I'm going to stick around for a little while and type up my notes. In the meantime, I'll leave the rest of the paperwork with you so you can get familiar."

I handed back the folder with the witness statements and settled in to read the scene report.

"Cait, I have a real bad feeling about this one. Like this is only the beginning." Vic said as walked back to his desk.

I read the scene report from the responding officer. A local physician, Karen Walters, had come across the body and called 9-1-1. When Patrol responded, they found the victim in a blood pool and several bloody sneaker prints belonging to Ms. Walters around the scene. She admitted to stepping in the victim's blood after almost stumbling over him.

Poor woman, I thought, *out on her morning jog, and she stumbles over a decapitated accountant. That's fucked up.*

I went over the rest of the details in the preliminary reports. I also noted the address for Carson Logistics, it was a swanky residential building on Monument Square, an odd place for an office.

My phone buzzed as I picked up the first photos, and my stomach dropped. I'd forgotten to call Gabe. "Shit!" I cringed as I answered. "I am so sorry."

"Where are you?" I could hear people in the background and

annoyance in his voice.

"I got called into work. Gabe, I'm so sorry; I forgot to call and cancel our lunch date. I just got wrapped up in the case."

There was a long pause.

"Gabe?" I probed.

"I'm here." He sighed heavily. "Look, I wish you had called. It doesn't matter. I'll see you later tonight." He hung up.

I blinked. "Fuck." I redialed his number. He picked up on the third ring.

"Hey, I said I was sorry. You're right. I should have called. I'm an asshole."

Gabe laughed. "Yeah, you are. Let's have dinner tonight, and then we can relax."

I started pulling on my ear. "Look, I'm on shift for the next five days, but I'll try. You know how this goes with a new case; I don't know where it'll lead."

He suddenly sounded concerned. "A new case? It wouldn't happen to have something to do with Jesse Caldwell, would it?"

"Yes." I drew the word out, brow furrowed. I worked to keep the concern from my voice. "Do you know him?"

"I got a call about ten minutes ago. We were supposed to meet with Carson Logistics this morning, but when we called to confirm, some lady named Ninetta said our point of contact had been killed last night."

I paused for a second. My boyfriend had just made himself a person of interest.

"Cait?"

"Sorry, just thinking. What is your schedule looking like today?" I dug out my pad.

"It's pretty open, at least now. Why? Still want to have lunch?" Clearly, he didn't understand the situation.

"No. I'd like you to come down to the station and talk to one of my team about your business with Carson Logistics. You said 'we.' Who was going with you?"

His voice turned suspicious. "Haimon Blackman, my VP from the New York office. Why are you treating me like some suspect?"

I dropped my tone, becoming deadly serious, "Honey, it's nothing like that. You had business with him the day after he gets murdered. Since you were going to meet with him, any information you might have could be useful."

"Do I need a lawyer?" He asked cautiously.

"Yes." Usually, I wouldn't recommend that, but I wouldn't let my boyfriend walk into a police interview unrepresented. "It's not that you're in any trouble. But, and I've told you a hundred times, never go to a criminal investigation interview without an attorney present. Also, please ask Mr. Blackman to join you." I softened my voice, then. "I love you."

"Love you too. I'll call you when we figure out a good time," Gabe said, then hung up.

3

I stared daggers at my plain white coffee mug. It looked like I'd stolen it from a diner—I had. It was the daily repository of the atrocious brown goop that we called in turns, 'the open case,' as in homicide by slow poisoning, or 'government coffee,' on account of the generic orange bags it came in. If there was worse coffee out there, I'd never tasted it. But caffeine was a critical part of my day, so I endured the protestations of my taste buds.

Resigned to the circumstances, I stretched in my chair and picked up the mug with a heavy sigh, prodding Victor with a silly British accent. "Oh, Victor, love, let me buy you a cup of coffee."

"The coffee's free, Reagan." His humorless demeanor was a little unusual, but I ignored it.

I sighed, grabbed his coffee mug from his paper-strewn desk, and headed for the breakroom. Vic's expensive shoes clop-clopped behind me, taking long strides to catch up.

"Hey," he snapped. "What the fuck?" The tone wasn't like him. He hadn't uttered a cross word toward me in two years, so I was somewhat surprised as he charged up.

I looked back at him. "What? I get you coffee all the time."

He slowed his pace a little. "Yeah, you're right. I'm just having a rough time right now. I think Donna's getting sick of my hours."

Donna, Victor's wife, was a school teacher, not in public service or medicine, so she didn't have the perspective on the kind of hours we had to keep. But, they'd been married for almost seven years, and as far as I knew, it was still all cake and roses. This was the first indication I'd gotten that there was trouble in paradise.

I tripped over a chair left in the doorway of our shitty breakroom and managed to catch myself on the crappy candy machine.

"Ow, shit!" I looked at my hand and back to the machine. My hand was fine, but I'd broken the keypad. No loss in my book, though. The only thing anyone ever ate out of there was the microwave popcorn that stunk up the floor—that and Funyuns. *Eww.*

"You alright?" Vic was digging into the refrigerator, which probably held more than a few science experiments

"Yeah, who left a chair there?" I dug out the implements of my destruction, namely the evil, poisonous coffee and a filter.

"Donna's been complaining about my hours all of a sudden. I mean, it's like it was okay for six years, and now, poof, I'm an asshole because I work the late shift." Vic rubbed his neck again, clearly exhausted.

"The phone rang last night at quarter after four. I got up to leave like I've done a thousand times before, and she jumped down my throat, telling me I needed to be home more. She also said she was getting tired of me leaving in the middle of the night every week."

"I don't know what to say. But I sympathize. This job is tough on relationships. But you've been together for six years. She knows the deal; she's probably just having a lonely period. Or—." I trailed off.

"What?" Vic asked, raising an eyebrow.

I opened the orange coffee bag and had almost dumped the contents into the filter when a very southern voice suddenly sounded from the doorway. "Aw, don't do that."

The speaker was a tall Hispanic man in a suit, wearing a

Boston PD detective's badge. He was easily six-foot-two and two-hundred twenty-five pounds. The Stetson on his head probably added a few inches more. "I have the remedy for what ails you, right here." He patted a black leather backpack.

Cowboy hat stepped forward and set his bag down on the table. I stood there, holding the open coffee pouch, and waited, an eyebrow cocked, curious, as he extracted two items of absolute beauty: a coffee grinder and a two-pound brick of Cafe Bustelo Dark Roast coffee, whole bean.

I imitated a swoon. "Oh my! You, sir, are welcome on this floor at any time."

He tipped his hat. "Detective Carlos Ramirez, at your service, ma'am. By the way, I'm looking for Detective Reagan."

I'd heard we were getting a new teammate; this must be him. "That's me. Call me Cait. And this is Detective Sergeant Victor Sebastian Alexander Adams." I held out my hand to Carlos and smirked as Vic grimaced. He hated his full name.

"Wow, that's a mouthful. Three double-barrel names not enough for your folks?" He gave us a broad toothy smile. "Cait. Victor. Nice to meet you." We shook hands. I could see the team was going to like him. He seemed to have an easy way that was endearing.

I casually dropped the government coffee pouch into the trash and put on my best South Boston accent. "Okay, kid, let's see what ya got."

Carlos plugged in the grinder and opened the brick of Bustelo. He waved it under our collective noses; the smell was amazing. Oh yeah, Carlos and I were going to get along just fine.

"Ahem." Vic waved his hand in front of my face. "You were about to say about Donna?"

"Oh, sorry. Is it possible she's pregnant?"

"Donna? No way, I—." He stopped talking, and I could virtually smell the rubber burning as he seriously thought about it. "Oh, shit! She had a Doctor's appointment last week. She didn't say why and she'd been acting weird ever since.

Crap, I've been an asshole."

"It's okay," I offered. "There's a lot of that going around. You might want to ask her about her doctor's appointment tonight."

Vic nodded, wheels still turning.

A moment later, the fabulous scent of good coffee wafted from the maker. I wondered if the machine would break down in the middle of brewing, just out of spite. To my shock, it just continued to perk away, and I rubbed my hands together in anticipation like some comic book villain. Up until now, I had believed that our coffee maker only had one setting, burnt. As it turned out, I was wrong.

We walked back into the squad area with fantastic coffee in hand, and I showed Carlos to the desk next to mine.

"You got a burner?" I asked as he began to settle in. A burner was a cell phone you bought with cash, near untraceable.

"Yep." He handed me the number. "Bought it the day I got into town."

Carlos opened the desk's top drawer and found the keys to the file cabinet underneath. He parked the grinder and coffee in the back of the file drawer then handed me one of the keys.

"Don't lose this." His tone was deadly, and it made me laugh. He raised his eyebrows. "I'm serious as a heart attack. I know you know the value of good coffee, and while I don't mind sharing, I don't want one of these guys sucking up all of it. Squad 2 nights, only, you know. And, if I'm not here, be sparing, please."

Carlos yanked the SIM from the crappy department phone and put it into a new iPhone, hooking it up to his computer and setting up access to his department resources.

"So I guess you're pretty tech-savvy."

Carlos continued setting up the phone as he spoke. "I had a stint in computer crime, mostly working child porn cases. But, I learned a hell of a lot about cell phones."

"I know the basics, but I'm glad I'm mostly computer stupid. I couldn't work computer crime. The child pornography would wreck me."

"It's not for everyone. I moved to the gang task force after two years in it, right about the time I found myself sitting in a family restaurant with my husband, trying to figure out which of the parents around me was sexually abusing their child." He pulled a framed photo of himself with a handsome black gentleman, both in tuxedos. Wedding photo, I assumed.

I pointed to the picture. "Is that him?"

Carlos practically beamed with love and admiration. "Yup, that's Marcus, the love of my life. We've been together for nine years. He works the ER over at MGH."

"Nice. He sounds like a good guy, handsome, too. Reminds me of a young Lawrence Fishburne."

Carlos placed the photo on his desk. "He gets that all the time. We met after I got shot on a bust."

I sat there for long moments, looking at the picture. I wondered if I would ever find someone like that, someone I could depend on and share my life with, someone I truly loved. I'd started wallowing a little in my own head when I realized that Carlos was saying something.

I jerked to attention. "Huh? Sorry, I was just thinking."

"I was asking if you have a girlfriend?" he repeated, taking me aback.

"No," I sputtered defensively. "I've got a boyfriend, Gabe. I'm not—I mean I'm straight. Not that it bothers me."

He smirked in a way I couldn't read for a second. "Sorry, I just assume everyone's gay until they say otherwise. Makes my world a little simpler."

I felt my face rapidly heat, so I tried to change the subject. "Alright, the rest of the squad will be here shortly. Carol is a tea drinker, but David will happily squander your coffee if you let him. By the way, they're both gay as well, so you'll fit right in. Carol calls us 'Squad Q.' I'm the 'honorary member.'"

He laughed at that, breaking the tension. "Perfect. Well, fine by me. So, you got a boyfriend." Carlos waggled his eyebrows.

I didn't want to discuss Gabe at that moment. My personal

life was too fucked up, and I had too much shit going on. Besides, I had no social life other than Gabe, romantic or otherwise. I was probably lucky to be with him. "Yeah, but it's —um—complicated."

"I bet it is," he said cryptically.

"What's that supposed to mean?" My eyebrow shot up. I got this kind of ribbing from Carol and David, but Carlos was the new guy. It seemed a little—familiar.

"Huh?" he asked, trying to look innocent. "Did I say that out loud?"

"Yeah, so I could hear you and everything."

"I need to remember that when I think, and people can hear me, it's because I'm talking." He beamed another smile at me, but if it was supposed to set me at ease, it didn't.

I sighed. My therapist, Jennifer, had suggested I try switching my thought process in situations like this—instead of following the feeling, force myself to react as if any offense was unintentional. So rather than running down the emotional rabbit hole that I was digging, I stopped. "Sorry, I'm not sure why I'm so uptight. Probably because my boyfriend and I are having issues right now. So, what brought you to Boston?"

"Why the reputation for amazing weather, of course."

I laughed. "Oh, it's amazing, alright. One winter not that long ago, we got three feet of snow in one day."

Carlos grimaced. "Ugh. Marcus and I are both in our late forties, and it's time to settle down. We want to find a surrogate and have a kid or maybe adopt. We want to be in a town where other people would accept two dads without much fuss. This seemed like the place. The weather is a bonus." He winked at me.

"Besides, I got sick of watching racist cops getting away with murder, sometimes literally, because of union pressure. So when the Governor signed the reform act here, we decided to move." Carlos referred to the Municipal Reform Act that limited the concessions government agencies could give to unions. It had been effective at getting some of the shittiest cops fired.

About that time, Detective Washington came in and squelched the discussion. "Hey there, you must be Carlos," she said and stuck her hand practically in Carlos' face. Carol Washington was a five-foot-nothing black woman who took after her West Indian mother. If something needed to be said, Carol was probably the one who'd say it.

"Yes, ma'am, that's me. Detective Ramirez, if you wanna be all formal like." He flashed that smile of his. I couldn't deny that he had charisma.

"Carlos, this is Carol, who I mentioned before. David should be here any minute." I glanced at the clock. It was quarter to two— more like any second.

Detective Mills didn't disappoint. He poked his ash-blond head up over the cube wall.

"Someone call my name?" Mills was the unit prankster. It was always his way to crack a joke or tape someone's desk shut. A few weeks ago, he left a black mug on my desk that read, 'Living Proof It's Better to be Pretty than Smart.' I could have killed him. I still hadn't figured out how best to get him back for that.

I introduced everyone and leaned back in the chair, sipping my coffee quietly while they exchanged pleasantries.

"Mills and Reagan, can you come in here for a minute?" The voice belonged to Lieutenant Bill Larson, the Homicide Division supervisor. David and I trotted into his office.

"Sit Down, please," Larson said, the star-shaped scar on his long face wiggling as he spoke. "I wanted to let you know that Carlos is taking the Detective Sergeant slot."

Mills spoke up before I could. "But, Bill, what about Carol? I thought she was taking it."

"She turned it down, flat," Larson said. I liked that Larson was a straight shooter who got right to the point, but sometimes a bit more sugar-coating wouldn't be amiss. "If you want to know why you'll have to ask her."

"What about Carl or Jamison or McFee?" I said, not willing to let it go that quickly.

"Stop. This is a done deal and not open for debate. I get it. It's a surprise, but I've made my decision. I wouldn't have hired from outside the department if I didn't think it was necessary. Now, get back to work. If you want to complain, send an email."

I pressed my lips together, and Mills sulked.

"Well?" Larson prompted when we didn't move.

"Yes, sir," We replied in unison and left his office.

I sat down at my desk and pouted for a minute. The idea of a detective from another department taking lead in our unit didn't thrill me. But hiring and politics weren't my job. I went back to my coffee and the Caldwell case files.

I gave the team a few more minutes to get to know each other and then got their attention. "Okay, guys, we can chat later. We need to meet with Vic's team so they can let our new case go and head home."

"Thank you," Vic called over the cube wall, exhausted and relieved.

We all migrated into the conference room and sat down around the table. We were joined by two of the day shift team detectives, Vic and a short, balding man who'd had one too many cheeseburgers, Tony Cardozo. I hated Tony. No two ways about it. He liked to play politics. Not because he wanted to make Detective Sergeant or anything, but mostly just to fuck with people. He and I had been in several arguments that probably could have come to blows if he'd had more stones. But that wasn't his way. He oozed around the department, acting like everyone's best friend, and then knifing someone in the back with the higher-ups.

He'd tried that shit with me when I was green in Homicide. Word had gotten around to me that he'd been criticizing me to Larson. So, I dragged his sorry ass into the ladies' room. I then explained to him that I would happily flush my career and plant his face on the linoleum floor if he didn't stop fucking with me. That was the end of that. Now he avoided me if at all possible.

Vic got everyone's attention. "Okay, so we're handing this off because we're all slammed, and Wonder Woman over here is down to one open case". Everyone else laughed, I gave Vic the finger. Everyone laughed harder while I tried very hard and failed to look mad.

"Okay, okay," Vic said to get us back on track. He went over the entirety of the case and then set down the files. There were no new details to speak of. Jessvin Caldwell, age thirty-four, was found murdered in the middle of the night by an ER doctor on her morning jog. Someone had stabbed Mr. Caldwell in the chest with an unknown object and decapitated him. The medical examiner's preliminary report was late, as usual. That was it. "Tony and I are cooked. It's all yours."

"Thanks," I said and sent them on their way. I flipped through the pages of the summary report and Cardozo's witness statement to get a perspective on everything done on the case.

"Okay," I said, "So Cardozo already talked to the witness. She didn't add any detail to her statement. We don't have much to go on, so we start with the victim. Jesse Caldwell has a mother in a home in New Hampshire, and his father is deceased. Ms. Carson and Ms. D'angelo knew him well. Now," I paused, rubbing my forehead. "I have a conflict on this case."

"A conflict?" Mills asked, his brow furrowed.

"Yeah," I swallowed and continued. There was just nothing for it. "Gabe had an appointment to meet with the victim this morning. I don't think it will lead anywhere, but obviously, I can't do his interview."

"Are you not going to hand the case off to one of us?" Carol asked.

"Can't," I said flatly. "You two already have three cases apiece. And Carlos is the new guy. He doesn't get a case until he's been here for at least a month. Besides, Gabe's not a suspect or a victim, just a guy who knows something at this point.

If that changes, let's make sure that we do everything by the proverbial book."

"Well, that's Gabe," Mills chimed. "Just a guy."

"Be nice," Carol said, slapping his shoulder gently. "Gabe can't help being a douche."

"Alright, guys," I chided, "knock it off. I know how both of you feel about Gabe. Please be professional. He should be coming in today with a lawyer in tow. Also, he has one of their reps from New York coming with him.

"Please review the case and get familiar. If anything comes in from Forensics or the ME, call me and let me know. I'm taking Carlos to the crime scene, and then we're going to interview the maid and Ms. Carson when she gets in. Any questions?"

Mills raised his hand. "If Mr. Wonderful gives me any trouble, can I shoot him?"

I flipped him off with a smile and grabbed my keys.

"Come on, Ramirez, we're off to Charlestown," I said as I walked out of the cube farm toward the stairs. "This'll be a treat. I hope you're hungry. Oh, and are you allergic to shellfish?"

"I haven't eaten darlin', so food would be good. And no, I'm not allergic."

"I hope you're gonna bring us a lobster roll." Mills called hopefully to my back.

"Not on your life, David. You should have been nicer."

4

"Aren't we taking an unmarked car?" Carlos inquired as we walked out to the lot on Tremont.

"No, we're not. Because of budget cuts, we don't have enough to go around." I'm not sure what it said about me that, at thirty-two, my car was my most prized possession—juvenile as that may be. My baby was a 2020 four-door Jeep Wrangler Sport with a stubby bumper, a twelve-thousand-pound winch, and a light bar that could bathe Fenway Park. This was no mall crawler; she was a rock-eating beast. I always told Gabe that I loved him more than the car; that was a lie. She was the absolute love of my life, no exceptions—okay, maybe my cat.

I heard Carlos' deep booming laughter from behind me. I looked back at him. He was nearly doubled over, his hat on the ground.

I gave him my most menacing glare of annoyance. "What's so funny?"

He took a moment to compose himself and started shaking his head. "Nothin'. Just—nothin'."

I waited as he picked up his hat and strolled to the passenger side, still laughing.

"Get in the fucking car," I snapped half-heartedly. "You know, I'm sorely tempted to leave your ass." I couldn't help but smile, though, infected by his childish glee. He just kept laughing and climbed in.

"At least it's not a fucking Subaru," I muttered, then jumped as a strange snorting sound came out of Carlos. Confident he'd had some kind of stroke, I watched him shake. "Oh Jesus, it wasn't that funny. And just so you know, she's a trail jeep, not some bro-dozer."

Carlos laughed even harder. "You just keep diggin'!"

"Hang on," I prompted as I flipped on the police radio.

"Victor 8-9-4," I said into the mic, giving my unit number to dispatch.

"Operations Victor 8-9-4." It was a woman's voice that I didn't recognize. Must be new, I mused. The job hadn't knocked the perk out of her yet.

"Victor-8-9-4. Code 10."

"Operations 8-9-4 Acknowledged."

I put down the mic and rolled down my window. It was a little chilly, but the sun was shining, and the air was clear.

"I run her off-road a few times a year," I clarified, resuming our conversation as I exited onto Tremont Street.

"Good for you. So, what's the plan?"

"Well," I responded thoughtfully. "First, we'll eat. Then, we can look at the crime scene just to get some fresh perspective. The tourists will be drawn to Salem this time of year, so close to Halloween. That means foot traffic at the Monument should be light. After that, it's over to the Carson Logistics office."

Carlos read over the reports and eyed the crime scene photos while I chauffeured quietly. After studying them for a few minutes, Carlos spoke up, a frown on his face. "My gut says we've got a serial killer here. I bet there are more murders we haven't uncovered."

I pursed my lips. "That's a pleasant thought." I didn't say more as I had to swerve to avoid a driver recklessly U-turning across four lanes of traffic. Shitty driving always tempted me to hit the siren, but I never did—not my job anymore.

"Folks always drive like that?"

"Yup," I answered. "We call them Mass-holes."

Carlos snorted a laugh. "That's pretty funny."

I smirked. "If our perp is a serial killer, then the method is just as important as the victim, maybe more."

"It's certainly a unique way to kill someone," Carlos said, still thumbing through the pages and photos. "The closest I've seen was one case where a woman murdered her husband with a chainsaw while he was in bed. Of course, he'd tried to beat her to death several times, so while I may not agree, I understood the desire."

"She get convicted?" I asked.

"Nope, a jury decided it was self-defense," Carlos responded pleasantly.

I was appalled. "Wait, he was alive when she got him with the chainsaw, right?"

"Yup."

"And they acquitted her?"

"It's Texas," Carlos said flatly as if that explained it.

We cruised for a few minutes more before I broke the silence again.

"So, any guesses as to why this particular MO?" I asked.

"Well, until we have more, your guess is as good as mine. I'm the new guy," Carlos pointed out. He closed the folders and looked at me. "So, what do you do when you're not working?" He was excellent at non-sequitur, now jumping into the get to know you phase of being squad lead.

I kept my answer superficial but polite. "I work out mostly: lift weights, practice Jiu-Jitsu and Muay Thai. I run every day as well— if I can, anyway."

Carlos' eyes never stopped scanning the streets as he spoke. "Sounds like between that and work, it doesn't leave much time,"

"There's enough," I countered a little defensively. "Gabe and I go out from time to time. Of course, he wants us to get married, but I'm not ready for that."

"No TV or movies?" he queried, watching me closely.

"I have WiFi and watch the occasional rom-com or sci-fi flick on the Internet," I replied, glancing at him. "I scarfed up 'Orange is the New Black' and 'Game of Thrones.' The last season of 'Game of Thrones' mostly sucked, except Arya Stark; she's my fave. I tried to watch 'Squid Game,' but I struggled to get past the idiot cop. Why so interested in my entertainment habits?"

"Just making conversation, Marcus and I go to the movies as often as possible. We're both movie buffs. Marcus minored in Radio, Television, and Film during undergrad, so he's always picking apart all the movies, talking about fifty-fifty shots or three-quarter shots. It's fascinating. Though, sometimes, it ruins the movie. You should have heard him go on about the cinematography in Citizen Kane and all the different things that Orson Wells did that had never been done before, like the deep focus lens. I had to stop the movie about twenty times to tell him to save it for the next time we watched it. He just loves that stuff."

"Sounds like fun," I smiled. "I'd like to meet him. I take it he doesn't talk about work at home?"

"Of course he does. We both do. But that's like daily decompression stuff. After a few minutes of that each day, we move on to other things."

I thought about that. Gabe and I never talked about my job. I was sure it bored him, or grossed him out, or both.

The rest of the ride over to Yankee Lobster was quiet. Most of the way, Carlos kept looking at me like Boston was out to kill him personally because of the potholes. Eventually, he gave up reading the case file and tried to relax. A few minutes later, I pulled into a space behind the restaurant.

"Hey," I poked Carlos, who now had his eyes closed. "Wake up."

"I'm awake," he grumbled. "Just resting my eyes."

"Uh-huh, well, rest them some other time. It's time you enjoyed a Boston delicacy, the 'Lobstah Roll.' Yankee Lobster has one of the best."

"You know, I don't generally eat a lot of wraps," Carlos griped as he got out.

"What?" I asked, an eyebrow cocked. "What are you talking about?"

"Wraps, I don't eat a lot of wraps, or rolls or that kind of thing. Though, I like burritos, beef burritos."

It was my turn to laugh. "Kid, are you in for a treat. It's nothing like that." I bounced my eyebrows and grinned wickedly.

The outside seating was nearly empty. Perfect, I thought. Close to the seaport, the easterly breeze blew in the smells of the ocean. The briny odor had always smelled like home to me, the conglomeration of moisture, salt, and subtle decay. It reminded me of fishing on the cape with my da.

Inside, Carlos looked at the list of menu items and frowned. "Seafood, seafood, and more seafood," he complained.

"What do you want to drink?" I asked, ignoring his protests.

"Just water," he said, now actually frowning.

"Two hot-buttered lobster rolls and two waters," I told the cashier, a pretty girl in her mid-twenties covered in tattoos to her neck. She acknowledged the order with a smile and handed us a block of wood painted to look like a buoy or maybe a boat fender with a big five stenciled on it. Then she gave us our water bottles.

It was too nice of a day to sit indoors, so I led Carlos back out into the autumn air. He frowned all the more when he realized we were sitting in the outside dining area.

"Kinda cold to be sitting out here, don't you think?" he said, rubbing the sleeves of his blazer.

"You're kidding, right?" I said with a knowing smirk. "It's sixty-five and sunny. You might as well get used to it now because winter is coming, Ned Stark.

"A few years back," I continued. "We had a blast of frigid arctic air that dropped the temperature to twenty-five below for two days, right in the middle of a nor'easter. Revere Beach flooded, and then the seawater there froze. It crushed over thirty cars on the street. It was a complete shit show."

"Iraq?" Carlos asked out of nowhere.

"What about it?" I replied evasively, trying to figure out where he was going.

"Your arm, it looks like a blast injury." He pointed to my scarred left hand.

I twisted my arm slightly. "Oh. Grenade."

"What happened?" The inquiry was innocent enough, but I suddenly couldn't breathe.

"Stop!" I said, probably too harshly. I took in a breath. "I don't want to talk about it. It was a bad day."

"Sorry," Carlos apologized. "I didn't mean to pry." He leaned back, and I could tell by how he looked at me that he was concerned. It wasn't rational, but I seriously wondered if he was concerned about my overall mental state. I had to admit that he might just be feeling a bit of sympathy, which I certainly didn't want.

"How many nights?" he asked cryptically a few moments later.

"How many nights what?" I shot back. Now I knew where this was going, and I didn't like it.

"How many nights do you wake up soaked in sweat, feeling like you can't breathe, reliving that day?" His demeanor was calm and understanding.

I didn't respond, but I could feel myself start to tear up.

"Look, I left Dallas because one of my squad got killed, and I felt responsible," he admitted with deadly seriousness. "It haunted me for over a year before I finally decided to get some counseling and get the fuck out of Texas.

"My partner and I were on our way to a scene in Richardson," he continued, "one of the suburbs. It was out of our jurisdiction, but the wounds on the victim matched another homicide we were working. So, I convinced Franklin to see the victim first hand rather than head home for dinner."

I could see the pain on his face, but I kept my mouth shut and waited for him to continue.

"Anyway, en route, on this little street near an elementary school, we see this guy running across covered in blood; at least it looked that way. So, I hit the siren, and we jumped out. We didn't get two steps before he was on Franklin. The dude was fast and strong. He'd ripped out Franklin's throat before I could move. Then he was on me. The guy was crazy. He started clawing and biting at me. While he was chewing on my shoulder, I pulled my piece and shot him three times in the chest. That got him off me so I could call for backup. But, the dude barely flinched; he just stood up and ran— *ran* off."

"PCP?" I asked, interested. I'd heard stories of people on PCP walking around on broken legs or taking multiple bullets before keeling over. The thought was chilling.

"No idea. He never turned up, no corpse, no hospital visits, nothing. The guy just up and fucking vanished. I put three nine-millimeter slugs in the guy, center mass—three! One of them, I was sure, was right in the pump. But that ain't the point. I had to face Franklin's wife and three kids after convincing him to make just one more trip—the trip that killed him. I still have nightmares, and I've had over two years of counseling. Marcus woke up with my hands around his neck one night a few weeks after it happened. It was bad."

"I'm so sorry." It was all I could say.

He cleared his throat. "So, try not to fly off the handle when I ask this. Have you seen a therapist? The war's long gone for you. My dad was ate up with PTSD for twenty years after Vietnam, and you don't need that. No one does."

I understood why Larson had made him Detective Sergeant. He was sharp, perceptive, and, clearly, very wise. He was also pissing me off with this 'I'm your buddy, let me help you' routine.

"Look, Carlos. I like you. But, Let's talk about something else."

"Okay, but one last thing. I am well aware of how hard it is when you're carrying baggage like that. Twelve years is way too long under that burden."

I looked at him blankly, trying very hard not to tear up.

"Now," he said, turning mirthful, "I think I see our food coming, which is good, 'cause I'm hungrier than a tic on a teddy bear."

"Tic on a teddy bear," I giggled. "I have to remember that. God, you are so country." And just like that, Carlos made it all better.

"Of course I'm country. My dad worked the rodeos. My mom wasn't a buckle bunny or nothin'. They were married before he started working the circuit. The point is, though, language and music are cultural, not racial. I speak fluent Spanish because my folks spoke it at home, but my English is all Texas, and my music is all country. It's who I am." He smiled broadly. It was evident that he was proud of his heritage—and his parents. And he was proud of being from Texas. I could relate. Boston wasn't just my hometown; it was in me.

The waitress walked up with our plates, the same woman who had taken our orders. She flashed me a bright smile and made eye contact. I didn't look away, but I blushed furiously. "Would you like anything else? More Ketchup or Malt Vinegar?"

"No thanks," Carlos and I answered in unison.

Carlos watched her closely as she headed back inside. "She look familiar to you?" Carlos asked.

"Not really." I looked back at her. Her walk was confident. I wondered if she was exaggerating her ass shake for Carlos or if it was natural. I had to admit that her tattoos looked sexy. I turned around to say something to Carlos but thought better of it when I realized what I was about to say. Carlos was lost in the distance anyway. I waved my hand across his view. "Hey, Earth to Carlos. Food."

"Yup," Carlos said, pulled from whatever he was thinking. "When you said we were getting a lobster roll, this isn't quite what I expected." In front of each of us was a hot dog bun, split through the top instead of the side, exploding with seasoned lobster meat and sprinkled with chives. I found it genuinely gratifying introducing people to great food.

Each plate had a side of fries with Ketchup, too. I tend to treat the fries more as an edible garnish than food. I mean, lobster, how can you go wrong?

"Trust me," I said. "It's awesome."

Carlos didn't need any more prompting. He dug into his lobster roll with gusto while I took a moment to watch. The man liked to eat, that was for sure.

"This is high cotton right here," he said around a mouthful. "So, tell me about your folks."

"Mine?" I said, also around a mouthful. I set down the roll, wiped my face, and took a drink of water, mainly to give myself time to decide what to tell him. "Well, my ma is fresh off the boat. She was born in a tiny village in County Mayo called Tourmakeady. It's in one of the Gaeltacht regions. That means they speak Irish rather than English as their first language. Now, she's a Linguistics Professor at Boston College focused on reconstructed Celtic and its correlations in Sanskrit.

"My da was an Irish Catholic cop from Southie; go figure. He tried to make me go to church, but Ma put her foot down when I was ten. He was a patrolman and about to join Homicide when a dealer shot him and his partner, one Lieutenant William Larson. Larson ended up in the ICU. Da came home in a box."

"I'm sorry for your loss; that must have been tough," Carlos said, empathy on his face.

"Ma grieved like any good Irish widow. She threw herself into social activities and dragged me with her. Then she started traveling back and forth to Ireland, visiting relatives. No matter how much I bitched, she never took me with her. I felt isolated. So, I grieved like a typical sixteen-year-old, acting out, cutting school, you know?

"When I was about to turn eighteen, I went to a recruiter and committed to the army. I told Ma it was so I could get some discipline in my life. Mostly though, I just wanted out from under my ma's thumb. Looking back now, I know she just didn't want to lose her daughter like she lost her husband, and trying to control me was one of the ways she felt safe. But, I just wanted to build a life of my own, and it seemed like the easiest way to get to a place to make my own decisions. Besides, my grades weren't going to get me into a decent school. I'm sorry, you were asking about my folks, and I veered it right into talking about me."

"How'd she take it?" Carlos asked, ignoring my apology. He was finished with his lobster roll and leaning back in his chair.

"About like you'd expect, Ma freaked. But what could she do? I was two weeks from my eighteenth birthday and had just graduated High School. After a day of calling our priest and not getting the answer she wanted, she just started yelling at me in Gaelic a lot. Then we didn't speak, even when the recruiter picked me up to report to MEPS.

"But, she came around as soon as I was gone. She wrote me letters a couple of times a week during my entire active-duty stint. When I came home after Iraq, she was right there with me through six surgeries and a ton of PT. And she didn't say a word when I joined the police force after college. I think she just knew I'd follow in dad's footsteps."

"Wow," he said. "That's a lot. My folks are also devout Catholics, but they're pretty cool. One day, when our priest found out that I was gay, he told mama he'd pray for me. She told him—and I'm translating here—'If you want to pray for him, pray that he comes home safe every night. Otherwise, save your prayers for those who need them. My son is a good man.' To my knowledge, he never said another word."

"I wouldn't expect that," I said, surprised. "I thought Latino families were usually a little less accepting. I mean, pardon my ignorance."

"Nothing to pardon; you're not far wrong. Bigotry against the LGBTQ community is still pretty heavy among Latinos and Hispanics, especially the men, but it's getting better. At least in the US, some of the younger generation are less invested in that machismo shit and are pushing the community to be more accepting. My mama, though, she's just a saint. Treats Marcus like one of the family and put papa in his place the day I came out. It was pretty funny. My dad told me that I should get some good pussy to make sure.

"Now, my mother is normally the epitome of Latin Catholic demureness. But, she turned to him, looked him straight in the eye, and told him that he should go out and get some first-class dick, just to be sure. I never saw my father turn so red in my life. I always wondered if it was because she pegged him or because he was angry. I'm sure I'll never know. I do know they argued about it for a while, but like anything else in the house, if it's important to mama, she wins; that's it."

We spent the rest of lunch chatting about work, with Carlos pretty much grilling me about the department, the squad, and different detectives. I told him about my last run-in with Cardozo. When I finished, he, again, looked like he was having a stroke as he laughed.

The waitress came by to check on us at that point, so I tried to see what Carlos was talking about that made her look familiar. She caught me staring and stopped to write something on a pad in her pocket, leaving it in front of me. I didn't bother to look at the paper, slipping it into my pocket— no need to give Carlos any more fuel for ragging me today.

The way we left the restaurant, laughing and swapping stories, you'd have thought we'd been friends for years, not that I'd first met him a few hours before.

5

After lunch, I notified dispatch that we were en route to Charlestown.

Carlos' demeanor turned a little impish as we crossed the bridge on Seaport. "So, you gonna call her?"

"Damnit," I grumbled. "I was wondering how long it would take you to say something. And, no, I'm not going to call her."

"What's her name?" Carlos prodded, goading me a little more with a twinkle in his eye. He knew the nerve he was poking.

"Nohemi." As we'd left the restaurant, I'd thought I'd been slick, glancing at the paper surreptitiously, clearly not.

I parked just south of the square, and we approached the memorial park. The Bunker Hill Monument is somewhat striking, a two-hundred-foot granite obelisk rising like a needle in the blue. It's honestly a weird design for a battle memorial.

"Well then," Carlos said as we walked up to the Monument. "Makes you wonder if someone might have been compensating for something. I bet whoever designed this probably had a hot-rod carriage, too." His wry tone made me laugh.

Around us, a group of tourists snapped pictures and read the various plaques, oblivious that, just hours earlier, blood covered the stones beneath their feet.

We shooed away the tourists with our badges, and I pointed back toward the southeastern corner of the surrounding park.

"Caldwell came from that direction. He would have come down across to the Monument here." I stood in front of the doorway to the exhibit lodge.

"According to Vic's preliminary, they towed a BMW registered to him from Concord Street, which is over there. So, whoever killed him was probably waiting right about here," I said, moving around to the northwest corner.

"What is that?" he asked, pointing to a door that led under the building. "Where does that lead?"

"It leads to the utility basement under the monument," I said. "What are you thinking?"

"It just reminds me of Washington, D.C. and all the tunnels running under the city. This," he pointed to the monument, "was obviously designed by Freemasons, just like D.C."

"Are you suggesting that Freemasons killed our victim?" I asked with a grin and a raised eyebrow.

"Ha, ha, Detective," he countered sarcastically. "Of course not; I was just curious. I know it's far-fetched to think there's a secret tunnel around her."

"That's not as crazy an idea as you might think. Right across the river, under my apartment building, is a tunnel originally used by pirates and smugglers. They run all under the North End. There are little nooks and crannies like that all over Boston."

Carlos looked around. "There aren't too many places to hide and watch someone around here. Over in the trees, maybe."

"Maybe, but it's a public park," I said. "Even if we figured out the observation point, I don't expect to find any evidence."

"Can't hurt to look," Carlos said, looking around.

I looked at my watch—5:15. "We've got about an hour of daylight left, and Ms. Carson will be back at six-forty-five. You think that's enough time to walk a strip?" I asked, indicating a type of search pattern.

"Sure, if we split it in half. The team might have missed something." Carlos looked at all the trees around the edge of the park. It was already dusk, and much of the park was in shadow.

"Hang on," I said to Carlos, and I jogged back to the car, returning with two flashlights, two pairs of gloves, and some evidence bags. "In case we find something."

I started at the northwest corner, flashlight in hand, and searched for anything relevant: footprints, a cigarette butt, a wrapper, whatever.

Not ten feet into my search, I came across a shoe impression in a small dirt area under a tree. I snapped a photo, putting my watch down next to the shoeprint for scale.

The shoe pattern was a little odd. It was larger than mine and made by a dress shoe with a pointed toe—European men's style, maybe men's size ten. I had no way of knowing if it was related, but the peculiarity of the impression made it intriguing.

The rest of the walk was fruitless other than some old candy wrappers. I suppressed my growing frustration with this case and returned to the lodge door.

A cold breeze blew through the park, making me shiver as the sun dipped below the horizon. Puffy clouds floated above, turning a vibrant pink in the sunset and mixing with the street lights, giving the entire park a magical quality. I remembered spending summer nights up here with my da, eating ice cream, and I tried to hold onto that feeling. But Carlos walked up, breaking the spell.

"Find anything?" he asked, looking just as disappointed in the search as I was.

"Just an interesting shoe impression and some garbage. You?"

"Nope, not a damn thing. You'd think that if you ran someone through and then cut their head off, you'd leave a pretty hefty trail of blood or something."

"Unless he wiped down the murder weapon," I said, staring at the empty space where the body had lain.

I pursed my lips and walked closer to Carlos, pulling out my phone. "So, look at this." I showed him the photo of the shoe impression. "I'd expected sneakers or bare feet."

"Huh," Carlos grunted. "It's odd; I'll give you that, but hardly a case cracker."

"No, but if we find a suspect at some point, it might tell us something—or maybe nothing." I glanced at my watch as we spoke—6:28 PM. On a whim, I pulled up a flight tracker on my phone and looked up Ms. Carson's plane. "Shit, they must have been hauling ass because the plane landed at six-twenty."

"Well then, we won't have long to wait," Carlos said, looking at his watch. "Figure thirty to forty-five to get her bags and go through customs. How long to get home from the airport do you think?" Carlos looked at me.

"Twenty-five, maybe thirty minutes," I answered automatically. "It's just across the harbor, but they will likely go through Chelsea to avoid traffic. She'll be in a private car, I'm sure."

"We should probably just relax on a bench somewhere until about eight. There," Carlos said, pointing to a bench near the building. We relaxed there, the file between us.

"Okay, so we know he was stabbed and decapitated," I said. "And, according to the preliminary report, the cut looked clean —a single strike with a blade."

"Yup, a sword of some kind."

I nodded. "So, what did they impale him with? And why? Whatever it was left a sizable hole; it wasn't a stiletto or a knife. It probably took a fair amount of muscle given the entry angle."

"Even more interesting is the lack of defensive wounds on the victim. He never saw it coming." Carlos sat bolt upright on the bench and pulled out the photos, thumbing through them until he found one. He pulled a pair of reader glasses from his inside breast pocket and put them on.

I eyeballed the glasses. "You weren't wearing those earlier."

"Nope, I don't need them to read. But here in a second, you'll see why I carry them." Carlos slapped the photo and handed it to me along with the reading glasses. "Look at the wound as close as you can."

I peered through the glasses. It took me a second to focus, but then I saw it. On the edge of the wound, stuck to the shirt, was a small brown line. It was no more than a smudge to the naked eye, but through the reading glasses, it became clear, a thick splinter of wood.

"Shit. You know, I honestly fucking wish the ME's office would work faster. I'd like to know what else we're missing." I looked at the photo again. "So let me get this straight. The guy was jabbed through the heart with a piece of wood and then beheaded. Who was this guy, fucking Dracula?"

"Puts an interesting spin on it, doesn't it?" Carlos said wryly. "Our perp either thought Caldwell was the un-fucking-dead, or he wanted us to think he did. We're dealing with one seriously deluded individual."

"That's fucked up."

"Yes, it is. We have some time, so let's just cogitate on that." Carlos leaned back on the bench to look up at the sky. I joined him in that endeavor.

I'd gotten shit sleep the night before, and the day was catching up with me; my mind started to wander. I thought about the last time I'd had a quiet moment like this with anyone. Honestly, it had probably been back in Iraq about a week before 'the incident.' As usual, the power had gone out in Mosul, and Morgan and I had been lying on a blanket, looking at the stars. The night sky had been positively vertigo-inducing.

Shooting stars had streaked across the night, and as each one passed, Morgan would say, 'that's one more wish.' I still wondered what she wished for. I also wondered why I hadn't had any moments like that with Gabe. I would have liked to blame him and his work schedule or his time with his idiot 'bros,' but I couldn't think of a single time I'd suggested we just lay outside together and watch the sky.

"Hey there," Carlos said softly. "Where are you?"

"Huh?" I said, shaking myself out of the memory. "Nowhere,

just thinking." I glanced around the park; it had grown deathly still. The tourists were all gone, and the shadows had closed in. It was all very dark and foreboding, chasing away my reverie. Honestly, I was a little creeped out now that we understood the MO better.

Carlos spoke up, snatching away the dark thoughts. "You know, Marcus and I took a vacation out to Big Bend National Park in Texas. You can see every star out there. It's like sliding past a giant river as the Milky Way moves across the sky. Our last time out there, we made love under the stars. It was beautiful."

I guess I wasn't alone in my appreciation of the night sky. Not that I'd ever made love under the stars. But, it was a beautiful thought. A pang of loss suddenly grabbed me. For a minute, I spiraled, thinking that everything in my life was tainted and ruined. Everything reminded me of Morgan or Iraq, or my da. It was a pit of sorrow that seemed endless. Then the brake lights of an SUV snapped me out of my negative thoughts.

"She's here," I whispered to Carlos, who looked up.

A black SUV sporting a livery tag was pulling up to the address we had for Ms. Carson. A woman in a black coat and a black hat exited the SUV, stalking toward the door in some haste. The driver got out and pulled a suitcase out of the back, following the woman I assumed was Ms. Carson. I couldn't see her well from the bench—just a figure walking into the building. My watch read seven-thirty-eight.

We gave the woman a little time to get settled, then we got up and strolled over.

6

Carlos whistled, looking between me and the enormous house, eyebrows raised. "There is a river of money rolling through this place."

The building, which had once been split into multiple apartments, was restored to its original glory as a single-family home, complete with a facade of 1860s-style brickwork. The entrance sported a beautifully crafted columned portico with double oak doors that looked damn solid.

"Says here," I commented, looking at the Carson website on my phone, "they've been in business since 1963, primarily handling shipping and receiving of aid packages and pharmaceuticals for various corporations and nation-states."

Carlos grunted in acknowledgment.

We strode up and rang the doorbell, one of those video do-lollies. A short, severe-looking woman with black hair in an understated, brown skirt suit answered the door. Vulturish eyes appraised us from within a late-middle-aged face, eventually resting on our badges.

"The Signora is expecting you; come in, please," she invited with a thick Italian accent.

"Pleasure to meet you," Carlos began but stopped when she didn't return his offered hand.

"Indeed. The pleasure is mine," she responded perfunctorily

while pulling the doors wide. "I am Ninetta, the housekeeper."

Carlos and I entered a grand foyer. Above, a lustrous, crystal chandelier cast bright motes across a circle of red Nordic runes embedded in the white marble floor. To our right, two enormous sliding doors of burnished wood hid another room, and to the left sat an open entryway to what appeared to be a library. Everything about the entrance screamed not just money but wealth.

The sparse furniture was both decorative and functional, reflecting opulence and practicality. A large picture mirror rested in a glittering gold leaf frame above a charming Queen Anne console table. Directly ahead, the marble floor rose in a staircase to an open gallery, flanked by a polished oak railing supported on exquisitely worked black iron balusters.

Typically, I'd have thought it ostentations as hell. But a single item in the room transformed it from a ridiculous, if somewhat minimalist, display of means to a comfortable living space. A rather ugly and worn little wooden bowl lurked on the console table with a set of car keys dangling over the rim. Looking thoroughly out of place and odd, they reminded me that this was a home, not an office. Someone lived here. Everything here had been chosen for personal reasons, whether deep or shallow. My gut told me that Marcella Carson had decorated this space for herself and no one else. And I was very interested in meeting her.

"And how should I announce you?" Ninetta queried, jerking me from my gawking.

Announce us? That was a trip. We were cops, not royalty, and it took me just a second to realize she was just asking for our names. "I'm Detective Reagan, and this is Detective Ramirez with the Homicide Department. We're here—."

She cut me off. "I know why you are here. Such bad business for Mr. Caldwell, just awful." Tear-filled lashes belied her well-composed facade. "I will tell Signora Carson that you are here." She disappeared to the second floor above.

I checked my appearance in the mirror, finding another

face there, one not entirely my own. It was me, but thinner, younger, and with short hair. I squeezed my eyes shut. When I opened them again, I found only my normal reflection, auburn hair still tight in its bun, and, thank God, no chives in my teeth.

"Hot date tonight?" Carlos asked, hat in one hand.

I stuck my tongue out at him. I was becoming more accustomed to Carlos' jokes, realizing it was his way to break the tension. At this particular moment, though, I'd have preferred another target. I was nervous enough as it was. Rich people intimidated me.

Ninetta waited until she reached the first floor before asking us to follow her up. She reminded me a lot of some of the women I'd seen going to church in my youth, the pre-Vatican II Catholic women who still wore white veils for confession and mass, prim and proper and quick to shoot you a nasty glance if you did something untoward.

The second floor was much more businesslike than the first. Beige walls met simple hardwoods here. Ninetta crossed herself as she led us past a room holding a messy office. Then, she stopped on the other side of a second doorway and motioned us in.

Next to a large executive desk stood a spectacularly attractive woman. To call her statuesque was an understatement. She towered over me. Her hair, like honey-dazzled sunlight, caressed a face of soft-looking, milky-pale skin, perfect and unblemished. Her blue-frosted irises flashed mesmerizingly with sharp intellect and movement. Below, a narrow, refined nose perched above soft, delicious-looking, blood-red lips that quivered slightly as she breathed.

She was dressed in an expensive-looking white blouse that admitted a tasteful hint of black lace-wrapped cleavage before sliding solicitously beneath the waist of a black pencil skirt. My eyes drifted down toward the edges of sheer silk stockings that traced her muscular legs, crossed at the ankles. They were like alabaster columns stacked delicately in shining black Louboutin pumps. My pulse thumped like a snare on a drumline. I was star-struck.

I inhaled sharply, only just turning it into a cough as butterflies lofted through me, tugging at my insides with something like—lust, maybe. I self-consciously tucked a stray hair behind my ear as I watched her gaze slide across my pedestrian frame, and I licked my suddenly dry lips.

Carlos cleared his throat and gave me a sidelong glance before speaking. I'd almost forgotten he was there. His eyes twinkled slightly but underneath sat a suspicious frown. Carlos turned back, entirely and perfunctorily professional.

"I'm Detective Ramirez, and this is Detective Reagan," he said confidently. "We're from the Boston Police, Homicide Division. We're sorry for your loss." She shook our hands. Her skin was cool to the touch and as soft as I'd imagined. It slid gently across my palm, and I suppressed a shiver as the hair on my arms stood straight up. I detected a hint of floral perfume and something underneath that was reminiscent of sandalwood.

Then she opened her mouth, and a crisp British accent flowed forth, a rich and beautiful alto, like silk flowing over bare skin. The fry in it reminded me of the blowing sands in Iraq. "Please, Detectives, sit down." She gestured to two empty chairs in front of her desk as she took hers. "I can't believe Jesse is dead. I just spoke with him yesterday."

Carlos got right to business, leaning forward in his chair. "Ms. Carson, we don't have a lot to go on in your co-worker's murder, and we'd like to understand who he was."

"Certainly, Detective, though I'm not sure what I can tell you."

I noticed that she had a wastebasket with several pink tissues next to her desk. It seemed she hadn't taken Mr. Caldwell's death easily, which was just as well. I didn't want to believe she was a killer.

"Jesse was smart, capable, a hard worker, and the best admin I've ever had. I don't understand why anyone would murder him. It's not like we're involved in anything even remotely dangerous here. Generally, we just arrange for shipping aid to under-served communities and poor parts of the world—blankets, pharmaceuticals, water, food, that kind of thing. May I ask how he died? The news didn't say."

"We're still investigating, Ms. Carson," I answered, deflecting the question. It seemed I'd finally found my voice. "Could Mr. Caldwell have been working on something personal or been mixed up in something that might have put him in danger?" She caught my eye and held my gaze a bit longer than was comfortable. I turned my eyes to my notepad, suppressing the burgeoning smile at the corners of my mouth.

"Not that I know of, Detective Reagan, and call me Marcella, please. Jesse was pretty relaxed. He generally left work, drove home, hit the gym, and was in bed early. Of course, Jesse had a social life, but it was tame, just dates and the like. He was pretty open with me about it, and we talked every day. I know he was between girlfriends at the moment and had been for a couple of months now."

My eyes were drawn to Marcella's mouth as she spoke, and I bit my bottom lip. I cleared my throat gently and swallowed hard. "Did he have any bad habits—drugs, gambling, things like that?"

"Goodness, no. And I would know. I have a nose for personal problems. Besides, even if he did, he can come to me if he needs money or is in trouble. I run a tight ship; I have to, but I'm not a slave driver or a tyrant. Jesse and I are friends, Detective Reagan, not just co-workers." She started to look more distraught as the conversation went on.

"Did he have any enemies, or do you know anyone who might want to harm him?" Carlos asked.

"Enemies?" Marcella directed her comments to me, though Carlos had asked the question. "He was an administrative assistant. What kind of enemies could he have? As for anyone who might want to hurt him, I know of no one."

"Was he working on any projects for you or unusual ventures at the moment?" Carlos asked, pulling her attention to him, thankfully. Her constant appraising looks had become a little nerve-wracking, flattering as they were.

"Well, we're in the process of shipping supplies to several Caribbean islands for storm relief, and he is peripherally involved with that at my request. He is, or was, keeping up with the process to make sure things proceed smoothly. Other than that, his work consists of keeping my schedule, answering my phone calls, acting as a business concierge for me when I need him, and keeping my world sorted. He is a good kid, and thirty-four is way too young to die." Her demeanor crumbled for a moment, but she recovered quickly.

"Jesse's father worked for my mother, who died in 1996. She had made sure that Jesse attended private school and paid for him to go to university. In 2000, Jesse's parents died in a car accident, and I, having taken over the business by then, ensured that Jesse's education continued. After receiving his master's from Brown, he returned to Boston and went to work for me. That was nine years ago." Pausing, she reached for a pink tissue and dabbed at her eyes. "I can't understand why anyone would kill him." As she said this last, I noted that Carlos' frown deepened. It was only for a second, but it was there.

Carlos continued to ask questions about Mr. Caldwell's habits, personality, friends, and enemies—covering the usual spectrum. I listened on and looked around the room. The far wall from where we sat held two bookcases stacked on a credenza. Between the bookcases was a small stone tablet with markings, like cuneiform. I couldn't make out any further details from my position, but it kept drawing my eye, and I had the urge to go over and touch it.

The books on the shelves fell into three categories, history, business, and, oddly, medical. A few ancient-looking texts surrounded a copy of Gray's Anatomy bound in brown leather, probably a first edition. The business books were all from the last forty years, primarily focused on general business or transport and logistics. The history books looked the most used. Many were older, but a few looked brand new. I tried to see if I knew any of the titles, but I was drawn from my observations by the end of Carlos' questions.

"Detective Reagan?" Marcella prodded. "Did you have any additional questions?"

"Yes, ma'am, just one. Did you read all of those?" I asked, gesturing to the books.

Marcella smiled broadly. "Yes, Detective, I have. And, please, call me Marcella."

"Even Gray's Anatomy?" I asked, skeptical.

"Yes, Detective," she responded, eyes twinkling with mischief. "Would you like to know what it says about the external carotid artery and its relation to facial blood flow?" I blinked, and her mouth pulled into a more cheeky smile as my face flushed, demonstrating that relationship very effectively.

"Sorry, I was just curious." I stammered.

She smiled again and then sighed. "Detectives, I just got off a six-hour flight from the UK, and I'm jet-lagged. Honestly, I need to get some rest. I'm happy to discuss this tomorrow, but I'm not sure what I can add. I need to go through it, but I'll happily provide Jesse's diary—sorry, calendar—and the list of projects he was working on for me. If you have a card, I'll call you tomorrow afternoon after I finish work, and you can come to pick it up."

I pulled a card out of my jacket and held it out. Marcella stood and walked around, offering her hand. She stepped with willow-like grace, so light that her heels barely clicked on the hardwoods, leaving me jealous. When I walked, I might as well be dragging my knuckles by comparison.

Carlos and I both shook her hands and turned to go. I wasn't sure, but she seemed to hold my hand longer, feeding me a warm smile as she did so.

"Detective Reagan?" she called to my back as I made to step through the door, and I hazarded a backward glance. Her eyes caught mine, and my pulse ramped again. She paused, drawing the lingering moment a little further. "If I think of anything that might be any help, I'll give you a ring."

"Thank you, Ms. Carson," I answered quickly, feeling the need to both stand there and escape. "That would be much appreciated." I decided for the latter and turned, hurrying after Carlos and Ninetta, feeling a slight flush.

Carlos and I waited to say any more until we got outside the building. I half expected him to start poking at me again and making jokes, but his face was serious.

"We need to be careful with that one," Carlos said. "She's dangerous, and she knows more than she's saying."

"What do you mean?" I looked at him skeptically. "She seemed nice enough. I guess she could be involved, but I'm not sure why she would be, especially if anything she said about Caldwell's work were true. Supposing it's murder-for-hire, I don't see a motive here. At least not yet. Besides, you don't hire a guy to decapitate someone unless you're sending a message. If so, the message would more likely have been for her, not from her."

"Oh, I'm not saying she's involved," Carlos said as we started back for the car. "I don't honestly think she was. And, you're right. It just doesn't look like your classic hit. The method of execution stinks of something more, like maybe a form of intimidation. But she's not saying everything.

"I used to know this guy who worked for the State Department some years back. One night, we were going out for beers, and he clued me into something about the government. If the government wants to ship weapons but doesn't want to be directly involved, they deliver them through a third party. He said that companies like this are just the types of organizations they use to move covert weapons and supplies. I almost guarantee that she's not just shipping humanitarian aid."

"Wow, conspiracy theory much?" I jeered. "We've just met the lady, and you've already convicted her of taking part in international arms smuggling." It seemed a little far-fetched.

"Oh, there's no smuggling about it in most cases. I'm sure almost everything Carson Logistics does is above board and on the level in both permits and taxes. But, there are laws against shipping munitions to certain countries. Even so, certain parts of the government feel it necessary to avoid those pesky laws from time to time.

"I'm not saying she's dirty. But, I can tell you that there's no way Carson Logistics has offices around the world and a headquarters in *the* financial office building of Boston if all they're doing is shipping humanitarian supplies. That's a cutthroat business, and margins are slim. Either that or they're smuggling drugs for the cartels, which I doubt." We walked quickly and made good time back to the car. We'd be back at HQ by nine-thirty if I hustled, and I might be able to find out how the interview with Gabe and his associate went. Just thinking about Gabe gave me a knot in my stomach, though.

"Well, at least you haven't convicted her of that. I guess I'll take your word for it." I said as we reached the Jeep. "How far do you want to dig on her business?" I asked as we pulled out of the parking spot.

Carlos looked at me incredulously. "Are you kidding? I don't. I just want to work the case where it leads. If it gets into an area like the arms trade, we need to talk the Lieutenant into bringing in the feds. Little people like us digging into international gun-running tends to lead to dead little people. I'll pass. I've got Marcus to think about, too. I'm a homicide detective, not ATF or ICE, and I like it that way."

"Do you honestly think she's dangerous?" I asked after the silence had stretched for a bit.

Carlos smirked. "I think her company ships guns and munitions, sometimes illegally. Anyone who has the stones for that kind of endeavor has the sack to do whatever is required."

Carlos was watching me like a hawk now. "You seem awful interested in what I think of the lady, so I'll tell you. She's rich, powerful, and well connected. That means she could probably squash either of us like a bug in the Mayor's office or with the Commissioner. She's also beautiful, smart, and very into you."

I felt that same flush and rush of butterflies start all over again. My mouth felt dry, and I croaked a little as I said, "What makes—" I stopped and cleared my throat. "What makes you think that."

"Oh, come on," Carlos said, "She practically stripped you naked with her eyes. You made a good show of not noticing, but I know you did."

My face felt hot as I drove. "Okay, fine. I noticed her checking me out, but she's involved in the case; it's not like I could do anything about it. Not that I would; I have Gabe."

"Yeah," Carlos said, "about that."

"Stop right there; I know what you're going to say." I yanked the wheel and pulled the car over, hitting the hazard lights.

"Look," I said, a little shakily. "I have no idea why I'm telling you this. But Marcella Carson wouldn't be the first woman I've been attracted to." There, I'd said it. My heart rate jumped, and my blood pressure dropped about twenty points. I leaned forward and put my head on the steering wheel, feeling dizzy. "Fuck," I said quietly.

"I wondered," Carlos said, the playful smirk gone. "As for why you're telling me, that's easy. I'm good at striking rapport. I'm a straight shooter and trustworthy. But this is something I can relate to, and you know that. Your attraction to women has finally caught up with you. Denying who we are is mentally exhausting. We all break sooner or later.

"Truthfully, though, it's not like you scream 'dyke cop.' Hell, I was just fucking with you earlier. But, if you're not sure about your sexuality, if this really is the first time you've considered you might not be entirely straight, then I'm sorry about messing with you. That was no bueno. It's no fun being confused. It can turn your entire world upside down."

"Dear Lord, I don't know why I'm having this discussion with you," I said, then blew out a breath to steady my nerves. "Please don't say anything to anyone. I don't think I can deal with this right now."

"It's not my truth to tell," Carlos said. "You need

to understand something else. Generally—and I repeat—generally, everyone who is gay knows better than to out somebody. But, darlin', I'll never say a word unless and until you say otherwise. If you need someone to talk to, you have my number."

"Thanks," I said, feeling only a little better. "I appreciate it. I'll call if I need anything."

"Just not on Friday nights," he replied, and the playful smirk returned. "That's Marcus' and my special dress-up night, and this week it's cops and robbers."

"Oh!" I exclaimed, "I do not need to hear this." We both laughed at that until we cried.

7

A dense, cold drizzle descended across the city as we made our way back to Schroeder. Carlos and I were quiet for the rest of the ride, and I was thankful for the time it gave me to suppress my anxiety.

Am I a lesbian? Is that why my relationships never work out? The thought pushed a lump of fear into my chest. It wasn't homophobia; it was something nebulous, like my life would spin out of control somehow.

I kept my life carefully balanced and compartmentalized. It was how I coped with my trauma. I had an apartment that was my space to be strong, weak, whatever I needed. I was competent at my job and respected by my peers, which gave me much-needed self-esteem. I had a boyfriend whom I kept where I needed him, so—. I paused mid-thought. *Is that how I see Gabe? Shit.* Before I could analyze it any further, we arrived at HQ.

While I parked, Carlos turned to me, and after a moment's thought, scratching his cheek, he said, "Do yourself a favor. Don't get involved with Marcella Carson."

I threw the Jeep in park. "Carlos," I said heatedly. "Just because I find her attractive doesn't mean I'm going to have sex with her. I wouldn't even know where to begin. Besides, I need to try to sort things out with Gabe. And more important than all of that, she's a potential witness in a homicide investigation."

Carlos rubbed the back of his neck. "I debated whether to say anything at all. But, I remember when I was a confused mess. I gravitated toward the first gay man I met. There was a certain excitement in it and a pretty overwhelming desire to 'know.'" He air-quoted the word 'know.' "Marcella seems nice, but, trust me, Cait, she's a predator."

I raised an eyebrow.

"I don't mean a sexual predator. Just that she strikes me as the type to relentlessly pursue what she wants. But, just so you know, I'm not the type to tattle," he continued. "This is just me looking out for you. Women like Marcella Carson can be very — uh — persuasive."

I barked a laugh. "I bet."

Inside the building, Carlos and I raced to the second floor like a couple of kids. With his long strides, taking the stairs three at a time, he easily outpaced me, and by the time we walked out of the stairwell, we were both a little winded and laughing. Sometimes, it's good to break the tension with a bit of clowning around.

"Hey," Mills said, looking at me. "Your boyfriend and his buddy never showed or called."

I had to pick my jaw up off the floor. "He what?"

"You heard me. No call, no show. I even called their office here in Boston, but neither showed there, either."

"But," David continued, ignoring my expression. "We did get a break in the Mass and Cass case. Your boy, what's his name? The homeless guy you usually see at the Common." Mass and Cass was how we referred to the corner of Massachusetts Avenue and Melnea Cass Boulevard. It was also known as the 'methadone mile' because of the methadone clinics along that stretch. Addicts often went there to score, shoot up, and then go to the clinics to avoid the crash.

"Daryl?" Daryl Cummins was a homeless vet I talked to from time to time. He'd been in the first Gulf War and had suffered from various health issues afterward. While the government debated whether Gulf War Syndrome was a thing, Daryl started using drugs to ease his suffering. Daryl was a good guy, but no amount of effort on my part had gotten him off the street. Over the last two years, he'd become my eyes and ears on the common late at night.

"That's him. He said he was down there trying to find some friend of his — Jo-Jo."

"Yeah, I know Jo-Jo," I said with a frown. Jo-Jo was a homeless woman I'd busted a few times for petty theft in my patrol days, an addict and, I thought, not good enough for Daryl. But the heart wants what the heart wants.

"Daryl said that he saw some dealer named LJ harassing our vic over twenty bucks worth of weed. By the way, we identified the victim finally; his name is Leon Davis from Memphis, Tennessee. We called his next of kin."

"That's great!" I said, thrilled that we had some movement on the case. We'd worked it to death the first three weeks, and then everything went cold. Honestly, I had never asked Daryl about it because he was never down that way, at least as far as I'd known. Dumb luck, I guess. "So, on the Caldwell case, neither Gabe nor his buddy Takahashi from Japan called at all? They said they needed to come in with a lawyer, but Kineda has those on retainer by the dozen. I don't get it."

Before I could comment, Larson hollered so loud it made me jump. "Hey, Reagan!"

"Fuck," I muttered and gritted my teeth, taking deep breaths to stave off a vision of Sgt. Holley's face screaming at me in the latrine as he held my face down on the floor. "Coming, Lieutenant."

"You okay?" Carlos asked, probably seeing me tense up.

"Yeah." I forced my shoulders back down. "I'm fine."

I walked into Larson's office and closed the door. "What can I do for you, Lieutenant?"

"Couple of things," he said, standing with his hands on his hips. "You need to tell your boyfriend that we need to talk to him."

"No shit," I said forcefully. "You think I don't know that. I expected him in today. Hell, I told him to come in today. He said he needed to find a lawyer."

Larson's eyebrows shot up. "A lawyer? What the fuck for?"

"Look," I said, not wanting to explain to the Lieutenant that I'd told Gabe to bring one. "I'll make sure he comes by tomorrow if I have to twist his fucking ear."

Larson sat down behind his desk with a heavy thump, clearly stressed out. "Please."

"Is everything okay?"

"No, it's not. It's like something straight out of a movie. Marcella Carson made one fucking phone call upstairs. So, I had to listen to the Commissioner tell me what a high priority the Caldwell case is." Larson took a breath, then a drink from a glass of water. I just waited, eyeballing the umpteen civic and law enforcement awards on the wall. "You must have made quite the impression on Marcella Carson because she's insisted on dealing with only you. What's worse, the Commissioner agreed."

Very persuasive, Carlos had said. "Okay, we can handle that. What else?"

"You will brief me on this case every three days. Email is fine. I don't want to be caught flat-footed with the Commissioner when she asks for a status."

"Yes, sir."

"And Reagan?" he said as I turned toward his door.

"Yes?"

"Don't fuck this up."

On that joyful note, I left his office. "Fuck," I mumbled again.

I looked at my watch — 10:05 PM. When I got back to my desk, I called Gabe's number on my cell. It went straight to voice mail. I ended the call without leaving a message. *Where the fuck are you?*

"Hey, Mills?" I called out over my cube. No answer. "Carol?"

"Yeah," she replied. She sounded like she was coming back from the restroom. "What do you need, honey?"

"Did Forensics send over their preliminary on Caldwell?" I rubbed my forehead.

"Yup, it's right here," she walked over and laid a fat, blue folder down on my desk. "It should be in your email, too. Let me know if it's not there, and I'll forward a copy." I checked; she was right. The report had shown up in my Inbox at eight-thirty. Someone over there had been working late on this.

"Thanks. And Carol? You're a good friend. I don't think I say that enough."

She smiled, looking a bit confused. "You too. Is there something you want to talk about?"

I thought about telling her exactly what was bothering me but instead said, "No, just wanted you to know."

I sat down for a minute and tried to read through some older case files, prepping for court, but I couldn't concentrate. My head was filled with visions of Marcella Carson. God, she was so—attractive. Not just physically beautiful, but everything. Her voice still sang in my head, silky with a hint of rasp. And it was clear she was intelligent, and those eyes, ice blue and penetrating. I tried to push her out of my mind and failed, so I stood and looked out the window, noting that the rain had stopped. Turning back to pack up, I noticed a post-it had been placed on my chair. It read:

I'll transcribe my notes from the Carson interview.
Better dreams tonight, I bet.
— C

What an asshole, I thought sarcastically and laughed as I left the building.

8

A light drizzle started again as I walked home from my parking spot. I clutched the files to my chest and hurried to the building, pulling open the door just as the clouds opened up and fat pelting drops began to fall. Junk mail jammed my mailbox until it was hard to open, all Chinese food menus, pizza delivery fliers, and one ad for a used car warranty. I threw them in the trash bin and almost missed the small manila craft-paper envelope buried among them. I turned it over and read the handwritten return address on the back.

Morgan Kennedy
486 Oakley Ave.
Chicago, IL 60636

All at once, my heart leaped into my throat, then dropped right into my gut.

"Damnit," I said quietly. "I don't need this right now." Part of me really wanted to tear away the crisp Manila paper, exposing whatever lay within.

Why was she writing after all these years? Did something happen? Maybe she misses me. Maybe—. Slow down, Cait; it's probably an anniversary invitation or something.

I put the letter in my stack of files and headed up the stairs.

A dark figure stood next to my door in the empty, pitch-black hallway. I dropped the files and drew out my firearm and pocket flashlight. Before I'd even raised my weapon, my flashlight lit on Gabe's face. He looked like shit.

I breathed a sigh of relief. "Jesus! Gabe, what the fuck? You should know better than to hover by my door like that in the dark. Do you want to get yourself shot?"

He had a weird, goofy grin on his face. "Aw, you wouldn't shoot me, honey."

"I almost did. You scared the shit out of me. Wait, what are you doing out here? You have a key."

"It's at home."

I smelled booze on his breath and scowled. "Are you drunk?"

"I've probably had one or two more than I should have, but I'm okay."

I moved to open the door, realizing he wasn't just tipsy drunk; he was headed toward falling down, passing out drunk. "Jesus, Gabe. How much have you had?"

Inside, I turned on the light, finally seeing him clearly. He looked like absolute crap. His dirty blond hair was mussed, and a day's stubble covered his square jaw. His face looked a little ruddy around his small nose. His tragically beautiful brown eyes were booze-watery and sunken. A dark bruise was blooming on his forehead.

"I was out with Brad and Anne. We went to that new tequila bar over on St. James. I had a few shots."

"That Lexical or Mezcal or whatever joint?" I'd seen the place a hundred times but never set foot in there. "Wait. Did you say Brad and Anne? Matthews?"

Brad was one of Gabe's old college buddies and worked for a local bottom-feeder law practice. I'd met him when Gabe and I had first started dating. Brad was an absolute prick. Brad had tried to feel me up under the table while Gabe was in the restroom. I'd left him with a red splotch and a bloody lip.

"Every time you go out with Brad, you get wasted. You're too old for this shit." I set my gear and keys on the table.

"Brad—," he started, then paused as he began to look green. I was sure he was going to puke all over my floor. He stifled it with a hard swallow. "Brad made partner."

"So I guess it's Sullivan, Stan, and Matthews, now. Lovely. Well, good for him. But did you have to get piss drunk?"

"I'm not that drunk," he said. And then, as if the gods themselves ordained it, he hiccuped. Then he laughed as if it was uproariously funny. I didn't laugh. I was fucking furious.

"Gabe," I stated calmly and firmly. "You can not be here. If you had come in and had —." Then, I had a revelation. "Wait. Did you hire Brad to represent you?"

"Yup," he said. "It jusht took me a whi—while—to get him on the phone becaush he wash in court today." His slurring was getting worse, splashing his words all over the place.

"Okay," I said, pointing at the door. "out. Now."

Gabe crossed the space between us and began trying to kiss me on the face, neck, mouth— pretty much anywhere he could. "Come on, honey," he said. "We haven't had sex in three w—weeks."

"Stop!" I attempted to push him off, starting to panic.

When he went after my shirt buttons, I slapped him.

"What — wha — you do that for?" he asked. His speech was now almost unintelligible. I'd seen guys do this before; they drank way too much, too fast, and got drunker even after they quit.

"Because I said stop. No means fucking no." I pointed to the door again, now on the edge of shouting. "Now get out, and I expect an apology in the morning. Go!"

Gabe walked to the door, looking like a kicked puppy. I felt a little guilty for hurling him out into the night, but I wasn't going to put up with this.

"Oh," I said to his back. "Make sure your ass shows up tomorrow for your statement. Bring Brad if you like, but if you don't show up, I will drag your ass down there."

"Fine," he said. "How am I supposed to get home? My car is — my car is — well, I don't know where my car is, but —"

"I'll order you a ride. Go wait outside," I said.

He turned around and flipped me off, slamming the door

behind him.

I groaned in frustration. *What the actual fuck?* I thought. As tough as my day had been, I had half a mind just to let him sit there until he threw up and passed out.

"Damnit, Gabe," I swore to myself.

I had seen Gabe drink before, but a wicked gross mental fit like this? Never. I chalked it up to Brad's influence. I ordered him a ride from my phone and waited on the veranda until it showed up. He flipped me off again as he got in.

Sighing, I walked over to the couch and sat down. Jabba was sitting up, looking at me expectantly. "Et tu brute? Et tu?"

I proceeded to scratch his belly, and he flopped down, sticking all four feet in the air. "At least you're not drunk, you little slut." I scratched him for a few minutes more and then stood to his griping meows.

"Sorry, buddy, I have stuff to do."

I grabbed a shower and changed into some pajamas. The heat was back on, thankfully. And, with the day's grime off of me, I set the files on the floor neatly and got to work.

Not far into my perusal of the documents, I eyed the cabinet next to the sink that held a single bottle of red wine. I usually didn't drink alcohol. I didn't know why. Somewhere along the way, I'd just become a non-drinker.

"Fuck it," I said a little loudly and got up.

Opening the bottle, I tried to let it sit. But after five minutes, I decided I didn't give a shit if it had time to breathe and poured. It turns out; it didn't matter. It was good, really good. I could feel my mouth respond to the dryness and the tannins. After a long drink, I leaned against the counter and sighed, holding the glass to my breast. It had been such a long day.

Still sipping my glass, I grabbed the bottle and went over to sit on the floor, and something occurred to me. I did a quick review of Patrol's initial report and the now neatly printed witness statement from Karen Walters. I knew it was late, but I called Karen Walter's contact number anyway on the off chance she might be awake.

It rang a few times and went to voicemail.

"Ms. Walters," I said, forcing myself to smile and sound upbeat. Many people don't realize that the minor inflections in vocal patterns caused by a smile can be heard. "This is Detective Reagan from BPD Homicide. Can you give me a call? I have a question about your statement I need to clear up. It's probably nothing, but I'd like to ask you about it as soon as possible." I left my number and hung up. A few minutes later, my phone rang. The caller ID said 'Fred Walters.' I snatched up my notepad and answered.

"Detective Reagan, Homicide." This woman had had quite a shock the night before, so I did my best to be soft and friendly.

"Detective Reagan?" Karen Walters sounded slightly nervous. Most people do when talking to cops. "This is Karen Walters. You said you wanted to talk to me about my statement?"

"Yes," I said. "I didn't see mention of a cell phone in our case files. Did you, by chance, have one on you this morning on your run?"

"Yes," she said. "I always run with it — for music."

"Did you take any pictures or video when you found the body last night?" I grimaced a little in anticipation. It was worth asking, as sometimes things like this got missed.

"If I say yes, do I need a lawyer?" she asked.

"You're always entitled to have a lawyer, ma'am. But your video could be relevant and help us find the killer. Supposing you did, though, I could really use a copy. If you send me a copy via text, it could be very helpful for my investigation."

"Just a second, Detective," she said. I heard some rustling, a thump, and some cursing. A few seconds later, my phone dinged in my ear, indicating an incoming message. "I just have the one video."

"You haven't posted it online anywhere, have you?" I asked to follow up.

"No," she said. "I really don't know why I took the video. I should probably just delete it."

"No!" I responded quickly and a little too loudly. "Sorry. Don't do that. What would be better would be if you could come to Headquarters and ask for Detective Jessica Doyle. She can get the data off your phone then and there in a forensically sound fashion. I can let her know you are coming."

"Okay, what time?" she asked, sounding slightly less nervous. "This is kind of exciting in a way. I've never been useful to the police for anything, ever." Typical, a man was dead, people in mourning, and she's excited that she gets to help. It was human nature, but it always struck me as wrong, somehow.

"Anytime between eight and four tomorrow," I said. "I'll let Jessica know you're coming."

"Okay. Thank you," Ms. Walters said.

At least she was polite.

"Thank you, Ms. Walters," I said as sweetly as I could muster and hung up.

I immediately pulled up the video on my phone. Ms. Walters had a damn nice phone. The video was crystal clear, not the grainy shit I expected. I scrolled through the video repeatedly, looking for anything; then, I found it. In the dirt, right where we guessed our perp was standing, sat one clear shoe impression, identical to the one I found by the tree. And then I spotted a second one. This time, it was in blood next to the body.

"Bless you, Ms. Walters, and whatever fabulous phone you carry," I said to myself quietly. "Fuckin' A."

I went back to the crime scene photos to see if I'd missed the shoe prints. I couldn't see how; they would have been obvious. Looking in the same spot, I could see a smear across the paving stones. Someone had probably tried to clean the blood off their shoe — likely Ms. Walters. There were no photos of the area behind the building. Either the crime scene unit missed the shoe impression, or someone had, more likely, ruined it. I shot a message off to Detective Doyle, letting her know to expect Ms. Walters and for what. I also included a copy of the picture I'd taken of the shoe impression I'd found earlier.

Taking a drink of wine, I scoured the rest of the paperwork, taking notes and refiling as I finished each page. It turned out that we were correct; the splinter that Carlos and I saw in the photo of Mr. Caldwell's chest wound was wood, a species of English ash.

Last but not least, I perused Mr. Caldwell's phone records, scanning the list of numbers, starting the morning before he died. I recognized one immediately — Gabe's. His number called Caldwell's four times that day. The last call was at eleven-twenty.

"Oh, Gabe, what are you into?" I whispered to myself, running my hand through my hair as my gut twisted into a knot.

What did I know about Gabe, really? He was thirty-five, an avid environmentalist, drove an electric car, and gave money to the ASPCA. He absolutely adored animals. He could be an asshole, occasionally, yes. Most of the time, though, Gabe was a saint. But, after a year, I didn't know his favorite food, his favorite movie, even his favorite sport. I knew where he worked and had met his parents. I also knew his favorite song was *Thunderstruck* by AC/DC. That was it.

Jesus, after a year, I know almost nothing about him. I am such a shitty girlfriend. Of course, now I know why. Sighing heavily, I stuffed that aside and continued.

Gabe was the last person to call the victim. He knew the victim's name before I mentioned it to him. Though, Gabe did explain that. He didn't show up to make his statement at HQ, hadn't even bothered to call. He came in drunk and acting way out of character. Sometimes people act strangely when under stress. Being caught up in homicide can make you very stressed. So can being unsure of your relationship, though. And if I was uncertain and confused, he probably was too—or maybe not.

Stop, Cait. You don't know Gabe's involved, and you're not objective.

Doug, our previous lead, often told me that a gut feeling, like the sinking one I had right now, was the evidence talking to you. I didn't like what it seemed to be saying.

Fortunately, the heavy rain had passed for now. The clouds were low, and a drizzle still drifted in the soft breeze. I stood and walked out to the balcony. Below, the street was mostly empty, but I could see a silhouette in the distance, maybe a block away, just out of the street light.

I had a sudden creepy feeling of being watched. All the hairs on the back of my neck stood up. I went back inside to grab my glass of wine. Nonchalantly, I strode back out and leaned on the railing. The figure was still there. It was impossible to see any details from my veranda. It could have been a woman, I supposed. I raised my glass in salute to see what they'd do. They just turned and walked away into the darkness.

"Well, that was creepy," I said to myself and lit up a smoke. I shivered a little as I did so. The temperature was dropping.

I waited a bit longer on the veranda to see if my visitor returned— they didn't. So, I returned inside and corked the wine bottle. With the case file organized, I picked it up to put it away. Something slid across the floor, and I looked back —Morgan's letter. I was too tired to deal with it tonight. I picked up the letter and stuck it under the same magnet as the unopened envelope from ten years ago.

Even emotionally and physically exhausted, I lay awake for about an hour, my mind racing, thinking about Marcella. I tossed and turned, unable to get my mind off her. Fantasies of kissing her drifted through my head, so exciting and terrifying that I couldn't think. I finally gave in and took half a Benadryl. And it wasn't very long before I yawned and knew no more.

9

She is standing before me—Marcella Carson, temptation incarnate. I am unsure how I got here, and I think this must be a dream.

The ankle-length red dress caresses the curve of her hips as it clings to her body. It is slit to the hip, and I can see the muscular calf and thigh of her left leg tantalizingly propped on a black patent leather heel. The cloth seems to shimmer in the shifting light. The bust of the dress just covers her breast and leaves little to my imagination. Thin straps cling to her shapely shoulders that flow into well-toned arms, milk-skin soft and inviting. The curve of her neck is perfection, each inch unlined and beautiful. I look at her red-stained lips, slightly parted on her breathtaking face, framed by golden hair. Her ice-blue eyes capture my gaze and hold me.

There is something wanton and lascivious within me. I am helpless. I can not think for the fear and excitement and lust that fills me, mixing headily into raging desire. I want this woman—like I've never wanted anything. Within me, a vast, desperate need reaches out for her.

I feel her fingers brush the back of my neck, and my body comes to life with a shiver — every hair standing on end. I am hot, flushed in anticipation as she presses in closer. Her breasts press against mine, and her long stocking-clad leg slides against my own as she leans in, her cheek against my face.

"I know you." Her words slide into my ears on a wisp of air, bringing a shiver to my spine. Around us, the world is a soft cacophony of swirling whispers, barely heard and indiscernible, but my attention is solely hers. She draws back, light fibrils of hair just tickling at the skin of my shoulder. Everything, every sensation, every sound she makes, is all clear as crystal. Her hand brushes against my bare ribs, startling me slightly. My heart is a rabbit in my chest, thumping away. I feel dizzy and lost in eroticism. God, I am so—. I am unable to finish the thought as she speaks.

"Tell me that you want this."

"Yes, please." My voice is small and submissive.

"Good girl," she whispers, and I feel a part of me let go, giving in.

Marcella leans in and brushes her lips to mine, soft and teasing. My lips part; my eyes close. The world becomes a dark well of sensation and sound and erotic pleasure. The strange whispers have ceased, replaced by the more prurient whispers of her dress sliding against her skin — and mine.

Finally able to move, I wrap my arms around her in desperation, drawing her closer, tighter. Her lips slide across my neck, followed by her teeth on my throat, nibbling. Again, goose flesh rises all over me, and I tilt my head back to give her better access, tangling my fingers in her long, luxurious blond hair. She nips and bites teasingly until finally slicing in with her teeth, sharp and stinging — painful. The bite brings a soft whimper from my lips.

"Oh, God." My voice is breathy and thin.

I feel a deep tug from within as if every blood vessel were being drawn away toward that one painful, pleasurable area at my throat. The noises of Marcella's attentions are wet, lubricious. I cry out in pleasure as an intense orgasm shudders through me, subsuming the pain and causing my knees to buckle. She buoys me in her arms and presses her lips harder to my torn flesh.

I open my eyes, heavy-lidded, and Marcella pulls back again, her chin coated in liquid red— my blood in her mouth and on her face, as it should be. I watch, bewitched, as bloody rivulets of my life slide down her throat onto her slightly exposed breast, crossing a faint scar near her collar bone. She leans in and kisses me again. I can taste the hot, salty iron of my own blood and something else, something thick and cool. My vision tunnels and my head swims as the world starts to grow dark. I would give her anything — blood, life, soul — as she holds me there, my body moving in convulsive pleasure. The experience is so intensely, deliciously carnal.

I can feel another orgasm welling up within as she returns to her ministrations, intent on consuming me.

✳ ✳ ✳

My eyes shot open and then squeezed closed as I arched my back in a wave of pleasure and stifled an intense moan into my arm. The orgasm was exquisite, long, and so powerful my legs shook.

"Holy shit," I breathed, giddy with fading excitement. "Well, that was — intense." I lay there for long moments, unable to move. The dream was so vivid, so profoundly physical. I could still feel the pulse of arousal beating through me, and I slid my hands downward between—.

My phone rang, still out in the living room.

"Really?" I implored to the empty air — "Un-fucking-believable."

I rushed out to answer the damn thing, legs a little wobbly. Then I saw who it was; I almost didn't answer it.

"Gabe." My voice was flat and stern.

"I'm so sorry."

"And?" I prompted.

"I'll come to the station today to give my statement." He sounded like a scolded child, and it was actually kind of adorable if a bit ill-timed. It was hard to stay mad at him, but I didn't let myself relent, not yet.

"Fine. Good. What got into you last night? You're usually not like that."

"It's this whole Carson thing. It's gotten into my head."

He suddenly had one hundred percent of my attention. "What do you mean?"

"This was a huge opportunity. Carson was looking for a new vaccine supplier for TCD. They're looking for a new vendor for influenza and some others. I had it in the bag." Everyone knew TCD; they were a humanitarian organization that managed and provided health care in the third world and combat zones.

Gabe sounded truly frustrated and angry. "Now, Caldwell's dead, and Marcella Carson isn't accepting any calls. That was a three-hundred thousand dollar commission for me. It was my first large-scale deal, and now it may not happen. If we can't get this done, we may lose the TCD account as well."

"Gabe," I interrupted, very soft and level. "I can't talk to you about this right now. You need to come to the station and lay all of this out."

"What? I thought you'd understand. This was going to get me into the President's Club this year. You know, the trip to Ibiza. We were going to have such a good time. Why are you being such a bitch?"

"Gabe," I said, again very level. "You're right; I've been a bitch for the last couple of days; you don't deserve that. But, I cannot talk to you about anything related to Carson Logistics. You need to go down to the station and give your statement to one of my teammates. Bring Haimon if you can, but you need to come down today, Haimon or no Haimon." I waited for him to respond.

"Honey?" he prodded, the concern rising in his voice. "What's going on?"

"Gabe, honey — " I paused and swallowed. "Please just promise me that you will go to the station between two and ten today and give your statement. I may or may not be there, but one of my team will take it. I do love you; I hope you know that."

The other end of the phone was silent. I couldn't say anything, and Gabe wasn't the type to understand my job and its restrictions. Like most suburban white kids, he had never had any significant interactions with the police. The whole affair made me feel like shit.

His voice turned desperate. "Okay, I get it. But, honey, I had nothing to do with this. You have to believe me."

"That's good then. Just go to the station and put this behind you. Then we can talk." I ended the call and immediately felt like an absolute piece of garbage. But there was nothing I could do. He certainly wasn't a murderer, and there wasn't any evidence to tie him to the crime, but it didn't look great, either. He just needed to go down and explain things. I hoped that would settle it.

How did my life suddenly get so complicated? It had gone from stable and probably a little too static to entirely out of control in twenty-four hours. My love life, my sexuality, maybe even my job, they all felt up in the air. I plopped down on the sofa and put my face in my hands. It didn't take long before tears sprang forth.

Jabba came and curled up in my lap, meowing and rubbing his face all over my arms and hands. I laughed a little at his attempt at consolation.

"Come here, buddy," I said through my sniffles, cradling him in my arms. "You'd make a pretty good boyfriend." I leaned back on the sofa, still stroking Jabba's fur, and tried to do what Jennifer taught me. I began breathing slowly from my abdomen — in through the nose, out through the mouth. Gradually, the tears stopped, but a feeling of hopelessness had settled into me, leaving me feeling tired. I didn't have to be on shift until two, so I decided that a bit of self-pity and gelato were in order.

A few minutes later, with a cat, a spoon, and a half-filled container of vanilla bean gelato, I sat in my bed drowning my sorrows. But, it didn't take long for me to finish the gelato and go back to sleep, leaving the container on the floor so Jabba could lick out the inside.

I was awakened about two hours later by Jabba's plaintive mewing and a somewhat hollow whap-whap sound. I got up to see what the little fur-ball had gotten into. What I found pushed aside my misery instantly. Jabba was on the floor, in a fit, his head stuck in the gelato container. The noise I'd heard was him running into things as he flailed around to get it off. I covered my mouth and started laughing.

I slowly removed the container from his head. "Oh, baby, you are the best cat in the world. But, honey, you are so dumb sometimes." I laughed again and trashed the container. I looked at my watch—11:28 AM. Time to get going, anyway.

I needed to do something rather than wallow in more self-pity. I had come to realize that work was my only escape, pathetic as that was. So I showered and dressed and headed to Schroeder.

10

Our whole corner of the floor was a ghost town, not that I expected anything else at just after twelve. Plopping down at my desk, I wrote a warrant for Gabe's phone records and sent it to the DA. There was nothing for it as heart-wrenching as it was to snoop my boyfriend's phone records. God, I need some coffee.

Even though Carlos' had given me carte blanche access to his Café Bustelo, I felt a little guilty taking it. But, a few minutes later, I decided it was totally worth it. And, by the time I'd finished my first cup, much of my morning misery was a long-forgotten memory. That was fortunate given who called me moments later.

"Homicide, Reagan."

"Detective Reagan?" It was Marcella Carson's beautiful British cadence. I could have happily listened to this woman read a dictionary, and gooseflesh immediately popped on my arms and neck.

I tried to mask my abrupt nervousness and be cool. "Yes, Ms. Carson."

"I have the copies of Jesse's diary, sorry, schedule, and a list of his projects along with relevant documentation. There is some information that I cannot disclose for reasons of confidentiality. I hope you understand."

I grabbed a pen from my desk, twirling it in my fingers,

as I recalled Carlos' comments on moving firearms for the government. "I understand. Anything you provide may help, though. Thank you."

"It's really no trouble, Detective."

"So, when will you be here?"

"I'm sorry, Detective, I am swamped today. But, I generally take tea at about three-thirty. Do you think you could come by and pick them up, then? I can have Ninetta fix something for you. I'm sure, on your schedule, you'd like a bite about then."

I almost laughed. *God, Cait, thirsty much?* Instead, I cleared my throat. "That'd be fine. I'll come by around three-thirty, then."

"Brilliant! I look forward to seeing you, then."

I felt a little flutter in my belly but forced formality into my voice. "Yes, ma'am."

"Detective, please, call me Marcella."

"Yes, ma'am," I replied, a stupid grin on my face, and hung up. I was so flustered and excited that I had forgotten to say goodbye.

Jesus, Cait, you're not going on a date. You're going to pick up evidence.

The next few hours passed dismally slowly. I confirmed that Doyle had received Karen Walter's cell phone, and then I did a case review with the team. I had trouble concentrating, though. My nervousness rose the closer I got to seeing Marcella again, and I kept losing track of my thoughts, remembering last night's dream. Finally, terrifyingly, the clock ticked over to three, and I left the building.

The ride to the Carson residence was pleasant. One could hardly call the place an office. I suspected Marcella Carson used the second-floor offices for convenience and a fat tax write-off.

Having swapped my stereo for the police radio, I'd resorted to listening to music on my phone, praising the wonders of noise-canceling earbuds. And, though it was cold, the music and sunshine had brightened my mood considerably. Stepping out of the car, I felt much more ready to take on Marcella Carson and her fabulous legs, last night's dream notwithstanding. I even found a parking spot along the square.

Keep it professional. I repeated the mantra over and over in my head as I walked. But, my bravado melted when I knocked on the doors, leaving bees buzzing about in my stomach. I wanted to see her again, maybe just look at her for a while.

Shit. I have a crush. Come on, Cait, what are you, twelve?

"Ah, Ms. — Um — Detective Reagan. Come inside, please." Ninetta's words were inviting, even if her face seemed almost hostile. "The Signora is in the sitting room." She led me through the sliding oak doors to a finely furnished sitting area. Two beautiful Queen Anne chairs sat opposite an expensive sofa. A small cherry wood table perched between the chairs sporting an exquisite porcelain tea set.

Marcella Carson sat in one of the chairs, the light from the burning fireplace giving her pale complexion a coppery shimmer. She was fingering her hair, expertly tied back in Celtic braids that must have taken her an hour to do. My simple ponytail felt ridiculous in comparison.

As I walked in, Marcella rose with feline grace, adjusting a red blouse of raw silk. Looking down at me from atop four-inch heels, she cracked a dazzling smile, inviting and, I thought, a little flirtatious. The sheer style on display was thoroughly intimidating.

I tried to keep my hand from trembling as I held it out. "Ms. Carson."

"Marcella, please, Detective. Ms. Carson makes me sound like someone's mother. How was your drive over? Uneventful, I hope?" Her voice slid through my head like velvet, so much better in person. She took my hand in hers, holding it just a tiny bit longer than necessary.

"Thank you," I offered as Ninetta poured me a small cup of coffee and offered me a seat on the sofa opposite Marcella. It smelled fabulous and tasted better—literally the smoothest coffee I had ever had. "God, this is amazing; what is it?"

"Kopi Luwak," Marcella replied, the corners of her mouth turning up. "It's Indonesian — considered the best in the world. Just don't ask how it's made." Her smile held a suspicious glimmer of some inside joke.

Marcella hoisted a thick accordion file into her lap from behind her, and I started to rise to pick it up. But she held up a hand, placing the file on the chair next to her. "Please, Detective Reagan, relax. We have time."

"Well, I don't want to keep you from your busy schedule," I responded in an attempt to cut the conversation short and escape. But, Marcella was having none of it.

"Jesse was one of my best friends," she countered. "I want to make sure you have whatever I can provide. Besides, we probably need to go over the projects here. Unless, of course, you have other things you need to do."

So much for that idea. I felt heat creep up my neck as I sat back down. "No, ma'am." I swallowed, and it sounded loud to my ears.

"Good, I cleared my schedule, so we could take the afternoon to work on this." Her face was impassive and damn hard to read.

Cleared her schedule? Swamped, huh.

"Okay, well, then, I have a few questions I'd like to follow up on before we crack open the information on the vic — Mr. Caldwell."

Well done, Cait, very sensitive.

"Please, Detective, it's Marcella, not Ms. Carson or ma'am or anything else. I insist." Her words were scolding, but she smirked as she said them.

"Sorry, Marcella, it's the force of habit — army and all that."

"Yes, your military service was quite impressive as I understand it."

I raised an eyebrow. *Did she pull my service record?* I shouldn't have been surprised, given what Carlos had mentioned about government contracts.

"It was a war. I was like any other soldier." I said it without inflection, hoping she'd get the hint and ditch the subject.

"Truly Detective? A purple heart, a distinguished service medal — you were nominated for the CMH as well, I believe." At my expression, she added, "please don't look so surprised. I like to know about the people with whom I deal."

"Sorry. It's not something I generally talk about with strangers," I admitted, deflecting her line of inquiry.

"I understand. I'm sorry. I was just curious." She looked genuinely concerned that she might have offended me. Watching her stick her foot in it made me feel a little better. She was human, after all.

I needed to get control of the conversation, so I played her interest against her. "I'll tell you what. Let's take the next few minutes to get to know each other — say, to the end of our coffee? Then, we can get to the business at hand."

"Absolutely! However, we've wasted most of the first cup on silly pleasantries and banter. I insist on a second." Ninetta appeared from nowhere and provided both of us with a fresh cup of coffee. Instead of a tiny teacup, she handed me a fat twelve-ounce mug. It was adorned with a cartoon vampire woman with bleary eyes and bedhead captioned with 'I'm not a morning person.'

I knew immediately that I was out of my depth. I had steered cold-hearted murderers into confessing and understood the tactics of manipulation well. Marcella had just worked me over like a rookie. I was willing to bet that she planned most of that exchange. Probably so she could suggest a little quid-pro-quo, Hannibal Lecter style. And, I'd walked right into it.

Part of me wanted to bail right then, and I raised the coffee mug. "Well played."

If I tried to back out now, she would dangle the file. If I tried to play coy in my answers, she'd think me impersonal and rude. Carlos had been right; she was used to getting what she wanted.

She raised an appreciative eyebrow and half-hid a smile behind her cup in a way that seemed to say, 'good girl.' *Is she flirting with me?*

"So, I saw a picture of your mother," I started. "I think you might forgive me for thinking that you budded from her like some plant pod."

Marcella's laugh flowed over me, rich and warm. "No, Detective, I had a father. I just inherited very different things from him. You're not the first to mention my likeness to my mother."

She set down her cup, and her face took on a faraway look. "My mother came from old money, and my father was more the adventuring type. Their relationship was brief, and he wasn't present for much of my childhood. I do remember him coming home once when I was about ten, I think. But he didn't stay long. A few weeks after he left, we found out he had been killed. His killers — well, that's a story for another time. How about you? What are your parents like?"

I looked at her, wondering how much to say. Usually, I kept a strict line between my work and personal life. On the other hand, there wasn't a rule that I couldn't get to know the lady. *Gasp, Cait, you might actually make a friend.* I decided to be candid.

"Ma is Irish, born in the Gaeltacht," I told her. "She's a linguistics professor at Boston College. My da was a Boston cop. He died when I was sixteen. That was a rough time, but Ma and I got through it. But, having just lost him a few years before, my ma had a fit when I joined the army. When I returned from my second tour, after—." I stumbled for a second, squeezing my eyes shut to banish an unbidden image of McCall laying dead on the evac chopper.

"Are you okay?" Marcella placed a cool hand on my forearm, voice filled with concern.

"Yes. Just a second." I cleared my throat and opened my eyes to find Marcella almost kneeling before me, holding a handkerchief she had produced from somewhere. I took it and dabbed at my eyes, trying to clear my throat again. "Sorry, this is why I don't talk about the war."

She said nothing, just waited patiently. Her eyes held me for a moment. They were the same blue eyes of my dream; every strand of her irises seemed placed as I remembered. And somewhere in those blue eyes, I saw a bit of understanding.

I took a sip of my coffee to wet my throat. "After the incident, Ma met me in Landstuhl at the military hospital. If there were recriminations in her head, she never voiced them. She just told me she was happy I was alive.

"A month later, I was re-deployed into an injured status and given desk duty at Fort Devens, walking guard duty and pushing paper for reservists. I was taken off active duty six months after that. So, I used my GI bill to go to college, and here I am."

"For what it may be worth, Detective, I'm no stranger to trauma, and I'm sorry you had to go through that." She sounded sincere, and I was suddenly very aware of how close she was. I gently moved my arm from under her touch.

"I'm sorry," Marcella apologized, standing and settling back to her chair. "That was inappropriate of me."

"No, Ms. Car—Marcella. It's alright." As she moved away, I felt genuine disappointment, and I took a deep breath. "So, this place, it's ginormous. Do you live here alone?"

"Well, Ninetta lives here with me." Marcella gestured toward a door in the back of the room. "She manages almost every aspect of my personal life. Other than that, I am alone."

She walked over to the doorway, looking up toward the foyer ceiling. Her voice adopted a soulful tone as she said, "I must confess, though, it is a lonely place. I travel so much for business that I rarely have time to date. I truly miss actual companionship. Ninetta is nice, and she's my friend, but —" She trailed off.

I couldn't figure out if she spoke to me or simply talked to get it out.

Her tone then shifted to one of pleasant invitation. "Come, Detective, let's get to work. I think the kitchen table would be best. We can spread out, and there is good light to work by.

Also, there are snacks."

I had intended to grab the materials and go, but now I didn't want to leave. While I hoped we might find a lead in the files, I had to admit that I just wanted to stay near Marcella for a bit longer. Somewhere in the distant reaches of my brain, alarms were going off, but I ignored them.

As it turned out, the kitchen was more expansive than my apartment. While I gawked, Marcella set the files on a small four-seat round table of expensive wood, polished to a shine.

"May I?" I asked as I drooled at the appliances.

"Of course, feel free to look around."

A large marble island dominated the center of the kitchen, surrounded on three sides by some of the finest appliances I had ever seen outside a professional kitchen. As I reached for the handle of an enormous Traulsen refrigerator that could hold at least three dead bodies, Ninetta stepped in front of me from nowhere.

"I am preparing something sensitive in there," she said quickly. "Please don't open it."

I grimaced in apology. "Sorry."

Ninetta didn't move, and I couldn't get past her to inspect the rest of the kitchen. So, I walked back to the table. "I'd kill for this kitchen. I mean, the cooking I would do. Just wow."

That peaked Marcella's attention. "Oh? You cook?"

I smiled broadly. "When I have a reason to."

She raised a sly eyebrow as if maneuvering me into a corner. "Do you have a favorite dish?"

"My mother charmed a great recipe for Bolognese out of the chef at Grassona's before he retired. It's amazing. Umm. . . You're not a vegetarian, are you?" I asked hesitantly. *Why did I care if she was a vegetarian?*

Marcella pounced on the question. "Why, Detective? Are you offering to come here and make me dinner? Of course, I accept. And, no, I'm not a vegetarian."

"Wait, what?"

"I'm sorry," she said with a laugh. "Were you not inviting me to have a home-cooked meal?"

"Uh. . ." I stuttered for a second. "Well, I-. Shit."

"Excellent!" Marcella clapped her hands. "I'm looking forward to it. What night?"

"I can try to do it Monday night."

"Pish," she said lightheartedly. "Monday it is. And don't think I won't come to find you if you stand me up."

Of that, I had no doubt.

11

We sat at the kitchen table, where she drew out several thick folders from the accordion file.

"When did you do all of this?" The material was mountainous. As a cop, I'm used to extensive paperwork, but I'd be hard-pressed to put this together from our files over several days, let alone in less than twenty-four hours.

"Well, some of it I had already, and rather than toss and turn with insomnia, I got to work. Though, if I'm honest, I can't think of what we might find in here that will help." She paused for a moment. "I want to thank you, Detective."

"For what?" I asked, a little bewildered.

"For putting this kind of effort into Jesse's case. I want to see his killer dealt with." Her eyes turned angry and hard.

It was a strange turn of phrase. Honestly, the whole afternoon had been a little weird.

"Marcella?"

"Hmm?" She was in the middle of arranging the files into neat stacks according to the starting month of each project.

"Please don't take this the wrong way. But you seem less grief-stricken than I would expect."

She looked up from the papers. "I'm older than I look." She sighed heavily. "I will miss Jesse, his quick wit, his grousing over relationships, his bad jokes. But you are correct. I'm angry, outraged, really. He didn't deserve this; no one does."

"I'm sorry, I wasn't questioning your relationship. I was just curious." I turned back to the work at hand.

"It's quite alright. I know it's your job."

The files weren't a jumbled mess, but despite Marcella's protestations to the contrary, she had been hurried when she'd put them together. We had to go through each one, ensuring the correct data was in the appropriate folder. On the other hand, Caldwell's schedule was entirely in order and ready for review. As I flipped through it, I found a few redactions, which I asked about.

"Those are confidential meetings with government officials, and I can't share them with you without a release from the agencies involved. I'm sorry."

"No need to apologize; it may not matter."

"I can tell you that two of them were just contract re-negotiations that had stalled. The third was an audit of materials delivered overseas, a shipment that had been stolen when it arrived. All three projects were closed and reports long filed."

As we worked, Ninetta brought water to the table, giving me an inscrutable look as she set down the carafe and glasses. I tilted my head in question, but she just walked out. It was odd, but I turned back to Caldwell's diary. As I leisurely turned the pages, I spotted a glaring and rather disturbing discrepancy in the schedule.

"That's interesting," I murmured to myself. "I have a question." I pointed to Wednesday's date, and Marcella leaned over my shoulder, pushing back her hair. I could feel her proximity. She was so close that her breath tickled my neck, raising goosebumps and causing me to shiver slightly. I found it both enticing and a little unnerving. *Focus, Cait.*

"Yes, what is it?" she prompted when I didn't say anything.

I swallowed loudly and cleared my throat before speaking. "Was Caldwell the type to not put something in his calendar?"

"No, that wouldn't be like him. He was very thorough,

almost meticulous." I could still feel her breath on my neck as she spoke. I tried to brush the feeling aside, but it drove me nuts and made my pulse quicken. I finally tilted my head, and she backed away slightly.

"That's weird then. Gabe said he and his boss had a meeting with him yesterday, but it's not on his calendar." I rubbed my arm a little nervously. Marcella was still so close.

"Gabe?"

"My boyfriend," I replied without thinking and then grimaced inwardly. I hadn't wanted to bring Gabe into our discussion. I felt guilty enough as it was.

"You didn't mention you had a boyfriend." She paused, scrutinizing me with those incandescent eyes. "Oh—" Her tone softened. "Is it not working out?"

I jerked my head around. "Excuse me?"

"It's just— you seemed upset. I can tell you're very dedicated to your work. Does Gabe support your career?"

Wow, she is forward, I thought. *And a little nosy.* "Sure he does." Despite myself, I couldn't keep the sarcasm out of my voice.

Her brow furrowed in sympathy. "That bad?"

"That's not what I—."

"Detective," Marcella interrupted. "When people are in a solid relationship, probing about their significant other usually elicits a different response. Your answer was tepid at best. I assume he's not thrilled with your career."

Shit, I am so out of my depth.

I felt almost naked under her stare. In one question, she'd nailed one of the most significant issues Gabe and I shared—at least the issue we fought about most.

"We've never really discussed it," I lied. "I assume Gabe's okay with it."

"Well," Marcella said, turning back to the paper. "I would be proud to have such an accomplished companion." Feigned innocence looked cute on her; she wore it well.

"Ms. Carson, if I didn't know better, I'd think you were trying to flirt with me." Two could play the innocent.

"Oh, come, come, Detective. Of course, I'm flirting with you. You're an attractive woman, and unless I've read my cards wrong, my advances would not be unwelcome. Besides, everyone loves a buff woman, as I'm sure you're well aware." She followed the statement with a sweet smile, but her eyes were fierce and penetrating. The bottom dropped out of my stomach.

I cleared my throat again and took a sip of water, careful to keep my face neutral. Marcella was right; I found the attention flattering, but it felt discourteous. Yesterday she had seemed distraught over Caldwell's murder, and today, she appeared to be taking his death in stride. Again it was odd.

"I just feel like we're disrespecting Mr. Caldwell somehow."

She seemed to think about it for a minute and then spoke gently. "Detective, I loved Jesse. He's been a family friend for years. But this isn't the first time someone I've cared for has died suddenly. Not even the second. I just don't grieve like most people. I haven't since my mother died. I think I'm just built differently. I do feel bad that Jesse is gone. As I said, I'm going to miss him." Her brow furrowed for a moment. "But, life doesn't stop because of absent friends, and no one in my family was ever one to roam the halls tearing at their hair. My mother taught me to keep my chin up and press on. I took that lesson to heart long ago."

I heard a much deeper pain hiding under her behavior, though. She was grieving for Caldwell, and I found myself relieved. Cold-blooded killers didn't suffer for their victims. I didn't want to believe Marcella was a murderer.

"Of course, I'm sorry." I reached out my hand toward hers but thought better of it and pulled it back. Marcella smiled appreciatively at the gesture but said nothing and looked back to the papers.

"Pretty women don't have to apologize in this house, Detective." She didn't look up, but I could see the edges of a suppressed smile on her face. "That includes you."

"Uh-huh," I said and laughed nervously. "I thought you Brits were all supposed to be understated and evasive."

She flashed me a coquettish smile. "I'm Swedish Detective. I'm sure you'll find we have a very different reputation."

"Please, call me Cait."

"You know, Cait, you may just find that reputation to your liking."

I fought the urge to react—and lost. The corners of my mouth crooked up at the suggestive remark.

We returned to business. I took notes on what she told me, but the more we plunged through the stacks of papers, the more it became clear that Marcella was probably right. There wasn't much here, but my mind kept returning to the missing schedule entry; it was tickling at my gut.

"Could there have been something else work-related that might have led Jesse into trouble?" I asked, hoping for another avenue to pursue. "Anything he was working on that's not here?"

Marcella blew out an exasperated breath and looked up, irritation plain to see. "That's unlikely. My company doesn't involve itself in anything illegal. We don't ship illicit substances. And while we do occasionally deliver military supplies, we do it according to U.S. federal law. Such shipments are very lucrative to the organization, but almost every dollar goes back into humanitarian work or charity. We're above board and pay all of our taxes. This isn't the Trump Organization or Blackwater, Cait; we're a U.S. Non-Profit that does important humanitarian work."

"I'm sorry; I didn't mean to offend you," I apologized. I had been trying to empathize, not piss her off.

"I'm not offended. But, any implication that we might be anything but legitimate and law-abiding here is a tender spot for me. Now, can I ask you a question in return?"

"If I say no, will that stop you?"

"Of course not."

I sighed. "Okay, ask away." I reached for my water to take a sip.

"Why are you with your boyfriend?"

I coughed and spluttered into my glass. I'm not sure what I had expected her to ask, but it certainly wasn't that. "I'm sorry?"

"Well, when I inquired about your boyfriend, you turned sarcastic, and I think you were less than honest about his perspective on your career. It must be hard."

"Are you always this nosy?" I wiped the water off my chin with a napkin. Her drilling had struck oil again. I was profoundly unhappy, and I knew it, unhappy with my past, my regrets, my boyfriend, my life. The truth embedded in the question stung and sucked the wind out of my sails.

"You didn't answer the question."

"I don't know," I admitted softly, abruptly feeling very small and very upset. Marcella didn't say anything for a few minutes, and I tried to compose my jumbled thoughts. "We should probably stick to the case."

"Detective, I really do think you are quite pretty. But moreover, you have a fascinating intellect and such a strong heart. You manage a job that is so cruel and demanding without support. And that seems wrong, somehow. I know I seem terribly forward, but I don't believe in dawdling. Time should not be wasted." She looked at me with compassionate eyes for a moment longer.

I didn't know what to say, but I felt so exposed like my chest was being peeled open to reveal my heart. I dared not look up. The hard-boiled Detective laid bare by the beautiful woman; it was so cliché.

"Have you ever heard of Karin Boye?" She asked quietly.

"'Let me live truly, and truly die but once,'" I quoted automatically and froze. Karin Boye was one of my favorite poets, but her work also held a terrible secret for me. And I just knew that Marcella Carson was about to rip my heart from my chest.

I briefly wondered how she was doing this and continued to

stare hard at the paper in front of me as if the columns of text might save me from what came next.

"*Önskan* is, certainly, one of my favorites," she said. "I do find it inspiring. The poem I was actually thinking of, though, is *Ja visst gör det ont.*"

I felt a lump forming in my throat. Translated into English, the title is 'Yes, of course, it hurts.' It was Boye's most famous poem, and I had read it often after leaving the army. It soothed the pain, reminding me that growth is always accompanied by hardship and loss. It had been a balm to my cracked and broken soul that had seen too much, too soon, and seemingly all at once. Now, my brain seized up at the mention of the title; I couldn't move, nor could I speak.

Marcella continued, quoting the poem in English, her voice soft, low, and sultry, almost—seductive.

"Yes, of course, it hurts when buds are breaking.

Why else would the springtime falter?

Why would all our ardent longing

bind itself in frozen, bitter pallor?

After all, the bud was covered all the winter.

What new thing is it that bursts and wears?

Yes, of course, it hurts when buds are breaking,

hurts for that which grows

and that which bars."

With a simple utterance, Marcella dragged me into a hot, dark, suffocating place, a place of screaming children and burning soldiers, a place of gunfire, and rape, and hurt. It encompassed the totality of pain, guilt, and loss in my life, forcing my fingertips into the tabletop, unable to let go. Those words, which I had relied on to help me get through day after day, had long since become an errant conjuration, summoning the horrors lurking in the black places of my head. I could barely breathe for long moments.

"Please, stop," I pleaded weakly when I finally found my voice. I felt very afraid for some reason, afraid to stay under her perceptive eyes and yet unwilling to leave. Light flirting had turned into an invasion. I know she hadn't meant to push me down into the abyss, but she had. And now, here I was.

Marcella leaned in close and put her hand on mine.

I looked at our hands, joined on the table, then back to Marcella and her lovely eyes. In a matter of a few hours, this woman had read me like a book and stormed the gates to my carefully structured life, giving the lie to it. And it scared me how suddenly and desperately I wanted her. I longed to touch her, to kiss her, to embrace her. We had just met, and, now, she was pulling me into her orbit, just like Morgan had in Iraq— a force of nature. But I couldn't trust my own feelings—feelings that I scarcely understood. So, I did the only thing I could; I panicked and ran.

"I—I can't do this," I stated flatly, frowning and pulling my hand from under hers. I stuffed everything back into the accordion file, snatched it up, and left without another word or a backward glance, gently closing the door behind me. Truly rude, I knew. But I had to escape, get some distance, and I needed air.

Sitting in the car, I drifted into a sea of embarrassment, anger, sadness, and want, filled with self-recrimination for crossing the professional line. I needed to pull myself back together and get back to work. Squinting through yet more tears, I fumbled out my keys to start the Jeep when my phone buzzed.

Carlos: Gabe is here. Blackman is a no-show.

Me: Let me know when you are done.

Carlos: Will do. He brought a lawyer. Some asshole named Brad.

"Fuck," I muttered to myself. "Gabriel Parkman, you are a dumb ass."

12

I turned off the car and sat in front of my apartment building, my head against the steering wheel; I had to think. Fuck, I needed to breathe. I was so off-kilter, panicked even. After a few minutes of hyperventilation and near abject terror, I finally pulled myself from the car and trudged up the stairs, my feet stepping in the smears of brown wood showing through the worn white paint.

What am I doing? I wondered as I collapsed on the couch. After a few minutes, Jabba finally padded from my room to curl up on my lap. "Huh, little man? What is your mommy doing?" Jabba stared at me with those orange feline eyes and purred, demanding attention.

I scratched the cat and thought briefly about Gabe. I was utterly disconnected from him. Even if he hadn't become a person of interest in the case, he and I had just drifted along in our relationship—going to dinner, hockey games, the odd movie, occasional sex, which was okay at best. It wasn't going anywhere. Maybe that was the problem. In my therapy sessions, Jennifer had suggested that I might be keeping everyone at arm's length to avoid becoming emotionally invested. She was probably right, and Gabe deserved better. He deserved someone that would take care of him, someone who wanted what he wanted, and someone who loved him the way he needed.

My phone buzzed with a text from an unknown number.

Unknown: Caitlin, I apologize for being so familiar.

Marcella, obviously. I rubbed my head in exasperation and responded.

Me: It's okay. I'm sorry for walking out. I just need to keep this professional.

Marcella: I can't say I'm not disappointed, but I understand. Please let me know if you change your mind. :heart emoji:

A heart emoji? God, she was persistent. I set down my phone and opened the accordion file, starting over with the list and paying particular attention to the projects from the last couple of months. There were only five that hadn't been marked as closed out before the summer. A pharmaceutical company tried to fleece Carson for HIV drugs destined for Nigeria. The company that held the patent wanted to charge Carson four times the US over-the-counter cost for drugs they weren't even manufacturing themselves — fucking bandits. That project was marked as a strictly internal charity effort, so no third parties were involved.

Next, the current government of Myanmar wasn't honoring import tariff agreements negotiated with the previous government — on hold for US State Department intervention.

The third project was arranging a shipment of blankets, foodstuffs, and essential medicines from various parts of the US to Boston for homeless veterans — noble. This was marked as an internal charity matter as well.

The fourth project was a joint cancer research effort with the Margaret Chastity Cancer Center. It seemed to be the project that Jesse spent the most time on. There were receipts for a dozen trips back and forth to Buffalo. It was another internal charity matter and not terribly relevant.

The final project was a stalled internal accounting systems project.

I dropped the files on the table in frustration. *Maybe Caldwell cut his own head off because he was sick of accountants,* I mused. It seemed to be about all he dealt with.

What the fuck am I missing?

Something was nagging at me. Then it struck me. It wasn't that I was missing something. Something was actually missing. There was no mention of any project or work related to new vaccine vendors for TCD. There was no mention of TCD at all. I found nothing on Kineda Pharmaceuticals, either.

I sat back in the chair again and drank some of my water. Marcella was correct; there wasn't anything in the files that pointed to the murder. But something was God damned well not there.

I shook my head. *What the hell is going on?* I snatched up my phone and texted Carlos.

Me: Gabe told me that Carson was looking for a new vaccine vendor for TCD. There's no mention of it in any of Carson's files here. He said that's why he and Mr. Blackman were meeting with them.

Carlos: Hold tight.

I went to the veranda and lit up a cigarette, watching the gray smoke drift away on the light breeze. Leaning back on the railing and glancing up, I could see Rebecca, my upstairs nosy neighbor, looking out across the street. I didn't feel like talking, so I moved back to the doorway, staying out of sight.

Rebecca was an extraordinary little, old Jewish lady who should keep her nose firmly out of other people's affairs. The emphasis was on extraordinary, though. Besides, as a homicide detective, I was always in someone else's business. So, I really couldn't judge her for that. Her husband, Eitan, a retired chef, had passed away a few years earlier, leaving her little to do but focus on others.

I liked Rebecca, though she held firmly to the belief that the Irish would be the death of civilization. I simply considered that part of her bigoted charm. Some things you have to overlook in people because they're too old to change and their influence on the world faded long ago.

"Well, hi, Cait? Fun night last night?" she asked.

Shit. "I'm sorry?" My cheeks started to burn.

"It sounded like you and Gabe were, well, you know, being—intimate," she said. "You were pretty loud."

"Sorry, Mrs. Weiss. Gabe was only here for a few minutes, and there was no nookie."

Rebecca's face was utterly skeptical. "If you say so." She ducked back inside.

I flushed with embarrassment. *Oh my God! Had I been moaning in my sleep? How fucking mortifying. Jesus.*

I turned away to finish my cigarette and make sure no one had heard our exchange.

As I finished my smoke, my phone rang.

"Homicide, Reagan."

"He's left the building," Carlos said from the other end. "Come on in, and we can talk about what we found out."

"On my way," I said quickly and hung up.

13

Carlos waited at his desk with the interview recording paused. "Well, you want to watch it or just get the reader's digest version?"

"How long is the recording?" I asked as I set down my gear.

"An hour and a half. I grilled Gabe pretty hard. His lawyer is an absolute asshole and an idiot. Where'd he find that guy?"

"Please don't mention Brad Matthews to me. I have a weak stomach."

"Oh, so you know the guy." It was a statement, not a question. It seemed Carlos had the same opinion of Brad that I did.

I gave him an icy stare. "Yes, I know him; he's one of Gabe's old frat brothers."

Carlos frowned. "Why don't you watch the recording for the full effect while I make us some coffee and return a couple of phone calls?"

While I watched the recording, Carlos returned with a mug of the good stuff.

"How much of this did you bring in?" I asked, gesturing with my mug.

He smirked. "Enough."

I skipped ahead in the recording, passing the perfunctory questions like 'state your name and occupation.' Gabe looked not just hungover but sick. Bags sat under his bloodshot eyes, and his blond hair was a flat, greasy mat. Gabe's complexion was pale, gray, and waxy—anemic. Brad, by contrast, looked the perfect picture of sobriety, brown eyes clear and black hair neatly parted and combed; that man could drink like a fish.

"So, tell me where you were on Tuesday night," Carlos started.

"You don't have to answer that," Brad interjected with a smirk. It was clear he was just trying to get the better of Carlos; show him who's boss. Carlos ignored him, as did Gabe.

"I was at dinner with Mr. Haimon Blackman, the Vice President of my division. We were at the Capital Grille in Chestnut Hill until eleven. After that, I went home," he said.

After scribbling some notes, Carlos asked, "Can anyone confirm your whereabouts after eleven?"

"You don't have to answer that, Gabe," Brad said again.

"Dude!" Gabe looked at Brad in annoyance, then turned back to Carlos. "No, I was at home alone. I did speak to my mother on the phone, and my cell phone records will confirm that."

Carlos continued writing. "What time was that phone call?"

"Detective Ramirez," Brad said. "I'm sure you can pull his phone records to find that. Presuming you can get a warrant."

Gabe just continued; Brad frowned. "I don't know; she called me at like midnight, I think, to tell me my dad is in the hospital."

Good boy, I thought, *just cooperate, and this will all be over.*

"Did you go to the hospital to see him?"

"No," Gabe said, face stoic, but I could hear his sorrow. "We don't get along. The guy's a prick."

Poor Gabe, no wonder he was so wrecked last night. He'd lost the deal of his career, assuming there ever was one. His father was in the hospital, probably pretty sick for his mother to call him at midnight. And I was treating him like shit. *I am such a bitch.*

"She had been trying to reach me most of the day but kept getting voice mail because Haimon — Mr. Blackman—had my phone," Gabe said quietly.

"Why did Mr. Blackman have your cell phone?" Carlos asked, eyebrow raised.

Brad opened his mouth to object again, but Gabe put a hand on his shoulder. "Brad, I didn't do anything. Let's just get this over with, okay?" Brad sat back quietly.

"Because, Detective Ramirez, he is the Vice President of my division. I work for a large Japanese company. When your boss asks you for something, you do it, and you don't ask a bunch of questions. Mr. Blackman did volunteer, however, that his phone wasn't working properly." Gabe looked much calmer now. His jitters seemed to have subsided, and I could see the confident man I'd admired when I met him.

"While I had told Detective Reagan that I had arranged the vaccine deal for TCD with Carson Logistics, that was all Mr. Blackman's doing. Last Friday, Mr. Blackman flew in and pulled me aside, saying that he needed me to take point on a deal." Gabe then outlined the TCD deal precisely as he had to me.

"On Tuesday, Mr. Blackman and I went to dinner to strategize on the account. He returned my phone then. I had seven voice mails from my mother when I got it back. I didn't listen to them, though, because she called me again shortly after Mr. Blackman returned my phone."

"Where is Mr. Blackman now?" Carlos asked.

Before Gabe could answer, Carlos looked at his phone. He held up a hand, stopping Gabe's answer, and typed out something. Then he went back to the interview. That must have been about the time that I texted him.

"I have no idea," Gabe responded. "Blackman wasn't at the office when I got there, and no one has seen him since Tuesday. Honestly, Detective, that is everything that I know about all this."

"So, Mr. Parkman, can you tell me honestly that you had nothing to do with Mr. Caldwell's death?" Carlos asked straight up.

"I had nothing to do with Mr. Caldwell's murder, Detective."

That was all I needed to see. The interview went on for

another hour, so I started fast-forwarding and I'd get any other details from Carlos later. I stopped the recording when something caught my eye.

Both Brad and Gabe were standing and looked to be arguing. I backed it up a little and hit play. "Brad, just go. I should never have brought you in here. You've been nothing but a frat boy all your life, and that's all you'll be, no matter how many university degrees you have. I can handle the rest of this myself."

"Gabe, I highly recommend —," Brad started, but Gabe cut him off.

"I said, get out. I can handle this. You're off the hook. It's recorded here, and I'll sign a release later," Gabe's voice was loud and firm.

"Good for you, Gabe; Brad's an asshole."

Gabe sat down, and Carlos began grilling him again. Gabe never wavered in his story for the rest of the interview. He added details, like what they ate for dinner and his business schedule that morning, but the main points didn't change. Haimon had set up the deal. Haimon had made the phone calls, and Gabe wasn't involved.

"Just one more thing," Carlos said, and I chuckled. He sounded a little like Columbo. "We have Mr. Caldwell's calendar, and there's no mention of a meeting with you or your company on Wednesday. How do you explain that?"

Gabe looked at Carlos impassively for a second, then he replied. "That's probably a question you should ask Ms. Carson or Mr. Blackman. I have no idea. Maybe he forgot to write it down."

"Okay, so let's go over this one more time," Carlos said once again.

Gabe finally lost his cool, banging his hand on the table. "No, we've gone over this a dozen times, and I'm done. So, I'm leaving. You know how to get in touch with me if you have any other questions, but I've given you enough time."

Gabe stood up and offered his hand to Carlos. "Detective, I

hope you find your killer. If for no other reason than so that I can have my girlfriend back." My mouth dropped. *Damnit, Gabe, you passive-aggressive prick.* He knew I'd see this.

I turned to Carlos, who was at his desk. "So?" I prodded.

"So, I think he knows more than he's saying," Carlos said, putting his hands behind his head and leaning back in his chair. "He's caught between a rock and a hard place. He works for one of the last keiretsus in Japan. He might know where his boss is hiding, but he can't tell us. He'll get fired, and I don't think he can take that right now. I think Blackman is our guy, though. I don't have anything to back it up, just my gut."

"You think Gabe's involved?"

"No," Carlos said sympathetically. "I don't think he had a clue that Caldwell would be murdered. Also, I don't know if you caught it, but he did say that Haimon Blackman tends to wear expensive brand name everything, shoes included. Though, he couldn't recall what kind of shoes Mr. Blackman was wearing the night of the murder."

I reached out and touched Carlos' arm. "Thank you," I said sincerely.

"You're welcome," he said. "But before you run off and call him, tell me about your date today."

I plopped the accordion file onto his desk. "Yeah, about that," I said. "You were right; Marcella goes after what she wants."

"Marcella, huh. You on a first name basis?"

"She insisted. Sorry."

"No reason to apologize. I think it's cute." He winked at me. "Regardless, you look none the worse for wear," he said. "So she must not have been trying too hard."

I grinned stupidly and tugged at my ear. "Oh, she was putting on a full-court press. I mean, she's a fucking barracuda."

Carlos just laughed. "Did you at least learn anything new?"

"Well, she's hot, lonely, and thinks I'm pretty."

"About the case, darlin', not your dating prospects," he clarified with a smirk.

"Well, she's convinced that Mr. Caldwell's death wasn't related to his work," I said, thinking about my exchange with Marcella. "Looking at the files she provided, I can't find anything that suggests otherwise. But none of it looks good for Gabe or his boss. The two people who most likely spoke to him last, and neither had an alibi. But I don't get why they'd do it at all. I mean, Gabe's a sales guy, coin-operated, you know. I'm not seeing what he would have to lose or gain by the guy's death."

"Hard to say," Carlos agreed. "But, I do know that people murder for two reasons when you get right down to it, money and sex. If there was a big deal to be had and Caldwell backed out, one of them might be angry enough to kill him."

I rubbed the back of my neck. "Well, Gabe did say that his commission alone on the deal was supposed to be three-hundred-thousand. But that would mean a huge deal, and Marcella seemed to think there was no deal."

"She might have been lying," Carlos said.

"That's possible, I guess. In the end, we've got nothing tying either of them to the murder. I want to talk to Blackman and hear his story."

"You and me both, sister. By the way, I found a witness in the Washington case."

"Really?" I said, a little skeptical. "Who?"

"Ms. Carlita Angelina Estrada."

I grabbed my notebook and thumbed through the pages. "I interviewed Ms. Estrada, but she said she didn't see anything. How'd you get her to talk?"

"I speak the language. She's from Guatemala, and my family's from Mexico, but we're all Latinos and Latinas in gringo territory, know what I mean? Anyway, she has a nephew in Austin whose in a spot of trouble. I promised to make a call for her." Carlos smiled widely.

"Well, hot shit. What did she say?" I asked expectantly.

"The man you're looking for is Aileas Mendéz. His street name is JJ." At my bemused expression, he held a hand up.

"Don't ask; she has no idea why they call him that, and neither do I. She'll be here at seven tonight to give a statement. The fugitive task force is already looking for Mendéz."

"Good job Carlos," I said.

"No," he said. "Good job, Reagan. Your notes and reports were spotless, making my work easy." I flushed at the compliment. "Don't let it go to your head, though. I'm pretty sure I can write a better report."

I smiled, wondering where he was going. "Oh, how's that?"

"I'm from Texas, darlin'. We do everything better there. Haven't you heard?" he said.

"Except pro football," I fired back with a grin.

"Ouch," he said. Let's be honest, though; there wasn't anything he could say.

I picked up my phone and dialed Gabe's number.

"Hey," Gabe sounded tired and defeated.

"Hey, I'm sorry all this has happened. Is your dad okay?" I asked.

"No, he's had a major stroke. The doctors say he's brain dead." I knew he didn't have a good relationship with his father, but I also knew that closure could be essential in those instances.

"Are you going to go see him?" I asked with more than a bit of disquiet

"Mom wants me to, but I'm not sure," he replied. I could hear the uncertainty in his voice.

"Would you like me to go with you?" I asked softly. "It might help you get through it."

"You don't mind?"

"No, Gabe. It's the least I can do. I haven't been a very supportive girlfriend lately," I said. That was an understatement. I'd been an absolute bitch. Gabe was hurting, and I had been so wrapped up in my shit that I hadn't even considered that something might be eating at him. "Where do you want me to pick you up?" I asked.

"I'm at my house. How soon can you get here?"

"I'm waiting on a witness to show up in less than an hour

and give a statement," I said. "Is that soon enough?"

"Yeah," he said. "Dad's on life support; he's not going anywhere. I'll let my Mom know I'll be by this evening. Please don't bail on me on this one," he said. It was just another kick in the gut. *Shit.*

"I'll be there," I said. "Eight-thirty at your place."

Ms. Estrada arrived at HQ at six-forty-five. Carlos sat her down in the interview room, and we both spoke to her. She fingered Aileas and about jumped out of her seat when Carlos said he'd spoken to the Captain in Austin, helping get her nephew into the scared straight program rather than jail. Carlos was good people. We bid Ms. Estrada goodbye and went back to our desks.

"Okay," I looked at my watch. It was seven-thirty. "I'm going to head out and take Gabe to see his father in the hospital."

Carlos gave me a sad smile. "That's fine. I'll go over the material you have here. If I have any questions, I'll let you know."

I followed Carlos back to the cubes and started slamming my stuff into my backpack.

Carlos looked at me, his voice very serious. "Darlin', try to relax. I know you're stressed. I'll take a look at them later, but I'm sure you're right. There's probably nothing in there related to the murder. Besides, I'm much more interested in your visit to Marcella-land."

"Oh, no. I told you. Marcella's a champion manipulator. When we stopped dancing around it, she was extremely candid — which I appreciated. I'm going to see my boyfriend now."

"Okay," Carlos said as I gathered my things. "Go take care of your boy. We got this, but keep your phone on."

"Always, Carlos." I gave Carlos a half-hearted smile and walked out of the building. As I got in the car, I took a deep breath to steel myself. This was going to be another long night.

14

Gabe lived in a cute blue duplex in West Roxbury. The house itself had a gorgeously manicured lawn. His mother, I suspected. I had a black thumb, so all I could do was admire the pretty flowers. Any plant I even looked at wrong was likely to die. There was still a dead cactus on my veranda. A badge of my failures as a gardener. I mean, who kills a cactus?

Like most of the homes in the area, it was single-family built in the nineteen-twenties, split to accommodate apartments. The first floor constituted Gabe's home. The upstairs was empty, dark, and ominous. The curtain-less windows reminded me dimly of a spider's eyes, all gazing down at the street for the next victim. I thought I saw movement, but there was nothing—a trick of the light, maybe.

Gabe was sitting under the small white-columned portico that served as cover for both doors. He stood and walked to the sidewalk as I pulled up. His stride seemed to have a slight limp to it.

I rolled down the window. "Hey, get in." Honestly, I couldn't come up with a better greeting. I could feel the strain between us in my gut. Gabe's face shifted between sadness and rage. That was something I could understand. His father, Richard, had beaten him as a kid —Gabe often taking the blows meant for his mother. His mother had refused to leave his father, though, being a good Christian wife or something like that.

If someone abused me like that, they wouldn't have to worry about me leaving. I'd toss them out, change the locks, and file a restraining order. Of course, that'd be after they got out of the hospital.

I'd met Gabe's father only once. The man tried to be intimidating, talking about how a woman should be in the home, not the police force—sexist pig shit. We had been at Easter dinner one year. After we left, I explained I wouldn't be going back a second time, and I wasn't kind about it either. I'd met men's parents many times over the years, but it had been the first time I'd actually sworn off a second meeting.

Gabe got into the car and closed the door.

"Hey, honey," I said, turning the key. "I'm so sorry."

"It's okay," he said, taking my hand before we could pull out. "I know your job is hard, and you've been having a tough time with combat stress, and I should have been more understanding. Dad's at Boston Medical Center."

"It'll be alright," I said with more confidence than I felt. "I know this must be hard." And I did. One of the worst things a person can suffer is the loss of a parent, even an abusive one. Humans seem to be hardwired to seek the approval of their parents or parental figures. It can leave an empty hole, full of need, never filled.

Gabe didn't respond; he just kept looking out the window, watching the cars go by.

"Are we in trouble?" Gabe asked after about ten minutes.

"What do you mean?"

"I'd like to know if you're thinking about leaving me," he said quietly.

"No, Gabe," I lied. "Besides, I don't think this is the time to talk about it." The last thing I wanted was to fight the way to see his dying father.

"Okay," he said and blew out a breath. I would probably pay for that lie at some point down the road, but I just couldn't break his heart — not right now. "I don't understand why I feel sad that my dad is going to die. I have hated that man for years.

But, here I am, going to see him in his final hours. He doesn't deserve that."

"No, Gabe," I said softly. "He doesn't. But you do. You deserve to close this relationship and have some peace from it. Also, I've known you long enough to know that doing the right thing is important to you. You're not just doing this for yourself; your mother needs you, too."

Gabe started to cry. In the entirety of our relationship, I had never seen him cry. He'd always been composed and relatively strong — a little whiny sometimes — but never distraught. Now I saw the scared little boy underneath all of that, peeking out. He always talked about the therapy I needed to handle my PTSD, but he never seemed to have a clue of his own need for the same.

"People just suck," he said.

"Yes, they do," I responded, understanding where this was going.

"My father was a bastard, and my mother stayed with him for forty years. I know she loved him, but how could she stay with him after all of the abuse? I just don't understand it. She was never there for me, and now I have to go console her over that asshole." Gabe ran a hand through his hair, pulling several loose strands out.

I glanced at the wad of hair in his hand. "Jesus, Gabe, you need to destress. You're so wrecked; your hair is starting to fall out, and you look pale and sallow. Are you sleeping?"

Gabe flicked the strands, watching them fall to the floorboard. "I'll be alright; it's just been a bad few days." He talked a good game, but his hopeless expression said otherwise. "Besides, you never take time off."

I wasn't going to let him brush this off. "I'm serious, Gabe. You look like shit, honey. What's going on?"

Gabe said nothing else. He just sighed and stared back out the window.

We arrived at BMC a half-hour later, and I followed Gabe to his father's room in the ICU. The nurse gave me a little static since I wasn't family. But, after I had explained a little of the situation and flashed my badge, she let me in. A little professional courtesy can go a long way. I can't count the number of nurses I'd pulled over for speeding or other minor infraction and then let go. I waited in the hallway as Gabe went in.

His mother was waiting inside, holding Richard's hand and quietly sobbing. Gabe put his arms around her. When she saw me, her expression changed to one of disappointment. While Gabe's mother wanted him to get married and have kids, she did not want him to do it with me. But, I thought, she'd resigned herself to the fact that Gabe had chosen me — even if I hadn't.

I watched the interaction between the two and thought about my mother. We had a different kind of relationship. Unlike Deborah Parkman, my mother was strong and independent. When my father died, she'd pulled herself together, organized his funeral and burial, and even arranged a nice Irish wake. She waited until it was all over to crumble, regularly disappearing back to Tourmakeady. I remembered many nights listening to her wail herself to sleep.

"Caitlin?" Deborah called from the room. "Could you please ask the nurse to come in?"

"Sure," I said, turning away from the room.

I walked over to the nursing station. An attractive young black woman in blue scrubs sat, typing on the computer. She twisted her platinum wedding band as she studied the computer screen.

"I'm sorry to interrupt," I said as graciously as I could. "But —"

She lowered her glasses and looked at me, and grinned. "You're not interrupting, honey. What can I do for you?"

"Room four," I said, smiling back. I knew I shouldn't smile at her with Gabe sitting grief-stricken in the room, but I couldn't help myself—the woman was pretty. And her warm smile made me flush a bit. "They're asking for a nurse."

"Oh," she said flatly, and her smile vanished.

She stood up, and we both walked to the door. As the nurse stepped into the room, Deborah put a hand on my chest, stopping me from entering. Gabe looked up briefly, eyes full of need and misery, imploring me to stand with him. Then, Deborah shut the door in my face as if I were a stranger rubbernecking an accident. I just stood there and closed my eyes for a moment, then I took a short breath, blowing it out in a rush.

What am I doing here?

I left the hallway and parked myself in the ICU waiting room. I watched, leaning in the doorway, as a few people walked into the corridor. One had the look of a respiratory therapist. It was nothing in particular; they seemed to have a way about them. The nurse I had met earlier walked up to me with a small paper coffee cup in her hand.

"Here," she said. "You looked like you could use it. They'll be getting ready to remove him from life support shortly."

I first thought it was coffee; then, I smelled the chocolate. I accidentally brushed her hand as I took the cup, and she smiled. I expected her to walk away, but she stayed, leaning against the wall next to me.

"Boyfriend and his mother?" She asked.

"Something like that," I said quietly, taking a sip of the hot chocolate, finding it the crappy, powdered kind but welcome nonetheless.

"Reminds me of how my partner's family treats me," she said, taking a spot along the wall to my right. "Like I'm not part of the family, and we've been married for five years. But, we have each other."

I didn't say anything; I just kept staring at the doors.

"Some people have a narrow vision of what's important. I'd think your boyfriend would need all the support he could get at a time like this." She continued leaning against the wall, arms crossed but turned herself toward me. "Though, when you walked in here, I had pegged you for his sister or a friend.

It wasn't until his mother shut you out of the room that I realized you were together."

"Huh," I said without inflection, continuing to listen and sip the hot chocolate.

"Does he know?" She asked. I didn't have to ask what she was referring to.

I looked at the floor. "No," I said quietly.

"How long have you known?" she asked.

"About a day and most of my life, depending on how I look at it," I said.

She laughed. "Yeah, that's usually the way it goes for us late bloomers. There's a whole world out there that tries to tell you what's normal. And it's, well, normal to try to conform to that. Word of advice, though," She said as she pushed herself off the wall with her shoulder.

"Hmm?" I said, still staring at the door.

"The longer you wait, the worse it will be. It doesn't go away, Detective." She started walking toward the doors.

"Is it that obvious?" I asked at her back.

"That you're a cop? Hell yes," she replied, still striding to the doors. "You coming? I still think he could use your support."

I sipped the hot chocolate and followed the nurse into the corridor. The room was open again, and a tall, broad-shouldered gentleman with graying hair and a crooked nose worked on one of the machines, the respiratory therapist I'd seen earlier. Gabe and Deborah were sitting next to the far side of the bed.

The nurse I'd been speaking with walked into the room. "Mr. Parkman," she said. "Would you like your girlfriend in the room with you?"

Gabe looked up. "Yes, please."

"I don't think—" Deborah started, but the nurse cut her off.

"Ms. Parkman," she said firmly. "This is a traumatic time for everyone, and I'm sure Mr. Parkman could use all the support he can get." And that was that; Deborah Parkman just shut up and stopped arguing. That's how good nurses dealt with troublesome families, no-nonsense and not above shaming them into compliance.

I walked into the room and put my hand on Gabe's shoulder. Neither Gabe nor Deborah were looking when the nurse winked at me.

A young man in a physician's coat stood before the bed. "I'm Dr. Vankateswara Patel, Mr. Parkman's attending physician." Doctor or not, to me, he looked about twelve years old.

"Detective Reagan," I said and shook his hand.

The overall process was short. Before we had arrived, hospital staff had determined that there was no brain activity. The stroke had been so severe that it had, essentially, killed Richard instantly.

I had seen this situation play out many times over my career as a cop. The first time, it had been a mother, Maria Alvarez, whose boyfriend had beaten her child to the point of imminent death. Maria's parents were Honduran and had been deported a little more than a week before the incident, during the previous administration's fucking anti-immigration push, leaving Maria, eighteen, and her daughter, six weeks old, behind. She struggled with the decision for hours. Ultimately, devastated and alone, she signed the order. That night, I didn't sleep a wink, thinking of the horror that would haunt the grieving mother. I had cried until morning. And, I had been so angry.

It was somewhat different with Richard. With zero brain activity, he was considered deceased. The life support was just a courtesy to give the family a chance to be involved with the termination of care. But, the effect was the same, another family in pain.

So, with all of the preliminaries over, the respiratory therapist looked back to Gabe, who nodded as his mother looked on in tears. I heard the familiar beep as the gray-haired gentleman deactivated the respirator and removed the ET tube. There was no other noise, no squealing alarms; all had been silenced beforehand. The last breath of Richard Parkman was a quiet sigh—a final, feeble exhalation. And just like that, a life was over.

Deborah came apart. Gabe began to sob, and even I teared up as grief filled the room. I pulled Gabe and Deborah both to me and let them express their misery in rivers of tears, one on each shoulder.

The nurse I'd been talking to, whose name I didn't know, gave me a sympathetic smile as she walked out of the room with the rest of the staff. I stood there, helpless, while Gabe and Deborah shook with sorrow.

I handed Deborah a handkerchief from my coat pocket. It was one that I carried for family members when they were giving statements about deceased loved ones.

"Thank you, Caitlin," she said, handing back the handkerchief. For what, I didn't know — bringing her son, giving her a tissue, letting her cry on my shoulder? So, I just smiled in sympathy and walked softly out of the room to wait for them, closing the door gently behind me.

The nurse from earlier came over to me. "You're a good person," she said in almost a whisper as she got close. I certainly didn't feel like one. She offered me a piece of paper. "Here's my name, number, and personal email, in case you need someone to talk to. I also run a local hiking group in town if you ever find yourself interested."

"Thanks," I said, taking the offered paper. "But I'm usually too busy for much of a social life."

She gave me a soft smile tinctured with sympathy. "That's a shame. I know a lot of my friends who would be happy to have you along. Anyway, let me know if you change your mind."

I looked at the paper before putting it in my pocket. The nurse's name was Anne. "I'll do that, Anne." I turned back to the room as Gabe and Deborah emerged.

Gabe had his hands in his pockets, looking dispirited and shocked. He gave me a brief hug. "I'm going to take Mom home and spend the night with her."

I looked at Deborah, tears burning their way down her face.

"Is there anything you need?"

"No," Gabe answered for her, his voice muted. "Thank you for suggesting I come and for bringing me."

"Of course." I gave him a peck on the cheek, squeezing his shoulders. "That's what I'm here for."

Deborah simply looked up at me, a hint of a bruise under one eye. Otherwise she was every inch the grieving widow.

"I'll be at home. Gabe, why don't you and I plan on having dinner tomorrow night."

"I thought you were working," he said, wrapping his arm around his mother's shoulders.

"I am, but I should be able to make dinner unless a new case comes up." I looked at Deborah again. "Will you be okay? Do *you* need anything?" I made it clear I was talking to her.

"Oh, don't worry about me. I'll be fine." She pulled herself up and sniffed, wiping her tears.

I turned back to Gabe. "I'll see you tomorrow, and we can talk about things, okay?"

Gabe didn't even answer; he just took his mother's arm and turned away.

I watched Gabe and Deborah walk out of the unit. As I did, I felt Anne's supportive hand on my shoulder. "You really are a good person,"

"Then why do I feel like shit?"

She said nothing because we both knew the answer.

15

It is just a month into my first deployment, and I am drunk. The anti-septic smell of the latrine sits caustic in my nose and sinuses. The toilet is full of dark brown liquor; my stomach roils. I pull myself up from the floor and stagger to the sink, washing out my mouth in the lukewarm water. In the mirror, Sgt. Holley's face appears, and terror squeezes my heart.

"Hey there," Holley's bass drawls. I think he's a misogynist redneck who likes killing. He disgusts me.

"What the hell, Holley! This is the ladies' room. You need to leave."

He grabs my wrist. "Now, come on, I saw how you were looking at me."

"Let go," I shout. "You're hurting my arm." No, no, no, this isn't happening.

Holley pulls me to the floor, banging my head on the sink. I feel warm blood on the back of my head.

"Shut the fuck up," Holley hisses, covering my mouth. I bite his hand hard, drawing blood.

"Ow. You bitch." My head rocks, banging against the concrete floor as he punches me repeatedly. I now see this nightmare for what it is, but I'm powerless to stop it or him.

He leans in with his fetid, whiskey-sodden breath. His spit lands on my belly as he yanks down my shorts.

God, why didn't I wear my BDUs?

Holley pushes me over. I try to pull loose, but he elbows me in the back of my head.

Please wake up! Please wake up! Please wake up!

* * *

I struggled to get loose of the wet sheets and drag my way off the bed. Dashing into the bathroom, I gripped the toilet as my stomach forced out what little was in it.

It took a few minutes before it dawned on me that my sleep pants were wet. The deep despair of shame clawed into me, dragging me down further. I sat like that for a long time, head pressed against the toilet seat, soaked and stinking with urine. My chest ached for any release from this misery.

I thought I should just put a bullet in my head for about the thousandth time. But, my mother couldn't take another loss.

"God damn it, why?" I cursed to the ceiling, rage filling me, not that God's sorry ass was listening. If God had been paying any attention at all, I wouldn't have been raped, and I wouldn't be so God damned fucked up. I tried, unsuccessfully, to stifle loud sobs bursting with heartache. Eventually, I stood, avoiding the mirror, unable to look at myself.

I took a shower and cleaned myself up, changing my clothes. Then I stripped the bed, putting everything in the wash. Walking numbly to the kitchen, I grabbed the pet stain remover and the little handheld wet-dry vacuum Gabe had bought me for my birthday. I couldn't keep the tears back as I cleaned the bed.

Why the fuck did this shit happen to me, I ranted mentally. *What the fuck did I do to deserve this?*

My pulse hammered in my ears. I wanted to scream and tear the house apart, but an irritating reasonable thought ground through my anger like sandpaper, reminding me that people were sleeping. So, like the fucking good girl that I was, after cleaning the mattress, I grabbed the spare comforter and slid to the floor next to my bed so it could dry.

"I fucking quit."

Defeated, I cried myself back to sleep.

I was awakened two hours later by the irritating ringtone I'd set for dispatch. I looked at my watch— 2:57 AM.

"Fuck," I swore. Three minutes later, it would have been a problem for Vic and the day shift. I sighed and answered the phone.

"Reagan," I rasped, throat parched. I'd left a glass of water on my nightstand, so I quickly gulped down a few refreshing mouthfuls.

"Detective Reagan, homicide requested at Humboldt and Seaver."

"Any details?" I asked.

"Three deceased," he said in a perfunctory fashion. "Two adults, one juvenile."

I closed my eyes and blew out a controlled breath. *Great, a triple.*

"Detective Reagan?" The dispatcher prodded impatiently.

"Yeah, okay." My voice was a little hoarse, and I rubbed the back of my neck. "I'll be there. Send me the address." I hung up.

I stared at the ceiling, putting my hand down to stroke Jabba's fur. He rolled over, exposing his belly, so I scratched his tummy. I could hear, just barely, a little purr through his little corpulent body. "Slut." I whispered hoarsely and stood. Jabba meowed in protest. "No, no. I have to go to work, you big baby."

I staggered into the bathroom and decided a second shower was in order. My muscles were sore and stiff. As the hot water cascaded over me, loosening up my muscles, my eyelids drooped closed. In contrast to my nightmare, unbidden thoughts of Marcella filled my head, images from the dream, intense and inviting: her shapely stocking clad legs gliding around me in the dim light, brushing against my own, her teeth on my neck. I let out a quiet moan of arousal.

My eyes flew open. *What the fuck is wrong with me? How could I even think of sex after a nightmare like that?* I finished washing and dressed.

When I arrived at the top of Humboldt Avenue, where it met Seaver, the entire block was sealed off at both ends by cruisers. I flashed my badge and pulled the Jeep up onto the sidewalk.

"Wow, this is not good," I commented as I surveyed six squad cars and two unmarked. The medical examiner wasn't here yet, of course. That was okay; they'd just get in the way right now anyway.

The far end of the block held news vans from the local affiliate stations. A few photographers were snapping pictures while local reporters spoke to the cameras. I could see Shandra Clark from channel 7 eyeballing me as she spoke among the crowded news vultures. Shandra fancied herself the next Bob Woodward or Christiane Amanpour. In reality, I considered her a muckraker on a mission to discredit the department. Shandra seemed to think that the entire department was full of lousy, racist cops waiting for a chance to shoot someone.

There were racist trigger-happy in every department that made the job damn near impossible for the rest of us. But they didn't represent all cops, not even most. Most of us just wanted to do a good job and go home at night. I found it easy to avoid 'use of force' complaints in my patrol days. When presented with a belligerent driver, I found it best to give them the citation and let them go. I never pulled my firearm in almost five years of patrol, not once. In the end, a fifty-dollar traffic ticket isn't worth someone's life.

I think that was why I didn't like Shandra. I felt like she painted us all with a broad brush. I hated how Shandra handled it, and right then, I wasn't feeling charitable.

I waved back at Shandra half-heartedly rather than giving her finger and headed over to the scene. I could see a few patrol officers going to the houses on the block, looking for witnesses. Three other officers were milling about outside, mostly watching the street. I recognized the officer on duty outside the building door.

"Hey, Nev. How's your Mom?" Neveah Campbell was,

literally, from the hood. She'd grown up in Mattapan, dealt with the crappy schools, the works. But, she'd carved out a life for herself that any parent would be proud of. Most cops from tough neighborhoods move elsewhere when they can, but Neveah and her mother still lived in their tiny two-bedroom apartment.

"She's good. She wants to know when you'll come by again for some home cooking."

"I'm not sure my waistline can handle her home cooking. Once I start, I can't seem to stop eating it. So, who was first on the scene?"

Neveah's voice trembled. "I was." Even in the dim porch light, I could see her pallor. "It's horrible. I've never seen anything like it."

"I've been there," I said supportively. "You're taking it like a pro." I'd have liked to place a supportive hand on her shoulder, but that would simply have been inappropriate for a host of reasons. Shit, I wanted to hug the poor girl and tell her it would be okay. She was only twenty-four.

"At least I didn't puke," she said, pointing to the remains of someone's dinner next to the front walk.

"Who?" I asked, looking at the goopy mess. "Please tell me it was Kenwood."

"Kenwood," She confirmed, giving me a half-smile that didn't reach her eyes.

I blurted a laugh. Mike Kenwood was an Officer in District B. He had this hard-as-nails, asshole exterior, but I had suspected there was a soft mushy center somewhere.

The exterior of the two-story residence was quite a mess. A shit-brown porch, suffering from significant rot, stretched across the front. Two front windows were boarded up. Looking at the age of the plywood, it was clear it'd been there for some time. The rest of the house was all peeling paint and warped siding. Around the side, I could see three rusting central AC units that looked like they hadn't worked in years. Shit, the house looked more like an abandoned building than a home.

This is what being broke in urban America looks like, and it sucks, I thought. Sighing, I pulled on some gloves and booties and stepped inside.

Standing in the hall, I was almost overwhelmed by the stench of blood and decay and immediately stepped back outside to get a clean breath. I could handle the smell itself, but the squeezing anxiety of an oncoming flashback had forced me to seek refuge on the porch for a minute. I jumped as I felt a hand on my upper arm.

"Are you okay?" Nev said.

I held up my hand to ward off any more questions while waiting for the feeling to pass. After about a minute of catching my breath, I turned to Nev. "The smell just reminded me of something — unpleasant. I'm alright."

Fuck! Now I look like I can't handle the scene.

The house was broken up into four apartments, two on each floor. The crime scene was on the first floor in the apartment to the right. Carlos was standing in the doorway, back to me, talking to an older patrol officer, clean-shaven and a little portly.

Beneath the bodies and surrounding them, a bloodstain soaked the carpet to the point of pooling. I could make out arterial spray on the couch and walls, even in the darkness. This had happened recently. The blood hadn't had time to dry thoroughly. Pressing my gloved finger to a spot, I found it tacky, confirming that assumption. The killer had eviscerated and cut the throats of both victims — their dead eyes were open, staring into nothingness.

"Mother of God," I said, coughing to avoid gagging.

"Yeah," Carlos said, acknowledging my presence. "It's pretty bad. I was just waiting for you before I walked the scene. But, look over there." Carlos had a flashlight and waved it around on the floor at something. I leaned further over to get a view of the spot he was gesturing toward. A bloody shoe print was pressed into the carpet. I'd be damned if it weren't the roughly same shape and size as the ones we'd found at our last crime scene.

"Son of bitch," I swore. "Same guy?"

"Might be," Carlos said, gesturing to the two bodies on the floor. "I don't get it, though. Caldwell was run through and decapitated. These two were cut open." It was a rhetorical question at this point because who the fuck knows.

"Where's the third victim?"

Carlos pointed forward. "Kitchen. Shot in the head. Nev said the heart was ripped out, Twelve-year-old kid."

"You ever seen anything like this in Dallas?"

"Nope," Carlos said flatly. "We did have a cannibal case once, but that's for another time."

I turned to the patrolman. "We have names?"

He flipped through his notes. "Josefina Rodriguez, her husband Danilo, and Josefina's daughter Acacia."

I sighed and rubbed a bead of sweat off my forehead with my forearm. "Okay, let's get this over with."

Carlos and I entered the scene.

Immediately I noticed the molding around the door was shattered. "He kicked or rammed his way in."

I couldn't touch the light switch for fear of smearing any prints, so we were stuck with flashlights. I made a wide berth of the victims to avoid the blood and any trace on the floor.

Carlos bent down to examine the bodies. "Looks like it happened damn fast. I can't see any defensive wounds."

I was dumbfounded. "How do you kill two people like this quickly enough that neither has time to react? Look at the Sofa. There's a void where they were sitting. They just slid off the couch to the floor, or they were pulled."

"Hell if I know. Two killers maybe?"

I swept the floor with my light, but only saw the one set of prints. "It's possible, but I don't see any other footprints. Nothing else indicates a second perp. And my gut tells me that this guy just kicked in the door and gutted them. The wounds look like single precise cuts. I don't see any jagged edges."

"How can you tell with all the blood?"

I bent down and tugged at Ms. Rodriguez's shirt. "The clothing, each shirt has a single slice, no dragging, no tearing, clean cuts. The necks look the same."

We stepped into the kitchen, careful to avoid the bloody footprint on the carpet. The lights were on. A twelve-year-old girl was sitting in a chair in front of a child-sized frozen dinner of fish sticks and mac and cheese, and she was very dead. I rubbed my forehead with my forearm, pushing back a sense of despair. "Fuck, she was just a baby."

Her head hung back over the chair, jet black hair hanging limply behind in two thick, blood-soaked braids. The back of her skull was blown open, and gore had dripped to the floor. Examining her face, I could see that she'd been a beautiful little girl with flawless light brown skin. I stopped and closed my eyes to catch my breath, unbidden images of the tiny Iraqi boy wearing the suicide vest burning in my head.

Carlos leaned close. "You okay?"

"Yeah, I just hate—" I stopped, sucked in a horrified breath, and blinked back tears. Across the floor was a series of bloody footprints. Each was the exact size and shape of the ones we'd found at the first scene. This time, I could see the logo that Doyle had mentioned.

One of the prints was smeared with a small bare footprint, and there was a bit of blood on one of the victim's feet. "Fuck," I swore, glancing down. "Look at her footprints over top his. He made her walk over here and sit down." I continued inspecting the victim closely, especially her wounds. "There's a single gunshot wound to the forehead. It looks to be a .380 or maybe a nine-millimeter. You see any casings?"

"There's one over to your left under the chair," Carlos said, walking around the table to get a better look. "Looks like .380 auto, good eye."

I took the compliment, though it didn't help the knot in my gut. The little girl's rib cage had been torn open, not cut. There was a lot of blood pooled in her lap. The splatter on the table was minor, and her legs, under the table, had some cast-off but not much else. "Looks like he took the heart after she died. Thank goodness for small favors. Carlos?"

"Yeah?" Carlos turned to look at me.

"What kind of strength does it take to do that to someone's rib cage?"

He shined a flashlight into the gaping cavity. "Like this? I have no idea. Every rib is snapped. So—" He paused, apparently doing some mental calculations. "I'd guess around four-thousand to five-thousand pounds. The only time I've ever seen damage like this has been in car accidents."

I looked around him. "I don't see any tool marks? Crowbar, rib-spreader?"

"None. But these look like nail prints in here. I think this was done by hand." I could hear the absolute astonishment in his voice.

"Not possible," I said flat-out. "No, way."

"Look for yourself?" He said, standing away and handing me the flashlight.

I looked into the chest cavity. My clinical detachment had finally set in, letting me see this as just another victim — at least for now. Just inside the rib cage, I could see what looked like fingernail impressions and what might be a smeared partial fingerprint on a bit of exposed bone.

I gasped as a palpable sense of dread squeezed my heart. "What on God's green earth have we gotten into?"

Carlos and I looked at each other uneasily.

"Let's finish the walk and go outside."

16

Outside, the forensics truck had just arrived; Doyle had been driving. I could see her auburn ponytail bouncing around as she gathered her gear. I just sat down on the stoop next to Carlos to wait, already exhausted by lack of sleep and the emotional toll of the scene. I was sick and tired of all of humanity. I'd worked a lot of cases in the last two years, and none of them had affected me like this. Of course, none of them had been this brutal.

"Well," Carlos said, arms resting on his knees. "It's official; we're dealing with a serial killer."

I ran my hands through my hair. "I don't need this right now, Carlos. I really don't."

"No one needs this, Cait. But it's the job, and we do it, no matter what."

One of the patrolmen walked up to report on the canvas. "No one saw anything except the upstairs neighbor. It looks like the other apartments are abandoned. The upstairs neighbor is Sharon Brian; everyone just calls her 'Candy.' She's been collared a few times for prostitution and possession."

I sighed tiredly and stood. "Where is she?"

"In my squad car." The patrolman pointed.

"Okay, thanks, I'll go talk to her. Did you get a statement?"

"Yes, but she won't come downtown. Just wants to know when she can go back into her apartment. I wouldn't want to sleep here knowing this had happened."

"Yeah." I put on my game face and strode to the car. 'Candy' was sitting in the passenger side, just watching everything. She had the shakes, probably withdrawal.

"Hi Candy, I'm Detective Reagan," I said as I got in. "I understand you were the one who called this in. Can you tell me what you saw?"

"So, I work over at Charlie's." Charlie's was a low rent stripper bar in Mattapan, known for frequent drunken and disorderly calls, a rough place. "I went home for some quiet time before my first appointment of the evening when I heard the back door slam. When I looked out, I saw some guy running around to the side of the building with a sword. It looked like he had something in his other hand, but I couldn't see too good."

"Any idea what kind of sword?"

"Not a clue; I don't know much about them." Her jittery hands made a curving motion. "Shaped like that. The guy was wearing a hoodie, so it was hard to tell much. He was tall and slim, not very big. When I saw the door, I wondered how someone so thin could do that. For a skinny guy, he must have been pretty solid."

"And you didn't see anyone else?" I probed, not sure what I was hoping she'd say.

"No, ma'am," she answered without hesitation. "There was no one else."

"Wait. You said he ran around the side of the building. Which side?" There was a clear avenue of escape through the backyard, so running to the side didn't make much sense.

"The right side? Toward the driveway." She pointed at the crumbling mess of concrete leading to the street. "I thought I heard the bulkhead doors, but they're locked."

"Did you see or hear a vehicle when he ran off?"

"No, nothing like that. Can I get back into my apartment? I really need—" She stopped, probably about to say she needed a fix.

"Not yet; wait here, please." I got out of the cruiser. The bulkhead rested against the side of the house next to an old rusting refrigerator. I grabbed three of the patrolmen, pointing to each of them. "You, you, and you. Come with me." I waved to Carlos, and he walked over.

"The witness said the perp ran around the side of the building, and she thought she heard the bulkhead. Carlos, can you take Officer Williams inside and watch the back stairs." Carlos nodded and went back into the building. Doyle and the forensic guys all scurried back out.

When we reached the bulkhead, I found a broken chain with a relatively new lock sitting next to it. I pointed to two patrolmen and soundlessly directed each to take a door handle of the bulkhead. The third man and I stood next to each, weapons drawn and pointed at the doors.

"Go," I whispered, and they yanked open the doors with the scream of rusted steel.

"Boston Police," I called into the dark—no response. My flashlight didn't shine very var, but there were footprints in the dust. I couldn't make out if they were the same.

I stepped down the stairs carefully, panning my flashlight around. The cellar was filled mainly with boxes. In one corner, a set of old wooden spiral stairs led upward.

The third officer, James, I think, came down behind me. I pointed to the stairs. He nodded, and I went to the left, around a pile of cardboard boxes and plastic crates. My heart hammered in my chest.

A rusty cabinet and a desk sat against the far wall. There was nothing else of note. I looked back over to Officer James, and he shook his head, indicating there was no one in the stairwell. The cellar was empty.

"Clear!" I shouted.

"Clear!" Officer James shouted back, and I holstered my weapon.

With the room secured, I paid more attention to the boxes. Most of them were file boxes of the variety typically used by law firms. They were all marked in one fashion or another with the name Schmidt, and the dust on them suggested they hadn't been touched in years. I tried the file cabinet drawers, but they were all locked. There was nothing here, yet my gut told me that the perp had come down here. I gave up and went back outside.

Carlos stood waiting at the top of the stairs. "Stairwell door's painted shut upstairs, but it's not locked or barred. The doorknob even turns. Find anything?"

"Nope. Just a bunch of boxes for some guy named Schmidt — business records, maybe. There were some shoe prints on the stairs, but the cellar looks undisturbed." I pinched the bridge of my nose, frustrated. "I don't know. Let's wait until forensics finishes with the scene. In the morning, we need to chase down Mr. Blackman."

Carlos blinked bleary tired eyes. "Yup."

"One other thing, as the lead detective for the unit, I need your approval to take this to the press. We need more eyes on this. We're getting nowhere fast."

After some coaxing, Candy packed a bag and went to stay with a friend. A couple of hours later, Doyle and the forensics team came out of the apartment carrying about two dozen bags of various sizes just as the ME showed up to take the bodies.

Doyle strode up to me, a gleam in her eye. She carried a small plastic evidence bag. "We didn't find much, but the shoe prints are an exact match to the last murder." She was practically vibrating to tell me what she'd found.

"Okay, Doyle, What's in the bag?" Her blasé attitude in the face of such vicious crimes was always disconcerting. Nothing seemed to affect her.

She hoisted the little baggie, looking like a kid with a new toy. "It's the bullet we dug out of the Kitchen wall, the one that killed the little girl. I can't wait to get it back to the lab."

I looked at her in annoyance. "Get to the point; what's so special about it?"

"Watch." She passed her flashlight across it. At first, I couldn't see anything. I was about to tell her so when I saw a hint of shine inside.

I grabbed her hand to hold it steady. "Stop. There."

"Detective," she said suggestively. "I didn't know you cared."

I ignored the comment. "What is that?"

"That, I think— and I won't know for sure until I get it back to the lab— is silver."

17

We returned to headquarters at about seven, tired and emotionally burnt. I called Gabe to see if he had a recent photo of Blackman.

"Hey, how's your Mom?"

Gabe spoke slowly, sounding exhausted. "I don't know, you'd think that she'd be relieved he was gone, given the way he treated her, but she's walking around acting like her life is over. She's sixty-two, you know, just past middle age. She's got a good twenty to thirty years ahead of her, maybe more. I just don't get it."

"And how are you doing with all this?"

"I'm okay. I just feel a little off-kilter. Dad's been the villain for most of my life, and now he's gone. I thought I'd be happy or relieved, but—."

I tried to be empathetic, but it came out sounding fake. "It sounds like it's put you on uncomfortable footing."

"Ya think?".

Tired and aggravated, I took a moment to calm myself before speaking again. "Sorry, I'm not very good at this."

"No, you're fine. I know you're trying. Thank you for being there for us last night."

Fuck. "Of course, I want to get together on Tuesday and talk?"

"Sure, I could use a break."

"Okay, good." I pushed my pen around on my desk and

leaned back, staring at the ceiling. "Meet me at my place around eight. I know it's bad timing, but when you have a free minute, do you think you could send me a picture of your boss? I need something more recent than his passport photo." I waited patiently for an answer as the line went quiet. Then my phone buzzed.

"That's the picture from the other night. It's the best one I have."

I looked at the picture. In it, Gabe was standing next to a handsome bearded man with black hair and eyes. He looked sick or something, though. His eyes were bloodshot, and his skin was pallid and waxy.

"Was he sick?"

"I think so," Gabe said. "He didn't eat a bite at the restaurant. When I asked him about it, he said his stomach was bothering him. Does that matter?"

"Probably not. I was just curious."

There was a short pause on the line, and I was about to say goodbye when Gabe spoke. "Cait?"

"Yes?"

"Are we going to be okay?"

I closed my eyes. This wasn't the time to discuss this. Gabe had just lost his father, and his mother was drowning in grief. So, I lied once more. "Yes, Gabe. We'll be fine. Go. Take care of your Mom. And thanks for your help."

"I love you, Cait."

"I know, Gabe. I love you, too." I rubbed my forehead and pawed at my eyes.

"Okay." He hung up.

I ran my hand through my hair and laid my head on the desk. "Fuck! Fuck! Fuuuck!"

After an appropriate few minutes of wallowing, I wrote up the BOLO on Blackman and sent it to the Fugitive Apprehension Squad. They couldn't arrest him without a warrant, but they could yank his ass aside and detain him for questioning. I didn't know who this fucking Blackman guy was, but his disappearance was pissing me off.

I snatched up my mug and decided to enjoy the self-flagellation of the office coffee. Detective Mills and Carol were chatting with Carlos when I reached the door in the break room. Carlos was telling another story of his time in Dallas. David and Carol were listening in rapt attention.

"So, the new guy comes in with no gloves on and picks up this little thing off the floor. It was about this long." He gestured to a length of about eight inches. "It had a cord and a little metal tip on the end."

I covered my mouth in shock as I realized what he was describing.

"So he says, 'What in the hell is this?' And she looks at him, and without so much as a hint of embarrassment, she says, 'It's a toy.'"

Carol and I laughed. Mills was clueless.

Carlos continued his story. "So he drops it on the floor and goes, 'Aww, did I just get you on me, or him?' And she said, without missing a beat, 'Probably him.'"

"Oh, God," Mills said, shocked, finally realizing that the 'new guy' of Carlos' story had picked up a dildo.

We all stared for a second; then, we erupted in laughter. Cops were a raunchy bunch sometimes. We used humor to deflect the emotional cost of cases like this.

I smiled at them as I stepped out of the doorway and headed for the coffee pot.

"Fresh pot," Carlos said as I scooted by him. "The good stuff."

I sighed. "I don't deserve the good stuff."

Carol was the first to jump on the comment. "Okay, Cait, what's going on? I've been watching you. You're always a little tense, but lately, you've been really on edge."

I looked at Carlos, nodding toward the door. "Detective Mills? Why don't you and I go see what's taking the ME so long?" He grabbed Mills by the arm and pulled him out, giving Carol and me the break room.

Carol looked around. "You want to talk in here?"

The break room was anything but private. To prove the point, one of the Fugitive Apprehension guys walked through to the refrigerator, carting his lunch and a light air of dip and gun oil. I poured my coffee and then did something I never do; I pulled out Carol's pumpkin spice creamer and poured a generous amount into it.

"Actually, no, let's grab the interview room if it's free."

Carol's eyes turned into dinner plates as she gave my coffee some serious side-eye. "Okay, You are not well. You never use creamer, especially pumpkin spice."

I strolled out the door and waved for her to follow. "Come on."

We grabbed an empty interview room, and I disconnected the recording equipment. Afraid my courage would fail, I didn't wait for Carol to sit down or even turn to face me. "I think I'm gay," I blurted.

She wheeled around. "I'm sorry?"

"I said, I think I'm gay." I looked down into my mug so that I couldn't see her reaction.

"That's what I thought you said." Carol pulled out a chair. "Come over here and sit down."

I did as she asked, and Carol took my now-shaking hand. I stared at the floor, the table, our hands, anything to keep from looking at her. I was afraid that she'd tell me I was a fraud, or going through a phase, or any of a hundred other dismissive comments. Lord knew I wasn't sure of anything myself.

"So, don't take this the wrong way, but what makes you think you're gay?" she asked cautiously.

Something about the question felt wrong. How does anyone know they're gay? You just are. My mind raced with how to respond to the question. I wasn't good at confessions, at least not my own. And, even though I had told Carlos, I still wasn't comfortable telling someone else that I liked women. Panicking, I started to rise. "Maybe this wasn't a good idea."

Carol pointed to the seat. "Sit down, Detective."

I sat but said nothing.

"Now," she continued, sounding more like a mother than a Detective. "Spill it. What happened?"

"Well—" My throat was a little dry, so I took another drink of coffee, swallowing loudly. "I've always found women attractive. But, until recently, I didn't put two and two together. You know?"

A slight grin cracked her serious expression. "So, come on. Who is she?"

"Um. Marcella Carson." I took another long sip of my coffee.

"Really? Not bad, Reagan."

I took a deep, cleansing breath. "Look, I'm not looking to go out with her. I'm looking to stay as far away from her as possible right now. But I have a crush on her, butterflies, nervous stammering, the works. When I'm around her, my brain goes on vacation. I can't think straight." I laughed nervously. "No pun intended."

"I see. Do Carlos and Mills know?"

I cleared my throat as tears fell over my cheeks. "Just Carlos. I haven't told David yet."

"So, you haven't told Gabe." It wasn't a question.

"No, I haven't. Hence the misery and indulgent self-pity. His dad just died; it's not a good time."

"Honey, you need to do this in your way, of course. We all do. But, there is no good time to tell your boyfriend you're a lesbian." When she said 'lesbian,' my head spun a little. It was all just so—surreal. Two days ago, I was with a guy doing 'couple stuff' and avoiding marriage conversations. And today, I realized I find women attractive. No, I was admitting I wanted to have sex with women. I'd always found women attractive.

Carol brushed tears away with her thumb. "Look, you take your time. But be careful. Sometimes men don't take this kind of news well."

I sniffed and grabbed a tissue from a box sitting on the table. "I know. You don't have to tell me."

She leaned back. "One last question. Do you think you

might be bi? As far as I can tell, you've been exclusively with men your whole life."

I had already considered that. "I don't think so. I know when a guy is good-looking, but I've never had these kinds of feelings for men. Men don't—" I struggled for the word.

"Make you horny? Get you hot?" Carol prompted playfully.

"I was going to say, excite me. Not like this."

"Well, then, what can I do for you?" She asked, still holding one of my hands.

"Nothing, maybe just be there for me to talk to."

"Of course, honey. You don't even have to ask; you know that." Carol set down her coffee, leaned forward, and hugged me. "I know this is hard," she whispered. "But you'll get through this and have a better life for it."

"Thanks." I felt not at all confident about that last statement.

Carol stood up and turned toward the door. "If you need anything, you know how to find me."

"Carol? One question."

She didn't even wait for me to ask. "Did I know you were gay? I thought you might be. But I wasn't sure. Oh, is it okay if I tell Janelle?" Janelle was Carol's girlfriend. They'd been together for a couple of years now.

I laughed. "Yes, you can tell Janelle."

Her entire demeanor changed, and she imitated a vapid teenager. "Oh my God! She is so going to freak. What about Mills? I really want to be the one to tell him."

"Okay, okay," I said, sighing. "Slow down. Yes, you can tell David, but please tell him to keep it quiet. I don't need my life becoming squad room gossip."

She closed her mouth and made the motions to turn a key and throw it away as she left the room.

And just like that, I'd told someone else. My life was still all over the place, but I felt like I'd exorcised something that had been eating at me. I felt like I knew who I was, and I could eventually figure things out. I also felt scared as hell.

When I returned to my desk, I found Vic reading over the ME report from the Rodriguez murders. A tiny brown Manila envelope was on his desk like you might use to give someone a house or office key.

"Hey." I touched Vic's shoulder lightly to get his attention.

"Oh, hey." He pointed to the envelope. "Doyle left that for you. She looked like a toy dog jumping for a treat."

I picked up the envelope. "Thanks."

"Oh, you were right, by the way. Donna's preggers." Vic's face broke into a broad shit-eating grin.

I winked and clucked my tongue. "Told ya."

"We're waiting until she's further along before letting other people know."

"A little Vic running around might not be so bad," I said, patting him on the shoulder.

"Vic? More like Victoria? I'm hoping for a girl."

"Well, congratulations. Good for you." I tried to keep the misery out of my voice. I found a post-it at my desk that my friend, Celeste, had called, so I called her back.

"Hello?" It was a woman's voice I didn't recognize.

"Hi, this is Detective Reagan; I'm looking for Celeste." I heard some laughter—well, giggling. Then the phone rattled around a bit.

Celeste squealed and laughed playfully in the background, then spoke into the phone. "Stop it! Sorry Detective. I'm on the cape with friends. I wanted to let you know that I have something you might be interested in. Can you come by my apartment Wednesday?" Celeste was an MIT grad who worked in Cybersecurity research. We'd known each other for a few years.

"Sorry, I'm on a case," I said.

"I know," she replied. "Hang on." There was some swearing in the background, a pause, and Celeste came back on the line. "Sorry about that. I saw you on the news last night. You're working that triple in Mattapan, right? I may have some information that's useful to you, but I won't be able to access it until I get back Tuesday night."

"Okay, I'll stop by on Wednesday then. What time?"

"Any time is good. Whenever. I'll see you then. Gotta go." There was another laugh, and the line went dead. I pulled the phone away from my ear and stared at it. Well, that was mysterious. However, Celeste had been pretty handy with what she called 'open-source intelligence' in the past, and she'd never come to me with something useless, so I figured I'd better see what she had. I made a note to see her on Wednesday.

I spent a few hours writing up my report from the Rodriguez scene before I remembered the little envelope that Doyle had left for me. Carlos had just sat down when I went to open it. Inside was a primarily intact bullet made of what looked like pure silver. A small scrap of paper in the envelope read 'Ag,' confirming it.

"Well would you look at that," I said.

Carlos looked up from writing his report. "Whatcha got?"

"It's the bullet they pulled from Acacia Rodriguez's home," I mused, still ogling the shiny slug. "I think we may have something of a signature here. Caldwell was killed like a vampire, and Acacia Rodriguez was shot with a silver bullet. Werewolf?"

Carlos snorted. "I guess. That's fucked up." He stood, looking about as excited as a Yankee fan at Fenway. "I'm off to go talk to the press."

"Have fun with that."

"I'd rather kick a turd on a hot day, darlin'," he said and walked away.

I laughed. *What did that even mean?*

18

Upstairs, in the Crime Scene Unit, we found Detective Doyle sitting at her desk looking at a grainy video showing Monument Street, just south of the Bunker Hill Memorial.

I waved as we approached her desk. "Hey, girl!"

Jessica looked up, flipping her long red-auburn hair back to reveal a gorgeous smile on her delicate features. I realized suddenly that, while she wasn't the goddess that Marcella Carson was, she was, in fact, stunning. *Was this the way it was? Was I suddenly going to see beautiful women everywhere?*

"Hey yourself, beautiful," Doyle said.

Carol snorted behind me and started to cough. I elbowed her in the ribs.

"So, what do we have from Tuesday night?" I asked, pulling over a chair from an empty desk so I could see her screen.

"Okay, so traffic cameras were a bust." She closed the window that she had been looking at and opened another file. "Our guy is one slippery character. A search of the local cameras came up with very little—nothing on gas station cameras or bank surveillance. We're still waiting on the video doorbell footage.

"However," Doyle continued looking excited. "Officer Best just sent this over. A rather security-conscious gentleman along Monument Square has several video cameras outside his home—like nine."

"Nine? Wow. Please tell me you have a good shot of the murder," I said, hopefully.

Doyle waggled her eyebrows. "Funny you should ask." She hit play and the screen filled with a perfect view of the monument. It must have been from an upper floor because it overlooked the trees. The timestamp showed 1:07:42 AM. As we watched, we saw Caldwell walking across the monument park. The footage was amazingly sharp, though the camera was too far away to pinpoint specific features.

"There! Pause, back it up three seconds." I spotted movement behind the exhibit lodge. "Okay, go forward, frame by frame."

The frames ticked by, showing a shadowy figure moving just behind the exhibit lodge, silhouetted in the ambient glow of the street lights. He was right where Carlos and I expected. It was too dark in that area to make out any detail.

Caldwell kept walking. As he reached the exhibit lodge doors, the figure stepped out of the shadows and hit Caldwell in the chest with his right arm.

"That's where he drives in the stake. Wow. Just one shot and backhanded. The dude's strong; he didn't even put his body into it."

"You think that's impressive, just wait," Doyle said.

There was a flash of something. Even slowed down, it was almost too fast to see. Caldwell's head clopped to the ground, then his body collapsed.

"Holy shit," I said, eyes wide.

"I know, right?"

In my excitement, I'd moved very close to her shoulder. Her hair smelled good, better than good; there was coconut and something more profoundly appealing. I blushed slightly as I backed away, blinking. If she noticed my discomfort, she didn't make any indication.

"Um," I stammered slightly. "Can you re-run that at full speed?"

"For you, anything." She flashed me a coy smile and caught my eyes with hers. I blushed furiously and looked away.

We watched again as Caldwell hustled down the walkway. The perp popped out from behind the wall, struck Caldwell with the wooden stake, released it, and then in a single, swift motion, pulled a sword from a sheath in his left hand, decapitating Caldwell before he fell. The precision, speed, and strength stunned me, especially since the man seemed so thin.

The killer put away his sword and then knelt over the body and pulled something from Caldwell's breast pocket — possibly his cell phone.

"Oh my God," Carol said behind me as the killer yanked the stake and, setting it aside, plunged his hand into Caldwell's chest. Then he picked up the stake, stood, and stepped back, his foot stepping in the forming blood pool.

"Can we get this any clearer? I can't see any detail of the perp," I said, focused on the screen.

"Only in the movies, I'm afraid. This is the best I can do," Doyle replied, leaning back with a heavy sigh.

While she spoke, we watched the perp take off, running back to the northeast and into the darkness. "That's it," Doyle said, stopping the video. "He just vanished."

Doyle walked us through the rest of the footage she'd compiled. The only other piece of interest was the same camera showing Karen Walters jogging up to the body, stumbling over it, and calling 9-1-1. Ms. Walters also took some video.

Doyle pulled up a picture of the event with several measuring lines. "According to my best calculations, given the motion, Caldwell's height, the angle and distance of the camera, and the other terrain features, your perp is around six-foot, give or take an inch or two. When he takes off, you can see a small bag flap against his hip, and I'm guessing that whatever grizzly trophy he took was in that."

"It was Caldwell's heart."

"Ick." Doyle stuck out her tongue in a gesture of disgust. For a split second, I wondered what it would taste like. I tried to banish the thought as soon as it came. I couldn't. *Knock it off,*

Cait.

Carol piped up from behind me. "Can you send that down to the team?"

"Yuppers." Doyle attached it to an email and sent it out.

We spent another thirty minutes going over all of the information that forensics had collected and analyzed. There wasn't much in the way of sound evidence, just the footprints, and the video. The entire time though, I struggled to keep my eyes off of Doyle's pretty hair and delicate mouth.

After we were done, I stood up and adjusted my blouse nervously. "Thanks, Doyle, that made my day."

"Glad I could help. Let me know if I can do anything else for you," she added with a wink.

Wait, is she flirting with me? Great, now anytime a woman says something nice, I'll wonder if she's hitting on me.

"Sure," I said. I returned her smile with a broad one of my own, and Carol and I left.

"Well, now," Carol said as we exited the stairs onto the second floor. "Did you catch that? Or do we need to sit down for another 'talk?'"

"Okay," I replied, turning to her. "Did you think she was coming on to me, too? I wasn't really sure. I figured she was just being nice."

Carol just laughed. "Oh, honey, you are so going to fit right in with the rest of us."

Back at my desk, I put in a call to a contact with TSA at Logan and had them send over a copy of Blackman's passport information. It took about thirty minutes, but when I got it, I was floored. He had to be our guy. His passport listed him as one-hundred eighty-seven centimeters tall and seventy kilos. That put him squarely into the right height and weight for our perp.

I looked at my watch. "Holy crap," I said. It was already twelve-thirty. Between writing warrants and our chat with Doyle, I'd lost track of time. There was a TV on in the conference room, and I could hear Carlos' voice. It was the press briefing, probably on the noon news.

I went into the conference room to see the footage. Carlos looked great as he described the nature of the case and the need for the public's assistance.

"Hey Carol," I called. "You want to get lunch?"

"Sure. Viga?" Viga was a little Italian deli-style restaurant over by the John Hancock building. It was further than I usually went for lunch, but I was in for Italian today. They had pretty good chicken parm.

My phone buzzed with a message.

> **Marcella**: I am going to the Common for a bite to eat. I thought maybe you might want to join me.
>
> **Me**: Sorry, working. Thank you for the invite, though.
>
> **Marcella**: I'll be there from one to three if you change your mind.
>
> **Me**: Okay.

"God, she's persistent," I muttered to myself.

Carol carol the phone from my hand. "Lemme see!"

"Hey!" I reached for my phone.

"Oh, no," she giggled. "You sit right there; I wanna read this."

I pouted, crossing my arms. "That's private. Do you want me to go through your phone?"

Carol gave me an impish smile. "No, but this is different."

"How so?"

"You're my trainee, now. I have to look out for your love life."

"Shh. Please keep your voice down." I looked around to see who had heard me, but everyone was heads-down in their work or on the phone.

Carol read through my exchanges with Marcella, all two of them.

Her eyes went wide. "Wow!"

I panicked. "What? What did she say?"

"You're right; she is persistent. She's messaged you all of two times."

"Well, you should have seen her at her house," I said, then immediately regretted it.

"Really? Was it good?" She had a twinkle in her eye and was obviously enjoying poking at me.

"Nothing happened," I said, feeling heat creep up my neck. "Good grief, she was just very—" I struggled for the right words.

"Sexy? Hot? Delectable enough to eat?" Carol finished for me, making me blush all the harder.

"No," I said, flustered.

"Bullshit," Carol exclaimed. "I've seen her photos. She's a fucking goddess, and you know it."

"That's not what I mean. I mean, she was extremely— straightforward."

"Oh, so you did find her sexy and hot."

"Yes," I whispered sheepishly, feeling weirdly okay with the admission. "But the Caldwell case."

"Is she a suspect, witness, or confidential informant?"

"No, but—." I reached for my phone again, but Carol pulled away.

"What I hear, she's just somebody the victim worked for. You should go."

"I can't," I replied, a little more forcefully. "Much as I might like to, the case could take a turn."

"How?" Carol said. "She has a cast-iron alibi for Caldwell; she was in London at the time of the murder. We have confirmation that she flew back the next day. On top of that, she has been extremely cooperative, has she not?"

"Yes, all that's true, but—"

"But, nothing. I'm going to do you a favor." Carol started typing on my phone.

"What are you doing?" I asked, eyes wide as she stopped typing and tossed it back to me.

"I accepted her invitation. She's expecting you at 1:30 by the rotunda."

I looked at the messages and rolled my eyes, groaning. "Why did you do that?"

Carol leaned against Carlos' desk and crossed her arms, giving me a motherly stare. "Because you need to make a friend outside of work and outside your—uh—relationship."

"I have friends; there's Dodge and Rebecca."

"Your martial arts instructor and your eighty-year-old upstairs neighbor? Those aren't friends. One regularly kicks your ass, and the other you feel sorry for because she's lonely."

"Fine," I said, still pouting. "But, I'm going to remember this."

Carol's face split in a wide grin that practically reached her ears. "I bet you will. Now, scoot!"

I stood up and walked away from my desk, giving her the finger as I did so.

"Reagan!" Carol called after me.

"What?" I demanded, turning around and catching my keys mid-flight.

"You're not gonna get very far without those. And, Reagan, if it doesn't work out, there's always Doyle." She made a dramatic fainting gesture.

Christ, could she be any less discrete? I flipped her off again for good measure and then left the building.

19

The splendid sun warmed the air, shining down around puffy clouds. Throngs of people milled about in rolled-up sleeves enjoying the unseasonable warmth.

As I approached the rotunda, I could see Marcella reclining on a vast green and black blanket; a small table next to her held a brown wicker basket. She lay with a single leg propped, a teasing touch of a garter showing under her side slit red wool skirt. Her blouse was untucked and partially open. Next to her sat a wide-brimmed black hat and a red blazer. She wore black stockings, silk for sure. The woman certainly knew how to dress.

I had a brief pang of guilt over Gabe, but I brushed it aside. *You're making a friend, Cait; you're not sleeping with her. Please, let this go better than last time.*

I walked up and stood in her sunlight.

"Hi, Detective," she said, eyes still closed. "You're late. Why don't you take a seat? And, take off those shoes and that blazer. It's too nice of a day to be wandering around fully dressed."

I gawked for a moment. Her angular face and flawless, milk-white skin contrasted amazingly with the flowing black silk of her blouse. When her beautiful blue eyes opened, she smiled alluringly, catching me staring. I looked away and sat down, removing my jacket.

Marcella sat up, pulling on the black hat and dark sunglasses, then opened the basket on the table next to her. She fished out a bottle of sparkling water and two crystal tumblers that threw spectra of light into the air. Then, she carefully handed me a delicate brown paper package tied with twine.

"Be careful with that," she said as she pulled out a second parcel. "It's a fine china plate, not some fast food wrap."

I rolled my eyes. "I'm not a heathen; I do know how to eat." I gingerly unwrapped the parcel, careful to keep it level. On the plate inside was some kind of open-face shrimp sandwich. The presentation was almost too pretty to eat.

Marcella handed me gleaming silverware. "This is räkmacka, also called räksmörgås. It's a common enough lunch in Sweden and best obtained at Melander's Fisk in Stockholm. However, you'll have to settle for homemade today. And, since we Swedes seem to have no clue that sandwiches should have two slices of bread, it is eaten with a fork and knife."

"Got it. Thank you so much." As I took my first bite, I tasted shrimp, cucumber, dill, lemon, and just a hint of some kind of spiced aioli. "Oh my God," I crowed. "This is fantastic. Give my compliments to Ninetta."

"Why would I do that?" she asked, a hint of flirt in her voice.

"Wait," I said, suddenly struck. "You made this?" Most wealthy women, in my experience, could barely boil water. Now that I thought of it. Most women of any stripe in my experience barely knew how to boil water. Any man who wanted a woman barefoot and in the kitchen these days might be risking starvation.

I savored the meal in both its simplicity and combination of flavors, wondering how she'd managed to deliver it looking so neat and pretty.

"I'm pleased you like it." Her eyes twinkled, and her face glowed in a way that made my stomach flip.

"Look, Marcella," I started, but she interrupted me.

"I was stunned that you accepted my invitation. Especially after you ran away yesterday."

"That's what I was going to say—"

"Please, Cait," she interrupted softly. "I know I was overbold before. I shouldn't have pushed you. I just thought —." Suddenly, the crisp, confident woman vanished, replaced by someone genuinely vulnerable. "I tend to wrap myself up in my work; piling on professional responsibilities helps me avoid loneliness. Truthfully, I would just like for us to be friends. While I find you quite ravishing—I will not lie—I enjoy your company just as much. You are intelligent, thoughtful, and vibrant. Please, let me make it up to you. Friends?" She put her hand out toward me.

I smiled sympathetically and took her hand cautiously. "I can understand wanting to make friends. I don't have many myself."

She raised an eyebrow. "Why is that? What I mean to say is that you are quick-witted, respectful, polite, and very pretty. I would think you would have many friends."

"Um, thanks," I murmured, a little uncomfortable at the praise. "I don't have any friends, really, not outside of work. I had friends in the army, but some of them didn't make it back, and of the ones who did, I just lost touch." It wasn't a lie. Rutherford had died, and I'd ghosted Morgan. "I usually don't have much time for socializing and it's hard to find friends who don't get uptight when you suddenly have to cancel plans for work."

"Well, we'll need to change that." Marcella poured glasses of sparkling water and handed me one. "To new friendships," she said, offering up a toast.

I clinked my glass with hers and took a sip without saying anything. It seemed that this friendship wasn't going to take much work on my part. She seemed content just to order me around and assume I'd be compliant.

"Tell me, Cait," she said, suddenly more serious. "Why did you accept my invitation?"

"Well." I felt heat creep up my throat. "You see—the thing is —I didn't."

She stared, bewildered. "You didn't? I have a text, right

here, stating you'd changed your mind and you'd love to have lunch."

"A fellow Detective decided that I needed to make new friends, so she hijacked my phone."

"So, you didn't want to be here?" she asked baiting me playfully.

"No," I said, suddenly flustered. "I mean, yes. I wanted to be here; I just didn't think it was a good idea."

"Why is that?"

"Right. So." My mouth immediately ran away, my brain in tow—again. "Here's the thing. I think you're stunning. But you're someone who's at least peripherally involved in a case. So, getting to know you, like, privately, is kind of a big no-no. And, I've never been good at keeping friends. Even in high school, I was an angry kid. So, I didn't have a lot of friends then either. I hung out with the boys, but that was either for sex or because we had common interests. I didn't do the whole makeup and dress thing. And I've been gay—I think—for like five minutes. You know?"

Fuck, Cait, Shut up.

Marcella burst out in peels of heartfelt laughter while I just blinked.

"I'm sorry," Marcella said through her hysterics. "Goodness, Cait—" She stopped talking as she made the most adorable snort of glee. Her hand flew up to her mouth, and her eyes went wide.

It was my turn to laugh, then. And there we were, both of us laying on our backs, howling, plates of rock-whatever jiggling in our laps. Not only did I like this woman, I liked her a lot. And, I was having fun just hanging out with her.

After we had finished laughing, we returned to our sandwiches and watched the other people walking by. A few somewhat questionable fashion choices passed, and one man in particular, in Birkenstocks and a leopard print pimp-hat, left us trying to hide our snickers.

"Can I ask you something?" Marcella said, her voice losing all of its humor.

"Sure."

She spoke gently. "What happened to you in Iraq?"

My smile vanished. "You have my file, I'm sure. It's all there."

"No, I don't. I did do some asking around about you, but I would never intrude on your privacy like that." She looked both offended and hurt.

"I'm sorry. I just assumed you would have pulled some strings or something. You said you like to know who you're dealing with."

"Well, you're not wrong, generally. But, the minute I met you, I believed you to be honest and forthright. I'm very good at reading people." She pushed an errant strand of hair behind her ear and looked at me sidelong. "So, will you tell me?"

I sighed heavily and closed my eyes for a second. "I really can't talk about it; please don't ask me to. At least not right now."

"Okay. Then let me ask another question. How long have you been carrying it with you?"

My eyes burned and a tear sprung forth, but I wiped it away briskly, sniffling. "Twelve years." I felt a hand brush against mine, and I looked down; in it was a handkerchief.

"Hang on to that. Why don't we finish eating so you can go back to work."

"Can I ask why you are so interested in my fucked up past?"

"I don't like to see good people suffer, I suppose."

It was an evasion, but I let it go. I wiped my eyes and dug back into my sandwich. Feeling a little melancholy, I kept quiet for a while as I finished the food. To Marcella's credit, she asked me no more questions, waiting for me to speak. I was about to tell her I had to go when a familiar face limped over.

"Detective, is that you?" It was Daryl, pushing his grocery cart full of aluminum cans. Many homeless collected cans to make a few bucks here and there. Daryl had dirty blond hair and a scruffy short beard. He was dressed in his old camouflage jacket, black sweater, threadbare jeans, and a new pair of sneakers. His husky baritone had a slight lisp for lack of teeth.

"Hi, Daryl." I offered him a wide grin. "I like your shoes."

He looked down, bounced on his toes slightly, and gave us a toothless grin. He pointed to my bare feet. "And I like yours."

I wiggled my toes in reply. I liked Daryl. Even with all of his challenges, he struck me as an honorable man with the best of intentions. And while I felt pity for his state of affairs, I wanted to preserve as much of his pride as I could. "Daryl, this is my friend, Marcella. Marcella, this is Daryl Cummins. He's a buddy of mine."

Marcella stood and walked over to Daryl, holding out her hand, much to my surprise. Most people were repelled by the homeless, considering them bums at best or dangerous at worst. Marcella had no fear of Daryl whatsoever, though.

"The pleasure is all mine; I'm sure, Mr. Cummins."

Daryl took her hand and then frowned as he pulled it back. Looking at Marcella with suspicion, he retreated a few steps back toward his cart. "You're the vampire lady," he uttered, refusing to meet Marcella's eyes.

"I'm sorry?" Marcella looked at him, clearly confused. She raised an eyebrow and mouthed the word 'vampire lady' at me with a questioning look, and I just shrugged.

"Detective," he said, glancing at me. "You should be careful who your friends with."

I was stunned. "Daryl, do you think vampires are real?"

"One killed Jo-Jo." His tone was very matter of fact with just a hint of sadness. And though he spoke to me, he continued watching Marcella, now seated.

"Wait, what? Jo-Jo is dead? What happened?" I asked, worried for him.

He finally turned to me. "Someone tore open her throat. The doctor at the hospital said it must have been an accident. BK and Dog found her down on the mile behind a dumpster." Daryl was referring to the methadone mile at Mass and Cass. "It took some work to get it out of him, but they said what happened. They said he was licking her throat, lapping up her blood like a dog. They wouldn't tell me anything else."

I frowned. "Wait, your not making any sense. Who are BK and Dog?"

He turned his eyes back to Marcella, still not meeting her gaze. "Just some guys. Can we talk over there?" He pointed toward the rotunda.

"Sure, Daryl." I made to apologize to Marcella, but she just nodded and waved us on as Daryl limped off toward the Rotunda, and I followed.

Irritated that Daryl had treated Marcella, who seemed perfectly lovely, with such disdain, I snatched Daryl's arm as soon as we reached the rotunda and swept him around. "Alright, Daryl. What's going on?"

"Jo-Jo is dead. BK said he and Dog saw someone drinking her blood over on the mile."

"Okay, and you said that someone called 9-1-1?"

"Yeah, Dog did. The ambulance showed up, and so did a cop. The cop said it must have been an accident. BK said it wasn't, but the cop didn't listen. That's what BK told me."

"Wait, BK told a police officer that Jo-Jo was murdered and no one called in Homicide?" I was incredulous.

He adopted a faraway look. "No one cares what happens on the mile. They don't care about Jo-Jo or any of us."

I was still skeptical of the whole affair. I didn't know any officer who would do what he was suggesting. "What else did BK say?"

"He said the man had a sword on his back. One of those ninja swords." That got my attention.

"Like a katana?"

"I guess. Anyway, Jo-Jo's dead." Daryl scratched at his nose, looking around nervously.

"Daryl?"

"Yeah?"

I glanced at Marcella who was watching us, face impassive. "Why do you call Marcella the 'vampire lady?'"

"That's just what some of the guys call her."

"Street guys?"

"Yeah, they all know who she is. She comes down here for lunch a lot. She used to feed lunch to a lot of us. Then, one guy, I can't remember his name, Jimmy, I think. Big guy, dark-skinned, long dirty dreads, he said he saw her kill someone. The next week, Jimmy disappeared. Now, no one talks to her anymore."

"Are you sure it's the same woman?"

"Well, I don't know if she actually killed anyone, but when the street talks, you listen, you know. I do know that's the woman they call the vampire lady. Do you think she's nice?"

"So far, she's been very nice to me." It was falling into place now. Street rumors were often taken as gospel when it came to who you should and shouldn't be around. It was a survival mechanism. Frankly, it worked most of the time. But, sometimes you'd get crazy shit like 'the vampire lady.' Sometimes the rumors were accurate, and sometimes, it was mistaken identity or a drugged-out haze. It was all its own mythology of sorts.

"Here, go get something to eat." I handed him a twenty, and he ambled away toward his cart, periodically glancing at Marcella suspiciously.

I walked back over to Marcella, who was packing up our plates.

"I'm so sorry," I told Marcella as I pulled on my socks and shoes. "He's a good guy, but apparently, you have a 'rep' among the transients down here. You've become the myth of 'the vampire lady.'" I made sure not to let any sarcasm creep into my voice. Homeless people don't deserve to be ridiculed. I knew none that were homeless by choice. In many cases, they were controlled by forces more powerful than they could hope to overcome, like the mental health issues hemmed in Daryl. The streets were the only place where his world made sense.

"It's okay, Detective. You might be surprised to find out that it's not the first time I've been accused of being the undead. Once, in London, a priest threw holy water on me." She chuckled a bit. "He was pretty horrified when I didn't scream and run away or burst into flames. I mean, look at me," she said, her tone turning a bit self-effacing. "Pale skin, skinny, low body temperature. What else would ignorant people think? The truth is, I have a physical condition that causes all this." She finished packing up her case and folding up the small table.

"I just figured you stayed out of the sun. And you're not the first person I've met with cold hands. A guy I went out with a few years ago whose hands were positively frosty all the time. It was a real turn-off in—" I stopped myself. She doesn't want to hear about your former sex partners, stupid. "Not that your hands are cold like his, they're not. It's just— " *Jesus, Cait, really?*

She bent over to pack her things. God, she had a beautiful ass, and my mind started to run away, me in tow. The urge to reach out and put my hands on it was almost overwhelming. She sensed my proximity because she stood upright, turned, and looked me in the eye.

"Yes, Detective?" A cocky smile played about her ruby lips. "See something you like?"

I flushed. I stammered momentarily. "I—I—uh—have to go back to work."

"Shame. I have work to do myself, too, though. A cargo ship lost power in the pacific and capsized. They rescued the crew, which is all that truly matters, but a half-million in cargo we were shipping went with it. But, I'm sure you don't want to hear about my woes." Her tone turned a little more intimate, and she looked me in the eye. "I enjoyed our time today very much."

I blushed like a schoolgirl, positively giddy at the compliment. "I did, too," I said dumbly.

She reached up slowly, almost languidly, and pushed a stray hair from my face, stroking my chin as she did so. "I'd like to see you again. Are we still on for Monday night?" Her forthright manner was so appealing—no games, no battles. While she could be coy, Marcella's true nature was very assertive, almost aggressive.

"No," I whispered. "No, we're not." I looked down at her lips, instinctively licking my own. My pulse started to race, and my breathing felt labored. A buzz of excitement filled my head. I watched as her lips turned into a frown, and she propped her hands on her hips.

"No?" Her tone was demanding.

"No, some crazy Swede I just met roped me into cooking dinner for her," I joked, smiling playfully.

"Good girl," she breathed as she stepped closer, the same smile tugging at her lips. A shiver ran down my spine. We were only inches apart. "Send me the ingredients you need for your Bolognese sauce."

"Yes," I whispered. I felt bewitched, lost in her frosty blue eyes, and a little weak in the knees.

She leaned in and kissed me, a light brush on my cheek from soft, cool lips that burned. Gooseflesh rose across my body, and I suppressed another shiver.

"Goodbye, Cait. I'll see you Monday night. Maybe sooner." Her voice was quiet and velvety and full of dark promises. Marcella turned away, gathered up the blanket, basket, and table, and left. Picking up my jacket off the ground, I watched her hips sway as she walked away, thinking of the hint of garter under the skirt.

Mary, mother of God, help me.

20

Carol sat at my desk, feet up, waiting for me. "Well? How did it go?"

I decided to understate the matter. "It was okay. She's very nice. You, by the way, are an asshole." But, regardless of how hard I tried, I couldn't stop smiling and blushing like a schoolgirl. I might as well have skipped into the cube farm.

Carol laughed. "Oh, you've got it bad. Is there a second date?"

Another flush crept up the back of my neck and pinkened my cheeks. "Okay, quit, two things. First, get out of my seat. Second, did you hear anything about a death on the mile last night?"

Carol gasped. "There is! Isn't there?" She started clapping her hands and hopping up and down. "That didn't take long. Look at you go."

"Carol! Stop." My whole body was burning crimson. "Now, I promise I'll spill everything—later. Please. Junkie? Last night?"

Carol raised an eyebrow and sighed. "Fine. Sure. Squad five picked it up. A junkie had her throat torn open and bled out. Wasn't a lot of blood at the scene, so they figured it was a body dump."

"Well, we're going to have to talk to them. The victim was Jo-Jo, Daryl Cummins' friend. He said two witnesses swore that she was murdered there by someone carrying a Japanese sword."

Carol's eyes turned into saucers, and she whistled. "Uh-oh."

"Yup, we need to find this guy. That's five bodies in three days." I blew out a breath and sent Benton, squad five's lead, an email letting him know that we needed to see his case files and why. He replied almost immediately, more than happy to hand the case over.

"I'm going to let Larson know that we're picking up the case."

"I'll go get the files from Dooley's team," Carol replied and walked off.

I went to Larson's door and knocked on it.

"Come in!" He snapped.

I opened the door and leaned my head in. "We're taking squad five's junkie; we're pretty sure it's the same guy as our other two."

Larson shook his head. "Okay, let Dooley know. Now get out while I work on these evals. Yours is in this stack, by the way, so don't fuck up." I rolled my eyes as I closed the door.

"I saw that," Larson yelled through the door. I shook my head and went back to my desk. I even threw Larson's door the finger as I walked.

I had just sat down when my phone buzzed with a gibberish text from Gabe. I texted him back, asking what he needed, but there was no reply. *Odd.* I thought and chalked it up to an accident.

Carol had already come back with a stack of case folders from Benton. Jo-Jo's real name was Charlotte Westfield, born in Annapolis, Maryland. Her rap sheet was relatively short: soliciting, drug possession, drunken and disorderly—nothing violent. I hadn't liked her because I thought she was terrible for Daryl, but that didn't matter anymore.

Whatever Daryl had been on about, Squad-Five had done an excellent job working the case. The witness statements would have been funny if someone wasn't dead. 'Witness claims a vampire, like Count Dracula, ate the victim.' *Good grief. Could this case get any more fucked up?* My phone rang.

"Homicide, Reagan," I answered.

"Cait?" It was Gabe, but his voice sounded strange, almost like a cry of anguish or pain.

"Gabe? What's wrong, honey?"

His voice turned on the spot, becoming enraged and growling. "I need you to come over here, right now."

I furrowed my brow in irritation. "Gabe? I can't. I'm working; you know that."

"You bitch. You need to get over here right now," he roared into the phone.

I blinked, taken completely aback by his sudden rage. "Gabe, what the fuck is going on?"

The line went dead. I tried to call him back a few times, but it went to voicemail. A sick feeling roiling my gut, I called the E-5 station, just a few blocks from Gabe's, and asked for a wellness check. They could get there far faster than I could.

I turned to Carlos, who was just rolling over. "Want to take a ride? Gabe just gave me the weirdest phone call. He sounded— unhinged. I need to go check on him."

"Sure, darlin'. You bet. Let me get my things."

Twenty minutes later, we'd turned along Weld Street and were about to pull down toward Gabe's when I saw the cruisers out in front of a small white house with a picket fence and a beautifully landscaped yard. "Oh, God!"

"What?" Carlos asked.

"It's Deborah Parkman's home." Panic snatched at my breath, and a creeping sense of dread crawled up my spine. The radio crackled.

"Victor 8-7-7. Full notification for Weld and Carlson, Homicide Requested."

I reached over and grabbed the radio in the cruiser. "Victor 8-7-7, responding. I need the victim's name for Weld and Carlson?"

"Victim's name is Deborah Parkman." My heart sank. *Oh, Gabe.*

"I can't go in; it's Gabriel's mother, Deborah." I shook my

head. This couldn't be happening. I didn't like Deborah, and she didn't like me. But I never wanted her dead, and I couldn't imagine what Gabe must be going through. I pulled out my phone and dialed Gabe's number. "Come on, honey, pick up." It went straight to voicemail. "Shit."

Carlos looked both irritated and concerned. "Jesus, Cait, what?"

"Gabe isn't answering. Look, obviously, I can't be involved in this one; you'll have to work it."

The radio crackled to life again. "Echo 2-1-4"

"Echo 2-1-4," Dispatch answered.

"I've got a guy walking down the street in a bloody shirt with a kitchen knife. Requesting backup to Weld and Russett."

I had an awful feeling rising in my chest. Carlos was already on it, though, "Victor 8-7-7 responding to Weld and Russett." Carlos hit the lights and sirens and peeled out, driving up on the sidewalk around the cruisers.

Just a few blocks down Weld, two officers stood, weapons drawn, yelling at Gabe to drop the knife. He looked terrible. His hair was disheveled, and he had at least a day's stubble. His white shirt and suit pants were torn and covered in blood. In his right hand was a bloody kitchen knife.

I leaped out of the car and ran toward the scene full tilt. "Hold your fire. Hold your god damned fire." I shouted. The officers didn't move, but they stopped yelling. One of them looked over at me.

I held up my badge. "I know this man. Let me see if I can talk him down."

They didn't lower their weapons, but one of the officers nodded.

"Gabe," I called softly. "Gabe, honey?"

He didn't seem to see me. He was pacing back and forth, muttering to himself. But I couldn't make out what he was saying.

I stepped a little closer, making sure not to get between the officers and Gabe. I didn't fancy getting shot if this started to go any further sideways. "Gabe, honey? What are you doing, sweetie?"

He stopped talking and looked at me. "Cait?" He squinted, and his eyes seemed to focus—just barely. He waved the knife at me. "You need to run."

"Gabe, honey? Put the knife down." I motioned with my hand.

"I can't! Don't you know that I can't?" He screamed at me. "I can't! He made me. He made me."

"Gabe, honey, you're not making any sense. Who made you? Made you do what, honey?" I took another step forward.

"Lower your weapons!" I shouted at the officers. "That's a fucking order! I'll take responsibility."

Finally, the officers drew their weapons down. If this went south, I was about to risk my career and, possibly, my life.

"Gabe. What's going on? What did he make you do?"

"I killed her, Cait. He made me kill Mom. He wanted me to kill you, too. But I was strong, and I don't want to." His eyes were wild, and he stank, even from this distance. Gabe slapped his head a couple of times. "Get out. Get out."

Gabe turned toward the officers as Carlos moved slowly past them. "Gabe, honey. Focus on me, don't look at them. I won't let them hurt you. Who wanted you to kill me?"

"Haimon!" he shouted. "Haimon! He's in my head. He wants me to kill you."

"Is Haimon talking to you now?"

"No, no, no." Gabe stomped his feet. I saw his left pinky finger was missing; it was just a stub, bleeding profusely.

Jesus, Gabe, what is going on?

"Hey!" I shouted, taking another step forward. "Eyes on me, honey. We can get through this."

He looked at me again, a touch of lucidity evident in his stare. "You have to run, Cait. I can't stop."

While I talked to Gabe, Carlos circled around and got behind him.

"Gabe, honey, talk to me. What can't you stop?" I took

another step forward. Carlos held up three fingers as he crept up.

3—

Gabe started to turn around.

"Hey, eyes on me, what can't you stop, baby?" I had to hold his attention if he was going to get out of this alive.

2—

"You don't understand. He's strong. So, strong. I killed Mom. I killed her. He made me."

1—

Everything happened at once. Gabe's eyes turned cruel and hateful, and he lunged forward, knife out. Carlos flashed forward. He was so fast that I barely saw the movement before he had Gabe in a bear hug, holding his arms to his side, feet dangling. I ran forward and wrestled at the knife. Finally, I slammed my knuckles into Gabe's fingers, breaking his hold on the blade and his fingers with it. Gabe screamed and then crumpled. Carlos felt him go slack and started lowering him to the ground.

The other two officers were still standing around holding their dicks.

"Call EMS!" I shouted.

I checked Gabe's pulse. It was thready. As I inspected him for wounds, I found a dozen or so bruises on his torso but nothing else other than the missing finger. "Jesus! What happened to you?" I muttered rhetorically. "Fuck."

EMS arrived on the scene about ten minutes later. Gabe was still unconscious; we'd cuffed him and laid him on his side so he could breathe.

I looked at Carlos as EMS took over, loading him into the ambulance. "BMC psych," I said to the EMT. "His name is Gabriel Parkman; he's had some kind of psychotic break. Let them know that he's under arrest and can be restrained if medically necessary."

The EMTs nodded and loaded him up, an officer riding with them.

"Carlos, I'm going to follow them in the cruiser. Can you get a ride back?"

"Yeah, darlin', you do what you have to. I got this. Are you going to be okay?"

No, dumbass, I'm never going to be okay again. I didn't say that; I just took him back to the scene and started the drive to Boston Medical Center. "Yeah, I'll be fine."

21

I strode into Gabe's room, pushing past a nurse who tried to block my way. He was strapped to his bed and seemed calm at first. But as soon as he saw me, his face twisted in rage, and he turned wild-eyed.

"I'm going to kill you, bitch," he screamed, thrashing violently against the restraints. "I'm going to kill you."

"Gabe, honey—" I started, but a nurse pushed me back.

"Okay, you need to leave, like, now!" She said firmly, and I backed out of the room as they sedated him.

A bit later, I watched him through the window, his chest moving up and down with the rhythm of sleep. "Good grief, Gabe, what the hell happened to you?"

"How is he?"

I turned at the soft British accent to find Marcella Carson standing at my shoulder. "I don't know. What are you doing here?"

"Someone named Carol said you could use a friend."

Fucking Carol, playing the matchmaker again. It was cute when she pushed me to go to lunch, but this was a step too far. *My boyfriend, or soon-to-be ex-boyfriend, or whatever he was now, was in the hospital, and she sends Marcella to comfort me?* I let out a heavy sigh and sat down on one of the plastic chairs in the hallway.

Marcella sat next to me. Brushing off her black slacks. "Do

they have any idea what happened to him?"

"No, Marcella, they don't," I snapped. "This morning, he seemed fine on the phone. He was taking care of his mother and asking if we would be okay, as a couple, you know?" I felt like absolute shit discussing Gabe with her after our little date on the common. But if it bothered her, she didn't show it.

"You feel guilty." It was a statement, not a question.

"Of course, I feel guilty. Whatever it was, it probably happened while I was gallivanting on the Common with you."

"Look at me," she demanded, and I felt an irresistible pull that drew my eyes to hers. It was almost frightening. "You are not to blame here. Whatever happened to him wasn't your fault, and you know that."

I hung my head and ran my hand through my greasy, blood-spattered hair. "I know, but I still feel responsible, somehow."

Marcella's tone shifted, growing gentle and comforting. "Your relationship was in a bad place. You as much as said so yesterday. When bad things happen to people we love, it's hard. But when bad things happen to people we love with whom were not on good terms, it's much worse. But, nothing happens for a reason, as much we'd like to think otherwise."

I looked at the tile floor, following the lines with my eyes. "I know. But I should have protected him."

She placed a hand on my forearm. "How could you have? This must seem terribly unfair for someone who has lost so much."

"Damn right, it's unfair." I stood up and started pacing. "What's worse, though. In addition to feeling like a shitty companion, I feel fucking relieved. Relieved!" My voice rose slightly. "Relieved that I have an excuse to let him go and move on. I am a terrible person."

"No, Cait, you're not," Marcella said firmly. She stood up and grabbed my arm to stop me from pacing. I tried to tear my arm away, but her grip was surprisingly solid. "You are a human being with feelings and emotions that can't be controlled. We have no control over anything, not even ourselves. Control is a fucking illusion.

"You didn't do this to Gabe. You didn't put the knife in his hand. You didn't even dump him. You wanted to, but you didn't. Gabe is a victim of a shitty turn in life, nothing else."

At that moment, I realized just how tired I was. I rubbed my face. "You're right. I need to go home and get some rest."

"No, Cait, you do not need to be alone. Is there someone you can call, your mother perhaps?"

"I can call her, but I need to go to the station first and make a statement."

"Bloody unbelievable." Marcella threw up her hands in exasperation. "No, you know what? You are coming home with me."

"I don't want—," I started, but Marcella stomped her foot.

"I don't care what you want. You need someone to take care of you tonight. If you're not willing to go to your mother's, I will do it myself." Her words rattled around in my head for a minute.

"What about the cruiser I drove over here?" It was a weak protest. Shit, I really just wanted to say 'yes, ma'am.' And, at that particular moment, hiding out at Marcella's didn't sound like the horrible idea that it probably was. I was just so fucking tired; I really couldn't think.

"Cáitlín?" I knew before I turned around that it was my mother, dressed in her usual jeans, sneakers, and a frumpy, oversized sweater. No one ever used the Irish pronunciation of my name but her, pronouncing it 'cotch-leen.' *Fuck my life. It was better than even odds that Lieutenant Larson had called her.*

"Conas atá tú?"

"Uafásach, Ma." I hugged her.

"Ma, this is my friend, Marcella Carson. Marcella, Ma." My mother frowned at me. "Sorry. Ms. Róisín Reagan."

"Marcella, good to see you again." My mother held out her hand.

Marcella took it, speaking in what I assumed was Swedish. "Róisín, hur är det?"

My mother responded in kind. "Bra, tack."

My mouth hung open. I hadn't even known my mother could speak Swedish. "Wait, you've met?"

My mother responded curtly, eyeing Marcella, making it seem like she didn't like Marcella much. "Yes, we've met."

They continued conversing in Swedish for a couple of minutes, and it seemed a bit heated. But then my mother breathed a sigh of relief, and they shared a quick hug.

"Okay," my mother said. "Ms. Carson has told me that you'll be staying with her tonight, and I'm glad. I was worried that you might be left alone. Bill didn't tell me what happened to Gabe, just that he was over here in the hospital and that you might need me. Goodness, Cáitlín, you look exhausted." She started fussing with my jacket and shirt, trying to make me look presentable.

"Ma, stop! Gabe tried to stab me an hour ago. I want to go home."

She let go of me and looked shocked for about a second; then, her eyes got hard. "That bastard, I'll kill him myself," she said through gritted teeth, staring daggers at his door.

"Ma, Gabe didn't know what he was doing. Besides, we're not dating anymore."

"You're not?" She did a one-eighty. "What happened?"

I sighed in exasperation. "It just wasn't working. I'll tell you later."

My mother grabbed me by my shoulders. "Now, Cáitlín, I don't want you to be all alone tonight. I mean it."

I rolled my eyes. "Okay, Ma."

"I worry." Her voice was almost a whisper, and remembered pain sparked in her eyes. "Promise me. I need to know you'll be safe tonight."

"Yes, Ma, I promise."

"Good." She turned back to Marcella. "Make sure she eats, stays safe, and gets a good night's sleep."

Marcella smiled beatifically. "Of course."

Ma turned back to me. "Cáitlín, are you leaving now? Do you

want me to stay here with you?"

"No, Ma, I'm leaving. It's okay. I'm going to take a few days off, so I'll call you later. I promise I'll be fine."

We said our goodbyes and I kissed my mother on the cheek, swearing to visit more often, about fourteen times. Then, like the force of nature she was, my mother swirled her way out of the hospital.

"I do like her," Marcella said appreciatively.

I turned on Marcella. "Don't ever do that again. Using my mother to manipulate me? That's low. And, for that matter, how do you know her?"

Marcella crossed her arms and stood, hip cocked as if waiting for something. After a moment, she said, "Are you done?"

I eyed her suspiciously. "Yes."

Her voice wasn't defensive at all, just assertive. "All I did was tell her that I was trying to get you to go home with me so you wouldn't be alone. I only said that because she said she was worried about you. She twisted it around as if it were a foregone conclusion."

That sounded just like my mother. I wanted to be angry with both of them, but I couldn't muster any feeling at all. "And how do you know her?"

"I once donated to your mother's department at the university. I just hadn't put two and two together." Marcella took my face in her hands. "Now, come home with me. I have three extra bedrooms on the third floor. You can have your pick, and I'll make you some tea."

Unsure how to react to the familiar gesture, I did nothing, and my shoulders slumped. Her cool touch felt so good on my cheeks. I had an image of me curled up in a bed with Marcella. It wasn't what she offered, but it was a nice thought. Then, I felt velvety lips brush my cheek, and Marcella spoke gently as if I might shatter into a million pieces.

"I may seem like the evil corporate bitch, but I'm not. I'm a caretaker. It's in my nature to look out for others. Come home with me, no flirting, no games, no invasive questions."

God, but that sounded so nice. Three days ago, the idea of letting someone else take care of me would have been unthinkable. I just wouldn't have done it. But I just nodded my head and walked out with her.

22

I climbed into Marcella's car, a black Audi Q4 eTron. I expected an Aston-Martin or Maserati, not an electric grocery mover. I wanted to make a snarky comment, but my exhausted brain couldn't find one.

I called Larson and requested time off, to which he agreed, if grudgingly. I didn't want to do it, but I was running on fumes, my life was in flames, and I just needed a break. I asked him to send someone to pick up the cruiser, then hung up, turning off my phone, yanking the battery, and putting it in my jacket pocket.

"Can we stop at my place? I'd like to pick up a change of clothes."

"Sure, anything you'd like," she said as she turned onto Storrow Drive.

I gave her my address in the North End and then leaned back in the seat to close my eyes. Sometime later, I jerked awake, feeling sweat beading on my forehead.

Marcella looked at me impassively. "We're here. Are you okay?"

"Yeah, I think I might have been on the edge of a nightmare, but I can't remember." I unbuckled the seatbelt and got out of the car.

It took a little longer than expected, but eventually, I trotted back down the stairs and got back into the car. "I am so sorry,"

I said. "I had to get my neighbor to watch Jabba the Hutt."

"I'm sorry?"

"My cat."

Marcella snorted with glee. "You named your cat Jabba the Hutt? Is he fat?"

"No," I said, feigning offense. "He's just big-boned."

"Indeed." Her voice was laced with skepticism. "You do know that big-boned is a euphemism for fat?"

"He's not fat," I pouted petulantly. "He's big-boned. It's not the same."

Marcella's garage had room for several cars, but there were only two. The Audi we'd just arrived in and an older BMW 3-series convertible.

"Huh," I said as we exited the vehicle. "Looking at your house, I expected there would be more cars, maybe a Ferrari or a Maserati."

"Despite what you might think, Cait, I'm not wealthy. Almost all of my money is tied up in my home and charity efforts."

"And your wardrobe," I muttered under my breath.

She threw me a lighthearted V-sign and said, "I heard that." I smirked tiredly, happy I'd finally gotten in a dig.

We stepped through a green steel door and into a small elevator. I noticed numbers for each floor on the panel. There was also a locked button marked B2.

"What's B2?" I asked, curious.

"It's the sub-basement underneath us. It is not a place for nosy detectives." She winked at me as she said it.

"Is that the drug lab? Or is it where you keep the bodies of your victims?" I asked playfully.

Marcella smiled strangely and shook her head. She pressed the button for the ground floor. The ride was short, and the elevator let out into a nook off the kitchen. Ninetta was preparing food when we walked in.

"Oh, thank you, Ninetta. We're starved, and Ms. Reagan will want to retire soon. Do we have a room made up for her?"

"Yes, Ms. Carson. The west bedroom is ready." Ninetta had a dark look on her face as she glanced my way. If I didn't know better, I would have said she was jealous.

"Delightful. The west bedroom has an attached bath where you can freshen up. Honestly, Cait, you look a bloody fright."

I looked down at myself and only now realized that broad smears of blood ran down my shirt and jacket. My right hand was sticky and coated from wrestling with Gabe's mangled fingers. I was covered. "Oh, God, I didn't realize." I began wiping nervously at my hand and arm.

Marcella pulled my hand away, taking it in hers. "It's okay. You're probably in a bit of shock. Do you have anything to sleep in?"

Shit, I had forgotten PJs. "No, I'm sorry. I'm not firing on all cylinders right now."

"Not to worry. While Ninetta is making food, I'll get you something to wear. Cait, if you take the elevator up to the third floor, down the hallway to the right, next to the back stairs, is your bedroom. Now, go take a shower; you'll feel better." Her tone was gentle, but it brooked no argument.

I followed Marcella's directions to the west bedroom. It was the size of my apartment. A queen-sized canopy bed sat against one wall. A door led to a bathroom with a large walk-in shower. Peeking around the frosted glass walls, I realized the shower had multiple showerheads. Still in the box, a fresh toothbrush sat on the marble washbasin, and fresh towels hung from a brass rack.

I didn't dawdle. Stripping out of my bloody, sweat-soaked clothes, I stepped into the shower and turned on every showerhead, scalding hot. I was instantly inundated, burning my skin. I didn't care. I needed to get clean.

I found soap, shampoo, and a mesh scrubby at the back of the shower, next to a fresh razor. Good grief, Ninetta didn't fuck around. She was like a concierge for a five-star hotel. I grabbed the mesh sponge and scoured Gabe's blood off of my skin.

Slowly, inexorably, as I removed the blood, shock faded with it. I leaned against the shower tiles and finally slid down, sitting in the scorching spray. I succumbed to a cold knot of pain in my chest and a sinking sense of sorrow. Deborah was dead, and Gabe had gone insane.

I lay under the spray for long minutes until there was a knock on the door. "Cait? May I come in?" It was Marcella, as expected. When I didn't answer, I heard the door open. "I've brought you some clothes."

I looked over at the door, it was open a crack, and I could see Marcella's delicate, pale hand on the doorknob.

My voice shook. "Um, just a minute." I tried to rise but found I didn't have the strength. My hands trembled violently, and I felt strangely cold. Moments later, tender arms pulled me into a soft embrace, and the flood of tears that had been threatening for days now fell like rain.

"Dear Goddess, Cait. What are you doing? This water is positively boiling." Marcella broke the hug and turned down the heat, hoisting me from the shower floor back into the water.

"Cait, honey, let's get you clean." The tender care in her voice only made me sob harder. Soft hands rubbed shampoo into my wet hair, scrubbing my scalp. I felt so small at that moment. I was naked in front of her in every sense. Wracking sobs jerked my body, and my thoughts vanished in a river of misery. I was broken.

Marcella finished washing my hair and pushed me under the water to rinse. The air seemed to turn instantly cold as she turned off the water and pulled my shivering form from the shower. Marcella's camisole was plastered against her skin, transparent with wetness, revealing perfect, beautiful breasts. Gazing up, I was captured by her blue eyes, inches from my own. Her lips were dark and full and red against her pale skin. My shivering stopped. I licked my lips almost unconsciously.

Marcella put a finger to my mouth. "No. Not here. Not like this." She pulled a towel from the rack, leaving one for me, and stole away on quiet feet.

I exited the bathroom, moving slowly, in a pair of drawstring pants and a t-shirt. The bed had been turned down, and a steaming mug of something that smelled vaguely of spearmint sat on the nightstand along with a BLT sandwich. A beautiful antique penshell lamp illuminated the room in a soothing ochre light.

Exhausted and defeated, I crawled into the bed and took a sip of the spearmint concoction. Marcella had made me feel so strange. I had been dazzled by her the day we'd met. Over the next two days, as I'd gotten to know her a little better, I found someone who was kind and compassionate, a caretaker, as she had said. But there was something more, almost as if my heart had been barely holding itself together, and as soon as it saw Marcella, it decided to fall to pieces. I tried to analyze the feelings, but I found myself too drowsy to think.

Eyeing the mug in my hands suspiciously, now about half empty, I yawned. Marcella wanted to make sure that I slept, I guess. I set down the mug next to the untouched sandwich and turned out the light. My thoughts drifted quickly into strange visions, and before long, I was asleep.

23

I wake to the soft chime of my phone — zero six-hundred. I am a light sleeper, always have been. Three AC units wail, delivering a comforting white noise. I cannot hear them; the noise plants itself in the back of my mind, something distant and remembered. Slipping soundlessly from under the blanket, I put my feet to the floor and stand. There are three beds: mine, one next to me, and an empty one across the room—Specialist Rutherford's. I feel a vague loss at the empty bed.

I turn and watch Specialist Kennedy sleeping for what has to be the thousandth time, her broad, soft curls slide, flowing over her pillow in a red wave. A sliver of buttery sunlight shines through a crack in the plywood. Moments later, it strikes her eyelids, and she turns, gracelessly flopping over onto her back. But it is not Morgan; it is Gabe. He launches himself out of the bed. His eyes are wild and bloodshot, and his skin is peeling off his body. The flesh of his face slides down, dripping in rotted clumps to the floor. An overwhelming stench of death and decay makes me gag.

"You bitch! You did this to me. You fucking bitch, I'll kill you, you cunt!" His voice is distorted and dark, mouth gurgling with black viscous fluid.

He flies at me, pinning me to the floor, hands wrapped around my upper arms, banging my head to the linoleum. Bits of Gabe are falling into my mouth in fat globs, tasting of rotted, decaying blood. I thrash and kick. A blood-curdling scream of pain, revulsion, and terror is torn from my throat.

*   *   *

I was jarred awake by a slap across the face.

"Wake up!" Marcella shouted at me.

"Ow! Jesus," I rubbed my cheek.

"Goddess, I'm so sorry, but you were thrashing and refused to wake." Marcella was straddling me, a painful grip on my left arm.

"You're hurting me," I whimpered, tugging weakly at my arm. She released it.

"Sorry, I was trying to keep you from banging your head on the headboard. I didn't know what else to do." Marcella looked horrified.

"What are you doing here?" My brain felt full of cotton, and my vision was blurred. I rubbed my eyes and slowly remembered that I was in her home. "I'm sorry, Marcella," I almost groaned with fatigue and started to turn over. I couldn't keep my eyes open as sleep began to take me. "What was in that tea? I'm so tired—."

"Hey, stay awake," Marcella admonished, shaking me back to consciousness. "The tea is nothing special, peppermint, lavender, and a touch of lemon balm. It's straight from the store, I promise." She picked up the tea and sniffed, then put a drop on her tongue. Then, frowning, she stood.

"Ninetta!" she hollered. She sounded almost enraged.

Ninetta hurried into the room in an old-fashioned nightgown. "Yes, Signora." She was trembling slightly.

"What is in this tea?" Marcella's voice was sharp and curt.

"Ms. Carson, you asked me to make some tea. In addition to the usual herbs, I added some Asian Valerian extract; it is much more potent than lemon balm or lavender. You said she needed sleep."

"I said help her sleep, Ninetta, not put her in a coma!"

"I'm sorry, Ms. Carson. It was my mistake."

Marcella dismissed her. "Okay, Ninetta, thank you."

"Anything else for you or the Detective?" Ninetta asked from the doorway.

"No, that will be all. Thank you."

Ninetta walked out of the room, shooting me a hateful gaze. I tried to understand it, but my brain just refused to function. Without another word, I turned on my side and closed my eyes.

Moments later, I felt Marcella slide into the bed next to me and envelop me in her arms. Without thought, I wiggled my butt back into her, snuggling closer. I was so tired and just needed to sleep this off.

"I'll stay here until you fall asleep," she whispered. The corners of my mouth lifted into a tired smile, and alarms sounded somewhere in my head, but I didn't care.

In the morning, but for me, the bed was empty. And it took me a minute of coaxing my addled brain to figure out if what I remembered had even really happened.

Asian valerian extract? My ass. Ninetta had dosed me with something; I was sure of it. The question was, did Marcella tell her to, or did Ninetta do it on her own. I couldn't imagine Marcella going to all this trouble to rufi me in her own home. Why? I'd almost thrown myself at her like a drunken prom date in the bathroom. Of course, that had been before she had stopped me. 'Not here. Not like this.' Yup, she had known what I was thinking.

A few minutes later, as the elevator stopped on the ground floor, I smelled the rising scent of frying bacon. *Oh, God, am I hungry,* I thought. The door opened, and I smelled not only bacon but something baking. While I didn't fancy another run-in with Ninetta's mysteriously hateful stare, I wanted to eat. I walked into the kitchen, wondering if Ninetta might try to poison me, where, to my surprise, I found Marcella cooking.

"Oh, good, you're up." She looked up at me with that dazzling smile as I walked in. "I assume you slept well, at least for the rest of the night."

I nodded and looked around with mild trepidation. "And where is Ms. Di'Angelo?"

"On an extended vacation."

"Please tell me that you didn't fire her." An extended vacation sounded somewhat ominous.

"No, of course not. She'd have had a fat severance coming, so I chopped her up and put her in the icebox. It was cheaper."

I blinked. Marcella's tone had been so flat, and the words delivered with such confidence I couldn't tell if she was kidding.

"Ha! That was for that remark about my wardrobe. She's First Class on British Airways bound for Italy. I sent her to visit her son and daughter-in-law in Florence for a few weeks."

"Okay, what did she put in my tea? I know what Valerian extract does. Marcella, I was drugged. Not with anything ridiculously high powered, but I was definitely sedated."

"She swore it was Asian Valerian, Cait," Marcella said, but the lack of indignation in her voice gave away her doubts. "I've known her for twenty years. For twenty years, she has been a consummate professional housekeeper. I have never had any cause to question her judgment or her word. So, let's leave it at that."

I learned several things about Marcella Carson in that exchange. First, she hadn't told Ninetta to drug me. Second, it scared her— enough to send Ninetta far away. Third, she was loyal as hell, given that she'd sent Ninetta out of the country rather than let her be arrested for poisoning a cop. Fourth, she was an expert at telling the truth while revealing nothing.

I decided that a bit of revelation was in order. If we were going to be friends, I had to believe at least that she was going to treat me honestly. "Marcella, I appreciate that you are protecting your friend. I might do the same for some of mine. But, I also know that she gave me a sedative, not an over-the-counter sedative, either. What was in my tea?"

"I don't know," she said, slamming a fork on the counter.

"I don't know what she put in your tea, but I can guess why. Ninetta has been my constant companion for twenty years. She's managed my home, a good portion of my finances. She knows all of my secrets, peccadilloes, and worries. I've confided in her for all of that time—."

"She's jealous," I interrupted.

"Yes, Cait, she's jealous." Marcella began cooking mushrooms and tomatoes in the bacon grease. "Is Full English okay?" she asked.

"Yes, that would be fabulous." I let the conversation go. People did stupid stuff all the time in the name of love and obsession. My presence here was a testament to that. Though, a paranoid part of my brain still thought this might all be some kind of setup. *God, am I that fucked up?*

Marcella served me some coffee as she cooked. I couldn't believe how different she looked. Her hair was up in a messy bun, and she was wearing a pair of striped pajama pants, a cropped t-shirt, and an apron that read 'Hail to the Chef.' I propped my chin on my palm and watched her move expertly around the kitchen.

When she finally finished and set the food in front of me, the grin on my face was practically shit-eating. The plate had bacon, eggs over easy, tomatoes, portabella mushrooms, and the one thing that went right through my stomach to my heart — black pudding, lightly crisped.

Marcella sat down.

"You are a goddess; you know that?" I said, scarfing down the black pudding, which was perfect.

She just smiled slyly. Now it was her turn to watch me, chin in her palm.

I swallowed a mouthful of food, feeling suddenly self-conscious. "What?" I asked, feeling a flush creep up my neck for about the thousandth time in front of her.

"It's just good to see you feeling a little better."

"I slept like the dead last night. I mean after—."

"I know. You have the most adorable little snores." My

stomach did a little dance as she smiled at me.

"Hey, I do not snore."

"How would you know?" she asked.

"Well, Gabe—," I started, then caught myself. *Shit.*

She stretched out her hand and placed it on my forearm. "It's okay," she said sympathetically. "It just happened. Do you want to talk about it?"

I sighed and looked back at my food. I realized I was angry at Gabe. He hadn't done anything, and I wasn't being fair to him, but I felt angry. I was probably just as mad at myself, but I was sick of putting it there. I needed a target, and he was convenient.

"You know, that's the funny thing. There's not much to say. Now that I have some distance, I realize that I kept him around because I thought I should. Well, that, and I didn't want to be alone," I said harshly. "I'm so angry at him. And I want to know why. I know I shouldn't be." I stopped and looked back up at her. "How can you sit there like that while I grouse about Gabe?"

"Because it's not my baggage." She took a breath as if pressing on over a precipice. "And, because I'm not insecure about myself. I know you need to work through a lot of things, but for whatever reason, I—." She broke off.

"You what?"

"I find myself very fond of you." She placed a hand on mine and looked down. "It's not something I've felt in so very long. I thought I'd lost the capacity." I was startled by the admission, and my cheeks flamed.

Marcella took off her apron and set it on the counter. "Finish your breakfast, I have a small place on the cape, and I'd like to take you there. So I need to prep a few things."

"Aren't you going to eat?" I asked, realizing that she hadn't.

"No, I'm not hungry." She walked out of the kitchen to the elevator.

I finished my food, washed my dishes, and dried them, leaving them on the counter. I wondered what to do, so I milled around a bit, but restlessness got the better of me. I took the elevator to the fourth floor, hoping Marcella wouldn't mind. The ride was relatively short, but Marcella was waiting when the door opened.

"No, no, no," she said playfully. "My room is a mess, back in the elevator."

So, we rode down to the third floor, and I got dressed. Then, we left for the cape, stopping only to move my car from HQ to my parking spot by the apartment.

24

Marcella's place on the cape was nothing like I expected. It was a small cottage in Eastham, tucked back down a narrow road with a gravel driveway. Compared to her home in Charlestown, it was positively tiny. There was no beachfront property or large estate—just a cute one-story house wrapped in gray painted shakes with an adorable red door.

"This is so cute!" I crowed as I climbed from the car. "I love it."

Marcella gave me a warm smile as she grabbed a large suitcase from the trunk. "I thought you might." I made to help her with the bag, but she had it well in hand, carting it easily one-handed to the door.

The house sported an open floorplan with a small kitchen, a half bathroom, a cozy living room with a fireplace, and a loft bedroom with a full bath above. Marcella turned on the heat and started up the stairs, beckoning me to follow. The loft was small, about the size of my bedroom. A queen-sized bed sat below a long window with a single nightstand.

"Marcella, there's only one bed here." I looked down to the floor below, wondering if I'd missed a door somewhere.

"Yes."

"Are we both supposed to sleep in it?" I asked, watching her open her suitcase.

"Yes."

I looked at her with feigned indignance. "Isn't that a little presumptuous?"

"I don't think so. I didn't hear you complain about it last night."

I laughed. "I was practically comatose last night. Fozzie Bear could have curled up next to me and gotten the same response."

Marcella threw a pillow at me. "If you want to sleep on the pull-out couch, silly, you may. But you'll find this bed *much* more comfortable." She leveled a playful smile at me.

"Speaking of sleeping, I didn't sleep last night, so I am going to take a nap." She started undressing, stifling a yawn as she did so. Not that I blamed her, beautiful as she was, but Marcella Carson was *not* body-conscious.

She stripped down to a camisole and her panties and climbed straight into the bed, not bothering to put anything away. I watched as she pulled back the covers on the other side. "Well?"

After picking my jaw off the floor, I stripped to my underwear and crawled in with her. We looked at each other for a long moment. Honey sunlight shone through the window above us, shining across Marcella's golden hair, which had fallen into her face. She blew out a breath, adorably pushing a few strands around to no avail.

I chuckled and reached over to uncover her shimmering blue eyes. Immediately, I felt lost in them.

"You look a little tired; a nap might do for you, too," Marcella suggested softly. "One in three nights sleep isn't terribly healthy."

I realized she was right, and as I stifled a yawn, I felt my eyes getting heavy. She kissed my forehead lightly, and I drifted off.

I awoke around three, feeling much more refreshed. Downstairs, Marcella sat on the couch. Her typically rigid and careful demeanor had vanished, replaced by something wistful and a little sad.

"Hey," I said, taking a seat next to her. "Why the maudlin

face?"

She gave a half-smile that didn't reach her eyes. "Sorry, I was just lost in a memory."

I placed my hand on hers, finding it warm to the touch. "Would you like to share it?"

She didn't answer, apparently still deep in thought. A mug sat next to her, full of what looked like wine.

"What are you drinking?" I wasn't expecting an answer to that either, at least not one I'd understand. In my world, wine came in red, white, and pink.

"The blood of my enemies," she joked, but there was little humor in her expression. Out here, away from the city, business, and her enormous home, she was a different person, no aristocratic air of self-confidence, only brooding melancholy and a sense of loneliness.

I returned to my original question. "Seriously though, what's the matter?"

Marcella looked at me, and her expression grew so severe that I thought her on the verge of some great confession. "Cait, I need to tell you—." She stopped and stood, offering her hand, clearly thinking better of whatever she'd been about to say. "You know what? Never mind. Let's go to the beach. And don't bother putting on shoes. Just carry them with you."

We walked along the shore south of Provincetown, a place of fond childhood memories that I'd visited many times. We picked up rocks and seashells and chatted. She told me about the places she'd visited: Paris, Milan, London, and others. I told her about growing up, bouncing back and forth between Boston and Ireland. She'd been to Dublin and had visited Tourmakeady some years ago but hadn't been there since.

Around six, we found a dry spot above the beach to watch the sunset. Marcella held my hand and leaned on my shoulder, saying nothing. A sense of euphoria washed through me, causing me to pull Marcella onto my lap in a bit of daring, making her laugh. As the gold light settled away behind the sea, cottony strands of cloud turned vibrant hues of pink and red like the sky from some fantasy painting. The moment was so beautiful that it drew tears from my eyes.

Marcella turned her face toward mine, blue eyes dark against the rising night. "Now," she whispered. "Like this." Then, she leaned in and kissed me. Heat rose inside me as I parted my lips and closed my eyes. Her breath tasted of peppermint and something coppery, almost like blood.

Her tongue, refreshingly cool, licked across my lips, and all of my worries fled. There was nothing but this solitary moment. Warm goosebumps charged across my skin as her hand stroked my face, finally finding the back of my neck and pulling me into a more intense, dazzling, and breathless kiss.

I moaned slightly with the enormity of my emotions. The joys of new love, my mother had once called it. But it wasn't just that; there was a sense of rightness and release that settled my spirit. The physical sensation of wanting her was almost indescribable. I wanted to be closer, nearer, within her. It was a need I'd never felt with anyone before. And I wasn't frightened.

I pulled back from the kiss, pressed my lips together, and spoke softly. "I'm falling for you."

A slight smile tugged at her mouth, but she said not a word. Instead, she pulled me into another breathtaking kiss, full of boundless need that rose within me. I wanted to make love to her.

I don't know how long we stayed there, wrapped in each other's arms. But, eventually, Marcella broke our embrace.

"Whew," she said with a bit of a laugh. "That was just—," her voice dropped to a whisper. "Beautiful. Thank you for this."

I tilted my head, confused. "You make it sound so final; please don't tell me you're dying."

She laughed loudly this time. "No, silly. It's just—" she looked away, embarrassed. "I feel things with you that I'd thought long gone. It feels like a gift."

We left the beach and drove back to her cottage, stopping along the way to pick up some live lobsters. Marcella insisted on picking up some wine. She hemmed and hawed over the selection and shocked me when she finally settled on a cheap Rosé.

"My, my, Ms. Carson, I think I'm seeing a completely different side of you."

"Well, I wasn't always the epitome of wealth and style you see before you," she replied, executing a childish curtsy in her frumpy brown sweater and rolled-up blue jeans, making me laugh. "I like the occasional pink wine." She winked black lashes and put the bottle in the cart.

Marcella Carson amazed me. She had seemed so confident, poised, and even a little old-fashioned. Here though, finally away from all her cares and out of her earlier brooding, she was still confident, but she was light and airy. The contrast was surprising and, in some ways, awe-inspiring. There was real power in knowing yourself that well, selecting the appropriate demeanor at the proper time, and having it all still be honestly you. Bewitched, it seemed, I felt like the proverbial moth to the flame.

Arriving back at her cottage, Marcella began making dinner. "I have a surprise for you. Go upstairs, put on a bathing suit, and follow the footpath behind the house. The pot will take a half-hour to boil, at least."

"What kind of surprise?" I asked with a hint of playful suspicion.

"It's magic. Go see."

I did as she asked. She had left me a simple black one-piece. My eyes bulged when I saw Versace on the label. Outside, it was damn chilly, having dropped into the forties. *What am I doing out here in this stupid bathing suit? The surprise had better be a fucking sauna.*

The short footpath behind the cottage ran on popcorn-block pavers through a small copse of trees to a tiny clearing. A small, gray shack sat within, maybe twenty feet square. The exterior matched the cottage in its cedar siding and bright red entryway.

Within, I definitely found something magical. It was positively humid and steamy, over seventy degrees. The entire interior was styled to look like a nighttime fantasy forest. Ambient light covered everything in dim illumination. The ceiling had a projection of a dusky starlit sky with occasional faerie-like lights darting here and there. Everything seemed so natural; the effect was mystical and romantic rather than chintzy. In the center was an oval pool of water set in dark stones, canopied by tree branches above. It ran about fifteen feet long by ten feet wide, bubbling and steaming. I dipped in a toe and found the water hot.

As I stepped into the pool, bubbles began to rush from the walls, making me jump. The pool's interior was lined in a dark pattern that I couldn't see well. I found a ledge along the edge and sat in the jets. *This feels so good.*

I heard the door to the shack open, and Marcella approached with two beach towels, two robes, and wearing the sexiest bathing suit I had ever seen. A black bandeau covered her chest, and a strap-sided bikini bottom covered the rest. She was stunning in the glowing light. As she stepped up, fireflies lit up the darkness of the 'trees' around the pool.

I waded to her and lifted her by her sides, setting her down gently in the water.

"You know, Cait, I can walk."

I lowered her into the water, and she splashed and giggled. "I know, but I'm happy, and it seemed the thing to do."

She held on to me, wrapping her arms about my shoulders and her legs around my waist. "I'm happy, too. This is so lovely, and so are you."

"I bet you say that to all the girls you bring out here."

"I've never brought anyone out here before."

That stopped me. "Never? How long have you had this place?" I was surprised that she'd never shared this

"It's been in my family since the eighties. I made this addition," she gestured around, "about five years ago after a bit of inspiration."

"And Ninetta never came out here?"

Marcella laughed as if the idea were preposterous. "No, she doesn't even know I own it."

I untangled myself and drifted to the center of the pool. "Well, it's wonderful. I could hang out in here forever."

"You know what they say, be careful what you wish for." She winked and pushed herself back into my arms. "You know, in my mother's village in Sweden, we had this old legend of a couple who had consummated their love in an underground pool near our home after pining for each other for many years. And, for a time, maidens of the village would go to this place to bathe in the hopes that they would soon find true love."

"And did it work?" I asked, feeling a little like she was yanking my chain.

"I don't know, but I certainly found my first love there." Her face cracked into a broad smile. "What about you? Where did you find your first love?"

I closed my eyes and spoke softly. "In the blowing sands of Iraq, though we never consummated it. I never even spoke of it, and I don't think she ever knew."

"Allt har sin tid." Marcella wrapped her arms around my neck and kissed me. I didn't ask what it meant; it didn't matter.

We left the jacuzzi a little while later and enjoyed a quiet dinner. Marcella only ate a few bites, opting to pack the rest in the refrigerator for later.

I noticed some logs and kindling next to the fireplace. "Does this work?"

"It does. Do you want to start one while I hit the loo?"

"Sure."

I heard brief retching from the bathroom as I lit some paper under the kindling. Moments later, she emerged as I placed more kindling and waited for it to catch. "You okay?"

"Yes, I'm fine, just feeling a little—off. I'll be alright." Something flashed across her face that I didn't catch.

We spent the rest of the night in front of the fire discussing, of all things, fine art. Marcella was a fan of Vermeer. She had some enlightening stories about the Dutch painter that she said she'd uncovered while in Delft. She was a little vague about why she was there and when.

Most of her stories revolved around the period of Vermeer's training and education in the arts. It was a time largely unknown, Marcella told me. One particularly salacious story involved a relationship in his teens with a married woman and something about jumping out a second-story window in a woman's dress to escape her returning husband.

"Have you ever heard of an artist named Sam Rueter?" I asked as the fire had burned low.

"No, I'm not familiar with her," Marcella replied, pushing an iron poker through the embers.

"When you have time, you should check out her work. I've always thought it was just beautiful. See if you can find a photo of a painting called 'sweater weather.' I think you'd like it."

Marcella nodded and kissed me lightly. "Come on, you, let's get to bed. I have to go back home tomorrow and take care of a few things."

We tucked ourselves into bed and made out for a while. She had the most uncanny means of hitting all of my erogenous zones that weren't between my legs, and by the time we settled down, I felt like I was drowning in arousal.

While we lay quietly in the moon's dim light, she whispered, "I'm falling for you, too." My heart seemed to stutter at the words, and I squeezed her close. I buried my head in her hair; it smelled of sandalwood. She tilted my head toward hers and kissed me chastely on the lips. She stared into my eyes. "You and I need sleep. There are things we need to discuss before we go any further, but that can wait until tomorrow."

"That sounds ominous," I said around a yawn. "Jesus, why am I tired. We didn't do anything today, and I even had a nap." I lay my head down, and before long, I fell asleep.

25

We returned to Charlestown early the following day. Marcella had been unable to sleep, so I drove us back while she snoozed in the seat next to me. I spent the time enjoying the sunlight and thinking about how badly I had it for the woman to my right.

The ride wasn't entirely pleasant. Heavy anxiety gripped me more than a few times as I thought of work and the team operating without me. They were busting their asses, and here I was, spending my night making out with a gorgeous woman. Then there was Gabe. God, I didn't even know how to feel about that.

Marcella was still sleeping when we pulled into her garage. She hadn't moved most of the ride. I gave her a nudge.

"Marcella, honey? We're back."

Nothing. She didn't move, make a noise, or anything, and she felt colder than usual. I felt for a pulse. Finding nothing, I began to panic. "No, no, no. Marcella, No." I jumped out of the car and ran around, opening her door. *Please, God, No.*

I had just opened the door and lifted her out of the car when she yawned. She fucking yawned. *What the hell. Jesus, she had a deep pulse.*

"Are you okay? I couldn't find your pulse, and it didn't look like you were breathing."

"I'm fine. Relax. I told you I had a condition."

"A condition? You were fucking dead."

"Cait, stop. Obviously, I'm not dead. I'm fine." She pulled herself from my grip and hopped up and down. "See. Fine." Then she pulled me into a hug. "I'm sorry I scared you. I should have been more forthcoming about the details." There was something in her demeanor, though, something she wasn't saying.

"Okay. You said we had things to talk about?"

"Later, let's get settled," she said dismissively, and we headed up the elevator. I frowned at her back but followed. Professional Marcella had returned, and I wasn't sure which I liked more.

After we had cleaned up and changed, Marcella headed to the grocery store to pick up the list of ingredients I'd given her for the Bolognese sauce. It seemed I would be making it tonight rather than Monday. I wandered around the house a bit, mostly being nosy. Curiosity about the sub-basement was eating at me, but I quashed it. I could have easily picked the lock on the elevator button, but I didn't want to break her trust.

By the time I returned to the kitchen, everything was arranged on the center island. Marcella had grabbed everything I had asked for, meats, vegetables, spices. The pasta even looked freshly made. There was also a rather fabulous food processor that I'd give my left arm for.

"So," Marcella said from behind, making me jump. In soft flats now, she was silent as the dead. "How can I help?"

I recovered quickly. "Well, you could chop the carrots and celery while I cut the onions and sauté them."

"It's an interesting recipe for Bolognese. I was surprised at the ingredient list."

"Well, it's a more modern interpretation. The carrots and celery balance the flavor, and the Calabrian chili's give it a little kick."

She pulled out a pair of knives, and we got to work. I cut the onions like a troglodyte with two left hands while she sliced the celery and carrots with the practiced strokes of a professional chef.

Marcella pushed a bit of carrot off her knife into a large bowl and leaned against the counter. "Anything else?"

"Nope, go have a seat and relax. It won't take long to get the sauce onto the stove, and then we can do whatever."

Marcella positioned herself at the table, watching me with unnerving intensity while I minced the vegetables in the food processor.

I smiled, suddenly feeling a little shy as she continued to stare. "I usually do this in my blender. This is so much nicer."

"You know, I didn't always live in a place like this. When I was a child, I lived in a much simpler home. My mother often cooked, though she didn't have any of the conveniences that I do now."

I dumped the contents of the food processor into the pan with the browning meat. "So, the spoiled little rich girl wasn't so spoiled?"

"Hardly. I may have attended posh schools, but my life was far from it as a child. What about you, Cait? What is it like having a mother from the Gaeltacht?" She pulled a hairband off her wrist and began putting her hair up, exposing her shapely neck and giving her a more relaxed look.

"Well, I grew up speaking Irish, for starters. From the time I was born until I was ten, it's almost all she spoke to me. It took me forever to lose my Irish accent. Of course, my mother can always find it again, usually when she says or does something aggravating."

Marcella snorted in amusement. "Really? That's adorable."

"Not when you're a teenager in Boston who doesn't want to be one of—" I paused and shook my head. I felt like I was remembering something important, but, whatever it was, it fled.

Marcella's brow furrowed. "Cait?"

"Yes. Sorry. Anyway, being the child of an Irish woman rather than an Irish-American woman is dramatically different. She is direct in her criticisms, but she lets me make my own mistakes. Even so, I feel like she armchair quarterbacked much of my life, but, all in all, we get along well. And, despite some of the challenges we had when my dad died, our relationship is solid today. I'm just glad she learned how to cook actual food. Maimeó boiled fucking everything. Yuck."

Marcella joined me by the stove.

"Would you like a glass of wine?" She asked.

I looked over my shoulder and right into her shining eyes. "Um—" I struggled for words for a second. "What do you have?"

She laughed, knowing my thoughts on wine, still holding my gaze. "I have lots. What would you prefer? Red or white? I don't have anything pink here this time. I prefer red myself."

"Red's fine," I almost whispered and cleared my throat. I turned back to the stove, face flushed. This was going to be a long night.

She handed me a fine crystal wine glass full of a dark red. I took a sip. It was good. I could smell a hint of forest floor and maybe raspberry. "Um, is this a Pinot Noir?"

She turned and raised an appreciative eyebrow. "Good nose. It seems you know more about wine than you let on."

"Hardly. Pinot Noir is pretty distinctive. My dad said it tasted like feet."

She laughed even harder. "Goddess, Cait, where have you been all my life? No one's made me laugh this much in years."

I grinned and turned back to stir the pot with a little bounce. Grinning, Marcella slid up next to me, wrapping her arms around my waist and taking a deep sniff of the simmering sauce.

"Oh, that smells amazing. I can't wait."

"So my mother says it's better than any Bolognese she's had in Italy. Having never been, I have to take her word for it."

"Well, I'll let you know," Marcella said with a wink. "How long does it need to cook?"

"Minimum two hours," I said, taking another healthy sip of wine.

"Well, let's go into the sitting room and chat then," Marcella offered, gesturing for me to go ahead of her. "Make yourself at home; I need to visit the loo first."

Leaving the kitchen, I watched Marcella walk to a blank-looking wall on the other side of the stairs. A section of the wall swung in with a gentle press, revealing a small water closet.

"Wow, that's cool."

"I felt a door here would look out of place. And yeah, it's cool." She stepped inside and closed the panel.

The furniture in the sitting room had been reorganized slightly. Marcella had turned the sofa to face the fireplace, and a low, cozy fire burned there.

I sat on the sofa and poked at the logs in the fireplace, enjoying the warmth of the blaze on my face. Retching sounds caught my attention, just as they had at the cottage. Was she sick? Maybe this wasn't such a good idea. A moment later, though, Marcella returned, wine glass in hand, looking perfectly fit.

"Are you feeling alright?"

"Perfectly fine," Marcella replied casually. "Why do you ask?"

"I thought I heard you throwing up again."

"No, I'm fine."

It was a lie; she had been throwing up, but she looked okay. She didn't look or act ill, so I assumed it wasn't a stomach bug, whatever the problem.

Marcella set her glass on the hearth and plopped down rather unceremoniously onto the Persian rug. "Come down here," she beckoned. "Let's relax by the fire and chat."

"Okay," I said, feeling a little weird. "Just so you know, I was never one for the slumber party thing, so this feels a little odd."

"Then you need to learn to relax." She pulled off her shoes showing perfect feet with manicured toenails in a deep red. "I forgot to ask, what do you do for fun?"

"Fun? Well, I don't know. I read, I guess. I like to work out. Muay Thai, Jiu-Jitsu, that kind of thing."

"I know that, as a child of Éireann, you have to suffer in sufficient quantities, but I'm pretty sure there's no prohibition on fun. None of that sounds fun. Do you like to go out dancing?"

"I used to, I think. But it's been so long since I've done anything like that. I'm more of the outdoor type, I guess."

"I love to dance. When I was younger, I took ballet lessons. I was trained classically, but I prefer contemporary ballet. Do you like contemporary?"

"I don't even know what the difference is," I said, feeling a little out of my depth.

"Well, classical ballet has all kinds of rules about what you can and can't do. All rather boring. Contemporary ballet is much more exciting. The choreography is always interesting, and the music is usually much more expressive. To me, it's like the difference between an architectural draft and a work of art. We'll have to go to one of each, so you can decide which one you like. So, Muay Thai, indeed? I saw a few bouts last time I was in Bangkok. It's pretty rough."

"I'm sorry, but you don't strike me as the type to entertain sports like that. I had you pegged for more the badminton or tennis type."

"There's a lot you don't know about me, Cait. My past is filled with all manner of indiscretions. Watching two men beat each other to a pulp is probably the least of them." She finished by dipping her finger into her wine and making a show of licking it with the very tip of her tongue, making me blush. "So, do you like music?"

I coughed to cover a shiver of excitement. "Oh, I love music — all types. Mostly, though, I listen to modern music. Lana Del Rey, Florence and the Machine, that sort. Though, and, don't tell my co-workers, I love opera."

"Opera? Really? Do you have any favorites?"

"Well, Carmen, for sure. Poor José, throwing his life away for a woman who used him and dumped him. My other is Le Damnation de Faust by Berlioz."

"I love them both. My favorite Carmen so far has been Jennifer Larmore. I could have just eaten her up."

"Me too. I can listen to her sing for hours."

We talked like that for over an hour—her quizzing me on my interests and sharing a bit of hers. Periodically I checked on the sauce, which was coming along nicely.

"There's some fresh made Tagliatelle in the icebox," Marcella said when I sat back down from checking the sauce for the last time. We had devoured almost two bottles of red wine, and I was feeling no pain. I couldn't tell if Marcella felt as buzzed as I was, but she had moved much closer to me as afternoon progressed into evening. At some point, she put music on in the room. The speakers were well hidden but delivered excellent sound. "How much time before the food is ready?"

I looked at my watch. "Well, it's been in for over two hours. It can be eaten now. Are you hungry?"

"Very," she said huskily. The way she looked at me told me she wasn't talking about food. It had gotten dark out, and she seemed even more beautiful in the fading light, and her eyes had a predatory fire to them that had been absent at the beach. Her movements became languid, deliberate, feline. She was, if it was possible, even more sexy.

"Why, Ms. Carson. If I didn't know better, I'd think you were trying to seduce me. And here I thought we were going to be —" My voice trailed off as she moved closer, so close that I could feel her breath, smell the wine—and the lingering aroma of her perfume.

My breath started to come a little shallower, and I felt faint. The room turned stifling as the sounds of Donizetti's *L'elisir d'amore* were sliding from the speakers, lulling me into a relaxed state I hadn't felt in—maybe ever.

Then, Marcella's silken lips fell upon my own. Her breath entered my lungs, hot and tangy with the alcohol. Every hair on my body stood up in a sexual rush. She started to draw away, but I reached up and put my hand on her neck, keeping her close, deepening the kiss. She pressed my shoulders down, breaking the kiss and pulling back. Her lissome movements were exquisite and flowing as she straddled my hips and cupped my face, drawing me into another deep passionate kiss.

My lips parted, admitting her tongue, and I whimpered in supplication as it stole aggressively into my mouth and swept across my own. My lips parted again, releasing a soft 'Oh' as she moved down and began to caress my throat with her tongue. Each swipe brought an erotic thrill that pooled between my legs. My hips began to lift against her, but she pushed them back down with one hand, moving her mouth to nibble at my neck with her teeth. Her right hand slipped into my blouse, brushing against the fabric of my bra, teasing and light. Both of my nipples stood up. *God, I want her.* A high-pitched whimper escaped my throat again, and she seemed energized by my surrender. Her arms were surprisingly strong, pulling me to her, holding my back away from the couch.

I sensed her teeth dragging across my neck, sharp and tantalizing and vowing delights to come. She bit at it teasingly, and I reveled in the pain.

Marcella pulled back, and I opened my eyes. A small drop of liquid lingered on her lips, thick and red. Dimly, a fleeting thought nagged at me, but I couldn't grasp it, make it stick.

"You're— " I breathed. "You're bleeding."

She leaned in and began to lick and suck at my pulsing throat again, uttering breathlessly, "It's not mine."

A cool sensation began drifting over me, and I tilted my head back. "Oh, God, please," I moaned, shuddering under her touch and the play of her mouth at my neck.

My fingers stroked up her spine, causing her to lift and arch her back. She shivered and let out a tinkling laugh, then she looked down, licking her lips. In the dim firelight, her half-smile looked different, filled with want.

I needed her to take me, consume me, love me. The depth of the feeling frightened me, and my fear only served to heighten my arousal.

She leaned in for another kiss. She pressed her lips to mine. "We should stop."

A hint of my own blood lingered on my tongue. I didn't want to stop. I wanted this. I wanted her. But, she pulled away and sat to my side, one leg still strewn over my own, breathing heavily.

I touched my neck, feeling a bit of warm, sticky liquid.

"Oh, my," she said, covering a smile and a bit of a laugh with her hand. "I'm so sorry. I think I might have drawn blood."

I pulled my legs under me as I drew my hand back. There was a small rivulet of blood there — nothing major. "I didn't even notice it. You know, I had a dream about you," I whispered, as much to myself as her.

"Indeed." It sounded more like a statement than a question.

"It was like this." I was still staring at the drop of blood on my hand. I knew I should be a little freaked out. But I couldn't summon an ounce of worry in the haze of eroticism and alcohol. What was a little love bite?

"You seemed to be enjoying it," she said seductively and licked the blood off my finger.

I turned my head to her, feeling very relaxed. "It's not a big deal; I've had worse," I said, drunkenly holding up my arm.

"You're a touch twatted, I think."

"I think I am." A touch of embarrassment settled in, but I brushed it aside. "Are you making me love you?" I sloshed.

She just raised an eyebrow. "I believe we should eat before we say anything more."

"You're probably right."

I tried to rise, but the room spun, and I stumbled. Marcella was right there to grab me and set me back on the sofa.

"Hang on a second, let me get something for your neck first." Marcella left and returned a moment later with a small bottle of a yellow paste-like substance and some first aid supplies.

"Wha—" I tried to ask but found my thoughts even slower and my tongue thick.

Marcella wiped down my throat with a gauze pad and

alcohol, causing me to jump.

"Ouch!" I complained. "That stings."

"Some hard-ass copper you turned out to be," she said with a crooked smile. "Whinging over a bit of alcohol."

Then she smeared the yellow paste in the same place and stuck a bandage on it.

"Come on," she said. "Let's get you fed."

Marcella guided me into the kitchen, where she finished preparing dinner. I just sat in silence, watching her cook. I had to jerk myself a few times to keep from nodding off. Wow, I *was* drunk.

"Eat!" Marcella demanded as she set down a healthy portion of food in front of me.

I dove into the food, absolutely ravenous and feeling more lively. Marcella had taken a small helping, not shocking, given her model-like figure.

"This is absolutely delicious," she cooed, taking a bite. "Just brilliant."

"Isn't it, though." I began to sober up as I ate. "I'm so sorry for getting drunk."

"It's not your fault. I forgot that you don't drink often, and here I was, just feeding you glass after glass. It's on me, truly. I won't lie, though; it was also kind of cute."

"Did you want this to happen?" I challenged playfully.

Marcella looked at me, puzzled. "Want what?"

"Us?"

"Want? No. I *intended* it. From the moment you walked into my office." She struck a seductive tone, and the predatory smile returned. "So, tell me about this dream you had."

I looked around the room to avoid answering. Having no ideas for an alternate topic, I took another bite of food to stall. I pointed to my cheek and made an apologetic face. *Look, my mouth is full. You wouldn't want me to talk with a mouthful of food, would you?*

She raised an eyebrow at the childish gesture. "It's okay. I can wait."

I swallowed. "Shit, I never should have mentioned it. Okay, so, the other night, after I met you, I had a—uh—sexy dream about you, or rather, us."

"Interesting." She set her fork down and just watched me with a hungry expression. "And what happened in this 'dream?'"

"Well, we were in my apartment, sort of, and you came to me, and well, it was very gothic."

"Gothic?" She leaned her chin onto her hand, eyes intent. "Do tell."

"You were in a very sexy dress, and you, well, seduced me." *God, I feel like a teenager.* "Then you were a vampire and drinking my blood. It was extremely—sensual." I shivered slightly at the memory. My face was on fire, and I hid my mouth behind my wrist to cover a creeping smile.

She sipped her wine, letting the glass dangle from her long delicate fingers. "Well, then, I hope you have more sweet dreams. Would you like more?"

I spat into my wine glass. "I'm sorry?"

Marcella snorted a laugh, "Would you like more food?" She stood and leaned close to my face. "Unless, of course, you'd rather something else." She picked a morsel of meat from my plate and placed it on her tongue suggestively, pulling it into her mouth.

26

After dinner, Marcella made us some coffee, and we returned to the sitting room. It had begun to rain outside, and there was a peal of thunder. I grabbed the edge of the sofa. I closed my eyes, breathing from my belly, slowly willing the vision of the alleyway in Mosul to dissipate.

Marcella spoke, soft and gentle. "Loud noises?"

I nodded quickly and held up a hand. When I opened my eyes, Marcella was watching me. There was no pity on her face, just concern.

"I can help you with that. I mean, really help you with that."

"And, how might you do that?" I hadn't intended to be snippy, but I'd had plenty of people make that claim over the years.

The fire had burned down to embers, and the room was extremely dark. Marcella lit a few candles, sitting cross-legged in front of the fireplace.

"Come, sit down with me, cross-legged, directly across."

"I've done things like this before—" I started, trying to forestall what would likely be a senseless effort.

"Not like this, you haven't," she said confidently. "Now get over here and sit down opposite me, cross-legged." The command carried a weight to it that I felt almost physically. Before I knew what I was doing, I was off the couch and in front of her, cross-legged, precisely as she'd asked.

Marcella tilted my head up at the chin so that I looked her in the face. "Now, look into my eyes."

I snickered and mimicked a bad Bella Lugosi. "Look into my eyes, Mina."

She slapped me on the arm lightheartedly. "Now. Cait. Be serious. Look into my eyes."

I snorted but complied, muscling the smile off my face. For the first time, I noticed slight black flecks glittering within her beautiful blue eyes. After a few moments, though, the blackness grew, engulfing the white. The fiery blue of her irises became all I could see before they slipped into a deep and vibrant red. It was like falling into a pool of blood-red light.

My breathing slowed and deepened, and the room temperature rose, becoming hot and stifling and dry. There was a vague sense of falling, succumbing to something powerful, intense, and tempting. Every muscle strung itself taught as the scent of diesel fuel and earthy dust filled my nose. A blistering wind blew through my hair. My breath came quick and overwrought, and I felt like my lungs were pressing against an immense vice. I squeezed my eyes shut.

"Take a deep calm breath," a familiar hypnotic voice echoed from somewhere near me. "You are safe. Nothing can hurt you."

My breathing eased.

"I will see what you see," the voice explained, dulcet and captivating. "Now, open your eyes and show me."

I lifted my lids. Morgan stood across the Humvee, pointing behind me, her mouth a scar of terror. I twisted around, heaving my M4 to my shoulder and firing in a single fluid motion. An armed insurgent fell forward, dropping his weapon. My thigh burned with a bullet wound, but Morgan covered me, killing the shooter.

"No, no," I sobbed desperately.

"This is just a memory," the voice explained, snatching away my fear. "You are safe."

Morgan and I ran down the dusty street. My leg burned,

screaming in pain with each step. I heard a shot, and Morgan grunted, face planting into the dirt. "Oh, please, no," I screamed.

"Shh. . . This has already passed. She lives." The voice suppressed my terror again.

I turned and fired, taking down another insurgent. Slinging my rifle, I hauled Morgan onto my shoulders, toting her heavy frame in a fireman's carry. The bumblebee whiz of a bullet zipped by my ear, followed by the rifle report. We'd gained a little distance.

I turned the corner, dashing up into the smoking door of the sniper nest. Twisting through the hallways, I searched, finally finding McCall was face-up on the floor, looking skyward, unseeing—dead. Holley lay next to him, cradling a ruined arm and howling. His hand bled everywhere, and I sneered at him, the fucking rapist.

I lowered Morgan to the floor gently, laying her flat and grabbing a bandage. I was lost in the memory now. I could feel the will of the voice, its thoughts and feelings—no, Marcella's thoughts, Marcella's feelings. I felt her fascination and sympathy. The emotions mixed with anticipation, like waiting for a storm to blow in.

I clamped Morgans' hands over her wound, holding the bandage down. "Pressure here,"

"What do you feel?" Marcella asked, level and tender.

"I can't lose her." My voice was desperate, and tears trickled down my face.

"Did you?"

"No. I didn't. Not yet."

"Reagan, the scope," Holley ground out through his teeth.

"What?" A split second later, I understood.

I took a line behind the rifle, hands coated in Morgan's blood. The aroma of the blood was intoxicating and arousing. No, that wasn't right. I saw the boy through the scope.

"Oh, no," I whispered before my training kicked in. "One hostile juvenile in a suicide vest." I guessed the distance and looked away from the scope for a wind gauge. An old chemise on a clothesline wafted gently in the distance. I had no spotter, so I took a swag at the range. "You should have to pull this trigger, you bastard," I spat at Holley as I adjusted the scope.

"Please stop," I whimpered, trying to wrest my will away from Marcella, trying to wake up, trying to make it end.

"Send it," Holley spat. "Shoot, God damn it!"

I forced myself to dead calm, gently squeezed the trigger between my racing heartbeats, and fired the weapon. The .50 cal bucked in a wave of thunder and terror. Plaster dust fell from the ceiling and rose from the floor.

"Okay, stop." It was a command full of force and control delivered in a gentle caress.

Everything stopped as if frozen in time.

"What are you feeling?" Marcella asked, her voice calm and clear.

"I'm enraged," I replied through gritted teeth.

"Why?"

"Because that bastard raped me. Holley stole my future and tainted it. And then he got to make me break myself."

"Did you fire because Holley told you to?" she asked flatly.

"No, I fired because the kid was a clear and present danger to the patrol. It was my job." My voice was more level now.

"And you did your job because it was a war," it wasn't a question.

"Yes."

"And you feel guilty about it," she said. Again it wasn't a question.

"Yes."

"Why?" The question stuck in my craw and pissed me off.

"Because it was a fucking kid. He never got a chance to live."

The vision dissolved into blackness, replaced by Marcella's gentle, coaxing presence, like a mother reaching out to her daughter as she learns to walk. It wrapped me in comfort and beckoned me to feel what she felt. Marcella pulled me into a deep embrace as a sense of forgiveness, mingled with love and acceptance, enveloped my soul.

It hadn't been my fault, just my bad luck. I had been an eighteen-year-old kid who had joined the army full of promise and ideals. I had been sent to war by an unfeeling apparatus that only followed orders. I had been forced to make an impossible decision that no one should have to make. I'd tried to be moral and righteous when there were no options for it, and it had gnawed at my soul ever since.

I still couldn't see anything; I was blind in her arms. But in my heart, there was understanding, recognition, and an inkling of forgiveness. For the first time, I recognized that moment for what it was— a tragedy.

I wasn't fixed; I knew that. But she had helped. She'd taken me into that horrible place and shown me it wasn't forbidden or insurmountable. There was hope.

My vision cleared, and I looked up at this goddess, this angel, this bright creature that had unearthed a hint of something I'd thought lost. I clung to her then and held desperately, sobbing and crying and shaking. I refused to let go as I loosed a torrent of pent-up despair and relief. Eventually, after I'd run out of tears, she disentangled my arms and stood.

"Come with me," Marcella said, voice filled with compassion, holding out a hand.

27

In the elevator, we rose in silence. So wrapped was I in my own conflicting emotions that I didn't notice the bell ring or the doors open.

"Coming?" Marcella asked, walking out of the elevator. Starting to find me again, I followed.

Beyond lay an elegant round sitting room with a chaise lounge. The soft sounds of rushing wind and leaves projected from hidden speakers and flickering ambient light gave the entire area a comforting feel, almost spa-like.

Above, a breathtaking painting adorned the domed ceiling. Two women in period dresses were lying on a forest floor, engaged in a passionate kiss; a trickle of blood slid down one woman's cheek.

Marcella continued through to a narrow hallway and into a darkened room beyond.

There comes a moment in a case where conjecture begins to give way to the evidence, and clarity comes to the investigator. This is when motive, means, and opportunity become tied to the suspect. As I stared at the painting for long moments, that clarity made my head spin. But such things didn't exist. It was impossible. I shoved the insane thought aside just as Marcella peeked back around the corner.

"Hey, are you alright?"

Pulled from my thoughts, I walked through the hallway.

The room beyond was positively palatial. A long sweeping window dominated the far wall, peering southward with a striking view of the city. Surprisingly, the rest of the room was appointed from a bygone century.

A monstrous canopy bed of luxurious dark wood shrouded in white linen sprawled against the western wall. On either side sat solid and expensive-looking nightstands of the same dark wood. A vast European rug of French designs covered most of the hardwood floor.

"You know," I said quietly, feeling a little less spent. "That bed is bigger than my apartment."

Marcella walked from the closet with a set of pajamas. A long streak of mascara was smeared down her cheek. I couldn't help myself; I started to laugh.

"What?"

"You've got a little something—" I licked my thumb and pushed it across her cheek, trying to clean it off, but only succeeding in making it worse. I gave up after leaving a fat thumbprint on her face.

She touched her cheek, much as I had when she'd kissed me on the common.

"You have such expressive eyes." Her voice was a whisper. "Like looking into the color of life."

I blushed, unable to respond. We stared at one another for a long moment, each with a hand on the small parcel of clothing.

Marcella cleared her throat and broke the spell. "I'm going to take a shower," she said and drifted back down the hallway, disappearing through a well-lit door.

The sound of the water spray filtered into the semi-darkness. The door was open, almost daring me to follow. I considered it but chickened out. Instead, I climbed into the bed and waited. I had started to drift off when Marcella slipped under the covers, and lightning lit up the sky outside. Thunder rumbled through the windows—special effects by mother nature.

Marcella's fingers began lightly caressing my hair, and I

rolled over, looking at her face in the dim room. She stroked my cheek. I closed my eyes and tilted my face into her palm. Marcella leaned in and kissed me softly on the lips. The kiss was gentle and unhurried but still left me a little breathless.

"You are so beautiful, just magnificent," Marcella whispered.

I could feel the flush of heat all over my body, aroused and a little embarrassed. Like a child, I held my arms tight to my chest as she ran her fingers through my hair. The soft scent of soap mingled with the deeper redolence that followed her, sandalwood.

"When you first walked into my office," Marcella continued quietly, "I was so enamored with your grace and confidence."

I snorted. "You're kidding, right? I felt like a deer in headlights."

"You concealed it well."

I snorted. "Not from Carlos." The corners of my mouth turned up at the memory.

"No, I expect it's hard to hide much from him. He seems very perceptive." She leaned in and kissed me again, and I parted my lips, admitting her tongue, which lingered teasingly on my own. She nibbled at my bottom lip as she pulled back, and my toes curled.

Marcella took my hands gently and unwrapped my arms from my chest, placing them softly on the pillows. She leaned in and kissed me once more. This time she was a little more forceful, and our tongues met. Immediately, my body responded as if I'd never been touched in my whole life.

I wrapped my arms around Marcella and rolled us over, pushing her on her back. My hands and my mouth explored her body. She was suddenly warm to the touch, but her skin didn't taste of salt or sweat; it was strange and impossible to describe.

As I ran my hands across the front of her hips, she shifted, making soft noises. I wasn't sure what I was doing. I just wanted to feel her body under my hands, lips, and tongue. I wanted to know every inch of her.

Marcella sighed and squirmed slightly, but she didn't open her eyes. I worked my way first down, then back up her body. I ran my tongue across one of her nipples and felt it harden underneath. I gently sucked at it, unable to get enough of her physical presence.

She stopped me and took me by the shoulders, gently muscling me onto my back while guiding my hands, wrists together, over my head. Her grip was like iron, and though not painful, it made me tremble.

"Do you trust me?" Marcella asked, whispering in the darkness.

"Yes." And, I realized I meant it. I don't know where it happened. Maybe after the common or after our trip to the cape, I'd thrown away my inhibitions. I'd let myself trust her.

Marcella released my arms and ran her hands over my body. The feeling was exquisite. I knew I should have been here all along. This is where I belonged. As she brushed her fingertips gently over my arms and legs, my trembling subsided, and my nerves calmed. "I want to try— everything," I said through a sigh.

Marcella peeled off my clothes, taking her time, and I tilted my head back in offering with a quiet moan. I tried to reach up and caress her back, but she pushed my hand down.

"No," she breathed in my ear, "lay back and relax." Her voice, while quiet and empathetic, was also a little playful. "It must be so hard being in control all the time."

I closed my eyes and relaxed into the bed. "Yes." My voice was just a whisper.

Her hands resumed caressing my belly and found all of the ticklish spots, making me giggle.

"My, you are sensitive. I'll note that for later." That sounded a little ominous. But before I could respond, Marcella's tongue began slowly exploring the creases under my breasts, and I sucked in a harsh breath. She moved up and kissed me again.

"Are you okay?" I could hear the smile on her face.

"Uh-huh," I said as she ran her hands across my hips and

around to the inside of my thighs.

Marcella slid down and began to run her tongue around the edge of my nipples. She was slow and deliberate, taking her time, making sure I felt every second. I squirmed slightly under her as my heart raced, and heat and wetness began to pool between my legs.

Her mouth finally found one of my breasts, and I bit my bottom lip to stifle another rising whimper. She bit gently, eliciting a gasp from me in an exquisite blend of delight and pain. Then, she coaxed me over onto my belly and traced every muscular line and soft structure of my body. Each stroke of her fingers found sensitive things I hadn't known I had.

As she drew her fingers up my spine, I arched almost violently, gasping in a kind of ecstasy I'd never felt before. It was virtually tickling torture, but I refused to pull away, wanting more. The total loss of control from such a simple action was breathtaking.

"Again," I breathed harshly, pleading. "Please."

Marcella ran her hands across my back, making me gasp with delight. I'd never known it was possible to feel pleasure like that before. She played at my spine, running her fingers and tongue over it. I arched up again, reveling in the complete loss of control. Eventually, I had to beg her to stop, unable to take anymore.

Marcella eventually tugged at my shoulders, coaxing me onto my back. Her face was filled with desire, and I pulled her back to me in a passionate kiss, desperate to have her against me.

A gasp pushed through my lips as her mouth found my breasts again. She was no longer being quite so careful or so gentle, and I loved it. She bit at my nipples, and a harsh whimper sounded from my throat. My moans became louder and more wanton as the rush of our lovemaking became more heated.

I knew I was lost. I would give Marcella whatever she demanded. I felt like I couldn't get close enough to her.

"How do you feel? Is it okay?" she whispered in the darkness.

"Yes," I breathed harshly. Unwilling to say more. My head was a tumult of powerful emotions. The fear was gone, replaced by a deep sense of affection. This was making love.

She leaned in and kissed me again as her expert fingers traced gentle circles around my clit and my hips lifted. She forced them back down, her mouth returning to its ministrations of my breasts, pulling my nipples between her lips, running her tongue over them, sucking on them, nursing them.

My breath drew indelicate cries from me as an orgasm began building. Marcella left my breasts and began licking her way down my abdomen, moving her hands to my hips.

"Please," I begged. "Don't stop."

Marcella used her tongue to caress the delicate corners of my thighs, probing downward, gliding toward my core. Then I gasped loudly as her mouth found my clit, and she pushed two fingers inside me, sliding smoothly back and forth, pressing against my most sensitive places. I panted loudly, needing air, as she pulled me into her mouth, sucking. All the while, her fingers moved within me, and my climax rushed upward. The threads of my thoughts unraveled in passionate cries of rapture. The building climax crested, forcing my hips off the bed again. And yet she continued, drawing it out. My body pulled like a bowstring, taught with tension as I came.

Chest heaving with exertion, I fell back to the mattress, shivers, and sweat running down my spine. Marcella glided across my sweat-slicked body up to my throat again, her hands playing at my outer thighs as she licked at my pulse.

I knew what she wanted, what she needed, what she was. "Do it," I panted in reckless desire, "Do it, please!" I tilted my head backward, ripping off the bandage and offering my throat. With her hand at the back of my neck, she lifted my head off the pillow and sunk her teeth into the flesh of my neck, a sharp, penetrating pinch that sliced me open, causing my blood to pour, claiming all that I was.

The brief pain vanished, replaced by a deep and vibrant sensual euphoria. An urgent sense of affection overwhelmed me, and I wrapped my arms around Marcella, entangling our legs and pressing myself into her body. My hands wrapped into her hair, clawing to be closer somehow.

I could feel an intense draw within me as if every blood vessel was trying to move toward my throat. My heart stuttered in my chest, competing with the power of Marcella's all-consuming pulls. Marcella shuddered erotically with each draw of blood. My body trembled then, muscles shaking with a sudden and violent orgasm. "Oh, God," I tried to scream, but it drifted from my locked throat as a high-pitched whisper.

As blackness began to cloud the edges of my vision and my body succumbed to a pleasant buzzing, my fingers flexed weakly at Marcella's back. I felt as if I were adrift in a sea of pleasing numbness, wafting in the bliss of orgasmic love and oblivion. The soft breath of death whispered from my lungs as my head lolled back limply against her grip. My arms slid away, fingertips slipping so delicately across her ribs. The blackness closed further.

"Oh, Marcella." It was just a breath, perhaps my last susurration. I wasn't afraid. I would die now, and I didn't care.

Abruptly, though, she pulled away with soft sucking sounds. Her lips pressed to mine, dripping thickly with my blood. The floundering recesses of my better judgment recoiled, but I was long beyond any control or care. I opened my mouth, allowing what she gave me to spill in, wanting it. My throat convulsed involuntarily, swallowing.

As in my dream, something thick and cool and salty flowed down my throat, and the buzzing malaise of my limbs receded, taking the suddenly burning pain at my neck along with it. My eyes closed, and I imagined I could feel a warm light drifting through every artery and vein.

"You are mine," Marcella's voice was suddenly thick and resonant, absent her usually bright intonations. The statement was deep and dark and full of shrouded promises.

I tried to respond, but I couldn't. So, I simply nodded quickly and pressed my lips together against the pleasant, thought-stealing warmth that flooded me. The sex had been mind-blowing, but her bite and what followed had been something beyond lovemaking, beyond lust. It had been wild and carnal and beautiful.

I opened my eyes and found Marcella looking at me with a cocky smile. I pulled her blood-coated face to my own, running my tongue across her throat to her chin, finally alighting upon her mouth in a deep, bloodied, resplendent kiss.

I lay there afterward for long minutes, eyes closed as she caressed me. The exquisite delight of her warm hand, playing across my muscles, tracing the corners and curves of my body, lulled me into a soft daze. She splayed her fingers, running them heavily down my abdomen and across my thigh.

I was finally able to move. I touched my throat gingerly. The flesh was sticky with blood but otherwise whole and seemingly untouched.

"How—" I started to ask, but she placed a finger to my mouth.

"So, setting aside the bite, which, I've heard tell, is addictive as hell, how was it?"

Deep emotion and speeding thoughts rollicked through my brain. I realized that I'd spent thirty-two years denying myself, and I felt a deep sense of affection and need for Marcella that seemed both irrational and right. Behind them rose a muted terror that I might become so addicted to her bite that nothing else would ever satisfy me, or it might kill me. That was suppressed by mild regret and self-recrimination over missed opportunities because I'd been too stupid to see that I was gay. More light tears slid from my eyes. Whether of joy or hurt, I didn't know, probably both.

I pulled Marcella to me and held her in an intense embrace, feeling an edge of desperation. "It was everything it should be," I whispered finally. I didn't know if the fondness I felt for Marcella suddenly was because of the bite, the sex, or what. "I love you," I said before I could stop myself.

Marcella looked at me, smiling appreciatively. "And, I you," she replied and kissed me again, lowering to the bed next to me. We lay there for long minutes, holding each other.

"My God," I said at last. "That's what was missing, all of this time."

"I'm glad," Marcella whispered, her breath warm on my ear. "When did you know?"

I knew what she meant. "The painting in the other room. But I didn't believe it until just now."

"And you're not afraid?" she asked quietly.

"No." And I wasn't. I wondered if I should be but pushed that thought aside and hugged Marcella close. "No, I'm not. If you wanted to hurt me, you easily could have at any time."

I thought for just a moment about what we had just done. It had never been like me to let go of the wheel like this. I had always been in total control of my life, afraid to allow one moment to go astray lest it all fall apart. But with Marcella, I had done just that. I'd thrown everything into the wind and let it land where it may, and it had been liberating. In the back of my mind, I was afraid that I'd never quite know who I was again, but that thought seemed so far away and childish. I did see that I wanted to be with her, and some deep need inside me had driven me to her, filling a space I had never known was empty.

"What are you thinking about?" Marcella stroked my hand as she spoke.

"Nothing, just how much better I feel. A week ago, I wouldn't have even considered doing this. I've broken a dozen rules, and I can't bring myself to care. I just want to be with you."

"Cait, there are some things we need to talk about," she started, but I pressed my finger to her lips.

"Later," I whispered. "Let us just have this moment, for now."

I released my hold and pushed Marcella onto her back. I

looked at her mouth, perfect ruby lips reflecting a beatific smile above her chin, coated in my blood. I kissed her again, tasting my cum and blood on her lips and in her breath. I ran my tongue, wide and flat up against her throat, bringing the remnants of my blood into my mouth. Now that I wasn't wholly besotted in the throes of passion, I could taste it. It was salty but not unpleasant, as I thought it might be.

Her exhalation of pleasure told me all I needed to know about what I was doing. I moved to her breasts, kissing her nipples, biting her hard, making her gasp and squirm under me. A desperate need to consume her swirled inside me. I needed to take her as she'd taken me. I had to taste her, to know her.

I wasted no time, and, perhaps too quickly, I slid my mouth down her abdomen to her sex to take her in my mouth. It was rushed and hurried, but a fierce need took me. I ran my tongue across her clit, pushing my fingers inside. As I slid them in and out, she reached down and guided my hand the way she wanted.

"There, across there," she gasped, and I felt her muscles tighten on my fingers. "Oh, Goddess, yes, there."

She moaned softly, sliding her fingers deep into my hair, pulling my head against her harder, mashing my lips into her. I continued plunging my fingers through her more quickly as I licked and sucked at her. She was a goddess, and this was how I worshiped her. She had taken all I was, and now all I wanted was to give her more. She tangled locks of my hair within her fists as she rode toward swift orgasm. The musky taste drove me to pull my knees forward for purchase and begin massaging myself. Her rising orgasm forced my own.

Her legs stiffened, and her knees locked as she cried out in ecstasy, pulling my hair and bucking against my face. My own orgasm followed closely behind; my screams muffled between her legs.

She released my hair, allowing me to breathe more easily, and I cried out loudly as I rode out my pleasure.

I lay my face against her leg, feeling exhausted. I could feel a real pulse against her now warm thigh, regular and fast. A few minutes passed, and the only sounds were my unaccompanied labored breathing and the thump of her heart.

Marcella propped herself up on her elbows, just smiling down at me. Then, she tilted her head back, and I could feel a bit of a shudder run through her. Weirdly, having pleasured her made me feel more complete. Maybe it was just dumb romanticism, but I felt like I had become something else, something more, something whole.

I crawled back up, pulled the covers over us, and lay my head on her breast. I listened to the fading heartbeat, slowing and slowing until it fell silent, but for a single periodic thump.

"What are you doing to me?" My voice sounded small to my ears.

"I don't understand," Marcella deflected with a touch of coquettish tease.

"Be serious, please," I implored gently. "Are you making me fall for you?"

She was silent for a second. "If by 'making,' you mean treating you like someone I care for, want to know, and think could be important in my life. Then, most certainly." Her words were playful, but her tone was serious. "I am fond of you, Cait. Your very presence is, at times, almost intoxicating. It has been a long time since I felt anything but friendly affection for anyone. But, if you're asking if I am doing something extraordinary to your senses or your thoughts or your feelings, the answer is absolutely not. I'm far too old and long away from those kinds of games."

"Okay, I just wanted to know if this was real."

"It is." Her reply was so gentle and loving.

Marcella and I changed the sheets and cleaned the blood off of us. There was so much more than I had thought. No wonder I'd been woozy. Dressed back in our pajamas, we crawled back into bed.

"Why am I not bleeding out?" I pointed to my throat as I

climbed back into the bed.

"We don't talk about it much because it's— unpleasant."

I just watched her with an eyebrow raised. This I had to hear.

"When we drink from someone, our bodies immediately change the blood into something life-sustaining. Don't ask me how it works. No chemist or scientist I've ever confided in has been able to make heads or tails of it chemically or biologically.

"When I kissed you, I forced a bit of that changed blood back into your mouth. You probably felt the warmth of it."

"I thought I had imagined that," I said, shocked.

"The same life-sustaining power it has for me works very effectively on non-vampires, causing a brief period of almost miraculous healing and a bit of euphoria. Sometimes, it can imbue humans with tremendous strength as it is absorbed. It will also help you replace the blood I took. But, by morning, most of those effects will dissipate, and you'll be exhausted.

"But, before you ask, you can't just stick a straw in my neck and get the same effect. I don't know why, but by the time it's oozing its way around my circulatory system, it loses all potency. It's just blood."

"How is that possible?" I asked, incredulous.

"It's a curse, Cait, not some viral infection. Several blood analyses found a mix of blood types, but it was completely human otherwise. If you just drank my blood straight from my body, it would make you sick, just like drinking large quantities of your own."

"That's weird and oddly fucked up," I said around a long yawn.

"It gets even weirder. I could feed you my blood if you were near death, but it wouldn't turn you. I have to want to turn you. And even then, it would likely not work. In ninety-nine percent of all cases, the recipient dies anyway or becomes a revenant."

I looked at her quizzically. "What is a revenant. I mean, I know the mythological description."

"It's a vampire with no real mind of their own. They are vicious killing machines, strong as any other vampire but single-minded in pursuit of blood. That's why turning is strictly prohibited in all cases. And I mean, all. Any vampire who turns or attempts to turn someone is put to death as a risk to the rest."

"Wow, that's draconian." Fatigue was seeping into my limbs quickly, and I stifled another yawn, shaking my head slightly to stay awake.

"It's survival, Cait," she said, tone flat. "None of us want to die. And there aren't nearly enough of us to save ourselves if the rest of the population turned on us. The council forbids it. Protecting our secret is the first and most important rule."

"The council?" I asked, curious but not shocked. Of course, there was a vampire council.

"That's what we call ourselves. There are three of us. Erik Schmidt, Nastasia, and myself. I will tell you that the others are what you might expect from a vampire of legend— cold, calculating, and ruthless."

The name Schmidt rang a bell, but I couldn't remember where I'd seen it. I shook my head again, trying to focus, but my vision grew blurry and extreme fatigue began to drag me toward sleep. "Oh! Can you turn into a bat?" I asked around my yawn.

"Of course, we learn that on the first day of vampire school,' she said, obviously fucking with me, then she spooned up to me and draped an arm across my mid-section. "Just so you know, it will take a little while for the changed blood to help you replenish your own. In the meantime, you should get some rest. There will be time enough for more questions later."

I heard what she had to say, but my eyes were too heavy and my mind too fogged. I had a million other questions, but I never got the chance to ask them as I fell asleep.

28

I jerked awake in the darkness with an odd sense of foreboding. Something felt off. The first time I'd had this feeling, Morgan and I had been ambushed. Something had told me to move the Humvee early, but I had ignored it. I'd never do that again.

Marcella lay next to me, sleeping or resting or whatever vampires do. I nudged her slightly; she didn't move. I almost pressed my fingers to her carotid artery but thought better of it and instead looked at my watch—3:38 AM.

I waited a minute more, but the nagging feeling that something was about to go down hadn't quit, and the hair on the back of my neck stood straight up. I took the stairs as quietly as I could down to the second floor. Just as I went to step out, I froze, hearing the whisper of voices below.

"Come with me; it's up here on the right." It was Ninetta, and she was coming up the stairs. I couldn't see her from my vantage point yet, but her voice was unmistakable.

"And the tablet is there?" Someone was with her, a man whose voice I didn't recognize. I held my breath, feeling like an idiot for leaving my service weapon behind. Thankfully, the light was out in the stairwell, and I could see the second-floor gallery clearly through a crack in the door.

Following Ninetta up the stairs was a haggard-looking Haimon Blackman, a katana in a red and gold scabbard slung to his back. In his left hand was a polished wooden stake, clearly made for its purpose.

I was about to return upstairs to warn Marcella when Ninetta opened the door to Marcella's office. A deafening alarm sounded throughout the building. Raised voices sounded from inside the office. I stepped out of the stairwell to hear better when Ninetta ran out, Blackman behind her with his blade drawn.

"Help me," Ninetta called out, and I started forward but stopped, shocked when Blackman's blade protruded from her chest like a spike. He said something in her ear, but I heard not a word over the howling alarm. Blackman pushed her body down the stairs and raced toward me, sword raised.

He was frighteningly fast and agile. I lifted my left arm, trying to get inside his blow and block it at the forearm, but I was too slow. The blade landed solidly on my arm— and stopped cold, impacting a titanium implant. Sharp pain stabbed through my arm from wrist to elbow, but I ignored it.

"Surprise, motherfucker!" I snarled and landed a vicious right hook to Blackman's jaw. His head snapped around and slammed into the wall cracking one of the studs, dazing him for a second.

The front doors exploded inward in a hail of splinters and brass shrapnel, leaving them hanging precariously and jerking my attention from Blackman for just a moment. Marcella stood in the doorway, fangs barred, still clad in her draw-string pants and Captain Carter t-shirt. In her right arm was a sword of her own.

Blackman leaped over me and the railing to the floor below, landing flat and easy. I charged after, landing hard on the marble floor and rolling into his legs, sending him sprawling. His blade and the stake skittered across the floor to the far wall.

An animal snarl sounded from Marcella's lips, and she charged forward, grabbing Blackman and flinging him across the room with one hand. He slammed into the wall, shattering the colossal picture mirror and the console table.

I pulled myself to my feet. My right ankle twinged, but the

pain died quickly, and the cut on my arm had already healed.

My eyes widened as Blackman pulled up on his hands and feet and lunged at Marcella. God, he was fast. But Marcella was quicker still. She slid under his charge and opened a wide gash in his leg, causing him to trip and slide across the room.

I rushed over to check on Ninetta. Her breathing was shallow, and her pulse thready. I had left my phone upstairs. *Fuck!*

Blackman had regained his blade and was back on his feet. The gash in his leg was already closing. Weapons clashed as they met again in the center of the room. Blackman's sword work was phenomenal. As Marcella chopped down with her short Gladius, Blackman charged right, slicing into left Marcella's side.

"Marcella!" I shouted, moving forward.

"I'm okay! Stay back," she cried as she turned toward her opponent. An arrow sang through the room and struck her in the sword arm. I looked toward the source. Two Asian men in black suits and ties stood in the open doorway. One carried a bow with two arrows in hand. The other held a long knife. I charged the one with the knife.

Knife-guy wasn't as fast as Blackman by any stretch, but he wasn't a novice fighter either. As I ran forward, he tried to time a strike with the dagger. But I had already ducked, landing a punch in his groin. He dropped like a stone, almost landing on me. God, I felt strong.

I rolled sideways and rag-dolled knife-guy, hoisting him in front of me. An arrow sunk directly into his throat, splattering my face with blood. The point of the arrow protruded so close it scratched my cheek.

Bow-guy charged forward, dropping the bow and his last arrow. He was competent, fast, and strong. What he wasn't was ruthless. He was working within a fighting structure. Most traditional martial arts were good against the uninitiated, but they were typically useless against a trained mixed martial arts fighter.

He landed a few solid blows on my arms and a solid kick to my gut. But, I managed to get inside his guard quickly and gave him a right hook to the jaw. Staggered by the blow, bow-guy stumbled. I shoved him right between Marcella and Blackman, who had just separated. Marcella didn't hesitate; she cut bow-guy across the gut and slipped her blade back to her right hand in a single, clean movement. Bow-guy sprawled to the floor, not moving, his blood pouring across the marble.

Blackman didn't need any prompting; he took off out the door. I scooped up the bow, knocking the last arrow. I didn't know more than the basics of archery, but sometimes, beginner's luck is all you need. I watched the arrow fly, sinking in under Blackman's right shoulder blade. It didn't even slow him down.

"Fuck!"

29

"Why?" Marcella murmured at Ninetta's side, pushing hair from her eyes.

"I— loved you. T—took care of y—you," Ninetta said, blood frothing in her mouth. "Why didn't you t-turn." Her eyes rolled up slightly before focusing on Marcella once more.

"You know why," Marcella said, thick tears tinged with pink dropping onto Ninetta's face. Ninetta's eyes closed, and a last whisper of air escaped.

My heart broke within the echo of Marcella's following wail. Her sorrow filled the room and left my face streaked with tears as sirens sounded in the distance.

Before moving to comfort Marcella, I checked the two men, confirming that both were dead. Checking for ID, I noticed both men were covered in intricate Japanese-style tattoos. Yakuza.

Marcella looked up at me, her face contorted in terrifying rage, making her look— demonic. "Who was that?"

"Haimon Blackman. At this point, I'm pretty sure that he murdered Jesse, too."

"Someone has broken our covenant and made progeny. I'm going to find out who, and then they'll both pay for what they've done." I saw the ruthless power flitting behind her eyes for the first time, and it terrified me.

Marcella looked back to Ninetta and shook her head. "She let her resentment fuel stupidity."

I wondered what their relationship had been to spark that much resentment. So much so that she'd betrayed her after so many years.

Marcella set Ninetta's head down and stood. "Do you know what they were looking for?"

"That weird stone tablet in your office, I think."

"I put it away when we got back from Eastham. I don't understand, though; it's a worthless hoax, both of them are. Or, at least that's what Schmidt had told me."

"What are we going to do about this mess?" I asked, gesturing around at the now blood-slicked marble and the two dead bodies.

"Why, nothing. Three men broke into my house and assaulted my girlfriend and me. They got more than they bargained for. It's open and shut, and I have an excellent criminal defense attorney on retainer." I wasn't sure I qualified as an actual girlfriend, but I couldn't disagree with her.

For my part, I didn't feel a bit of guilt. These weren't teenagers who didn't have a chance to grow up because they got involved in gang violence. These were grown-ass men who'd attacked us unprovoked. I had an incredible sense of satisfaction rather than horror when I looked at the carnage. These men had broken in looking for trouble, and we'd given it to them.

"You're right," I said finally. "Fuck 'em."

The first police cars arrived on the scene a few minutes later. By then, Marcella had found another t-shirt, and we were both sitting on the front steps of the building. Marcella had her gladius in her lap, and I was smoking a stale sweet-cigarillo that Marcella had dug out of a drawer somewhere.

We were interviewed by one of the responding officers, a rookie named Shipley, who looked us both up and down and shook his head. His facial expression left no doubt that he didn't like what he saw.

Fuck you, too, I thought but chose to stay quiet while Marcella explained the whole mess.

"Detective Reagan?" One of the officers, a short Latin woman, stepped out of the doorway. "I'm officer Alvarez. Ms. Carson tells me that you were here when everything started. Can you fill in the details prior?"

I took a deep breath. The cat was out of the bag now anyway. "Sure, Ms. Carson and I were out on the cape yesterday and returned this morning." The officer started scribbling away on her notepad. "At 7:30 PM, we retired to bed. I woke and headed downstairs at 3:38 AM. I heard Ms. D'Angelo and Mr. Blackman walking up the stairs. Since Mr. Blackman is a likely suspect in a murder case, I decided to wait to listen to what they were saying.

"Unfortunately, I wasn't able to make anything out. They went into Ms. Carson's office. When they opened the door, they set off the house alarm. Mr. Blackman then stabbed Ms. D'Angelo for her trouble and pushed her down the stairs. Then he came after me as I stood outside the stairwell door." I pointed up the stairs to the left.

"About then, Marcella came through the busted front doors, and Blackman charged her. I followed him downstairs and got into it with his two accomplices. That guy," I said, pointing to bow-guy, "shot that guy in the neck, narrowly missing me. Then, he wandered in between Marcella and Blackman and got cut down. I shot Mr. Blackman with the same arrow, and he ran away. It's that simple."

While Alvarez wrote all that down, my team showed up.

"Hi, guys," I said, waving. Carlos didn't even acknowledge it. He went right after Marcella.

"This is your fault that she's mixed up in this shit, you fucking leech."

Fucking leech? I filed that for a much later conversation as I leaped up between Carlos and Marcella.

"She's a grown woman, Detective, and she can make up her own mind," Marcella shot back hotly.

I turned to her. "You," I said sharply, "do not need to defend me; I can take care of myself."

"And you," I turned back to Carlos, "need to simmer down. I'm here of my own free will, thank you very much. If you have a problem with it, we can discuss it later, or you can take it up with the Lieutenant."

Carlos looked down at me, and I'd swear he growled. His brown eyes looked flecked with gold.

Aw, fuck. Everything suddenly became apparent, and I felt a sharp stab of fear. But, I recovered quickly. Fuck this; he wasn't my dad. Shit, I'd just met him six days ago.

"Carlos," I said through gritted teeth. "Now is not the time. You have a killer to find. Now, go inside and do your fucking job."

"This isn't over," Carlos said, voice low and menacing.

"Oh, yes, it is, and don't you forget that," I shot back, in a low growl of my own, poking him in the chest. "No one, and I mean, no one, tells me what I can and cannot do no matter who, or what, they are."

Carlos looked at me, frowning in disappointment, but he didn't say anything else. Instead, he stepped inside to work the scene. Carol walked by after Carlos, mouthing the words, 'I'm sorry.'

I shook my head and turned back to Marcella. "I'm sorry. Maybe it's best if I leave."

"Pish, Cait, that's ridiculous," Marcella said, sounding at first perfectly fine. Then, her voice shifted to soft and a little sad. "You can leave if you want to, but I'd rather you didn't. I don't think I want to be alone right now. Besides, you've done nothing wrong, and neither have I. Detective Ramirez is just running on his instincts right now. He'll cool off."

"Okay," I said, but I wasn't so sure.

"Detective Ramirez?" Marcella called through the doors. Carlos turned and walked over.

"What?" he snapped.

"Detective, I'm sure that you feel I'm responsible for all of this— this mess. But, I assure you, I have no idea why that madman broke in here."

Carlos stepped back outside the building. "Look," he seemed a little calmer, and though his eyes were still hard, the gold flecks were gone. "Let's talk about this over here," he said, gesturing away from the front door.

We walked to the curb with him, out of earshot of the other officers. "What are you doing here, Cait?"

"Just what you think I'm doing here. Duh." I probably should have been trying to defuse the conversation, but damn it, I was pissed.

"What did you do to her?" Carlos demanded of Marcella.

She snorted in derision. "Absolutely nothing, Detective. As she said, she's here of her own free will."

"Carlos," I reassured. "She picked me up at the hospital after Gabe tried to murder me. We went to the Cape for an overnight girls' night, not that it really is any of your business, and then we came back here early this morning. I stayed here because I didn't want to be alone, and frankly, I like Marcella. She's been absolutely lovely."

"You know what she is, then," he said, voice finally returning to some semblance of courtesy.

"I do. The fact that you knew before I did is a whole other matter, though," I said straight-up. "You might have told me before all this. Not that it would have mattered one bit."

"Cait, she is dangerous." He looked at Marcella. "No offense, honey."

"None taken, love," Marcella replied with an air of perfect decorum.

"Wait, and you aren't?" I asked, not believing where he was going. "I saw your eyes. That makes you a little sus in my book, too, *honey*."

Carlos stopped and blinked. Then he pursed his lips. "Cait, I'm not like that."

"Like what? You're a fucking werewolf, aren't you?"

Carlos looked around, lowering his voice. "Jesus, Cait, keep it down. You can't just go around shouting shit like that."

"He's right, Cait," Marcella said impassively. "You need to keep that to yourself."

Carlos sighed, staring at me like a disappointed father. "I'm not going to talk you out of this, am I?"

"No," I said firmly.

Carlos turned to Marcella. "You will make sure she's aware of what she's getting into." It was more a statement than a question.

"Of course, I will, Detective," Marcella said gravely. "And, for what it's worth, I care about her as much as you do, though neither of us has known Cait for very long."

Carlos closed his eyes and pinched the bridge of his nose. "Fine. Tell me, Ms. Carson, what do I need to cover?"

"Just a few minutes of video out front," Marcella said. "I'll take care of the rest."

"Alright. Cait, I've only known you for a few days, but you're fast becoming like another sister. Please be careful."

"I will. It'll be fine," I said with a confidence I did not feel.

He started walking away looking for all the world like a parent who had just found out their child has some awful disease— like he suddenly had to adjust his expectations, and he wasn't happy about it.

"And Carlos?"

He turned back.

"I feel the same about you. I still have your back."

"Oh, more than you know, darlin'. More than you know," he said cryptically and went back to work.

Now, what the fuck did that mean?

30

Amidst the crush of cops, lawyers, repairmen, and more lawyers that followed Monday morning, the department put me on administrative leave, per policy, but it didn't last long. So, I bounced back and forth between Headquarters, my apartment, and Marcella's. Jabba was a little put out that I wasn't home more, but I mollified him with a few cat treats as I stopped in periodically.

The video footage from the doorbell camera only showed the entry of Blackman and his henchmen. There were no images of Marcella at all. Carlos' handiwork, I suspected.

While manipulating the criminal justice system bothered me deeply, what might happen to Marcella if her true nature were discovered chilled me far more. Human beings happily visited all manner of atrocities on each other. What might they do to a vampire?

It didn't change the facts, anyway. Three men broke into Marcella's house with murderous intent and were met with lethal defensive force— end of fucking story. I was not at all guilt-ridden about the outcome.

After the fuss had died down, I took a minute to check on Gabe. He had been transported to Bridgewater State Hospital, where visitors weren't allowed. After talking to his transport detail, I'd learned that he'd been catatonic for most of the trip from BMC. But, at one point, they'd had to restrain him. He'd begun banging his head against the van wall, screaming about his 'master.' I decided that when I found Haimon Blackman, I would ram a stake so far up his ass that he'd be spitting splinters. Assuming Marcella didn't get to him first. Still, the vast well of guilt that I seemed to have in inexhaustible supply gnawed at me whenever I thought about him.

Monday morning had been a slog once the rush of the changed blood had worn off. Her feeding, followed by the fight, had ultimately left me exhausted and somewhat sick. Marcella fed me hearty meals and gave me iron supplements to combat the fatigue. It helped a little.

Marcella looked pretty haggard herself by Tuesday evening.

"Are you okay?" I asked as I lay in the bed, watching her standing at the window. "You look exhausted."

"I'll be fine," she whispered in the dark. "I just need to feed and start sleeping during the day more."

"I get the feeding part, but sleeping during the day?" I nudged, finding an opportunity to learn more about her condition.

"Cait, even the power that comes with my age has limits. If I don't feed regularly, at least a couple of times a month, I get ravenous. Not getting enough rest and activities like last night can worsen the hunger. I don't want to kill anyone. That person is always someone's sister, or mother, or daughter. It's worse if I don't sleep during the day. Bottled blood keeps the hunger at bay, briefly. But the blood is incidental. We drink the life from people; the blood is just a medium."

"Wait, we lose years of life?" I began to imagine myself an old hag at thirty-three.

"No, nothing like that. Normal people have an inexhaustible supply of whatever animates them, at least until they die. It goes beyond simple biology. I can't explain it to someone who's never experienced it, but it isn't just the blood that sustains us."

"Well, if you're really that run down, I'm right here. I'm tired, but I'll be okay." Though I wasn't at all sure, that was true.

"No, Cait. I took more than I should have on Sunday. If I don't give you time to make more blood, you won't be worth much to anyone. I'm going to go out for a few hours."

Suddenly I felt a twinge of something ugly— jealousy. Did I not want my vampire girlfriend feeding on someone else? I frowned, wrestling with the feeling.

Marcella read my expression. "Cait, my life is very complicated. I don't want you becoming some blood doll or pet that I feed on whenever the mood strikes me." Her tone had changed, becoming gentle, and I realized she spoke from experience. "I want us to be together as equals. You can't just offer yourself up every time I need blood. That isn't going to work."

I thought about that. "But, I'm not sure I'm comfortable having an open relationship."

"What do you mean?" She turned and sat on the bed next to me. The moonlight silhouetted her stunning figure and gave her hair a silvery cast. I could just make out half of her face as she took my hand. Her fangs were fully extended, and her eyes burned eerily in the dark with a faint blue glow of their own. It was both frightening and exciting.

"When you feed on me, there's always a sexual component. It's really like nothing I've ever experienced," I explained. "I'm not sure I like the idea of someone else enjoying that but me."

"Cait, since the advent of vampires as the tragic villains of Gothic stories, the myths around us say that we very sexual creatures. We represent forbidden passions and dark desires. And it's not far wrong. As much as I try to reject that view, some things can't be helped." She stroked my hand and leaned in to kiss my lips, letting one of her fangs play across them.

"It's one of the things," she began kissing my chin and running her tongue down my neck, "that I cannot deny."

I felt my heart skip a beat as she passed her lips across my throat. Her hand slid into my pajama bottoms and stroked at my inner thigh, and I whimpered at the touch.

"I won't be long, my love," she whispered, vanishing into the darkness and down the stairs.

"Fuck!"

I sighed loudly, sexually frustrated. Eventually, I forced myself to roll over, and it was a testament to my fatigue that I fell asleep quickly.

About six hours later, around three in the morning, I woke and dragged myself out of bed to find Marcella reading a book in the sitting room. Rather than disturb her, I opted to try to work out. There was a small workout area off the garage. I assumed it was for guests because I couldn't imagine what a vampire might need with a gym. Inside there was everything I could ask for: a complete set of free weights, a heavy bag, a speed bag, and a protocol bag. It was heaven, and after an hour of boxing and lifting, I headed to the kitchen to grab some food.

"Hey," I called out. "You going to read all morning?"

Marcella walked into the kitchen in her pajamas, dragging a faint scent of stale cigarette smoke and blood.

"Can I ask?" I prodded cautiously.

"Of course, you can, my dear. It's not something I mind." She sat at the kitchen table to watch me cook my eggs and grits.

"I'd like you to tell me about your night. Who you met, how you fed, everything." I knew I was just begging for the green monster of jealousy to claw at me, but it was something that I wanted to be open between us, not some dirty little thing we both pretended not to know. I wasn't sure if I could deal with it, but I wouldn't disrespect myself by pretending it wasn't happening.

"Well, I went to *d-bar*. I found a nice young woman named Stephanie, an accountant at a local firm. She hates living with her mother. She is black, very dark-skinned, from Nigeria, I think, and lovely. Truly, she was beautiful."

I absorbed that as I dumped the two over-easy eggs into my bowl of grits and salted and buttered everything within an inch of its life. For her part, Marcella didn't blink or offer any apologies as she continued to describe the rest of the evening.

"We left together and went back to her place. Stephanie's mother has a condo in Back Bay with a deck overlooking the Charles. The view was extraordinary. The lights of Cambridge playing across the river have a sort of magic to them. Anyway, she drew me into her bedroom. Stephanie was pretty, but her taste in decor was for shit."

Marcella's eyes began to flicker away into an almost trance-like state. It was mesmerizing watching her face drift from fond remembrance of an event to arousal. Her nostrils flared slightly as she inhaled to speak, and her eyes dilated.

"She smelled of Chanel and faintly of the cheap curry sauce, the kind you get from a jar. The slightly aphrodisiac spice of Vodka wafted in her breath. Her lips were soft." Marcella rose slightly in her seat, a feral, savage look playing on her features. My breath quickened, and breakfast lay forgotten in the bowl, fork still in my hand. Marcella reached across the table, taking the fork.

"I ran my tongue down her neck, and she moaned underneath me." Marcella's voice became thick with hunger and desire. My own emotions tumbled between arousal and stabbing jealousy.

Marcella set the fork down and took my hands, looking at me directly. Her eyes were fully alight now, burning with lust. I could almost feel the young woman's skin on my tongue and smell the perfume and alcohol. I was falling into Marcella's gaze, and my mouth parted slowly. The difference between my imaginings and Marcella's memory blurred away. I felt what she had felt, saw what she had seen. Her flawless memory became mine.

I literally *felt* her fangs extend. The experience was my own now.

I bit into the delicate, flawless, ebony skin. Stephanie trembled at the initial pain, then settled as salty warmth and brightness cascaded over my tongue. I moaned softly.

In the present, my tongue ran over my lips, trying to get at the phantom drops of blood. Marcella's hands were between my legs, sliding up my inner thigh, spreading them as I gave myself to the vision and rapture. I felt a power welling inside as I told young Stephanie how beautiful she was.

Marcella was kneeling on the floor, lapping at my wetness as my breath heaved in my chest, building to the crescendo—and then I came. I remembered the light and heat of Stephanie's blood, the drip of it on my neck, the ecstatic expression on Stephanie's face as she called out my name weakly.

'Oh, Marcella,' Stephanie cried.

"Oh, Marcella," I cried as my hips moved. I clawed at the table and Marcella's hair as she slid her fangs into my upper thigh. My breath tumbled in and out, awash in the euphoria that siphoned away all thought, and I came again and again in a swell of wetness and sweat and blood and tears. And then it was over, just a droplet of blood coursing down my leg. Marcella hovered over me, forcing my mouth open, dribbling my blood back into me, erasing the signs of her passing.

I snatched at the back of her neck, pulling violently closer and forcing my tongue into her mouth, probing for the drops of my blood. Again. God, I wanted it again, the salty warmth of life. And then it was gone, leaving me trembling from head to toe in the chair, gasping in jerking spasmodic breaths.

Marcella pulled away and rose, slowly walking to the sink and gingerly picking up a dishtowel. My head lolled a little as I watched her, drunk on her beauty and the afterglow. I buried my hand in my hair and threw my head back to get air. I needed air. I still felt flooded with her emotions. I couldn't think; my head buzzed in both need and satisfaction.

I looked down as Marcella knelt in front of me in a pantomime of supplication. She wiped the blood from my thigh. Her hair obscured her face, but soft, tinkling laughter reached my ears.

"Is it always like that?" I breathed, finally filling my lungs with life-giving oxygen.

"On a shitty day," she said and chuckled. "With you, it's so much more."

"What did you," I swallowed loudly, "just do to me?"

"I'd think that'd be obvious. I drew your mind into my own as I remembered the experience." Her tone was slightly superior, almost cocky. "I can't feed on you like I did little Stephanie every time I need it. You'd waste away quickly." That phrase, 'little Stephanie,' reminded me of the power of this creature to whom I'd bound my heart so quickly.

I was still a little breathless. "But you just—."

"Only a few drops," she interrupted, anticipating my response.

"Oh." I tilted my head back, letting the buzzing in my brain subside.

Eventually, a pinprick of reason began to assert itself. Marcella's life, her very existence, required her to feed on multiple people. There was no way I could reliably meet all of her needs, and if I wanted to be with her, I needed to adjust to that. A niggle of jealousy still burned inside me, and I tried to stomp it out.

"I just never thought about the differences," I mused. "I guess it never occurred to me that a relationship with you wouldn't be monogamous."

"It's what I was trying to tell you, Cait." She stood and pulled me up off the chair. My legs buckled slightly, but she steadied me. "Oops, there you go. That young woman, Stephanie, she was just— ." She trailed off, looking for a word that I couldn't supply. Victim? Prey? Snack? It was all too weird.

"If you were a vampire, you'd understand the difference between claiming someone and loving them."

"I guess it'll take some getting used to." My reply was noncommittal, but as much as I tried to crush the toxic green demon, it wouldn't die.

"You can go ahead and finish your breakfast. I'm going to shower and change; then, there's something I'd like to show you before you start your day." She rose and started for the door.

I looked at her sideways. "Like what?"

She stopped and turned back, meeting my eyes. "I'd just like for you to know the real me, so to speak."

"Okay," I said slowly. "Is this not the real you?"

"It is. But there is more." She turned and fled up the elevator.

I scarfed my breakfast, and Marcella didn't get very far into her shower before I joined her. She shaved her legs as I stepped in between the main showerhead and her back.

Marcella gave me a sidelong glance. "Um, darling?"

"Yes, dear."

"It's unwise to get between a vampire and her hot water, and especially when she has a lethal instrument in her hands." She waved the razor at me.

I laughed. "Are you going to gut me with your Gillette Venus?"

She shook her head and got back to shaving. However, I stepped out of the spray, watching the rivulets of water slide down her back. Switching legs, she stood for a second, and I could see a small scar near her left collar bone. I stopped scrubbing my own body and pursed my lips.

"What?" she asked, looking at my expression.

Mixed feelings swirled in my gut, swiftly turning dark. I had seen that scar in my dream, but how could I have known about it then. My eyes went wide. "That scar."

"What about it?" she asked, now looking concerned herself. "Tell me, what's wrong?"

"My dream wasn't a dream, was it?" She'd come to me, seduced me in my sleep-addled brain. "You put the whammy on me that night, didn't you?"

"The whammy?" she asked, looking confused.

"The night I had the dream about you drinking my blood — before we started dating. It wasn't a dream, was it?" My voice started to rise. "You came into my house; you drank my blood, and you did it before we— we—" My head was spinning. I rinsed off the soap quickly and stepped out of the shower, covering myself with a towel.

Dear God, why? Why did this keep happening to me?

"Cait!" Marcella followed me out of the shower, dripping, naked. "Stop!" A dizzying power passed through me, snapping my head toward her. I looked down instinctively, feeling suddenly submissive.

Damnit.

"Cait," she said, more softly this time. "You need to calm down. I'm sorry. I—." She knelt before me. "You're right. I—." She kept breaking off, clearly upset, and my anger wavered. "Please, don't leave," she begged. "I can explain."

It was heart-wrenching. Under all of her composure and fun-loving nature was a deep well of loneliness, not all that different from my own. But the rage wouldn't subside.

"How could you?" I whispered.

"I wish I could say something that would make it better. Yes, I came to you that night. I influenced your senses, making it seem like a dream, but you have to know that I didn't force you to do anything."

"How can I know that?" I asked desperately. "How can I trust you? You violated me! You took my blood, and you made me feel— things."

She looked at me in horror. "No! I never made you feel anything. I wanted to tell you when we were at the beach house. But I was afraid you'd react this way. I mean, I knew it would come out, but I was already so—." She stopped for a second and looked into my eyes. "So in love with you." It was a whisper.

I clutched the towel around me. "I was raped my first month in Iraq, Marcella. Can you imagine how I feel right now?" My voice was shrill, even to my own ears.

"I'm so sorry. I—I hadn't known that."

I had never seen her look so broken before. I asked the only question that I wanted an answer to. The question that would make or break us, right here.

"Why?"

She looked at me, and I could see in her face that no answer she gave would be what I wanted to hear. I steeled myself.

"Because," she started and then stopped to compose herself. "Because I have been alive for over a millennium. I've become accustomed to just taking what I want. You are beautiful, and I felt a spark of attraction. I reacted as I always had, claiming what I wanted regardless of the price it exacted on my—."

"Victim?" I suggested unhelpfully.

She paused, then soldiered on. "I was as drawn to you as you were to me. I could think of nothing else. But I didn't know then that I would fall in love with you."

"That's no excuse," I snapped. "Tell me the truth; have you been controlling me this whole time? Manipulating me?"

She looked up, aghast. "Goddess, no! You saw what it did to Gabriel. His mind is permanently broken; no one can help him. That kind of control destroys the psyche. You'd be a drooling puddle by now." She looked away and shivered, then whispered, "I would die first."

My resolve cracked, looking at Marcella's desperation. A war began in my head. I'd happily gone along with the dream, hadn't I? Didn't I bear some responsibility here? I shoved that aside. That way, as they say, lay madness. But if she wanted to control me, she could have just grabbed me and made me forget. Maybe she should have.

No! I need to get out of here, I thought, *before I let this go and become a victim again.*

Marcella spoke, voice almost inaudible. "Cait, you don't understand. Can't understand. I—."

No matter what I said, what she said, or how I rationalized, I couldn't let go of the feeling of utter violation.

"I can't. I—I just can't," I said finally.

I dressed and left the house. Looking back from my ride-share, I saw her in the window, hand pressed against the glass, expression pleading. The pain in my chest hurt so bad I could scarcely breathe. I wanted to stop the car, to run back and hold her and tell her I was sorry. Instead, I jerked myself back around as the driver pulled away.

Fuck.

31

I slammed the door to my apartment in frustration and threw my bag on the floor. "Fucking vampires!" I shouted. "God damn it!"

I had been ready to burst for the entire fourteen-minute ride from Marcella's.

"Language," came Rebecca's muffled voice through the ceiling. I just shook my head. *Fuck you, Rebecca,* I thought bitterly, then realized how early in the morning it was.

Jabba was in his usual perch on the couch, and he just raised his head to look at me accusingly.

"What?" I said, staring right back at him.

He rolled off the couch like a furry slug and sauntered over, rubbing against my legs. Large tears fell across my cheeks as I picked him up. I had been crying quite a bit in the last few days. And now that I was home and Jabba was in my arms, my anger subsided, leaving a yawning pit in my stomach.

I couldn't make any sense of my feelings. Every fiber of my being was so pissed off. Marcella had made me feel wanted and cared for and—loved. But I felt like I couldn't trust those emotions anymore.

I set Jabba down on the sofa, forestalling his inevitable complaining with a few belly scritches. I needed a drink. I poured myself a glass of wine and stepped onto the darkened balcony with my aged pack of stale cigarettes.

Immediately, the hair on the back of my neck stood up. I looked down the block toward the lamp post, but no dark figure stood watching me. I thought I saw something on the rooftop across the street for a second, but there was nothing —obviously just nerves. I pushed the feeling aside, and my thoughts inevitably drifted back to Marcella.

She had been kind, caring, and supportive— especially when I had needed it most. She had an almost uncanny way of knowing just what to do and say. I smiled to myself as I recalled her sliding into bed with me on Friday night, unasked, just knowing that I needed comfort. I felt a touch of something giddy as I thought of tucking myself closer to her.

Damn it, I thought. *I fucking miss her already.*

'Tell me that you want this.' Marcella's words from Wednesday night echoed in my head.

God damn it, why are all of my relationships a fucked up mess?

As upset as I was, it didn't take long for more sullen feelings to descend, making me feel isolated and tired. I went into the bedroom and stripped, crawling into bed. My hair still smelled like sweat, but I couldn't muster the energy to care. "Fucking vampires," I muttered to myself. It wasn't long before I was fast asleep.

Later, my phone woke me.

Marcella: Please, Cait, I'm so sorry.

Marcella: Please answer me? Please tell me this isn't over.

Marcella: Cait, I know I fucked up. Please answer.

There were several other messages like that, each seeming more desperate than the last. I set my work phone down and noted a message waiting on my burner.

Celeste: Come by today. I need to show you this. Anytime is good. I'm at home.

I got dressed and looked at my watch— 8:35 AM. There was

plenty of time to get a cannoli and coffee.

Despite the long line at Modern being out the door, the man in front of me was a fucking dawdler. His logo emblazoned jacket, spare tire, and mom jeans just shouted tourist. He kept hemming and hawing about what kind of espresso drink to order.

I busted out a thick Southie accent. "Ya' gotta order, kid. The line's out the door, and we don't have all day." There was scattered laughter from the line as we waited.

The man turned around, redfaced. He looked to be an overprivileged, poorly dressed southern businessman who had too many guns, worshipped a military in which he'd never served, and only respected cops when they were being used as a bludgeon against people he didn't like.

Given my shitty mood, I was spoiling for a fight, but he just grumbled and ordered a black Americano. There were a few snickers and some hateful stares as he left.

I took no time ordering my usual cannoli and coffee. Outside, I took a few bites, but it might as well have been made of ash for all I could taste it.

God, I'm depressed.

The last time I felt this awful had been when Morgan had left for Montana. We had been staying at my mother's, waiting on discharge paperwork, which Morgan got, and I did not. To this day, I still don't understand why the Army chose to discharge her and have me re-assigned. But who the fuck knew how they came to decisions?

I'd found Morgan at the front door, bags packed, waiting for a cab. I had panicked and blocked the door.

"I thought we were getting an apartment together," I'd said, voice shaking. "What are you doing?"

"Cait, I want to, but I can't. I'm going back to Montana. I need to sort out my head."

When her cab had arrived, we had been only inches apart. I looked at her mouth, wanting so badly to kiss her goodbye, but all I did was hug her with my one functional arm. I never saw her again.

Weeks later, when she dropped the bomb on me that she was getting married, I had felt betrayed, like I'd been right on the edge of something incredible only to have the person I trusted most snatch it away.

This sucks.

I threw away the rest of my cannoli and dumped the coffee, unable to bring myself to eat with this rock in my gut. I needed to get my mind off of Marcella, so I went home, picked up my gear, and headed to work early.

32

"Hey there," Carlos greeted me as I sat down, making me jump.

"Umm—hey," I said, looking at him askance.

Carlos looked hurt. "Darlin' don't be like that. I'm as safe as anyone here."

I sighed heavily. "Sorry, this is all new to me. And I'm not sure which way is up right now."

Carlos turned to face me fully. "Everything alright?"

"I'm fine," I said, fatigue creeping into my voice. "You warned me, and I didn't listen."

"Uh oh, what happened?" His beard had become a little unkempt in the last couple of days, and I suddenly felt guilty about my absence.

"Oh, I don't know, Carlos. We've just hit a rough spot."

"Already?" He sounded surprised. "I thought you were in love, or, at least, heavy lust."

"I was. I am. Shit, this sucks." I lowered my voice as I brushed my hair and pulled it back into a ponytail. "She fed on me."

"Well, that was bound to happen. Did it freak you out?"

I rested my elbow on the desk, chin in my hand. "The feeding? No. That's not the issue. I had this dream last Wednesday. It was very—uh—." I paused, blushing, unable to find a word other than erotic. "Anyway, in the dream, Marcella came to me in the night and fed on me, and I let her. But,

AOIBH WOOD

it turns out, it wasn't a dream. She swears she didn't make me do anything I didn't want, but I know she made me forget whatever happened afterward because I just woke up in my bed. I feel violated. At least, I think I do."

"Cait, you need to remember what she is," he admonished in hushed tones. "I told you she would be relentless in getting what she wanted. I also told you not to get wrapped up with her—"

I bristled at his tone. "I don't need a lecture. Besides, I'm not sure you're one to talk. I assume you knew what she was and didn't tell me."

Carlos scowled in annoyance. "Cait, I couldn't; it's forbidden. And, I won't feel bad about that. Now, what have you decided to do?"

"Nothing," I said flatly. "I haven't decided anything. I left her house this morning and haven't talked to her since."

"Ouch," Carlos said.

"Well? I didn't know what else to do. She lied to me. When I first told her about my 'dream,' she asked me to tell her about it as if she hadn't been there the whole time."

"Look, I'm not trying to tell you what to do, but if I were you, I'd cut her the fuck loose. They're manipulative in the extreme. She might seem nice enough, but even if she's sweet as pie, that relationship works only if she turns you. Do you honestly want to live forever?"

I thought about that. It might be cool and exciting to see history unfold on a grand scale in front of your eyes, but then there would be duplicity, fighting not to be discovered, and of course, the eating habits. Most importantly, how serious can you consider any relationship when you know the other person will wither and die as you stay young. "No, I guess I don't."

The whole experience sounded dehumanizing. It made me think about how lonely Marcella must be. And here I thought I couldn't feel any more miserable. But the way she'd pursued me, manipulated me, and brought me into her orbit had been, as Carlos had said, relentless and almost effortless. It was both flattering and terrifying. So terrifying, though, that it made me worry that she might dispense with all pretense and turn me into her little pet like Blackman had done Gabe. *Did I honestly believe that?*

She seemed so sincere. Of course, that was part of the problem. I'd seen people guilty of some of the most cold-blooded murders deliver Academy Award-winning denials. Working Homicide could give one serious trust issues. I pushed those thoughts aside.

Carlos stood. "I need some coffee; want some?"

"No, I'm good," I replied and went to talk to Vic.

Vic looked at me in undisguised amusement. "Well, hello there."

"Okay, go ahead, Vic, get it out, now." I gave him a playful 'bring it on' gesture.

"So, Marcella Carson, huh?" He raised a suggestive eyebrow. "I mean, if you're gonna bat for the other team, you could do way fuckin' worse."

I laughed half-heartedly. "Very sensitive, Victor. The other team? Really?"

"Well, I didn't realize you were what? Bi? Gay? I mean, I know Gabe wasn't the love of your life, but I thought—" Vic grimaced, realizing how he sounded.

"Where are we with the case?" I asked, switching subjects.

Vic pushed an armload of files toward me. "Carlos and I found two cases, going back about two weeks. They seem to match our killer's weird as fuck signature. There's a case in Lowell. Lowell CID is working on that one. The lead on that case is Detective Cahill—"

I interrupted. "Lynn Cahill? I know her; she's a bit of a hard-ass with a good sense of humor. I also know she gets along with her team but would like to strangle the men from time to time."

"That's her," Vic continued. "The details are in the file. The other case is in Quincy, a headless body, but I'm not sure about that one. It looked drug-related."

"We also found some other strange cases going back about eight weeks though that you should look at. I have no idea what to make of them."

"What are they? Do they seem related?"

"I'm not sure, but my gut says something is going on here that we're missing. You remember that woman who washed up on Revere Beach about two months back?"

"Vaguely, it was all over the news. As I recall, she washed up right in front of Antonia's Restaurant. I thought she drowned." State Police had the case along with the Coast Guard. I couldn't remember the victim's name.

"Nope. The official cause of death was exsanguination." That got my attention. He opened one of the folders to a stack of photos and reports. "Throat was torn open. She bled out before she ever hit the water." My pulse sped up, and my breath came a little quicker.

Victor continued grimly. "It gets worse; there are three others just like it, one in Salem, one in Chatham, and one in Falmouth. What the hell is going on here, Cait?"

"I wish I knew." I felt the lie on my lips, but there was some truth. I certainly had no idea who was feeding on people. It wasn't Marcella; she was way too careful. "Why didn't state police flag those as possible serial killer crimes?"

"No clue," Vic said. "Bad day in the analysis group? Your guess is as good as mine."

"Well—," I started and then stopped when I realized I was about to say I'd ask Marcella. *Where the fuck is my head?* Then I had a thought.

I walked back to Carlos' desk and leaned in close. "I think I need a smoke; why don't you join me?"

"Don't smoke, darlin'," he responded without looking up.

I put a hand on his arm. "It looks like you're taking it up today."

He got the message.

We took a walk down Ruggles Street toward the

Northeastern University campus. I waited until we were well away from the building before I spoke.

"Okay, so, what's Blackman's endgame here?" I asked.

"I've been asking myself that all week." Carlos took off his hat and ran his hand through his hair. "It doesn't make a lick of sense. I'd really like this case to go away, unsolved, and soon. But Blackman won't stop dropping bodies left and right. I can tell you every werewolf in Boston is looking for him."

"That's my point. Whatever he's up to, he must believe it's huge and going to change everything. He's acting like he has nothing to lose. He commits a series of gruesome and messy killings and then tries to steal some tablets from Marcella. If what Marcella has said is true, then piercing the veil of secrecy around the existence of preternatural creatures comes with the ultimate price, and he doesn't seem to care."

"That rule is sacrosanct," Carlos confirmed. "I've only been a werewolf for a short time, but I've already seen it enforced once. One of our number here in Boston was seen changing. It was an accident, but it didn't matter. They don't fuck around, Cait."

I was shocked. "They killed him?"

Carlos' tone was deadly serious. "Both of them. Like I said, The Vestry don't fuck around."

"God!" I was appalled that they'd kill a human for witnessing it. Even if they told someone, who'd believe them. "What's 'The Vestry?'"

"Werewolf council of sorts, far more strict than the vampires. Being a werewolf comes with a certain level of control problems from time to time. Without The Vestry and the group leaders, we'd have been outed and, probably, exterminated long ago."

"Wait," I said, suddenly not liking where this was going. "Am I in danger?"

"Right now? No. You're under Marcella's protection."

"And how is that? How does your council even know about Marcella and me? Did you tell them?" I snapped.

Carlos stopped and took me gently by the arm. "I didn't have to. Marcella marked you as Imperium Persona almost the day she met you. It shocked the hell out of me. The Vestry is already asking me about you."

"I'm not a fucking controlled person."

"Imperium Persona doesn't mean that—at least not anymore. It means that you are 'in the know' and Marcella has taken responsibility if you fuck up. If you spill the beans or expose us, it's open season on both of you. And, Cait, she can't take it back—ever. I can't believe I'm saying this, but you shouldn't blame her for that. The minute they saw you in the park together having lunch, you were on the Vestry's radar."

I was incredulous. "Wait, someone was spying on us?"

"On Marcella? Of course. The Vestry is always watching them. If Marcella hadn't put you under her protection, you'd likely be dead, and I'd probably have been given the order."

Damn, I was in way over my head. "Would you have carried it out?"

"Cait, I have a husband, and the Vestry has people everywhere. Let's say I would have hoped there was a way to avoid it. But, if it's between you and Marcus—" He didn't have to finish the sentence.

"Okay, so there's the Vampire Council and the Werewolf Vestry. Any other groups I should know about?"

"None that I know of." He turned us back, walking quickly toward HQ.

"I can't believe my ass is hitched to Marcella's," I griped as I huffed to keep pace with the tall man. "Can you slow down, please? My legs aren't as long as yours."

Carlos slowed down and then stopped. He took one of my shoulders gently and spoke. "Cait, can I be honest?"

"I prefer it."

"Fine," he said, and his eyes grew hard. "It's time for you to grow up."

"Hey—," I protested, but he cut me off.

"No, you need to listen to me this time. Larson says you

have the makings of a great detective, and I agree. But you need to get your shit in order. You need to go back to therapy and get your head sorted about Iraq and whatever else is rattling around up there. On the surface, you're this hard-as-nails bitch, but underneath, you're a frightened little girl. And, you're off the map, with us, darlin'. You're gonna need your wits about you.

"I know you didn't ask for this, but here you are, so buck the fuck up and get to work. Pull your personal life out of the shitter. That's what made you easy pickins for Marcella. And, for God's sake, don't go back to her; she is bad news. But, you'll need to make nice with her because she's all that's between you and the noose, and I can't protect you. Werewolves don't get to declare Imperium Persona; there are too many of us to manage that."

I hadn't expected him to dress me down, and it shook me to my core. I wanted to say something, anything, but I couldn't find my voice. He didn't wait for me to come to my senses either. He pulled me into a quick hug and then walked away down the sidewalk back toward Schroeder, leaving me standing there, wondering what the fuck just happened.

33

The walk back to HQ felt more like Shackleton's march than a quick jaunt outside. The wind blew miserably cold and pushed through my zipper, adding to my soul-crushing depression.

Back at my desk later, I started going over the mountain of information Vic had so thoughtfully provided.

First on my list was the case from Lowell. The victim, a 'Jane Doe,' was found in a beat-to-shit, abandoned building off Morrissette Boulevard. There wasn't much left of her. She'd been burned alive, which was— horrible. Her heart was missing, too. That wasn't the strange part, though. According to the scene report, portions of a giant reptile were mixed in the remains. Unfortunately, there was significant cross-contamination in the DNA samples, and no identification was forthcoming. There were no witnesses, no leads, and no video.

I marked that file with a post-it labeled 'possibly related' and continued. The case in Quincy involved the decapitation of a known heroin and oxy dealer. The beheading had been postmortem, and the heart was intact. Head was never found, though. Again, there were no witnesses, leads, or video. I set that one aside as probably drug-related.

Finally, I looked at all three of the exsanguination cases. All three looked like vampire bites, at least as I understood them — the carotid artery was torn open. Someone was snacking on our turf. I couldn't say it was Blackman, but unless it was Marcella. I stopped my train of thought. No, no way. Marcella wouldn't leave this kind of a mess. She was just too meticulous. You don't hide as a vampire in Boston for over fifty years by being sloppy.

I sat back. I could still see Marcella's face in the window, pleading. I shoved the thought violently out of my head before the waterworks started again. I had things to do.

My burner phone buzzed, and I looked at it.

Celeste: You coming by or not?

Shit, I'd forgotten about her.

Me: Yes, I'm at the office finishing up some things. Be by around 5:30. Is that okay?

Celeste: Sure, see you then, hot stuff.

I rolled my eyes. Celeste was a near-constant flirt. I put away my phone and rounded up the team. I found Carlos in the breakroom making coffee with David and Carol. Vic had already left for the day.

"So, how are things with your blond goddess, hmm?" Mills inquired, waggling his eyebrows as I entered.

"Don't ask," I snapped a little more harshly than intended. Mills moved back as if I'd bitten him.

"Geez, Reagan, what's got your twat in a twist?" he asked, hoisting his coffee cup to his lips.

I sighed. "David, I'm sorry; it's been a tough two days. I'll be fine, I'm sure. Anyway, can we get together in the conference room? I need to play catch up."

"Sure, I'll gather everyone up."

The team moved to the conference room, where we huddled.

I gestured for Mills to start. "Alright, David, what'd you find out."

David began reading from his notes. "Well, Haimon Blackman was born in New York and was an avid environmentalist. Tokyo police arrested him at twenty-one for participating in an anti-whaling operation in the antarctic, boarding a Japanese factory whaling ship to bring attention to the practice."

I whistled. "That's a pretty bold move, given that the Japanese government subsidizes the whaling industry."

David continued. "Well, he spent nine months in prison. After prison, somehow, he managed to stay in Japan and make his way into Waseda Business School to earn an MBA. Usually, a school like Waseda wouldn't take someone who'd so embarrassed the country. Blackman has connections."

"What kind of connections?" Carol asked, one eyebrow raised.

"I'll get to that. After leaving Waseda, Blackman joined Kineda Pharmaceuticals in their sales department and worked his way to VP. He became a mentor to a young American salesman helping gain a foothold in New England, Gabriel Parkman. Sorry, Cait."

I just nodded for him to continue.

"Haimon Blackman was a rising star at Kineda. His family, however, was another matter. Blackman's father is connected with the Yakuza presence in New York. He has an extensive rap sheet: prostitution, illegal gambling, drugs; you name it."

Well, I thought, *that explained the two men I'd fought at Marcella's on Monday morning.*

"So, maybe we're looking at this the wrong way," I blurted after Mills had finished laying out Blackman's background.

"What do you mean?" David asked with a shit-eating grin I couldn't understand. He looked like he was about to bust out laughing. The others were also suppressing snorts of amusement.

I stopped and tilted my head. "The fuck, guys?" I asked, scanning the group.

David gestured at my coffee mug in amusement. I looked down. Somehow, the little shit had replaced my plain white mug with one that said, 'I like Big Busts, and I cannot lie.' It sported a graphic of a patrol officer's hat sitting on two enormous breasts.

My face blushed about fifty shades of red before settling on just the north side of the garnet. The levity of the joke infected me, and I was reduced to hysterics, laughing uncontrollably. "Nicely done," I said through heartfelt glee.

"Damn, David! I think you broke her," Carol said, watching me. That just made me laugh more.

After a few long minutes of much-needed fun, I pulled myself together—mostly. "Okay, the joke's over," I said as firmly as I could muster. "Let's get back to it. And David?"

"Yes?"

I shot Mills the finger. "Fuck you; you know that?" Mills beamed and sat back down.

"Okay, what about Kineda. What do we know about them?" I asked.

Carlos took over from Mills. "They have a line of vaccines for various illnesses, mostly from mergers and acquisitions. The FDA just approved their research for a new series of cancer drugs."

Something suddenly occurred to me, and I turned to Carlos. "So, again, do you think we might be looking at this wrong?"

Carlos tilted his head. "What do you mean?"

"Okay, so we've been treating this case like it's just some guy on a killing rampage—that he's delusional. What if we look at it differently? What if he's targeting these people for some mundane reason."

Carlos shot me a warning glare, but I ignored it. "This might be something far more simple than it seems. Let's set aside the crazy methods of homicide and see if the victims have anything in common."

"We already did that?" Mills groused. "We came up with bubkis."

I plowed on. "What about health issues? Blackman works for big pharma. Jessvin Caldwell was spending a lot of time at the Margaret Chastity Cancer Center in Buffalo. Marcella said it was for charity work, but what if *he* was the charity."

Mills looked at the Rodriguez case notes. "Acacia Rodriguez was treated at the Margaret Chastity Center for Cancer Research for inoperable glioblastoma. When she left, she was in full remission. My uncle died of a glioblastoma just last year. As far as I know, there's never been a good way to treat that."

Carlos studied me intently across the table, but he seemed more interested than alarmed. "So you think it's just someone using an unapproved treatment, and now they're cleaning up?"

"Maybe, but it seems so sloppy. On the other hand, the weird methods of killing might be to throw us off. Regardless, I think we could have a real break here. Mills, can you and Carol see if you can get the information from the Cancer Center on Rodriguez's treatments? Also, check to see if Caldwell was being treated there too. If it turns out they've been on any drugs from Kineda, let's find out who else is on the list."

Mills and Carol filed out of the room. I stayed put and waited for Carlos to speak up.

"Cait, we're treading a dangerous line here," he warned, voice low.

"I know, but the case isn't going to go away magically, and we can't just ignore it. As you said, bodies are piling up. We can't bring Blackman in alive, but we need to find out where he's likely to strike next. Also, I have a friend who thinks she has information for us. I'd like you to go with me tonight."

"I can't," Carlos said, grimacing. "It's my anniversary with Marcus. What about Carol or David, if you need backup."

"No, it's not that. I would have wanted you there in case something developed. But, it's nothing I can't handle."

"Okay, so call me if anything happens. I promised Marcus I would leave at ten sharp unless another body turned up."

I sighed. "Can I ask you to keep your cell handy?"

Carlos nodded as we returned to our desks. I needed to prep for next week's court date in the Washington murder.

About a half-hour later, a man's voice disturbed my review of the Washington case notes. "Detective Reagan."

I found Agent Matt Reynolds of the FBI looking down at me; lips pressed thin. I smiled broadly. "Agent Reynolds, how are you? Is this a social call, or do I need a lawyer?"

Reynolds was a relatively handsome older man in his early forties with salt and pepper hair, a mild gut, and a military bearing. During my patrol days, the department had assigned me to the tactical team supporting an FBI sting operation to break up a child pornography ring. The case had sucked, but Reynolds and I had become fast friends.

"This is a business call, Reagan. We just want to chat for a minute." Despite his friendly manner, his expression looked tight.

"Interview room?" I asked, eyebrow raised.

Carlos looked over. "You want me to call a union rep?" Carlos' expression made it clear he wasn't a fan of the feds.

I stood. "No, I'll be fine," While it was against my usual rule of not taking an interview without a lawyer, I felt I'd get more from them without representation. If it went somewhere I didn't like, I could end it.

In the interview room, another man joined us. "This is Special Agent Reese," Reynolds said, gesturing to the short, stocky fellow.

I stared at them for a moment before I spoke. "What can I do for you?"

"How well do you know Marcella Carson?" Reynolds placed a rather thick file on the table.

"If you're asking that, Matt, you know. So, why don't you just cut to the chase? What's this about?"

"I can't get into that. How long have you two been—together?"

I laughed at the euphemism. "We're dating, Matt. And I've only known her for about a week."

"Okay, so we have some concerns that have been brought to our attention, and we need your help." Matt was a money guy, so I knew already that these 'concerns' were related to either money laundering or embezzlement.

I interrupted him. "Matt, look. I haven't seen anything out of the ordinary. The woman has a nice house and drives a decent car. We looked into Carson Logistics and Marcella, too. She pays her taxes, and everything looks above board. So what is going on?"

"That's just it; we're not sure. I need your commitment to keeping this confidential."

"From Marcella, you mean. Fine." It felt uncomfortable, but I wanted to see what Matt was on about.

"Eight weeks ago, we were contacted by Jessvin Caldwell about irregularities in the accounting." The mention of Jesse made my stomach do flip-flops, but I held my expression in check.

"It's not so much money that's missing; it's inventory bound for charities in Boston. The materials never made it.

"We're not talking about a few pairs of jeans, either, Cait. Sixty tons of canned goods, for example, just in the last two months. Forty large-scale saltwater filtration units worth over a half-million dollars disappeared less than a year ago. Cait, thirty million dollars worth of inventory has gone missing, and no one at Carson seems to know where it went. All of them were orders for pet charity projects run by Ms. Carson."

Reynolds opened the file and showed me a list of purchase orders approved by Marcella. Then he showed me a field report. According to a dozen field agents, all the charities received only a tiny percentage of what was ordered by Carson Logistics.

What the actual fuck?

"Okay, so this proves she signed for the orders and someone, possibly her, purloined a sizable chunk. But according to these invoices, the goods were paid for by Carson Logistics, not the charities themselves. So, it's not actually theft, is it? I mean, Reynolds, it's her company. She can kind of do whatever she wants with it. What proof do you have that she's doing anything with the goods? Are there bank statements, large deposits, foreign accounts, what?"

"Right now, there's nothing. If she's selling the stuff, it's not obvious where she's putting the money. We've traced every account, subsidiary, and holding company she owns, has stock in, or walks by. And this is where we need your help. Don't you think it's odd that Jessvin Caldwell talks to us about accounting irregularities, provides us with all this material, then he's murdered?"

Hell yeah, I thought it was fucking odd. But, something didn't add up, literally. "It's hard to prove embezzlement without a money trail. Right now, all you've got is an inattentive CEO of a private company who signed off on some questionable invoices. And, I'm certainly not going to help you nail my girlfriend."

"Come on, Cait. Don't be naive. Marcella Carson is dirty, and we're going to put her in cuffs. Best case, we nail her for tax fraud and embezzlement. Do you honestly want to be swimming in those waters? They get pretty deep."

Oh, you have no idea, I thought.

"Look, Matt, I get it. You've got a case to investigate, and so do I. You forget I know this game. You don't have enough for a solid indictment, so you're trying to use my career as leverage for me to dig up dirt on her. But, Matt, let me ask you this. What would you do if I came to you with something this thin on Peggy?"

Reynolds frowned, twirling his pencil. "But, you said you'd only known her for a week. And besides—"

"Let me stop you right there." My expression turned hard, and I scowled at Reynolds. "I don't know what you were about to say, but let me save you some trouble. This discussion is over unless you want to detain me. In which case, I'll call Marcella and have one of her flesh-eating attorneys crawl up your ass."

I got up and stalked out of the interview room. *Fucking assholes.*

"So, what was that all about?" Carlos asked as I packed my stuff.

"Fuck if I know. The feds are looking into Marcella. I have something I need to do."

Carlos squinted at me suspiciously. "Where are you going, Cait?"

"To find this bastard and end this fucking case," I said harshly and walked out.

"Don't do anything stupid, Reagan," Carlos called after me. I ignored him.

34

The traffic between Schroeder and Celeste's place was thick, and it took a good hour to get there. I was glad of the delay, though. It gave me time to think about my encounter with Reynolds and Reese.

The FBI thought Marcella was embezzling from her own company. One requirement in such a case was that the money or resources had to be used for non-business purposes. From what I knew of financial laws, her most significant risk was tax-related, but I wasn't an expert. Carson was big enough to have a few skeletons buried, but the feds had to have something solid to go as far as they had. Hassling me was a risk unless they had more of a case than I realized. I rubbed my face and paid attention to the road.

Celeste lived on the first floor of a two-story home in Brighton. Outside on the sidewalk, someone had free-cycled an easy chair. I considered it for a moment, trying to decide if it would sit well in my apartment, but decided against it. Go to the easy chair, and before you know it, you're in a walker. I wasn't that old yet.

"Is that a real gun?" the speaker was a young heavy-set white boy with brown hair. Beside him stood a thin African-American girl with tight braids. They were both maybe eight years old.

"Of course, it is, dummy," the girl said caustically. "She's a cop."

I smirked. Kids were the same all over.

"Huh-uh, she's a girl, and girls aren't cops," the boy said.

"What cave did you crawl out of, Noah," she snapped back at the boy. "Just because your dad's a pig doesn't mean you have to be one."

I bit my lip to stifle my laughter. Maybe kids weren't the same all over. Noah had better quit while he was behind.

"Yes, I'm a cop," I said, pulling back my jacket to show the badge clipped to my belt. "And yes, it's a real gun. And, no, you may not touch it or hold it; you shouldn't even look at it." The boy pouted, but I ignored him, continuing to Celeste's door.

Celeste opened the door as I knocked, a large bag of lime-flavored tortilla chips in hand.

"I heard you and the crotch-goblins talking," she said with a smirk, inviting me in.

"Hey, ease up on the kids. You were one yourself once. I remember arresting your crass ass at the ripe old age of sixteen."

Celeste Laughed. "True. And I will be forever grateful for your help with the apartment and the job, not to mention getting me off with the DA."

"And your first-semester tuition, and telling your parents to stuff it over your transition," I finished.

Celeste turned a little defensive. "Hey, I did well with it. Who'd have thought that stupid sixteen-year-old would turn into this stunningly beautiful MIT grad student in just three years?"

"I did, and I'm damn proud to have been a small part of that."

I gave her a quick hug and realized she'd had her top surgery. "Hey, new boobs, how do you like them?"

"Oh, yeah." She hefted her breasts. "Still doesn't feel like me yet. The doc said it would take a few months before it felt natural. I sleep on my side, but I'm afraid they'll settle funny or something."

I laughed. "I'm sure they'll be just as uneven as mine. How

have you been otherwise?"

"I'm doing well. Jim and I didn't work out. He took a job with some douche-bag online magazine in California. That's why Erin and I went to the beach."

I didn't know Jim or Erin. Celeste had a touch of ADHD, so she tended to babble a bit. I found it endearing if challenging to follow.

"Want a chip?" She held out the bag, so I took one.

"Sorry to hear about you and, uh, Jim." I didn't want to have a half-hour conversation about Celeste's love life, and I didn't need the salacious details, which she would be happy to provide.

"Yeah, no loss there. Hey, what's with the biker dyke look? I like it," she grinned and waggled her eyebrows suggestively.

"Huh?" I looked down. I looked like a butch in my jeans, leather jacket, boots, and, shit, no bra. I flushed with mortification as I realized I'd gone into the station like this.

"Wait." Celeste's expression turned suspicious and inquisitive. "Did you? Oh my god, you did! Didn't you?"

My whole body was a deep shade of red, but I played dumb. "What are you talking about?"

She gasped dramatically. "You're fucking a woman!" She about jumped off the couch with glee, clapping her hands. "About time!"

I closed my eyes as my face burned. Celeste had this unnerving sixth sense about my personal life that drove me nuts. When Gabe and I first started dating, Celeste had told me about a dream she had that I went to work in pharmaceutical sales before I'd mentioned it. It was fucking creepy.

"What does my outfit have to do with my eating habits?" I deflected with a bit of humor. "Honestly, Celeste." I laughed nervously and couldn't meet her eyes.

"You're kidding, right? Just look at you? No slacks, blouse, no blazer. And," she wiggled her eyebrows, "no bra. Jesus, Cait. Welcome to the family, honey. Please tell me you're not exclusive." She gave me a mischievous look. "But, are you like a lesbian or bi or what?" She was an excited puppy with a new toy.

I decided I wouldn't get anywhere until I answered her questions. "Okay, so I met this woman, Marcella Carson."

"Oh. My. God. *The* Marcella Carson? I saw her at a charity event last year. She is un-fucking-believably gorgeous. They call her the 'vampire lady' on the street, did you know that? Go Cait! Banging the smokin' hot vampire lady. Nice." She gave me a thumbs up.

"Okay, you want to hear the story or not?" I asked in annoyance and total embarrassment.

"Yeah, yeah, okay," she said, leaning forward. "Oh, wait. Are you working today? You are, aren't you?"

I sighed heavily at the interruption. "Yes."

"Wait, hang on; one sip won't hurt you." She darted out of the room into her kitchen and came back in with a mini-bottle of champaign, which she immediately uncorked with a pop. "First swig in celebration of your coming out!"

I took a very short draw on the bottle and coughed as the bubbles tickled my nose. While drinking on duty was a definite no-no, there were worse offenders on the force. The bottle started to fizz over, so I shoved it back into Celeste's hands. She simply guzzled down the rest.

"Wooh!" She set down the empty bottle, eyes watering. "Okay, okay, I'll stop. How did you two meet? Wait, was it that Caldwell guy that was all over the news? And what's with that new Detective? He is so hot."

"Stop. Focus. Carlos is gay and married, and I can't discuss any open cases, you know that. But she sort of swept me off my feet. We spent Saturday on the cape."

"Wow, that is so exciting and romantic. Oh, that reminds me, I want to show you something. Come over here." Celeste got up and made little prancing steps of excitement over to her desk. I followed; I did *not* prance.

"Okay," she said. "So, check this out." Celeste pulled up a map of Boston. Tiny blue and orange dots were wheeling around the city.

"Each of these dots is a cell phone. If it's not secured well, any smartphone will send out beacons looking for WiFi access points it recognizes. For example, yours is always looking for 'Jabbas Palace.'"

"Yeah, that's the name you used when setting up my home WiFi."

"Exactly. They do this all day, every day. So, we have this set of sensors we've placed all over the city, right? Follow me so far?"

I scowled at her in irritation. "Yes, I know a *little* bit about how my phone works."

"Okay, so when our sensors receive these beacons, they log everything about them and feed them to an AI algorithm. That means artificial intelligence, by the way."

"I know what AI is," I said wryly. "I don't live under a rock."

"Okay, right. Now, newer phones try to hide their identity when they beacon, making it harder to identify them, but the phones beacon the same WiFi network names repeatedly. After a while, the AI teases out which phone is which. Does that make sense?"

"Okay, I think I get it. Each phone tries to call its home. Your program records these— beacons?"

She nodded.

"Then your HAL-9000 munches on that data and links the beacons to the phones. That allows you to track where a phone goes."

"Right, now we don't typically know who the phone belongs to, but—." Celeste trailed off, waiting to see if I was following.

"But you can track each phone when it enters your coverage areas."

"Exactly, you got it. See, you're not nearly as tech stupid as you claim."

"Har, har, Celeste. My brain is on fire right now, trying to keep up. Anyway, what does this have to do with my case?"

"Cait, I checked our sensor data, and you need to see this."

She turned to the screen.

She centered Charlestown on the little map, and I could see tiny dots lighting up in various colors. She clicked a button on the screen marked 'save filters' and then selected some esoteric numbers from the list.

All of the other dots vanished, leaving only one in bright orange. That dot hovered around the monument for a bit, finally moving down the street and disappearing. A timestamp in the corner of the screen showed Wednesday's date at 01:04. She fast-forwarded the animation, and several blue dots appeared in Charlestown. Then they went away too."

"What—" I started to say, getting excited, but Celeste shushed me.

"Just watch."

The map zoomed in on the corner of Humboldt and Seaver. Again, the orange dot appeared down at one end of Humboldt, and then it moved up to the house where the murders had occurred. It disappeared a few seconds later. The timestamp was about the time of the murders there, as well. Once again, later, another half dozen or so dots, all in blue, showed up at the scene. This time a dot of green appeared.

"Wait, those dots are phones? And, the orange dot was at both scenes?" I asked.

"Uh-huh, and this guy has a shitty phone," Celeste said, beaming with pride. "By the way, the green dot is your burner."

"And you can track these where?"

"Almost the entire city," Celeste replied with a bright smile.

"Why does it disappear then?" I asked.

"Well, either he's turning off the phone or moving into a space with no coverage."

"But you said you have coverage all over the city, right?"

"Yup."

"So, he must be turning off his phone."

"That's possible, but why would he turn it on just as he's about to commit a crime. That makes no sense. There is another possibility, though. As I said, we have sensors all *over* the city."

"Holy shit. He could be going underground! That's why there's no footage, and the fugitive squad can't find him. He uses the sewers or old tunnels. Celeste, you are a fucking genius." I scooped her out of the chair and gave her a bear hug. "I could kiss you."

"Okay, okay! Shit, Cait. Work out much? Jeez!" Celeste groaned, holding her ribs as I released her.

I was positively ecstatic. "Is any of this legal?"

"It's one hundred percent legal. There's already court precedent."

"Fucking A." I grinned in triumph and gestured to the screen. "If that orange dot appears again, call me. This is just the break I need to nail this bastard."

"Who is it?" Celeste asked.

"I can't tell you that, you know that. I need you to do something else for me."

"Sure."

"God, Celeste, you are such a lech. No, neither of them involves you taking off your clothes. When you see that phone again, after you call me, I need you to call my lead, Carlos Ramirez." I handed her my card with Carlos' number scribbled on it.

"Of course. Anything else?"

"Nope, but if you ever need anything, you know where to find me. And, thank you."

"Of course, Cait. Anything for you, hotness." She winked flirtatiously.

35

A few hours later, I sat parked at the Humboldt crime scene. Celeste had called, letting me know she'd picked up the perp's phone again.

It was eerily quiet, and the battered house was completely dark. A gloom had settled over the building, giving it a creepy, haunted vibe. Drawing my service weapon, I chambered a round and returned it to my shoulder holster. My phone buzzed. It was Celeste.

"Reagan, Homicide."

"I see your phone; the bad guy just disappeared into the house a second ago. I couldn't get Carlos on the phone. I'll keep trying."

I looked around to make sure he wasn't creeping up on me. "He's going to get away; I can't wait for Carlos. Okay, if you don't hear from me in an hour, call 9-1-1 and give them my badge number. It's on my card. Text me if his phone reappears."

"Cait, please be careful." Celeste hung up.

The exterior looked even more dilapidated and hateful than the night of the murders. Now, the windows were *all* boarded up, giving the impression of sleeping menace. There was already a notice of non-occupancy on the door. I stepped inside—the entire building stank of stale decay and death.

Candy's place was empty; she'd moved out in a hurry. Old

newspapers and a few ragged boxes littered the floor.

The other apartment doors were locked tight, so I stepped into the Rodriguez's place. I drew out my small hand flashlight, which barely seemed to penetrate the dark, casting a dim spot against the wall. The living room reeked, and I passed through it quickly.

After what I'd learned at Celeste's, I suspected there was a tunnel in the cellar that we'd missed, probably a remnant of the underground railroad or prohibition. As if on queue, I heard the sound of a metal grating on concrete from the cellar below.

By the back door, I found the cellar entrance. It was still painted shut, so I quickly cut at the paint around the edges of the frame with my folding knife.

I gave the door a gentle shove; it moved slightly. I pushed harder, and it creaked as it opened louder than a busted chainsaw.

Fuck! I thought.

The boards whined under my weight with each step until I finally gave up all pretense of stealth. Heart hammering in my chest, I moved down the stairs quickly, clearing as much of the basement as I could in a single sweep as I rounded the final turn. There was a faint woody smell to the basement coupled with something earthy, almost like incense.

My chest heaved, and the breath through my nose seemed to rasp impossibly loud. I clamped down hard on a rising feeling of panic. I'd cleared pitch-black tunnels in Iraq where I knew people were waiting to kill me. The thought of Blackman being down here, though, scared the fuck out of me. *Some combat-hardened bitch I am,* I thought. *Scared of a fucking basement.*

The boxes were still here, and they blocked my view to most of the cellar— not ideal, too many places to hide. My pitiful flashlight left vast shadows that seemed to move and shift as I did.

On my left, just past the bulkhead entrance, I heard a brief rustle of something and a skitter. I turned my flashlight toward it— just a few boxes, in front of them, a child's shoe. Whatever it was, it sounded too small to be a person. *Dear God, Marcella, I really hope you were fucking with me about turning into a bat.*

To the left of the boxes were the rusty water heater and a dilapidated oil-burning furnace I hadn't paid much attention to last time I was down here. The furnace looked like it hadn't worked in years. The piping for the oil tank was rusted through. Through the break, I could see black tar-like bits of oil. I wondered if the tank had any oil in it. I tucked the fire possibility into the back of my mind.

I took a deep breath and a moment to steady myself. It's just a fucking cellar, Cait. I turned to my right and could see straight to the cabinet and the desk. I pied the corner of the boxes stacked in the center. The entire basement seemed empty. I pressed forward to the other end of the stack and found nothing. No one was here. I holstered my weapon and covered my flashlight with my hand to concentrate on my hearing.

An almost inaudible whistle reached my ears from my right. I uncovered my flashlight and pointed it toward the sound— the cabinet. I walked forward and started feeling around the edges. Another skitter sounded above to my left. I jerked my light in that direction— still nothing.

My pulse was now hammering in my neck, and I could hear my own raspy breath. I tried to calm down and felt around the edges of the cabinet once more.

A burst of warm, moist air flowed up the wall from behind it, smelling of earth and decay. I pointed my flashlight down at the base, illuminating scratch marks on the concrete floor.

Examining the feet, I found it was on old rusted casters. I heaved on its side, and it slid gradually and very loudly out. I found a rusted plate propped against the wall behind it that didn't sit quite flush with the floor.

I placed my hand next to the narrow opening at the bottom of the plate, feeling as if something might jump out and grab me. But, with some effort, I pushed the steel plate and moved it enough to see inside.

It was a small tunnel, big enough to low crawl through. The tunnel burrowed straight into solid rock and seemed to go on for some distance. I pushed harder on the steel plate, and with several complaining groans, it finally moved aside enough for me to fit inside. I'd dealt with places like this before, more often than I cared to because I was smaller than most men and fit in places they usually didn't. It made me the tunnel rat of my patrol group from time to time.

I looked at my watch. It had been twenty minutes and still no Carlos. I waited another couple of minutes, but impatience got the better of me, and I did something I was pretty sure was supremely idiotic. I crawled into the tunnel.

Inside, it was claustrophobic and positively sweltering by comparison with the chilly cellar. The tunnel floor was dirty and poorly worn, making the going slow. I counted each pull of my arms from when I entered to track how far I'd gone. After a few feet, the tunnel sloped sharply downward. My arms started to hurt from the effort of low crawling, but I ignored them and kept my flashlight pointing forward as much as possible. Fuck, it's dark in here.

I was starting to sweat now. "409. . .410. . .411. . ." My breathing became labored, and I'd been in here for about ten minutes; mental math told me I'd traveled about 275 feet.

A few feet further, the tunnel opened up onto a wide ledge with about four feet of clearance. I peered over the edge into a yawning circular pit of inky blackness. I couldn't see the other side. Old ropes dangled from hooks and pitons embedded in the cave wall, indicating a bridge here at some point. Slowly, stiffly, I started to rise to my haunches but stopped when I thought I heard something.

I waited. The seconds seemed to tick by interminably slowly. Nothing. I finished getting to one knee, and I heard it again, clearer this time. It was like a slow skittering of a thousand legs. It was coming from the depths of the pit. I drew my weapon and released the safety, pointing my flashlight below, but it was too dark, and whatever I heard seemed too far away. The skittering continued conjuring a rising panic in my gut.

My mind began to race with insane possibilities, a million tiny spiders, a giant millipede, the creature from 'Alien.' I took a deep, ragged breath to calm myself, and then I saw something move at the edge of the light, a spot of gray. Whatever it was circled up the walls of the pit, rising slowly. I had a sense of something large and ponderous making its way toward me.

"Fuck me," I whispered.

I dove back into the tunnel, crawling painfully and slowly on my elbows. Periodically I stopped and faced the flashlight backward to see if I could glimpse it. The skittering was now inside the tunnel behind me; I was sure of it. In addition, I heard an inhuman screech which gave me quite the incentive to pick up the pace. The sound was almost indescribable, metallic and grating. I heard a huffing sound now, too, just under the echo of a thousand tiny fingernails scratching against the walls. I still couldn't see anything, but it was coming.

"Fuck. Fuck. Fuck." I tried to crawl faster. Was that one-thirty-eight or two-thirty-eight. In my terror, I'd lost count, leaving me clueless to the distance back to the cellar.

From ahead of me came a screech of metal and a bang. I realized the huffing sound was breathing and that whatever followed me was huge. "Shit. Shit. Shit." I crawled as fast as I could.

More crawling and another glance back brought me a flash of gray in the black. I rolled over and pulled my pistol, aiming between my legs. Praying not to blow off one of my toes, I squeezed the trigger.

The report of my weapon was deafening. The thing screeched in pain, and an afterimage filled my momentarily light-blinded vision. I saw something with a round mouth the size of my head filled with backward-curved needle-like teeth.

I peddled backward, back up the slope I'd descended earlier, smashing my hand on a small rock when I reached the top. I watched my flashlight tumble uselessly down the grade.

"Shit!"

Now I was truly blind. But I was at the top of the incline, so I was close. I could make it. Hope flared in me as I realized that if I could reach the cellar, I could get clearance and be able to maneuver. I kept pushing backward. The dim light of my fallen flashlight winked out. I scrambled back as fast as possible, almost crab walking and scraping my head against the ceiling. Then all hope fled.

My back came up against something hard. The steel plate was blocking the exit again. I was trapped in here.

"Help!" I screamed. Tears were starting to come down as panic took over. "Help! I'm in here!" I fired back down the tunnel, emptying the clip of its remaining rounds. I saw something disgusting and worm-like in the muzzle flashes. Legs on the bottom and sides of the creature scratched at the walls, pulling it toward me slowly. Its gibbering mouth was a round opening full of thin needle-like teeth. The skin looked wet and slimy, and some kind of dark gray tongue-like proboscis slid between the teeth onto the floor. I didn't see any eyes. I banged the back of my head on the steel plate until I saw stars. It was all I could do; I had no leverage. No matter how hard I braced my feet and pushed, the plate wouldn't budge.

I yanked my feet back, banging my knee against the ceiling of the cramped tunnel as something touched my right shoe. Fumbling my spare clip out of my shoulder holster, I slid it home just as something wet, warm, and slimy slipped up my right pant leg.

A shiver of revulsion and terror slid down my back. Before I could aim and shoot, though, it latched on to my right thigh just above the knee, and my leg screamed in agony. I scrabbled at my right leg, trying to dislodge it, dropping my weapon, but I couldn't get purchase. My hands came away sticky with blood, and I screamed again as it dug in further.

An inhuman roar and tortured metal sounded behind me as the steel plate came away, and strong arms pulled me out of the tunnel. Whatever had my leg detached with a disgustingly wet sucking sound. The thing didn't pursue as Carlos hauled me out of the tunnel and fired his .45 at it. It either didn't like the cold or was much more hurt by the .45 than my 9 mm. I heard its scream vanish into the darkness as it scrambled away. I collapsed into Carlos' arms in relief.

"Oh God, thank you," I said, squeezing him tightly. He stroked my hair once and then summarily dumped me on the floor, jarring my leg.

I grabbed my injured knee. "Ow! What the hell?"

"What the fuck did you think you were doing?" Carlos yelled. "Have you lost your god damn mind?"

I looked down, chastised. "I was looking for Blackman."

"Darlin'," Carlos said, a little quieter but just as firmly. "There are things in this world that you can't even imagine. Like that, whatever that was. You know better than to go chasing down a perp without backup."

I held up a hand, squeezing my eyes against the throbbing in my leg. "Stop yelling at me, please."

"Cait, he's a fucking vampire," Carlos continued, still furious. "They are strong, fast, and slicker than snot. You cannot take him on alone. How'd you end up in that tunnel anyway?"

"I heard someone pull back the cabinet down here. When I found the tunnel, I thought Blackman had gone down there. I tried to wait, but it was taking too long, so I went into the tunnel. I tried to run from that *thing*, but someone had closed the plate on me."

"No shit. Why would Blackman send you down there rather than kill you outright?" Carlos asked.

"I don't know. He probably figured I had backup coming, and it was more convenient," I posited, considering the circumstances. "If your pursuer is likely to off themselves, you don't get into a confrontation with them; you just wait."

"Maybe. But, Cait, you need to understand vampires have

unfathomable motives. They've been alive forever, and they don't think like normal people. Next time you decide to go screwing around, make sure you fucking have backup. This kind of reckless shit is going to get you killed."

"You're right. This was stupid," I said, blowing out an exasperated breath. "But, I called you, and you didn't pick up, and I didn't want Blackman to get away."

"I told you. It was our anniversary. We were busy." He picked me up off the floor.

I pushed him off, collecting my gun and limping toward the stairs.

"I would have expected Marcella to come to rescue you. You know she can sense where you are and when you're in danger after feeding on you, don't you?"

"Yes. She told me." She hadn't, but I wasn't going to tell him that. Besides, even if she could, she lived across town; how would she get to me?

"Not until after she bit you, I bet."

"Hey," I snapped, turning to face him, one hand on the wall. "The werewolf doesn't get to lecture me on the dangers of my vampire paramour. It's not like you were forthcoming."

"That's not fair. I couldn't say anything, and I told you why."

"Yeah, I know," I said, feeling much wearier all of a sudden. "Look, Carlos, I admit it. I'm falling in love with her, and I can't help it. Even after—" I trailed off.

"Even after what?"

"Nevermind." I hopped my way up the stairs.

When we got back outside, I saw a candy apple red Dodge Charger sitting next to my Jeep. "That yours?" I asked appreciatively.

"Yeah," he said. "She's mine."

"Nice car," I said, trying to divert his attention.

"Cait," he said, stopping at my Jeep. "Tell me the truth. Are you really in love with her?"

I paused for a second and then pulled open the door to the Jeep. "I think I might be. We had an argument, and I stormed out, but I couldn't stop thinking about her. I've got a knot in my stomach over it."

"Look, darlin', you need to understand more of what you're dealing with. Think about all the things that make you human. I'm talking about the deep biological shit, the chemical reactions. Oxytocin makes you feel love. Too much testosterone makes you aggressive. You understand?"

I nodded, but I didn't understand. "Where are you going with this?"

"Vampires don't have body chemistry. If she loves you? Ask yourself, where does that love come from? She doesn't have Oxytocin floating around in her system. So, how can she love?"

"Carlos, other than the one night, she's been nothing but gentle, kind, and caring. I don't know where her love comes from, but I don't doubt that she loves me."

He sighed. "How can you be sure? Vampires are consummate snowball artists, and they have infinite patience."

"Why are you meddling in my relationship, Carlos?"

"I'm not trying to meddle, damnit!" He blew out a calming breath. "I am just warning you. You are much more fragile than the company you keep. Just try to stay safe and remember that."

He was right, of course. I needed to be more careful.

"Now," Carlos demanded. "Let's get your leg looked at."

Carlos and I left the scene and stopped at the Boston Medical Center Emergency Room. It took two and a half hours to get seen. A nurse cleaned the wound and shot me up with an antibiotic and rabies immune globulin. At least they put a bandage on it. I got the usual bit from the nurse on infection signs and aftercare; then I left. They tried to give me crutches, but I told them no. I could walk fine. Afterward, Carlos walked with me out to the car.

"I'm sorry," I said. "Thanks for coming to my rescue."

"You're welcome. It's not a problem. "

I got into the car and rolled down the window.

"Cait? Do you think she's worth all this?"

"Yeah, Carlos," I answered without hesitation. "I do. You should see how she is with me. I've never had anyone be so completely loving before."

Carlos shook his head in disbelief. "Take care of yourself, Cait. And tell Marcella if she doesn't treat you right, I'll be on her like a tick on a hound."

"Yes, dad," I said, giving him a half-assed salute as he walked away.

Fuck me; I need to call Marcella tomorrow and patch this up.

36

"I'm hit!" I drop to one knee. My leg burns with the bullet wound, but it is the wrong leg. Behind me, Morgan's M4 fires, taking down an insurgent. The explosion in the sniper nest rattles my ears, and we run down the dust-strewn street. Heat blooms then sputters as the buildings melt into deep black basalt canyon walls—a bone-numbing cold clamors over my skin. I turn, expecting to see Morgan go down from a bullet wound in her abdomen, but she isn't there. I am alone. I search, looking all around, but I can't find her.

Behind me, four insurgents are scrambling toward me on all fours. Their forms turn misshapen, the flesh peeling away in globs of black oily fluid as they flow into strange shapes. Each is different. One is small and spider-like, looking at me with terrible and sad child's eyes of deepest brown. One slithers on a thick black carapace, twisted into a creature mixed of insectile and serpentine features, a great maw of needle-like teeth splitting its torso. The third skitters forward on five human-like arms, flattened and ghastly with interlocking black plates of armor. The last appears almost human, almost feminine, with shining black skin, like patent leather or latex. Short tentacles bud from its body, each ending in poison-dripping needle-like tips.

I turn and walk backward, firing, scoring hit after hit. The bullets sink in, but the wounds close up behind. The beasts don't even slow.

"Dráti!" screams a voice to my left. The word is foreign, alien, strange, but I know it means 'run.' The speaker is a woman with black eyes and gray-tinted skin, tall and robust.

A short golden spear hangs from her back, and a strangely stylized bow dangles from her fingers. Beneath the spear, crosswise, is a full quiver patterned in angular knotwork. The woman's thick legs pump as she snatches my hand and pulls me along. I repeatedly stumble from the leg wound, but she pulls me forward. Her face keeps morphing back and forth, flowing like water, into Morgan's and then into someone else. A name drives into my head like a hammer strike, Déra. I drag my hand to my mouth.

"I miss you," I whisper as I struggle forward. My steps are slow and ponderous, like walking through water. God damnit, I can't move forward.

Somehow, we wind our way among the blackened ravine walls. The deep red light of the sun reflects into the space, painting our faces in demonic crimson. Ahead of me, a massive black sphere, the gateway, hovers at the end of what I realize is a box canyon. We reach the black doorway; through it, I can now see the blasted landscape beyond. My companion turns. "Hélít!" she screams. Go!

I hesitate; I do not want to leave her. The gray woman is firing arrow after arrow, each one strikes home, bringing down the spider-like creature in a single shot and dropping the snake-thing with two more.

She shoves me backward into the blackness, and I land flat, not on the dirt of the canyon, but in a bed of sandy pumice. Before me, I can see her firing at the other creatures as more of the spider things begin dropping over the canyon walls.

"Dráti," she shouts again over her shoulder. She cannot see me in the darkness, but she knows me too well, knows that I would rather die than leave her. But this was why we came here, and this is how it must end. The shining feminine-bodied beast pounces on her, an arrow still in its chest.

"No!" I scream.

"Run, Cait." I turn and see a sixteen-year-old version of myself with short hair. She looks just like me, but she is not me.

I am confused, but I turn, running into the darkness, my right knee aching and wet with slick black ooze. The creatures are right behind me; I'll never make it.

* * *

I erupted from a restless and miserable sleep screaming at the top of my lungs. My right leg throbbed, pain spearing through my knee. The bandage seeped with a deep blackish-red stain, and I unrolled the dressing gingerly. Something caught my eye, like a vein bulging just under the skin. *What the hell?* I touched the bulge, and it slithered up my leg, disappearing deeper into my flesh.

"Ohmygodohmygodohmygod!" I went into the bathroom and pulled out my first aid kit. Rummaging through wildly, I found bandage scissors and forceps. I cut the gauze cleanly and quickly, pushing down the rising panic and bile in my throat. Peeling the bandage didn't burn as I expected; the skin was numb, which I decided was worse. There, under the gauze, was a red circle of holes just above my knee, precisely as the night before. But whereas they had been red and splotchy, they were now a necrotic black ring. The skin in the center had peeled away, leaving an open wound of sickening rotted flesh. Sticking out of the rot was a milky-white, wriggling worm-like thing covered in pus and rotted blood. Goopy black slime and dark red blood ran with the yellow pus in viscid rivulets down my leg; a horrible stench of decay assaulted my nose.

I shivered in disgust and fought not to vomit. I pulled at the slimy thing using the forceps, but they clattered to the floor as dagger-like pain shot up my leg into my chest. My head swam, and I dropped, vomiting. Mixed in with last night's dinner was bright red blood. I knew this was bad, but I couldn't think. My body convulsed and heaved.

I tried to rise, but the room spun, twisting my vision into a weirdly doubled image full of haze and black fog. My leg refused to support me, so I dragged myself back to my room, dripping a trail of foul-smelling black and yellow liquid across the hardwoods.

"Shit! Shit! Shit!" I gritted.

On my nightstand was my phone. I fumbled, trying to find the right buttons. It took three tries, but eventually, I found what I hoped was Carlos' contact in the list and dialed.

"Mmm, hello?" Carlos sounded tired.

"Carlos. . ." My voice sounded small, even to my own ears.

"Cait? What time is it?"

"Help me," I said weakly. I let out a desperate whimper of pain. "My leg—hospital." My head throbbed, and spots started to swirl in my vision.

Carlos' voice shifted, filling with panic. "What's going on?"

"Oh God, Carlos, it hurts. EMS."

There was a brief pause. "Okay, darlin', hang on." I heard the thumping of footsteps and the click static of a radio. "This is Detective Ramirez, officer down." I listened as he gave my address, and the dispatcher responded that EMS was on the way.

"Can you get to the door?" Carlos asked me.

"Ungh. . . No," I said through clenched teeth. "Door's locked."

"Is it safe to enter?" Carlos asked.

I nodded my head before realizing he couldn't see me. "Yeah." I groaned as the agony shot through me again.

"Dispatch, tell EMS the officer is incapacitated, and the door is locked. It is safe to enter."

Dispatch acknowledged.

"Do you want me to stay on the line with you?"

"Mmmhmm," I whimpered.

"Okay, let me get dressed." I heard rustling around and a thunk as he set his phone down.

At that moment, every muscle in my body seemed to contract at once, jerking my arms and legs spasmodically out, spreading eagle, causing me to lose my grip on my phone. It went sliding across the floor under the bed. Painfully I curled back up into a fetal position, and I could see several of the little worm things pushing beneath my skin. Every muscle in my body screamed with agony, and I shrieked with them.

More and more distantly, I could hear Carlos' voice. "Cait? Cait? Hold on, darlin', they're coming."

My vision swam, and I vomited again, gagging on my own sick, and darkness closed in.

I woke in a hospital bed. I felt good, like drugged up good, and I could hear the beeping of monitors. My skin itched, and I rubbed my left arm. I looked around and felt wrong somehow. I could only see out of my right eye. "Hello?" I called to the room. My voice sounded distorted, and my tongue felt thick.

"Hey there," I heard Carlos' warm Texas drawl from my left. "How ya' feelin'?"

I popped a thumbs up from my right hand because my left hand wouldn't move. I thought that was odd amid the haze of sedation. "Wha... Wha..."

Carlos moved around to the right side of my body, where I could see him. "Some kinda parasite the doc said. When they brought you in, you were having convulsions, so they sedated you for treatment. Try to relax. The docs are working on this. They managed to pull out half of one of the little critters and send it off for analysis."

I had given up on intelligible speech and made a motion with my right hand like writing. I also started crying, but I didn't know why. I tried to tell Carlos that I didn't understand why I was crying, but an incomprehensible mumble came out.

"They've got you on a Dilaudid drip with some anti-parasitics. Hang on," he said, "I'll get some paper." He left the room.

The pink and purple hues of sunset told me it was late. I had been out most of the day. In the distance, I spied a pinprick of black that seemed to be sucking up the clouds around it. I tried to focus on it, but it was hazy, and everything was growing darker. My back spasmed, forcing out a grunt. Pain ran the length of my legs, beating back the Dilaudid. I heard several pops from my back as fire shot through my breast and stole my breath. The heart monitor squealed as my world spun, and the room faded.

37

I open my eyes, aware of the vision but unable to influence it. A black fog swirls around me, and black crushed pumice and ash cover the ground, falling from my back as I sit up. A hot breeze blows through the white shift I am wearing, searing my skin. There is no sun, moon, or skyward source of illumination that I can see. A dim, sickly-yellow ambient light surrounds me as if I'm the source. I start walking forward.

After a time, the thick, dense fog parts, revealing the glow of flowing magma maybe a hundred yards away. A pinprick of bright white winks in the distance, around which the burning orange glow of the magma beyond twists and distorts, like looking through the edge of a lens. It reminds me of the twisted lensing of a black hole I've seen on TV.

I continue forward; the hot wind smells of sulfur and recent decay and raises the hair on my neck. From behind comes the sound of something, immense and fast, scrabbling on the dirt. I whirl around but see nothing. Retracing my steps, I find large three-toed, feline-looking footprints in the black ash. Something is out there, stalking me in the infernal landscape.

I realize this dream is like no other I've ever had. I am conscious and fully aware, but I have no control over my body. It's as if I am a passenger inside someone else, along for the ride. Every sound, sight, and smell is sharp, more like a vivid memory. A sharp rock digs into my palm as I stumble. I feel the pain in my hand, my dirty, delicate, pale hand. I tear off a piece of my shift and wrap the fabric around the wound.

Something else is nagging at me. A wrong feeling I can't put my finger on. I push it aside. The anxiety is palpable, but it seems strangely remote and diffuse, more like the first breath of fear on my neck than actual worry.

The ground isn't featureless; I stand on a rocky slope covered in gritty black pumice that scratches the soles of my feet. I decide that downslope, toward the blinking light, is the best direction and continue walking. Distantly, a wail of sorrow sounds, and another echo of distress courses through me. My arms are smeared with grainy, black filth. I rub at the dirt, revealing more pale skin beneath.

"Aoife!" hisses a wheezing voice from behind me. I spin, looking back, seeing only black, inky fog.

"Aoife!" Fear begins to claw at my thoughts as I pick up my pace, stumbling again along the uneven ground.

After what seems hours, the ground levels out, and the sandy cover deepens, making walking more difficult. The last remnants of smoke between me and the blinking white light are gone. It is a perfectly circular portal or window that shows into a hospital room in the distance. I long to run to it, but I stop. To my right stands a burned and charred sapling. Next to it hovers someone, or something, in a black shroud. I move a bit closer and make out a pale face with green eyes—my eyes. It has my face, cold, vampiric. It blinks slowly behind the veils. Long slender fingers tipped with dagger-like nails drop from within the mantle, tensing.

In an instant, it darts forward, alighting on me. I can feel its cold hands burning me and something enveloping my chest, clutching. I gasp at the freezing sensation. Tendrils of its smoky fingers push into my nose, making me gag.

"Cait," it screams, high and raspy and alien. "You left me! Why did you leave me!" Something inside me ignites, hot and bitter, consuming my fear and panic. I give in to the madness and the tempting power. I encircle the writhing thing with my arms; blue-black fire burns across my skin, tracing my veins. My flesh itches as

bits of power are drawn in from the oily smoke. The hot ecstasy of control and raging violence pulls a broad smile to my lips.

"Oh! Mother Darkness, Yes!" I cry as I feel the power bruised and angry peeling off me. My eyes burn, blinding me, but I care not. I push harder at the fire, willing it to grow and burn and sear. I drive on with my will until I can bear it no more. I squeeze my eyes shut and utter a guttural growl of rage, forcing the fire into the imposter with all that I am. The power, now a swirling mass of black, blue, and purple, cascades off and around me, consuming the doppelgänger.

* * *

My breath came in ragged gasps, and sweat coated every inch of me. The hospital gown felt like sandpaper against my arms, and I was shrouded in absolute darkness. "Aoife," I whispered into the black, and a deep sense of loss tumbled through my chest.

The sound of movement to my left caught my attention. "Hello?" I croaked through parched lips. I felt a cup pressed to my mouth, gently tilted, and dribbling cold water down my throat. Tiny bits of crushed ice slid down my chin. "Who's there?"

"Shh," a soft feminine voice whispered, and a cool silken hand caressed my cheek. The fingers were smooth and smelled of flowers and—sandalwood.

"Oh, thank God," I breathed as relief flooded through me. She was here. She had come for me.

"I'm here," Marcella said softly as she brushed away the sweat from my forehead and cheeks with a washcloth. "Please, Cait, I am so very sorry. I came as soon as Carlos called me."

A terrifying realization coalesced, and I pawed at the bed rail. "I— I can't see," I stammered as alarm bubbled over and squeezed my heart, forcing it to buffet against my ribs. My respiration became short and ragged, providing no air. "I can't breathe," I gasped in fear. "I can't breathe." Alarms on the devices around me sounded electronic screeches.

"Easy, deep breaths, love," Marcella's soothing voice said, invading my consciousness, calming my mind, helping me force back the fear, and slow my breathing. I felt her presence within me as if she were wrapping my emotions in soft cotton, dampening their control and bringing me back to sanity.

I tried to reach out both arms to her, but only my right would respond. The terror began to rise again, but Marcella's influence pushed it back down.

"I can't move my arm? Marcella, I'm scared."

She shushed me, lowering the bed rail and pulling me into her arms. The silk of her blouse stuck to my sweat-soaked skin. I slumped against her, unable to move.

Gently, she whispered to me. "You've been here two days, unconscious since yesterday. While you were out, I took the liberty of collecting Jabba and taking him to my home. I hope you don't mind; I didn't know how long you'd be here."

"Thank you, that was very thoughtful."

Marcella continued. "He's quite pampered at home by Robert, Ninetta's replacement, though he has quite a bad habit of rubbing up against Robert's pants legs, leaving them rife with orange fur."

I laughed, but it only caused my ribs to hurt. "When did you get here?"

"Carlos called me right after your first seizure. I collected Jabba and got him settled, then came straight here. By the way, you need new door locks." She spoke slowly, in relaxed tones. It was a little like listening to a female David Attenborough. "I spoke with your doctors. It took some cajoling, but they finally told me what they know."

'What they know,' not, 'what was wrong with me.' That didn't sound good.

"And?" I asked, a tingling starting to rise slowly up my left arm.

"You're infected with an unknown parasite. The doctors

don't recognize it. They've taken two samples and sent one off to the CDC. But there's been no response yet. I had a look at the thing and called a friend, and she says she's seen this before."

"Who?"

"A physician friend of mine," she said evasively. "She might be able to help you, but you'll need to leave the hospital, and soon. I can't bring her here." I was struck by just how delicate she was in her tone. Now that I was paying attention, I could hear her fear.

"Marcella, I'm really scared. Am I dying?"

"Cait, the doctors have tried two different high-powered anti-parasitics, but they haven't had any effect other than to make you weaker. The parasites are infiltrating your nervous system. According to the neurologist, if we don't kill them soon, it will affect your autonomic functions, and the hospital will have to put you on life support. And yes, eventually, you will die.

"But, my friend, Bian, thinks she can fix this." Marcella's tone turned pleading. "Cait, even if you hate me for the rest of your life, I want you to survive and be happy."

Her words were like a slap. "I'm so sorry, Marcella. I was angry, hurt, and afraid, but I don't hate you. I never could. I'm sorry I left you like that. I should have said something. I should have told you I was coming back. I should have—." A sudden fit of coughing stymied my rambling.

"I'm going to ask you to sign yourself out of the hospital against medical advice."

I held on to her as she cradled me in her arms. "Okay, what do I need to do?"

She turned my head, and I felt the soft cool flesh of her lips on mine. "Phillip will handle it."

Phillip, as it turned out, was Marcella's attorney. He advised me against leaving and then explained my rights. It took almost a half-hour, but the doctor finally brought me a liability release form. While I wrangled with that, Marcella went and collected my Jeep. This Bian person lived off the beaten path, and her Audi wouldn't make it. With Phillip's help, I signed it. Marcella returned and helped me dress in some warm clothes.

Less than an hour after I'd regained consciousness, I was in the passenger seat as we raced south along I-93.

"Where—." I started, but a sharp pain snatched away my breath as every muscle in my body tried to contract at once. A stabbing, cramp-like sensation tore through my stomach. Then, it ceased as suddenly as it started, leaving me retching.

"Please—," I said through gritted teeth as another spasm shocked my body.

"Just hold on, honey, we'll be there soon," Marcella said, voice desperate. "Which one of these switches turns on the sirens?"

"Use lights only. Third switch," I gasped out, chest heaving with exertion. Marcella grabbed my hand as my muscles seized again. Under my pain-intensified grip, I felt the crack of her fingers breaking. "I'm— sorry," I wheezed.

"Undead, love. I can take it." Her voice was calm, but she peeled her hand loose anyway. I didn't have time to worry about it further, as every nerve in my body burned, and my skin felt like it was being flayed. My eyes rolled back, and my back spasmed harder. I heard a tremendous pop. I moaned out as a fit of physical pleasure blossomed behind the convulsion, only to be replaced by pain once again.

After what felt like hours of muscle spasms and wracking pain, the darkness took me again.

38

When I next became aware, my hands and feet were damp and ice-cold. The soft movements of water sloshed around me as Marcella walked almost waist-deep in— something.

"Where—." I couldn't find the next word in my head, and my mouth wouldn't function. It was like being aware of language but not remembering how to speak.

"Are you okay?"

I understood Marcella well enough, though, and shook my head.

"We're in Hockomock swamp."

I smelled burning, and it made me think of a rectangular tower of bricks billowing smoke. It took me a few moments to find the word 'chimney' in my vocabulary. I lost the English word and scrambled to find it again, unable to, finally grasping at childhood Irish. "Deataigh." *Smoke.*

Marcella held me closer. "Tá."

"I—no—," I tried to speak.

But, before I could hear Marcella's response, the seizures began anew, ripping another piercing scream from my throat. My chest ripped with pain, and I couldn't get air. Panic swarmed my senses just before I blacked out again.

I gasped and coughed in the darkness, feeling Marcella's mouth on my own and tasting the copper tang of blood as her breath filled my lungs.

"Oh, thank the Goddess." Marcella's voice filled my ears. I wanted to tell her that I loved her and was sorry for running out. I tried to hold her one last time and to see her. I tried to breathe in her scent and lay in her arms. My body didn't respond. The fear banging away at me changed nothing; it was just there, pressed into my skull, crushing down on my psyche.

"It's your only option, Marcella. She's dying." It was a foreign voice with a slight Asian accent, female, odd, and sibilant. "You started this."

Marcella's voice sounded of fear and remorse. "I can't do it again, not to her."

"Then she dies," the other voice replied coldly. "You started this, Marcella."

"I know." There was a pause. Then I felt Marcella's breath on my ear. "Cait, I do not know if you can hear me. I love you; please forgive me." I felt her lips on my throat as she bit into my neck, tearing me open. There was no following euphoria; an ungodly pain danced through my blood vessels like streaks of electric light. I couldn't breathe. My left arm ached, and my chest squeezed tight. My body convulsed repeatedly.

Oh, God! It hurts! Please help me.

After just a moment, the excruciating pain gave way to the dizziness of hypoxia. Endorphins flooded my brain, bringing on a sense of deep calm and love. I was dying, and it was okay. I'd be gone in a few minutes, and all this would be over. Numbness permeated me, quieting my thoughts, allowing me to focus on a strange noise—my heartbeat. It thumped slower —and slower—and—

Thick, syrupy blood, hot and salty, filled my mouth. I gagged first, then swallowed. The sensation of drowning overwhelmed me as I swallowed and swallowed, but there was still more. Eventually, Marcella relented, and I coughed weakly, feeling the warm blood on my lips. I snatched Marcella's arm, overcome with the need for more. I bit into the bleeding wound before it could close. I could feel the blood flow into me, renewing me.

Marcella whispered again through her soft sobs, "Please forgive me, Cait."

An injection pinched into my thigh, straight into the ghastly wound above my knee. Needle-like lances of pain shot from my leg like bolts of lightning, blistering through my chest and every limb; blood spewed from my mouth as I screamed. My head felt like it would burst, hammering and hammering in time with my erratic pulse. I roared in pain, legs shaking, back twisting, convulsing.

"What's happening to her?" It was Marcella's voice, remote and echoing.

"I don't know, but they're digging out, look."

My vision cleared, snapping into focus. Marcella hovered above me, my blood on her chin and a terrified expression on her face.

"Help me," I whimpered through gritted teeth, limbs flailing as agony enveloped each nerve ending. Like a wave of electric shocks, it spun out from places all over my body, driving through me. My skin bubbled and blistered, scorched and dry. I could hear the flesh cracking like burnt wood as I twisted. My teeth rattled as I gritted them hard against the pain. Like insidious little drills, tiny white worm-like parasites pushed from inside my legs, arms, and chest, even out of my cheek. Blood seemed to run over the length of my body, and a wheeze erupted from my throat, almost like a hiss. Screams were torn from me as my flesh burned from within. Then, finally, blissfully, thankfully, darkness claimed me once more.

Sometime later, a ponderous sound like shifting sand coaxed me to consciousness. Every part of my body felt strained and torn. It was as if every muscle had tried to rip itself asunder and very nearly succeeded. A woman in a green shirt was pouring a sour-smelling liquid into a plastic container to my left. To my right, Marcella sat in a chair, head down.

"Marcella?" I whispered hoarsely.

A moment later, she looked up slowly. She was worn; pain and worry haunted her eyes.

"Marcella?" I prodded again.

She launched herself to my side. "Cait! Do you know who I am?"

"Of course," I croaked hoarsely, throat burning.

"What do you remember?" she asked, looking at me.

I scrambled in my thoughts for a fleeting image, a memory of someplace— and a face, pale and delicate.

"Something—. I don't know. You carried me through the water, and now I'm here."

"Oh, thank the Goddess. You were dying. I had no choice. I'm so sorry."

She moved over next to me and began to kiss my face and hands. My wrists were bloodied and raw, as were my ankles. But I was alive, and I could see and talk and move. I might actually be okay.

"Cait, honey, this is Bian. She helped me save your life."

I looked toward the other woman and blinked, rubbing my eyes, unsure what I saw. Bian wasn't a woman, at least not in the human sense, and she was magnificent. Her upper torso was roughly human-shaped but flowed seamlessly into the long body of a snake— very long. It seemed to wrap around the entire room. Her backside was covered in moss-colored and emerald scales, which blended into a light yellow on her front.

Bian's face was reminiscent of a human woman, framed by long luxurious-looking raven-colored hair. A blue forked tongue flicked out periodically, tasting the air. Her arms were almost human, terminating in delicate-looking hands with long, thick, claw-like nails. The front of her torso protruded, breast-like. It all gave her a feminine and yet, profoundly alien appearance. Her scales were so small and delicate on her abdomen, chest, and face as to look smooth, almost like human skin.

"You're beautiful," I breathed, watching the muscles ripple beneath as she moved.

The snake-woman didn't answer; she just slithered across the floor to my side and began examining me roughly.

"Well, you seem healthy enough. But, we'll have to keep an eye on you. Say ah," she said, sounding for all the world like any general practitioner.

I did as she asked, allowing her to examine me.

"Well, then, that's just fascinating."

Marcella stroked my sweat-soaked hair, looking worried. "Um, Cait, honey? I think you're going to be okay, but you might need to prepare a little."

Bian arched up, rising to an impressive height, rummaging into a box on a makeshift shelf. She moved with seemingly no effort, languid and graceful. When she lowered back down, she handed Marcella a small hand mirror.

"It's probably better if you show her."

Marcella held the mirror to her chest. "There have been a few —um—changes. Maybe it's not the best—."

"Gimme," I said, feeling weirdly playful.

Marcella handed me the mirror. For a moment, a different face appeared, the same young woman I'd seen repeatedly, but it vanished just as quickly. My face looked ashen, and my skin was flaky, as if sunburned.

I tilted the mirror to look into my mouth, which felt— odd. My canines had grown to a more extended point, not unlike Marcella's when she extended them. I ran my tongue across them, closing and opening my mouth; it didn't seem to affect my bite. My tongue, however, was the strangest of all; it was dark blue and forked— just like Bian's.

"Dear God," I gasped, touching at the dry flakes on my face. "What the fuck happened to me?"

"I—," Marcella began, but Bian cut her off.

"We don't know everything. The English name for the creature that infected you is simply the 'white worm.' You are the first ever to survive such an infection, at least as far as I know. I'm going to examine these parasites." She held up a specimen jar, displaying an inch-long grotesquely pale worm-thing wriggling inside. "They burrowed out as soon as we applied the poison, and it's the first time I've had a chance to look at them with modern equipment."

"Help me over," I gasped, suddenly and thoroughly nauseated. Marcella rolled me to my side, and I vomited. A bit of blue-black goo spewed onto the floor, then nothing. After a few agonizing minutes of dry heaves, I rolled back, sucking in deep breaths. "I'm so sorry. I just feel— a little sick. That was inside me?"

"Yes, but the infecting parasites are very susceptible to neurotoxins. Lucky for you, I have that in abundance." She opened her mouth much more expansively than I'd have thought possible, fully displaying two long, stiletto-like fangs.

My head became fuzzy, and I lost my train of thought. I reached out to Marcella, flapping my hands for her to come to me like a little kid. I felt— drunk.

Marcella laughed and then yanked me up into a hug. "I'm so sorry," she whispered. "I've never cared this much for— for anyone. What have you done to me, Cait?" Her words were breathy and desperate.

"Same thing you've done to me," I whispered in reply and squeezed her close, our fight over the 'dream' and what she'd done long forgotten.

Bian turned out the bright overhead light, dimming the room considerably. My eyes adjusted instantly to the darkness. Flickering wall sconces filled the room with eerie yet comforting light. Marcella lifted me from the table and carried me to a stone pool that occupied a good quarter of the barn-like cabin. Marcella placed me into the shallow water. It was warm and clean, with gentle currents flowing from one side to the other, and a low hum of a pump sounded somewhere nearby.

A set of old wooden stairs descended from a loft above, ending close to the large bath. Next to the kitchen where I had been lying moments ago sat a small laboratory that looked fairly complete, at least from the standpoint of my high-school chemistry expertise. A large wood-burning stove sat in the other corner of the house with a small teapot on top.

Bian was both beautiful and wondrous, and I could finally

see just how large she was. Her body filled much of the available space. If I'd had to guess, her lower part had to be at least ninety feet long. I longed to run my hands over it, wondering how it felt.

"Is— is she a Naga?" I asked, still feeling very intoxicated.

"We prefer the term Nehtra," Bian said, working over a small lab table, with her back to us.

The word seemed to fit, feeling like it described her. I knew that the term was ancient in the deep recesses of my thoughts. I thought maybe I'd heard it when I was a child, perhaps in one of my mother's lectures.

Marcella brought over a three-legged stool, and after ensuring I was secure, she stripped and joined me, setting shampoo, soap, and a mesh scrubby next to a metal cup on the edge of the basin.

"Ow," I said as I twisted my head a bit further than my angry muscles wanted to allow. "How did you—"

"How did we save you?" Marcella finished. "I'll explain after we're done. Just rest for now." Deep remorse showed in her eyes, but my thoughts were thick and slow. It didn't take long before I'd forgotten I'd even asked the question.

I settled in and let her bathe me, letting out a little laugh of embarrassment when she reached my legs.

I giggled. "I need to shave those."

The corners of Marcella's mouth turned up, but she said nothing and proceeded.

Sitting with my legs in the warm current was like feeling it for the first time. The flow was like liquid silk continuously sliding across my skin. I dipped my head as she poured warm water across it, washing away the remnants of soap.

Her hands pushed through my hair in unhurried, tender strokes, working the shampoo to a lather. It was all so hypnotic, and I waved my hands under the water, feeling it swish between my fingers, suddenly wishing they were webbed.

As Marcella scrubbed at my arms and shoulders, great

long strips of skin peeled away, revealing milky-white skin underneath.

"Did you—" I started but again lost my train of thought.

"Hmm?" Marcella prodded, pouring a cascade across my head. I closed my eyes, feeling the warm water and soap slide down my face, my throat, across my breasts. Though Marcella had helped me in the shower at her home, I had never before known the pleasure of being bathed by someone else, not as an adult. It felt like a supreme expression of love.

I heard every drop of water falling to the pool below, each distinct and whole— gifts of affection.

Deep drug-like euphoria continued to cloud my thoughts, and I turned bodily toward Marcella, laying my head on her chest. I squirmed in the intense sensations and rubbed my cheek against her breast.

"I love you," I said dreamily, still pressed against her skin. "Join me in the water; it's heavenly."

Marcella put her hand under my chin and very gently turned my face toward her. She covered one eye and then the other, expression serious.

"Bian," she called. "Come over here, please. Is this what I think it is?"

Bian was looking down into my eyes a moment later, and I could see her eyes were slit, like a snake's, with yellow irises that glittered in the flickering sconce lights.

"She's blood drunk," Bian said, her tone again scientific and cold.

Marcella frowned and something passed across her face I couldn't read, spaced out as I was.

"It's okay. I'm fine," I said languidly. "Right. As. Rain." My head lolled a bit as I looked back at Bian. "Wow, you are so pretty. How do you stand being that gorgeous?"

Bian ignored my comment and continued to assess my state. "All we can do is let her rest. You should probably take her upstairs to sleep it off. It's not a good time."

"Oh," I said, grinning. "I don't want to sleep; I have better ideas." I ran my hands over Marcella's arm and Bian's abdomen, feeling the strange musculature underneath.

Bian flashed a smirk and moved my hand away. "I can't wait to see how embarrassed she is in the morning, though. That'll be a treat."

"Hey," I complained drunkenly. "You have nothing to be embarrassed about. I think you're hot. I mean, you have, like, super sexy scales. And they're so green."

"Oh bloody hell," Marcella said, rolling her eyes and picking me up. "Time for you to get some sleep."

"Are you gonna sleep with me?" I asked, making the most lascivious look I could muster.

"Of course, I am, darling. Let me take you to bed." Marcella returned the look and then threw me over her shoulder.

"Woo! That's more like it." I felt a sharp pinch in my butt. "Hey! something bit me!"

Before we reached the top of the stairs, my eyes grew heavy, and I fell asleep.

39

The blinding morning light showed through the skylights. I felt as if I'd been reborn somehow. My thoughts were clearer than I could ever remember. I flexed and stretched, reveling in the feeling of wholeness that permeated me. Though, there was something—making me rub my arms nervously. It felt like vague anxiety, a strange antsiness that crawled under my skin.

Marcella was still asleep, and I opted not to wake her. With all that had happened, she had to be running on fumes. For that matter, after the last few days of no food, I was starving. My body practically glowed in the brilliant light. I looked at my skin and sat back down on the bed. *Dear God, what have I done?*

Head in my hands, I drew in a deep breath. I checked my pulse, finding it slow but strong. Maybe it wasn't what I thought. I tried to dismiss my anxiety. I needed to speak to Marcella and understand what was happening. I turned and moved to wake her but decided against it. She needed rest. We could talk later. I dressed in a pair of drawstring pants and a t-shirt I found next to the bed.

Bian was awake and looking into her microscope when I walked down the stairs, clumsily stumbling over her—body?—tail?—as I reached the bottom.

"Watch your step, hon," she said, holding up a finger, face still pressed to the instrument. "Sit down at the table. I'll be with you in a moment. I do have food for you, but this is just fascinating."

I looked around the kitchen area and didn't see any cooking, just a plate on the counter with a few non-breakfasty foods. I sat down at the table and waited.

Bian pulled away from the microscope. "I think these things have recombinant properties."

"Wait, recombinant, as in genetically recombinant?" That was frightening; what else might they do to me?

"Yes, it would certainly explain your tongue."

Before I could inquire further, Bian slithered over and placed the plate in front of me. "Here you go, try that."

"Applesauce and two sliced bananas? I thought you were a carnivore."

She gave me a hard stare. "Very much so, but you're on the brat diet until I say otherwise." Her overall size made her very intimidating, especially since she could pull up a significant portion of her bulk to tower over me, which she did.

"Hey, I'm not a brat," I whined.

Bian laughed. "Bananas, Rice, Applesauce, and Toast. B-R-A-T. I want to make sure your tummy can handle human food."

"I feel fine—" I started to say but stopped when I looked back at Bian's stern face. "Whatever." I wished everyone would stop treating me like their kid sister. It was getting beyond annoying. I dove into the food ravenously. Bian watched as I scarfed down the food before returning to her lab work.

"God, these bananas are so flavorful. where'd you get them?"

Bian turned slowly, looking at me askance. "Define flavorful."

"I don't know." I swallowed. "Like banana, but more. There's also an earthy taste that I can't place. I can't really describe it."

Bian slid over and tilted my head back a little forcefully. "Open your mouth, Cait. As wide as you can."

I did as she asked, feeling my jaw click strangely, though not painfully.

"Hmmm. Can you open wider?" Bian tugged, and I opened

freakishly wide, drawing my lips taught. She poked inside with a penlight and then wiggled my lower jaw, which moved disturbingly freely.

"Fascinating," she said. "Your jaw has unhinged, and you have a vomeronasal duct here. No venom glands, though, pity."

I closed my mouth and rubbed my jaw, feeling it click back into place. "What is a ver—whatever duct?" I asked though I didn't hear the answer as I was wracked with stomach cramps. I charged to the sink and retched up everything I'd just eaten. "Shit, this isn't happening," I muttered to myself, returning to the table and pushing away the plate.

Bian acted as if I hadn't moved. "It's how snakes smell. If there's a vomeronasal duct, there's a vomeronasal gland. Consider that a gift. Things will taste a bit different, but you'll appreciate it in the end."

My confusion must have been evident on my face as she pulled me to the door and opened it. "Now, stick your tongue out, wag it up and down quickly, and pull it back in with a breath."

"What?" I asked, feeling stupid.

"Do as I say, girl!" She stared at me in annoyance, crossing her arms stubbornly.

Feeling ridiculous, I did as she asked. My tongue flicked out and back in, impossibly fast, just like a snake's, and my nose practically exploded with odors and scents. I could smell the water, the earth, something skunk-like to my right, something like a wet dog to my left, and twenty other things I couldn't recognize, all packed together.

"Holy shit!" I exclaimed, pushing the door closed.

Bian smiled a wide, alien, snake-like smile. "Give it some time, and you'll be able to pick out individual people just by their scent. Pretty cool, huh?"

I freaked. "No, it is not cool! I'm not a fucking lab rat. I'm a person. This is my body we're talking about, and all of these changes are terrifying. I don't know how far they'll go."

"A forked tongue isn't a bad thing," she said, arms crossed.

"For you! You're a fucking creature of legend. I'm human. I'm not supposed to have a fucking forked tongue or scales or a ver-whatever duct. I'm not supposed to have fangs or be a poster girl for skin bleaching. If it goes too far, what am I supposed to do? I won't be able to do my job. Jesus, my mother will never understand any of this, regardless. And what am I supposed to say to my boss? I'm a fucking cop. Interacting with the public is what I do. I don't want to be driving a desk for the rest of my life because witnesses can't stand to look at me."

"Cait," Bian roared.

I froze, my voice dying on my lips.

"We saved your fucking life." The sibilance in her speech increased.

Bian rose, towering over me, and her voice turned hissing and raspy, full of menace. "You died right there on that table, and we brought you back! Yes, there were side effects! I could strangle you right now if it's too much to bear!" She snatched me by the throat faster than I could see, forcing me to gasp for air.

Marcella flew over the railing from the loft and dropped to the floor, half-dressed. "Bian, honey, let her go. She's just in shock."

"No! Not until she answers me." Bian's eyes were cold and hard, the pupils mere slits.

"What was the question?" I gagged out.

"Would you rather be dead," she squeezed harder, "or alive?"

"Alive," I choked, pulling at her claw-like hand. Christ, she was strong.

"Then start acting like it and stop whining," Bian spat as she shoved me roughly to the floor.

Marcella ran over to me. "Are you okay?"

"Yeah," I croaked, rubbing my neck, though I was most definitely not okay.

Bian slithered out of the kitchen area and into the pool, pulling all of her bulk into a neatly wrapped coil and disappearing into the center somewhere. Water sloshed over the basin to the floor. I could see her sparkling, alien eyes peaking between her coils, staring at me in annoyance.

Marcella helped me up. "Back home, she was worshiped as a goddess and treated with respect. Try to remember that. She is trying to help, but she doesn't have the same sensibilities about compassion. In the end, she's not human and doesn't think like us. It's not your fault or hers. She's just different."

"No, it is my fault!" I retorted, voice angry. "I did something, as you said, monumentally stupid. Now I'm paying the price, and I don't know how to handle it. Like some brat, I'm taking it out on other people."

I walked over to the pool, climbing into the warm water, pajamas and all. Bian was still watching me through the coils, so I lay my chin on her massive bulk and looked back at her glittering eyes. "I'm sorry. I didn't mean to offend you or seem ungrateful. I'm just scared."

A delicate, clawed hand slid gently between the coils and touched my hair. "Once, little girl," Bian began softly. "I wandered the jungles of my home without fear. For over ten thousand years, each day knew that I was the unchallenged queen of my domain. I had sisters who looked up to me and loved me. And I had magic, real magic, that could save or damn a soul. Then, all of that faded. The magic disappeared, and my sisters began to die until only I remained. Now, my world is this fucking hovel in this forsaken frozen swamp. I'm forced to hide to survive, wary of every idiot human who wanders near. I know what it is to be afraid. I, too, am sorry." Bian's tail end slid through the water and around me, pressing me gently against her in what I could only imagine was the Nehtra version of a hug. "We are, all of us, desperate to survive in a world being raped to death by the blindness of mankind."

I stayed there, laying in the muted flow of the water and the warmth, head against her coils. My fear and anxiety fled, and a deep sense of peace settled in.

I took Bian's hand and stroked her arm; she didn't resist. I traced the semi-diamond pattern of scales that rode a narrow channel along her arm. They were softer than I expected, the surface so supple.

This magnificent creature lay before me, full of power and beauty, and I'd scarcely spent a second appreciating who and what she was, so concerned was I with a shitty life that I just had to get back to.

Eventually, drained by my emotional turmoil and lulled by the warm water and the press of Bian's body, I slipped into a magical daydream of a vast jungle. Thick sheets of warm rain fell in fat drops across my naked body. I lay on a rock overlooking a broad green valley. And, nowhere were there dead children, or rapist soldiers, or lost loves, only peace.

I must have fallen asleep again as I awoke to find myself lying next to the pool, Marcella standing over me.

"How long was I out?" I asked through a long yawn.

"About two hours," Marcella replied softly. Bian was out of the pool and futzing about her little lab station next to the kitchen. I tried not to think about weird substances in the lab and the food she'd made just feet away.

I yawned again. "God, why am I so tired? I slept like the dead last night, and I felt great when I woke up earlier."

Marcella ignored the question. "Here, I bought these for you." She held out a bundle of clothes and a pair of black booties. All of the clothes looked expensive. I didn't recognize all the labels, but the shoes were Manolo Blahnik.

"Where'd you get these?" I asked, setting down the bundle next to the pool.

"I bought them on Tuesday while I was out. While you were sleeping, I had Robert drive them down in his Land Rover." Marcella stepped into the tub and began to scrub herself with the soap.

"Robert?" I queried, rubbing my eyes, then remembered. "Oh, right. New butler."

Bian started slithering around, uncoiling herself as she did so, slowly making her way toward us as I stepped into the bath to wash.

"I need a bigger house," Bian griped as she continued to get herself untangled. It turned out most of her body had been coiled up by the woodstove, and I was reduced to hysterics watching her grump her way around, unraveling like a yarn ball.

"Hey, it's no laughing matter," Bian chided playfully. She made an exaggerated grimace as she unwrapped her bulk from around the table.

I rubbed shampoo into my hair as Bian slipped her torso into the pool, followed by several feet of her length. She rose from the water with a mischievous gleam in her eye, and Marcella suddenly grabbed me from behind.

I tried to shake loose as soap dripped into my eyes. "Hey, what the hell?" I found out moments later as ice-cold water splashed down on me. I threw myself further into the pool to get warm, bumping up against Bian's thick body.

I sputtered and fussed as I surfaced. "What is this? Some 'things that go bump in the night' hazing ritual?"

"No, Cait," Marcella said through gales of laughter. "It's just a spot of fun to lighten the mood. But, you better start learning to go bump in the night if you want to hang out with us." She and Bian erupted in fresh guffaws. They were entirely too entertained with their own humor.

"I go bump in the night just fine, thank you very much," I said with a pout, grabbing the soap. "I haven't heard you complaining," I muttered. They both whooped and convulsed in their unabashed glee at my peevishness. Soon, I was laughing along with them.

"Bian, honey?" I said after I'd dried and dressed.

They both turned, and Marcella whistled. "Wow, you are fucking lush in that outfit. I was right about the shoes, too."

"Thank you. Though these shoes are going to get ruined, you know that. They're completely impractical for my job. As I was saying, though, Bian, do you have any other food here? Something I might be able to eat?"

"Well, there are some mice and a few rats in cages in the

cellar," she replied with a very snakelike wink.

I made a sarcastic laugh. "Haha. I mean human food."

"No, I haven't eaten a human in forever," she said and started laughing all over again. She tried to make an evil face, wiggling her tongue, but it just looked silly.

Marcella slapped her on the shoulder and climbed from the pool, leaving the entire space to Bian, who pulled more of herself into the water.

"Be nice, Bian. Cait, hang on. I'll get you something."

I sat down at the table and waited for Marcella to finish dressing. She opened the fridge, plucking out an object that I recognized immediately. My tongue played over my lips unconsciously as I gazed at the full blood storage bag. I shivered with a weirdly, almost aroused excitement, and I ran a finger across my bottom lip.

Marcella poured some of the blood into a tin cup. "How are you feeling?" she asked, watching me intently.

I looked away from the blood with effort. "I don't— I don't know," I stuttered, distracted by the smell and taste of blood in the air. "I—" My mind seized up. All I could think of was the blood, and I swallowed reflexively.

Marcella smiled beatifically. "It's okay, honey. Let's see how you do with this. We need to know how far the change has gone."

"The what?" I whispered, distracted, unable to keep my eyes from the cup.

"Cait, please know that I didn't want to do it, but you were dying. I had no choice." I barely heard her, and she slid the cup to me.

Instinctively, I lifted the cup to my lips. I could smell the coppery-iron tang of the blood, and my adrenaline spiked. Hesitantly, I took a sip. It tasted of iron, but the salty nature lingered most. It was so good. My body reacted, and a shudder passed through me. My breath came short. I swept my tongue instinctively across my mouth, collecting the thickening drops. Insatiable need flooded me, overwhelming all thought.

I had to have more. I snatched the cup violently off the table and gulped down the contents as fast as possible. Just a few swallows and it was gone.

"More," I gasped as I reached for the bag, but Marcella pulled it away.

I slammed my hands into the table and barred my teeth instinctively. A very snakelike hiss boiled from my throat. She was between me and the blood, and I was going to get it. I jumped at her.

"Stop!" Marcella thundered, and I dropped to the floor involuntarily, unable to look up, terrified.

Marcella cupped my face gently and turned it toward her. "Cait, It's okay. Come back, honey."

I hissed again, baring my fangs, but I didn't move otherwise. She shushed me and caressed my cheek.

Marcella spoke again, voice motherly and coaxing. "Cait, dearest, come back to me. It's alright."

My lip quivered, and hot tears burned down my cheeks. "Oh —" A lump formed in my throat, closing off any further utterance.

"Shh. It's okay," Marcella said, pulling me in close. After a minute, she pushed me back and examined me, wiping the tears away with her thumbs. Bian glided over, sliding the rest of her bulk around much more gracefully than before.

"It's given her a flush to her cheeks," Bian noted, turning my head left and right. "She'll be done soon."

"Yes," Marcella confirmed. "But, I think we knew that already. Caitlin, we need to talk."

Trembling, I sat down at the table. Marcella retrieved more blood and filled two cups, handing me one. I forced myself to take small sips of the blood with substantial effort.

Marcella reached out and stroked my arm. "There you go, small sips, love."

I continued drinking the blood. Bian dropped a box of tissues in front of me; they landed with a light thwack. I pulled one and dabbed at my eyes, noting that each tear left a tiny spot of pink.

"Cait," Marcella spoke gently. "I'm sorry. I just couldn't let you die."

A deep angry part of me wanted to know why I'd been so reckless—so fucking idiotic. But, another emotion wormed into my thoughts. I loved Marcella, and I wanted to be with her. Now, I could. Maybe we wouldn't grow old, but we could have the little house on the cape if we wished to, supposing I didn't accidentally depopulate the area in my blood lust. But did I want to be with her for eternity? It was a sobering question for which I had no answer.

Marcella and Bian watched me as, I'm sure, all of these thoughts played across my face.

I took my last sip of blood; then, I used my finger to lazily spoon out the last of it from around the edge. "There's no way back, is there?"

Marcella's voice was gentle but left no doubts. "I'm sorry, no."

"Will I have to quit my job, do you think?" It seemed silly to ask, but I loved my work. And, right now, the idea of losing my job felt like losing everything.

Marcella looked at me sympathetically. "No, you won't have to quit your job; it will be fine. People will assume you're just naturally pale."

"Carlos is going to have kittens," I said dismally.

"Carlos will be fine, after a fashion, at least."

I put my hand on hers. "How am I going to tell my ma?" I said it in all seriousness, but it sounded so stupid it made me chuckle.

Marcella snorted a laugh as well and then covered her mouth. "I'm so sorry. I know it's not funny, but—."

I started laughing too because it was hilarious. "It's like a line out of a vampire movie."

"Your girlfriend is a vampire; wait 'til I tell mama," Marcella said with a perfect southern accent, followed by her adorable snort of a laugh.

"Fuck my life," I said, blowing out a resigned sigh. "I guess it could have been worse; at least I'm not a zombie."

"Revenant, honey," Marcella corrected.

"Whatever."

40

"What the hell, Reagan?" Carlos almost shouted in the interview room when I returned to work.

"It was an accident!" I wished Marcella had come up with me, but she'd been away too long and had to attend to business matters.

"No," Carlos said, "two cars running into each other on a busy street, that's an accident. Eating the prize in the box of cracker-jacks, that's an accident. Being turned into a fucking —," he lowered his voice, "vampire is not an accident."

His tone was starting to irritate the fuck out of me. "What the actual fuck are you bitching about, anyway? You're the one who called her."

"And what about your next physical?" Carlos demanded, ignoring my protest. "How will you explain that pallor, your lack of a heartbeat?"

"I can drink right before my physical. I'll seem right as rain physiologically," I said.

"Except for your tongue, and your skin and your—" Carlos had his arms crossed. He was pissing me off with how smug he looked, pointing out how fucked I was.

"It's not my fault, Carlos. Did you fucking want me to die?"

"You know that you'll have to drink from the living eventually. You can't survive on stale blood for much longer."

I'd have blanched if I could have. I'd forgotten about that.

Carlos misread my expression. "You didn't know. That bitch!"

"Fuck, man! Ease up! She saved my life. I know I'm not ready, but we haven't had much time for anything else. I didn't ask for this!"

"Well, you better start making time before you kill someone. I hope you're happy that you've joined the land of the leeches." Carlos slammed the door as he left the interview room.

Ouch, that one hurt a lot—especially coming from Carlos. I sat down in the chair next to me, stunned. *Fuck.* I forced back tears, blinking them away, and stood. *It doesn't matter. I have a job to do, and I am bloody well going to do it.*

I opened the door and stomped to Carlos' desk. Leaning over, I put my face in his, voice low. "Better a leech than a flea-bitten, mangy asshole."

Carlos looked at me like I'd slapped him. Then he just shook his head and laughed. "Fuck you, Reagan, you know that?"

"I know," I said, suddenly feeling a bit better.

Carlos stood and wrapped his tree-trunk arms around me.

I sniffed. "I'm sorry; I didn't have a choice in this."

"I know, darlin'. I know. I shouldn't have said that. I'm just scared for you, that's all. You've stepped into a world that's wilder than a June bug on a string."

"Tell me about it. A week ago, my biggest worry was how to tell my boyfriend I didn't love him." I let go of Carlos and sat down at my desk.

I didn't sit long because Carol came over and threw a bullet-resistant vest at me.

"What happened to you?" She asked, eyes wide. "Never mind, tell me later. We've got him. We've got his ass. Fugitive is already on the way."

"Got who?" I asked.

"Blackman," she replied and stalked off. Carlos and I looked at each other.

"Oh, shit," I said, eyes wide. "It'll be a slaughter."

I checked my service weapon, thanking all the gods there

were that Marcella and I had stopped to pick up my gear before heading over. Ten minutes later, we were flying through the streets of Boston.

According to a couple of patrolmen, it had turned out that Blackman had holed up in Gabe's empty house. He'd been spotted by some of the guys from District E-5, right around the corner from Gabe's. Carlos stepped on the gas, trying to get there before anything happened.

While Carlos drove like a bat out of hell, I contacted Detective Freyer on the tactical frequency. "Freyer, you need to hold until we get there."

"Copy that. We're already in position, Reagan. How long?"

"Two minutes, Freyer," I tried to keep the desperation out of my voice.

"You've got two minutes," Freyer said. "Then we're going in."

"Freyer, you need to wait."

"Two minutes Reagan," he said with finality.

"Freyer— Freyer." He'd switched frequencies. "Shit, Carlos, hurry. Blackman will tear through them like tissue."

"I know," Carlos said, both hands gripping the wheel and eyes glued to the road. The engine of the overbuilt Ford Explorer roared as he turned out of a roundabout, and I grabbed the Jesus strap for dear life. Carol was in the back, eyes wide, using both hands to hold onto my seat. Lights and sirens or no, Carlos was doing nearly ninety down West Roxbury Parkway, only slowing enough not to send us into oblivion at each turn.

"Can you please slow down?" Carol shouted. We ignored her.

"Can you take him?" I worried that fighting Blackman might fall on me, and I didn't feel one bit stronger than I usually did.

"Maybe," Carlos replied. "Is he a good hand-to-hand fighter?"

"I don't know," I replied, remembering his fight with Marcella. "But, he's fucking aces with a blade."

"Cait." His voice turned grim and low. "You need to be careful. If anyone gets a whiff of what you've become, there'll be a heap of trouble."

"What the hell are you two talking about?" Carol called from behind us.

"Carol, I'll explain later," I hollered as Carlos took the next roundabout on damn near two wheels. "Please just make sure you have your seatbelt on, and you stay back when we get there."

"Cait, so that you know, the feds are already looking into us."

"You and me? What for?"

"No, as in people like us," Carlos lowered his voice so Carol couldn't hear. "I don't aim to be a slab of meat on anyone's exam table. You have to be Cait the human, not Cait, the almost vampire."

On a whim, as we rounded the last roundabout and Carlos slowed down, I felt for my pulse, not finding it at all. "Correction, that's Cait the vampire," I corrected in a whisper.

How the fuck we were going to bring Blackman in without exposing everything? I had no idea.

Rather suddenly, the world exploded into a cacophony of color and light, almost blinding me, strength suffused every limb. Sundown had arrived.

"Fuck!" I swore and clamped my eyes shut.

"What?" Carlos asked, startled, jerking the wheel slightly and slowing further.

I opened my eyes, viewing everything with perfect clarity. The night was in glorious color, every star in the sky visible through the ever-present light pollution of the city. "Keep going, don't slow down. I'm fine."

We rolled to a stop at Gabe's house, and I spotted movement on the second floor.

Carlos and I stepped out of the car. He handed me an M4 from the trunk, along with a magazine. I checked the magazine, slammed it home, and chambered a round.

A dozen officers in tactical gear ringed Gabe's house. Mills and Vic were at the front door.

"Freyer, get them away from there!" I yelled, running forward, but it was too late.

Everything seemed to happen at once. Mills knocked one time and took in a breath to identify himself. The front door exploded outward. Mills flew into a squad car twenty feet away, sandwiched between the vehicle, and the door knocked off the hinges.

Blackman pushed his blade through the gap in Vic's vest like lightning. Vic crumpled. He continued down the steps, plowing through the remainder of the fugitive unit faster than they could move out of the way.

I raised my rifle and stalked forward, firing at Blackman. He was fast, but now, so was I. His movements no longer seemed like a blur, and I could get a bead on him. I hit him with four shots center mass— no misses. It was all I could manage without hitting the other men around him or sending high-velocity rounds into the neighboring house. Headshots were out of the question. Blackman staggered but kept moving, slashing at the Fugitive team as he went.

Carlos darted forward and dove for the vampire. Blackman spun away from the charge and took a swipe at Carlos, narrowly missing. I waded in, delivering a bone-shattering kick to Blackman's midsection. It seemed I was much stronger than I realized. The kick lifted the short man off the ground and sent him into the tactical van, six feet away, leaving a rather remarkable dent. He dropped to all fours for a second, eyes wide. I raised my rifle to shoot him in the head, but I wasn't quick enough. He launched forward, impaling me on the katana. I elbowed him in the face, knocking him back. He took the sword with him and raised it, looking to take my head off. But Carlos bowled him over, and the two went down in a heap. Blackman came up first, taking off at a sprint. I shot after him, hard on his heels.

We charged down Parklawn, across a small stand of broadly separated trees, turned up West Roxbury Parkway, and headed north, effortlessly passing local traffic. A car spun out in front of me to avoid hitting Blackman, and I was forced to speed vault over it. I came down with more momentum than I anticipated and staggered for a second.

Blackman stopped suddenly, then pivoted and kicked the back end of a passing Jeep, causing it to swerve right into me, head-on. It launched me back into the trees. Fortunately, I landed on the ground rather than impaled on a branch. But, both of my legs were well and truly banjaxed. I sat up, banging the earth in frustration. The pain subsided quickly as the bones reset themselves and the wounds closed.

I stood and walked out of the tree line as soon as I was able. The Jeep that hit me was gone. *Asshole,* I thought.

I was almost a half-mile from Gabe's. I jogged back to the scene. There was a bloody hole in my jeans and one in my shirt, but no wounds to match. The shoes were covered in blood. *Fuck, how am I going to explain all this?*

I looked at the radio still attached to my belt and replaced my earwig. The radio was still working. God, these things could take a fucking beating.

Freyer was calling 'officer down' on the tactical channel. I waited for the traffic to clear on the channel and called in.

"Victor 8-9-4 Victor 8-7-7," I said into the radio. The tactical channel was encrypted so that we could speak relatively freely.

"Cait, are you alright?" Carlos sounded panicked.

"I'm fine. How bad is it?" I replied, more worried about the state of the team.

"It's bad. Mills is dead, and Vic is in bad shape. We have five others down, all with survivable wounds. Where are you?"

"Walking back, I chased him down the street, but I got bumped by a car. I'm not injured," I made sure to keep my report vague but truthful.

Two ambulances sped past me, full lights and sirens. The scene at the house was a horror show.

A tarp covered Mills, and the EMTs performed CPR on Vic. I could tell by the amount of blood on the ground around him that he wasn't going to make it. Carlos was helping with downed officers. I started taking supplies from the EMTs to care for the wounded who weren't already being helped.

It wasn't long before three more ambulances showed up, followed closely by four press vans from local news. I handed off the last officers who needed care to the EMTs and sat down on the curb holding an alcohol wipe. My hands were covered in blood.

I brought my hands to my mouth reflexively, almost licking them. The urge was powerful and frightening. I ripped open the wipe and started wiping the blood off. *Damnit.*

It was then that I noticed the entire fugitive team was wearing body cams, per policy. If Carlos were right, the feds would be all over this with me right in the middle of it. Having to quit my job would be the least of my worries. I also realized that every last officer still conscious, except for Carlos, was staring at me accusingly.

I just sighed and lowered my head. Seemingly miraculously, a pack of cigarettes appeared before my face.

"Here, you look like you could use this." I recognized the voice as belonging to Shandra Clark from Channel 7. She was bent over, cigarettes and lighter in hand, wearing a sweater, jeans, and a pair of flip-flops. I took a cigarette and lit it, taking a long drag. It was a menthol and tasted awful, but the throat hit was worth it. And, strangely enough, it helped quell the hunger slightly.

"You're not supposed to be here," I said, blowing out a puff of smoke but otherwise not moving.

She pulled out a cigarette and lit up next to me. "Looking a little pale, Detective."

I tried to be polite, but my words came out bitchy. "I can't be seen talking to you; thank you for the cigarette, now go away."

"I think talking to me will be the least of your worries. I count at least ten body cams around here in plain view, and you were running at automobile speeds."

I looked at her with suspicion. "How do you know that?"

"I watched you from my front porch. I live right over there." She pointed across the street a few houses down toward the corner of Weld and West Roxbury. I had run right past her front door.

"No way you and your hot girlfriend can cover this up." Her voice wasn't scathing or mean; she was just stating the facts. How she knew about Marcella and me, I didn't want to guess at that particular moment.

"It doesn't matter," I said.

"Yes. Well, I'll buy you some time, at least."

When I didn't respond, she said, "I'll let you get back to it, then." She then stood up and walked back down the street. "Sorry to hear about Gabe," she called back consolingly. "He did seem like a nice guy."

"Thanks," I muttered, taking a last drag off the cigarette and putting it out.

I was so fucked. Marcella was, too. She'd said that technology would drive us underground. I just didn't realize how soon.

41

"Did you fucking know?" Detective Freyer screamed in my face. "Did you fucking know what we were up against?"

I wasn't sure how to respond. My emotional state was tortured and twisted. In one instant, I could feel an urge rising in my chest to grab Freyer and suck out every last glorious drop of blood. The next, my eyes burned as I thought of David flying through the air into the squad car like a rag doll and Vic bleeding out. I looked again at Freyer's throat; I wanted to tear it open. I stomped hard on the feeling and stood, turning my back to Freyer.

Freyer pulled us into the conference room and read us the riot act as soon as we got back. Then he had zeroed in on me.

I thought for a moment whether to lie. But I couldn't think of anything believable. And, frankly, the team deserved better than that. I'd charged down the street like Captain fucking America after the Winter Soldier, passing cars doing forty. I was screwed on so many fronts. It sucked when you had rules to play by, and the enemy didn't have any. It was all too easy for them to use that against you. But, abandoning those rules is how people justified putting children in suicide vests.

Everyone had seen Blackman cut through a half dozen men and kill two of our own. They'd blame me, no matter what, at least in the short term. That's how cops were.

"Hey!" Carlos shouted, getting everyone's attention. "How

about you back off and cut her some slack. She's almost died, watched her boyfriend try to kill her, and, now, two of her best friends are dead, both good detectives."

I stood up and put a hand on Carlos' shoulder. "It's okay, Carlos," I muttered. "Yes, Freyer, I had an idea. I'd seen him fight at Marcella's the other night. I'd warned the officers that night that he was dangerous. I don't think I understood just how dangerous."

"That's not going to fly, Reagan. Blackman ran you through with a three-foot sword, and you walked it off. Then, you took off faster than a fucking thoroughbred at Suffolk Downs. If I hadn't seen it with my own eyes, I wouldn't have believed it."

"If you calm down, I'll explain."

"Reagan," Carlos warned.

"You shut up." Freyer spat at Carlos. "If I find out you knew about this too, I'll be kicking your ass."

"Just try it, muchacho," Carlos stood up, towering over Freyer and growling right in his face. "You wanna go, little man?"

Shouts sounded from around us, half of them wanting to see the two of them go at it, the other half trying to break up what was becoming a scuffle.

An ear-splitting whistle sounded through the conference room, and everyone stopped.

"Knock it the fuck off!" Larson stood in the doorway. "All of you sit the fuck down, right now." Everyone backed away from each other, but no one sat.

"Reagan, let's talk about this in my office."

"No," I said firmly. "These guys need to know what they're up against."

"Are you sure?" he said, giving me a warning look.

"Yes," I said. "I know what I'm doing."

"Yeah, Lieutenant, she knows what she's doing," Freyer mocked.

"Shut the fuck up, Freyer!" Larson shot back at him. "We all make mistakes. You are no exception." Freyer looked hurt.

Freyer had been one of the survivors when his team had served a no-knock warrant gone bad. Internal Investigations cleared him, but we all knew he'd fucked up.

"Fine," Freyer said, throwing his arms out in a 'let's have it' gesture.

"It's easier to believe if I show you," I said. I extended my fangs and reached over with one arm, picking Freyer up by his vest. I held him off the ground, dangling over the floor. Everyone except Carlos slid back about four feet. Carol was looking at me like I'd grown another head.

"Holy shit!" Freyer exclaimed, pawing at my arm. I set him back down and pulled my teeth in. Larson looked a little spooked. Of course, the only person who didn't react was Carlos.

"I'm— special," I said, dodging the word. It was okay, though; one of Freyer's guys was kind enough to fill it in.

"Madre de Dios!" Soledad breathed, eyes wide with fear. "You're a fucking vampire! My mama said they were real, but I didn't believe her. Holy shit!"

"Yes, I'm probably going to be outed nationwide tomorrow, so it's not going to matter. And I'll be killed. So, you see, Lieutenant, the best thing I can do is tell them what they're facing."

"Did you know about this?" Freyer asked Carlos.

"Yes," Carlos said. "But I knew she was forbidden to tell anyone, so I didn't say anything. It doesn't matter that Blackman was the first to break the rules; she did too when she tried to run him down."

"How do you know so much about it?" Freyer asked, looking suspiciously at Carlos.

Carlos ran his hand through his hair. "I've known vampires were real for years, but who would have believed me. Besides, we all have secrets of our own. Some of us have cheated on our spouses. Some of us have done other things we're not proud of. She tried to get everyone away from the door, but it was too late. That's why we asked you to hold until we got there. Cait was trying to keep all of us safe."

"How's that?" Freyer asked, incredulous.

"They'd kill you too if anyone found out you knew," I told him. "And someone here would spill the beans. At least now, you don't have to worry about it. It's all on me. They can't hush this up or cover it up. Now, I have an idea for how to fix this, but everyone in this room needs to keep this to themselves. I've been on the force for seven years and part of this team for two. I've been there for all of you at one point or another. I didn't ask for this. It was imposed on me only yesterday, and it sucks." A few of the guys snorted at the unintentional pun. "But, I'm the same person I was on Friday, so please help me out here." My eyes welled up a little, but I refused to cry. "I don't want to die, and as you've seen, no one here can protect me."

"Bullshit," Freyer said, doing a one-eighty. "I may be pissed off, but we protect our own Reagan."

"They'll kill you, Freyer, and anyone assigned to any protection detail. You saw what just one of them did, and I plugged him four times with my M-4."

"Who is 'they?'" one of the other Detectives asked. Bird, I think her name was. I didn't know her well, but we'd never disliked each other. She looked terrified of me now.

"The vampires have a council. I'm not sure I can call them evil; I've never met them face to face. But they're all hundreds of years old, and none of you would stand a chance against one of them, let alone all. Besides, it would all happen gradually, each team member offed, making it look like a run-of-the-mill murder or an accident." I knew I was embellishing, but I was also trying to save their lives.

"Now that there's evidence—" I continued, but a dozen phones started buzzing at that moment.

"Turn on the news," one of the men said.

Larson grabbed the remote off the tabletop and flipped the TV. Shandra Clark was on the screen. There were a few loud boos from the men behind me.

"Hush!" I hissed. *Fuck. What else was going to happen?*

"Sources say that this evening around nine, the Boston Police were serving an arrest warrant at this West Roxbury home. If you remember, Doug, we're only a few blocks from the scene of a murder that happened just a few days ago." The feed switched to footage showing EMS loading an officer into the back of an ambulance, then Shandra's voice returned.

"A couple of witnesses swore that one of the officers took off on foot after the perpetrator and was passing cars on West Roxbury Parkway." Shandra made her voice sound like she didn't believe it.

"I understand you were on the scene, Shandra," Doug Myles said from the news desk. "What did you see?"

Cut back to Shandra near Gabe's house. "Well, I didn't see any super-cops, if that's what you mean. But there was a shootout here, and several officers were injured. We've received reports that two officers were killed during the incident."

Bless you, Shandra, I thought.

"I believe the mayor is about to give a statement," Shandra said, and they cut over to the Mayor moving in front of a camera with the Commissioner and the Chief Superintendent. The mayor began to speak.

"It is with a heavy heart that I come before the people of Boston to report that two officers were killed in the line of duty tonight while serving an arrest warrant. We will not be releasing the names of those officers at this time so that we can notify their families. I now turn it over to the Commissioner. She will provide further details and answer questions."

The Commissioner cleared her throat. "Tonight, in the service of a warrant for the arrest of Haimon Blackman, who is wanted in connection with four murders, Mr. Blackman was able to escape from the Fugitive Apprehension Unit. During his escape, Mr. Blackman wounded six officers and killed two others. We would like civilians to be on the lookout for Mr. Blackman. If seen, he should not be approached; call 9-1-1. Mr. Blackman should be treated as armed and extremely dangerous.

"I will take questions at this time."

"What about the reports we've heard from multiple witnesses of some kind of super cop?" Wow, I was the first question off the bat. Not even questions about the other officers who were injured. That was fucked up.

"We don't know what witnesses thought they saw, but if we had a super-cop on the force, we certainly wouldn't be hiding it. Any other questions?"

My phone buzzed, and I looked down. I stepped out the door, mouthing to Carlos, 'Marcella.' He nodded and stepped up in front of the door behind my exit.

I hit the answer button and cringed. "Hey."

"Are you okay?" Marcella sounded more worried than upset.

"Yes, I'm okay. But Blackman killed one of my best friends, and I'm pretty sure I'm going to be fired."

"First, you're not going to be fired," Marcella stated unequivocally. "I'm just glad you're okay."

"I'm sorry, Marcella, I fucked up."

"It was bound to happen eventually. Honestly, we've been lucky it hasn't happened before now. I think you did the right thing. Blackman is a rogue, and we need to take him down before it gets any worse. We've had shit like this before, and we've always managed to blow it off. It'll be looked at as a hoax." The line was quiet for a few seconds.

"Marcella?" I prompted.

"Sorry, just thinking. Anyway, I should have stayed with you, but I can't be everywhere at once. I wasn't prepared for this to happen right now, but we'll have to make due. How are you feeling? Are you hungry?" Her voice was laced with concern.

I took a breath. The desire for blood had been rising rapidly since my chase with Blackman. I rubbed my arms, feeling the antsiness crawling under my skin. "Yes, but I'm okay for now," I lied.

"That won't last. Come as soon as you can, and don't

dawdle."

"Okay."

"I love you, Cait. I won't let anything happen to you. This is as much on me as it is on you."

"I love you, too."

We hung up, and I turned around to go back into the conference room and almost walked into Lieutenant Larson. "Come on," he said. "Let's get this over with."

We walked into his office. He shut the door. "Good job today."

I blinked. "I'm sorry?"

"I said, you did a good job today," Larson repeated. "I'm just sorry you didn't catch the bastard."

"I'm not fired?" I asked.

"Fired? For what?" he asked me, one eyebrow raised. "Cait, you've been with this department for seven years. Your service record has been exemplary. All I've seen from the footage was that Blackman plowed out of the door and cut down six officers. Then you and Carlos, with no concern for your own safety, tried to take him down.

"Then, you, again with no concern for your own safety, took off after him. You didn't kill Mills or Vic; Blackman did. Those guys know that." Larson pointed toward the conference room. "And don't mind Freyer, you heard him. We protect our own."

"But, Bill, I'm a vampire. Doesn't that bother you?"

"It might if you were the first I'd run across, but you're not."

The hunger began to pound on my senses. "You'll have to share that story at some point."

"At some point. Now, get out there and find this bastard. I can't bring him down without you."

"Yes, sir." I breathed a sigh of relief as I left Larson's office. A teary-eyed Detective Doyle was standing outside the door. She threw her arms around my neck and pulled me into a hug, pressing into me in a way that felt more intimate than the moment demanded, but I didn't pull away. Instead, I pushed my face into her neck, unable to stop myself.

"I'm so sorry to hear about David and Vic," she whispered in my ear. "It's terrible." Her pulse was next to my mouth, and I could hear her heart beating in my ears like a drum. She smelled— oh, so good. I could feel my fangs lengthening as inappropriate thoughts filtered into my head.

Just a little taste.

I jerked back and nearly ran away, grabbing my things on the way out.

42

I pulled into the parking garage under Marcella's at about midnight. My thoughts obsessed on Jessica Doyle— the beautiful way her luscious auburn hair drew my eye to her precious throat, her pulse beating under her skin, the smell of lavender and jasmine in her hair. I'd stopped three times during the drive, desperate to turn back, to find Jessica and claim her. It was more than enticing; it was an almost irresistible urge tugging at my chest, my emotions, my sex. My mind repeatedly clouded with thoughts of her burning with passion underneath me as I smeared her blood across my lips and kissed her. The vision played in my consciousness, causing me to stumble as I exited the car.

A distant part of me fought for control, but it was feeble, weak. I staggered to the elevator, mashing the call button repeatedly.

"Come on, come on. Please." The last word came out as a whimper as I leaned against the elevator door. Underneath my skin and the banging beat of the hunger was the tiny voice of my terror. Mixed in the arousal and predatory need roiled fear and hopelessness.

The door opened, and I fell inside. Gentle, pale, feminine arms caught me. I looked up into the unfamiliar green eyes of an unknown vampire and pleaded, "Help me." My hands were quaking, and shivers were running down my spine.

"Shh," the woman said. "Marcella is worried sick." Her voice should have been soothing, but it was grating.

I bared my fangs and hissed at her. "Shut up!" I struggled to get loose; I needed blood. I clawed at her face and chest, tearing great rents in the fabric of her shirt and leaving long scratches on her flesh. They bled slightly before healing, and I licked at them, desperate. But the blood was dead, cold, empty, and I spit it to the floor.

The elevator dinged, impossibly loud. She picked me up roughly and carried me into the kitchen like a rag doll. I could smell the blood as soon as we walked in. It was close— so close.

"Marcella!" the unknown vampire called nonchalantly. "She's back."

"Oh, thank the Goddess. Elizabeth, get her to the table." Marcella rushed into the kitchen as the green-eyed vampire dumped me rather unceremoniously into a chair. Marcella slid a cup in front of me. "Cait, I'm so sorry. I shouldn't have left you like that."

"You need to take better care of your toys, M."

"Shut up, Elizabeth. Not now." Marcella's voice was harsh and sounded like bristles on brass.

I looked at the cup of blood. Now that it was in front of me, I fought for control. My whole body trembled as the hunger drove me to lean toward the cup, and I jerked back. Holding on, barely, muscles clenching in my arms, I bit into my lip to keep from just pouring it down my throat. Pink tears, tinged with blood, flowed down my face, dripping off my chin and onto my chest.

Finally, I picked up the cup with two shaking hands, tremulously bringing it to my lips. The first sip was like sex in a drop; the relief flooded into my very being. The blood was almost warm. But then, control fled, and I upended the cup, gulping and licking out every drop, my tongue snaking out to find the bottom.

I looked up to Marcella, feeling so much like a child. Her eyes scraped away my defenses with utter compassion, and a soft hand slid through my hair. Lain so painfully bare, I started to weep. All of the sorrow, grief, self-pity, and horror I had inside just spilled out in a torrent of ear-splitting, wrathful sobs.

Marcella sat on the floor and pulled me into her lap, wrapping me in a powerful embrace. She anchored me to her as I shattered like glass on marble.

For days, I had been in shock with terror piled on tragedy: parasites, vampires, Gabe, Mills, Vic. I had no more room for any more pain, and now, I could see him, a little boy named Ahmed Hadi, looking at me from across the room. His liquid brown eyes pierced my being, shaming me—the little boy who had never had a chance to live before my bullet ended his life. Memories, dulled by time, were now crystal clear. I had no words for the suffering that coursed through my heart and pushed into the cracks of my soul. So I howled my grief to the universe, raging against an uncaring God.

Elizabeth stood next to us. "I'll call you," she said to Marcella and turned to go, but she stopped. She bent down and ran a hand through my hair, pushing aside errant strands. "Not too different than I was at first."

Marcella continued to rock me. "No, she's not."

"I'm sorry, Cait. It shouldn't be like this." Elizabeth stood. "Goodbye, Marcella. We're even, now." She strode from the room.

I heard all of it, but it would be much later before I comprehended, so lost was I in my head. Marcella and I sat there for almost an hour. She didn't coo or shush or say anything. She simply held me in her arms, rocking me, waiting. When I had run out of tears and lamentations and miserable desperate screams of hurt, she handed me another cup. I drank it slowly, cradling it with still trembling fingers. Emotionally exhausted, I looked at Marcella's face.

"You did good," she whispered. Her expression was one of approval—not a hint of judgment.

"Did I?" I asked, my voice small, child-like.

She chuckled. "Oh yes, the state you were in? When you

staggered out of the elevator with Elizabeth, I felt awful. I hadn't realized how far along you were when we were on the phone. Goddess, I should never have left you alone."

"He killed them, Marcella. He killed Mills and Vic. David Mills was one of my best friends—one of my only friends. And Vic's wife, Donna, just found out she's pregnant with their child." I put my arms around her and buried my face in her collar.

"Come, Cait, let me take you to rest." Marcella picked me up as if I weighed nothing, carrying me to the elevator and up. She was my love, my life. I'd die for her without question. I was hers.

We arrived in her room, and she lay me on the bed, covering me with the blanket. And though I was neither hot nor cold, that simple act of compassion filled me with profound comfort.

"Rest, my darling," she said, and the echo of command filtered through the words. I didn't bother to resist. My eyes shut, and I was no more.

There were no dreams, no visions, no conscious or unconscious thoughts. There was no awareness of the passage of time. It was blissful oblivion, so far beyond sleep, like somehow being unmade, all my parts removed and laid to rest until needed.

"Wake up," Marcella commanded, and my eyes flew open. Every part of my being felt comfortable and whole, feelings settled and clear. The rage and anger of the previous night had scattered. I didn't know if it would continue, but I felt—safe. Since my father had died, I felt whole inside for the first time.

Fatigue overwhelmed me as the morning sunlight burned through the window. I was about to pull my head down under the covers when Marcella pulled the blackout curtains across the enormous picture window, shrouding the room.

"Here, drink this, and then rest more." Marcella handed me another cup of blood, blissfully warm. I downed it quickly and rolled over, licking my lips.

"Tonight, you and I need to go out so I can start showing you the ropes. So get rest."

"Okay, mom," I joked tiredly, yawning reflexively and nearly dislocating my jaw. "Who was the woman that brought me up the elevator?"

"Elizabeth Tyler, she's an old friend. She was dropping off some things I'd left with her in London, returning a favor."

"Oh. She looks a lot like you. She's stunning."

"Yes, dear, it seems you have a type." Marcella's tinkling laugh descended on me, making my skin prickle, as she stroked my cheek, and a touch of contentment filtered into my fogged and sleepy brain. Then, I slipped away again.

43

Later that night, having slept to sundown, I sat on her bed and looked out the window, admiring the stars. It had been a long day. I laid back and closed my eyes. The hunger returned immediately. My skin felt as if it were burning. My eyes felt tired, and I could almost, but not quite, taste blood on my tongue. It was agonizing. Visions of Doyle and her precious neck swam through my head. I thought about calling her. I had her number.

I jerked as Marcella interrupted me. "Come into the bathroom; I need to do your makeup."

"Fine!" I snapped.

Marcella looked at me, but instead of getting upset, she just smiled beatifically. "Come now, darling. Let's get that hunger under control."

I marched into the bathroom with her, and, with me seated before one of her vanities, Marcella began applying my makeup. Like her wardrobe, it was high-end stuff. After she had finished, I looked in the mirror. I looked— beautiful. She had even managed to tone down the sheen of my skin. Then, she grabbed a hairdryer and gave me a blowout. By the time she was finished, I was agape at my appearance. I looked— glamorous. For once in my life, I didn't think my eyes were the color of swamp water. They were deep like green-brown glass, windowing the world.

"See, Cait," she said, looking over my shoulder and smiling appreciatively. "You are truly worthy of the catwalks of Paris and Milan. I'd certainly give you a shag."

I laughed nervously at the comment. "You've already given me a shag."

"Well, then I'd give you another one. Okay, let's get dressed. I have a surprise for you," she took my hand and dragged me to her closet.

Marcella had set aside a generous portion of it for me and filled it with clothing. I tried dressing in my usual conservative work wardrobe, but she would have none of it.

"No, no, white's not a good color. Here, put this on." She handed me an outfit. I had no problem with the black silk top, but it took a minute to struggle into the tight leather pants and over-the-knee boots.

Marcella bit her lower lip. "Perfect, except—" She stepped into me and nibbled at my throat, undoing three of my buttons. "We're going dancing, dear, not to a criminal interrogation."

I rolled my eyes.

"Come," she said, holding my hand. "Leave your badge, gun, and cell phone." I did as she asked with the gun and cellphone but pushed my badge into a pocket. One never knew.

We ended up at a bar called Leslie's. It wasn't a lesbian bar, per se; there are none in Boston—I blame assimilation. But there were many gay women inside, some enjoying fairly involved displays of affection.

As we entered, I resisted the urge to flick my tongue. Even so, I could taste the excitement in the air, literally. Pheromones and sexual attraction had a flavor to them. It was enticing, and the hunger immediately yanked at my attention, the palpable need making my skin crawl. It seemed to have a mind of its own, knowing where I was and, more importantly, why.

"Do you feel it?" Marcella shouted over the music.

I nodded vigorously as Marcella led me to the bar, her body language making it clear that we were 'just friends' tonight.

"Now what? I'm not much of a cruiser."

Marcella spoke into my ear. "First of all, look at me and focus. Filter out the rest of the noise. You need to learn to do this."

I faced her, and she began speaking. I tried to listen to her directly, but that didn't work. I could hear Marcella's voice in the cacophony of shouting and the banging drum-beat of the DJ, but she was too faint to make out. I closed my eyes to listen. Around me, the noise began to separate itself into individual words, phrases, and conversations. As I concentrated on each conversation, the music settled itself into the background. It was still loud as hell, but the voices became clear.

"I'd like a martini, dirty." The voice belonged to a woman who sounded to me in her early twenties.

"I need ID, kid." That was the bartender.

"My husband can't fuck to save his life," a woman whispered further down.

"Can you?" another woman shouted. I didn't think it was the same conversation, but the coincidence was funny.

"Oh, my God," a woman gasped in ecstasy. Was that the bathroom? Eww. Who has sex in the bathroom? I wasn't one to knock people's proclivities, but I wouldn't do it. Sex in a public place eeked me out.

"So, eventually, you should be able to hear me, and when you can, open your eyes and look at me." I opened my eyes, and Marcella's voice rang crystal in my ears. "Good girl," she said, and I smiled. Even though I could hear Marcella, I was also aware of many conversations. I didn't block them out, but they became unimportant— background noise.

"I thought we were going dancing," I said sardonically.

"We will, later, if there's time. Now we need to find you a suitable donor."

"You mean victim?" I said flatly.

"No, you remember how you felt when you thought it was a dream?" That poked a bit of a nerve, but I nodded.

"It'll be similar, but there'll be no domination until it's over."

"So you're saying I'm going to seduce someone and then

whammy them to forget I fed on them?"

"Absolutely! Clearly, you understand." Marcella seemed supremely confident in my abilities. I was not.

"I'm not sure who you think you turned, but—."

Marcella interrupted me. "You'll take to it naturally, trust me."

She glanced around and spotted someone, then leaned in, still looking. "Behind you, against the far wall, is a woman in a gray tank top, jeans, and biker boots. She's been scoping you since you walked in."

I took a moment to order a drink and had to remember to speak up for the bartender. I looked around the bar, dangling my glass of scotch from my fingers. I saw the woman Marcella was talking about. Looking to be in her mid-twenties and fit, she had short dirty-blond hair in a pixie cut. Her boots were knee-high motorcycle boots, and her jeans were ripped. She was cute—hot, really.

I glanced at her, smiled, and then turned back to the bar. "I feel a little guilty right now," I said and drank from my scotch.

"You can't feel guilty about survival, Cait. I won't let you hurt her, and she'll enjoy her evening. I promise."

She wasn't getting it. "Not about that, at least not yet. I'm getting ready to flirt with a woman, and you're right here."

"Cait," Marcella said with all seriousness. "You're one of us now. Love is love, which will never change, but sex is sex, and blood is blood."

"But I've always been a one person at a time lover. I don't think I can change that." I was suddenly getting a little uneasy, and an ugly touch of jealousy began to rise.

"Me too. And that's okay, but you need to see this as more about feeding and less about sex. Does it bother you that I might be a little flirty with someone else? After sharing my night with Stephanie with you, does it still bother you?"

"No. I get why you have to do it. But it's different—."

"When it's you. I get it. Think of it as more of a game of flirting. We're here to enjoy our evening, and this is part of it.

Trust me, it's enjoyable, and you don't have to feel guilty, as long as you don't—." She trailed off.

"Kill anyone. I know." I downed my scotch, which felt like dropping a rock into my stomach.

"Yeah, you're going to regret that later," Marcella said with a laugh. "Next time, don't drink anything before you feed. It's not going to cause a real problem, but you'll find the experience is better in the long run."

Why did she have to be some damn cryptic? But I already knew the answer. This was like a training patrol. She wanted me to make mistakes so that I didn't make them later when she wasn't around.

I ordered another scotch, top-shelf this time. Carrying the glass, I walked through the crowd to the other side of the club where pixie-cut was standing, and the hunger seemed to take on a life of its own. The music permeated all that I was, each bass note pumping into my blood. Every step became a statement of predatory intent, like a cat stalking its prey. I slid through the crowd with preternatural grace, and they seemed to part for me. Lust and wanton power fueled me now. I could feel an aura of sexuality flowing off of me in waves, causing heads to turn as I passed. I ignored them, intent on my target.

Marcella was halfway across the bar, but I could still hear her. "See, relax, and it will just happen. Did I mention you look so fucking hot right now?"

A cocky smile parted my lips at the compliment. Now, very close, I held out the drink to pixie-cut. She took it and raised the glass. "I'm here with my girlfriend, but thanks for the drink."

I put my arm on the wall next to her and leaned close, smiling like the monster that I was, all dark promise and seduction.

"Are you?" My breath brushed through her hair, blowing the strands about. "You've been over here alone for quite a while." I could feel the heat of her body, and I heard her heartbeat quicken. Intense satisfaction filled me, knowing that I was turning her on with so little effort.

"I don't like to dance," she shouted over the music— a lame excuse. "She's on the floor with one of our friends." I could feel the underlying tension in her tone. The way she said 'friend' suggested they were anything but.

I leaned just a hair closer. "Which one is she?"

Something floated at the edge of my consciousness, previously unnoticed. There was no good way to describe it, but it felt like soft sand sliding against my thoughts. Instinctively, my consciousness touched back. It was like slipping into something private and enticingly forbidden— a peaceful space in pixie-hair's mind that had no defense. I felt her desire for me, and it was becoming more intense by the second. Beneath that desire stirred a harsh feeling — jealousy. Pixie-hair's eyes turned dreamy, and I realized it was something I was doing—automatic, reflexive. My will was reaching out, tentacular and dark, drawing up her most wanton needs. It wasn't something I controlled; it just— was. And I decided I liked it.

"The blond in the pink dress," she said, pointing lazily toward the dance floor. Pixie-cut looked at me, her expression shot through with lust. I had utterly snuffed out her will. The power trip of that was heady and intoxicating all on its own. The desire to claim this creature, this woman, was dark and powerful. I needed to take her to the heights of pleasure, then consume her.

I finally spotted pixie-cut's girlfriend on the dance floor. 'Dress' was a generous description of what she wore. It was a body-contoured little thing that ran from her ass to her shoulders. It covered the critical parts, but it screamed sex. She was pressed against another woman in black skin-tight pants and a yellow crop t-shirt. The two of them were very, very close.

Marcella was over at the bar, clearly listening to every word and smiling like the cat that ate the canary. The guilt and unease I'd felt earlier vanished, and I understood what she had meant. It was a game. I was the hunter now, and this woman was my prey. The burning need of the hunger stubbed out my conscience like a dead cigarette. She was mine, and it was already all over.

Pixie-hair's girlfriend embraced her dance partner and laid quite the lip lock on her. Pixie-cut stiffened and made a face of irritation and disgust. Her eyes turned toward mine, and I could almost see the obscene thoughts racing behind them.

"Seems like you're alone, now," I whispered seductively and licked her ear gently.

She downed the scotch. "Let's go," she said.

I drew a predatory smile and let her lead me to the door. I looked to Marcella, but she wasn't in her seat.

We didn't get far down the street before pixie-cut pulled me into an alley and kissed me, probing my mouth with her tongue desperately. She pulled away for a second and put her hand to her lips. *My fucking tongue. Shit.*

"I'm into body mods; they have their uses," I said with a wink and slid my flat, blue, forked tongue up to touch the end of my nose. She gasped slightly and pulled me in for another deep kiss. The hunger roared, but I drew the encounter out, enjoying her kiss and feeling her tantalizing need rise to an uncontrollable urge.

I nibbled at her ear and listened to her moan quietly. She pulled my hand to her breast, and I caressed it gently. She wasn't wearing a bra, so I used my thumb to stroke her erect nipple, eliciting a series of muffled noises from her throat.

So sensitive had I become to her pulse that I felt it beating against my tongue as I ran it wet and wide across her neck. I could feel her heat and desire both physically and mentally as I brushed against her mind again. I thought to push into her thoughts to heighten her arousal, but her mind was open and seemed to be almost clawing for me to control her. I shoved my hands into her pants, massaging her toward climax.

Then she moaned loudly with unbridled lust while I tore her throat open to drink in all that she was. She gave a modest whimper of pain, but then she sighed, and her body relaxed into me, shivering with pleasure. The blood tasted divine, so different from the stale goop I had been drinking. She tasted pure and sweet, like lust and want and surrender. My body quivered in pleasure as I drank, and drank, and drank. After a few moments, I felt something new— a brightness, a heat, a warmth. It was the sparks of her life, settling into me, consumed to keep me alive. Her blood, a dark, sinful delight incarnate, filtered through me, taking me to the crest of pleasure and then over.

I wanted more, though, to own her, possess her, and take all that she was. I didn't want to stop. I knew I should stop, that I should let go, that she would die— was dying. She was lost in her heat, clawing at the back of my shirt, bunching the fabric in her hands in orgasm after orgasm. Her hands became weak, but I didn't stop. I couldn't get enough. Alarm bells were ringing in my head, but still, I drank. One of her hands dropped limply to her side, and still, I drank.

Finally, a soft hand pushed at my forehead, and a voice, quiet as a whispering breeze, spoke. "Stop. You'll kill her."

I didn't want to stop, but the pressure from Marcella's grip became more insistent. Finally, I released the girl.

"You feel the warmth?" The voice said. I nodded lazily, feeling a little drunk on the life's blood of this young woman, now pulsing beneath my skin.

"Return a bit to her," Marcella said.

The pixie-haired girl leaned hard against the wall, hanging on to my shirt and panting weakly. Blood spilled slowly from her throat— too slowly. I cupped her face and felt the changed blood rise to my mouth. It was tasteless, and I pushed the cool, viscous substance between her lips. She swallowed and then gasped. I watched in awe as the gash in her throat stopped bleeding altogether and closed.

The thrill of power was heady— terrifying. What was I doing to this poor child? But, God, her response when I bit into her was so beautiful—here—in the dark alley where no one could see. I was the beast, the monster of both nightmares and tantalizing, wet, needful dreams, and I loved every glorious drop.

"I know you feel her mind," My senses now felt less clouded. But, the hunger remained. God, this young woman was beautiful. I could have this whenever I wanted. I could call her to me; all I had to do was find her, feel her.

"What do I say?" I asked, grasping for some way to explain the blood on my chin and her neck.

"You have time," Marcella whispered in my ear. "Look at her and think about it. But remember, if you tell her something that conflicts too heavily with her reality, you can break her."

What the hell do I say to explain the feeding away?

I found the same gentle space that was the core of who she was, but I could think of nothing. I released her thoughts.

"That was so good," I said.

"Oh yeah." Pixie hair replied.

"I'm sorry I got a little carried away."

"Are you okay?" She asked dreamily, her eyes starting to become focused. She looked up at my face and drew back, letting me go and staggering slightly.

"Am I okay? Are you okay?" I asked and then realized my fangs were still extended. *Shit. I suck at this.*

"Are you going to kill me?" There was no fear in her blissed-out expression, just curiosity.

"No. Now, are you okay?"

"Are you kidding? That was the most intense sexual experience of my life, and you're asking if I'm okay?" She touched her neck, finding the skin whole and unbroken.

"Seriously, are you okay?" I asked again.

Pixie-cut just nodded, hooked an arm around my neck, and turned me to the wall, kissing me passionately and unbuttoning my pants. She reached her hand into my panties. God, I was still so turned on and, suddenly, so wet. I was about to push her off when Marcella whispered seductively in my ear.

"It's okay, Cait, I don't mind." Marcella was standing at my shoulder, but pixie-cut seemed not to see her.

The pixie-haired girl began working me toward my own orgasm, moving down to kiss my neck. I looked at Marcella, gliding back into the dark, watching me. I orgasmed quickly, my eyes slamming shut as I moaned lasciviously. It was like fire running through me, and my knees felt a little shaky as the climax seemed to go on and on.

"Oh, God," I whispered.

Afterward, Pixie-cut pulled out a cigarette and then held out the pack. "That was unreal. By the way, I'm Pauline."

I took the cigarette and the offered light, drawing in a deep drag. "I'm Caitlin," I said, and she moved back in front of me, licking at my chin.

"Wanna go to my place?" Pauline breathed, leaning back against the wall.

I blew out a puff of gray smoke. "I can't; I've got to be someplace else. Another time perhaps?"

"Definitely," she replied, backing away unsteadily. "Don't worry, your secret is safe with me." She grabbed my neck and kissed me deeply before walking away.

As soon as Pauline was out of sight, Marcella swooped in and pressed her lips to mine. "You are so sexy," she said. "That was not too bad."

"You're kidding, right? I was completely out of control," I admitted. "I almost killed her."

Marcella hung her arms around my neck. "That's why I'm here. You did rather well. But, next time, retract your fangs."

"Yeah," I said sheepishly. "I figured that out."

"Also, you need to think a little quicker on your feet. She had a little blood on her shirt. It didn't need to be explained at all. She probably wouldn't have noticed if you'd licked the blood off of her neck. And carry one of these." She held up a packet containing an alcohol wipe.

"You could have given me that advice to start with," I said, lips pursed.

"Failures are how we learn, darling. You'll remember it

better for next time."

"I know. You know, I practically dominated her will from the start."

"That's instinct, and it will take time for you to learn to quell it."

"I—I'm not sure that I want to," I confessed.

"Cait," Marcella said, turning very serious. "They're people, not just food. I didn't think you, of all people, would have trouble remembering that."

We started walking back to the car, and I was surprised by a powerful urge to go back into the club and do it again. Stopping, I wrestled with what Marcella had just said. It wasn't like me to take advantage of someone, especially after I'd stomped all over Marcella for precisely the same thing. But, I couldn't bring myself to feel bad about it, and I couldn't figure out why. And that was bothering me a lot. I should feel guilty or something. Maybe, hopefully, it would hit me later.

I looked toward the bar and watched Pauline's girlfriend in the pink dress stumble out, clearly drunk, looking around. Pauline was long gone, it seemed. I decided to wait and see what she did. A naughty little part of me wondered what she might be like compared to her girlfriend, but I pushed that thought away. What I'd done to Pauline was surely going to upset me later, and I didn't need to add to it. But, the temptation was strong.

Pauline's girlfriend stumbled down the street from Leslie's, and a guy next to a van tried to chat her up. He grabbed her and pulled her into the van when she kept going.

"Oh, hell no," I said and tore off toward the van at full tilt, springing up on my toes in the heeled boots.

I reached the van before it got up any speed, throwing myself into the driver's side door. A painful shock jarred my shoulder, and I fell, knocked to the ground by the impact. The van jerked right and hit a parked car head-on, stopping cold. The steam of a busted radiator whistled through the grill.

I picked myself up and ran around to the back, yanking open

the doors. Inside, I found three men, the driver, and two others pulling themselves off the floor. Next to the two kidnappers in the back were Pauline and her girlfriend. I didn't hesitate. I yanked the first man out of the van and knocked him roughly to the ground.

Marcella rounded the van. "Sit," she ordered. The man I'd chucked out sat down and didn't move.

I snatched the other two men out, dragging the driver out over the seat and whacking his head on the ceiling. I smelled the blood of the cut it left on his head and licked my lips.

With surprising speed and clarity, I found the spaces in their minds that were the core of who they were. Unlike Pauline, their minds were far from gentle. They were greasy and crusted with anger and amorality. "Sit down and stay quiet," I commanded.

They did as they were told. Marcella snatched a phone out of one of the guys' pockets and called 9-1-1. While she was on the phone, I carefully checked in on the girls, bringing them both through the van doors.

A small crowd had gathered outside the club, snapping pictures. I ignored them and used my badge to move them away from the crime scene. Marcella gave me a disapproving look but said nothing.

Pauline was a little dazed and bleeding from the back of her head. Her girlfriend was drunk and staggering but uninjured. As soon as I set her on the sidewalk, she turned and puked all over one of the men. He jerked around but did not stand. I knew the situation was serious, but I had to stifle my laugh.

When three patrol cars rolled up a few minutes later, one of the men recognized me.

"You working vice tonight, Reagan?" he asked, waving at my outfit.

"Fuck you, Delauder," I answered, giving him the finger. "I'm out dancing with my girlfriend, and we happened to catch these assholes in the middle of a kidnapping."

"Where'd the blood come from? You hurt?"

"It's hers." I pointed to Pauline. "She's got a cut on the back of her head." Marcella gave me the alcohol wipe, and I started cleaning my face.

We were on scene for about an hour while we made statements and ensured that Pauline and her girlfriend, Jenny, as it turned out, had a ride home. Jenny tried to hug Marcella and me, but we waved her off. She had vomit on her dress. Pauline walked up to me and put her arms around my neck.

"I thought I recognized you. You're that cop I saw on Twitter," she whispered as she hugged me close. "Thank you." She planted a soft kiss on my cheek and then looked at the side of the van, whistling. I peeked around the vehicle and realized I'd crushed in the I-beam behind the driver's door.

"You should have a doctor look at your head," I told her.

Pauline just waved her hand dismissively. As she took Jenny's hand and they climbed into a patrol car, she glanced back appreciatively.

Marcella and I went back into the bar, and I cleaned myself up in the bathroom sink, getting the rest of the blood off me. Then we returned to the Jeep.

"How do you feel?" She asked.

"Like a fucking superhero right now," I replied, totally jazzed by the rescue.

"Okay, well, that's good because what I have to say next will be a bit of a letdown."

"Okay?"

"I told you to leave your badge at home," she said sternly. "What do you think will happen if you're interrupted while feeding and drop it accidentally. You can't 'whammy,' as you say, more than one person at a time, so you might have to run. Next thing you know, you're up on charges of, at best, attempted murder. Now, you need to follow my instructions."

"Yes, ma'am," I said sheepishly. She was right; I'd been stupid. But, in my defense, this was my first time. But hadn't I just whammied two guys at once? It felt like it, but maybe one had just obeyed because the other did. I couldn't be sure.

"Anything else?"

"Listen to the little voice that tells you that your donor is done. Otherwise, they'll die, and you'll be miserable. Now that you've fed, you, I assume, felt when your donor had given all she could, as I did. Pay attention to that because I won't be there to rescue you next time."

"Okay." That scared me. The training wheels were coming off after one go? I didn't know if I was ready for that.

"Also, never be seen leaving the bar with your donor. Make an excuse for the ladies' room and meet them outside. It makes for fewer witnesses and less suspicion later if something goes wrong. And, finally, don't ever feed in public like that again. Stick to a private place, preferably their apartment or hotel room, not your own. That way, you're less likely to be interrupted. If you want them to live, they'll need changed blood. How will you provide that if someone interrupts you and stops your feeding? Your donor will bleed out."

"Christ, there are a lot of rules."

"Yes, Cait, there are. This takes time to learn. Fortunately, I'm a pro." She winked at me. "That's enough for one night. There's something else I need to show you."

44

As we drove back to Marcella's, my feelings about what I'd done had become much more ambivalent. The strange high I'd felt had subsided, and I began to feel very guilty.

Pauline had been a sweet young girl, but she'd been in pain, and I had taken advantage of that. Setting aside the fact that I'd had a sexual encounter with a stranger in an alley something I had never thought I'd do. I felt like, somewhere along the way, I had assaulted her.

"Don't overthink it, Cait," Marcella said as she drove.

"I can't help it." I stared dismally out the window at the passing cars, my finger worrying at a bit of condensation.

"You didn't choose this. None of us did, really. I can be honest enough to say that I'd have done it anyway had I been told what I'd become. But I was out for vengeance." Her voice grew gentle, and she placed a hand on my leg. "Cait, if you don't feed on the living, you will become a killing machine. You took the least harmful option."

"I just wish there was a better one."

"Well, you could find a pet," Marcella said distastefully.

"Does that mean what I think it does?"

"You find someone, groom them to trust you, tell them what you are, and keep them as your walking juice box."

"What happens when one of these 'pets' gets pissed off, jealous, or suddenly gets the John Wayne's and decides to report their 'master' to someone."

Marcella looked over at me, and her expression made it clear that such events only had one outcome.

"I see."

"You're less than a day from your transformation, so you'll need to feed often. Bagged blood will tide you over, but it lacks the actual life that sustains us. After a while, it won't sate the hunger at all. But, try to remember that young girl—"

"Pauline," I clarified.

"Yes, Pauline. Her experience with you tonight thrilled her. As far as she was concerned, it was exciting and fulfilling, and she walked away uninjured and happy. You didn't even have to lie to her in the end.

"On top of that, if you hadn't been there, she probably would have left the bar anyway, and then she and her girlfriend would have very likely ended up raped and murdered. Everyone won, except the bad guys. Exorcising your guilt over the encounter is a small price to pay for all of that."

While I digested that, Marcella continued. "I am glad, though, to see that it bothers you some. I was worried that you might get hooked on the power trip, and I speak from experience when I say that's easy to do."

It was hard to argue with her, and it mollified my guilt somewhat. I tried not to think about how much I had enjoyed the power over Pauline, the pleasure I had given her and received in return. But, my mouth quirked in a satisfied smile anyway. I had become the beast I had feared—and I liked it, which scared me.

"Marcella? Every story I've ever read about vampires has missed the mark."

She smiled knowingly and prodded me to continue. "Go on?"

"They all focused on the battle against the blood lust of the hunger. But the real battle is against the power we have over others. It—" I paused, considering my words. "It feels *so* good."

Marcella kept her eyes on the road, turning us out of

downtown and circling back toward Charlestown. "I'm glad you recognize that because it will get the better of you at some point. It always does."

That was a pleasant thought. I gazed out the window, looking at the buildings lining Storrow Drive. Somewhere up there was Stephanie's apartment. I wondered, if I came to Stephanie in the middle of the night, as if in a dream would she deny me? Probably not. And I found that idea incredibly tempting. "I'm so sorry about walking out over the dream. I didn't understand."

Marcella glanced over and patted my arm sympathetically. "It's okay, Cait. How could you? It is all part and parcel of what we are. But you should know that I feel bad for what I did."

"I know," I said. "Where are we going?"

"I told you, I have something to show you."

We pulled up to the house and parked the car in the garage. Instead of going inside, we left through a small door to the street and headed down Mt. Vernon toward the Navy Yard.

"Marcella? How often will I need to feed? On the living, I mean."

"Right now, probably a couple of times a week. It's hard to say."

"Twice a week?" I exclaimed. "I don't know if I can do this."

"We just talked about this, Cait. You don't have a choice, and it's not like you dosed Pauline with Rohypnol and then left her to figure out how badly she'd been raped. She walked away, knowing what you were and wanting more. Just because the bite causes an almost orgasmic ecstasy doesn't make it sex."

I wasn't convinced. "You're just rationalizing."

She whirled on me, raising her voice. "Yes, Cait! I'm rationalizing as I've done for fifteen hundred years. I love you, and I don't want to lose you. If you keep looking at this like you've raped someone, you'll drive yourself mad. Eventually, you'll commit suicide or, worse yet, stop feeding and kill someone indiscriminately. It's a shitty choice, and I wish you didn't have to make it. But there's nothing for it."

Marcella scowled in frustration. Then she took my shoulders gently, her eyes gazing into mine. "Take heart in that you are trying to learn how to make this as easy as you can on everyone involved. And, again, try to remember that tonight, you saved two women from a fate worse than death. Your existence is justified by that fact alone. Sometimes, we just have to weigh the positives with the negatives. This isn't like shooting a child to save your patrol. No one died tonight."

That got me. I'd been in worse situations and been forced to make worse decisions. I had another question, though. "Did you feel at all jealous?"

She'd slowed our walk to talk this out, and I was grateful. "No, Cait, I didn't feel jealous. Feeding is a carnal thing of lust, power, and need. Like I told you, love is love, but sex is sex, and blood is blood. Don't confuse the latter two with the former."

Marcella gently pressed me against a wall next to us, delivering a passionate kiss that made my toes curl. I relaxed into her embrace, tasting her mouth on mine. When she broke the kiss, I felt lightheaded and covered in gooseflesh. I hadn't known I could still get lightheaded. It was nice.

"That is from a place of love," Marcella whispered and then pulled me down the street.

At the bottom, we walked under the Tobin Bridge, and I could see the entrance to the Navy Yard across the street. The masts of the USS Constitution, just visible over the buildings, gleamed in the floodlights that surrounded her. Under the bridge sat a large pair of metal doors set into the concrete, which opened easily and quietly. Inside, a vertical street elevator rose to meet us.

"Mind the gap," Marcella said with a smirk as we boarded the lift.

The descent was short, only about fifty feet. Beyond the elevator lay a monstrous concrete storage area, probably thirty-thousand square feet, and filled with pallets of crates and boxes.

Marcella hit a switch on the wall, and overhead lights came

on with the sounds of thunking breakers.

"Wow, I had no idea this place was down here," I said, looking around. "This is like—."

"The warehouse from 'Raiders of the Lost Ark?'"

"Exactly! What is all this?"

Marcella gave me a knowing smile. "Blankets, purified water tanks, dried and canned foods. Fruits are stored in a refrigerated unit over there along with various types of fresh seafood." She pointed toward the far left.

I looked at the closest pallet, stacked high with white boxes, and I could just read the words 'FEMA' and 'Shelter' through the cling wrap. "Are these FEMA emergency relief tents?"

"Yes, they're all expired per the manufacturer, so I was able to buy them cheaply."

"What is all of this for?" The volume of supplies here was shocking. Now I knew where the missing supplies had gone. But, I still had no idea what happened after they left this place.

"Come on. It's just a little further."

We walked across the floor to a set of double doors directly opposite the elevator. Beyond was a long hallway lit by rusted and ancient industrial lamps. Surprisingly, the walls were clean and dry, and the floor held no dust. It seemed to be in regular use and sloped downward almost immediately.

As we walked further, maybe a few hundred yards, odd smells assaulted my nose and lit on my tongue as it flicked out. I detected a faint scent of brine and saltwater underneath a thousand fragrances of earth, flowers, and rot. Below all of that was the faint smell of woodsmoke.

"What does it smell like to you, I wonder?" Marcella asked absently, and I smiled at how well-suited we were.

"Honestly, in some ways, it reminds me of home and my time on the water with my da. I smell butterscotch, honeysuckle, tilled earth, and something like freshly mown grass. I smell blood, too, but I don't think it's human blood. Also, someone is cooking something heavy with pepper and ginger." I was getting used to this new sense. Somewhere ahead came the voices of dozens of people, just a whisper in the darkened tunnel to my newly attuned ears.

"That's impressive. I think I might be a bit jealous. I don't smell any of that except for the tilled earth, grass, and some of the flowers, but I couldn't pick them all out like that. Even the blood is too faint for me to smell at this point."

"My tongue has other uses," I said with a wink. And we walked on.

We came to a door, beyond which was nothing I had ever expected— a forest. Giant firefly-like creatures flitted among a collection of thirty-foot oaks. On closer inspection, I realized they were tiny, nude, winged women—pixies. A soft ambient glow filled the room. High above us, the ceiling was painted in iridescent paint, giving the impression of the night sky. Regular breaks in the tree canopy revealed enormous lights, currently off. It was breathtakingly beautiful as if I'd stepped out into a fairy tale world.

The air was warm and summer-like, and small ponds littered the chamber. Amidst the trees sat small huts.

"Are those real trees?" I asked, reaching toward one.

"Yes, but don't touch them; they're occupied," Marcella said cryptically. As soon as she had spoken, a slender hand shot out of the tree and grasped my wrist. I felt a tug at my consciousness, similar to our own vampiric influence. A young woman of perhaps twenty slid through the tree bark to stand before me.

She was soft and round and beautifully proportioned. Her eyes were a mixture of brown and green like my own but almond-shaped and inviting. Long chestnut hair hung about her naked body.

I felt the brush of a mind on my own, and my thoughts turned almost pornographic. The trance was broken, though, by Marcella's touch. The girl stuck her tongue out at Marcella and stepped back into the tree.

"Are you okay?" Marcella asked with a bit of a giggle.

"Uh— yeah," I said, looking back at the tree, seeing what

looked like a girlish face in the bark. I did a double-take as it seemed to wink salaciously at me. "What was that all about?"

"Dryads occupy the trees. They can't hurt our kind, but they consume the life force of normal humans, much as we do. Rather than blood, though, they use sex, and they are insatiable. It's unwise to consort with them; their powers of persuasion are, ah, formidable. Though, they usually lose interest in us rather quickly. The huts are for the brownies, and over there," she gestured to some caves in the far walls, "we have caves for the redcaps."

"Wait, redcaps, dryads, brownies? These are all Faeries?" I asked.

"Fae creatures, yes," she said. "They used to live all over Europe, Britain, and Ireland. Now I keep them here hoping that I can find a place for them where they'll go unmolested."

I could see into some of the huts as we passed, and I realized that, while they looked like wooden huts, the interiors were made from various things, chief among them being parts of the FEMA tents I'd seen earlier. Several had small cookstoves and other simple conveniences.

"How do you keep all this alive?"

"Above us are full-spectrum sunlamps activated in time with the sunrise. In addition, heated air is pumped from above via those vents." She pointed to several dark recesses in the ceiling. "As for food, they all share the duties of cooking, gardening, and cleaning."

"There must be remote places to go that are better for them." I couldn't believe there was nowhere to hide.

"If there were, I'd send them there, but humans have claimed the entire fucking planet, and any temperate open spaces are occupied by territorial creatures, such as werewolves and the like."

A man, about two feet tall and oddly proportioned, walked over. His head, hands, and feet appeared much too large for his diminutive body. On his head, he sported a red mushroom-like cap. His mouth was full of sharp teeth.

"Hello, Ms. Carson," he said in a perfect British accent.

Marcella shook his hand. "Hello, Salloweye. How have you been?"

"Same as always. The wife is wondering when you'll stop in for dinner again. She misses adult conversation, and she said something about continuing your discussion on— post-modernism?"

"As soon as I can, you know that I am busy. By the way, Salloweye, this is Cait Reagan, my girlfriend."

"Aye." Salloweye stuck out his hand, and I shook it with a wide smile. He returned it with a toothy grin. "So are we gonna eat this one like the last one?"

"No, Salloweye, you can't eat this one." Her deadpan delivery made me wonder if they were kidding.

"She's the only one that gets to eat me," I interjected with a cheeky wink.

Salloweye stuck a sausage-like finger under his little hat and scratched for a moment. Then, after an awkward silence, he busted out in peels of thunderous laughter, too deep for his small frame. Marcella, for her part, looked absolutely mortified.

"Oh, you're gonna fit in just fine around here," Salloweye said. "Ms. Carson, please do come by soon. My wife won't shut up about those art books, and she's got some new paintings she wants you to see. She'll drive me mad soon."

"I will, Salloweye, as soon as I'm able." We bid him goodbye, and Marcella gave him a kind smile.

Salloweye tipped his cap to Marcella and patted me on the thigh. His laughter receded as he walked back into the little underground forest.

"He was kidding about eating people, right?" I asked Marcella after I thought he was out of earshot.

Marcella laughed. "Only partly, from what Salloweye tells me, humans used to be quite the delicacy. Cait, you really are a natural. You have a way of endearing yourself to people: your friendship with Daryl, Bian just loves you, and now Salloweye.

It is so gratifying to watch."

"I never considered myself that way. Most of the guys just think I'm an icy bitch at work."

She kissed me gingerly on the cheek and then took my hand, leading me on. "They're guys. Now come along."

"So, that's a redcap?"

"Yes," Marcella said. "We have a population here of about thirty. Salloweye's clan had dwindled from several hundreds when I found them. According to him, they are the last of them, so I brought them here. It was better than just waiting for their habitat to be destroyed."

The trees gave way to a tiny village, and numerous redcaps and brownies approached Marcella with lists of needs and various blessings. She took it all in stride, stopping to chat with men, women, and children whose only crime, as far as I knew, was that they looked different.

"Where did they all come from?"

"Mostly from Europe, though camp three is where the Lamia live. Being a reclusive set, they live alone."

"Wait, Lamia? Like Medusa?" My interest was now thoroughly piqued.

"Somewhat, but the baleful gaze is just a myth, and they don't have snakes for hair. They look like shorter versions of Bian. I managed to pull them from the Paris sewers. Don't ask me how they ended up there; I have no idea. But, they've literally nowhere to go to avoid discovery."

"How many people live here?"

"In this community? Two-hundred-four at last count. There are a few expecting mothers, so the number may have changed."

"Expecting mothers?" I hissed. "Oh my God, Marcella. What is the infant mortality rate like down here?"

"Very high; one in three won't make it." Her voice was neutral, but I could see the pain in her eyes.

"What about medical care?"

"I have a doctor who comes in every so often to help, and

I take some to him when I have time. But that's not nearly enough. There are eight other camps like this, and I just can't keep up with the need?"

I stopped and stared at her, thunderstruck. "Wait, you did all this? I spent a summer in college interning with an emergency crisis contractor overseas. This is a heavy lift. We spent over a million dollars just to build schools and shelters for a village of fifty. You said there are nine of these total?" I whistled in astonishment.

Marcella looked around, sounding embarrassed. "I had a great deal of help, and it was a very long hard slog. Now, we're out of space. Eventually, people will start dying, or they'll be discovered, and that could be worse. I'm at my wit's end trying to keep this working.

"It started small, but habitat destruction, logging, and pollution continue unabated. Before I knew it, over a thousand people were living down here in these slums. That's the real reason I started Carson Logistics. So I could find a way to provide for these people. With twenty lifetimes of experience, I thought I'd be different from every other 'white savior,' but I'm not. And now they have nowhere to go. I've just made a mess. Humans, on the surface, are destroying everything in their path and all I can do is try to prolong the suffering. It's hellish." She rubbed her face and covered her mouth.

"How long do you think before it's untenable?"

"A year, maybe two? Assuming no one here gets an infectious disease."

"What happens then?"

"I don't know, Cait. I'm terrified for them. If they go to the surface, it's almost assured they'll be persecuted and just as likely murdered or hemmed up in some kind of internment camp. Look what Hitler did to the Jews, or Roosevelt to the Japanese, or Trump to Latin children; it's fucking despicable, and they were human. Just think what they might do to poor Salloweye and his children."

I watched her in sympathy and wonder. I hadn't realized

that she was supporting an entire city beneath Boston. She wasn't just providing medical care for the sick; she was feeding, housing, and, I suspected, educating a thousand or so people. I knew the logistics of such an undertaking; it was staggering.

"How are you managing for money?" I asked.

"So far, we're fine, but eventually, the expenditures will become so large that I can no longer hide it from the board. Even though a lot of this comes from my own resources, I couldn't have ever provided this without the company's help. It's all booked to various charitable efforts for taxation, but essentially, I'm embezzling from my own company to support this."

I had a sudden thought. "You know," I said, looking around. "I have an idea on how we can turn this around and possibly make it work. Tell me you have some records of the people living here."

"Yes, we've kept records of immigration and birth almost since the beginning. Almost everyone living down here was born here."

"Who else knows about this?" I asked, curious how much help we might find.

"Just a handful outside these communities. The other vampires all know. I couldn't have done this without bargaining for their help. Of course, they all think I'm mad. Ninetta knew, and so did Jesse. I have a couple of trusted people at the office. And, now you."

"Is anyone down here acceptable enough to people on the surface to serve as a sympathetic spokesperson?"

Marcella looked at me, and it seemed the light went on. "Oh, yes," she said, and her face cracked into a cautious smile. "I think I have just the person.

45

We walked further through the camp and stepped into another tunnel that was as neat and tidy as the one running from the warehouse. We passed three side passages that ran off the tunnel in various directions; Marcella indicated that those were closed off because of instabilities. The scent of salt and brine became more pungent—an alluring song filtered through the tunnel, almost hypnotic.

Marcella touched my shoulder, pulling me out of my reverie. "You'll need to stay focused in here, Cait. The song you hear can affect us, and you can fall under its spell. I'll keep you safe, but I don't fancy getting wet."

"Who is that?" I asked, suddenly extremely curious.

"You'll see."

At the end of the tunnel was another chamber, about half the size of the first and decorated very differently, mimicking a tropical beach on a sunny eighty-degree day. The ceiling above was animated with puffy clouds. The floor was covered in sand except for a group of ten bungalows along the wall. One of them held a young human-looking woman with blue-dyed hair at a high-end computer. The rest of the cavern was filled with women from every ethnicity in various states of dress, though most were nude. All of them were fit and beautiful.

In one corner was a small open lagoon-like pool under several sun lamps. The walls around it were painted like a tropical seascape. I couldn't see into the lagoon itself, but it was undoubtedly the source of the mesmerizing music.

"Okay, what's with lesbian beach blanket bingo?" I asked, still dazzled by the display of beautiful skin.

Marcella laughed. "They're mermaids, Cait."

My eyes went wide. "Real mermaids? You're shitting me."

"No, I am not, and these are the last of their kind, at least as far as I know."

"I see seventeen, and I think there are some in the pool. Is that it?"

"Twenty-two in total." Marcella looked as if she might cry.

The young woman I'd seen on the computer walked up to us and wrapped Marcella in a tight hug.

"I wondered when you'd be back," she said smiling. "Who's the gorilla?" She pointed that last comment at me. I supposed, compared to her skinny ass, I was built like a gorilla. But I didn't appreciate the comparison.

"Gretchen, please mind your manners," she said. "This is my girlfriend, Cait. Cait, this is Gretchen."

"Hi Gretchen," I said, putting my hand out. She didn't take it; she just waved. "You have a girlfriend, Marcella? Wow. I thought by now everything had shriveled up."

"Gretchen! Honestly," Marcella protested and popped Gretchen on the butt playfully.

I tried to stifle a snort of laughter and failed. The kid was precocious, that was for sure.

"Well, it was good seeing you, and it was nice meeting your gorilla friend." Gretchen dodged another butt slap from Marcella. As she walked off, Gretchen stuck her tongue out at me. In return, I flicked my tongue up to my nose and winked. She flushed deep red and hurried away. I grinned in triumph.

"Don't mind Gretchen; she's brilliant but precocious. She doesn't get much socialization that's not on social media or video chat."

"Um," I said, looking around at the encampment. "Forgive my ignorance, but it's a wide ocean out there with hundreds or thousands of uncharted islands. Why are they here?"

"The reasons you'd expect, pollution and overfishing. Microplastics are harmful to humans, but they are potentially deadly for these women. So, everything they consume has to be carefully monitored. The lagoon water has been specially treated to strip out pollutants, and the air is pumped down through multiple filters. We have to make up for the lack of other natural minerals in different ways, primarily through their diet, which is farmed, frozen, and shipped.

"If they wished, they could go topside and stay there, eating human food, living human lives, and in short order, they'd become almost human. They might even live relatively long lives if they were careful about their bathing and eating habits, but they'd still die far too young.

"I'm looking into something more extensive to relocate them to an island in the Caribbean potentially, but there are other risks even if we could solve the pollution problem. Could you imagine the exploitation they'd suffer if they were discovered?

"It's things like this that tax my faith in people. Humans consume their way from crisis to crisis, only working hard on a problem when it bites them in the proverbial arse."

I shivered at the idea. I could easily see the US Government using these kids as guinea pigs for experiments or, worse, turning them into killers for the Navy.

I pulled off my boots and socks, enjoying the feel of the sand as we walked toward the lagoon. A gentle heated breeze blew from a vent on one wall. All the place needed was a few palm trees. Several sets of eyes followed us. More than a few eyed me suspiciously. I tried to ignore them.

"I could spend a week down here, just enjoying the atmosphere."

"I should think so," Marcella said playfully.

"Why, Ms. Carson, are you suggesting that my motives for such an excursion would be less than pure?"

Marcella's demeanor turned to mock primness. "Most certainly not. And I have never stayed down here for more than a few minutes, myself. No, ma'am."

The mermaids in the lagoon looked very different from my expectations. Princess Ariel, they were not. Their skin appeared smooth, their bodies sharklike. Black, soulless eyes watched us with predatory intent. Razor-sharp teeth filled their mouths, and their hands ended in vicious claws. Their upper bodies still resembled humans to some extent, but it was just a passing likeness—except for their faces. Other than their teeth, their faces were beautiful.

As it turned out, the singing came from a group of three sitting on the rocks in the far corner. Unlike either Gretchen or those in the water, the singers were different, halfway transformed. I asked Marcella about it.

"This is their usual form," she said, pointing to the water. "But, they are shapeshifters after a fashion, similar to werewolves. Unlike most werewolves, mermaids have no control of their shapes once submerged in saltwater."

One of the mermaids swam up to us and pulled herself halfway out of the water. Swiftly, her upper body transformed into that of a beautiful woman probably in her late twenties, the spitting image of Gretchen, except her hair was dyed pink.

"Hi Marcella," she said, propping herself upon a rock.

"Speak of the devil; this is Kaja," Marcella said.

I leaned down and stuck out my hand. "I'm Cait. I met your sister."

"Yeah, I saw you talking to her," she said, shaking my hand politely. "You're that vampire cop I saw on the Internet. That was so cool. Can Gretchen and I get an interview with you at some point?"

"An interview? I suppose. Are you a journalist?"

"Really? Oh my God, this will push our subscribership through the roof."

"Hold on," Marcella said firmly. "Cait and I are thinking of a way to make that possible, but that may take a bit. So you'll have to wait."

"Marcella, Cait's trending right now. We need to jump on

this."

"I'll see what I can do," Marcella said noncommittally.

We bid our goodbyes to Kaja and Gretchen and headed for the door. A deep sadness suddenly struck me as I looked back. Despite how friendly Kaja and Gretchen were, I wasn't stupid enough to think they were 'nice people.' Mermaids had a reputation for luring sailors to their deaths. And, given that their song was still pressing on my thoughts, it was probably well earned. But they were sentient beings, and we'd ruined their habitats. They were going extinct.

"You know, if protected, they'll live at least a hundred and fifty years each, and almost a hundred of those will be child-bearing years. Any human man can mate with them. They can survive." I placed a sympathetic hand on Marcella's shoulder, and she sighed heavily. It sounded like she was trying to convince herself more than me.

"If it weren't for the pollution, they'd be a robust lot. In the meantime, like the redcaps and brownies, many of them hold down remote jobs and help with the expenses as best they can. Gretchen works in remote video editing, and she's quite the prodigy at it. She and Kaja have a YouTube channel called The Mermaid Twins, where they laze about in the lagoon and pick apart movies they've seen. It's quite funny. You should watch it. There's a PO box delivery for them a few times a week with newly released movies sent by the studios. Their review of Disney's 'The Little Mermaid' had me pissing myself."

I stifled a laugh. "You're kidding, right?"

"No, I am not." Marcella smiled, but it didn't reach her eyes. Her desolate expression told me all I needed to know. This level of support was unsustainable. Something had to change outside this little haven. "They're not going to make it, are they?"

"No, Cait, probably not. We need serious research into some way to protect them against the ravages of pollution. Something that doesn't involve—all of this." Marcella gestured at the carefully purified artificial cavern. She ran a frustrated hand through her long blond hair, and I could see tears floating on the edges of her lashes.

I looked back at Gretchen, suddenly enraged at what people were doing to the planet. It seemed like such an insurmountable problem, not because it couldn't be done, but because humans were a stupid lot. We were handed a paradise, and all we knew how to do was destroy it.

46

We spent the remaining hours of Tuesday morning making out after retiring to the bedroom. But, both of us drifted off in the middle as the sun rose. It wasn't a terrible way to fall asleep, but it was kind of funny. One moment, we were hot and heavy; the next, we were ostensibly dead to the world.

I woke early for some reason. Nothing seemed out of place, but I couldn't get back to sleep. I looked at my watch—1:00 PM. Outside it had rained at some point, leaving ice dangling in the bare limbs like drops of liquid light. The scintillating patterns of afternoon sunshine sparkled and shifted as the branches swayed in the wind. Frost covered the ground below, leaving me feeling as if I were standing in a bowl of silver mist lit with a million prisms. My senses were so different now, so vivid. Every day things had become extraordinary, and extraordinary things, like this view, had become beguilingly beautiful. I could have stood there until sunset, but my musings were interrupted as my skin began to crawl, and a violent shiver ran down my back. I sighed heavily— the hunger.

Down in the kitchen, I pulled a fresh bag of blood from the Traulsen, chuckling at the memory of Ninetta trying to keep me out of it that first day. I still hadn't asked Marcella where she got the blood; I wasn't sure I wanted to know. After my encounter with Pauline, the cold blood tasted stale and listless.

It was a little like finding yesterday's coffee in the car the following day. But it satisfied my hunger for the most part. "Well, this sucks," I said to the air as I drank.

"Sorry, ma'am, but we haven't anything fresher," a man's voice said from the doorway, causing me to jump. I turned to find a tall man, at least six-foot-three, standing in the doorway. He filled out a black three-piece suit complete with a tastefully striped tie of blue, yellow, green, and red. Beautiful green eyes sparkled from under his business cut of thick red hair. He looked like a movie version of something between an expensive butler and private security.

I walked over and offered my hand. "You must be Robert."

"And you must be Ms. Cait," he replied with a voice like warm chocolate. "It's a pleasure to make your acquaintance." He took my hand and kissed it.

I wasn't interested, but the gesture made me blush all the same. No one, and I mean, no one, had ever kissed my hand before in introduction. "Wow, you are a smooth one, aren't you? It's nice to meet you as well. And, you are quite wrong, Robert; I see something much fresher right here in front of me." I winked and went back to the table to finish my blood.

Robert cleared his throat. "Rather droll, ma'am. Would you prefer me filleted or roasted?"

I laughed at the joke and then imitated a British accent. "Excellent riposte, sir. I think we'll get along splendidly."

"Goodness, I'm sure we'll do fine if you never do *that* again."

I stuck my tongue out at him, wiggling it, then dropped into a brogue. "Yeah, I made bags of the accent, for sure. But ya don' need to eat the head off me."

"A bloody mick, brilliant," Robert muttered, and we both chuckled. I noted a bit of swagger and military bearing as he took off his suit jacket, laid it carefully over the chair, and walked to the coffee maker.

"Where did you serve?"

He sat down across from me. "Garmsir, Afghanistan. Royal Marines. You?"

"Mosul. Two tours. Left me with a gammy arm." I held it up. "Blown up in 2009. But it could have been worse."

He tapped his right leg. It made the plastic thunk-thunk sound of a false limb. "Certainly could have been."

"I'm sorry," I said with genuine sincerity.

"Not to worry. The replacement's pretty good. I can run on it very well, though I won't break any records. So, onward I march, I suppose."

A kindred spirit, I thought. I suspected his service record played a part in Marcella hiring him.

"Indeed," I said, lifting my cup in salute. Robert poured himself a cup of coffee and sat down with me.

"Isn't there some kind of rule against fraternizing with the household?" I asked, really just joking.

"It's frowned upon. But I don't care about all that. Marcella didn't select me because I adhere to silly customs. I'm an experienced soldier, and I'm a guild member. But, also, I have known Marcella for a few years and am well aware of what she is. It makes things— simpler." He leaned in conspiratorially. "And she pays above rate," he whispered.

I laughed. "I bet she does." I poured more blood into my cup. "To old friends, departed and gone." I offered another toast.

Robert returned it. "To old friends."

I drank the rest of my blood, feeling the bees crawling under my skin finally recede. "Can I ask how you and Marcella met?"

"Sure, you can ask." He joked and took a sip of coffee. "Seriously, though, I was down on my luck after being discharged, and Marcella found me drinking away my misery at a pub in Crowthorne. The next thing I know, she's convinced me to dump the booze and go to University. I got a degree in hospitality at Cornell here in the US and then worked for a few wankers back home. For a while, I even worked for her friend Elizabeth. Don't know if you've met her."

"Only briefly," I replied, sipping from my cup.

"Yes, well, Elizabeth got herself into a pickle one night and needed help disposing of a body. I agreed to help her, but then she tried to wipe my memory with that mental thing you do, except it didn't work." He tapped the side of his head. "I didn't let Elizabeth in on that fact initially, though eventually, she figured it out. Turns out, I'm immune. It's a rare gift, apparently."

My eyebrows shot up. "That's fascinating. May I?"

"Sure, yeah, give it a go."

I looked Robert in the eye and tried to pull his thoughts into mine, I could feel him, but the soft spot that should be at the center of his mind wasn't there; it was solid and impenetrable. "How did Elizabeth not know that it wasn't working? It's like trying a whammy a brick wall."

"Marcella says that Elizabeth isn't very good at it. Worse than most. I guess that's why she couldn't tell."

The elevator opened, and Marcella stepped into the room. "Oh, good, you've met. Wonderful. So, how are you getting on?"

I grinned and barked a laugh. "Suckin' diesel. We're kindred spirits, I think."

"I thought you might be," Marcella said, grabbing a glass from the cabinet. "So, what did you talk about?"

"Well, Robert was filling me in on Elizabeth's shortcomings in the whammy department."

Marcella laughed. "Yes, she's somewhat hamfisted when it comes to that. On the other hand, she has a nasty ability to clamp down on a person's will and snuff out their senses. It works on humans and vampires alike."

"Well, that's handy."

Marcella poured some of the blood into her glass and sat with us. "Unless you're the one she's using it on."

"Fair enough." I didn't bother to argue the point. I barely knew the lady.

My phone buzzed on the table shortly after Marcella had finished her blood and headed back upstairs to get a shower.

"Homicide, Reagan."

My mother was on the other end, and she sounded nervous.

"Cáitlín, are you alone?"

I hopped up from the table, holding up a finger to Robert, indicating I'd be back in a moment. Once I was in the sitting room with the door closed, I continued.

"Okay, I'm alone. What's wrong?"

"I need you to come to see me at my office. Don't bring Marcella." Now that I was paying attention, I could tell her voice was shaking.

"Mom, tell me what's going on."

"I will, but I need you to come over right away. And be quick about it. Don't tell Marcella you're coming."

"Okay, okay. I'm on my way. Let me get dressed. Mom, by the way, before we see each other, there's something I need to tell you."

"Cáitlín, you can tell me whatever you like when you get here, but please hurry." She hung up.

I stared at my phone in confusion. I'd never had a call like that from my mother, so I hurried upstairs to find Marcella just stepping from the shower. I didn't waste time with a shower and got dressed.

"Everything okay?" Marcella asked as I was gathering my gear.

"Yeah," I said. "There's something I need to do today. I'll be back in a bit."

"You want me to come with you? It'll only take a moment —."

"No," I interrupted. "I need to take care of this myself. I won't be out long."

She looked at me suspiciously, but I ignored her and left, taking the stairs to the garage.

47

I struggled with a feeling of dread as I climbed the steps of Lyon's hall. Stepping out onto the third floor, I could see that my mother's door was open, and a brunette co-ed was leaving. I ducked my head slightly, not meeting the girl's eyes as she passed.

I stopped just outside and took in a deep breath before entering. This was going to be complicated.

My mother was sitting at her desk, pouring over a sizeable, ancient-looking tome of a book. She looked up and gasped, jumping out of her seat and hurrying over to me.

"Cáitlín, what happened? You're so pale." She touched my face, her thumb stroking my cheek as if she were trying to rub the odd color off of it. "And so cold. Oh, God, no. She turned you. Damn that woman!"

My eyes went wide. "Ma? How do you know?"

My mother swallowed hard. "Sit down, dear; let's talk."

I started to feel a little shaky as she pulled her chair around, and we sat in front of her desk, face to face.

"Cáitlín, I have known what Marcella is for many years."

My eyes widened in shock. "What?" My brain ran in a hundred directions at once, and my anxiety rose. "Ma, has she been watching me this whole time? Did she do this to me on purpose?"

My mother closed her eyes and blew out a breath. When

she opened them, the deep sadness was beyond anything I had ever seen in her face, not since Da died.

"Ma, what is going on?"

"Your father—" she started, then stopped, blowing out another heavy sigh as tears welled in her eyes. "Cáitlín, I know you love your father, but you have to know, he wasn't the man you thought he was. And he got himself into some serious trouble."

I pulled a handkerchief from my pocket and handed it to her with a shaking hand. "What do you mean?"

She sighed. "At this point, you're likely to find out eventually." She collected herself and wiped her tears. "Before you were born, your da was involved with the Patriarca's."

"What?" The Patriarca's were an infamous crime family in Boston. I couldn't believe that my father had been mixed up with them.

"It doesn't matter. Erik Schmidt, one of the—"

"I know who he is," I interrupted. "Why is this the first I'm hearing of this?"

"Because you were a child. What good would it have done to tell you after he'd died? You loved him. I didn't want to ruin that."

"So you let me believe a lie?" I shot back. "How was that supposed to help?"

"Cáitlín, you weren't supposed to be involved in this."

"Involved in what? What does any of this have to do with Marcella or me? And why would you say something so shitty about Da?" I demanded, raising my voice, a deep rage building inside me.

"He wasn't your da!" My mother shouted, then she gasped and covered her mouth.

I shrank back, speechless. "What?"

She composed herself and calmed. "Our marriage was troubled. Michael was cheating on me almost from the start."

I blinked.

"The year before you were born, I discovered his

indiscretions. So, I returned to Tourmakeady, and I ended up having a fling with Donny Moylan."

I ran a hand through my auburn hair. "Uncle Donny?"

The man we called 'Uncle Donny,' my favorite of ma's friends, had taken me to Limerick to shop on one of our trips to Ireland. As I thought about it, something began to nag at the back of my mind, something I should remember, but I couldn't grasp it. Before I could think on it further, she continued her story.

"Yes, dear. And it was the worst mistake of my life."

"What are you saying? Did you not want me?"

"No! Don't be ridiculous. I love you, and so did your da. Donny didn't want kids, and he was perfectly happy with the arrangement. Your father was thrilled for us to be back together. He swore he'd treat you like his own daughters! And he did," She paused, and her face fell. "'til it all went wrong. I promise you; I didn't know what he'd done."

"Mother? What is it? What did he do?" Before she'd answered the question, though, something else occurred to me. "That's why Larson said I wasn't the first vampire he'd run across. Wait, daughters?"

She brushed past the question. "He and Michael were going to be indicted when the FBI came for the Patriarca's. Erik got them out of it. I didn't ask how at the time. But, I found out later that, in exchange, they had promised to hand you over to Erik at some point."

"Oh, my God! Why?"

"I'll show you in a minute. When Schmidt came for you, Mike and Bill reneged. A week later, they were both shot." She trailed off.

"The night Michael was killed, Marcella came to me, and she offered to keep you safe." Tears were running down her face now, and she sobbed. "I was desperate. I knew what she was, but I didn't dare turn her down. Schmidt was coming for you."

I didn't know what to do. So, I sat very still. "And what did she want in return?"

"Nothing. She's never asked for anything." She started to shake.

"So, was that what you were talking about in the hospital—when you switched to Swedish?"

"No, not exactly. She protected you from Schmidt for sixteen years. So when Gabe attacked you and Marcella said she wanted you to come home with her, I knew she'd protect you again. But, it never occurred to me that she'd turn you. I didn't know, mo chroí." She put her face in her hands and began to cry again.

I pulled her into a hug and shushed her. "It's okay, Ma. You only did what you thought was right." I didn't know what else to say. My mind was reeling. Mike Reagan wasn't my father. My mother had known who Marcella was. She'd been keeping this from me for years. What else had she not told me? And Marcella! She'd known who I was from the start. "Ma, I have to know. Why did Marcella bring me into her life? Do you have any idea what her game is? She says she loves me, but—all this. I don't know anymore."

After a long few minutes, she stopped sobbing and wiped her eyes. "I don't know, child. But I don't think courting you was part of her plan. I've spoken to her since, and she seems sincere if very torn about the situation." She then held out her hand. "Come with me, Cáitlín. I'll show you why Schmidt wants you."

We crossed campus to Higgins Hall and entered the imaging lab. An Asian man in a lab coat with safety goggles on his head was staring at a giant smoking drill. Next to it sat a fire extinguisher. On the bench in front of him rested the tablets Marcella had mentioned. The air reeked of ozone, burnt electronics, and smoke.

My mother crossed over to him. "Hi, Kenji. This is my daughter, Cáitlín. Cáitlín this is Dr. Kenji Imai."

He removed a thick glove and wiped his hand on his jeans, offering it to me. "Hi, your mother has told me a lot about you. She's very proud."

I took his hand, and Kenji paused for a moment. He seemed like he wanted to say something, but the moment passed, and he released my hand.

"Any luck?" My mother asked Kenji.

Kenji studied me for a moment, then answered. "No. I've tried everything. This is an industrial drill with a diamond head that I borrowed from the materials lab, and it didn't even scratch it. Nothing I've tried will hurt them in the slightest. They look like granite, but it's some kind of material I've never seen."

"Are you trying to destroy them?" I asked, looking first at the smoking drill and down at the tablets. This close to them, I felt something, almost like they were calling.

"Yes," my mother answered. "Marcella asked me to."

I looked at her, surprised. "Marcella did? Why?"

"To protect you."

Confusion played across my face. "What do you mean?" I reached out absently and touched one of the tablets. There was a flash, and I jerked my hand back. It felt like placing my finger in a light socket, almost electrical. "Ouch."

Kenji grabbed my hand and looked at it; it was unharmed. "Wow, they haven't done that before. What did you do?"

"I—I don't know. I just touched it."

"That's what I mean. That's why Schmidt wants you," my mother said. "Kenji, show her the rest."

Doctor Imai walked over and picked up the small tablets, placing them under some kind of sophisticated camera. As he did so, he began to make idle chit-chat. "So, is your mother just as bossy at home as here?"

"Hey!" My mother protested.

I laughed, deciding I liked Kenji. "Absolutely, worse even, I'm sure. She was a slave driver when I was a kid."

"I was not," my mother muttered, pursing her lips.

Kenji turned on a monitor, showing the feed from the camera. The tablets appeared with complex pictograms hovering just above their surface. "What are those?"

"Oh, that's probably the coolest thing. So the marks in the tablets aren't a language; they're angular reflectors of some sort. We shifted the frequency of the light sensors in the camera to cover a wider portion of the spectrum." He spun in his chair, looking at me. "The engravings reflect more wavelengths than we can see with the naked eye. We're looking at the regular spectrum plus infrared, turning what looks like simple tool marks into that elaborate cartouche. It's remarkable. I've studied every kind of imaging known to man, and I can't make heads or tails of it. We can't even take a sample of the material to see what they're made of."

I gestured to the pictograms. "Can you translate that?"

"I already have," she answered softly. "But we'll get to that in a minute. Kenji, are you sure these are safe to touch?"

"They should be. There are no indications of radiation."

I reached out and touched the stone tablets. They gave me the same mild shock, but it quickly settled into a tingling sensation. A streamer of energy quickly spread between them, coalescing into a purple and black whirlpool. It was eerily silent, and the lights in the lab dimmed slightly.

"This feels weird," I said, then gasped as my entire body lit up inside like a Christmas tree. Bolts of energy shot through my blood vessels, causing my muscles to clench and unclench. Strength permeated every part of me, and I felt almost invincible. The hunger rushed in, forcing my fangs to extend. My thoughts twisted with rage, hatred, and a desire to destroy everything.

I sensed Kenji's and my mother's minds near me. My mother's mind was strangely shrouded, and I could only feel the surface. It was much like Robert's, though more a deep pool than a brick wall. I pushed deeper, hearing her whimper.

Let her scream. I thought callously. She'd left me to Marcella. She'd done this to me. She'd abandoned me, the bitch.

I had a flash of myself again, with short hair, looking about fifteen, but I couldn't hold on to it. Kenji's mind was chaotic and jumbled like some growling beast, all instinct and baser thoughts— food, water, sex. I snatched at it but couldn't get hold of anything. Then another mind opened before me, seemingly far away, like an echo in a canyon, almost a reflection. My mother screamed and clutched her head. Before I could probe further, Kenji yanked me away. The rage receded, along with the rush of power, leaving me with a deep feeling of remorse. "Oh, God, Ma, I'm so sorry. I don't know what came over me."

My mother stood up, leaning hard against the table and breathing heavily.

Kenji had returned to his screen, staring, mouth agape. "Wow, look at this."

"I don't see anything," I said, trying to figure out what I was missing. "It just looks like a black dot at the center of the energy stream."

"Look at it at ten-times magnification with the light emissions masked out." He selected part of the image and blew it up. A shiver of anxiety ran through me. There, in the magnified photo, was a circle. And within that, I could see something I'd only seen in my wigged out visions when I had been dying; a blasted volcanic landscape precisely as I'd dreamed it.

"Oh, God, it's real." I clamped a hand over my mouth.

"Yes." My mother said, looking at me askance.

"That place. I've been there. Or at least I've dreamed I've been there. It's hard to explain." I reached out and touched the screen as if my fingers might pass through it, naming it just a horrible dream.

"Cáitlín, that place, it's a hellscape. There are things there that we can scarcely imagine. And these tablets are designed to open a gateway to it. According to the tablets, it's a source of magic. The kind of magic we tell stories of. But it is also a place of unspeakable evil."

I stared at the tablets. The urge to touch them was powerful, but the awful feeling that followed stayed my hand."

My mother tugged at my sleeve, getting my attention. "Are

you okay?"

"No, mother, I'm not." I pointed to the screen. "What does that say."

"It's a prophecy of sorts. Along with the description of a ritual." My mother began to recite the writing in English.

"Do not open the black gate, the place of the Avra, closed by the Mother of Darkness, the Phantom Queen. The beasts of hate lay within.

On one side is the life of a child; on the other is the death of the world. Bonded by two birthrights, she shall decide the fate of all. The dark ones come for knowledge and power. The older shall find the younger in pain. The magic of the world will be renewed."

My mother finished and touched my face. "You are the only one who can make them work. That's why Schmidt wants you."

My mother read through the rest of the tablets, describing a ritual that involved some kind of device bathed in the blood of power, whatever that meant.

Just as my mother was finishing explaining everything, my phone rang. I answered it. "Reagan."

"Cait?" It was Carlos. "I need you to come to Schroeder. There's something you need to see. Right now."

"Okay, I'm on my way. I'll be there in twenty."

"Mom, that was Carlos; I have to go."

"Before you go—" She paused, collecting herself. "There's something else I need to tell you."

I rolled my eyes. "I'm not sure I can take any more. Tell me later, okay? I need to get to work."

"Okay, come by the house after work." I bid them goodbye, giving my mother a hug and a peck on the cheek. Then I left.

* * *

Carlos wasn't at his desk, so I browsed my email, waiting for him to show up. It wasn't more than a few minutes when Agents Reynolds and Rees accosted me.

I tasted Reynold's scent in the air, recognizing his shitty cologne instantly. "What do you want, Reynolds?" I asked without looking up.

"We need to talk." His tone was demanding.

"No, Reynolds, we don't. If you want to talk, here, call this guy." I pulled Phillip's business card out of my wallet. He could go through Marcella's lawyer.

Reynolds took the card and set it back on my desk. "We know."

I smiled crookedly and continued going through my email, waiting for Carlos. I still didn't bother to look at him. "Know what?"

"What you and Ms. Carson are," Reynolds said ominously.

"Lesbians, Agent Reynolds. It's okay, you can say it. Also, I don't think it's been illegal in Massachusetts for some time." I did turn to look at him, then, smiling sweetly.

Reynolds' face flushed with anger. "That's not what I mean, and you know it."

I didn't bother to play with him. Instead, I reached into his head and latched onto his will, snuffing out any agency, snagging Rees at the same time. I had been right; I could do it.

"Gentlemen, there is no such thing as Vampires. Furthermore, I don't know anything about Marcella Carson's business, so you need to leave and forget you saw me today." Both men turned and left the building. It was about as subtle as a sledgehammer, but it worked and got them out of my face. I wasn't sure if I would pay for it later, but I didn't care. I was sick of people being in my shit.

"Fuckers!" I muttered as I returned to the screen.

"Hey," Carlos said somberly as he walked up with a cup of coffee. "I just saw Reynolds and Rees. What did they want?"

"No clue. I sent them away. What are you doing here on your day off?"

Carlos raised an eyebrow, then frowned. "Sent them away? Did you—"

I looked up at him. "Yes."

Carlos' frown deepened. "Do you think that's a good idea? Glamor can have some nasty side effects."

"I don't care," I said, casually looking back to the screen. "I'm sick of those guys crawling up my ass and trying to strong-arm me."

"Hey!" Carlos shouted, causing me to jump slightly. "Those are people, Cait. You can't just go around fucking up their heads as you see fit. Or, did you forget what happened to Gabe?"

"How could I forget, Carlos. But, fuck, man. If Reynolds and Reese want to play hardball with me, I'll play hardball with them."

Carlos shook his head. "You've changed, Reagan. And not entirely for the better, I don't think. This is what I was afraid of. You're becoming like them."

"Fuck you, Carlos. I'm finally feeling like a whole person after years of suffering. Maybe I'm just sick of being a fucking doormat for everyone."

Carlos sighed. "I don't want to fight with you. But, you should give some hard thought to why you suddenly seem to think it's okay to push people around at your fuckin' whimsy."

I closed my eyes and sighed. "Fine, I'll think about it. What is it you wanted me to see?"

"The footage that TSA sent us verifying Marcella's entrance."

"Why? Did we miss something?"

Carlos took another sip of his coffee and pulled up the video on his computer.

I looked over his shoulder, watching several people pass

through passport control. Carlos grabbed the mouse and scrolled to where Marcella first walked up. As the border agent asked her questions, the bottom dropped out of my entire world. The person standing at the counter looked very much like Marcella Carson, amazingly so. But it wasn't Marcella Carson; it was Elizabeth Tyler. I wanted to throw up.

"Who is that?" Carlos asked, placing a hand on my arm.

"One of Marcella's friends, Elizabeth Tyler. Fuck, me."

Snatching up my phone, I almost dialed Marcella's number. Instead, on a hunch, I grabbed my burner and dialed the number Celeste had given me for Blackman's phone.

"Hello?" It was Marcella's voice. I couldn't think. I couldn't move. "Hello?" She said again; then, there was a long pause. "Oh, Goddess, Cait? Wait—."

I hung up. "Fuck this," I said and marched into the conference room. A dilapidated old wooden desk sat in one corner that had probably been there since Lazarus died. I snapped off one of the wooden legs and stalked toward the door.

Carlos grabbed me before I got very far. "Slow down, now, darlin'. We don't know what this means."

I jerked loose. "Yes, we do, Carlos. It means that she killed Caldwell and that the phone I chased down that fucking tunnel was hers. It means that she infected me and turned me on purpose." I dropped back and hissed at him, baring my fangs.

Carlos shot forward and grabbed me around the arms again, dropping his coffee and knocking the makeshift stake from my hands.

"Let go of me," I said, but there was no fight in it. "Let go." I beat at his chest weakly, tears flowing down my cheeks.

Carlos held me still. "You can't kill her, Cait. It'll be open season on you. The Vestry and the Council will call you rogue. You won't last a day."

"Why, Carlos? Why is this happening to me?" I pushed out of his arms and sat down in one of the chairs.

"Come back to my desk," he said cryptically. I got up and

followed him. He handed me some tissue, and I wiped my eyes, looking miserably at the pink tears.

"What have I done to myself?"

He dug into his bag for something but apparently couldn't find whatever he was looking for.

"Fuck it," I swore. "I at least need to find out why she did all this. I loved her, Carlos, and this is what she did."

"Okay," Carlos pulled me into an awkward hug, and for a moment, it felt like he was feeling my ass. "Go talk to her, but don't do anything stupid, and be careful."

48

I drove recklessly, lights and sirens blaring through rush hour traffic. I made the entire twenty-minute drive in just over ten. Jumping out of the Jeep as I parked in front of the building, I stalked toward Marcella's. So focused was I on my burning anger that I missed the white panel van on the corner.

The hood came down fast. Strong arms grabbed me and wrestled me into the van. All of my senses were extinguished before I could respond in any meaningful way other than thrashing wildly. *Elizabeth,* I thought. *I guess she's working for the other side.*

I felt nothing, and, honestly, I could have been like that for days. Eventually, though, the veil of shadow draped across my thoughts lifted, revealing a bare concrete cell. At one end was a thick steel door. The cell was eight feet or so long and maybe three feet wide. A light embedded in the ceiling provided the only illumination.

A thick steel cuff and heavy chain bound me to the wall. I yanked at it and was rewarded with stabbing pain. Long steel pins penetrated the flesh anchoring the cuff to my arm. If I wanted out, I'd have to rip my forearm off.

The cell itself, otherwise, was a featureless concrete block. I shifted on the floor, and something dug into my back from the waistband of my jeans, a slim card-like device with a light on it. It was a portable GPS tracker. The range was limited, but it meant someone knew where I was. Someone would find me. *Bless you, Carlos.* I slid the tracker into my back pocket.

"Hello Detective, my name is Schmidt," a voice said from beyond the door. "I believe you're feeling quite hungry, ja. We took the liberty of draining you some before putting you in there."

"You can go fuck yourself," I spat. "I know you don't care, but you've kidnapped a cop. I wouldn't give a rat's ass for your life at this point."

"Such language, my dear, I promise you'll not be harmed as long as you tell us what we need to know."

Keep him talking, I thought. "You don't need to go through all this. If you wanted directions or something, you could have just asked."

"They said you were prone to use humor. Good to see my information is solid. But, I need more than directions around town. Perhaps you'd be so good as to tell me where Marcella has hidden the tablets?"

"I have no idea. I guess you'll have to get it the old-fashioned way."

"Oh," he sounded almost gleeful. "I was hoping you'd say that. We have ways of making you talk." He laughed at his humor, and his footsteps receded into the distance.

I sat there for quite a while with the hunger burning under my skin, and I rubbed my arms unconsciously. It wouldn't be long before the shivers started. Exertion would make the situation worse, so I slept.

Sometime later, as night fell, I opened my eyes, yanked awake by the sudden influx of strength. Pulling myself gently to a sitting position, I saw a pretty female vampire with black hair and brown eyes standing in the doorway. She was dressed in 'basic bitch' wear: grey fleece leggings, brown riding boots, and a brown sweater, complete with white puffy vest. She sipped from a steel camp cup as she watched me. My tongue slipped out involuntarily, and I tasted blood. I'd half expected pumpkin spice.

After a minute of staring at me, she finally spoke. "They call me Nastasia."

"That's nice," I said snidely, giving her the finger.

She took another sip of the blood but said nothing.

"So, that's it; you're going to starve me until I talk?"

She raised an eyebrow and smiled over the cup as she took another sip. "Not exactly. We believe another incentive would be more effective." Nastasia stepped out of the doorway as two men threw a young girl into the room. She looked no more than seventeen. I could hear the girl's heartbeat racing and smell her fear.

"Enjoy your snack, Cait," Nastasia crowed from beyond.

The hunger roared within me, and I backed away from the girl, eyes wide. I covered my mouth with my fist and pressed my lips together.

"Stand by the door," I ordered, stomping as hard as I could on the urge to take her right then and there. My fangs extended, and my vision tunneled in on her.

As gently as I could manage, I asked her name.

"Katie," she said as she pressed against the door.

"Of course it is," I muttered, shaking my head. "Good girl, Katie. Stay where you are. Right now, I can't get to you without tearing off my arm. Do you know what is happening?"

Katie nodded. "Are you a vampire? The others told me you were." Her voice was so soft, so innocent, so frightened. I could sense her mind. It would be so easy to soothe her fear. But to do so meant loosing the hunger. It would only be a little bit, but I was terrified I'd lose control.

"Yes, Katie. My name is Cait. I will sit over here on one wall, and you stay by the door. Understand?"

"Okay." She sat down cross-legged, as directed.

"That's so that I can't reach you. I haven't fed in a while; being near me is dangerous." A violent shiver ran down my spine, and I started fidgeting. "Now, I'm not a bad person, and I didn't become this by choice. They want something from me that I can't give them." I knew this arrangement wouldn't last

373

long, but the talking was calming her fear and thus lowering my excitement. "I'm a cop. I've sworn to protect the public, and I don't want to hurt you."

"If you bite me, will I become one of you?" she asked. I tilted my head at that. It was an interesting question to ask. She was frightened, but the excitement I tasted in the air wasn't the terror I'd assumed; it was anticipation. She wanted to be turned. I had a momentary pang of sadness, but the hunger tore through it like tissue.

"No, Katie. That's not true. Now, how old are you, kid?"

"Fifteen." She had a bit of the street about her. They'd probably grabbed her near one of the homeless shelters.

"Where are you from?"

"South Boston, near Dorchester."

"I figured. Grew up in Dorchester myself. Parents?"

"What is this? Twenty-questions?"

"Look, kid," I snapped at her. "I'm trying to get to know you. It'll help me stay sane. The people who put you in here will let you die. They are going to let my hunger make me kill you. Don't you get it? The only thing keeping you alive is knowing who you are. It makes you a person and not just the walking equivalent of a drink box."

She shrank back slightly, and I realized that I was almost snarling at her. A few more feet of chain fell out of the wall, giving me enough slack to reach the door, enough to reach little Katie, enough to feed. "Fuck," I whispered.

"Detective Reagan, just tell us what we want to know, and we'll take her out of there." The voice was female, the accent English, deeper and richer than Marcella's, with a street quality. I was pretty sure it belonged to Elizabeth Tyler.

Katie stood then and started banging on the door, screaming in tears. "Please, I just want to go home."

Tears of rage and sympathy flowed down my cheeks as I listened to her pitiful cries. I shook with the effort of staying still, biting my lip.

Katie continued to plead. "Please, pick someone else. I want to go home. I have a little sister; she needs me."

I launched forward and grabbed Katie, wrapping my hand around her mouth. "Tell them nothing," I hissed. She struggled for a second, and then I finally broke down and allowed my will to settle onto hers. I twisted her fear into a deep sense of caring centered on me.

She stopped struggling and turned, burying her face in my chest. The tears still flowed, but she was quiet.

"I'm sorry, kid," I whispered, straining for control. "I'm so sorry."

"Cait, we'll take her home unharmed if you just tell us what we want to know."

I was having trouble thinking clearly. "What is it you want to know again?"

"Where are the tablets?" the voice asked. They followed a pretty standard enhanced interrogation playbook, one I knew well. Unfortunately, it was a playbook that often worked.

"I don't know," I replied flatly and heard footsteps as several people walked away, closing another large door somewhere.

"Are you going to kill me?" Katie asked, voice shaking and tiny.

I said nothing but shook my head no, placing a trembling finger to my lips to silence her. I pointed to my ear and the door. She seemed to get the message.

I leaned in very close to her. The hunger sang in my veins, desperate to drink. I set her in the back corner of the room, away from the door, and released my mental hold. To her credit, she did not move or scream, and I motioned for her to cover her eyes.

I stepped to the length of the chain, feeling the spikes in my arm tug painfully. I began to pull at the chain, grabbing at the edge of the door and digging the fingers of my right hand into the steel frame. The metal creaked and dented under my grip as I used it as leverage. The pain was excruciating, and I screamed in rage and agony as the spikes tore into my arm.

The door flew open, and a well-built male vampire tackled

me to the floor. I pushed my arm back into the steel sleeve and wrapped the chain around his neck in one swift movement, jerking sideways, disconnecting his spine. He continued to struggle, head canted at an impossible angle, and I dug my fingers into his neck, tearing his head from his shoulders. I ran back to the door and yanked at the chain with everything I had. My arm tore at the elbow with a sickening ripping of flesh and cracking of bone.

I fell to the floor, the stub pouring blood. I scrabbled forward but slipped. Slender arms grabbed my shoulders, trying to drag me out.

"Get away!" I snarled at Katie, causing her to run back. "I don't want to hurt you." I pulled myself forward and looked out the door. Beyond the cell, a dark hallway ran left and right. Safety lights burned sickly yellow in the darkness. I didn't get far before several vampires dragged me back inside, removed the dead vampire, and snatched Katie away, slamming the door behind them.

"Honestly, Detective, was that absolutely necessary?" Schmidt called through the rust-covered steel, voice snide and condescending. "I think you've earned punishment for your charge. Don't worry, though; we'll save some for you."

"You fucker," I whispered, knowing he could hear me. "I'll be the one that kills you, you fucking Nazi." His steps down the hallway stopped.

"Detective, I was not, nor have I ever been, a member of the Nazi party. I supported the allies during the war and even saved your precious Marcella's life. So, if you'll please dispense with the slurs, that would be appreciated."

"You're still an asshole," I muttered and dragged myself to a corner, huddling, my back to the door.

49

I pressed my face against the cold concrete. My body burned, and agony raged in my savaged arm. I laughed out loud, not that anything was funny. My emotions were out of control. What good is deep breathing when you no longer need oxygen? Thick tears like glycerin slid down my cheeks, each one banging in my ears as it plopped to the floor. I clawed at the wall with my good hand and cursed my sensitive ears as Katie's screams echoed into the darkened room.

My tongue flicked, pulling the velvet-copper taste of blood into my mouth. I tumbled into a vivid half-dream, walking through Leslie's, eyes on Pauline.

She leans against the wall in her painted-on jeans and leather boots. Her shirt clings to her young body, contoured by her soft, round breasts.

"Looks like you're alone now." I lick her ear suggestively, and Katie's beautiful young eyes stare back at me, hungry with desire.

I tried to banish the image, squeezing my eyes shut, but it wouldn't leave.

"Oh, God," she says as I lick at her throat, mesmerized, in the throes of lust.

"No, no, no," I whimpered as if the hunger could hear me. "You can't have her."

"Dear God, anyone, please let me die."

My throat grew tight, and my shoulder muscles taught. I

barely noticed the pain in my arm as the last of the blood in my body completed its grisly task, pulling new flesh and bone to order.

Katie's ecstatic intake of breath sounded from somewhere beyond the door.

"You bastards!" I shouted against the burning need within me. I had no more tears, only rage for another child I could not save. The door opened, and rough hands thrust Katie's limp body inside.

Before I could rush the door, they closed it and dropped the crossbar. I looked at Katie, black hair spilling across the blood-soaked floor. Her throat was torn open, draining her blood to the ground.

I dropped to her side, fighting against the screaming, pulsing hunger.

"Please," Katie whimpered. "I don't want to die."

I looked to the door. "Anyone, please help me!" There was no answer.

I battled furiously against my instincts, trying to put pressure on Katie's gaping wound, but it was no use. Her heart hammered, a massive drum driving through my body.

My vision distorted, and I realized that it wasn't Katie; it was Pauline. I shook my head, but Pauline remained.

"Come to me," she beckoned, smiling sweetly. Her voice was hollow and echoing, but I did as she bid. I dipped my head into the crook of her neck and drank deeply. Her hand grasped at my hair, weakly caressing through it while her blood, a flood of salt and ecstasy, filled my mouth. I shivered as the hunger took its final hold, forcing another long pull against her throat until the last of her light burned bright within me.

My arms shook, lifting my heavy, near immovable body away from Pauline, but it was Katie, lying on the floor.

"Oh, God!" I pleaded with her as I opened her mouth and tried desperately to get my body to release changed blood. But I had been so starved my body had consumed it before I could bring it forth. I ran my bloody hands through my hair. I didn't know what to do. They'd made me kill her. "Why?" I screamed.

"Please, don't die," I whispered as tears, real and thin, rained from my eyes to her face. Finally, with no other ideas, I reached up and tore open my own throat, letting my blood flow into Katie's mouth. *Please, turn,* I thought. *Please, turn. Please, be okay.*

For long moments, nothing happened, and I thought her dead. Then a grip, solid and powerful, slapped to the back of my neck, pulling me downward. Katie's eyes flew open, but there was nothing of the young girl within them. Her tongue slipped out and caressed the skin of my neck and chin, sweeping away the blood— her blood— that coated it. She bit down, new fangs descending into my flesh, tearing and pulling at my throat.

I pressed my hands to her shoulders and pushed away. She lurched unnaturally from the floor, burying her face in my neck and tearing at it again to reopen the closing wound.

I staggered, falling backward, but she held on, taking more blood, and I began to drift away.

It took a moment to martial my sluggish thoughts, but I pushed her off, sending her sailing to the corner of the room. "No!"

She rolled up, snarling and watching me, an animal waiting to strike.

The hunger still rode behind my eyes, and my emotions still tumbled through my head one after the other, fear, loathing, excitement. Now that I'd fed, I wanted a fight. Katie began stalking toward me, a predatory gleam in her narrowed eyes, still growing fangs bared. I marveled at the speed of her change, not instantaneous, but nothing as slow as mine. Katie hunched down, bunching muscles to strike.

"Stop!" I commanded at the top of my voice, shocked to feel the power within me rise into the command. She obeyed, flinching back to the corner. I stalked over imperiously and turned her head to face mine, eye to eye. All she had been lay submerged within a sea of wanton need for blood.

Oh, God, I thought. *She's a revenant.*

Until now, the concept was only a story. Revenants were terrible beasts craving only blood, like zombies. But the truth was far worse. This creature before me was flesh and blood and whole. It wasn't just some horror that skulked the night. Katie was still in there, somewhere, lost, the essence of her shrouded in the curse. I could feel that essence buried within, hurt and alone.

I reached out and cupped her face, holding her under my influence. It wasn't wholly slack; there was recognition of a sort there.

I caressed the poor child's head, and she bowed it before me. She wasn't an unthinking monster or a beast at all. She needed blood and lacked much agency beyond that.

"Can you speak?" I asked, knowing that she had undoubtedly understood my command.

"Y-y-y," she stuttered, but nothing coherent came out. Most of the Katie I had met was suppressed or gone, but she had understood the question.

"Sit."

Katie obeyed, sitting cross-legged, as you might expect from a kid her age. Her face was blank, and she worked her jaw involuntarily as her canines finished lowering into fangs. I sat down across from her.

You fucking bastards, I thought. *I will kill you all for this.*

I closed my eyes and reached out into the empty gulf that was Katie's mind. Deep within, I could feel the core of who she was, gentle and pliable. Even deeper still, I pushed. She started to move in front of me, squirming. My hands struck out in a flash, grabbing her arms, keeping her seated. The touch of my hands seemed to strengthen the bond between us.

I slipped through the fog of the curse into the space within. Distantly, I could hear Katie's whimper of pain. It was hurting her, I knew, but I needed to know. I wasn't sure exactly what I was doing. The only time I'd experienced anything like this, I had been on the receiving end.

The blackness resisted, not wanting to let me in. I pressed against it and heard another sob echo from Katie's lips. But, for just an instant, I could feel a warm light of purity and wonder pulsing beneath the dark. It reached out, and there was a spark of connection for just a millisecond.

There were no memories, just a few images, but there was a budding personality, beating and alive. She was like a newborn, possessing many traits, ready to learn but bereft of identity. The darkness became more insistent, and Katie's cry of pain became a wail. I drew out of her mind quickly, panting unconsciously.

Revenants were vampires like any other, but they had no will because they had no memories. They hadn't the mental strength that a lifetime of experiences would give them, girding them against the ravages of the accursed hunger.

Katie wasn't gone; she was a child, regressed from where she had been. I could help her. She could grow again. There was some hope.

I held out my arms, and she curled within them. "Rest," I said gently, feeling the power of command flowing through my words. Her eyes closed.

I sat there for over an hour like that, with Katie lying in my arms. The emotions I had been pushing aside now threatened to overwhelm me. It wasn't the fear or the panic. Those were long gone. Instead, I felt a deep sadness for the poor child within my lap, resting in a sleep that mirrored death. I closed my eyes to rest with her. There was no point in staying awake.

50

I woke as Elizabeth Tyler strode in. I couldn't decide if it was surprising or inevitable. She carried two blood storage bags and a large plastic tumbler. Ah, I thought cynically, so it's time for good cop.

Four vampires, all with blades, waited for me to make an untoward move. They needn't have bothered. I knew my odds of escape at this point.

"Nastasia and Schmidt are such barbarians," Elizabeth said as she opened the bag and poured a cup. "None of this was necessary. I told them that." It had been Liz I'd heard earlier. She placed a finger to her lips in a shushing gesture and said, "I'm Liz."

I played along. "I've heard of you. Feeding time, is it?"

"Yes." She knelt in front of us.

"Wake up, Katie," I whispered. Katie's eyes opened, and she turned her face toward Liz and the cup of blood she presented. Shocked, Liz fell back on her rump.

"I thought she was dead," Liz said.

I stroked Katie's hair. "No. Please feed her first."

Liz handed the cup of blood to Katie, who took it and began to drink heavily. Then Katie did something even more to Liz's evident surprise. Katie offered me the cup, still half-filled. I took a small sip and pushed it back to her. She continued to drink, not like some animal, but like a small child with a cup of milk or juice, two-handed. It might have been cute if it hadn't been so tragic.

"How did you do this? She's a revenant."

Katie held the empty cup out, licking the blood from her lips and teeth.

"It doesn't matter. If they touch her again, I'll kill them all."

She barked a laugh. "Bloody hard to do from in here."

I ignored the comment. "Are you going to give us the rest of that blood, or are you leaving?"

She refilled the cup with the remaining contents of the first bag and stood pacing a bit. This time I went first, drinking half of it before giving the rest to Katie.

Liz stopped and turned. "Where are the tablets, Cait? Just tell me, and I'll make sure they send you home."

"No, Liz," I said firmly but gently. "That's not how this works."

Liz snorted, cocking a hip and staring at me, incredulous. "Oh, still loyal to your lady love? She's not worthy of it."

"And why's that?" I asked derisively.

"You aren't the first person she's done this to, you know."

"What, she trapped you in a tunnel with a ravenous beast that almost killed you?"

Liz turned and snapped. "No, she infected me with the bubonic plague!"

"What?" My response was a little loud, and Katie stirred in my lap. I shushed her, stroking her hair.

"Oh, yes." Liz's tone had shifted, becoming softer, friendlier, and she sat down next to me, pushing the chain and bloody cuff aside. "Marcella met me in 1665. My marriage had been arranged when I was twelve, and I had three children."

Liz paused as if lost in thought. "Marcella brought me under her shadow quickly."

"Well, you look great for having had three kids," I commented glibly.

"Why, thank you." She winked at me. I didn't bother to tell her that I wasn't flirting or looking for a friend. She continued.

"When Marcella and I met, I was twenty-seven and a great deal heavier. In any event, we started a rather torrid affair. Then, a few months later, I came down with the plague. It wasn't suspicious at the time. The disease was running all about England."

"Then how did you know she'd done it?"

"Marcella keeps rather meticulous journals. These days, they are locked in her basement along with her various treasures." She stood and walked to the door, making a show of banging on it. "Can we get someone to clean up in here and a chair or two, please?"

I was more than a touch skeptical. "So, she actually wrote down in a journal that she poisoned you?"

"Yes, she placed infected blood into my wine. I suffered horribly for three days before Marcella told me that she could save me. Of course, I already knew what she was. I'd known almost from the beginning; we believed in such things back then. But I begged her to save me anyway. I didn't want to die."

I didn't say anything, looking for any indications of deception, but there were none. Until that moment, I'd held out a slim hope that Marcella hadn't known what was down in the tunnel. I was starting to wonder who was worse. Schmidt and Nastasia, who had tortured a fifteen-year-old girl, or Marcella, who had manipulated me from the beginning and then fed me to the literal master in the cellar.

"It gets worse. Two nights after I was turned, she left me all alone, at home— with my family." Liz's expression grew dark and pained.

"Oh, God!" I hissed in shock and horror.

"Yes. I couldn't help myself. I killed my husband and all three of my children. And she let me blame myself. Worst of all, I think, now, is the fact that I followed her like a puppy dog for fifty years after."

"Why would you do that?"

"Because I thought she'd saved my life. She had rescued me from a loveless marriage, rescued me a second time from the plague, and then supported and loved me when I'd been tearing myself apart over my children— the husband I was less concerned with."

As a captive audience, I was forced to listen, but if she spun a lie, it was damn convincing.

"Usually, she finds someone she can trust and keeps them around until they leave, or eventually, die, like Ninetta. But, over the last hundred years, she's turned six other people in defiance of council rules—a council that she sits on."

"Six? Why haven't you stopped her?" I asked, utterly baffled by the fucked up politics of these people.

"Because we can't, Cait. She can make any one of us commit suicide or kill one another with a word. She's that powerful."

Liz paused and took the empty cup from Katie, dumping the last of the first bag into it and handing it back.

"Did she tell you that you made her feel things she thought long dead or some shit like that?"

I didn't answer. I didn't have to. I was sure it was plain on my face.

"She did, didn't she. 'Oh, Elizabeth, my love, I am drunk upon thy presence and thy grace.' Sound familiar? I bet you just intoxicated her."

I stifled burgeoning tears. I was so tired of all this— completely worn out. I'd been victimized in one way or another all of my life. There was literally no one I could trust. My da had sold me out to these nutjobs. My mother, God, my mother had sold me out to Marcella. And Marcella, in service to whatever twisted fantasy she had, had turned me into this monster. "Why? She didn't need to do this. I didn't want any of this. I just wanted—."

"Love? Yes, Cait, I know. I was the same. I'd spent twenty years, almost, pining for the one thing I couldn't have—the love of another woman. In truth, though, I'm not sure that she doesn't actually love you in her own mad, twisted way. When you came staggering into Marcella's place, overwhelmed by the hunger, she and I had been arguing about you. She had expressed genuine remorse over what she'd done. And, I felt so bad for you that night, but there was just nothing I could do."

Liz's arrow had hit the mark. The worm of betrayal slid into my heart, gnawing its way home.

"I'll never understand this. I'm a nobody, just some kid born in Dorchester."

Liz bent down and stroked my hair, looking into my tear-filled eyes. "No, Cait, you're not just a nobody. You're special."

"Those fucking tablets. You know what, you can have them. They're in the imaging lab at Boston College, Higgins Hall."

Liz looked at me, genuine surprise painting her features.

"Please, just don't hurt my mother or Dr. Imai," I pleaded.

Katie fished out the remnants of blood from the cup with her finger and stuck it in my mouth. I hugged her to my chest, knowing that a single innocent life was worth the world.

Liz gave me a sad smile and stepped out, closing the door behind her.

51

Without watch or sun or moon, I had little concept of the passage of time. But I hadn't felt the rush of fatigue that came with sunrise, so I knew it hadn't been too long.

Katie and I sat in the corner of the room. We were playing a child's game. I would make a face or raise an eyebrow, and she would mimic it. After a few rounds, I stuck out my tongue and wiggled it. Katie seemed to notice that mine was different, and it fascinated her.

I stuck it out again, and her hand shot out, grabbing my tongue and pulling it to its limit.

"Hey—." I tried to say around my tongue, and she let go, laughing a childlike giggle. The bloodthirsty, mindless revenant laughed.

Katie's eyes turned bright, and I saw a hint of something flow through them. "K—K—," she stuttered, and it was gone.

"Katie?" I queried, watching her closely. But she seemed not to recognize the word. I smiled sadly and pushed a strand of her matted hair behind her ear. It occurred to me that she might be better this way, blissfully unaware of her life before, absent any memories on which to base judgment. Carlos had been right; I was a hard-as-nails bitch on the outside, but my insides were fucking marshmallow.

Elizabeth knocked at the door. "If I open this door to feed the two of you, will you be difficult?"

I struggled for control, but my emotions were too raw, too wild. Finally, I pushed out a few words. "I'll try not to."

In the meantime, I was trying to square the intimacy and vulnerability I had seen in Marcella with what Elizabeth had told me. Marcella was so beautiful and strong. She was dynamic and capable. I just couldn't imagine that she would twist me around like that. Was she manipulative? Sometimes. But a game player? I hadn't thought so. It was infuriating, and I couldn't find any resolution to my feelings in my ragged state.

These guys weren't pros at coercion. But, they understood my relationship to the hunger better than I did myself. Had I been human, I might have held out, but how could I battle them and my curse when I didn't understand the latter hardly at all?

Elizabeth opened the door and walked in with a tall blond Ken doll of a man. Katie stood and looked at me, and I nodded.

Whatever Elizabeth had thought about Katie's condition, any thoughts she might have had about Katie being anything but a revenant fled as soon as she latched onto the blond blood doll. She went at him with ravenous hunger, tearing into his flesh and dropping him to the floor. After about thirty seconds, he looked extremely pale.

"That's enough!" Elizabeth shouted, but Katie ignored her.

I looked up languidly. "Stop, Katie."

Katie released him, letting his head bounce on the floor.

Elizabeth looked at me coldly as two men, whose scent I didn't recognize, came in and dragged the Ken-doll out.

I just snorted. This was so insane. Liz spoke in exasperated tones outside the door.

"He'll live, thank God. Bring Donna in." Elizabeth returned through the door with a brunette in a dark red velvet dress.

"Nice color choice," I said sarcastically.

"You think so," Donna said, turning in a circle. She was a pretty girl. The dress she wore hugged her body closely, revealing a curvy figure. I couldn't bring myself to care much, though. This was all functional. Katie and I needed our strength, and I needed to be able to think. The hunger had been gnawing at me, again, steadily.

I stripped off my shirt and handed it to Elizabeth. "Be a dear and hold this for me, will you?" I was sick of being covered in blood all the time. I'd been so blasé about what I'd become, so tied up in the emotional drama, that I hadn't considered all the effects.

Blood used to be something I saw as part of the tragedies I investigated. It had been disgusting and gross. Now it was not only a need but something I reveled in. After feeding, that first kiss, passing the blood back to my victim, had felt addictive. Feeling my victim's heart pump with the power I'd returned to them, hearing them as the changed blood heightened their sexual pleasure, it was a heady trip, for sure. But, this experience had soured that. I just wanted to be clean.

Donna strode over to me and threw her arms around my neck.

"Tell me what you need," she whispered in my ear. The blood lust tore through my senses and thoughts, stripping away my doubts and depression. I could hear and feel the anticipatory rise in her pulse and respiration. I could taste her arousal in the air.

I buried my nose in Donna's hair, smelling her scent. She carried an aroma of apples and cinnamon. I was spellbound instantly.

Donna pressed her mouth to mine, sweeping it with her tongue. Like Pauline, she pulled back and touched her mouth in an almost identical unconscious movement. I stuck my wide blue tongue out to its maximum length just over my nose, feeling weirdly playful—in the mood.

"Oh, my God," she breathed. "We need to talk later."

I was too excited by the thought of blood to respond. The idea of sliding her dress up her supple thighs drove itself into my head. My emotions were all over the place now. And it had only been a few hours since I'd fed on Katie. *Dear God.*

I bent into the nape of Donna's neck and proceeded to feed.

The blood was pleasurable, and Donna shivered beneath me, hitching with ecstatic breaths.

"Yes. Oh God, yes," she cried. "Take it." She threw her arms around my head, knotting my hair in her grip. Donna began to grind her hips into me, one leg wrapped around my ass.

I drank hard, and her cries became weaker, still ecstatic, but more pitiful, too. Her grip slackened, and her legs buckled. I lowered us gently to the ground, but I didn't stop. I could feel her consciousness fading, but I still didn't stop. If I knew one thing, this woman was an addict. It was atrocious; it was wrong. I loved it.

Liz pulled at my shoulders, and I ended it, forcing a bit of changed blood into Donna's mouth.

I stood, the hunger more than sated for the moment. "Bring me something to clean up with." Liz started to look obstinate. "Please," I added quickly.

Donna's wound had closed; she would live, I hoped. It was the closest to angry, public sex I had ever gotten in my short life.

The two men carried Donna out as Liz left and returned with two buckets of water, soap, and a washrag. "Here, you can clean up." Liz nodded to Katie. "Cait, I'm sorry that they did this to her. She didn't deserve that."

"Thank you for the supplies, but you need to remember that 'they' includes you." I stared at her accusingly, and she actually looked chastised. It might have been an act, but I didn't think so.

Liz just stood there while I stripped. I washed the blood off of my chin and the few dribbles that had slipped into my cleavage. Then I called over Katie. Her shirt was soaked through, so I took it off her and began to wash her down. Katie stood quietly, watching as I washed the blood off her hands, face, and chest.

I turned back to Liz. "Can we have a change of clothes?"

There was an exasperated sigh, and she left. The door opened a few minutes later, and Liz handed me some clothes.

For Katie, she held out an ill-fitting dress that was too long. She gave me a shirt and a pair of jeans. I palmed the GPS unit as I changed.

Liz came to take the bloody clothes, and I grasped her hand gently. "Thank you. There are things on the other side of the gate. It may not work out the way you plan."

She said nothing, but there had been something in her eyes.

Katie and I sat away from the blood on the floor, propped against the wall. If I'd had to guess, I figured it'd been no more than a half-hour when I heard another steel door groan open and close, followed by a hint of sandalwood in the air.

"Marcella?"

"Cait? Are you okay?" She was close, the cell across the hall.

"Not so much. How did they get you?"

"Blackman, he ambushed me with a stake. It was total luck." She sounded irritated like he was a fly she'd meant to swat and kept missing. "Have they hurt you?"

"No more than you have, darling." I spat the words like venom.

"What do you mean?" A whisper of fear slipped into her voice.

"You lied to me. You manipulated me. You've been playing on my emotions from the start. That's what I mean. You know you could have told me anything, including the truth, and I would have followed you into hell. Instead, you fed me this bullshit story about being alone and all the feelings you felt that you'd lost the capacity to feel."

"Liz," she whispered hoarsely.

"Liz," I confirmed. I didn't dare mention my mother and what she'd said. "She told me how you turned her. I also know you killed Caldwell and trapped me down in the tunnel with that—that—thing."

"Cait, wait, you don't understand—"

"No!" I shouted angrily. "I'm still talking. I thought I'd been chasing Blackman, but it was your phone that led me to the Rodriguez place, wasn't it? You experimented on her, and you murdered her. A twelve-year-old girl Marcella. You tore out her heart. What kind of monster are you?"

There was a long period of silence. "I'm sorry, Cait. I don't expect you to understand. Jesse and I fucked up. We were trying—."

"Trying to what? Make more vampires?"

"What? That's ridiculous. It had nothing to do with that. Acacia's parents came to me and begged me to help their little girl. She was eleven years old and had already faded away. They'd written an application to the American Cancer Society for help with treatment costs, and Acacia's doctor had just thrown it in the trash. We weren't just randomly experimenting on people. Acacia's parents knew what I was doing and understood the risks. I'm not Joseph Mengele. We were trying to find a cure for fucking cancer. I was trying to help Jesse, and Kaja, and Gretchen—all of them. But the Vestry discovered her, and they insisted that I kill her. They gave me no choice. It was her, or—"

"Or what?"

Marcella was silent for a moment, then she spoke. "It was her or war. There aren't nearly enough of us to survive that."

I wasn't about to let her off the hook, but then Katie shifted closer to me, leaning against my arm.

"Who's in there with you?" Marcella asked, forestalling my planned diatribe.

"That's just Katie, the fifteen-year-old girl they made me turn. Let's just say she's not all here at the moment."

"Oh Goddess, Cait. Did they leave her in there with you? Are you safe? Is she chained?"

I rolled my eyes. "No, she's not chained. She's sitting here quietly. I'm looking out for her until I can figure out how to help her."

"Cait, you need to be—."

I lost it. "And you need to shut up! You don't know everything, you condescending bitch. These people absolutely hate you. And, frankly, I'm beginning to understand why. Why did you lie to me? Just, for once, be honest? How long have you been planning this? How long have all of you been watching me?"

"Since you were a child," Marcella whispered, resignation in her voice. And there it was, confirmation that she'd known exactly who I was when I'd first met her. "Your father promised you to Schmidt when you were ten years old. You and your sister." Her voice was flat, but underneath was an ocean of regret.

"What? I don't have a sister."

You could have heard a pin drop for the next few moments; then I caught the scuff of a shoe from the other side of the door; it was Liz. "Tell her the rest, Marcella."

"No, she's not ready, Liz."

"Not ready for what?" I asked. What else could they possibly say that would be worse.

Elizabeth replied first. "Not ready to hear just how awful it really is; what Marcella really did to you."

"Liz, don't," Marcella pleaded. "It's not that simple."

"Come now, Marcella, isn't it?"

"Liz, please, don't." Marcella was begging now, tears distorting her plea.

"You could make me stop," Liz said to Marcella.

"You know I won't," Marcella answered, defeated.

Liz opened my cell door and waved for Katie and me to step out. For an insane moment, I thought it was a trap, a kind of 'shot trying to escape' thing. But I brushed the thought aside as stupid. We stepped out of the cell. Steel doors barred each end of the hallway. Along each wall were three identical doors to the one I'd just exited.

Marcella's fear-filled eyes showed through an open slot in the cell directly across from ours. Fat tears flowed over her lashes.

Liz walked us over to the door. "Show her the rest, Marcella. She deserves to know."

Marcella whined, almost childlike. "Why are you doing this, Liz?"

Liz didn't answer.

I stepped up to the slot, looking at what little I could see of her face. "What is she talking about?"

"Caitlin, you need to understand something. I've changed. After I show you this, it may not seem like it, but I have. We've been on this crusade to save us ever since our ability to turn others began to fade. I thought that survival was the most important thing for a very long time."

My rage waivered again as I listened to her pitiful tone. I tried to tell myself it was for show or that she was only upset because she got caught, but I couldn't bring myself to believe that.

"Enough pre-amble," Liz demanded. "Show her!"

"No, Liz. I will take the time to explain. You all owe me that for getting us this far." Marcella's tone was hot and brooked no argument.

Liz rolled her eyes. "Fine."

"Cait, I won't belabor this. I promised your mother I'd keep you safe, and I succeeded for sixteen years. I kept Schmidt busy looking for the tablets all that time, playing out a long shell game. But then Schmidt finally discovered where they were. I was able to get to them first, but he became relentless, pulling together everything he needed.

"I had intended to approach you directly, but then Jesse lost his shit and turned me in to both the feds and Schmidt."

I crossed my arms, looking at her eyes through the slot in the door. "So Liz provided your alibi while you killed Jesse."

"Yes." There was a genuine sadness in her voice. For what, though, I wasn't sure. "After that, it was easy enough to have Larson assign you to the case."

"But, then why lie after you turned me? I asked you point blank, and you lied to my face."

"Because I didn't want you to think I—."

"What? Was a murderer? Jesse knew the risks, just as I do. I wouldn't have blamed you. You didn't have a choice. Or did you?"

"No." She said flatly.

"Then why did you trap me in the tunnel with that thing?"

"I was looking for information on this place. You showed up, and I panicked. I knew you'd survive for at least a few days if it infected you."

There was absolute silence for a moment as the truth sunk in. Up to this point, I'd held out hope that she hadn't done it, that maybe she didn't know it was me, or it had been a mistake of some sort.

Marcella continued. "I came back to the house a few minutes later, but Carlos was skulking around outside, and I realized it was too late."

I leaned my head against the cell door.

"Cait, I know. I'm sorry." She reached her fingers through the slot. "Liz is right, though; you should know the rest. But you'll hate me when it's over if you don't already."

A deep sense of emotional fatigue washed over me, and I touched Marcella's hand. "Honestly, I just want out of here." I turned to Liz. "Can't you just let us go? I gave you the tablets."

"Unfortunately not," Liz replied. "They still need you."

"Because I can activate the tablets."

Liz nodded.

Marcella released my hand. "Liz, I need you to show her. I can't do it."

Before I could ask what she meant, Liz placed her hands on my face, turning my eyes to hers. I felt the tug of her mind. The pull was weak and gentle, it didn't have Marcella's force, but I could tell she was trying to share a memory. I could have shaken it off and probably should have, but I relented, and she swept me away into her gaze.

*　*　*

I see everything from Liz's point of view. She is standing outside the restroom at the church. Marcella is in front of her, speaking with a young woman in hushed tones, a woman I recognize. It is my mother, and she has been crying.

"Look into my eyes, Róisín."

"No. I can't do this."

Marcella grabs my mother's face. "Look at me."

My mother's face goes slack as Marcella's will washes over her. "You will forget what she told you and that we were ever here. Aoife was never born. You will forget her. That's all you need to remember. Your husband died in a drug deal gone bad."

I can see the struggle playing across my mother's features. "No —" she says, resisting Marcella's influence.

"Yes! You will forget we were here. She belongs to me now. Michael promised both of them to us. Michael died in a drug deal gone bad. Now stay."

"No, you bitch. Where is my daughter?" I can't help but feel impressed as my mother stares down a fifteen-hundred-year-old vampire, throwing off her influence like a prom dress.

"Yes, unless you want one of them to die. You don't get it, Róisín; I'm their only hope."

My mother stops, horrified.

The door to the bathroom opens, and a young girl steps out, no more than sixteen. The image is surreal. I am looking at myself as a skinny kid in a black dress, long hair in a tight braid. Marcella turns to young me and captures my will instantly.

"Your mother told me what you said last week. You will forget coming out to your parents. You will forget that discovery about yourself until the time comes. I will let you know when that is. You will forget we were here, and Aoife; she was never born."

"Yes, ma'am." My voice is droning, automatic, emotionless.

My mother pulls me to her breast, cradling me.

"Marcella, stop," Liz says. "You can't do this."

Marcella spins on Liz, enraged. "I have no choice, Liz. There's no other way."

"You're mad. Think about what you're doing. You know what? I'm having no part of this." Liz turned, stalking away.

"Liz, stop. You still owe me, and you know what will happen if

you betray me again." The force of her command halts Liz in her tracks, and I am very aware of the dangerous line Liz is walking as I come back to myself.

* * *

Tears were streaming down my horrified face as Liz looked on with genuine compassion.

"Why?" My voice was a choked sob of devastation. "Why would you do this to me?" Katie began to growl, looking at Liz with cold, heartless eyes. I shushed her with soothing strokes of her hair.

"I am so sorry, Cait." Marcella's voice was quiet— small even.

"You took away my identity. If I'd known then what I know now, I might not even have been raped. My life has been shit for twelve years because of you!" I suddenly felt cold, and my whole body began to tremble. "Why? Why any of this?"

"It was a different time, Cait. Liz and I were different people."

Liz chimed in. "Speak for yourself, Marcella. I begged you to stop."

I looked at Liz. "Who is Aoife? That name, it sounds so familiar, like I should know it."

Her expression was coaxing, waiting for me to make some monumental connection.

I struggled to remember why it was important, but it wouldn't come to me. The name kept bringing me back to a single inexorable memory. My father and I were at Arnold's restaurant, on the cape, for my fifteenth birthday. But it was strange. Almost like I was someone else watching myself participate. I watched myself eat ice cream, but I had a short, sort of butch cut instead of my long auburn hair. The same image of myself I'd seen in my dreams. I was wearing a—. Then it hit me; it wasn't me.

Daughters, my mother had said.

My mind exploded with a thousand memories: memories

of hopscotch, jump rope, and singing, memories of a secret language that we had shared, a sort of shorthand, memories of a sixteen-year-old girl who looked just like me, screaming for help from the back of a car. I had just watched her disappear, unable to remember who she was.

I couldn't control my sobs as I stared away, unseeing, my thoughts stuck on the image of my sister being stolen away in the back of a black Mercedes. My knees buckled, and I choked on the sudden revelation, finally stuttering out a broken "Oh my G-God." I looked at Marcella. "You took her. You stole my sister from us."

Liz was crying now, and tears floated at the edge of Marcella's lashes. Even Katie, so lost in her head, had knelt, hugging me tightly.

Marcella dared to try to apologize. "Oh, Cait, I'm so sorry. We didn't steal her. It was all wrong—."

A cold rage blew through me like a winter wind, and before Liz could react, I'd risen, yanked up the crossbar, and dragged Marcella from the cell, pinning her to the wall.

"You're Sorry?" I screamed. "Sorry? Do you have any idea what you crazy bitches did? You destroyed my life!" The anger was hot now, and Marcella crumbled, tears flowing like rain. I wasn't done with her, though, not by a long shot. I clamped my hand around her throat and dug in with my fingers, choking off her voice. Blood spilled past my knuckles. "Where is she! Where is she! I'm going to kill you. I'm going to—"

A shot rang out, and Marcella's head rocked backward. She dropped like a sack of sand.

52

"Marcella!" I screamed, dropping to her side, cradling her bloody head. Liz grabbed me and yanked me up roughly. Looking back down the hallway, I saw Schmidt, a pistol in his hand. But I could do nothing further as Liz and another vampire cuffed me. Two more vampires I didn't recognize caught Katie and cuffed her as she kicked and struggled violently.

"Thank you for keeping her busy, Detective. I had no idea how we would have kept her contained without your distraction."

I struggled, but Liz and the other vampire held me tight, and I turned a questioning gaze to Liz. She said nothing, and her stare was blank, giving little away, though tears still flowed on her cheeks.

"You fucking sleaze!" I shouted at Schmidt as they dragged us away. "I'll be the one that kills you. Do you hear me? I'll be the one that kills you!"

We were led out of the cellblock, down a short hallway to a pair of thick steel doors. Liz muscled past Schmidt, leading us into a large chamber, bumping him roughly on the way in. "Get the fuck out of my way Schmidt. I'm not sticking around for this. I've had enough. You got what you wanted; now I want to be as far away from you fucking psychopaths as possible. I've paid my debts to everyone these last two weeks.

I'm done."

"Fine, Elizabeth. Thank you for being so helpful."

Liz threw him two fingers and stalked back out the double doors.

That fucking bitch.

Beyond the door was another narrow hallway that led into a large, almost amphitheater-like chamber. Around the room was a broad ledge of rock about ten feet up, upon which stood about thirty people, all vampires. Schmidt had been busy.

A large brass tripod sat over a low flame in the center of the room; I could smell blood wafting from it.

Schmidt's little helper, Nastasia, was sitting on the edge of a small dais rising above the tripod, dangling a leg. She still had her tin cup in her hand, twirling it around one finger, over and over. Behind Nastasia, unrestrained and looking very calm, stood my mother.

To either side of the dais stood large curved stone columns of some gray metal. The same style of marks I'd seen on the tablets embossed the columns. In the center of the brazier, hovering just above a swirling pool of bubbling blood, was a small metal sphere plated in what looked to be gold. Gyroscopic circles turned and slid around it slowly. I was baffled at how the blood didn't cook, coagulate, or separate in the heated brazier. Hell, it didn't even steam. I felt a much deeper dread that something far worse than I could imagine was about to take place.

Schmidt nodded to them curtly. "Nastasia, Róisín, is everything ready?"

Nastasia just nodded and took a sip from her cup. Then, she cracked a crooked, malicious smile at me.

My mother smiled at Schmidt sweetly. "Of course, my dear."

I looked at my mother, brow furrowed in puzzlement. "Ma?"

"It's okay, Cáitlín. It will all be over soon," my mother replied. Something about the way she said it frightened me beyond measure. She then proceeded to pull the tablets from a silver case next to her, placing one on each of the bookstands.

"Why are you helping them?" I asked plaintively.

She turned slowly, smiling beatifically. "To make things right, of course. Your father failed in his duties, so I am completing the task." Her voice was droning, and her eyes were empty.

Shock and horror shot through me. "What did you do to her, Schmidt?"

Schmidt looked at me, his face painted with a self-satisfied, malignant smile. "I—suggested that she help us."

The vampires pushed Katie to the center of the room and led me to the dais. Schmidt stood in front of me, the mocking grin still on his face.

I looked back to the assembled vampires, wondering just how many people they'd turned to revenants and consequentially murdered to get this many functional vampires. Regardless, we were out-gunned and out-manned, and, at this point, I just wanted to get all of us out with our lives because we were well and truly fucked.

Blackman and two other vampires dumped Marcella's body roughly into the center of the room, just in front of the dais. Blackman secured a gag around her face, cuffed her arms behind her body, and walked to the dais. One of the other vampires held a shotgun to her head. Now that I was examining her, I could see the bullet fragments pushing from under her skin as the entry wound began to close. A moment later, her eyes fluttered open, locking Schmidt with a hateful stare.

Oh, thank God!

Schmidt looked at her and then back to me, a cocky smile on his face. He stalked off the platform, his shoes clanking across the metal grating as he strode down to Marcella. Without slowing, Schmidt slapped Marcella across the face, the force of the hit whipping her head around and, almost, but not quite, dislodging her gag. He took a moment to right it and tighten it, and it took all the self-control I could muster not to yank at my chains.

While Schmidt was staring at Marcella, as if on a whim, Katie struck out with her foot and caught him right in the groin, lifting him several inches off the floor. It wouldn't hurt him for long, but he doubled over in agony from the strike.

"Katie, stop!" I exclaimed through my laughter.

Katie looked at me and blinked. "Scum!"

Nastasia chuckled. "Seems she has your number, Schmidt."

Schmidt looked up, a mixture of agony and annoyance on his face. As he turned his back on her, I saw the glimmer of a malicious smile wrinkling Marcella's eyes.

"The great Marcella Carson," Schmidt began. "The Savior of us all. I have had to put up with you for over three hundred years, your arrogance, your demands, your stupidity. All you had to do was give us one of the girls, and we could have done this a dozen years ago. But no, you hid Aoife away from us and then refused to hand this one over as we agreed."

Schmidt continued. "We could have controlled the planet and stopped this insanity. But you decided it wasn't our place, and what Marcella decides, we all just accept."

Marcella, to her credit, didn't make a sound. She just watched Schmidt's little rant. Though, if looks could kill, Schmidt would have been turned to ash by Marcella's baleful gaze. I noted that Blackman wasn't paying any attention to Schmidt at all. He was watching me. I smiled inwardly at that. *I've got something for you, asshole,* I thought. *You just wait.*

"Hey, Schmidt," I called. "I thought we were past the part where you explain your evil plan. This is where you're supposed to quit monologuing and tell us that we're all going to die."

Blackman punched me in the stomach, dropping me to my knees, where I stayed.

"Fräulein Reagan," Schmidt said in that same snide and condescending tone. "I don't think I'd be the one making jokes right now if I were you. I had planned for the final sacrifice to come from Marcella, but little Katie will do just as well—better, in fact."

"You bastard!" I cried, yanking at my cuffs.

Nastasia reached under the dais and pulled a pair of goggles from a bag hidden under the dais structure. "Here you go, dear," she said as she handed them to my mother, who placed them on her head.

Schmidt walked back over to me and yanked me in front of the tablets. "Activate them, now!"

"I have no idea what you're talking about."

Schmidt snapped, backhanding me to the floor. Marcella and Katie both jerked but were rewarded with a whack to the back of the knees with the butt of a shotgun.

"I am done playing games with you, Cait!" Schmidt screamed, spit flying in my face.

My mother's head dropped, and she refused to meet my eyes.

"I will make this simple for you." Schmidt snarled. "If you do not activate them, Detective, I will have no use for any of you. I will kill your mother, but not before I kill young Katie and Marcella."

Katie started to stand, but I shook my head as one of the vampires cocked a shotgun and pointed it at her head. Katie knelt back down next to Marcella and then did something odd; she leaned against her, placing her head on Marcella's shoulder.

Marcella tilted her head, resting it briefly on Katie's. There was something in that simple gesture that struck me, and, whereas a moment before, I might have been tempted just to let Schmidt kill her, I thought maybe what she'd said was true. Maybe she'd really fallen in love with me. And after what Schmidt had said, perhaps she had been trying to protect me. I realized I couldn't let her die, angry as I might be with her.

I sneered at Schmidt. "Fine, uncuff me, and I'll do it."

"You know," I said as Nastasia started unlocking the cuffs. "if he gets what he wants, you'll be just another threat to him."

Nastasia laughed. "I'm over eight-hundred years old, dear. I invented mind games."

"Yes, well, you may be eight-hundred years old, but Schmidt has all the classic signs of malignant narcissism. So, you might want to keep an eye on that, just sayin'."

"Enough!" Schmidt said. "Nastasia, go kill the little girl if Cait doesn't activate the tablets."

Nastasia stood bolt upright from uncuffing my wrists and stared daggers at Schmidt. "Do not presume to give me orders, child. Cait will do as she's told, won't you, Cait?"

I shrugged at Nastasia, giving her a smug smile, saying, 'See, told ya.'

I stepped up and placed my hands on the tablets, and they lit with purple light, though, this time, the stream of energy flew to the golden orb in the brazier rather than coalescing between them. The blood in the brazier began to draw up into the sphere, turning the light a deep, ominous crimson. My mother began to chant.

"Trisores deiwas, pehúr, dagome, woder, ósmí dworis haregos."

There was no slow build-up. One moment the feeling of the tablets was just a buzz in my fingers, then my body jerked, and I froze. I became almost, but not entirely, a passive observer as another personality fused with my own. Ungodly power raced through me as it continued raising gooseflesh on my skin. A hot wind from nowhere blew through my hair.

My mother's chanting shifted from something unintelligible to words I understood, beckoning Mother Darkness, the Avra, and the Phantom queen to open the black door.

I screamed as something infiltrated my consciousness. On one side, the vampire was dark and full of predatory delights. The creature invading my mind, though, was something much worse, demonic, chaotic, and evil. My thoughts turned alien and malignant.

My mother chanted the ritual into its fifth verse. The ball began to pulse, and a deep thrumming filled the cavern. My mother, the evil bitch who'd helped strip me of my identity, completed the second triplet of the song, the *shómen*, the ritual of opening.

A word spilled from my mouth. "Rhendos!" The tablets rose off their stands, hovering in the air for a moment, then they exploded in a swirl of purple and black fire.

My head keened as the sliver of another reality began to form around the golden ball. Schmidt, Nastasia, and Blackman drew closer, thinking to basque in the power of the budding portal. I drew a crooked smile. "Mr. Blackman, be so kind as to kill Schmidt." My words were flat, almost polite, but the vast well of power now open to me ensured he'd obey. They had all been fools to believe that they could control this or understand the forces they were playing with.

There was a swift flash of metal, and Schmidt's head fell to the floor, followed by his body. Liz charged in and knocked over the two vampires guarding Katie and Marcella. Before they could recover, she'd unlocked Marcella's cuffs.

Realizing what had happened, Blackman darted forward, sticking his blade into me and twisting it painfully. He kicked me in the chest, and I flew through the air, sailing across the room. It all happened too fast, so I didn't have a chance to see his face when he realized I'd grabbed hold of the sword, yanking it from his grasp.

I twisted in the air, skidding across the stone on all fours and sliding to a stop next to Marcella.

"Yup," I said through gritted teeth as I pulled myself up. "That hurt." I pulled out the sword and breathed a sigh of relief as the pain vanished.

"You know, we are going to have a serious talk about trust and honesty when we get home," I said, getting the first strap on Marcella's gag loose. "Though, I really should just kill you right now. Actually, I think I will." I stood and raised the blade, rage-filled and eyes narrowed, as the beast in my head scrabbled for control.

Marcella's eyes widened, and she grunted around the gag frantically. "Mmph, mmph, mmph!"

I couldn't understand her. "What's that, dear? You're sorry for fucking up my entire life? Why Marcella, thank you so much for being so contrite, but it's too fucking late. May Mother Darkness have mercy on your soul. Because I will not."

53

Liz's pale hand landed on mine, stopping it mid-stroke. "Cait, stop. This isn't you."

"Get off me," I shouted, jerking loose, as something tickled at the back of my senses. I swung the sword backhanded and took the head off one of the vampire guards who was just rising from the floor.

"I could kill all of you with a word," I shouted to the room. Something in my mind rebelled, though. What am I doing? I snatched at every powerful, happy thought I could find, Aoife and me playing together, Marcella and I embracing on the beach, anything.

My thoughts spun chaotically. I couldn't hold on to anything for any length of time. I could feel myself slipping away, subsumed in the depths of a raging monster—a real monster. My emotions shifted once again, angry, torturous, sadistic. I was going to kill them all and tear them apart. *What do I care? They cannot stop me.*

"Cait!" Marcella shouted, finally loose from her gag. Her voice snapped my head around. Hatred filled me as I looked at her, but she grabbed my face. Immediately, I felt her presence deep in my consciousness, piercing and cold. It was like a spike in my mind. I cried out in horror as every awful experience, every terrible feeling bubbled into me, and I fell into a heap.

"Pull yourself together; it's the tablets. They're evil. I'm so sorry I did this, but we have other problems. Please, Cait. Get. Up."

I shook my head, trying to push aside the crushing depression and helplessness I felt. The assembled vampires began jumping down from the ledge above. I didn't see Blackman anywhere, which was deeply worrying. That guy was too good with a blade.

I turned to Marcella. "Can't you just order them to murder each other or something?"

"It doesn't work like that," Marcella replied. "It only affects one of them at a time."

"Shit, then we're fucked." I counted just over thirty vampires.

Nastasia began marching in our direction. She didn't speak, didn't taunt, didn't make any demands. She just stalked toward us with absolute confidence. If I was being honest, it was a little intimidating, and the closer she got, the more nervous I became.

Someone hit me from behind, knocking me prone and causing the Katana to skitter from my hand. Before I could rise, Blackman darted past me and snatched up the blade.

All of the power I'd felt from the tablets had largely faded, leaving only my hand-to-hand skills.

Blackman and Nastasia were staring us down. Several of the other vampires had drawn weapons as well, eyeing Marcella, seeing her as the greatest threat. My mother's eyes were still closed, chanting.

"Mother!" I shouted. "Stop!" If she heard me, she did nothing.

Nastasia smiled wickedly and tensed to strike, probably convinced that we couldn't fend off this many vampires at once. They would have been correct a moment before, but then everything changed. Howls sounded from outside in the passage. And, while Marcella was formidable, the ninety-foot-long Naga charging through the doorway was a fucking wrecking machine. I hadn't known anything so large could move so fast. I didn't get much time to appreciate it, though, as Nastasia charged forward with a powerful one-two punch, followed by a rain of blows.

I blocked several, but she got in a few body shots. God, she was fast. In all my time in Iraq, as a patrol officer or as a Detective, I'd never fought hand-to-hand in the field against a competent opponent. After her first few shots, I figured I had a good measure of Nastasia's skills. Liz stepped up next to me, and Nastasia hesitated, but I waved Liz off. "Go help Marcella; I got this." I smiled and squared off with the eight-hundred-year-old Russian.

Bian slithered back out, leaving a dozen bodies and many more groaning figures in her wake. It was way too cold for her to be down here long.

Nastasia ran forward, raining down blows against my arms. She even launched a vicious kick at my ribs which I ate, though it picked me up and tossed me into the wall. Fighting a vampire was so different. I couldn't take a lot of hits like that. I straightened up, my bones mending almost instantly, and leaped back quick as lightning, bringing my knee into her chin as I jumped. Nastasia's head snapped back, and she launched backward, flying into one of the dais supports.

I didn't wait for her to recover; I ran forward and kicked out at her prone form, getting a stiletto in my calf for the trouble. I screamed with pain as she tore the knife through the muscle in my leg, doing no permanent damage but spilling precious blood all the same.

Shit!

I backed off, yanking out the knife and letting Nastasia pull herself up while my leg healed. Behind her, my mother continued her chanting. The clockwork orb was spinning faster now. Blue-black strokes of lightning and smoke danced between the columns, and a steady glow began to light the runes, one by one, bottom to top.

I had no choice. I had to stop her. "God damnit. God damnit, mom, please stop," I cried. But she didn't seem to hear me, so I did the only thing I could. I threw the stiletto at my mother. The blade seemed to sail in slow motion, tumbling end over end. Then it just stopped inches from my mother's outstretched palm and fell to the ground.

Nastasia stepped into a punch and grabbed my throat, digging her fingers into my neck. I could feel the pressure as she started pulling against it, trying to lift my head from my shoulders. I drove my right arm down across hers and pulled her in close, head butting her multiple times in the nose.

She snarled in my face, fangs extended. I was no actual match for her strength, it turned out. She picked me up, running and driving me into the wall, knocking me almost senseless.

Carlos, partially transformed, plowed into Nastasia, taking them both to the floor like a pair of titans locked in battle. Carlos' long teeth tore into Nastasia's neck, and arterial blood spewed across the floor.

I looked around. Werewolves had poured in the door, and a chaotic battle raged amongst us all. The vampires were physically stronger, but they couldn't match the ferocity of the werewolves who were rending them with tooth and claw.

Marcella was slicing her way through a group of vampires. Around her, four dead bodies lay. Katie was nowhere to be seen, and Blackman wasn't in the corner where Marcella had kicked him.

"Cait! Forget Nastasia!" Marcella called. "Stop your mother before she opens the gate!"

"Shit," I swore and started toward the dais, but a flash of movement to my right caught my attention. I'd found Blackman. He had Katie run through with his katana. The words of the prophecy rang in my ears.

On one side is the life of a child, on the other is the death of the world. A woman bonded by two birthrights shall decide the fate of all.

Blackman pulled the blade from Katie's gut and raised it, ready to strike a killing blow. I had no choice, not really. I wasn't going to sacrifice another child for the sake of someone else's fucking war.

I leaped at Blackman's back. The world seemed to slow down precipitously, and my vision went completely red as my body exploded into a red mist, twisting across the distance in an instant. One moment I had been leaping toward Blackman, and the next, I was standing behind him.

I didn't pause to consider what had just happened. I delivered a sharp kick to Blackman's side before he ever knew I was there. Ribs were pulverized as he flew through the air, slamming into the wall with a grunt. I didn't wait for him to recover before I barreled in on top of him, delivering strike after strike to his head, staving in his face.

"You motherfucker," I screamed as I beat him, knuckles covered in blood. "You. Mother. Fucker." He stuck his blade into my side and twisted, but he missed my heart, and I ignored the searing pain, hitting him again.

A tumbling werewolf bowled into me and knocked me off of Blackman, wrenching me free of the blade.

Marcella was screaming at Carlos, gesturing toward the dais, but she couldn't be heard over the screaming squeal of the spinning orb. I grabbed my ears, feeling the air pressure in the chamber suddenly increase. Time seemed to slow down; the fighting ceased, and the room was layered in an eerie silence. A twisting distortion like gravitational lensing grew from between the columns. The spinning orb burst into a circling cloud of black smoke, shining from within with a bruised blue and purple light.

Blinding light flashed several times as concussive thumps filled the air, the blasting pressure wave throwing us all backward against the chamber walls. I drew myself back up and turned to see Katie scrambling toward me, arms behind her back.

My eyes went wide as a massive hole in the universe swallowed the dais and my mother— the black gate was open.

I screamed. "Ma!"

You could have heard a pin drop in as it seemed the entire world took in a long, deep breath. Power flooded through me, healing my wounds and filling me with ungodly strength. The battle began anew, intensified by the burst of magic flowing into everyone.

In the depths of the black gate, I could see the blasted volcanic landscape of my nightmares. Beyond the gate, black, spider-like shapes darted and moved across its surface.

I charged toward the portal as, abruptly, my mother stood up and dusted herself off.

"Run!" I screamed, but it was too late. Something enormous, black, and powerful scooped her away with a scream.

"No!" I cried. Something darted past me impossibly fast. Before I could react, Elizabeth had shot through the portal and leaped into the air, pulling my mother free from the winged beast. I ran forward as Elizabeth carried my mother's limp and bleeding form back through the gate.

"We have to get out of here. Something's coming!" Elizabeth cried.

Over Liz's shoulder, I could see the black spider-like things skittering across the basalt plain, frighteningly fast and heading right toward us.

I looked to the ensuing carnage. Carlos and his wolves were still fighting. Marcella sprawled on all fours; a black mist composed of irregularly shaped bits of— something— circled, cyclonic around her. Within, I could catch glimpses of Marcella writhing in agony, growing larger and larger. Then she stepped free of the black smoke, hugely tall now, great black bat-like wings protruding from her back. Her long hair had turned deepest black, seeming to absorb all light. She looked like an angel of death or a demonic creature of old. She was beautiful and powerful and terrifying.

It was ancient magic, and it flowed through us all. Under my skin, I could feel the roaring hunger, the curse flowing within my veins. I dropped to the ground, stunned by its power.

I sensed Blackman's presence before the blow landed, but there was no way I could move. When the impact didn't come, I turned to find Marcella looking down at me, Blackman's headless torso in her hand, a grisly smile of satisfaction on her face.

Marcella turned away, wading through the amassed vampires, swatting them like so many flies. Long claw-like fingernails rent flesh and bone alike as she cut them down like wheat.

I found Katie, finally, and lifted her from the floor, shattering her shackles as if they were made of peanut brittle.

Gooseflesh popped all over my skin, and I turned back toward the portal. The spider-like shapes were looming much closer.

"Stop!" I bellowed, my voice filling the chamber. Dust and small pebbles rained from the ceiling. The clamor and howling ceased momentarily, and all eyes turned toward me, small and bright and burning. "Let them go; we have to get out of here."

"We have to close it!" Marcella shouted as a hot, violent wind blew from the portal.

"You can't," Elizabeth shouted back. "It's self-sustaining. The orb is gone, and so are the tablets, destroyed when the gate opened. You need another set to close it."

Marcella didn't have time to respond as five-foot-tall, five-foot-wide monstrosities poured from the other side of the gate. Each ran on six legs ending in long, razor-sharp sword-like points. I could see mouths on their undersides filled with spiny teeth that seemed to grind together like gears as they jumped through the air, landing on anything they could. One landed on Marcella's left wing.

I grabbed Blackman's discarded blade and sliced into the spider-thing on Marcella. A Black soupy ichor leaked out, smelling of a foulness I couldn't describe. Marcella flung the thing off into a corner where it spasmed and died.

"We have to get out of here," I shouted to Marcella as the creatures crawled about, taking down some of the vampires. I ran to the door, pulling Katie behind me. "We don't have the weapons or manpower to fight this battle. We need to get out and barricade the exit."

Marcella looked at me. "How am I supposed to fit through the door," she shouted as she swatted away another of the spider things. The noise was deafening.

"I don't know. You didn't do this?" I shouted, pushing Katie out of the room.

"No! I have no idea what this is!"

I took another swipe at a spider thing, but it dodged back. "Well, concentrate or something!"

"What?" Marcella called back, tearing at another spider. It had one of its bladed legs stuck into hers.

I cut another spider-thing down. "Try imagining you are yourself again and believe it." It sounded stupid, but I had no other ideas.

Marcella kicked another spider thing back into the gate and then closed her eyes. At first, nothing happened, then there was a crack of bone, and she whimpered softly as her form violently shifted back to normal. She was naked, still covered in blood and ichor, but it was her.

My eyes widened in shock. "Shit! I can't believe that worked."

Marcella pulled herself up off the floor, looking exhausted. "You and me both."

The spider-like things were all around us now, charging in.

"Fire!" a voice called from near the door, and the spiders began to drop like— well— flies. I looked back, finding Freyer and a group of officers, armed with M4s, firing at the creatures. They moved forward as a unit, clearing a path toward the gate, giving us room to retreat.

"Everyone out! Now!" I screamed over the gunfire. Nastasia was gone. Apparently, some of the vampires had decided discretion was the better part of valor and fled; the rest were dead.

A spider jumped on one of the officers, impaling him through the chest. I tore it off and threw it, scooping up the officer and his weapon.

"Katie, carry him!" I said. She didn't seem to comprehend, so I threw him over my shoulder and fired backward, one-armed. Eventually, we were able to make a fighting retreat.

A spider landed on my back, grazing my shoulder and knocking me to the ground. The officer I was carrying fell forward through the doors. I grabbed the spider and tried to throw it off, but I just couldn't. It was like every ounce of my strength had fled.

Marcella cut threw it with a blade she'd picked up somewhere along the way. I started to gasp for air, and my arm was bleeding profusely. I pulled myself up against the doors and fired the remaining rounds from the M4, downing two more spiders.

More spiders poured through the portal as Carlos yanked me out and slammed the door shut.

Spent, I collapsed to the ground. Carlos picked me up and launched himself down the hallway. A scrabbling and pounding sounded at the door behind us. Fortunately, for all their hideous appearance, the spiders were just numerous, not particularly strong.

We burst through a side tunnel and into the cold. And I could feel it. I was in jeans and a t-shirt in thirty-degree weather. *Shit.* I started to shiver.

We were in a section of the old Tremont subway line that had been abandoned years and years ago. Behind us, Marcella slammed home the final door of the facility, and we did a headcount. Miraculously, we had all survived, including the werewolves. Freyer and I were huffing and puffing. My shoulder still hadn't healed, and I wasn't feeling all that great.

Katie sat on the ground next to several werewolves, now all in human form. Carlos was giving them orders, but I couldn't concentrate on them. My whole body hurt, and my head throbbed.

Liz was standing away from everyone, apparently keeping her distance. She had a dejected look on her face, and I put a hand on her shoulder.

"Thank you," I said and gave her a gentle squeeze.

Marcella marched over and snatched me into a hug of her own, and I screamed in agony. My ribs were broken. Marcella let me go as I gasped in pain. I looked around; my mother looked terrible. She had a gash across her belly that was bleeding profusely from the right side. Katie looked none the worse for wear, but she was covered in black syrupy ichor.

"We have to go," Carlos said, picking my mother up off the ground.

Marcella leaned toward me, but Katie picked me up, hissing at Marcella as she did so.

We emerged from the tunnel at Eliot Norton Park. On the southern edge was a line of cars and a tractor-trailer. I could see Bian's head peeking around the trailer doors, motioning us to hurry. We looked like a nudist camp run amok in downtown Boston with the naked werewolves, now in human form, charging across the park toward the cars.

54

The werewolves had scattered off in different directions. Someone had taken Bian back to Hockamock, but I never saw who. Frankly, after a couple of days of the council's hospitality, I was cooked emotionally. Physically, I felt even worse, literally sick. My joints ached, and fatigue racked my limbs. Sinus pressures had taken residence in my forehead. I was breathing shallowly, gasping for air, almost hyperventilating. I shivered with a fever, too. Something was terribly wrong. Vampires don't get ill. Scariest of all, though, my heart was pounding in my chest.

The ride back to Marcella's seemed to take forever, and I began to panic, unable to draw in enough breath. Finally, as we rolled into the garage, I gasped for air, and Marcella, eyes wide with fear, carried me to the elevator.

"Something's wrong, dear," I wheezed dazedly.

"It's okay, Cait. I've got you." The panic in her voice was unmistakable, though. Something about my appearance had rattled her.

Marcella rushed me into the kitchen, laying me on the long counter. Carlos had taken my mother to the hospital.

I shivered weakly as I lay on the chilly marble. "I'm so cold." The panic that had been rising subsided, and my eyes drifted closed. My thoughts became leaden and disjointed. All I wanted to do was sleep.

"Cait!" Marcella shouted. "No, no, honey. You can't go to sleep."

Marcella held a cup to my lips. I took a sip and tasted the blood. My body rebelled, and I rolled sideways, puking red and black blood all over the floor, the remnants of Donna's blood.

"Thas naw goo—," I said, tongue thick, swollen, and sluggish. With some effort, I opened my eyes and saw Katie staring down at me, a deep furrow on her brow. Her hand stroked my face, but it felt distant, and a warm numbness permeated my body. I let my head loll to the side again, eyes closing.

There was a pinch first in one arm, then the other—needles.

Marcella shook me. "Hold on, Cait. This will help."

I opened my eyes once more. Marcella was holding a bag above her head marked O-Neg. She was squeezing it for all she was worth, pushing the blood into my veins. Liz stood next to her, holding a bag of clear fluids, also squeezing. Someone lay a blanket over me, and in a few minutes, the numbness and buzzing in my head fled, leaving behind a dull ache all over my body. Finally, the bliss of sleep began to take me.

"Cáitlín, child?" It sounded like my mother's voice; I had to be imagining it.

"Yes, mother," I said softly, eyes still closed.

"Stay with us, honey, please. I can't lose you."

"Okay, Ma," my voice sounded small, like a child's.

I woke later, in our bedroom, as I'd come to think of it, to find Katie curled up and resting next to me. Marcella sat on the edge, staring out the enormous window. I tasted her sandalwood scent; it was heavy in the air. Outside, it was mid-day, and the stark winter sunlight streamed into the stuffy room.

I pushed down the covers and tugged at the sweat-soaked, blue button-down pajamas sticking to my skin.

Marcella turned to me, placing her cool hand on my face. The look in her sad eyes was devastating. "I'm so sorry, Cait."

I didn't know what to say. I loved her, but I couldn't get past what she'd done to me, to Aoife. I stared into those frost-blue eyes, desperately wishing I could go back to her house on the cape, before I'd been turned, before all this shit happened, and before I knew.

"Is she still alive?" I asked finally.

Her voice was so soft, mired in regret. "Yes. Liz knows where she is; I don't. We arranged it that way so Schmidt couldn't find her. We split you up. Given it was just two of us, it was easier to protect you alone and hide your sister."

"But why did you make me forget her?" I needn't have asked, though. I already knew the answer.

Marcella sighed and turned back to the window. "So that you wouldn't go looking for her. Your mother we could trust, but you were sixteen. We were certain you'd track her down at some point, and it would all be for naught."

"But, why did you turn me? Why did you send me down into that hole?"

"Because I let my heart get the better of me. When you entered my office, I did find you captivating. You were beautiful and strong and so vibrant. I couldn't help myself. I— I wanted you."

"I don't understand."

Marcella turned and ran her hand through my matted hair. "When we met in the park, Schmidt's people watched us. I had led him straight to you. It wasn't long before I realized I wouldn't be able to stop Schmidt; too many were against me. You could have activated the tablets if you had been human, but I am certain it would have killed you, and I couldn't bear to lose you."

"But—"

"But, why the tunnel, the parasites, all that?" she finished for me. "Simple, really. I didn't want to be your villain. I wanted to be your hero."

"Liz was right. It was like you did to her?"

"In a way, I suppose, but my motives were purer this time, I think."

I ran a hand through my hair, fingers catching among the tangled, matted mess. "So, now what?"

"Now, you go back to a normal life, and I leave you be."

My eyes flew open, and I jerked up painfully. "What? No." I moved my aching legs to the edge of the bed. I realized I couldn't feel her presence. It was like suddenly going blind. That vampiric sixth sense upon which so much relied was just silent. I felt isolated. I tried to brush it off, but I couldn't shake the terrible sinking feeling in my gut. "Marcella, what's happened to me?"

"You're cured. As near as I can guess, your interaction with the tablets unwound the curse from your soul. You're human again, Cait. You can have the normal life I wish I could."

I felt suddenly desperate, and anxiety clawed at me. "No. We can still be together. I'm still alive; I'm still here."

Marcella's tone took a hard edge to it. "How can you say that? Look what I did to you? I took away your life. I stripped away your identity. I broke your world. I am a monster."

"No, you were trying to protect me. You made mistakes, and it all got fucked up. But that's what happens to people in love. They fuck up, but they move on."

She stared at me silently, stroking my cheek.

"Well, say something," I begged.

Marcella hugged me close. "Let's get some food into you and see how that goes."

Marcella helped me to the kitchen, propping me up while we were on the elevator.

"I know what your thinking," I said softly. "But you can't. Please, don't."

She didn't argue; she just held me close and kissed my forehead, which was worse than if we'd fought. It meant she wasn't going to entertain anything I would say. She'd made up her mind.

She made me a breakfast of toast and eggs, then sat quietly, watching me eat it, face impassive. When I finished, I took a deep breath and told her exactly what I thought of her fucking contemplations.

"I can't stop you from dumping me, but it's bullshit. How can I have a normal life now, anyway? I can't. Not with what I know, with what is out there, and yes, with what you did. Besides, if it's because I seem cured, you could turn me again. And with the flood of magic back in the world that I can still feel, I might add, you could probably do it instantly.

Like a gentle pulse under my own, I could still feel the magic, beating warm and alive. I didn't know what it meant, but it meant—something. "The risk would probably be low that I'd become—"

"Cait," she interjected quietly. "You don't want to live forever; you never did." She raised her voice passionately then. "And there is no fucking way I'm going to deprive you of the possibilities you deserve, finding that someone who will live with you, love with you, and grow old with you. You have the second chance I never had, and I won't take that away from you."

"But," my voice sounded small. "But, I just found you. What the fuck am I supposed to do now? If you leave me, I'll have no one."

Tears welled up in my eyes and spilled over, running down my cheeks, dripping off my chin. "You just can't." I buried my face in my hands as the sobs came.

"Cait—."

"No!" I snapped and moved to stand, a little unsteady. Marcella caught me, pulling me into a deep embrace. She tilted my head up, and I looked into her eyes. "I wish you wouldn't hate me so much," she said, and I felt the brush of her mind against my own.

I jerked my face away. "No, you don't," I shouted, struggling to get free. "You don't get to take this away from me. Leave if you want, but I won't let you take my love. I won't." She grabbed my chin and pulled my face back toward hers, holding my arm painfully. "No!" I cried. "I won't let you. Please, Marcella, don't take it away. Don't make it bad. Don't make—."

I was wailing now, hopeless.

Her will settled over mine like sackcloth, and I went limp in her arms, captivated by her gaze. I loved that feeling; it was peaceful, with no decisions, no responsibility.

"Oh, my love," I said, the words deep from my heart but unbidden.

"I wish—," she started, but some deep part of me rebelled suddenly, and I furrowed my brow, furious. Hot anger flashed through me, breaking her mental hold.

"I said no!" I shouted and pulled at her arm. I wasn't going to let her do this. She couldn't leave. I drew her to me with my free hand, kissing her deeply. I nibbled her bottom lip and swept her mouth with my tongue.

"Stop it, Cait," she said as she pulled away, pushing me back. "It's over. Stop acting like some slattern."

It was like a slap. I knew she didn't mean it, but it still hurt.

"That was shitty, even for you, M," Liz said from the doorway. *How long had she been standing there?*

I took the moment of distraction to break loose from Marcella's hold and stalk out of the room. "You fucking bitch." I whispered through my tears.

The clothes Marcella had bought me still hung in her closet, and though I hated to take fucking anything from her right now, I had nothing else. So I dressed, ready to leave.

I tried to rouse Katie, but she didn't move.

"Fuck, what am I going to do with you?" I asked her sleeping form.

"Wake up!" Liz's command was clear, and though it lacked Marcella's power, I'd felt it. I'd had no idea she shared that trait with us—well, Marcella anyway. And I didn't understand how I could still feel it if I was cured. Glamor was different, speaking directly to the mind of the victim. Vampiric commands were raw power, overwhelming the will. I should have only felt the former, not the latter.

Katie stirred and stood. She was in a pair of rolled-up linen pants and a tank top.

"Come on, Katie. We're leaving," I said, headed toward the elevator. But she didn't move. She sniffed at the air and looked at me with a predatory gaze, baring her fangs.

"Oh, shit!"

Katie leaped at me. Fortunately, Liz was faster and managed to get between Katie and me. "Stop!" Liz shouted, and the power of the command forced me to my hands and knees, gasping.

"Cait?" Liz queried, turning toward me. "Are you okay?"

"Yeah, can you be a little more directed with that?"

"That's interesting," she said. Then, she donned a sly smile, quirking one corner of her mouth. "Strip!"

I started lifting my shirt and then realized what I was doing and stopped.

"Hey," I snarled hotly. "That's not okay."

"That is so fucking fascinating." Clearly, her wheels were turning, and I felt I needed to leave right then.

"Probably the remains of the curse. I must be in some kind of vampire remission. Obviously, Katie is hungry, you'll need to help her feed since I can't, and Marcella is going to run the fuck away." My voice was hard and full of resentment.

"Don't worry; you and I will manage Katie together. And, go easy on Marcella," Liz said. "She'll probably figure out her fuck up here in a year or two. She's just trying to protect you."

"Me? Oh, no," I spat. "She's protecting herself. I have a fucking dangerous job anyway. She's not saving my life or anything. She's running away to protect her own feelings so she doesn't have to face me after what she did to me. Don't you fucking dare say it's about protecting me. You, of all people, should know better."

I walked over to Katie, who seemed to recognize me this time, and hugged her. I collected Jabba and found his carrier in Marcella's closet. After he was loaded, I headed for the elevator.

Liz blocked the way for a moment, placing her hand over the call button.

"Liz, please. I appreciate that you want us to figure it out, but after everything, she's probably right. Maybe we need some time apart."

"You don't believe that any more than I do. But, fine," Liz said impassively. "Have it your way. But, she will come back to you eventually, hat in hand." She stepped aside.

I walked by and pressed the elevator call button. I heard Katie step into the sitting room, and Liz put her hand on my shoulder. "I'm sorry, Cait. I know we're not mates or anything, but I've been where you are right now—with Marcella, I mean. If you need to talk, you know where to find me."

"I may take you up on that." Liz's tone was so sincere that, on a whim, I gave her a quick one-armed hug. "Thank you for saving my mother."

She returned it with a squeeze. "You're welcome. I just hope she's okay."

I swallowed hard several times and blinked back more tears. We got off on the first floor, and I found Marcella sitting in the kitchen nursing a glass full of blood.

"Well," I said with as much dignity as I could muster. "I'm going, just like you want." I could tell from her dismal demeanor that this was the last thing she really wanted, but I wasn't going to play games.

"Okay," she said softly. "Carlos called. Your mother is out of surgery, and it looks like she'll be okay physically, but Carlos is worried about her mental state. You should see her."

My shoulders slumped. "I will. And, Marcella, for what it's worth, I love you."

Tears spilled over my lashes again as I took the stairs to the garage, not wanting to stand awkwardly by the elevator where she could hear me cry.

EPILOGUE

One Month Later. . .

I looked at the stack of boxes, wondering how, after the last fourteen years, all that I owned fit into such a small space, minus the Jeep down the garage. On one hand, it had been easy to move out of the apartment. On the other, the sum total of my possessions fit into six boxes. It was pretty pathetic.

"It's kind of sad," Liz said from the doorway, mirroring my thoughts, sipping from Marcella's 'I'm Not a Morning Person' mug.

I looked at her. "Isn't it, though?"

"Not the boxes, Cait. That there's a perfectly gorgeous California king on the fourth floor, and you're staying down here."

I shook my head in disbelief. "Liz, we've had that conversation."

"Just friends," she finished for me, smirking devilishly. "I know, I know. At least step one of my evil plan is in motion. I finally got you to move over here rather than staying in that dungeon you called an apartment. Good God, that place was bloody depressing."

"Hey, that place was fine for me for four years. It wasn't that bad."

Liz walked over and sat down on the bed. "Cait, it was dreadful. All it needed was a rack and an iron maiden, honestly. Besides, your little furball seems much happier over here."

"Speaking of which, where is my baby?" I hadn't seen Jabba for hours.

"In the TV room, curled up with Katie, watching a movie."

"Is everything ready for my mother?" I asked, changing the subject. "She gets out of rehab tomorrow, and she's still not fully recovered. We need to make sure we can take care of her."

"Yes, her room is right down the hall and ready to receive her. Robert has some experience with the mentally disabled, so he will be able to help." She took another sip of blood from the mug. "I'm sorry Schmidt fucked her up. We'll find a way to help her."

"Yeah. Okay, G-Great," I stuttered, losing my concentration as I tasted the blood from Liz's mug in the air. I watched as Liz drank and licked tiny drops from her lips; it was mesmerizing. My tongue flicked out, bringing more of the scent to my vomeronasal duct. God, it was so tempting. I shook myself.

"Are you okay?" Liz asked, watching me. She moved her cup left and right, and watched as I followed it for a second. I shook myself again.

"Yeah, I'm fine. Probably just memories."

"You want to try it? See what happens?" Liz asked.

I didn't bother to answer. I reached out and grabbed her mug, taking a small sip. It was cold, salty, and thick with the appropriate coppery tang. But there was no feeling at all. No hunger to be sated roared in my consciousness. The blood was just—blood.

"Oh, well, good to know," Liz continued. "Anyway, I met Gretchen and Kaja, and this reporter friend of Marcella's, Shandra?"

I barked a laugh, interrupting her. "Shandra is a friend of Marcella's? That's a shock."

"I don't know; she seems nice. We've brought the Channel 7 producers down to the camps, and they're working with Gretchen and Kaja on a half-hour special. Gretchen said not to worry about the interview. She said you were 'old news.'"

I laughed at that, too. That sounded like the precocious little twerp. "That's fine. I didn't want to do it, anyway."

"On an unrelated note, Lieutenant called again. He wants you in on Wednesday."

I laughed. "Well, that's too bad. I'm on leave for the next two weeks, so he'll have to wait. Besides, he's got his hands full with the feds and that hole in the world we left behind."

"True. Though, he seemed pretty insistent that you call him in the morning." Liz finished the last of her blood and set her mug on the nightstand. I noticed for the first time that she had a tube of lotion in her other hand as she patted the bed. "Come here. Strip off that sports bra and lay down on your stomach. I want to show you something I learned overseas."

I raised an eyebrow but did what she asked. I had an idea of what she had in mind, and I was all for it.

I wasn't stupid; I knew she was trying to seduce me. And, frankly, I was tired of pining over Marcella. I would probably never get over her, but Jennifer had been right; it was okay to move on. I just wasn't ready, not yet.

Liz squeezed a bit of the lotion into her palm, the tube making a somewhat rude noise. Then, an involuntary groan escaped my lips as she began her magic, massaging my lower back muscles.

"You know, I think I see what she saw in you," Liz said. Her voice was husky and low.

I closed my eyes and finally began to relax into Liz's ministrations. "Mmmhmm. Go on."

"Good God, you really are beautiful, Cait, but I'm sure you know that." I didn't, but I let her go on. "Now, I would never want to make you do something you don't want."

I rolled my eyes. "Good to know, just please don't stop," I grunted as she massaged up my spine.

"If you want me to leave, you just need to ask," she said, working her thumb into a particularly stubborn knot under my shoulder blade.

"Yep," I groaned in agreement.

"Aren't you worried about the gate?" Liz asked as she began to work my glutes. "You have a nice rear end."

I blew out a breath. "Knock it off, Liz. And—" I groaned as she hit a kink in my right thigh. "No, the gate isn't my problem anymore. All this paranormal shit was giving me hives anyway."

Liz slapped my butt. "Now, Cait? Honestly? I give you hives?"

I laughed. "Sorry, I just meant the politics and the skullduggery. You're plenty nice in small doses."

Liz gasped in mock indignance. "I'm hurt. I've been nothing but lovely to you since—"

"Since you trapped me in a fucking concrete cell and let Schmidt torture me?" I let out another groan of pleasure as she worked my other thigh. "Oh, God, I needed this."

"Well, that was before I knew you. And did you just use the word skullduggery in a sentence? You've been around us too much, I think."

"Yes, despite the muscular exterior—" I moaned as she hit another knot, this time in my shoulder. "As I was saying, despite my appearance, my vocabulary extends beyond the monosyllabic. And, are you saying your compassion only extends to people you know?"

She stopped and grew very quiet for a moment. I turned my head to look at her.

"Only people I trust," she said softly, and the corners of her mouth crooked in a sad smile.

"Why would you trust me? I swore at one point I'd kill you."

"Because you tore off your own arm to save a child you scarcely knew. It's hard to find someone that dedicated to doing the right thing, Cait. Truthfully, the more I think about it, the more inspiring it seems."

"Turning your back on your sinful ways, are you?" I asked, jerking my thumb toward my back. "Keep going."

"Hardly, darling." Liz sounded a little choked up. "Just—oh, shut up, Cait."

Liz went back to work, and I said nothing else for the next half hour as she massaged my back, working out the kinks like an expert. She had probably been doing this for a hundred years, so I was in good hands.

Eventually, she leaned forward, and I felt her breasts pressed against my back, soft and cool. "How does that feel?" she whispered. *When had she stripped off her shirt?*

"Lovely," I said tiredly, eyes feeling heavy-lidded.

"Oh, no, you don't," Elizabeth said, running a finger down my back, causing me to gasp loudly and arch. "Oh, my! We are sensitive, aren't we?"

"No," I whimpered. "Don't you—"

Her tongue, wet and soft, ran up my spine, causing me to jerk spasmodically and pulling a harsh, aroused breath from my throat.

"That was not okay, Liz," I said with a laugh. I began to lift, trying to get off the bed, but she jerked me onto my back roughly, pinning my arms. A wicked smile split Liz's beautiful face as her fangs extended.

"No," I breathed, my eyes wide with terror. "Don't."

"Too late, little girl," she murmured, leaning down.

"Please, Liz, stop," I whimpered as her grip tightened painfully on my wrists. I struggled against her as she leaned in, licking my neck. Then her will washed over mine, and I felt as if I were falling into darkness as the world around me dissolved, leaving only her eyes, those beautiful green eyes.

For a moment, I wanted her so badly, but I shook off the influence quickly. Robert had been right; she sucked at glamour. But, unable to break free physically, I turned my head and closed my eyes, waiting for the inevitable. A gentle kiss pressed to my cheek, and Liz lifted. She was still straddling me but left my hands free.

"Whew, I'm sorry, I got a little carried away," Liz said cheerily as she lifted off of me, moving to stand next to the bed.

I jerked myself up and backed to the corner of the bed, hands shaking, fighting the instinct to curl myself up very small.

"No, I'm sorry. I wasn't trying to be a tease; I just—."

Liz's eyes widened in sudden realization, and sympathy crossed her face. "Oh, God, I had no idea." She placed a hand on my arm.

"Yeah, well, now you know," I said. "And it sucks." My emotions spun jumbled as feelings of arousal and attraction warred with fear, shame, and mistrust. Slowly, I stretched out my legs and forced myself to uncoil.

"Yes, it does," she said. Her voice was low and sympathetic, and her face spoke volumes about her own experience. "Have you ever spoken with someone about it?"

"No." I had told Jennifer it had happened, but I hadn't recounted any of it, not ready to open that can of worms at the time.

She placed her hand on mine. "Would you like to?"

Before I could think about it, I just started blabbering, the words tumbling out.

"It was in 2008. I was deployed to Iraq for my first tour. I had just finished my first patrol, and we were all sitting around drinking. After we'd been having fun for a while, a couple of guys joined us. One of them was named John Holley; he was a Marine Scout Sniper. He had classic good looks, you know: square jaw, cleft chin, black hair, blue eyes. He kept making eyes at me the whole night, and I was pretty drunk, so I was probably being a little flirtatious."

Liz sat and listened, pulling one leg under the other. It was strange how much of Marcella I saw in Liz. It was also refreshing that she was so *not* like her. Where Marcella was demanding and pressuring, Liz was coaxing and respectful.

"Anyway, I began to feel a little queasy. I wasn't an experienced drinker, you know? So, I went into the latrine and puked my guts out. And that's where Sergeant Holley found me. I didn't like him. He liked killing." I snorted in derision. "He got off on being a sniper and 'the pink mist' or some shit. Anyway, I told him to leave, but he pushed me down, banging my head on the sink."

"I thought he found you puking."

"No, sorry, I skipped that part. When I finished puking, I went to the sink, and that's when he came in."

"Sorry, I shouldn't have interrupted. I was just making sure I understood. Please continue." Her voice was gentle and supportive.

"So, he pushed me to the ground, and I cracked my head on the sink." My voice had started to shake a little. "I tried to call out, but he—." I stopped, taking a breath and swallowing hard. I could feel pressure in my eyes. Liz held up a finger and then brought me a glass of water from the bathroom.

"Here," she whispered.

"Thank you," I said. "I'm sorry."

"No, you don't have to apologize. Keep going, please."

"Are you sure? You look—." I could see the pain in her eyes as I spoke, and I knew she was reliving her own trauma, maybe more than one. I took a drink of water.

"I'm sure. Keep going." She placed her hand back on mine as I set down the glass of water.

"Anyway, I tried to scream, but he punched me and banged my head onto the floor. Then, he pulled down my pants, and he—." I broke down into sobs, and Liz put her arms around me.

"Shh, I'm here. You're safe with me." Her hold was gentle, and I wanted to sink into it, but I pushed away as a rush of anger boiled inside of me.

"No, I need to get through this. It's been ten years, and I haven't been able to talk about it with anyone, not ever. He flipped me over and pulled down my shorts. I wasn't wearing any panties at the time, having just come out of the shower before the party. I just remember wishing I'd had more clothes on, you know? To make it harder for him.

"Then, he—uh—." My head was spinning. "He raped me," I whispered. "He put himself inside me. And I couldn't—." I began rubbing my hand reflexively on my legs as if I could wipe the memory away.

"Anyway," I said, voice trembling. "I reported him. Morgan

went with me."

"Morgan?" she asked.

"Specialist Kennedy, my would-be girlfriend at the time, though we were never—. Anyhow, when I went to report it, they just said it was my word against Holley's. They didn't bother to do a rape exam. He was never charged or even given a slap on the wrist. A year later, I was deployed to the same post with him. The ironic thing is that I ended up saving his life. We were in his sniper nest when a grenade came in. If Morgan hadn't been there at the time, I would have just let us both die."

Now that I'd said it, I felt nothing, neither relieved nor miserable. In movies, there are moments when the hero spills their guts to someone, and suddenly, now that trauma is out, they are all better. I call them 'Good Will Hunting' moments. They don't exist. Dealing with trauma means re-living it repeatedly until you process your feelings. Eventually, if you're lucky, it becomes a faded memory that never goes away but doesn't ruin your life anymore. I had a very long way to go to get to that place with the rape.

I ran a hand across my face and looked at my watch— 2:07 AM. I gave Liz a gentle hug. "Thank you for listening, and please don't think I don't appreciate it. But I'm suddenly exhausted. You can stay or go. It's okay, but please don't expect anything."

Liz stood but said nothing as I fished a t-shirt from the dresser, turned out the light, and crawled into bed. A few moments later, the light in the hallway went out, leaving me in darkness as Liz closed the door.

I had thought she'd left until she slid silently into the bed, her cool flesh pressed against my back. I didn't speak or protest; I just closed my eyes.

❋ ❋ ❋

I woke to an empty bed around nine the following day,

and I staggered down to the kitchen to forage for breakfast. The elevator dinged, and Liz walked out, freshly dressed but looking a little peaked.

"Hey," she said. "We don't have much for food in this house, did you know that? So I picked up some coffee and a fresh cannoli for you. I also stopped by the store and got you some breakfast food." She held up a pastry box and a coffee cup from Modern.

"Oh, baby, you are speaking my language," I cooed.

"Oh, is that all it takes," she said with a smirk.

I bit into the cannoli and spoke around a mouthful. "It takes more than a cannoli—"

"Hello," Liz said, interrupting me, looking at the table. "What's this?"

I had left Morgan's letters from my refrigerator door there, and she picked them up, eyebrow raised.

"Those are private." I went to snatch them away, but she moved her hand preternaturally fast and put an arm out to block me.

"I'll say. This one here is over ten years old and unopened. And it still smells of—of perfume." She flipped them over, looking at the return address. "Are these from the same girl that you mentioned last night?" Liz wiggled her eyebrows. "Wow, Cait, you have taken useless lesbian to new heights with this."

"So I've been told," I quipped. Unable to stop her, I crossed my arms and watched her cut open the first letter. My cheeks flushed as she leaned against the island and read it.

"Oh, my," she whispered. "Um, Cait, why didn't you ever open this?"

"Because she chose a man over me, Liz. She got married, and I never forgave her for abandoning me; that's why."

"Oh, Cait," Liz whispered, hand over her mouth and shaking her head. She looked like she was in shock. Liz's eyes were even a little wet. "This is just fucking tragic. I mean, look at me." She wiped her eyes with a thumb and held out the paper. "You,

Kitty Cait, should more promptly open your mail."

I snatched the letter from her at the mention of Morgan's pet name for me, and I almost fell to the floor as I read it.

Dear Kitty Cait,

I couldn't help but notice that you haven't been returning my calls. I think I know why and I can only hope this letter reaches you. So, if you listened to my voice mails, you know by now that there was no wedding. I couldn't do it. I don't love Clay, and I never could.

Now comes the hard part. I couldn't ever love Clay because I'm in love with you. There, I said it. I wrote it down for all the world to read. I am in love with my best friend. I am hoping that you'll call me after you get this and we can talk. I am hoping that the reason you stopped returning my calls is the reason that I think it is. I am hoping that you'll call me back and let me know that you feel the same way I do. I am hoping that you can forgive me for leaving you in the state you were in. I wanted to kiss you and tell the cab to piss off, but I was afraid.

I have an interview next week with the Chicago PD. Please, please, forgive me and call me. If you don't, just know that I think I'll always feel this way for you.

Love,

The fire-haired goddess extraordinaire

"Fuck," I swore loudly

I sat at the table and read the letter three times over. I didn't know whether to laugh or cry.

"It fucking figures," I whispered.

"What does?" Liz asked.

"That, in my fucked up angry brain, I'd chosen to cut her off and ended up cutting off my fucking nose to spite my face, that's what."

"Okay, well, yes, that was a colossal fuck up, darling; I can't lie. And there's no fixing it." She waved the second envelope at me. "Or is there? Aren't you just the least bit curious about what she has to say after ten years?"

"I'm fucking terrified, is what I am. I'm a total bitch, a total asshole, a fucking idiot," I admonished. I put my face in my hands and screamed in frustration.

"Yes, all that may be true, but—." Liz waved the second letter at me again.

I looked at her for support as I took it, and she just nodded, grinning like she knew what was inside.

I started opening it but stopped. "What do you think it is?"

"I have no idea, but this is too dramatic and delicious to pass up. It's like a soap opera. So come on, open it." Liz was practically vibrating with excitement.

"Have a lot of experience with soaps?" I asked as I tore open the envelope.

"Over sixty years of Coronation Street," she said indignantly. "I've seen every episode except last week's, so fuck off and read the bloody thing."

I unfolded the letter.

Hey Kitty Cait,

Been a long time. I can't believe it's been ten years since we've talked. I've been doing well. I've spent the last three years on SWAT for the Chicago PD, but I'm feeling it's time for a change. I put in for an open spot on the Fugitive Apprehension Unit in Boston, and I got the job. Shocking, I'm sure. Not having heard from me in ten years and suddenly poof. But I didn't want you to get blindsided. I was hoping we might get together and maybe bury whatever is between us. You were my best friend, and I'd like to have her back.

I've been out there a few times. I even saw you stomping out of the Homicide Lieutenant's office. You looked pissed, so I didn't think it wise to approach you. It was funny, though; you walked right by me. You probably wouldn't have recognized me with the scar and the short hair. You looked just as I remembered you. Maybe a little more buff than the day I left. The day I screwed up.

I asked one of the detectives about you, a guy named Tony. He said you were a first-class bitch. Attagirl. Well, here's to hoping! See you soon.

With Love,

Morgan

"Holy shit," I whispered, handing the letter to Liz, who just squealed in delight.

Cait and Marcella will return in *Black Mirror. . .*

Coming 2023

ABOUT THE AUTHOR

Aoibh Wood

 Aoibh Wood has been a practitioner in the cybersecurity space for over 17 years and has worked in technology for 35 years. Blood Rituals is her first novel. She lives in New England and is a strong believer in the power of women and our ability to support each other.

COLLABORATIVE LEARNING IN
STAFFROOMS AND CLASSROOMS

The Primary Curriculum Series

This innovative series promotes reflective teaching and active forms of pupil learning. The books explore the implications of these commitments for curriculum and curriculum-related issues.

The argument of each book flows in, around and among a variety of case studies of classroom practice, introducing them, probing, analysing and teasing out their implications before moving on to the next stage of the argument. The case study material varies in source and form – children's work, teacher's work, diary entries, drawings, poetry, literature, interviews. The vitality and richness of primary school practice are conveyed, together with the teacher expertise on which these qualities are based.

Series Editors

Mary Jane Drummond is Tutor in Education, University of Cambridge Institute of Education. and Andrew Pollard is Professor in the Faculty of Education, University of the West of England, Bristol.

Series Titles

ASSESSING CHILDREN'S LEARNING
Mary Jane Drummond
1-85346-198-9

COLLABORATIVE LEARNING IN STAFFROOMS AND CLASSROOMS
Colin Biott & Patrick Easen
1-85346-201-2

DEVELOPMENTS IN PRIMARY MATHEMATICS TEACHING
Ann Sawyer
1-85346-196-2

THE EXPRESSIVE ARTS
Fred Sedgwick
1-85346-200-4

THE HUMANITIES IN PRIMARY EDUCATION
Nick Clough, Martin Forrest, Penelope Harnett, Don Kimber, Ian Menter & Elizabeth Newman
1-85346-342-6

LITERACY
Margaret Jackson
1-85346-197-0

PERSONAL, SOCIAL AND MORAL EDUCATION
Fred Sedgwick
1-85346-291-8

PRIMARY DESIGN AND TECHNOLOGY
Ron Ritchie
1-85346-340-X

PRIMARY SCIENCE – MAKING IT WORK
Chris Ollerenshaw & Ron Ritchie
1-85346-199-7

WORKING FOR SOCIAL JUSTICE IN THE PRIMARY SCHOOL
Morwenna Griffiths & Carol Davies
1-85346-341-8

COLLABORATIVE LEARNING IN STAFFROOMS AND CLASSROOMS

Colin Biott and Patrick Easen

David Fulton Publishers
London

David Fulton Publishers Ltd
2 Barbon Close, London WC1N 3JX

First published in Great Britain by
David Fulton Publishers 1994

Note: The right of the authors to be identified as the authors of this
work has been asserted by them in accordance with the
Copyright, Designs and Patents Act 1988.

Copyright © Colin Biott and Patrick Easen

British Library Cataloguing in Publication Data

A catalogue record for this book is available from the British Library

ISBN 1-85346-201-2

Typeset by Harrington & Co.
Printed in Great Britain by BPC Journals, Exeter.

Contents

Acknowledgements   vi
Introduction   1

Part One: Belonging and Contributing

1   Children Learning to be Together in Classrooms   7

2   Children Learning to be Contributing Members
    of Classroom Groups   35

3   Learning to Belong and Contribute in Staffrooms:
    Student Teachers as Temporary Staff Members   67

4   New Staff Members Learning from the
    'Memory Bearers': Teachers' First School
    Christmas (with Anne Spendiff)   93

5   Experienced Teachers Planning Together:
    Belonging or Contractual Membership?   110

Part Two: Developing Collaboration through Enquiry

6   Becoming a Good Response Partner (with Jo Fawcett)   131

7   Developing Learning Partnerships in Classrooms:
    Peer Tutoring and Advisory Teaching
    (with Julia Smith and Jo Ann Buczynskyj)   144

8   Children Working in Groups to Solve
    Real Problems (with Karen Haggis)   162

Part Three: Collaborating and Learning

9   Collaborating to Learn and Learning to Collaborate   183

10 Understanding and Promoting Collaborative
    Learning   203

References   210

Dedication

This book is dedicated to all the people with whom
we have worked and learned collaboratively,
and to our friends and families:
Sylvia, Catherine and Anna,
and
Wendy, James and Abigail.

Acknowledgements

We would like to acknowledge, with gratitude, the help of
the following teachers and colleagues who contributed case
study materials for this book: Meg Barber, Debbie
Collinson, Jo Fawcett, Jo Ann Buczynskyj, Karen Haggis,
Julia Smith and Anne Spendiff.

We also thank Madeleine Atkins, Catherine Clark, Gill
Morrow, Mick Clough, Malcolm Eves and Alan Stoker who
worked with us on previous projects from which we have
drawn.

The cover photograph was taken by Ken Etherington, and
is used with the permission of Alison Bishop and Harlow
Green Infant School, Gateshead.

Introduction

When children start school they join an accidental collection of separate individuals of their own age, and they begin to learn what is acceptable and what is unacceptable in a context of both established rules and emerging ground rules which arise when they work and play with other children. At the same time as they experience challenges of community life, children also become aware that schools concentrate mainly upon individual achievement, sometimes even emphasizing lack of it. Very soon they have to come to terms with being tested and judged separately, having their own progress measured and being made to feel different from others. This is just one of many tensions that characterize school life. Children experience a complex weave of imposition and choice, individuality and interdependence, formality and informality and peace and turmoil during ordinary school days. Sometimes they are expected to work privately and silently and at other times they are required to do things together. They have to learn to juggle their self-interests with the obligations and demands of being members of a class or group.

Teachers may also experience similar tensions as they balance their individual concerns with the expectations and obligations of staff membership. They work apart from each other for much of the day, they are appraised separately, and they sometimes compete with each other for extra salary allowances. At the same time, they are often obliged to plan and review in teams and they sometimes choose to work and learn together informally because they find it beneficial.

It is not surprising, then, that much worthwhile collaborating, in both classrooms and staffrooms, is unanticipated and spontaneous, whilst that which is planned and pre-organized often yields superficial activity of little consequence. For this reason, attempts to improve collaboration require more than lists of suitable activities, packs of appropriate materials, comprehensive guidelines about arrangements or coherent policy statements. These all have their places, but serious attempts to improve collaboration are helped more by investigations of what happens when people actually work and learn together in specific schools. Systematic studies of this nature can take us beyond misleading impressions which derive from intermittent and ad hoc observations of surface behaviour, and overheard snatches of talk. Close analysis of children's and teachers' interaction can yield surprising insights into patterns of collaborative learning and help towards a better understanding of the progress of individuals, pairs and groups. In this book, we have introduced a number of case studies drawn from investigations which teachers have carried out to research and improve their own practices. Whilst they are a weak substitute for your own enquiries, we do hope that readers will be able to review their own experiences in the light of the evidence we have offered.

We have selected our cases to convey and explore some of the uncertainties and complexities of collaborative learning and at the same time to show how it can seem ordinary and familiar. For this reason, we have tried, in four main ways, to represent a broad range of ways of working together in order to show its perplexing complexity. First, we have not concentrated solely on formal groupwork with set exercises, either in classrooms or staffrooms, nor have we started with a single definition against which to judge the way children or teachers have tried to learn together.

Second, we have included both children's and teachers' learning in the same book. As well as providing additional breadth, we think that this will also help teachers to reflect on their own experiences of collaboration with colleagues as well as on their work as teachers of children. It also underlines that what teachers think and do to promote collaborative learning in their classrooms will relate partly to their own social experiences as well as to what they have read in libraries or been taught during courses. A major part of our own professional knowledge of collaboration has been gained through working and learning with other people: through accumulated insights and by making associations between the particular and general. Learning from social experiences is multi-faceted, multi-directional, fragmented, inconsistent, ambiguous and contradictory.

Third, we have focused on a range of contextual features of collaboration. We considered the extent to which patterning of behaviour was, at one extreme, formally imposed by a teacher on children or by a headteacher upon staff, and at the other extreme, how far it emerged from interactions which were initiated by the children or teachers themselves. Other researchers have worked at various points along this continuum. Galton, for example, has been concerned mainly with teacher-initiated collaborative groupwork which he has defined as an activity 'where all the pupils in the group are expected to work together to produce a single outcome' (Galton and Williamson, 1992, p.11). Towards the other end of the continuum, Hart (1989; 1992) has investigated spontaneous collaboration which was initiated by the children themselves and which was often associated with getting help for individual work rather than starting shared tasks. This form of collaboration was found to be much more 'fluid, fleeting and difficult to pin down' (1989, p.5). This broader notion of there being many different situations and opportunities for children to cooperate and collaborate, suggests that teachers need to pay attention to children's overall experiences of working together in classrooms. For example, Rowland's (1984) year-long observation of a class of children caught the spontaneity of much of their shared learning and showed how children controlled their own participation in group activities which they started themselves, and Dowrick's (1993) comparison of different kinds of paired work between 6- and 7-year old children also helps to widen the lens through which we interpret children's opportunities to learn together. Dowrick used the terms 'sidework' and 'associative interaction' to describe activities in which children worked separately, but beside each other, to complete the same tasks. They were able to talk with their partners and he found that, for some pairs, there was more cognitive conflict and higher order talk during 'sidework' than when both partners had to work jointly at each task.

We also considered another contextual factor: the relative strength of expectations and norms of collaboration in different settings. Hart (1989) advocated that encouraging 'collaborative learning is, in effect, a process of developing the class as a learning community, rather than being simply a matter of choosing, for a particular task or activity, between individual or group working' (p.22). Like Hart, Nias has also studied both direct and indirect ways of building a sense of community in schools. Nias *et al.* (1989) have coined the term 'culture of collaboration' to describe a sense of community which enabled staff of some primary schools to work and learn together. They found that collaboration involved the interdependence of the individual and the group, for the enrichment of both. Teamwork on tasks overlapped with social interaction, and in a later study of 'whole schools' (Nias *et al.*, 1992) collaboration was seen as having both practical and symbolic purposes:

> when teachers and other staff worked with one another they demonstrated that they could, at least from time to time, do so productively. In this sense, collaboration was more important as a symbol, even a celebration, of interdependence than it was for the instrumental gains that it brought. (p.113)

Even so, it would be naive to imply that all people would be expected to collaborate, or avoid collaboration, to the same extent in any classroom or staffroom. Hall and Oldroyd (1992), for example, have shown how collaborative relationships may be 'restricted to certain interactions within a wide social situation marked by contradictory goals' (p.105). Like Galton and Williamson (1992), they also draw distinctions between cooperation and collaboration. Whilst Galton and Williamson refer to task demands and outcomes as distinguishing features between them, Hall and Oldroyd point to varied degrees of choice, commitment and amount of effort which are put into pooling ideas and learning together.

This brings us to the fourth feature of the book. We have tried to represent a range of personal perceptions and individual meanings that people make of collaboration, partly in relation to the extent to which an activity is seen as risky, partly to how demanding it is felt to be and partly to do with whether or not it is seen as meaningful and worthy of special effort.

It is intended that this book will convey the value of systematic enquiry and the use of evidence and feedback in teachers' reflections, judgements and decisions about how to improve their work. Its sub-text conveys the message that many teachers are developing deep understanding of how to encourage and teach children to be 'positive, participative citizens with the motivation to join in' (NCC, 1990). What is more, they are doing this whilst having to cope with a bombardment of slogans and glib solutions about how to make children grow up to be disciplined and respectful. At a time when some people beat drums of doom about contemporary society and schools, it matters that teachers are confident about how they work and learn together and how they promote and foster children's participation in classroom learning communities.

PART ONE

Belonging and Contributing

Chapter 1

Children Learning to be Together in Classrooms

One afternoon, I was sitting in a classroom observing children aged 7 to 8 years. I was sitting alone at a desk writing field-notes, when a girl came and sat beside me with her book in her hand. I stopped writing and turned towards her, anticipating that she would ask me to read what she had written or would say that she was stuck. Without looking at me, she said, 'You can do your work, if you like'. I turned back to my field-notes and she started to write in her book. We sat together like that for some time, not talking but comfortable in each other's company.

We have recalled the above incident to remind ourselves of a significant feature of school life: that children work for most of the time in the constant presence of other people. Even when children work on individual tasks they usually do so in close proximity to others. Classroom life offers a perplexing and sometimes frustrating mix of privacy and public action. Openness and cooperation may be encouraged one day, but on the next, a teacher may expect that work will be kept private, and anything else will be called copying. Even a friend at a neighbouring desk may ask for help, then resist unwelcome intrusion soon afterwards.

Some adults still recall public rebuke embedded in apparent help, their skin prickling as they waited for a teacher who was standing over them to start drawing attention to their mistakes:

> '"Right", says the teacher in a quiet voice, "I see you've made a mistake." Then, speaking in a loud, public voice, "How do you spell receive ? ...John, you tell Colin how to spell it. ...Good lad ...did you hear that ? ...Right then, well don't forget next time... or you will receive a severe blow on the bonce ! ...Alright now, stop laughing everyone and get on with your work."'

A likeable teacher often used to do that. It seemed fair because we all seemed to have our turns to laugh and to be laughed at. Maybe it wasn't really fair, but it was done with benevolent playfulness. Most of the children also seemed to like to know about each other's mistakes. What with that, and with the possibilities of copying, it is not surprising that we sometimes kept our arms around our work. Some people have carried a fear of negative judgements from school into adulthood and they still avoid revealing their work for others to see. Those who went on to become teachers put children's pictures over the windows of their classroom doors.

The proximity of others in classrooms is so obvious that its consequences are often ignored, and insufficient effort is put into trying to understand how the social organization of work in classrooms may influence children's personal and social development as well as affect their progress on set tasks. Children will experience different kinds of formal arrangements for working with others. These are likely to range from set exercises to be undertaken separately whilst sitting alongside others, through taking part in group activities with or without a teacher present, to being part of a collective audience receiving direct whole-class teaching. There will be times when arrangements will be imposed and directed by a teacher and other times when children may initiate their own activities and manage their own participation, either during lessons or in breaks between them. Sometimes children will choose who they will sit with or work beside, whilst at other times they may have little or no say in the matter. There will be variations in how they are expected to work with others, in what they are asked to do together, and for how long they are expected to do it. The prospect of being removed from a group may even be used as a threat of punishment, as in the warning, 'If you go on like that much longer ... you'll have to work over there by yourself'. In order to build a broad base for our discussions of collaboration in classrooms and staffrooms, we shall start, in this first chapter, by exploring how children both shape and respond to the social conditions in which they work and learn.

Working and learning with others in classrooms

We shall begin by exploring informal and spontaneous forms of working and learning together rather than with formal groupwork which has been the main emphasis in many previous accounts of classroom collaboration and which we shall address in the next chapter. We shall concentrate first upon how young children learn to be together in pairs and loosely knit groups with changing participation, illustrating our points with field notes describing interactions between children in the 'writing corner' of the reception class in an infants school.

Much of the writing about collaborative learning describes pre-arranged groupwork imposed by teachers. Galton and Williamson (1992), for example, have recently categorized group work in primary classrooms into four types: seating groups, working groups, cooperative groups and collaborative groups. Their classification is based upon the nature of the 'task demands' and the intended outcomes of children's work:

Type	Task Demand	Intended Outcome
• Seating groups	Each pupil has a separate task	Different outcomes from different assignments
• Working groups	Each pupil has the same task	Each pupil completes same assignment independently
• Cooperative groups	Separate but related tasks	Joint outcome from different assignments
• Collaborative groups	Each pupil has the same task	Joint outcome, all pupils share the same assignment

(after Galton and Williamson, 1992. p.10).

This is a helpful categorization of how teachers attempt to

impose patterns of social interaction on children's behaviour, but it does not account for any of the kinds of spontaneous working together which children might initiate themselves. Underlying it is a succinct, operational definition of collaborative group work which, according to Galton and Williamson, 'involves all children contributing to a single outcome'. However, more than a decade of research at the University of Leicester has shown that this is, in any case, quite rare. They have identified some enduring contradictions of seating and working arrangements in primary classrooms. At the beginning of the 1980s, the ORACLE study (Galton *et al.*, 1980) showed that whilst the most common style of classroom organization was for children to sit in groups, only 9 per cent of class time was spent on cooperative or collaborative work. It was individual activities which took up 80 per cent of the children's time. At the end of the decade a study in small primary schools (Galton and Patrick, 1990) showed a similar pattern. Children were seated in groups for 56 per cent of the time, but they only worked in groups for 5 per cent of the time. They worked individually for 81 per cent of the time, even though they sat at individual desks for only 7.5 per cent of the time. Notably, few differences were found between infant and junior classrooms.

A great deal of emphasis has been placed upon the extent to which children concentrate on tasks and on levels of distraction. This perspective on group work is evident, for instance, when Yeomans (1983) advocates its use as a 'kind of organisation which allows them [children] more contact with their teachers' (p.104), and when Barrow (1984) claims that if we want children 'to learn things and produce responses of quality - it follows that we will need to structure and play an active part in that group work' (p.123).

Since the large-scale studies referred to above, Galton has conducted a number of small-scale studies in contrasting classrooms. He has explored the meanings which both teachers and children make of group work (Galton and Williamson,1992). He has also involved teachers and children in the research and has provided more telling insights into the complexities of how children work and learn together. He has shown how teachers' approaches and concepts of group work are value-laden. As well as revealing how teachers try to shape children's working relationships,

Galton's more recent studies have shown the influence of each teacher's values and beliefs about teaching. These fruitful investigations have not only identified emergent patterns of children's and teachers' participation but have also explored, with the children and teachers, how these might be interpreted. We shall return to Galton's case studies of formal group learning in Chapter 2, but first we shall consider what happens when young children interact spontaneously and informally during periods when they are given a relatively free choice of what to do.

We have been interested in what we might learn from investigating apparently formless and spontaneous interactions between children which, by their nature, may only be understood in retrospect through sustained study of classroom action. We do not assume that such activity will necessarily be unstructured and unimportant simply because it falls outside a teacher's direct control. We are aware that the label 'structure' is usually reserved for explicit and formally documented activity in schools, such as 'the curriculum structure' or 'the school management structure'. Similarly, when the term 'structure' is used in relation to classroom management, it is associated mostly with patterns of activity which are shaped and controlled by teachers. The term 'unstructured', or even 'structureless', is more likely to be used to denote apparently formless interactions which seem to occur in corners and recesses of classrooms.

We use the term 'structure' in its fundamental sense to refer to regular and enduring patterns of behaviour in classrooms and staffrooms. It then becomes apparent that preplanned or 'imposed structure' is just one aspect rather than the whole area of our concern. Salaman (1980), for example, has argued that the analysis and description of structure is central to the study of how people work in all forms of organizations. The concept of 'structure' has a long pedigree and researchers have tended to employ two main perspectives in investigating its origins and effects: imposed and emergent. The distinction between imposed and emergent structure is worth mentioning because it helps us to avoid confusing 'official' or, in this case, teachers', definitions of classroom organization, with the analyses of actual behaviours and events. Official accounts are problematic because, as Salaman has argued, 'members of organisations themselves [like teachers and children] tend to perceive their jobs and activities in terms of their conception of what they ought to be doing' (p.57). For this reason, patterns of children's working relationships in classrooms have been explained according to the structures which are apparent when viewed in terms of teachers' and/or researchers' main priorities.

We want to emphasize that classrooms which seem formless and haphazard to a casual observer, because teacher direction is not obvious, may actually be structured and worthy of systematic and concentrated attention. For example, 'teacher-directed structures' and 'child-initiated structures' coexist, sometimes at variance with each other and sometimes congruently. Classroom structures may also shift and change in unplanned ways, as when teachers modify their actions in line with changes of moods and unanticipated events. Perhaps this piece of writing distilled from teaching and observing teachers will illustrate what we mean:

There's a Dog in the Yard

It was good when we first started.

Miss Hetchins had said she liked our teacher's
New tie,
And he was in a good mood.

He was sort of
Half smiling
        and half singing,
To himself.

We were in groups
Again
Doing 'Floating and Sinking'
Again,
With these corks and plasticine and things
In these washing up bowls.

When we knocked our dish over,
He smiled and said,
Mop it up
And fill it up,
In a singing sort of voice.

When Doddsy and Burnsey knocked their dish over, and
Judy dropped her jotter in the water,
He talked to them, quietly
Like when that inspector came.

I think he wouldn't have minded,
When we spilled our water again,
If Melanie's little sister hadn't brought that note
About the staff meeting at lunch-time, and
'Has anyone lost these gloves ?'.

He looked dead cross, and
He muttered something to himself about
Bank and cash
And lunch-time.

'Right, put your dishes away, and
Gather around this one on my desk,
With your hands
On your heads'.

We all watched Alison floating a piece of paper,
Except for Peter Bell
Getting the cork from Grahame
And Burnsey nipping Jane.

'Right, go to your own seats.'

We had to do drawings,
Off the board,
Of dishes and things.
And the teacher walked up and down looking
Dead bored.

He looked out of the window, and he said.

"There's a dog in the yard !'

'It might be a rotweiller.
I'd better tell the caretaker.'

And then he went out into the corridor to talk to the other
teachers who'd got bored with their lessons as well.

And I had to write,
Naughty people's names
On the board.
(Colin Biott)

Case Study : You can use a lot of Blu-tak

In this first case study we show how Debbie Collinson, a
teacher of 4- and 5-year old children, tried to identify some
features of the emergent social structure of children's working relationships, At the time of the study, the children had
been in the school for only ten weeks. On five occasions,
during a seven-day period, she tried to detach herself for
between ten and 15 minutes in order to make field notes of

what was happening in the 'writing corner' of her class-room. The 'writing corner' is enclosed on three sides, with one wall on which children can stick their drawings, writing or notices. The children have free access to this area which contains books, writing equipment, a desk and a tape recorder. The starting points for her observations were chosen opportunistically in moments when her attention was not being sought directly by any of the children and when she anticipated, intuitively, that it was possible to snatch ten or 15 undisturbed minutes. Despite some interruptions from children wanting immediate attention, she was able to sustain the field noting, for about 15 minutes, by sitting at a particular desk: a signal she used to indicate to the children that she wanted 'to do her work' for a while.

FIELD NOTE   Monday 9 November, 2.40–2.55 pm. Writing Corner.

1   John, Abbi and Laura go in. John copies words from wall. Abbi and Laura argue over Naomi's dictionary. Abbi comes over and says it should be in the drawer. I remind her that Naomi has gone and it can be used for play. Abbi takes it back and says to Laura 'the teacher says I can use it'. Laura picks up a book. Abbi makes a book using paper and a stapler.
   Laura announces that they're playing schools. John and Abbi agree to play. 'Go outside and wait quietly', she says, and John and Abbi go outside the corner and stand in line. Laura pretends to ring the bell and calls the class numbers out. They don't move until Laura says, 'Class Two'. Laura makes them sit down. Laura tells them what they are going to do today–'number jobs, writing jobs and a painting job, and then you can chose'. Laura shows them some flash cards and asks what sound it is. They repeat what Laura says. John gets up and comes to ask me if he can go to the toilet – he goes. Grace comes in and Abbi and Grace make a book. They start writing their names.'Remember tall letters and short letters' says Laura. John comes back and Laura wants to know where he has been. Laura looks at Grace's and Abbi's writing and gives it a star. Grace reads a book. Laura points to some words in her book and asks her what they begin with. 'Well done, you have tried hard', says Laura to Grace when she is finished. Laura now claps her hands and says it's playtime. Grace and Abbi start to go out but Laura reminds them to tidy up first. All leave.

FIELD NOTE   Tuesday 10 November, 1.30–1.40 pm. Writing Corner.

Ben, Leanne and Ross go in. Ross picks up a teddy bear and starts to play a tape. Leanne starts to choose a book and Ben makes a book. Stuart comes in and asks Ben what he is doing. 'Flying a kite' says Ben. Stuart says he's not, he's making a book and he starts to make one himself. They argue over the stapler. 'I was here first', says Ben. 'We've got to share' says Stuart. Ben uses it first. Ross starts to record a song – making it up. 'Make a quiet song' says Leanne. Ross ignores her. Leanne goes out.

John comes in. John starts to copy words from the wall. Ben comes to show me his writing and says he's going to do the pictures next. Stuart shows Ross his book. Ross reads it backwards (right to left). Stuart shows him the correct way. Ben returns and says his book is better 'because my writing is neat '. Stuart says it's not. They argue. Both come over to me and I say that they are both good books and they go back. Ross replays the tape. In the background Stuart and Ben's voices can be heard – they now want to record. Ross says they can't because he was first. They say he's got to share. Ross picks up a book. John shows me his work and decides that he wants to take it home. Stuart and Ben start singing. Ross joins in – 'you can't because it's our turn' – Ross goes out. Leanne comes back in. She tells the boys to tidy up because 'it's a disgrace in here'. Stuart and Ben ignore her. Leanne tidies up. Ben says 'anyway it's your jobs today'. Stuart and Ben come out. Leanne starts copying from a book.

FIELD NOTE   Thursday 12 November, 2.25-2.40pm. Writing Corner.

Jonathan and Edward are making books. Ed is reading. Grace is listening to a tape. Ben enters. Ben picks up Ed's pen – they argue. Ben chooses another. Grace tells them she 'can't concentrate'. It is quiet now. Ben copies from a book. Jonathan looks at the pictures and asks Ben to read it. Ben starts to make up a story. 'You've got to turn the pages over' says Jonathan. Ben turns over at least three. Jonathan calls for him to come back and 'read properly'. Ben ignores him. Jonathan reads on his own. Grace tells the boys to tidy up because they are messy. They ignore her. Ben comes back and tells them to tidy up because it's playtime. They do. Writing corner tidy except for paper on the floor. Ben tells Jonathan to pick it up. Jonathan tells Grace to pick it up. She does. Ben tells her to put it in the bin because there is no name on it. Ben orders others in tidying up - 'pick the book up', 'those pencils shouldn't be there'. Others follow. All leave when Ben says it is tidy.

FIELDNOTE   Friday 13 November, 2.10-2.25pm. Writing Corner.

Ed and Ross argue over the teddy bear. Ross wins and takes the bear to read. Ed sits and listens. Leanne copying alphabet. Ross reads the alphabet to the bear. Laura enters and starts to write a letter to her mum. Ed is playing with a cassette. He pulls it out. Ben comes in – 'if it's broken you'll be in BIG trouble'. Ed mends it quickly. Ben makes a notice and starts to tell everyone what it says. Nobody listens. Ben says 'this notice says everyone must listen to me'. Laura , Ed and Ross look up. Ben puts it on the notice board. He uses a lot of 'Blu-tak'. Leanne tells him he should only use a little bit. He ignores her.

Leanne says that she will come and tell me. He takes some off and goes out. His notice falls off the board.

Leanne goes to tell him. Ed and Ross go out. Ben comes back in and says that someone has pulled it down. Leanne explains. Ben uses more Blu-tak to put it back. 'Told you it needed a lot' Ben says. Leanne asks what the notice says. 'You can use a lot of Blu-tak', says Ben.

Leanne goes back to her letter. Ed and Stuart come in and play with the tape. Trouble with tape. Leanne comes to tell me that the boys have broken the tape. I go over and find that the pause button is stuck – easily mended. Leanne seems disappointed, Ed and Stuart are relieved. Leanne reads her letter to everyone.

John comes in and starts to make a list. He asks Stuart to write his name on it – he does. Then he asks Ed and Ross. Leanne asks to write her name on it. 'No it's only for boys'. 'That's not fair'. She writes a notice and sticks it up. She announces that it says 'boys have to do hard work in the morning'. All the boys protest and say it's not fair, and they begin to argue. I go over and say that the list and the notice are both unfair. The notice is taken down and John lets Leanne write her name on the list (reluctantly?).

Leanne says she will read. Asks everyone to sit cross-legged with arms folded while she reads the story. After a while everyone does. She asks them if they are listening. She reads the story, holds up the book and points to the pictures.

Ross reading Fat Cat Book made by the class. John is writing a letter. Ross reads to Ben and then they try to find their stories. Ross, John and Ben look at other class books to find each other's work. They compare writing 'My letters are the right way round' says Ben. 'But mine are smaller', says John. They leave the books. Ben picks up the telephone – 'Robbers in the house, put them in jail' – he's playing policemen. He writes on a piece of paper. Ross asks him what he is doing. 'Making a list of naughty people to take to jail'. Leanne sticks up a notice. She says it says 'Everyone has to go to the dentist' (she has just been).

All quiet for two minutes. Ben says 'This is a police station and you have to be good'. Grace comes in and reads. John makes a treasure map. He explains to Grace where to find treasure. Grace goes out. Ben, with his list in his hand, asks people if they have been naughty or good. All reply, 'good'. He comes to ask me. 'If naughty you get a X, if good you get a star'. Ben says that everyone in the class has been good except Grace. Grace has been throwing sand on the floor – she has to go to prison. I get a star. Grace goes back to the writing corner. Ben tells her to tidy up the sand. She ignores him. Ben says 'You'll go to prison if you don't'. Grace still ignores him. Ben says 'I'll tell Mrs C'. Grace goes to tidy up. John sticks up the treasure map so 'everyone can find the treasure'. Leanne and John tidy up (without being asked).

By making field notes in this way, the class teacher was able to assess the progress of specific children and to find out about their relationships with others. She was also able to discover some patterns in the children's interactions and to learn about the emerging social structure of her classroom and of the 'writing corner' in particular. Three themes were identified in these episodes :

- children's use of rules, authority and control,
- their concern for getting it right, being praised and showing others to be wrong,
- their strategies for involving others.

Use of rules, authority and control

Even though the teacher was sitting at a distance from the children, her authority was appealed to both directly and indirectly. For example, when Abbi and Naomi argued about the use of a dictionary, Abbi went to the teacher and got her assent. By doing so, she was able to make her point of view unchallengeable (9 November). More subtle, but nevertheless effective, were Ben's instructions about tidying-up (12 November). The teacher said, 'his language, phrases and almost his tone of voice are the same as I use'. Ben succeeded in getting others to tidy up. Similarly, other children seemed to have learned to use the oblique controlling function of some of their teacher's phrases, like 'make a quiet song' (10 November) and 'can't concentrate' (12 November).

During preceding weeks, the teacher had taken many opportunities to emphasise that it is good to share and to take turns. When analysing her field notes she thought that the children were sometimes using, even perhaps manipulating, ground rules to 'share' and 'take turns' in order to get their own way. They were learning how to negotiate within the legitimate social framework of the classroom at the same time as they conformed to expectations and showed themselves to be her kind of pupil.

Tuesday 10 November.

Stuart comes in and asks Ben what he is doing. 'Flying a Kite', says Ben. Stuart says he's not, he's making a book and he starts to make one himself. They argue over the stapler. 'I was here first', says Ben. 'We've got to share', says Stuart.

Stuart and Ben start singing [into a tape recorder]. Ross joins in. 'You can't because it's our turn'. Ross goes out.

The children negotiated for control over such things as turn-taking, tidying-up, fairness, sharing and noise reduction.

They were learning how to manage their own participation with others. They made use of ground rules which permeated the classroom and which were reinforced constantly by the teacher. Some ground rules had become part of the fabric of the classroom and they became the focus of bargaining, trade-offs and compromises, whether or not the teacher was present in the group.

As well as using the teacher to settle disputes and appealing to ground rules about fairness and sharing, the children also used written notices and took on authority roles such as teacher and policeman to legitimate their bids for control. These tactics figured prominently, and the latter also revealed how children often attempted to start cooperative activities by initiating a game. We shall return to this point when we discuss the children's strategies for involving others.

Concern for getting it right, being praised and showing others to be wrong

The children sometimes sought recognition at the expense of others. Their main claims to status seemed to be from showing that others were wrong or from doing things correctly themselves. Ben, for example, claimed that his book was better than Stuart's because his writing was neat (10 November). This led to a dispute between the two boys which they asked the teacher to resolve. On 15 November, Ben and John compared their writing and then left their books amicably to try to start a new game. It seemed to be fair when Ben said that his letters were the right way round and John pointed out that his were smaller.

Some of the children were eager to point out the mistakes of others and to draw attention to unacceptable behaviour. It is pleasing when others get into trouble, as when Leanne told the teacher that the boys had broken the tape recorder. She seemed disappointed when the teacher found that it was not broken, but that the problem was overcome simply by releasing the pause button. Later, Ben conveyed the significance of breaking the tape recorder when he saw Ed playing with it and said in a censorious and dramatic manner, 'if it's broken you'll be in BIG trouble!'.

This incident with the Blu-tak also illustrates, delightfully, how the authority of a displayed, written notice overcomes a previously invoked local ground rule about not using too much Blu-tak.

Friday 13 November.

He (Ben) uses a lot of Blu-tak. Leanne tells him he should only use a little bit. He ignores her. Leanne says that she will come and tell me. He takes some off and goes out. His notice falls off the board.

Leanne goes to tell him. Ed and Ross go out. Ben comes back in and says that someone has pulled it down. Leanne explains. Ben uses more Blu-tak to put it back. 'Told you it needed a lot' Ben says. Leanne asks what the notice says. 'You can use a lot of Blu-tak', says Ben.

Strategies for involving others

Sometimes children's attempts to talk or share are interpreted as interference and rejected. This happened, for instance, when Ross wouldn't let Ben and Stuart join in his activity with the tape recorder (10 November). When Ben and Stuart did start singing with him, he told them it wasn't their turn and walked away from them. Many attempts at working together started awkwardly and didn't last long, as when Jonathon and Ben were reading together until Ben turned over too many pages and they argued briefly before returning to separate activities (12 November). The children sometimes resented the distraction or discomfort of having others in close proximity when they were trying to work alone, as when Grace tells the other four children in the writing corner that she can't concentrate (12 November).

Sometimes gender differences caused problems. The most notable incident was on 13 November when John was making a list and he asked Stuart to add his name. When Leanne heard that, she wanted to add her name too, but Stuart told her that the list was only for boys. Grace responded by using the authority of a notice to say that all boys had to do hard work in the morning. This had a dramatic effect and the boys protested so vociferously that the teacher moved in to say that both the list and the notice were unfair.

Starting new games was a key strategy for getting others to do things with you. Sometimes it worked successfully and sometimes it didn't. There was willing participation, as in the positive response to Laura's announcement that 'we're playing schools', and to Leanne's request for everyone to 'sit cross-legged with arms folded' while she read a story to them. There was also an example of a game being played even when other children were not willing participants, when Ben picked up a telephone, took on the role of a policeman and declared the writing corner to be a police station. This continued smoothly for a while until Ben tried to involve Grace in his game. Ben said that everyone in the class had been good except for Grace and that she had to go to prison for throwing sand on the floor. Grace refused to comply, and she also ignored his next order to tidy-up. It was only when Ben threatened to tell the teacher that she reluctantly tidied the corner. It seemed that when he was thwarted in his claim to power in his imaginary game, he then turned to use the threat of the real power of the teacher.

After these interpretations of what was happening in the writing corner, we look at how much the children were learning about the functions of writing, and secondly, at what they learned about working together.

Learning about the functions of writing

It is clear that the teacher had provided a specific context and framework for the children to learn to use writing to communicate. It seems inappropriate to categorize the activity exclusively as either direct or indirect teaching or as individual or group learning. For young children to learn about the function of writing they need to experience a strong sense of audience and a context in which they can use writing for real purposes. At other times, the teacher did arrange more formal group exercises in which children became obedient, but less genuine, readers of each others' writing. That kind of arrangement was useful, but it could not have offered the same learning opportunities as this spontaneous interaction in the writing corner. In the episodes recorded above, the children were learning about the social functions of writing. They used lists and notices to claim power to affect each others' behaviour, and they usually got immediate feedback from each other.

Learning about the functions of writing was a social process inseparable from the experience of working, playing and learning together.

Learning to work, play and learn together

Returning to Galton and Wiliamson's classification of groupwork, we can now see that the 'task demands' and 'intended outcomes' of these episodes cover three of their types. There are times when pupils were engaged in separate tasks, times when their separate tasks were related and times when they were working together with others on the same task, however briefly. What is also important is that the children structured their own tasks. Some were individual and others were undertaken jointly with varying degrees of sharing. Returning also to the key concerns of some earlier research, it would also be difficult, and perhaps only marginally useful, to try to judge what happened according to criteria of 'time on task' or 'distraction levels'. It is interesting, however to think about the extent of 'remote control' which the teacher retained over these children when she was not taking part directly in what they were doing. There are some discernible patterns and some regularities which the teacher came to recognize as deriving from the way she organizes and runs the whole classroom. The emergent structure of children's interaction in the writing corner is embedded in the context of the school and classroom and its rhythms, twists and turns are shaped by whoever is in there at the time.

The children are, in effect, learning to negotiate and to get their own way within the framework of both explicit and implicit ground rules of the classroom. The micro-politics of the writing corner are discernible, for example, in the ways in which power is sought and used. For instance, pleas for others to share and take turns seem to be used by some children to get their own way, imaginary roles are used to take authority to affect others, and lists and notices are used to bargain and try to control what is happening.

For these reasons, interaction between the children is not smooth-running. Conflict arises for the children because of the instability and unpredictability of what they do and say, and between the teacher and children because of the difficulties of trying to disentangle the simultaneity and complexity of what is happening. Sometimes the children try to reduce or lessen conflict and sometimes they enjoy it and try to add to its drama. Conflict is endemic in classroom episodes such as these, and it is educative for the pupils to learn to cooperate in real situations in which they have to cope with disagreements and discomfort. The place of conflict in collaborative learning is discussed more fully in Chapter 9.

At a time when 'assertiveness training' classes are appreciated by many adults, it is salutary to notice how young children learn to be in control of situations. Working and learning with others is not about being 'nice' all the time. Being with others sometimes requires such things as saying 'No' without feeling guilty, disagreeing and then forgetting disagreements, stopping people from interfering and being able to complain without being resented. Collaboration and cooperation are not the same as compliance.

This is one of the reasons why it is often uncomfortable for teachers to give children enough scope and time to learn these things. Disagreements between people usually seem unpleasant to those who overhear or observe them and, in addition to coping with noise and fuss, teachers may find it especially difficult to know when to stand back and when, and how, to intervene. For example, in the case study above, the teacher, Debbie, thought on reflection that she could have responded differently to the gender dispute. She could have encouraged Leanne to make a list of girls and John to put up a notice saying that girls had to work hard. Nobody would have been wrong then. On the other hand, she chose to try to reduce sexist behaviour by saying it was unfair.

There can be a tyranny about children's loosely knit groups, and there may be a fine balance between giving time and space for children to have educative experiences of negotiation and allowing time to be wasted through aimless squabbling and intimidating aggression. This is one of the central dilemmas for teachers who try to understand children's relationships and who try to promote classroom learning communities in which both collaborative learning and individual achievement are valued. We have already made the point that learning to be with other children in classrooms is not smooth-running, and because of this, McNeil (1988) has made the point that there is a tendency for schools to displace their main goal of encouraging quality learning by the ritual of seeming to do so. For example, difficult classes might be kept under control for much of the working day by setting individual work, by standing at the front of the room teaching and orchestrating the whole class, by reducing movement and by banning talk.

We should not underestimate the skill and energy needed to create the kinds of classroom conditions in which children learn to be constructively assertive and cooperative members of purposeful learning communities. It is important for children to learn through a mixture of individuality and interdependence and to benefit from a combination of privacy and fellowship, but it can be exhausting, wearing and stressful for teachers to cope with the instability and unpredictability which emerge.

The following anonymous case study illustrates some of the problems in trying to create a purposeful learning community in difficult circumstances in an urban school.

Case Study: creating a classroom learning community in difficult circumstances

It was the third week of the Autumn term and an experienced teacher, who had just moved to the school, was beginning to get to grips with his new class of 8-year old children, known in the staffroom as the 'wild bunch'. He found them to be generally difficult to motivate and he said that a lot of the children behaved in a 'surly and defiant' manner. There was an undercurrent of aggressiveness. There also seemed to be a general lack of confidence - 'They wouldn't do things they thought they would fail at, and, if pressed, some of them have run out of the classroom in the past.' For example, children often tore their own and others' pictures.

The teacher wanted to create a more positive learning environment. Whilst direct, whole-class teaching and enforced control over individual work would be part of his pedagogy, he thought that the children should also be given opportunities to have a say, to take responsibility and learn to work with others. Some problems could be alleviated temporarily through confrontation, but with some children any apparent gains were merely temporary. He knew he couldn't achieve results quickly, and he started to do three main things to work towards better learning conditions in the longer term.

First, he sought the support of other adults. He wanted the children to be able to talk with adults at moments when they were working well and when they had produced things which pleased them. Many of them seemed to have defensive and hostile attitudes towards adults, and he tried to change that. He discussed his strategy with the headteacher and she agreed to help as well as arrange for a support teacher from an urban primary project to work in his class-room for four days each week for a period of three weeks.

Second, he tried to emphasize good features of children's effort and work, and positive aspects of social interaction such as sharing, helping a friend and tidying-up. He encouraged them to make their room a better place for everyone. At the same time, he aimed to make minimal or subdued responses to undesirable behaviour. This was par-ticularly wearing and it took a great deal of self-control and will power.

Third, he rearranged the classroom so that different activ-ities could take place simultaneously, so that children could move about and so that he would be not be the focal point through being at the front of the room for so much of the day. The presence of another adult in the classroom would help to ease but not eliminate the strain involved in this change.

To help with the enquiry, I observed six classroom ses-sions and recorded discussions with the teacher and sup-port teacher. During one of the discussions the teacher said:

> I remember in the first couple of weeks – one Friday – I'd had enough. I didn't feel like going back into the classroom. It was only because [the support teacher] was prepared to give a lot of time – timetabled virtually every day – that we overcame the problem. I felt I needed somebody to talk to – just about behaviour problems, just about having to share with someone – because when you are on your own the responsibility is so immense – and you think to yourself – 'I'm not doing the job properly here.' There are big pressures on you. So I needed someone, not just to support me in the classroom, but to sup-port what I was doing really.

Both the class teacher and the support teacher emphasized the underlying importance of their 'shared philosophy' in achieving a successful partnership. They had begun with a set of common principles, but what mattered more was that they modified, adapted and redefined their actions and ideas strategically, according to their reviews of what was actually happening. This required a lot of talking and a lot of practical preparation. They were redefining and recon-ceptualizing their task in the light of their interpretations of specific circumstances, constraints and conditions. In the introduction to this book, we said that we wanted to try to show how children's and teachers' collaborative learning are sometimes deeply interrelated. The two teachers in this case were strengthening their own beliefs in working and learning together at the same time as they were fostering and promoting the conditions for children to benefit in the same way. They talked together:

Teacher (CT)	Dinner-times, after school - [the headteacher] was quite involved.
Support teacher (ST)	We also did a lot of talking in the classroom - ' Oh look at that – or how can I improve that?' – while the children were there.
CT	There were all sort of things going on after school and dinner-time and it took a lot of time.
ST	It was virtually every lunch time and ....
CT	every night. Yes, it would develop, I mean, I would identify a problem – in the classroom and we'd start talking about it. We identified certain behaviours, and had a look at strategies. We really knew that we needed not one, but thousands of different ones, and we'd have to keep trying. It was the time it took. The head gave a lot of support, tremendous, yes, I mean it was hours, sometimes until 6.00pm just discussing what and how. But it was vital for me to discuss it. I needed to know that someone was supporting me in what I was doing, or trying to do. If I hadn't had the support I'd not have got through that first term.

The teachers did not formalize their classroom partnership, in the sense that they would take on separate tasks or fulfil separate functions. They both worked in a similar way, talking with individuals or groups of children and responding to situations as they arose. They were also modelling the kinds of spontaneous, purposeful interactions they were encouraging. They seemed to be able to handle parallel and sometimes competing tasks and conversations, showing the kind of high tolerance threshold needed in a lively classroom. Unlike many other examples of relationships between support teachers and class teachers we have observed, they often seemed to share overall class management and direction. Either of them might speak to the whole class at any time when something interesting arose, and children would ask either of them for help or for permission to do something. In order to work so responsively and spontaneously, they also knew that they would need to have adequate resources available :

ST   You've got to be so prepared for every eventuality that you are spending the whole night beforehand, aren't you, working on what you are going to do. You need all the resources there to let the children follow their interests as they arise....

CT   So one of the big things we used to talk about – one of the things the Urban Primary project team helped with was the management of resources. We decided to have a lot of practical input, because the traditional 'sit-down' wasn't working. I remember [the headteacher] saying 'there is always something that is going to interest children' – but it needed two teachers in the classroom and it needed resources.

One thing which did interest all the children, and gave them a more positive sense of whole-class identity and membership, was the hatching of some eggs. The teacher had brought an incubator into the classroom:

CT   The ' birth of the chickens' – we turned a corner then. It was something to be proud of in the school. They had such a poor reputation and had four or five different teachers. When we had the chickens it got around the school and children were coming to see them. 'Oh, they're chickens'. It wasn't the total answer, but it was as though something exciting was going on. Something to be proud of instead of being known as the 'wild bunch'.

The birth of the chickens helped to engender a sense of shared wonderment, a feeling of togetherness in caring and a pride in belonging to the class that had the chickens that everyone else wanted to see.

The teachers introduced a system of badges as rewards for 'sharing' and 'helping a friend' to try to emphasize the kinds of behaviour they were encouraging. Basic social rules were being established and prioritized. Importance was attached to tidying-up and to making decisions about what work to do. Sometimes groups were encouraged and helped to work out job descriptions and to plan their own activities. Photographs were taken of children working purposefully, especially when they were working with other children. These were labelled and displayed in the classroom, and then used at key moments to start conversations with children about good things which they had done. Every opportunity was taken to raise the self-esteem of the children.

Because of some of the children's general wariness of unfamiliar adults, and especially because of their suspicion of adults in 'official' roles, I had avoided initiating conversations, asking questions or imposing myself upon them during my first visit to the classroom, preferring to wait until the children wished to talk with me or to involve me in what they were doing. They did know that I had come from the university to watch how they got on with their work together. The first session included the only long period in which the teacher talked to the whole class from the front of the room. Some children were volunteering to chew disclosing tablets and to observe the patterns of plaque on each others' teeth. The relaxed manner of the headteacher was evident when she came unexpectedly into the room and participated in the lesson by chewing a tablet and then talking informally with some children about what was happening. None of the children spoke to me that day.

In the second session, during which the support teacher was also there, I observed the children moving freely from place to place. After about 45 minutes, the children were completing their main tasks and then I was approached for the first time by a boy who held out a ball of fur with legs sticking up in the air and asked me if I wanted to see the hamster. Three minutes after that, a girl brought her work to show me. She said, ' I've been cutting-out all of those and I'm still not sick of it yet'. We talked for some time about how she had designed the badges and what they were for.

During the rest of my visits, I was made to feel welcome and part of the class community. As I entered the room, one day, a boy said:

> You can sit on my chair if you like ....
> This is my transformer [a model he had made].

He sat with me for a while as we talked about his model. His partner, who had helped to make the model, also came across and sat with us. We talked about how they had made it, and about what they were going to do to improve it.

While we were talking, Phillip, who had been disturbing and loud in the previous session, was given a sticker for good work. I saw him take the sheet of stickers from the drawer and he came over to me and leaned comfortably on the desk. It was the first time he had spoken to me. 'Which one do you think I should pick?', he asked. We started to talk about the different stickers and about his work and what he was good at. As we looked through his work and talked about it, we counted the stickers he already had. He hadn't realized that he had five of them and five is the number you need for a badge. He jumped suddenly to his feet and shouted with delight. He ran across and disturbed the class teacher who was working with another child. The social rules which the teacher was trying to establish were often being broken like this, in unanticipated ways and without malice.

I was often drawn into children's activities. The children were respectful and friendly and I wasn't afforded any special status as this extract from my field notes shows:

> 'Do you want an apron ?' 'Yes, OK, thanks', I said, taking the rolled up ball of cloth. 'Right, will you help us ?' Two children tied my apron and we went to work on a machine to move marbles. Soon, two others came over and the five of us tried out some ideas. The support teacher came across to where we were working. 'Can I show you something?' 'Sorry to take you away, but...'. I went with her and one of my fellow marble machine engineers came too. We read a poem that two girls were writing.

I noticed many incidents when children moved to sit beside friends and then continued to work separately. Sometimes one would help the other or they would work together on a practical activity. Many of the paired and group activities were spontaneous rather than formal and pre-planned:

> A girl noticed a boy sitting by himself at a tape recorder into which he was reading a book. The tape recorder formed a fixed activity point and there was usually someone there during my observation periods. The girl took her chair and moved beside him. The pair continued reading together.
>
> A group of three boys were testing a machine they had made. Two others saw them and came to watch the tests. They joined in the discussion about ways in which it might be improved.

The teachers also talked to each other spontaneously and periodically in the classroom: comparing impressions, sharing enthusiasms, giving things to each other or involving children in showing and explaining their work. They also emphazised working with others whenever possible. For example, if one of the children asked a teacher if he or she could start a new activity, the teacher often asked who he or she would be going to work with. When one of them noticed a child who did not seem to be involved in any activity, they would be more likely to say, 'Who are you working with next?' than 'What are you doing?' or even less likely, 'Get on with some work'.

Even with two teachers in the room, such were the constant demands of this difficult class, and the enormity of the challenges that the teachers had given themselves, that both of them frequently felt numb at the end of sessions. After the period of intense support, the class teacher worked alone for the rest of the term, apart from one session each week when the support teacher returned. By the end of the first term there were few serious behaviour problems, but there were still many minor difficulties with some children. The two most difficult boys caused problems in different ways. David seemed to want to be on his own and he avoided work most of the time and Phillip tended to shout and disturb others, even when he was working with enthusiasm and with interest. The following field note extract, written in the classroom shortly after the incidents observed, illustrates their behaviour:

10.56. The teacher is sitting beside two children talking with them, stopping periodically to respond to a few others who have come to him for help. He looks across the room and says in an even-toned voice, 'Kevin take your hat off, please', and then continues to talk with the girl beside him. Two boys are standing beside him now, waiting for attention. At this point Phillip shouts loudly and points to the clock he is making, 'Is that 5 to 11?'

He has been working behind the teacher, but now he comes across to interrupt the conversation between the teacher and a girl, ignoring the two boys waiting for attention. The teacher answers in a quiet voice and then continues to talk with the girl. Phillip returns to his table and shouts 'Where's the pen?' but he finds it immediately, and before anyone could respond.

I felt uneasy about Phillip's aggressive manner and strong but nervous presence. I was also struck by the assured way that the teacher had not let Phillip's interuption affect the tone of his conversation with the girl. There was a general air of quiet patience in the room, and Phillip had not changed it.

11.02. The teacher has kept moving around the room to sit beside different children, some of whom have attracted his attention and some of whom he has chosen to speak to about their work. His voice has been quiet except for a few incidents where he has spoken across the room in a more 'public', but still even and relaxed manner:

'Are you working by yourself or with someone else, David?'

'Why don't you two take that piece of card over there where there is more room?'

'Are you working with Robert, David'

'Tidy-up, before you do any more, please.'
'That looks good, I like that...take your coat off...it's very good. Have you...'.

11.05. The teacher is now in a corner, talking with two girls, when Phillip comes over to him. 'Mr...is that 5 to 11?' The teacher tells him that it isn't.' Hey, Kev man it's wrong man.' The teacher shows irritation for the first time.' Oh, Phillip, PLEASE!'

Phillip goes across to Kevin and when he sees how Kevin has made pointers for his clock he shouts, 'Hey, that's good that Kev'. David comes across to see what Kevin has done. Phillip says, 'Look at these soldiers [for clock hands] I think I'll make them for mine' and then he hurries back to his seat.

David seems aimless. The teacher asks him if he is going to work with Phillip. He gets no answer and he then asks Phillip if he is working with David.

11.10. David has still not settled to any work. He watched Phillip for a while and then he saw a dog in the quadrangle. He told Phillip and he came to look. Two others joined them. They opened the window and called to the dog. The teacher told them to have a look and then to sit down. The teacher got up himself and walked over to see the dog. The four boys went to their seats and none of the other children showed any interest in the dog.

11.14. Phillip takes a break from making his clock and goes to stand beside the teacher who is talking to two boys about their mathematics work. Then he follows and listens while the teacher says positive things about a girl's work at the back of the room.

11.16. The teacher seems to be easing his back and stretching his legs now. Five children soon gather round him and he starts listening to one of them. David has gone to sit with Phillip, and Phillip asks him to draw a figure 6 on his clock for him. Phillip watches and then he yells excitedly 'Yes!' and he goes to show it to the teacher.

12.00. The bell rings to signal lunch-time and the teacher's tone changes. It is commanding and aimed generally and impersonally at 'the class'. 'RIGHT...FIRST TWO READY IN SEATS. TWO READY...COME ON...FOUR READY...'. The change seemed to prepare the children, almost military fashion, for lining-up and being representatives of the class in the rest of the school. It seemed to emphasise, at the same time, a change to a more 'public image' for their teacher: a kind of commanding, rule-enforcing presence around the school.

This field note conveys the kinds of dilemmas, tensions and ambiguities of classroom life which cause teachers to experience mixed feelings of pleasure and despair. Teachers have to judge themselves simultaneously against both long- and short-term criteria and as a consequence they are continuously fluctuating between self-doubt and assurance. In this case study, clear improvements were being made in the classroom environment and in the quality of the whole learning community, yet the teacher was concerned continuously about the behaviour of a few individuals and its effect upon the progress of the whole class. The teacher's clear intentions, conviction, persistence and resilience were often tested in relation to two main concerns: first, to generalized images of well-controlled, quiet, smooth-running classrooms and, second, to standardized notions of children's attainment. These can weigh heavily on the mind, and can introduce doubts which make teachers question their own judgements and easily divert their attention from interpreting the specific task in hand.

The teacher's sense of being judged by colleagues for the control of his class, meant that he remained concerned about his children's behaviour in 'public areas' of the school. This is evident both in this extract from a later discussion:

> There are certain rules outside the classroom that put pressure on you as a teacher – walking to the hall, for example, or walking to the yard or walking from the yard into the classroom – because you know other teachers see you there. That's their guide as to how – it seems simplistic to say it, but that's basically it – they don't have any real contact in the classroom - occasionally they might come in for two or three minutes – but you can't tell what a classroom is like in two or three minutes.
> You come out into corridors and into a different place really – but the children know that, too.

and in the ways in which he ended lessons by giving orders with military clarity as he prepared the children to become model pupils and got himself ready for the role of rule-enforcing corridor supervisor.

Turning to tensions between notions of generalized standards of behaviour and the progress of individual children, we can see how challenging Phillip is to the teacher. During the period described above, Phillip was interested in making a model of a clock, but he was having difficulties reading the time and he didn't trust his own ability to draw a good enough figure 6: one which he would be proud to show to the teacher. His progress was slow but he did get a little bit further forward. He sought and received help from the teacher and from David, and he was inspired to try to draw soldiers (for clock hands) after he looked at Kevin's clock. He watched and listened as the teacher talked to some other children, but he often shouted in a disturbing way, and, although he sometimes waited for his turn, he also interupted some conversations. He sought 'official recognition' and although he wanted to have stickers as rewards for his work, he also had an annoying tendency to yell out his delight when he did something good.

The teacher was trying to create a cohesive community and a classroom environment in which both Phillip and David would learn to be able to work and learn with others as well as to make progress as individuals. He did not want to label any child as deviant, and during that period, the teacher typically tried to avoid making negative responses to these two boys whose behaviour was often a challenge to him. It is tempting to make noisy children work by themselves in corners of the room or beside the teacher's desk, but instead, this teacher tried to get them to work with others. Phillip's interaction with others was disturbing even though it was fairly effective. David was being cajoled into doing some work with someone else, but he tested the teacher's patience by his indifference. He seemed to do little of consequence, apart from draw a six for Phillip and see the dog in the quadrangle, but the teacher was prepared to wait for David to make his own mind up about what to do. Under the circumstances, it would have been so much easier to set a task for David, and to keep him in his place, but this would have diverted the teacher from his original intention of encouraging initiative and self-determination.

This brings us to one of the themes of this book, that of the growth of the self in social settings. The teacher had thought that, although they behaved differently, both Phillip and David expected failure in the classroom. David's reluctance to commit himself to a task and to express what he was thinking, and Phillip's noisiness and aggressive manner, seemed to mask their insecurity about what they could achieve. Changes in self-image do not happen quickly, and one of the principles guiding the teacher's approach was that he should be consistent in how he responded to them. This did not mean that they could get away with anything, but he had to be able to show that he disapproved of their behaviour without disapproving of them as people.

Teachers who try to create classroom learning communities are usually concerned about maintaining and raising the self-esteem of individuals. The idea that self-esteem affects a child's capacity to learn to cooperate with others has been addressed by Borba and Borba (1982) and Canfield and Wells (1976) who have devised a number of activities to help teachers to improve children's views of themselves. It is also a key dimension, along with interdependence and cooperation, in an approach to global education which has been developed through the Global Education Centre at the University of York. This project has used the concept of an 'interactive workshop' to describe an enabling classroom environment for children, and one which creates conditions for collaborative learning.

Conclusion

In this first chapter, we have tried to show the importance of helping children to learn how to work and learn with other children in classrooms. In order to create the conditions for collaboration, teachers not only set group tasks, but also strive to build classroom learning communities in which spontaneous help and support are possible most of the time. The two case studies we have selected have conveyed the energy, skill and commitment of the teachers, whilst also indicating that classroom learning communities are not 'smooth-running'. In the first case, we saw how the processes of learning about writing were intertwined with early social learning in a class of 4- and 5-year old children. We also saw the importance of understanding the ways in which children learn to negotiate and bargain within the framework of class ground rules. In particular, we reminded ourselves of the place of assertiveness in the growth of the self in social settings.

The second case study showed some of the difficulties of trying to create a classroom learning community amongst a class of 8-year old children which had been known previously as the 'wild bunch'. The teacher sought, particularly, to make an impact on the collective and individual self-images of the children.

The teachers represented in these case studies had different concerns, but what they had in common was a desire to gain deeper understanding of the nature of their task of creating collaborative learning communities in their classrooms. They were engaged in action-research enquiries to create better conditions for children to learn and to help each other to learn. Both had also created opportunities for themselves to learn collaboratively. They sought the support of other teachers to help them to collect or interpret evidence and to think about what to do next.

What we have tried to show through both case studies is that:

- It is important to try to create conditions for collaborative learning by making opportunities for children to support, help and work with each other spontaneously and informally. This takes us beyond teacher-initiated group-work in which all children are expected to contribute to a single outcome. It raises questions for teachers about the kinds of behaviour which they see as acceptable and legitimate and about the ways in which explicit and implicit ground rules and values of their classrooms influence children's interactions.
- One of the features of classroom learning communities will be that they will reflect the rhythms and dynamics of the settings and the people in them. They cannot be implanted or created according to templates taken from elsewhere.
- In order to try to make sense of emergent relationships, it is necessary to collect evidence and look closely at the ways in which children participate in classroom communities. Intermittent and ad hoc impressions may be misleading, especially when it comes to trying to understand the mix of self-interest and concern for others.
- There is likely to be some instability and unpredictability about interaction between children as they learn to negotiate and bargain for resources, attention and control. Cooperation is not built simply upon obedience and it is important to understand the constructive possibilities of disagreements and conflict in learning.
- For both children and teachers, participation in a classroom learning community provides opportunities for the growth of self and social competence. Teachers who try to promote collaborative learning communities also try to find strategies to maintain and enhance the collective and individual self-esteem of children.

Chapter 2

Children Learning to be Contributing Members of Classroom Groups

I was talking recently with three 9-year old boys whose teacher was involved in a project linking schools and industry. Their class was divided into small companies and each company had a system for recording, filing and retrieving information about its activities.

'You're a company are you?' I asked them.
'Yes, I'm the manager', said one.
'I'm the deputy-manager', his friend said.
'And I'm the vice-deputy-manager', said the other.
'Oh', I asked, 'you are all managers are you?'
They nodded, and I asked what managers do.
The reply was immediate. 'They give out the jobs that nobody wants to do... you know, things like writing and that.'
' How do you do that ?'
'Well... we always take turns... because that's fair.'

In this chapter, we continue to explore what it means to be part of a classroom learning community by concentrating mainly on children's participation in groups which have been established by teachers to work on set tasks. We have already argued, in the previous chapter, that formal group work is only one amongst many of children's other experiences of working and learning with others, and so before looking at formal groups we shall remind ourselves of some features of the social context in which task-oriented group activity takes place. In particular, we shall consider two parallel and interlocking social structures of the classroom: the structures of the child/peer culture and the structures created by teachers for their pupils. If we are going to try to understand how children learn to be members of task groups, we should first try to understand what it means to a member of their own peer-groups and then to think of how this relates generally to the membership demands of being a pupil in a classroom.

During a school day children are likely to experience a complex weave of attachments with varying degrees of informality and formality, of transience and stability, and of choice and imposition. Relationships with others will include personal friendships and self-chosen groups, some of which may extend beyond the school day. Children will also spend time in imposed working partnerships and groupings, in groups labelled to suit administrative arrangements such as 'second sittings' and 'packed lunches' and be reminded that they are part of the 'whole class' and the 'whole school'. Children will experience groupings which differ in size, purpose and duration, and which may engender mixed feelings of belonging, obligation and even estrangement.

Each child's involvement in a classroom learning community is supervised continuously by teachers, and permeated by judgement and evaluation, and Pollard (1985) has shown how children develop collective strategies to cope with the obligations and social expectations of the role of pupil. For example, his study of the child culture of primary schools described playground games and activities which fell outside of adult definitions of acceptability and which took place in areas which were difficult for teachers to supervise. Some of these games continued and others were evolved for playing during working periods in classrooms. In one infants school, for example:

> There were several under-the-table games including shoe-swapping and playing with small toys such as plastic cowboys. The greatest refinement was 'Boogie Thomas', which was a game of tig played with pieces of paper torn from a wax crayon: the child hit by the paper was 'on' and would then throw the next piece of paper. Clearly, these types of activity very much reflect the children's own collective strategies for making school fun in their own terms, despite the 'sensible' injunctions of adults. (p.46)

Being part of a classroom learning community, for both children and teachers, is about personal interests as well as having to cope with the role expectations of pupils and teachers. For children, it is about trying to belong in two parallel and sometimes interlocking social structures: the structures of the child culture and the structures created by teachers. An example of such a link between the two structures is evident in the comments quoted at the beginning of this chapter, when the boys used established protocol of fairness and turn-taking from their own friendship group to find a legitimate way of 'doing what managers do' during their school-industry project activity.

Belonging as a member of the 'child culture'

The main underlying theme of the child culture is friendship, a form of relationship which according to Rubin (1980) fosters a 'feeling of belonging and a sense of identity' (p.37). Davies (1982) has related the importance of friendships at school to the alleviation of vulnerability and the growth of social competence:

> To be alone in a new place without friends is potentially devastating. To find a friend is partially to alleviate the problem. By building with that friend a system of shared meanings and understandings, such that the world is a predictable place, children take the first step towards being competent people within the social setting of the school. (p.63)

This suggests that social competence is learned through being with friends and being able to act on shared understandings about such things as when and how to make a claim, when to be assertive or when to complain as well to respond, share and cooperate. For instance, Sluckin (1981) found conventions and ritualized patterns of behaviour amongst children in playgrounds, which were cued by well established signals and terms like 'bagsee' and 'pax', and Opie and Opie (1959) had previously described many national forms of protocol, with regional variations, in what almost amounted to a children's 'code of oral legislation'.

Pollard (1985) claims that the child culture looks in two directions at once. Looking externally it is a source of support, security and esteem, which insulates children, to some extent, from adult domination. On the other hand:

> if we look internally, child culture acts rather differently to provide norms, constraints and expectations which bear on its members. Thus although it is enabling in one respect, it is constraining in another, and we have seen that the social system of children is itself structured and represents a context in which children seek to establish their competence and a positive identity. (p.50)

Woods (1983) showed how concerns about status are an integral part of children's relationships and their views of their own and others' competence, and Pollard has argued that child cultures are not homogeneous and, as a result, sources of status vary. Pollard uses extensive data to illustrate the importance of differentiation processes which take place in specific school contexts largely as a result of chance factors such as class composition and grouping arrangements. During his fieldwork with 11-year old children he identified three types of friendship groups. Two of these groups had their own names – 'good groups' and 'gangs'– and the third he called 'jokers' to highlight its particular character. Children belonging to these groups had common ways of seeing themselves and members of other kinds of friendship groups. From our point of view, and in relation to the themes of this chapter, the key value in Pollard's work is the way that he used distinctions between friendship groups to analyse children's classroom participation. He found that children's strategies for coping with the existence of two social systems in the classroom – the official system represented by the teacher and the children's own social system – was patterned around the goodies, jokers and gang characteristics.

Differences between the friendship groups hinged around their main reference points in the classroom. The goodies main reference point was the teacher whilst the gangs directed their actions mainly to the peer group. The jokers, however, showed flexibility and skill in bridging both systems by making school fun along with rather than against the teacher.

In developing his analysis, Pollard identified children's concerns in relation to six 'interests at hand', four of which related to facets of self-image and two which he called 'enabling interests':

Self	*Enabling*
Maintenance of self-image	Peer-group membership
Enjoyment	Learning
Control of stress	
Retention of dignity	
(After Pollard, 1985, p.82).	

All children tried to manage and maintain their self-images in ways which were advantageous to them. The good groups saw themselves as kind, quiet and friendly; the gangs regarded themselves as rough and tough; and the jokers thought they were clever and good fun. Enjoyment, having a laugh and having fun were the kinds of rewards which were sought from supportive interactions and which, at the same time, confirmed membership and security. Gangs tended to like the excitement of 'causing bother' and 'mucking about' in lessons. Good groups emphasized enjoying lessons and getting pleasure from teachers' jokes. Joker groups got excitement from activities which were less disruptive than those of the gangs, such as passing notes and drawing in jotters and they also drew satisfaction from having a laugh within lessons, but usually with teacher participation. In these ways, each group was able to gain enjoyment in ways which were supportive of its reference values and each individual's self-image.

The children in different groups also found different strategies for controlling stress. For all children, potential stress arose from the power of the teacher, from constant evaluation, and also for some, especially the 'good groups', from concern about peer conflict. Some other sorts of stress were introduced by children from time to time as a source of enjoyment and as an antidote to routine or boredom.

Jokers, for example, got a lot of their fun and enjoyment from:

> juggling with the risks of 'getting done' by teachers. If their judgements were correct, then routine teacher reactions would not result in much stress. Indeed, spice and zest would be added to classroom experiences from such exploration of the limits without serious sanctions resulting. (ibid., p.85)

The defence of personal dignity and the preservation of self– and peer-group-esteem is mentioned as another constant interest-at-hand. Children resented being 'shown-up' or 'picked-on' by teachers or other children, and intergroup rivalry had both defensive and aggressive qualities. As well as having to cope with evaluative comments from teachers, children also had to deal with teasing, name-calling and fighting amongst themselves.

Pollard shows how it is important for children to feel part of, and to be seen as full and competent members of, their peer-group. At Moorside, one of his case study schools, he noted how:

> enjoyment, laughs and 'great times' almost exclusively derived from interaction between children and their friends with or with-

out the positive participation of the teacher. A positive audience was thus crucial and could be guaranteed only by the secure membership and solidarity of a peer-group. (ibid., p.88)

Clearly, peer-group membership serves to protect self-images and to help children to cope with the range of curriculum and pedagogical demands which they meet in the classroom. Whilst the central underlying demand upon children is that they satisfy teachers' and parents' expectations that they will learn, the more obvious and immediate requirement is that they participate fully and do their best at all times. Pollard found that children were assessing the interrelated costs and benefits of trying to learn, on the one hand, with maintaining their peer-group membership on the other. Gang groups tended to see many lessons as a waste of time and 'their perceived academic failure meant that learning did not seem to provide anything more than a very limited means of enabling them to cope with their situation' (p.89). At the same time, good groups put up with boring activities which were seen as good for them, and in any case they wished to avoid compromising their identities with teachers. It was the joker groups which were most successful at juggling the relative and simultaneous obligations of membership of their peer-group against those of the class or task groups: 'their success at learning earned them credit with teachers and parents with which they were able to relax and cultivate laughs' (p.89).

Nick Hornby (1992), who would probably have belonged to one of Pollard's 'joker groups', catches the way that his own sense of social competence at school was associated with life outside it. In *Fever Pitch*, his book about being a football fan, he describes how his interest in football and collection of stickers of famous players made school such a comfortable place to be:

The benefits of liking football at school were incalculable (even though the games master was a Welshman who once memorably tried to ban us from kicking a round ball even when we got home): at least half of my class, and probably a quarter of the staff loved the game.... The main thing was that you were a believer. Before school, at breaktime and at lunchtime we played football on the tennis court with a tennis ball, and in between lessons we swapped soccer star stickers. ...And so transferring to secondary school was rendered unimaginably easy... and though my performance as a student was undistinguished (I was bunged into the 'B' stream at the end of the year and stayed there throughout my entire grammar school career), the lessons were a breeze. (pp.22–23)

He says, seemingly tongue-in-cheek, that he is aware of the downside of his obsession on his personality, relationships and emotions , but, then says:

> ... If you can walk into a school full of eight hundred boys, most of them older, all of them bigger, without feeling intimidated, simply because you have a spare Jimmy Husband [soccer stars sticker] in your blazer pocket, then it seems a trade-off worth making.(p23)

Nick Hornby went to an all–boys school and in this extract he is writing about his memories of 1968. Today there are other passions and crazes which meld the child community. National and international media and marketing is used to promote topics which soon permeate schools up and down the country. We have had Mutant Ninja Turtles and, at the time of writing, pictures of dinosaurs from *Jurassic Park* are to be found in many school trays. Young children achieve status from being able to recite complicated names of obscure creatures.

The topic which bound Nick Hornby's friends together and conferred a measure of social competence also genuinely bridged the adult and child cultures. Sometimes local passions bridge these cultures too. For example, Newcastle United's championship winning season in 1992–3 and the later stages of Manchester's Olympic bid reached across age groups and genders.

Whilst these potential sources of common interest offer opportunities for sharing and provide a a sense of belonging for some children and sometimes help adult-child relationships, they may also engender explicit rejection as well as more implicit forms of detachment, estrangement and alienation. As we argued earlier, child cultures and adult cultures are not homogeneous. Before going on to discuss children's membership of task groups we want to emphasize the importance of the child culture whist avoiding over-simplified notions of membership patterns.

Children's membership obligations as pupils

Being a pupil, as well as a child, brings a complex mix of obligations, constraints and opportunities. It means, for example, being part of a whole class unit, being a separate individual and being part of any small group a teacher arranges during each day.

Belonging to a specific class, and to a school, brings a

sense of 'official membership' and of being a representative pupil. Many teachers are anxious about the conduct of their classes when they are in 'public places', such as corridors and assemblies and to emphasize this, children are often identified as Mrs Bates' or Mr Mercian's class. Children soon learn that they are expected to behave in ways which will bring credit to their teacher, and that poor behaviour brings down the reputation of the whole class. The second case study in the first chapter was about an experienced teacher who moved to a difficult urban school. It showed how he tried to modify the internal classroom culture with the help of a support teacher, yet the field notes also show how, at the same time, he tried to prepare the children to behave with unquestioning conformity in the corridors at breaktime. One of his habits was to change his own manner to be brusque and commanding at the end of a lesson.

Inside the classroom, being a member of the whole class often means being part of a participatory audience, listening mainly to the teacher and answering questions. It brings a sense of being orchestrated, requiring attentitiveness, responsiveness and an ability to recognize cues. It is shaped partly by ground rules and contextual conventions about such things as 'showing hands', and not talking when the teacher is talking, and partly by implicit signals communicated through facial expressions and body language. One of the themes of this book is the relationship between being an individual and being a member. As far as being a whole class member is concerned, children can usually learn how to look an integral part of a smart and attentive body of pupils so long as teachers are clear and unambiguous about what they seek. What some pupils also learn, especially Pollard's 'jokers', is that you don't necessarily need to express your individuality or peer membership through rebellion or confrontation. You can, for instance, use expressions of boredom and tired body movements to try to bring a whole class session to a close, you can divert a topic onto more interesting ground and hopefully you can try to get some laughs, preferably with the teacher. One of the key learning points is that you can be assertive without being aggressive and you can influence events without risking being labelled deviant.

Another aspect of being part of a whole class is to be a member of the informal classroom work culture. For example, periods of time set aside for individual work may offer opportunities in some classrooms for brief and fleeting collaboration between children who seek help or who want to compare, show and share what they are doing. As we said at the beginning of the book, individual tasks are carried out in close proximity to other children. Some teachers try to prevent talk between children, but many accept, or even encourage, informal interaction so that children can feel a sense of being members of a learning community through both social and work-focused talk. Bossert (1987) has shown how such peer group and friendship structures are affected by the teacher's classroom task organization. He found that in classrooms where recitation–style teaching was prevalent, children's friendship patterns were stable and exclusive to those with similar performance levels. However, in multi-activity classrooms, pupils formed friendships on the basis of hobbies or tasks, changing groups as interests shifted. Children in the latter style classrooms were willing to work with each other in groups, but in the former the children had competitive attitudes and preferred to be in segregated work groups based on performance.

This brings us to another form of membership experience which children have when they are allocated to groups by teachers, given set tasks and expected to get on amongst themselves for specified periods. In some classrooms children may be asked to work in a number of such groups during a week at school, the groups changing from subject to subject or according to ad hoc seating arrangements or to criteria which the teacher uses to judge what is likely to be appropriate at the time. This means that groups may be matched or mixed ability, single or mixed gender or race groups, and may or may not correspond to existing friendship patterns. In view of this, and of what we have said above about the child culture (particularly children's strategies for enjoying themselves and maintaining their self-images and dignity) we should not expect that their participation in group work will be straightforward and focused entirely on the task.

In the second part of this chapter, we develop and illustrate our line of argument by concentrating upon what happens when teachers establish children's groups, set specific tasks and then ask those groups to 'get on by themselves'.

We are referring to those occasions when teachers divide a class into, say, five or six groups and then move around the room paying intermittent attention to each group. We have found evidence, both from analysis of our own teaching and from enquiries with other teachers, to suggest that we should be cautious when making judgements about children's participation in groups merely from the impressions we get from spasmodic listening and observing. Too often, we have been misled into making superficial interpretations of what is happening and, at the same time, we have missed important aspects of participation and learning.

Children learning to belong and contribute as members of task groups

Despite research studies which have pointed to its rarity over the past decade (Galton, 1981; HMSO, 1983; Mortimer *et al.* 1988; Tizard *et al.*, 1988), claims continue to be made for the value of group work. For example, collaborative learning in groups is seen as an integral part of the National Curriculum, and an essential aspect of some of the programmes of study. It is therefore important that we should look closely at children's experiences of working and learning in groups. In particular, we should try to understand ways in which children learn with and from others and how they might contribute effectively to group learning to benefit both themselves and others. In this section of the chapter we explore what it means to be an active or 'contributive' member of a group.

In order to work towards clearer understanding of 'contributive membership', we begin by comparing the ways in which two 10-year-old girls worked on a task as part of a group of six children. The teacher expected that one of these girls would take the role of the leader of the group and that the other would be a willing participant, making only modest contributions. Evidence from an audio recording of the group led to some rethinking, not only about the two girls, but also about what it means to be a leader or a member of a group which has been established for a specific purpose, and for a short period of time.

The group of Year 6 children was building a model bridge, and the recording was made during an action-research project in which four pairs of teachers, from different primary schools, were investigating their approaches to group work in their classrooms. The teachers were committed to using small group work with all children in their classrooms. As such, they differed from three other broad categories of teachers which Cowie and Rudduck (1988) have called 'non-users', 'occasional users', and 'divisive users' who use group work only with some pupils, say the lower or higher achievers, but not with others.

As well as leading some discussions and activities, the committed teachers also gave the children frequent opportunities to work in small, self-directed groups without being present themselves. The action-research project was undertaken to investigate the ways in which the children participated and shaped an activity once the teacher had set the task.We were studying what was happening when children worked in groups without continuous teacher presence. Teachers brought tape recordings and transcripts to the action-research group and before we listened to the recordings, those who knew the children usually talked about their expectations and about how they had anticipated that a group might work together. In this particular case, the teacher thought that Jane would be a leader. Her written work was often the best in her class and she was seen as having a consistently responsible attitude towards work. Alison was expected to take part willingly in the activity, but not to 'take the lead'. The teacher described her as a popular girl who was average for her class when it came to individual work. During the actual lesson, the class teacher had moved around the room, talking and listening to each group, and observing each of six groups occasionally. This had not caused him to question his ideas about the two girls. As expected, Jane seemed to be taking the lead and Alison was involved and interested throughout the session when the group was building a model bridge strong enough to hold a toy car and wide enough to span a river.

We then listened to the recording and we noticed that Jane had read the instructions card to the rest of the group. She used an officious manner for this, which she carried into most of her other contributions, giving an impression of being 'in charge'. For the rest of the time, however, she was impatient and negative. She resisted other children's attempts to improve the design of the bridge or to test ideas.

Alison, on the other hand, was concerned about the quality

of the bridge. She kept asking whether it would be strong enough, refusing to be satisfied despite others' attempts to persuade her that what they had already done would be good enough. This helps to reiterate the point, made in the previous chapter, that being a willing member is not simply being compliant.

Alison   Would they [toy cars] not fall off?
               When they came over there would they not crash?

Simon   Just put some stuff...

Jane   Whey no!

Jane, especially, seemed in a hurry to get the job finished, but Alison wanted to improve the bridge and she was not prepared to be discouraged.

Jane   Then all you do is put the cars on
               and paint it and that...

Tracey   Then it'll be like the real thing.

Alison   Well, would it be strong enough ?

Tracey   Whey aye.

Jane   For matchbox cars it will.

Kevin   A stick going through there?

Tracey   But that'll have to be where?

Alison   Unless we put like...and we'll have to
               stick that down, because that might come off.

Jane   Oh, man, all you have to do when you've
               glued it, is to staple it and then paint over
               the top of it!

Alison wanted to try different strategies. She showed the others what she would like to try, and eventually Lisa and Tracey did respond and they tested out some ideas together:

Alison   You could bend the ends so that it would
               be easier to make the bridge...know
               what I mean?

Lisa   Unless you bend the two ends that way,
               and when you stick it down it'll be
               balancing like that.

Alison   That's what I mean. More inwards.

Lisa	Like that should I? Go on then try it. You bend it. You cannot bend it properly.
Tracey	There. That's alright like that. Then we could stick them things down. We'll need the wood though. We'll still need the wood to keep it up. Where are we going to get it from?

Throughout the activity, Alison posed questions, raised doubts, thought aloud and seemed to increase possibilities of reflective work. She was assertive and persistent, rather than aggressive, She invited comments from the others and at one point she even seemed to check herself mid-sentence to change an imperative into a tentative idea:

then you have to... you could put yellow lines at the side.

From listening to the tape, we noticed that Alison had sustained her positive influence throughout the activity. On the other hand, Jane had tried to reject ideas prematurely, to dismiss questions and to block reflective, exploratory thinking. She had been impatient when different ideas were being tested. This raised questions about how we should think about children's involvement as group members. As well as being surprised about having underestimated Alison's contribution to the group, we also recognized how easy it is to oversimplify the notion of leadership.

We began to cross-check our tapes and we found other examples where children, like Alison, were contributing in different, and often unexpected, ways to the quality of their groups' work. We also found that some children who appeared to be leaders were merely bossy. They liked to read out instructions or give turns or allocate tasks to others. We started to think that the concept of leadership was of limited use in describing children's involvement in temporary groups. How many leaders could a group have, in any case? Perhaps, when teachers say that there are a number of leaders in their classes, and when football managers say that a good team has a lot of leaders, they are actually talking about responsible, active and contributing members who take initiatives, accept responsibility and are concerned about others as well as themselves. Rather than looking for qualities of leadership we should be fostering contributing membership. It does seem to be a legitimate, clear and practicable aspiration to aim for *all* pupils to learn to be responsible, active and contributive members. It is certainly better than encouraging the dominance and bossiness of one or two.

We shall go on to discuss the practical benefit of this shift in conceptualizing children's involvement in group tasks in relation to contributive membership rather than leadership. When it comes to giving feedback to children about their contributions to the processes of their group's work, we felt we needed a broader, yet better focused, framework of criteria from which to draw. The action-research processes were helping us to derive our criteria of 'contributive membership' from evidence of what children were actually doing.

To illustrate our move away from the concept of leadership and our emphasis upon membership, we have chosen an episode from an activity in which a group of five 10-year old boys struggled with the task of deciding what objects they would take with them, if they were to live on a desert island. This activity was being used in a sequence of lessons on classifying and using generic terms for the categories. The group had 'got bogged down' and was making little progress when Chris, John, David and then John again, tried to find new angles on the task. This episode is very brief and it ends as the group is willing to accept John's idea to project itself imaginatively into the task. First Chris posed a new question:

Chris	Think of a day at home. What everyday things do we use?
Paul	What I use...I use loads of things... I use binoculars and everything.
John	I use my football.
David	I know but you won't think of that will you. That's useless that.
John	If you play football all you'll use is a pig's bladder, or a coconut...but it would be painful using a coconut. In any case, why are we talking about that?
David	We've got to think of something useful.
John	Imagine we are on a desert island and we are stranded...

Neil	We haven't got anything at the moment.
John	I'm canny hungry at the moment...
David	Suppose you've got five wishes.
John	I'm canny hungry right... [an interuption at this point]... I'm quite hungry at the moment...so, like, if I imagine myself on a desert island.
Paul	I would be hungry...
John	Well you'd have your coconut with you... Just imagine we'll not talk for a minute right... Right, we'll just imagine, not one of us, us here...and we're hungry...and we're on a desert island.

(At this point the boys closed their eyes and started to imagine being on the island.)

We suggest that it is better to think about contributive membership, than to try to identify a leader or leaders in this group. Even in this short extract from their discussion, Chris, John and David offer new ways of approaching the task. We think it would be unhelpful, in relation to giving feedback and to fostering further collaboration, to assume that John is the leader because his suggestion is carried out whilst other ideas are not. Paul, for example, responds willingly and appropriately to both Chris and John, by answering Chris's question and starting to imagine being hungry to share feelings with John. With this kind of evidence of contributing membership it is possible to give specific feedback to these boys rather than make generalized remarks about the whole group. We are certainly not suggesting that checklists be devised and ticked or that elaborate records should be used, but that feedback is given casually, and carefully, within the spontaneity and informality of the primary school day:

> Oh, by the way Paul, I was listening to the tape of your group yesterday, and I noticed how you all imagined being on the island. I thought that you helped everybody to concentrate after John suggested it. How well do you think that you worked together?
>
> Your idea about the five wishes was interesting, David. It gave the group more choices of how to approach the task. What do think about the way that you made the list?

This kind of feedback will help the children to start thinking about their own contributions and to increase their understanding of what working in groups might entail. Most teachers are aware of the importance of chance remarks in building relationships with and amongst children All of us have been children, and those of us who are also parents know how a teacher's casual comments can sometimes worry or upset a child or, conversely, raise his or her self-esteem, interest or motivation. For this reason, we do not think that collaboration will be advanced by drawing attention to negative examples. In the case referred to earlier, for instance, it is likely to be better to talk about Alison's contribution openly and informally, and so draw Jane's attention to what is valued, than to tell Jane that you thought she was being unhelpful to the group. To dwell on weaknesses is inappropriate in a field of activity which needs to be fostered with a spirit of optimism and enthusiasm, but also of realism rather than Pollyannaism.

The following example shows how 'contributive membership' is complex and multi-dimensional. It is interesting to look closely at the transcript and to try to work out the contributions of each of three girls and two boys who have been allocated to this group. In particular, Mark seems to show extraordinary resilience to maintain his positive involvement in difficult circumstances. The children, aged 10 and 11 years, had been given an assignment, by the teacher, to build a structure which would support a marble 80cms from the ground and at least 20cms out from the centre of the structure. The transcript numbers have been included for reference in the discussion which follows. The whole transcript was numbered from the beginning and the extracts have not been re-phased.

The activity involved estimating and measuring, but the teacher was disappointed, at first, to find that the children were not sketching alternative ideas in order to persuade others to accept them. From subsequent review, three factors seemed to prevent the testing of alternative ideas: a time limit of 45 minutes had been imposed; an 'official' competition had been arranged between the groups; and each group had only had one set of materials. At the outset the two boys wanted to build a pyramid structure, but the girls did not accept the idea.

1	*Brian*	Make a base first.
2	*Gillian*	There's four pieces [of card]. Roll some up. Then cut out two half circles. That'll be for the stand. It's like making a card doll.
3	*Sara*	Make a half circle.
4	*Mark*	Use the sellotape as a half circle.
5	*Julia*	I thought we might do that. Make a half circle stick that on there, and bend that over until it stands.
6	*Sara*	It's got to be 80cms.
7	*Julia*	But that's only the stand isn't it.
8	*Brian*	Make a pyramid with a piece out there for the weight, and put another piece out there and put the plasticine on there.
9	*Sara*	That's just cheating. We've got to have something sticking out.

Even at this early stage, alternative ideas were not being discussed. Gillian and Sara had taken the materials and Brian was trying to find out what Sara, in particular, was already doing with some of the card, before any joint decisions had been made:

12	*Brian*	What are you doing there?
13	*Sara*	It's like a little dish thing.
14	*Brian*	What are you making it go with?
15	*Sara*	That's for the marble.
16	*Sara*	Make a half circle. Bend that over. If that's sticking up and that's at the bottom of the stand. Bend something over that way so that the structure can stand upon there. The marble will go on there.

At this point Gillian announced that she had an idea. Again she began to work on it rather than try to explain and justify what she was going to do. She ignored Brian and Mark, but she was being supported by Sara and Julia as they watched what she was doing.

| 17 | *Gillian* | I've got an idea for the stand. |

18 *Mark*	Why not make a pyramid?
19 *Sara*	I know, make a massive circle.
20 *Mark*	What with?
27 *Mark*	We've only got 40 minutes you know.
28 *Sara*	Make Gillian's stand. it's a good idea. Make a stand – two half circles.
29 *Mark*	I'm going to make a pyramid.
30 *Julia*	You can't do it by yourself.

Gillian continued to build the stand and Sara and Julia watched and helped her, adding comments and suggestions. Mark and Brian were finding that they couldn't influence the others at this point.

30 *Julia* (cont)	Use a ruler to cut it in half [the card]
31 *Sara*	You have to measure the radius. You should have a compass.
32 *Julia*	That's about the middle. A bit farther over Gillian.
33 *Mark*	She's not listening.
39 *Mark*	I don't know what she's doing [referring to Gillian].
40 *Julia*	It won't stand up.
41 *Brian*	She's [Gillian] got it all wrong.
42 *Mark*	Wasted good card.
43 *Julia*	Only three sheets.
44 *Brian*	But three sheets could make all the difference.

Gillian carried on building with Julia measuring and Sara estimating. Mark was doubtful about the idea and by this stage Brian was just watching in a detached way. Gillian (67) asked for guidance from Sara.

58 *Gillian*	Measure how long the card is first.
59 *Sara*	Say, 30 cms.

60	*Julia*	It's 22.5 cms.
61	*Sara*	Just say 30. Two of them is 60. Cut that. That's about 20.
62	*Mark*	It's not going to work.
63	*Julia*	27cms.
64	*Sara*	It doesn't matter, leave it to Gillian. There's 2 cms wrong there. So you'll need it like that. Just cut it off there. stick them together and roll them into one long roll.
65	*Mark*	Plenty of sellotape here if you need it.
66	*Gillian*	That's enough.
67	*Gillian*	Which way are we going to roll it – that way?
68	*Sara*	Not long ways.
69	*Julie*	Put splits in the bottom and let it slide down.
70	*Sara*	I know, we'll have to wait until we've rolled it up.
71	*Mark*	I've got a funny feeling it's not going to work.
72	*Julia*	We're just trying it.

As the structure began to take shape, Gillian decided to change the cross section of the column (83), Julia thought of a way to attach the column to the base (84), and then Gillian thought of a set of three support members to join the column to the base in a tripod arrangement. The base was giving problems, since it was bending and it would not lie flat.

83	*Gillian*	Make it a square. Make a square long thing.
84	*Julia*	We need two slits in the bottom.
85	*Mark*	I've got an old ruler. How big has it got to be?
86	*Sara*	What are you going to do with that?
87	*Gillian*	Make like a pyramid. Make a totem pole.

A little later, Sara had another idea (103). Mark helped her and, seeing this, Julie reminded him that the girls had done most of the work (110).

103	*Sara*	Bend it like Christmas cards.

Bend it in. Sellotape it on there.
Draw around the inside like that.
Then fold the corners in like a triangle.
Then stick it on there.
We'll have little flaps to support it.

104   *Mark*   But what are we going to use for the triangle ?

105   *Sara*   This.

106   *Mark*   I'll get the scissors. Only one sheet
of card left. Cut the base and put a slot there.

107   *Julia*   Use this ruler to score it.

108   *Sara*   Half that and double it.

109   *Mark*   Is it working yet ?

110   *Julia*   Just about. We've done most of the work.

Despite the reminder that he was still seen as an outsider by Julia, Mark began to contribute ideas. Prior to this he had made encouraging remarks or offered to get things for the girls which he thought would be useful.

115   *Mark*   We might be going the wrong
way about it. Stuff something
down inside it for the weight.

123   *Mark*   Remember the old crippled
woman with a walking stick.
Stick one piece of card on there
and stick it to the table.

At this point Mark (like Sara, 103) used the kind of image which Ollerenshaw and Ritchie (1993) like to hear children use in primary science group work to illustrate and communicate their ideas. He watched what happened next and he was pleased when he saw how Sara built the stand. He even called her a genius at this point.

130   *Julia*   That bottom's not flat.

131   *Mark*   Why not make a stronger base.

132   *Gillian*   What are you doing?

133   *Sara*   Building a stand.

134   *Mark*   You're not making a tripod.

135   *Sara*   Make three...stick all of them
on the corners. It should stand up.

136   *Mark*   You're a genius.

Even though Mark has not had his hands on the materials, by now he is collaborating with Gillian, Sara, Julia as they turn to the next part of the task.

141 *Mark* I told you my way about making a
stand for it... with an arm on. It'll work easy.

142 *Julia* I hope it works.

143 *Mark* We've used up all the card.

144 *Sara* At least it's worked.

145 *Gillian* I know why it won't stand up.
Because it's got too much weight
on one side. Put some sellotape on each side.
The arm is going to weigh more than the
sellotape. Put the arm on one side and the
sellotape on the other.

146 *Mark* Put the arm there and get another
piece of paper like this to even the weight.

We have chosen this example to illustrate, again, the usefulness of the concept of 'contributive membership' and to show, at the same time, the limitations of 'leadership' as a criterion for judging children's participation in task groups. Gillian takes control of the materials and it seemed that she led the group, doing most of the actual building of the model with the others commenting, suggesting ideas and generally following her. However, this does not take us far. We found that it was more fruitful, both in terms of enhancing our understanding of group work, and in making practical decisions about how to foster further learning for each child and for the group as a whole, when we began to think about how each of the participants contributed to the quality of the work. Gillian did contribute in ways other than doing most of the building. For example, she did sometimes think aloud and ask questions. Julia gave precise measurements (60, 63) and pointed out problems (130) and Sara often summarized and supported the ideas of others.

Mark's contributive membership within the group is particularly heartening. Despite the early rejection of his ideas and regardless of some further attempts to exclude him, he continued to be supportive and encouraging to the others (65, 125, 136). He introduced his ideas tentatively, sometimes as questions, and he always celebrated the collective successes of the group. Brian, on the other hand, became detached. Unlike Mark, he did not show the disposition or the social skills to cope with conflict, and he was easily excluded by the girls.

However, in the next example of a group of two 8-year-olds – two boys and two girls – who are making a list of useful objects to have in a lifeboat, Steven was supported even though his ideas were unacceptable and rejected. Some of Steven's comments had been flippant and he had mainly tried to make the others laugh. Lesley was particularly patient and supportive even though she kept asking him to stop being silly:

48 *Steven* You could chew trees.
(laughter)

49 *Lesley* Don't be silly, Steven.

Later in the discussion, Lesley responded to another unacceptable idea without being discouraging.

76 *Steven* I would take a bed because you might get frozen.

77 *Lesley* Yes, but it's a desert island...you will never
get frozen...it's hot ...but still...

Lesley started encouragingly with the word 'yes' and her phrase 'but still', spoken tentatively, opened rather than blocked further comment. Helped by this, Steven felt able to justify his suggestion and in the following discussion the principle of 'making things' is made explicit.

78 *Steven* There might be storms.

79 *Peter* Well, you could build a hut,
and you could live in there; and you could
live in a hut and be as
warm as anything Steven.

80 *Lesley* Yes ...and...

81 *Steven* ...But where would you sleep?

82 *Peter* On a bed. You could make fur...
out of skins of animals...

83 *Lesley* Yes, skins...and...palm leaves.

84 *Peter* See.

85 *Lesley* You could use palm leaves to lie on.

86 *Laura*   I think that's a good idea... not to
take a bed... 'cos you can really
make things.

Remembering what we said earlier about the child culture,
it is significant that humour was interwoven with the task-
focused talk throughout the discussion. Later, Peter made
them laugh again, by mentioning the kind of luxury item
which can be taken to Roy Plomley's desert island:

119 *Peter*   Take...er...a bucket and spade. (Laughter)

120 *Lesley* Don't be silly. Peter. I know we
could make sandcastle. (Laughter)

121 *Steven* It would be fun.

122 *Lesley* Be serious... we need...

123 *Laura* A bucket and spade.

124 *Lesley* Stop being stupid, Laura.

Peter then made another suggestion and, after a long pause
for more thinking, Lesley summarized their progress. In
doing so she also categorized their list of objects into
weapons and 'things to show the way'.

125 *Peter*   Get some fish hooks.

126 *Lesley* We wouldn't need fish
hooks 'cause sticks...

127 *Peter*   We could make them.

128 *Lesley* Sticks... sticks... and then dig
them into the fish and bring them out...
yeah, but what else could
you bring?
(Long pause)

129 *Lesley* Well, let's see what we've got.
We've got a knife, and axe,
a gun and maps...there's one more thing...
er...we've got some weapons
down...we've got something to show
our way back.

Key characteristics of this mixed-ability group were its
capacity to maintain cohesion and to refocus its attention
onto the task after diversions. Its style of interlacing fun

with serious discussion was a major factor in its success, in the same way that Pollard's 'jokers' were able to operate simultaneously within both the child culture and the teacher-dominated culture. In the extracts quoted here, Peter, especially, shows both the social competence and the cognitive capacity to fulfil the expectations of both the teacher and his peer-group.

Like Prisk (1987), who noticed that children in her groups stopped taking responsibility for their own group management once she rejoined a group, teachers in our action-research projects have often commented with pleasant surprise upon how well children take responsibilities in self-directed groups, referring frequently to how some children do the kinds of things that they would have done themselves if they had been present. These comments have been made during close scrutiny of group processes, which have also thrown some light on two features of group work which had raised doubts when they had been noticed in the hurly-burly of the classroom.

First, children sometimes seemed to lack commitment and, at times, group activities would seem to degenerate into squabbling. It was discouraging for teachers when they saw that children seemed so detached or when disturbing disputes, laughter and other kinds of excitable behaviour seemed to come from all sides of the room. Second, tasks often seemed to be accomplished quickly, suggesting that they had been dealt with only superficially. Faced with such discomfort and apparent lack of depth, less resilient teachers had tended to opt for safer arrangements, sometimes allocating the role of leader and expecting one of the children to control the rest.

We have tried to show the doubtful value of assuming that designating a child as a leader of others will solve control problems or enhance the learning potential of a group. We have also seen that group activities are prone to variation in direction, depth and intensity of engagement with the task. Tensions build up and they are usually relieved in some way, sometimes by recourse to the child culture and sometimes to the structure of the task. Groups can lose direction and then, when it is least expected, troughs of shallow, shapeless talk may be followed by peaks of genuine, collaborative learning with a clear sense of purpose. It is surely educative for children to solve the inherent prob-

lems involved in group work in different kinds of circumstances. If they are denied this experience, then, like the less
resilient teacher, children will carry on preferring to work
alone or to hide within a whole class for as much time as
possible.

What, then, do we mean by temporary, contributive
membership of classroom task groups? It differs from peer-
group membership in two main ways. First, it is unlikely
that membership of a temporary task group, established for
a brief one-off purpose, will bring a feeling of belonging or
a sense of identity unless the group is made up of existing
friends. Yet, as in other kinds of classroom activity, some
children will be seeking the support and security of their
peers in order to cope with task demands. In the case of
group work, however, it is particularly unfortunate when
children feel vulnerable in relation to their peers as well as
indirectly in relation to the teacher's power. This sometimes
makes learning with others an uncomfortable kind of activity for some children, like Brian above, when they find
themselves allocated to uncongenial groups.

Second, unlike more enduring friendship groups, the sole
reason for the group's existence may be the completion of a
task in a set time-scale. In this sense it is more like a team
than a group, and being part of a team requires that members make a contribution towards the result or product. For
this reason, children's contributive membership may be
bounded and procedural. Silence is the most obvious form
of non-contribution, but being silent in a group does not
necessarily mean a child is not taking part and learning
from the experience. Nevertheless, silent children usually
concern teachers and they try to help them to take a more
active part in group talk. Drummond's (1993, p.69) account
of her pleasure at a 6-year old child's progress illustrates
this:

>...for nearly a year Eve attended weekly discussion sessions with-
>out speaking. She listened, certainly, and responded with laughter,
>and other signs of appreciation to the contribution of her friends;
>but never a word did she utter.
>
>Late one autumn afternoon however, after the close of our dis-
>cussion period, the tide turned. We had been discussing 'stripes',
>the theme of a current exhibition of children's work displayed in
>the lobby outside the room where the sessions were held. Eve had
>been as silent as usual. But as we walked back to her mobile class-
>room however, across the playground, we passed the window

> cleaners at work. Eve tugged at my hand and whispered in my ear 'ladders have stripes'. This achievement, which was celebrated throughout the school (with, we hope, appropriate tact as well as enthusiasm) was just the beginning of the apotheosis of Eve. She became, in her own way, one of the leaders of the group she worked with: other children listened carefully to her ideas, which varied from the accurate and penetrating to the wildest flights of fantasy. The range of her linguistic powers (in spoken language – she was not reading or writing independently) grew, quite visibly, week by week.

Drummond catches the unexpected burst of growth in Eve's social competence as well as her linguistic powers. We would prefer to think that she had become a contributive member rather than 'one of the leaders of her group', but this is a minor point and what is notable is that the impetus for her sudden progress arose spontaneously outside of the organized group setting, after the activity had been formally concluded.

How can teachers foster children's belonging and contributing in collaborative groups?

We shall not attempt to offer a blueprint for promoting and fostering contributive membership of groups even if we could think of one. Consistent with the aim of the book we shall try to derive some guiding principles and some examples of the kinds of anticipated problems which we think teachers are likely to encounter. Before doing this we shall draw upon a recent book on groupwork (Galton and Williamson, 1992) and on an earlier volume in this series which explores approaches to assessing children's learning (Drummond, 1993).

Galton and Williamson (1992) have made an extensive and detailed review of the literature on group work from the USA and the UK. From this they have drawn six general conclusions and pointed to two key remaining questions which have shaped their own recent work. What has been learned so far is, first, that group work does improve children's self-esteem and motivation when they are encouraged to work towards a shared outcome or make individual contributions to a common goal. Second, 'groups function best when they are of mixed ability but such groups must include pupils from the highest ability group within the class. Where possible they should also be representative of gender and racial differences within the classroom.' (p.42). Third, children perform in different ways according to the nature of tasks. Levels of conversation are highest during 'action tasks' involving practical activities, and exchanges are more intermittent but also more sophisticated during 'abstract tasks'. Fourth, problem-solving tasks with clear, testable outcomes tend to generate a greater degree of collaboration than more 'open-ended tasks'. In the latter, pupils tend to be satisfied with the first solution offered, and they also seem to assert rather than hypothesize or raise questions. Fifth, pupils need to be taught how to collaborate and they need to know what is expected of them. They also need feedback followed by further discussion with the teacher. Sixth, it seems useful to think of group work as a two-stage process involving initial and subsequent interactions and then to use different strategies for supporting each stage.

Galton and Williamson then point to two areas of concern which remain. First, whilst the research suggests that children's self-concepts are crucial if they are to take on the 'ownership' of an activity and run groups on their own, little is known so far about pupils' perceptions of working in groups. Second, research offers little guidance for teachers about how and when to intervene and when not to intervene in a group's work. These questions formed the basis of their further work in ORACLE II and then in a more recent action-research project.

In the ORACLE II study, children's perceptions of group work were collected through recording their responses to cartoons of practical tasks and of discussions with and without teachers present. Four interpretations were made from the data collected. First, they revealed children's uncertainty about what to do, especially in the early stages before a group developed a sense of solidarity. Second, children expected teachers to look for and correct mistakes or accuse them of 'not getting on' quickly enough or of 'fooling around'. Third, children often lost ownership of what they were doing when teachers got involved, and fourth, they preferred practical tasks where there was less ambiguity about purpose than more abstract discussions when they doubted whether the teacher would accept their ideas.

Overall, the children expected corrective feedback from teachers and they were concerned about getting things right. At the same time, Galton had recorded children's reliance on the teacher in his fieldwork diary. However, one teacher (referred to as Jean below) had being singled out as different from the other teachers. This led to a small-scale project with Jean and another teacher with a contrasting style. This project has yielded important insights into a teacher's role in facilitating collaboration in children's groups.

Whilst both teachers operated what Galton and Williamson call a 'two-stage' approach, they used different strategies. Norma began with a 'guided discovery' strategy, working closely with the children to demonstrate and offer advice when they encountered difficulties. She expected that the children would gain confidence and take more responsibility for the task as the lesson progressed. Jean, on the other hand, used the opposite strategy. She withdrew initially so that the children would start to rely on each other, and only when collaboration had begun to develop did she become increasingly involved by raising questions and challenging ideas. From the analysis of filmed episodes in their classrooms, Galton and Williamson suggest that Norma's approach fosters pupils' individual identities at the expense of their social identities. This results in what they call 'cooperative activity' in which each pupil contributes towards a joint task. In contrast, Jean's approach fosters pupils' social identities at the expense of their individual identities. They found that her groups did engage in collaborative activity in which pupils made contributions to a single outcome.

Galton and Williamson support their argument with extensive, illustrative extracts from transcripts, interviews and fieldwork which show that Jean's approach provides 'freedom within a framework':

> She makes it clear that she expects the children to work collaboratively together but, recognising the risks involved, limits the range of issues or activities with which they are confronted. She argues that this makes them more confident and, as a result, they tend to engage in more collaborative activity where they share abstract ideas and where they work together towards one joint outcome. (p. 111).

Like the teachers featured in Chapter 1, part of Jean's approach was to develop a relaxed classroom ethos with mutual caring between herself and the children. She tried to show herself to be at risk: to 'show myself failing at times or struggling at things and tell the children how I feel about it' (p.113). In turn, the children engaged willingly in activities which had unclear outcomes, because they were confident that she would not 'misinterpret their faltering first efforts in negative ways' (p.119). Galton and Williamson noted how she avoided dealing with pupil behaviour at a surface level (eg, noisy class, pupil not paying attention) which would have pushed her into being the 'boss figure'.

This, in part, also helped to overcome a common dilemma that children often experience in dealing with teachers: that of having to learn the difference between arguing a point and 'answering back' or taking time to formulate ideas from reflective discussion whilst also 'getting on with the job'. One of the boys in Galton and Williamson's study conveys that dilemma:

> If you are in a group and you are all writing out different things for about half an hour and she comes up and says, 'How much have you done? 'and you say, 'Nothing' and you get done and we are discussing really.(p 113)

Jean communicated and modelled the high value she placed upon collaboration. She set out to help children to get better at listening to each other and discussing disagreements and she was not put off by the faltering nature of some children's learning. When her groups had developed a sense of identity she commented on the quality of what they were doing rather than correcting their mistakes. Galton and Williamson refer to this as giving 'critical' rather than 'evaluative' feedback. A key point to emphasize seems to be that collaborative learning can be fostered most successfully when a teacher's relationship with the children promotes mutual respect and when it engenders trust based upon consistency in the teacher's procedures of observation, participation and feedback.

In an earlier volume in this series, Mary Jane Drummond (1993) tells how she fostered collaborative group work as headteacher of an infants school. She arranged weekly group discussions for up to 45 minutes with children aged $4^1/_2$ to $7^1/_2$ years. Five key principles seem to be embedded in her accounts of what she did. First, the weekly discussions were events which had a simple routine, with the recording of contributions on large sheets of sugar paper being described by Drummond herself as a much appreciated ritual. Second, the children's task was explained as a simple fourfold process: 'to think of their own ideas, to tell each other their ideas, to listen to each other's ideas, and to question and comment on them' (p.62). Third, the topics were negotiated between the children and herself. Fourth, every opportunity seems to have been taken to celebrate achievements – mainly by displaying the sheets recording the content of discussions in corridors for other children, teachers and parents. Fifth, as the children's linguistic strengths were revealed, the topics changed from concrete and down-to-earth things towards abstract concepts such as 'movement' and 'silence'.

The idea of being a contributive member seems to have been communicated clearly to the children as giving ideas, listening, questioning and commenting; a kind of procedural responsibility for a bounded period of time. At first, Drummond suspected that it was a competitive rather than a collaborative spirit which moved the children to listen so intently to each other's contributions, but over time she said that the outcomes exceeded her wildest dreams. Her initial intentions had been modest but she soon realized that she was looking at significant learning. She has described some of this learning in detail and gave examples from lists of children's creative ideas which she had written on sugar paper. There are two alternative ways to convey this learning. One is to give her summary of types of learning and the other is to quote one of the accounts. The latter seemed to have so much life and vibrancy that it provides a fitting end to the chapter. We have chosen her description of the discussion of 'movement' to catch both the spirit of the learning and her own excitement as she witnessed it.

They had already listed under moving things cars, eyes, people, all the different animals, motor bikes, vehicles, all the different vehicles, wind, rain, clouds, the moon and the world but not the sun. The first suggestion for 'non-moving things' was the 'sunshine', and heated debate followed. When the sun goes in, where does it go? What is it that moves or appears to move? Debbie was insistent that the sun did not move and 'the sunshine' was allowed to stand at the top of the list. The next suggestion 'this school' was promptly ruled out by the consideration of an earthquake – it could move then!

The earthquake clause, was applied to many suggestions, which were, after a while, recorded as 'the bricks of a house that isn't in an earthquake', 'a road that isn't in an earthquake', even ' a coffin in the earth that isn't in an earthquake'. To get out of this difficulty I suggested 'Sheffield' – 'we don't have earthquakes here'. Debbie responded with 'Yugoslavia', which Nancy generalised to countries. Harking back to the solar system, Bryony suggested 'outer space'. Controversy started in earnest with Nancy's suggestion of 'Tuesday'. We wrote down all seven days of the week while we tried to decide. The sheet ends on a note of genuine indecision. 'We think "tomorrow" but we are not sure', and a scribbled note along the side of the page records Sarah's comment as we left the room, 'Time doesn't move...' Debbie challenged her to look at her watch, but Sarah stood her ground...I was silent – in admiration and respect. (pp.67–8)

Conclusion

When trying to make sense of how children participate in task groups, it is helpful also to think about their own friendship groups. Friendship groups offer opportunities for children to learn social competences in situations where they feel that they can act upon shared understandings of how to be both cooperative and assertive. Children's friendship groups develop strategies to maintain collective esteem. For some children this can fit comfortably with the demands and obligations of classroom work, but other children may use various tactics to insulate themselves from adult domination. When individuals weigh the costs and benefits of participation in task groups arranged by teachers against preserving their self-image and enjoying themselves with friends, some will find it unproblematic and others may find it very difficult. In this sense, membership of friendship groups in classrooms can be both enabling and constraining.

We should consider the extent to which childrens' participation in group work is a source of support, security and esteem as well as being socially, creatively and intellectually challenging. Group work is particularly demanding, because it affects children's social identities as well as their individual identities. In some task groups, for example, we have seen that children can be vulnerable to domination or rejection by other children.

When it comes to judging children's participation in task groups, we have found that impressions gained from intermittent observation of surface behaviour can be misleading. On the other hand, close analysis of children's interactions in groups can lead to surprising insights into individuals' contributions and overall patterns of learning.

We have argued that 'contributing membership' is a more fruitful concept than leadership when assessing the ways in which children enhance the quality of their collective work. Furthermore, as most group tasks are undertaken in bounded time by contrived, temporary groups, what can be realistically expected is a kind of procedural or bounded form of contributing membership. We think that this form of participation can be taught, or at least effectively learned, given favourable conditions. Drummond (1993), for instance, has described how young children were taught to listen, question and respond to each other's ideas.

It is also important that teachers try to create a favourable classroom context by modelling and placing high value on collaboration. This means listening to and discussing disagreements, not interpreting children's ideas or actions in negative ways, not expecting first ideas to be right, but showing oneself to be uncertain and spending time thinking together with children about topics in which asking questions, 'wondering if' and seeking alternatives are more appropriate and helpful than being correct or getting it right.

It is unwise to try to offer prescriptions for group work, and in this chapter, as in the book as a whole, we have tried to show how teachers have conducted investigations into their own practices and modified their work in the light of what they have found. Chapters 6 and 8 and the first part of Chapter 7 take up the theme of improving children's group work and learning partnerships. We shall return to suggest some broad guiding principles in Chapter 10. Before that, however, we shall explore, in the next three chapters, how teachers themselves experience and conceptualize belonging, contributing and learning in staffrooms at different stages of their careers.

Chapter 3

Learning to Belong and Contribute in Staffrooms: Student Teachers as Staff Members

They knew how I liked my coffee and by the end of my 'block' (a six-week placement in a primary school) the teachers acted as though I was one of them and they didn't keep any staffroom talk from me.

The staff were cliquey and made me feel like an intruder. After the first week I never went in the staffroom at all and I ate my sandwiches in the classroom. The advice was very patronizing –'Oh, it doesn't get any better you know'. (Year 4 BEd students talking about their final placements in primary schools.)

In the first two chapters we explored how children learn to belong and contribute as members of classroom communities. In this and the following chapter, we consider how teachers learn to become members of their profession and staff members of school communities. For teachers, just as for children, schools are made up of a complex weave of privacy and public work, individuality and interdependence, formality and informality, voluntariness and imposition, and turmoil and peace. Like the children they teach, teachers also have to learn to juggle their separate and individual interests and responsibilities with the obligations and demands of membership of small task groups and whole staff teams. As a starting point for exploring what it means to be a member of staff, we shall focus firstly upon new entrants to the profession, in the same way that we looked, in Chapter 1, at 'novice pupils' learning to be with other children in a reception class. Staffrooms can be as demanding an environment for students and new teachers as classrooms are for young children. In this chapter, we shall show how learning to belong and contribute can either be a comfortable or a daunting experience for students, depending upon existing staffroom relationships and what established teachers do to help or impede their introduction to the adult world of a school.

Recent proposals to increase the time allocated to the school-based element of initial teacher education could provide better opportunities for students to learn about belonging and contributing as members of a school staff. So far, however, most institutions and researchers have paid more attention to processes by which students might improve their classroom competences. This has meant that most discussions about partnerships between schools and training institutions have addressed supervision strategies and emphasized interaction between two individuals – student and mentor – within the confines of a single classroom. At the same time there has been a tendency to ignore or undervalue the significance of the whole school as a learning context. This is an unfortunate omission because longer placements will probably help students to learn more about the nature of schools as workplaces for adults.

Year after year, students return from stints of teaching practice to express surprise about how important the staffroom was in their placement schools. Prior to their placements they will have been preoccupied by the demands of preparation for classroom teaching, and it is only when the placement is completed that they review 'the luck of the draw' and compare their experiences in favourable and uncongenial staffrooms. Students find that they have learned a great deal of positive and negative things about schools in ad hoc and informal ways during the working week. What is learned sometimes contrasts sharply with the brief explanations they have been given about general school matters and 'official' arrangements. Yet, the idea that students learn about schools through being told is mentioned in a recent HMI report (HMSO, 1991, para 33), which indicated that school management, organization and staff relationships have often been addressed through discussions with the headteacher or a senior member of staff. From students' reviews of their placements, it does seem, however, that unplanned learning about these things has far outweighed headteachers' talks and information sheets about them. In a similar vein, Tickle (1989) has also noted that informal support from staffroom colleagues is often valued more highly by beginning teachers, than supervisory advice from people of higher status.

For this reason, students' opportunities to learn about staff membership and their experiences of staff relationships are likely to be too unpredictable and uncertain to be covered by generalized documentation. Placements are intended, in any case, to allow students to experience the work environment as it really is. Learning about adult relationships in schools, like learning in classrooms, cannot be accomplished in ideal conditions. Sometimes, other adults working in schools may be just as undermining and awkward as the children the students are teaching. Students would not be helped to learn about schools as workplaces if problems were smoothed out in advance or if artificial circumstances were specially contrived. Further complications arise because the ways that students are treated will depend partly on how they conduct themselves and how they are perceived by the permanent staff who regularly meet there.

This chapter draws mainly upon a case study conducted with a cohort of 87 students after their final primary school placement of six weeks, during a four-year course. Whilst most had only limited opportunities to engage in formal teamwork with other staff, they all learned a great deal about informal ways of working and learning with others. They were particularly sensitive to patterns of social relationships and they were able to work out whom to approach for support and whom to avoid. They encountered teachers who 'raised their spirits' and those who attacked their self-esteem, those who shared and those who were possessive and competitive. Amongst the adult communities of schools they said that they had found individuals who they thought were dogmatic, insecure, and jealous of others' success, as well as admirable people who were enthusiastic, open-minded, willing to explore new ideas and interested in talking with others about what happened. Sometimes they suffered from being labelled, patronized and undermined, whilst at other times they were consulted and involved in conversations. Some school staffs were insular and unwelcoming to outsiders whilst others were open and pleased to have new people in their midst.

In the previous chapter we looked at ways in which children might develop a sense of membership by learning that they belonged and could contribute in a classroom community. We argued that feelings of belonging help children to identify with their peers, to build shared understanding, to reduce vulnerability and to foster the growth of social competence. We then tried to show how this form of social competence is essential if children are to contribute to collaborative learning activities by being constuctively assertive as well as responsive and cooperative. For the same reasons, we suggest that learning to be a staff member is a key dimension of becoming a teacher. It is beneficial if students are able to experience feelings of belonging and are able to contribute to the adult community of the school. Before looking in more detail at what our students learned about staff membership, we shall discuss why we think that this should be an important part of teacher education.

Why is learning to be a staff member a key dimension of becoming a teacher?

Several recent studies have stressed the importance of adult relationships in schools. Nias (1989), drawing on extensive interviews with primary teachers, has shown that even in schools where teachers operate with a maximum of autonomy and a minimum of interaction, their own classroom teaching is affected by what other adults do and say in the school. She argues that:

> ...many of the frustrations which primary teachers suffer arise from the perpetuation of the false expectation that the job of teaching involves a relationship with children alone. They are not generally prepared by their training or by the conventional wisdom of the profession for the fact that participation in the life of the school is inseparable from teaching itself. (pp.112-13)

There are at least two interrelated ways in which membership of a school staff is experienced by teachers. First, there is the expectation or obligation that they will contribute along with colleagues to various kinds of task groups which plan, develop and review the work of the school and, second, there is the extent to which they experience mutual support which helps to spread and ease the stresses and strains of the job. Just as children develop collective strategies to cope with the obligations and social expectations of being in the roles of pupils, so do teachers learn collective strategies to cope with the demands of their work. Like the children they teach, teachers work in interwoven social structures created partly by themselves and partly by management and organizational arrangements and processes. Underlying both are deeply embedded historical factors which shape the social organization of their work, the nature of teaching as a profession and of schools as workplaces.

Recently, and especially since the 1988 Education Reform Act, there has been been a rapid and substantial increase in teachers' formal obligations to work together on such things as curriculum review and the writing of annual school development plans. Anticipating the introduction of a national curriculum, Richards (1987) forecast that it would be 'no longer reasonable for teachers to cope individually and unaided'; he went on to say that:

> individual self-sufficiency is undesirable in any case in view of the importance of continuity of experience and reasonable consistency of approach from class to class within the same school. (p.194)

Since then, debates about the benefits and problems of staff collaboration have shifted somewhat from concerns about the isolated and individualistic nature of teaching towards problems arising from enforced, imposed or 'contrived collegiality' (Hall and Wallace, 1993; Hargreaves, 1991). The positive and negative effects of imposed staff collaboration on planning is a key theme of Chapter 5 of this book in which we look critically at the claim that experienced teachers might become empowered through meeting their obligations to collaborate with their colleagues in writing school development plans. Teachers' contributions to task-oriented aspects of staff activities are no more straightforward than children's contributions to imposed groupwork in classrooms. The nature of people's participation in group activities depends to some extent on whether or not they perceive those activities as a legitimate, practicable and meaningful way to spend their time when judged against other competing priorities.

Formal involvement in 'official' teamwork is, however, only one of the ways in which teachers might contribute to the development of their schools. Nias *et al.* (1992) have shown that formal, planned approaches to whole school development and informal patterns of staff interaction coexist and may or may not complement each other.

Informal interaction is clearly seen as a key element of school development because it involves processes through which teachers learn likemindedness and extend and deepen the things which are held in common. Similarly, Acker (1991), whilst being aware of problems of imposed collegiality, found evidence that primary teachers were striving collectively to interpret the demands of the Education Reform Act mainly by helping each other to cope creatively and to develop sensible ways to do what was expected of them. These kinds of collaboration are mainly informal and they are embedded within 'normal' working days. As Nias (1992) has noted, working together and learning together can be difficult to separate.

As well as shaping school development, informal aspects of membership are important and worthy of careful attention in initial teacher education, because of the emotional dimensions of teaching and because of their potential for relieving stress-related health problems. Tickle (1991), for example, has provided evidence of the significance of the emotions of learning to teach during his recent research with new teachers:

> ...excitement and elation as well as anxiety and anger, satisfaction and success as well as fear of failure, were aroused by the experiences of classroom events, staffroom relationships and contacts with parents or LEA personnel. Feelings fluctuated erratically; contrasting ones sometimes coexisted; at times they were uncontrollable and controlled; at other times they seemed unstable and explosive. Making sense of this element of the learning equation was at least as important for each teacher as understanding how best to 'teach'. ...the emotional aspects of their learning had a direct relationship to technical and clinical competences. (p.322)

Tickle has claimed that an understanding of the self and the management of emotions are essential aspects of competence and should be an explicit part of initial teacher education. He has suggested that this would help to alleviate the surprise experienced by new teachers when they realize how important it is to learn to deal with their own emotions in teaching. Students should know that they are not alone in experiencing feelings of anxiety. Tickle suggests that 'the equation of the establishment of competence with suffering would at least have been a shared professional problem' (p.328).

Yeomans (1992) has also argued that recent contractual

changes and organizational demands have meant that 'the skills and understandings of collaborative professional relationships are now too important as ingredients of professional life in primary schools to be ignored by teacher educators' (p.21). He defines staff membership as:

> the capacity of an individual to recognise, understand, accept as legitimate and adopt the staff's culture, including the meanings that the group's rituals and symbols carry for its members as expressions of shared values and attitudes. Membership also implies that the individual has been accepted as part of the group, and that once accepted the new member's own behaviour expresses and may shape the staff culture. (p.21)

In earlier work, Yeomans (1986) referred to full membership as 'hearing secret harmonies'. He identified three phases of 'listening for harmonies', 'hearing harmonies' and finally 'polyphony', which convey the capacity to integrate personal, affective dimensions with task demands and with the collective, tacit values of the staff as a whole. He has cited two aspects of complexity which arise from the small size and relatively flat hierarchies of primary schools. First he notes how the small size means that interactions between teachers are frequent, if sometimes fleeting, and so their personal and professional concerns are rarely kept separate. Secondly, he claims that flat hierarchies mean that leadership and membership roles are not easily distinguished.

This matches what we said in the first two chapters about children's experiences in classrooms. We tried to show that the merging of personal and task concerns and the combining of membership and leadership experiences in what we called 'contributing membership' are both key themes in classroom life. We argued that contributing membership is a more fruitful concept than leadership for understanding children's participation and for developing collaborative learning in classrooms. Like Drummond's (1993) point about Eve being one of the leaders of her group (referred to in our previous chapter), Yeoman's also makes the point that any teacher can be a leader regardless of his or her position in a school's hierarchy and that there may be several leaders and forms of leadership within a school staff.

We have shown earlier that all children might also contibute in different and sometimes unexpected ways to improve the quality of their collaborative work, just as teachers are expected to do as staff members.

Case Study: Experiencing temporary staff membership
during placements

A small-scale enquiry into primary BEd students' experiences of temporary staff membership during their final
placements was undertaken at the University of
Northumbria in 1992. It was an integral part of a course
unit on staff relationships and educational reform. As a first
step, an open response questionnaire was given to 87 students one week after they had completed their final placements of six weeks. The students were invited to write
about the things that made them feel like staff members and
those which did not, and also what they they thought had
contributed negatively or positively to relationships they
perceived amongst the permanent staff of the schools.
Other sections covered how they had learned from teachers
they admired and the extent to which they thought they
had contributed to a school as a whole.

A summary report was given to the students and, following discussions of it, they listed points they thought would
help them to have better experiences in whole schools. For
this activity, the students divided themselves into 15 groups
ranging in size from three to nine. This activity preceded
seminars in which they discussed literature about adult
relationships, processes of whole school development in
primary schools, and the effects of educational reform on
staff membership in schools.

Yeomans' notion of 'temporary staff membership' was
found to be meaningful to most of the students, with 63 out
of 87 saying that they had felt like staff members most or all
of the time, and a further 19 experiencing a sense of membership for some of the time. In contrast, only five students
had not felt like staff members at all during the six week
placement. One section of the questionnaire asked them to
list those things that had made them feel like members and
those which had not. This yielded 334 positive items and
145 negative items with most students saying that they had
a mixture of positive and negative experiences. Preliminary
analysis of the students' writing revealed three main over-
lapping issues:

- overall sense of belonging or exclusion;
- general staffroom atmosphere and learning informally
  from other teachers;

- being responsible, contributing
  and having a wider role in the school.

Overall sense of belonging or exclusion

Sixteen students had felt excluded from, or unwelcome in, the staffroom. Some of these students did continue to go in there but they had felt uncomfortable for the whole of the placement because of social awkwardness over such things as coffee arrangements or because conversations stopped or changed when they entered the room. Some had used the staffroom very little or not at all. One student wrote:

> I wasn't taken to the staffroom and so I never had the opportunity to go there. This was because my teacher never went to the staffroom herself.

In contrast, many other students reported being welcomed into staffrooms, making comments such as,

> they knew how I liked my coffee
> by the end of my block the teachers acted as though I was one of them, and didn't keep any staffroom talk from me.

Nineteen students also mentioned being invited to social events outside school. They had been invited to go to the pub on a Friday lunchtime, and to join in the staff nights out.

Whenever students were given support by teachers other than their class teachers this increased their feelings of belonging in the school. They appreciated approachable people with whom they could discuss things and they also said they liked informal visits from teachers and heads who just 'popped in' to see how they were getting on.

A major source of regret for 31 students was that they felt they had been excluded from formal staff meetings. Overall, 66 of the students had not been invited to attend any staff meetings at all, and, of these, 58 had been aware of meetings taking place. As one said, this was a little insulting

> especially when I had to creep in during one to collect my coat.

Of the 21 students who had attended staff meetings, 11 had contributed opinions or ideas. Two-thirds of the meetings had been about curriculum policy, planning and review and the rest were about forthcoming events such as carol services, Christmas productions, parents evenings, fund raising and school outings.

General staffroom atmosphere and learning informally from other teachers

This section is divided into two parts. The first outlines students' views about general staffroom atmosphere and staff relationships and the second part describes the qualities of teachers that students admired, and from whom they learned informally.

Students were sensitive to atmosphere and appreciative of friendliness:

> Basic manners and politeness can make a big difference.
> It is a great advantage if the teachers actually like each other.

Unfortunately, 17 students had been left with negative feelings about general staffroom atmosphere:

> Like staff in any occupation, some members disliked each other. There were obvious conflicts in the staffroom. Certain staff never entered the staffroom and staff talked about each other. There was bad cohesion of staff, due to pressures of assessment.

Students' interpretions of staff relationships are discussed more fully later in this chapter, and the main point to emphasize here is that their treatment by experienced staff in the schools had been varied. In some cases, the students had felt that their 'student status' had been constantly emphasized:

> other staff members audibly referring to me as 'the student',
> head introducing us to the parents and the children as students,
> constant talk of when you leave.
> the class being referred to in assembly as the permanent teacher's class, and me sitting there with them.

Their own sense of 'low status' was sometimes reinforced by the actions of other adults in the school:

> The school secretary refused to pass on any messages to me or ask me for any information which concerned my class.

Labelled students felt rather like the 'free dinners' or the 'readers' who are making slow progress and have to troop off to special lessons. One student referred simply to,

> bad mannered staff who made no effort to communicate – [it was as though they thought] – she's not important, she'll be gone in a couple of weeks – we'll just ignore her.

In contrast, many others had been treated as colleagues and called by their proper names, rather than 'the student', both in casual conversations and in formal announcements to the whole school. Whilst 15 of the students had felt undermined, over-ridden and patronized, 31 reported having been respected, trusted, confided in and made to feel equal with other adults in the school. They mentioned numerous examples:

> Hearing other teachers' problems.
> Small talk with other teachers in corridors.
> Being on good terms with office staff and domestic staff.
> Auxiliary staff asked me for instructions.
> Other teachers asked my opinions about which books to buy.
> Confided in me about the children.
> The headteacher asked for my comments on a new child before he had consultation with the parents.
> They treated me like a teacher, asked my advice and permission, we also discussed weekly plans.
> Discussed ideas, good points, problems, etc. with several teachers not just my classteacher and they would ask my opinions as a teacher.

Yeomans (1992) has claimed that most students also seem ideally placed to be participant observers of staff relationships in their placement schools. As he suggests, some did seem to have:

> the advantage of becoming a legitimate, accepted and natural part of most staffrooms, as students they are relatively invisible and so may hear, see, learn and begin to understand how staff membership is expressed, but with the relative detachment of an outsider (p.23)

As well as describing their own feelings, the students were asked to list what they had observed that they thought had contributed positively or negatively to existing features of staff membership in their placement schools. Overall, they made 250 positive and 135 negative statements which were subsequently categorized into three themes: general relationships between teachers; established teachers' working relationships; and the ways in which headteachers related to the school staff.

It was apparent from this list that students were observing some of the turmoils and tensions as well as some of pleasures of relationships at work. Sometimes they described incidents which conveyed graphically the meaning they were making of the concept of membership:

> A teacher suffered a bereavement and was visited and given flowers
> One teacher kept picking on children from another class for minor matters, knowing it's deliberately against the policy of that class teacher
> There was some fighting about who should put the kettle on. It went on for six weeks.

Some descriptions caught the tensions of the adult world of the school:

> During the time of the 'block' the school was rehearsing for a Christmas play. The rehearsals depended on staff availability and hall availability. As a result, very short or no notice was given about the rehearsals and schedules had to be changed. A comment was made by a permanent member of staff whose class was involved, but she was personally not, that the first they knew of the rehearsals was when a child was knocking on the door to inform them that they were waiting for her class in the hall.

The following positive and negative aspects of staff relations were mentioned by students (numbers in brackets indicate numbers of mentions):

Positive	Negative
All staff use the staffroom (14)	Some staff do not use staffroom, leave school early, avoid interaction with other teachers (18)
Arrange social events school (15)	Staff cliques and factions (14)
Rituals of togetherness such as cakes on birthdays (7)	Persistent tea/coffee disputes (4) Divisions between junior-infant, nursery whole-school, different union memberships, smokers-non smokers different views of policy/practice (19)
Rapport, caring friendships, respect (40)	Discrediting, gossiping (19)
Humour, joking (4)	Problems of dominance, dogmatism, insecurity (15)
Personal support, interest in other people's ideas (34)	Career jealousies (3)
Welcoming to outsiders (6)	Not welcoming to outsiders (4)

When the students mentioned working relationships between staff they were mainly positive. Examples included staff having discussions, in places like corridors, corners of the staffroom or each other's classrooms, about plans, expenditure, timetables, resources and topics (47 mentions), having small informal meetings to arrange teaching links (27) and working together on special events, clubs and assemblies. The negative observations of informal working relationships included possessiveness over resources, keeping ideas to themselves and not sharing (15), competitiveness over display, and tensions arising from different attitudes towards standards of discipline in the school (3).

There were equal numbers of positive and negative references to the influence of headteachers upon staff membership. Dominance, lack of interest in staff and unwillingness to spend time in classrooms were contrasted with enthusiasm, intelligence and encouragement. For example, one headteacher was seen as a good staff member himself because of the ways in which he mixed with the staff, joined in informal conversations and was aware of what was going on in the school.

Teachers from whom students learned informally

Preliminary discussions with students had revealed that they had learned informally, in unplanned ways, from teachers they admired. They said that they learned mainly by positive example and so, in part of the questionnaire, they were asked to describe the qualities of up to two teachers they admired. Unfortunately, ten students had not seen any admirable teachers, but the other 77 students gave a total of 98 teacher descriptions. It is to some extent misleading to isolate separate qualities because students seemed to admire combinations of hard work, easy disposition, flexibility and accessiblity rather than, say, pure dedication or constant lightheartedness. Two students made contrasting comments about the qualities of the staff as a whole, which illustrate the 'luck of the draw' in placement allocations:

Could not help but admire all the staff for the amount of teaching and level of teaching achieved under the difficult social conditions which were evident.

There was no teacher who I admired – the atmosphere in the school was one of repression fear and anxiety. The staff never appeared at ease, and there was nothing I found I could admire in any of them.

There were three main sets of qualities mentioned by students. First, it was the general dispositions of teachers which students said they most admired. Second, they referred to ways that admired teachers kept up-to-date, tried new things and discussed what had happened with colleagues – factors also identified by Little (1982) following research into staff relationship in schools in the USA. Little referred to high 'norms of experimentation and collegiality' amongst the staff as workplace conditions of school success. A third set of qualities described teachers' ways of relating to children both 'around the school' and in classrooms. Interestingly, students' descriptions of teachers' classroom abilities were usually framed in terms of motivating, encouraging and gaining the interest of children rather than about techniques or results.

Many of the teachers who were admired were 'socially outgoing, lively and had a sense of fun'. Such people mixed well and 'raised the spirits of others'. Some of those described 'talked a lot' and started conversations, especially with newcomers. Others were seen as 'easy to approach', thoughtful and quietly spoken. Students admired helpful and supportive teachers like the ones who

> invited me into her classroom after school to discuss displays
> offered me literature on the topic I was covering,
> helped me to set up activities;
> talked to me as though we were both professionals.

Students also admired and learned from teachers who got on well with all other adults in schools, including nursery nurses, parent helpers and dinner ladies. They admired some teachers' rapport with parents. In addition to being caring, helpful and willing to cooperate with colleagues, the admired teachers talked with other teachers about ideas and problems –

> didn't have a sense of one's own power but accepted advice from others, and also seeks advice;
> not frightened to discuss problems they were having with certain children.

McLaughlin and Yee (1988) have also identified this willingness to share, rather than hide, problems as one workplace characteristic which creates opportunities for teachers to make teaching more than just a job through learning together and having a sense a developing career.

Student teachers also admired hard work, energy, enthusiasm and dedication. This was expressed often as teachers' willingness to learn new things and to put in extra work –

gave up a lot of time for school events
spent a great deal of time over the summer holidays sorting out the classroom

and sometimes as an indicator of caring about children –

tried to provide out of school activities for children who would never have an opportunity to do things.

Whilst many of the students' observations were about things which teachers did or said which improved social cohesion amongst the staff, some of the experienced teachers were admired because of their willingness to assert their convictions in the face of disagreements. This adds support to the speculation of Wooldridge and Yeomans (1992) that professional diversity will enhance the training culture of a school. Some were –

very straight discussing views if unhappy;
able to voice opinions;
an individual and not a stereotypical teacher.

One, for example

did not readily accept situations, but argued against them for reasons related to the promotion of school policies.

Some were described as up-to-date,

ambitious and experimental with new ideas

and others were admired for their practicality:

he knew what he was on about

or

didn't have any up-in-the air ideas about schools.

For some students this even overcame age differences:

trying new ideas even though she had been teaching a long time.

The abilities most admired in classroom expertise were teachers' abilities to make good relationships with children. Students referred to differentiation of tasks for individual children, class organization and control, interesting and exciting lessons and pupils' tasks, and good display of children's work: by far the most frequent references were simply to 'rapport with children'. The admired teachers cared about the children who in turn respected the teachers. Admired teachers had:

> the ability to identify the needs of individual children;
> flexibility/diversity of ideas, adaptation to working with many different children;
> treated the children fairly and looked for their best qualities;
> the ability for excellent observations of children's capabilities.

Their class control was characterised by –

> a balance between discipline and friendship;
> quiet control, rarely had to raise her voice;
> firm with the children but kind and encouraging.

The students themselves were being assessed partly through the use of an observation schedule listing a range of skills, but items on that list were mentioned by only three students when they described admirable teachers –

> ability to introduce and conclude activities,
> very precise with explanations;
> pausing and selecting during questioning, decisive.

For the most part, it was flexible, adaptive and participative approaches which were admired most, although one student did describe a teacher who she admired for her organization, whilst seeming to doubt her overall approach –

> All the teachers tended to run very formal classrooms, with no wall display, but they were extremely well organized. My classteacher heard all the children read everyday – 25!

Being responsible, contributing and having a wider role

One of the ways in which students felt they contributed and had some degree of identification with the whole school was through being trusted to play a full, active role in school activities. This even included having a share of chores such as 'doing yard duty' and impicit obligations such as 'helping with school parties and fund raising'. Twenty-five students mentioned being involved in special events and daily routines like assemblies, as well as being asked to deal with incidents like arguments between children or looking after sick children. Fifteen students reported having had full and sole charge of their own class and a further five had covered for other teachers by taking responsibility for different classes in the school. These duties had all been cited as positive indicators of being trusted as contributing staff members. It is perhaps not surprising to learn that final-year students were finding it as encouraging and motivating to be given a full teacher's role as children do when they are given jobs like giving out the rulers and tidying the cupboards. It also seems to signify belonging as well as contributing. The students also mentioned filling in record books, marking the register, sitting with the class in assembly, being included in the staff photograph and having access to resources, as giving them a sense of being a staff member.

Some students, however, were denied opportunities to experience general responsibilities. They recalled

having to mark the register in pencil or not at all,
not hearing children read because the teacher wanted to continue her own system which was quite complicated,
being constantly monitored by the head or classteacher and never being allowed to have the class to myself;

Some incidents made them feel merely temporary and unimportant:

the class teacher always took the children out at the end of the day to meet their parents,
being told to do my own thing for a topic and not follow the planned topics of the school,
not being informed about children in my class being in trouble,
not being given information about what was happening in the school which was given to other teachers.

Another factor frequently mentioned was the extent of the students' involvement with parents. Whenever students met parents they were positive about the effect on their professional identity:

I was introduced at the parents' evening as a teacher and not as a student;
parents asked me about their children and were very friendly;
parents addressed letters to me as the classteacher;
I liked being involved in the parents evening in the classroom when parents came to see the teacher and I was asked for my opinion.

However, twelve students had felt excluded from formal parents' meetings.

Some students said that they had also introduced new ideas to the schools. Interestingly, the proportion of students who thought that they had contributed in some way to the school staff (45 per cent) exceeded the proportions of those who said that they had been able to attend formal staff meetings (24 per cent). They mentioned having given new materials and worksheets to teachers, helping with displays and demonstrating their approaches to classroom organization. The following comments illustrate the range of contributions :

gave ideas to a teacher who had an HMI to visit his art lesson. Ideas on progression, organisation etc.
gave new ideas on mapping skills related to follow-up work after four visits,
discussed ideas for a word bank with reception teacher, based on topics throughout terms
discussed positive and negative points of 'Breakthrough to Literacy' and discussed providing a reading environment for the class,
gave practical ideas about how to encourage maths through games
gave teachers copies of my own worksheets
teachers were interested in various maths games and activities which I'd made. They borrowed them in order to copy them.
I demonstrated new IT software.
I set up a technology area.Other teachers came to see it
I was asked to look at a language corner area and give advice. Teachers were interested in my ideas.
I rearranged the furniture to establish a writing corner for the children
I shared practical ideas on how to display maths work.
I provided science work and photographs for school science display for an adviser's visit.

Students' ideas about improving school placements to increase their sense of belonging, contributing and learning as temporary staff members

After preliminary analysis of separate responses, outlined here, an overall summary of their views was presented to the students themselves. They worked in 15 small, self-chosen groups to make suggestion about what could be done to help them to learn more about becoming staff members during placements. The following ideas were suggested (ordered according to the number of mentions):

• More personal interest from the headteacher (12 groups). Students suggested that they would like headteachers to take regular, formal and also personal and informal interest in them, giving advice, acknowledgement, praise and encouragement (and possibly even stories from their own teaching practices)

• Clearer expectations and better information (12 groups). This was a plea for being better informed about what is going on in the school, and especially about things which would affect the student directly, such as a secondary school student coming into the class for work experience, a parent coming to collect a child early, or a change of arrangements for the use of the hall. Connected to this was the need for clarity of expectations about courtesies for all people involved : the class teacher, student and college tutor. Examples given were about expectations about yard duties, assemblies and meetings, the use of forenames and other aspects of the general etiquette of being a student in a school.

• Increased opportunities for attendance at formal staff meetings and extra-curricular activities (11 groups). Students said they would appreciate being invited to whole staff meetings, training days and extra-curricular activities. One group thought that explanations could be given if it was felt inappropriate for some reason to invite a student to a specific meeting.

• Visits and information prior to placement (ten groups). Students suggested that they should have the chance to meet the whole staff at school events prior to the placement period. Another suggestion was to have a set of policies, school routines and general information in advance of starting the placement.

• Play down student status and avoid labelling (nine groups). Students would like to be known and called by their proper names at all times in the school, rather than 'the student'. They would like to be seen as 'new teachers' or as 'visiting teachers' by all adults in the schools, the children and the parents.

• Attention to relationships between the student and the whole staff (seven groups). The point was made that students would like to be introduced to all staff personally. They also would like all adults in school to know why they were there and for how long.

• More clarity about the student's place in staffrooms (seven groups). Related to the above point, students' places in the staffrooms should be clarified, including coffee procedures, who washes up, and, if it matters, the seating arrangements. An extra seat could be added and a mug brought in, if necessary.

- Clarity about use of resources/facilities (seven groups). Some groups thought that they should be informed about the procedures and ground rules for getting access to facilities and resources that are centrally available to all staff.
- Attention to allocation of class teachers to students (five groups). Two groups made the point that class teachers should only have students if they genuinely wanted them and are keen to support them, and that the headteacher should always choose ones who would benefit the student rather than vice versa. Students should not be seen as 'a helping hand' or allocated to reluctant teachers to 'shake them up'.
- Increased time for activities other than teaching their own classes (three groups). Some students said they would like to see an increase in non-teaching time which should be well-planned and maintained. This would give the chance for the student to learn about and be included in aspects of school life other than teaching their own class.
- More access to curriculum leadership (two groups). Some students suggested that they might be given time to work alongside the curriculum leader in their specialist subject to learn more about the role and whole-school development.

A number of other issues emerged from this enquiry which could be given further thought, at this time when primary school placements are likely to be extended, and training partnerships between the schools and universities and colleges are being modified. There are a two particular issues which do seem worthy of urgent enquiry and action.

First, there are implications for how training institutions create partnerships with whole schools. In addition to existing schemes to train mentors to work individually with students on their classroom teaching, some attention should also be given to whole schools as learning contexts for students. Whether or not they are officially allocated to the task, all teachers in a school may be influencing what and how students learn about belonging and contributing and what students come to understand about how a 'whole school' works. For this reason, professional development programmes for heads, mentors and university staff should include some work on school cultures, formal and informal whole-school development, and on the ways in which students and newly qualified teachers develop their professional identity as part of a school staff. This process of learning to be a teacher, like learning to teach, is far from straightforward. There are many problems hidden, for example, behind the newcomer's apparent compliance with obvious aspects of being 'teacherly' such as dress and ways of disciplining pupils who misbehave in corridors.

Secondly, students also need frameworks for making critical sense of their experiences of temporary staff membership during placements. As Wooldridge and Yeomans (1992) suggest, they should become educated about schools as workplaces rather than merely acculturated into one particular setting. Learning opportunities for individuals will be 'hit and miss' depending on the luck of the draw when schools are allocated, and so students need to be helped to learn from both good and bad experiences. For this reason they need time to analyse, both individually and collectively, their experiences of working and learning with others.

Yeomans (1992) has tried to structure student teachers' experiences of collaboration during their course at Bedford College. Since temporary staff membership on placements only gives students limited access to a school staff at work together,

> their course must also give them surrogate experiences to develop and exercise the skills of effective group membership. If collaboration can become part of the course culture, expressed through experiences on the course as well as part of course content, it may become an accepted part of the way we do things as students and ultimately as teachers. (p.23)

He advocates that students should have collaborative experiences during their whole course, in stable groups about the size of a large primary school staff. He suggests that tutors can then help students to develop insights into the nature and culture of groups and what this culture means for primary school staff membership. Activities are arranged so that conceptual growth and first-hand experiences are mutually reinforcing. The key ideas are :

- the significance of the self in the experience of staff membership;
- the relationship between the self and the group;
- the influence of the group and its culture in shaping individual behaviour;
- the role the individual plays in maintaining that culture;
- the individual nature of each primary school's culture and the ways that it is manifested through its norms, symbols and rituals.

Yeomans describes a case study of groups of 12 or 14 students of different backgrounds and ages which met for several hours each week. Cumulatively, the students came to understand what staff membership means, through discussions of their experiences in schools and reflections on their own group and their participation in it. Three extracts from his field notes illustrate first, an early stage of group formation, second, how collaboration was tested at a later point and, third, how students came to see aspects of membership in their final year:

An early stage

The group is asked to organise itself to carry out a collaborative investigation involving taking different but complementary roles in preparing a joint report . They have to decide how to share out the roles between themselves. One sits in determined silence, two others offer competing ways of organising the group. The tutor listens, but seems not to be helping. Another student comments loudly that it is all a waste of time and asks why the tutor wouldn't say how he wanted the task done. Eventually several members opt for one strategy and everyone joins in with varying degrees of commitment.

Later in the week we meet again and I ask the group to think about how well it is working. One of the dominant members comments that not everyone has contributed equally to the fund of ideas. The tutor suggests that members can contribute in different ways, that all members have equal rights to a share of the group's attention, but may choose not to use it. The previously silent member then talks about how difficult she finds it to get used to the apparent violence of some of the arguments in the group, an experience she had not had at school. She confesses she was finding some of the mature students intimidating. In response they admit they are worried about writing essays. (Yeomans, 1992, p.2)

It is something of an irony that future primary school teachers require skills of collaboration and a willingness to work and learn with others, yet so many of the students entering teacher education realize that, when they were pupils, their schools undervalued collaborative learning, engendered reliance upon the teacher and emphasized individual achievement.

In this next example, the tutor is trying to get the group to develop its own identity using strategies similar to those of Jean in Galton and Williamson's (1992) case study quoted in Chapter 2 of this volume. Like primary teachers whose work is included in the other case studies in this book, the tutor found progress was not rapid and constant.

Testing collaboration

The group has a week in which to organise itself to plan, carry out and display the products of a thematic study derived from some aspect of the local environment. Members must agree and structure a theme, assign roles, make arrangements to co-ordinate individual work and agree their timetable.

The tutor offers help as needed, but the group confidently declines. Within a day a male mature student confirms to the tutor that they are to study the effects of change in the local country park, and that jobs have been assigned. During the week, conversations with various group members suggest that the same mature male is being too dominant, some members are working hard and meeting regularly, others have been inconspicuous, one has disappeared completely, and the outcome is likely to be sparse in content.

By Friday morning all except the missing member (who had been ill) are gathered with their contributions. Two previously inconspicuous members bring three successful products of their researches at the record office, another contributes skilfully taken photographs of the wildlife now in the park. A sub-group has collaborated on a series of models to illustrate the change from iron-age settlement, to gravel extraction to country park. Another member offers her speculative poetry. Individuals discuss and prepare the mounting and layout of the display, seeking and receiving advice on the best alternatives. A layout plan is produced, discussed and modified as they work. Individual effort is imperceptably co-ordinated and the final outcome is visually impressive and intellectually rigorous. Yet there are still students who say they can't see the point of it all. (Yeomans, 1992. p.28)

The final comment shows how some future teachers continue to deny the value of collaborative and experiential learning. Yet the tutor continued to foster their understanding of the micropolitics of negotiation and of the ambiguities and uncertainties of working together on a set task. Their reflections upon resentments and misunderstandings as well as on their successes helped to promote group cohesion without moralizing or implying that real collaborative working and learning is always harmonious.

Throughout the course, Yeomans was encouraging the students to consider the meaning of seemingly trivial or ordinary events and incidents, which he illustrates with the following example :

Seeing and perceiving

Fourth year students return from their final term in school. The experience is being dissected in the group. The subject is the contribution of the staff culture to effective functioning as a whole school.The focus is the significance of symbols and rituals in conveying shared values. Students reflect on their recent experiences and offer their perceptions. One describes the major role of a vase of flowers during changes in one primary school. A close knit, well established staff, with a deeply rooted collaborative culture, was sorry to see its head leave, but anxious to continue the minor rituals which expressed their commitment to the school. One such ritual was the appearance in the school entrance every week of a vase of fresh flowers, put there by one of the most established staff, and accepted as part of the everyday scene. A new head came and there seemed to be every reason to continue this custom. The flowers disappeared during the first week, and there was puzzled concern but no explanation. When events were repeated in the second week, concern became anger, expressed as the main topic of staffroom conversation. The new head said she had removed the flowers, and didn't want them put in the entrance.

This important piece of staff history had been shared with the student in a staffroom whose members were united against the head as a consequence of that incident. The head had been in the school for a year, but now only entered the staffroom for formal meetings. (Yeomans, 1992. p.30)

This account brings us back to another of the key themes of this book: that it is through interpreting ordinary, everyday interactions that we shall best understand how collaborative learning might be fostered in both classrooms and staffrooms. There are strong connections between the infant school teacher's observation notes of 4- and 5-year old children, quoted in Chapter 1, and Yeomans' notes on student teachers in this chapter. Both were observing their learners, collecting evidence of interactions and then giving critical feedback without trying to paper-over conflicts or tidy-up the messiness of the learning. Both were trying to create the conditions in which collaborative learning could flourish.

Both the case studies in this chapter were from participative research projects in which the researched learned with the researcher. They were undertaken as an integral part of course programmes which were based on principles of enquiry-based teaching to enhance students' understanding of group and staff membership. The next chapter also reports on a participative research project with eight new teachers in their first year of work.

Conclusion

In the first chapter of this book we tried to show how it is important for teachers to create conditions for children to belong and contribute in classrooms, so that they would make individual progress and also learn how to support each others' learning. In this chapter we have attempted to remind teachers of how favourable or unfavourable conditions might also influence student teachers' opportunities for belonging, contributing and learning in staffrooms.

Arrangements for school placements tend to emphasize classroom supervision and focus upon relationships between individual students and designated experienced teachers. They often neglect to take account of the whole school as a learning environment and so misjudge the significance of its effects upon students' developing personal and professional identities and on what they learn about schools as workplaces for adults.

What students actually learned about staff relationships and whole schools from watching, listening and taking part far outweighed, and sometimes contradicted, what they were told or what was written in documents.

Most students felt generally welcome and able to contribute in their placement schools but some felt excluded and were given the impression that they had little to offer when it came to the day-to day operation of the school. They were affected by ordinary everyday events and processes and the ways they were treated by other teachers. Their self-esteem could be raised when they were treated with respect and trusted to do duties such as yard duty or to help with a fund-raising activity, just as young children, and their teachers, might attach importance to tidying cupboards and giving out pencils. In contrast, some felt undermined and socially and professionally awkward because of chance remarks which conveyed doubts about their capabilities and sense of responsibility.

Students learned informally and incidentally in unplanned ways from experienced teachers they admired, many of whom were not designated to support them. They mainly admired positive dispositions, conviction and abilities to create good relationships, to motivate children and to create good learning environments in classrooms.

It is important that our future teachers should have positive experiences of working and learning with experienced teachers in schools for three main reasons. First, if they are to develop the dispositions and professional competences to contribute to teamwork and also to help to develop schools through relationships with colleagues, then they need to learn in contexts where they feel that they can belong, can contribute and that what they are doing is worthwhile.

Second, because the management of personal and emotional dimensions of teaching is an essential aspect of competence, it is important that students learn to teach in favourable contexts supported by a staff of experienced teachers who help to relieve the stresses and strains of the job through their everyday interactions with each other.

Third, because the foundations for collaborative learning are laid more by social experiences than by reading about them in libraries, students should have opportunities to reflect upon their own working and learning relationships in staffrooms. They will then be in a better position to create supportive learning communities in their classrooms.

Chapter 4

New Staff Members Learning from the 'Memory Bearers': Teachers' First School Christmas

(with Anne Spendiff)

This chapter, like the previous one, explores how new entrants to the teaching profession learn to be staff members of schools. In Chapter 3, we showed what student teachers learned about the adult world of primary schools from spending six weeks as temporary staff members. We now move on to see how new members come to work and learn with a school staff during their first year of work. We draw mainly upon Anne Spendiff's case study of newly qualified women teachers as they became full staff members of primary schools in 1992–3. From a series of seven semi-structured interviews and discussions with eight women teachers over the whole school year, we have chosen to emphasize their experiences of their first Christmas in schools because of the ways that it throws into focus some general issues about belonging, contributing and collaborating. Christmas is a time for planning and carrying out celebrations collectively, and for teachers it is also a time of pressure to meet deadlines and to produce work for 'public' display and presentation. Schools have their own traditions and ways of making their own 'school Christmas'. New members watch and listen and the existing staff show and tell the newcomers what to do. Although little is written down, much is learned from the 'memory bearers' who have been through it all before.

There is little time to pause and new members can't stand back and watch. If they find that they lack resources, many teachers spend their own money to buy them, such is the will and determination to do their best for themselves, the children and the school. New members of staff take part and, at the same time, they learn to be part of the whole, contributing their own touches within a framework of established traditions. Because of the need to get on with their tasks and because of the focused effort and influence of the whole staff group, even the significance of the head-teacher, as the main referral point of authority for the new teachers, seemed to diminish at Christmas.

Christmas provides a special context for collaborative learning. In the introduction to this book we drew a contin-uum from spontaneous, informal collaboration initiated and controlled by children or teachers for themselves, at one end, to imposed requirements for them to work togeth-er on set tasks like science experiments or school develop-ment planning, at the other extreme. Christmas is also a contrived festival which has evolved from a mixture of old midwinter custom, less-old church ceremonies and even more recent commercial influences, yet in many cases it feels important and bigger than the school and the people in it. For the schools in this study it was essentially about collectivity and it offered potential for children and teachers to create and take part in activities like carol services and plays which were held in high regard in the local communi-ties.

Case Study: Teachers' first Christmas

What I needed, it seemed to me, was a sort of personal Christmas organiser, something I could reach for in October and keep by me as a guide all the way through to the point where the last of the Christmas left-overs have been dealt with.
    On paper a detailed plan of action can look quite simple and straightforward – but plans on paper can easily lull us into a false sense of security...Have you allowed for those last minute panics that only Christmas can create? (Smith, 1990)

This case study is draw from research into the staff mem-bership experiences of new women teachers in their first year of work. It is a qualitative feminist study involving a sequence of semi-structured interviews and group discus-sions with two groups of newly qualified women primary school teachers. By coincidence the data-gathering timetable scheduled a recorded group discussion in the middle of the schools' 1992 Christmas preparations. I had planned to hold discussions comparing paid work with teaching practice, and questioning the gender balance in school staffs: the iniquities of so many men in senior positions. Instead, I got Christmas.

The study is not written in the tradition of feminist polemic, but seeks to 'correct both the *invisibility* and the *distortion* of female experience' (Lather, 1986, p.68) by *describing* what it was like for new women teachers to be part of school Christmas for the first time (Du Bois, 1983).

The teachers who took part in the research had begun work in the previous September and our discussions focused on the stresses and the pleasures that they experienced: where they found support, how they learned what it means to be a teacher inside and outside of the classroom, sources of anxiety, and the impact on their home lives. Preparing for Christmas added to the pressures. One teacher said:

> It's the end of a very stressful and long term. You're getting to know children – and that in itself is stressful...You're desperately trying to get a foothold, a hold on their lives...by the time you're getting them to settle down, there's Christmas and therefore they're up high again...There's so much going on outside your class. You're no longer in control.

The Christmas data are illuminating for two reasons. First, they throw some general issues into sharp focus. The difficulties and pleasures of collaborative working, and of being a new member of staff, become evident in the light of the heightened expectations of staff, pupils, parents and community at Christmas time. Second, analysis of the data has caused me to question the nature of the learning that goes on at this time. Teachers say, 'nothing gets done' meaning that the National Curriculum is, at least partially, abandoned. But other learning does take place, and the sense of belonging to a community, for teacher, pupils and parents, is very strong.

It is important to record two omissions from this chapter: all the schools I studied were in predominantly white English communities, so the experience of teachers in communities shared by black and/or ethnic minority people have not been recorded. The class background of the teachers and of the school pupils and their communities varied and I have described the communities where this background appears to me to be significant to the issues raised.

The second omission became evident when I compared the Christmas data with the other data I gathered, and it concerns the role of the headteacher in the school. In general, though not at Christmas, the teachers named heads, more than anybody else including mentors, as sources of support. They were seen as authorities; teachers expected Heads to observe them, to 'check' what they were doing, and to encourage and advise. If heads failed to do this, the teachers felt undervalued. In the Christmas data, the significance, even the presence, of the head was greatly diminished. Occasionally a teacher mentioned the head praising a display or a concert, but in general the heads were not mentioned at all. So, while selecting the Christmas data does raise some general issues of interest to new teachers beginning work in the Autumn term, it does not raise all of them. Perhaps the most significant absence is the importance of the head as a source of authority and a referral point for new teachers. The apparent *absence* of the head's influence may be significant, and I shall return to this later.

This chapter describes three aspects of group working and learning which are evident in all the data and which became particularly significant at Christmas. The first aspect concerns how staffs planned together for Christmas, and for other events, and identifies some of the features of collaborative and non-collaborative working. The second section covers how new teachers learned what to do at Christmas. School Christmas is a good example of the special occasions that teachers learn to cope with in the first year of work. Third, I consider the significance of Christmas as a learning event and I draw some conclusions about the nature of Christmas and the opportunities for group learning that it offers.

Preparing for Christmas

Arrangements for Christmas varied from school to school, and in each school they reflected to some degree the different organizational patterns adopted generally.

All of the schools held staff meetings, although not all decisions were made at them, and the newly qualified teachers did not always feel able to participate in decision-making processes. Participation appeared to increase as time went on, but several teachers were still feeling unable to contribute very much to the Christmas planning. The teachers said that they liked *clear* decision-making procedures, rather than *formal* ones. Informal ones were satisfactory, so long as the newcomers knew what they were, although it took longer to learn about informal procedures than formal ones.

The smallest school, consisting of four staff, only held staff meetings for important issues, and the teacher in that school commented that 'it's almost like a staff meeting all the time'. In contrast, one of the larger schools, with 24 staff, had a complex system of meetings.

> You put your name down for what (curriculum) area you want to be part of...like English, Maths or Science...then the next set of subjects, like history or geography, that band, and then it's things like parental involvement, field study, special needs.... Within your little sub-groups you decide what you want for the school within the policy and the sub-group then puts it to the staff as a whole...(and) the head... Each group gets allocated money from the budget as well.

This larger school also had weekly staff meetings, unit meetings, and unit coordinators' meetings, and the new teacher liked the system.

New teachers were particularly aware of their lack of experience of school Christmas and their feelings of inadequacy in relation to other teachers' experience influenced their ability to participate:

> It's not as if I had any experience of Christmas anywhere else, as a teacher who'd been in teaching for quite a long time would have had. They have ideas, but I didn't have any because I haven't been involved before.
> I find I just say nothing. It's very occasionally that I ever say anything in a staff meeting. I just sit.

The latter comment was made in November 1992. By February 1993, the same teacher was using staff meetings to change the staff's perception of a boy generally perceived to be naughty:

> The whole time he was always getting wrong... so I'm trying to get away from that...I'm even doing it in staff meetings... so it won't go on next year... . Just since Christmas there's a massive turn-round.

Extra staff meetings were held in all the schools to plan the Christmas events. However, everything did not always go as planned:

> They had a... meeting of junior teachers to decide who was going to be responsible for the art, for the music, for the drama... two or one persons in charge of that. And then, as far as Christmas parties go, the three in the age range get together and discuss it. And as far as decorating your own classroom, the mentor is in my age group and I'll speak to her about it.
>
> I think sometimes the organization of Christmas on paper seems adequate, but it's when that organization actually comes into play that problems arise, and that comes back to individuals ... . If you want to put a display up and you haven't got the resources, it's only natural that you get uptight, if you see somebody else putting up a super display using resources that you would love.
>
> In our school we all got together to say what we were going to do, but then people started to do different things. So you go away and do your own thing yourself.

The main difficulties seemed to arise from lack of resources, feeling excluded from events, and from responsibilities not being clearly delineated.

For one teacher, Christmas revealed how staff ceased to collaborate when there was pressure for resources:

> You realize the people who will hoard...the people who will rush down first – who know exactly how to get what they want, the ones who will share, the ones who won't share...I was going mad to (the auxiliary) saying 'I don't know how to get anything in this school'. In my classroom I've got nothing for Christmas at all, and everybody else seems to. [One colleague]'s got a Christmas tree, a crib, the lot, and I haven't – not one thing. I was saying, 'How am I supposed to get all this stuff? Am I supposed to wish for it and never get it?'.

One solution the teachers found was buy their own materials and subsidize the school out of their own pockets:

> I buy my own resources in, like bulk orders and bulbs and things like that. I don't bother putting a chitty in because then they belong to me and I keep them in my class.
>
> I buy my own everything now. Absolutely everything. Scissors – and that's dreadful I know – I just put my name on everything and then no one can say 'Whose is it?'.

This solution solved the immediate problem, although other schools had developed an ethos of sharing which had more of a long-term effect, and which extended from materials to skills and ideas:

> Everybody shares everything... We know some people are more artistic than others, so their displays are always wonderful. If you want to get an idea, you go and have an look in their classrooms...you go up and pinch ideas. They have a way of mounting things or displaying things in a different way that makes them look really effective...[There is no] hoarding of worksheets or anything.

The importance of feeling able to *contribute* to a group was outlined in the previous chapter. The new teachers found that it was one thing to feel that one belongs to a group from whom to seek or accept advice; it was another to feel that one could make a contribution.

> I didn't know the Christmas carols. Somebody said, 'Oh, we'll do this one because that will lead on to that.' Well, I didn't know what the words of the Christmas carols were, so I wouldn't have been able to place them in order. Next year maybe I'll say a little bit more, but the year after I would have more of an idea. It's just because I don't know that I can't – and if I don't know, I wouldn't voice my opinion.

Even when they did feel confident in their abilities, teachers were still sometimes reluctant to contribute because they thought that more experienced teachers would have little confidence in them:

> I found that very difficult, to have to take a back seat, because I gave (my colleague) the idea, and from there she's taken it her own way and I found it very difficult to sit back because she's done it before quite a lot of times and she feels I'm new, so I shouldn't really know what to do. And I keep offering these ideas, and I feel like, every time I do it, I'm offending her by giving her these – and I know I can do that because I've already done it on a teaching practice.

On occasions when new teachers overcame their reluctance to contribute they met with new problems concerning the negotiation of power sharing:

> We had a rehearsal on Monday evening and there were three teachers there, and we all were finding ways to get up to say what we wanted the children to do. It was ludicrous. It was stupid, really. But we were all dominant people, I suppose... .One angel would say something and I would get up and say something, and then I would sit back down, and then another angel would say something and [another teacher] was there.

When I raised this point in discussion with new teachers, several thought that the problem was that no-one was in overall control:

> Alison Everybody does a bit in it in ours, so maybe it'd be better if there was one manager.
>
> Anna So nobody coordinates it all?
>
> Alison No, but everybody wants to have their say in it. Everybody wants it to go their way, but they wouldn't stand up and say 'Could I – ?'.

Fleur	And the more people that are in it, the more staff members that are involved, the more negotiation must be in that situation. If there were only one or two people involved, the dialogue must be easier.
Anna	There's not the communication between adults, is there?
Fleur	No – because we're all dominant within our own classrooms really, I suppose that's what it is – you all lead a group every day and therefore to take a back seat...
Alison	I don't say anything. I just let them get on with it.

Fleur's suggestion that teachers find it hard to give up control in collaborative relationships because they have to be in control in the classroom, it is true, has serious implications for staff who are trying to establish collaboration. Teachers have choices in these situations. They can try to take control, allow other people to take control, or negotiate (either openly or manipulatively) shared control. In some schools, this negotiation can be carried out successfully. The teacher who worked in the school with only four staff described how this can happen:

> We were working a lot together. We all had to plan the display – that was all linked up, the corridors and the hall and everything. The children all contributed to that. The parents were in a lot doing various things – the Christmas Fair. And we had carol services – we had a carol service at the church and it just felt like a really nice time.

Social events among the staff sustained feelings of sharing and collaboration. One school had this very well organized:

> Each Unit comes to see each other Unit. So we watched Unit 2's and that was lovely and we went down to Reception and watched them and the Nursery. There was so much food and drink and wine and mince pies in the staffroom and Christmas Dinner and a pizza because it was somebody's birthday. We were eating and drinking in there. There was a Christmas spirit to things. And a lot of people just had carols playing on tape recorders in classrooms. Each Unit did something for the other Units. We did coffee and mince pies. Upstairs did sherry and canapés...Unit 2 had a coffee morning...Reception had something that they set out – just for the staff to go to. Either a lunch time, or a playtime or after school. We had a staff Christmas night out.

It is not surprising that this teacher described Christmas as 'hectic' and 'mayhem' and said that she used 'worksheets in abundance'. She also enjoyed it all, in spite of being tired.

All the teachers had domestic commitments of some sort and all were preparing for Christmas for their families at the same time as the school's Christmas. The data do not, in fact, reveal the interaction between school and domestic Christmas arrangements, although at other times the teachers talked generally of family and friends and the necessity of finding a balance between domestic, social and professional commitments.

The teachers found a number of ways of coping in schools and, in all cases, of overcoming their resource difficulties, putting on the plays, parties and concerts, and meeting deadlines. The activities and demands, however, while often enjoyable, left teachers feeling tired and sometimes tetchy. The decision-making processes were complex, and individuals and groups negotiated, argued and agreed over the best way to do things.

Occasionally, the new teachers felt excluded, and this was part of the general feeling of exclusion they were experiencing as new teachers because of their perceptions that other teachers knew more than they did. Part of the process of learning to belong involved learning how their particular school did things and this theme is explored in the next section.

Learning about what to do at Christmas time

During their first recorded interview with me, in the previous summer, the teachers expressed some concern about the difficulties of learning about school procedures. Once they started work, they learned in a number of ways: one picked things up by coming in to school to talk to the auxiliary in the term before her job started; one spent half a day with the deputy head going through paperwork and routines; but most of the learning was done informally during ordinary working days. Everyone identified people who would willingly answer questions and respond to requests for help, although these people were not always the ones formally designated as mentors.

The Christmas experience contrasts with what the new teachers said about their relationships generally. They usually referred to one individual, who could be a curriculum or year coordinator, a mentor or a head, and they saw these people as sources of authority or affirmation. These relationships, whether supportive or supervisory, were one-to-one and private. They were also seen as *sustained*. However, the relationships established to deal with Christmas were temporary, formed within groups and their outcomes, at least, were public.

None of the teachers said they sought help in written communications, school handbooks or policies. One teacher had received a lot of information from the LEA about other things, but said:

> They sent a big package of materials, which I haven't used ...because a lot of the things were irrelevant, because I'd already found them out...what is the name of the caretaker and the name of the cleaner and things like that. Other things I'd already done at college, so it wasn't really relevant. And then, to be honest, it was about (an inch) thick and I haven't really had time to read through it. I do keep intending to, but I never seem to have the time. It's more helpful, actually just to sit and talk to people.

Other teachers agreed that talking, observing and discovery were their main methods of learning:

> You fumble through. That's all. Oh yes, I fumbled and eventually got there... Things like: Is the hall locked?, Where the apparatus is. What PE stuff have they got? Who's in the hall when?
>
> [My mentor] dealt with [a discipline problem] really well... It was good because she showed me maybe how I could've done it.
>
> I thought I'd send [a Christmas card] to each child. [The mentor] said send one to the class otherwise it can get out of hand... I put a message on the back to each of them.

The teachers valued the opportunities for observing other teachers' practice very highly, but in some schools it was difficult to create those opportunities because staffing levels did not permit them. Even if staffing levels would permit, there are no opportunities to be a disinterested observer of Christmas. The teachers often did not know what was required of them, although one felt that she had learned from the harvest festival which had been earlier the same term.

> When we were practising for harvest festival, I didn't know what to expect... There was going to be a practice for harvest festival and I didn't know what part I should do, or anything, or where the children should go, or how many times we did it, or how quickly they would learn it. I didn't know any of that. But now we're going to be practising for Christmas, I feel all right about that because I've had that experience beforehand.

Christmas and harvest festival are examples of the ceremonies and events which were particularly important to
the teachers in their first year of work. Other examples were
staff meetings, parents' evenings and assemblies
Procedures for these ceremonies were rarely documented,
and even in schools where development planning was
advanced, noone mentioned written instructions or records
to which new staff could refer when they wanted to know
what to do at Christmas. Oral and visual communication
procedures were used throughout the year, and their
importance was particularly evident at Christmas. The procedures were stored in the memories of experienced teachers and passed on by word of mouth and example. Some of
the Christmas traditions, like Mary's white and blue clothes
and the ox and ass, are not even in the Bible. They are not
written down in readily available handbooks and guidelines, but are retrieved from memory every year.

Sometimes people's memories differed and the new
teachers received mixed messages about how to deal with
Christmas.

> It was a panic because it was my first one and I was so enthu-
> siastic about it all because I was so excited. In fact, I was more
> excited than the children were because you're not allowed in
> on teaching practice because you get in the way... The staff
> kept saying 'You've got to calm down–don't mention it too
> soon, because you'll have the children so excited and you'll
> regret it in the end'... At the same time, I was being told that
> the staff were on at me about 'Haven't you started practising
> songs for the Christmas concert?

Mary Daly has reminded women who have been feminists
since the 1970s that we are now 'Memory Bearing Women',
that we carry with us the history of the modern women's
movement (Daly, 1993, p.10). Schools have their memory
bearers too, and in primary school staffs, many of them are
women.

Women frequently bear the main burden of work
involved in organizing Christmas. Women generally deco-
rate the churches, plan, shop for and wrap presents, write
the cards and cook the food. In primary schools, the staffs
knew what to do; they did not need the head's permission.
The experienced teachers set things in motion, and the
newly qualified teachers watched, and learned the
Christmas traditions. Organizing the family Christmas was
not an issue for the women teachers, perhaps because they

know what to do there too. In schools there was pressure for time and anxiety about getting everything done, but there was no bewilderment, no unfocused panic, because one of the purposes of the public ritual was to teach people (new teachers and pupils) how to carry out the public ritual. The heads (like Joseph), the passive yet authoritative father, watched and approved.

Learning how to deal with a new experience can involve a number of processes. Christmas was a good example of the teachers' experiences of learning how to be a member of staff. Sometimes they asked what to do; sometimes they were told without being asked; sometimes they were told contradictory things and had to work out avenues for themselves. Generally, they watched and listened and experimented. They may have turned to written material for the words of carols or prayers, but never for procedures and routines. Some Christmas traditions are ancient, pre-Christian even, and some are newer than that. The *means of preserving* these traditions are old indeed, for they are the *oral* traditions, which we learned from our mothers and teachers and keep in our memories, and which are manifested in the stories we tell the children. I, and my mother, and the teachers and their mothers belong to a group of memory-bearing people who preserve and maintain, and sometimes create, the Christmas traditions, and we present them to each other, and to the children, at the annual public and family events, the ritual dramas which constitute Christmas. I turn next to these events and ceremonies.

Christmas ceremonies and children's learning

> Christmas simply isn't Christmas without a trifle.
> (Smith, 1990, p.191)

> Christmas won't be Christmas without any presents
> (Alcott, 1977, p.9)

Trifles and turkey, cakes and carols, the treasured tree decorations and the familiar routines all form part of the social construction of Christmas for many people brought up in the Christmas tradition. Christmas is constructed in schools in particular ways too, although it is one of many similar events (and perhaps it is the most important) where teachers feel that their work is on show. The new teachers expressed considerable anxiety, and a need to learn, about school routines for public events: harvest festival, parents' evenings, Christmas and assemblies were all mentioned as being particularly difficult to cope with. Some of the difficulties concerned the amount of work involved in planning these events, and the consequent tiredness. In some schools, stresses created friction. The ceremonies were public: the teachers' work was on show to colleagues and to parents, and there were opportunities for judgement and criticism:

> It's part of you that goes up. It's what you can do.
> I did the Epiphany Mass when we first came back and I couldn't enjoy the Mass because I was screwed up because I didn't know whether the bidding prayers that my children had written were suitable ... .The church ... was packed. They know whose children were doing the prayers.

On the other hand, the public events are also an opportunity for affirmation. The same teacher said, of a parents' evening:

> I went home dancing. I've felt...more confident since then...I seem to be well thought of, but I think you always like to have that reinforced from different sectors... We're like kids, we like praise.

The sense that other people were judging them featured strongly in the teachers' accounts of their work generally and of Christmas in particular. Parents and pupils were perceived as having certain expectations that had to be met, both in terms of present giving and public performance:

> They always have to do a Christmas card; they always have to do a calendar; sometimes... a little present to take home ... You've got to do this... You think 'Oh God, not again'... How many different ways can you do an Easter card or whatever else? (The nursery nurse) said 'Oh, that's not enough. They've only got four things to take home' ...it was like a production line...the parents think they've been working hard...even though the teacher's done it.
> We had to involve every single one...the toy parade, you know. The innkeeper's daughter. We've got everything. Snowbirds – they're all involved. They've got all their costumes...their own part. It's a big thing.

Some people saw an opportunity for collective celebration, involving the whole community in the school district. This happened both in a small village school in an affluent area –

> There's not much else gets done, mind. At least, not in our school there isn't. It's all just Christmas display really. That's the most important thing – and the play, and the carol service, but the rest of the weeks seems to just go out of the window.

> But then, our head's of the opinion that the Christmas thing,
> and celebrations like the harvest festival which takes loads of
> preparation as well – she thinks that's all just part of being a
> member of a community celebrating things together, so she
> thinks it's very important anyway.

– and in an inner-city school, where a performance is produced every term, and the new teacher also saw this as an opportunity to do something for the people living locally:

> The parents really – you want to do something for the parents... On a night-time performance that didn't start until six,
> they're queuing up at 5 o'clock... It's just a cheap night out for
> them, of entertainment. They're just desperate. The grans and
> everybody. The hall is packed to burst and it's nice for them to
> see the kids doing something – it's nice for the kids to get
> dressed up.

Some people had difficulty in finding the money to participate in Christmas, although many struggled to do so in order to feel part of it all. One of the newer Tyneside traditions is Fenwicks' windows: a city centre department store devotes its window display to animated tableaux depicting Aladdin's Cave or Santa's Winter Wonderland. The trip to see Fenwicks is one of my family's traditions and we admire the decorations and the artificial snow and the considerable skills of the model makers. The local paper generally features photographs of children's faces, wrapped in woolly hats and mufflers, animated by the magic. After we've seen the show, we can go into the store, where we will have the opportunity to speak with Santa himself. One teacher took her class:

> When we took them to Fenwicks, the parents all had to pay
> their own money...£1.50. For a lot of them, that's quite difficult
> because they're unemployed.

They made the effort though and found the money, because it is important not to be excluded from the group of parents who take their children to see Fenwicks windows. Excluding people, particularly children, from the groups involved with Christmas events, is seen as a cruel thing to do. One school chose only the 'best' children to appear in a Christmas concert, and the teacher said:

> The amount of my parents who said that their child wasn't in
> the concert, and when I mentioned it to the staff, they said,
> 'Well, we did consider that before, but you do want the best,
> and you can't hear the quiet ones.' It seems so unfair and it
> really seems to hurt the children.

The parents' view was that Christmas should involve *all*, and not simply *the best* children. This view contrasts with some other school activities, such as the competitive sports that take place in some schools, and raises the issue of whether one set of values operates throughout a school, or whether opportunities can be taken by staffs to question values and to decide which ones they want to apply at different times.

The teachers' main complaint about their work at this time was that nothing else gets done, apart from the Christmas preparation:

> It was hectic. It began very early: we began Christmas first of December...you've got so much to organize – concerts, carol services. It was as if the curriculum was dropped... You couldn't really do any work with them anyway because you'd start something off – Right! we've got to go for hymn practice – Right! rehearsal – Right! it's getting costumes organized. It wasn't like real teaching. I enjoyed it.
>
> I think being in a [Year] 6 class as well. We are always expected to have the ablest children – to do jobs... I don't think I've had a full class because, the poor souls, they were moving staging equipment all of the time... They were far more responsible than I would ever have given them credit for. So – yes, it's a valuable experience, though frustrating in some respects, but I think I've learned from it. I've learned you can't kick against the system.

This teacher's perception that her class became more responsible at Christmas time represents a recognition that some change was indeed happening within the children. The change, though, was seen as being brought about by the process of organization rather than through the content of the Christmas story. The models teachers present to children in this story are of virgin motherhood, passive fatherhood, and the powerful male who will either save the world or commit infanticide. Many of the teachers, however, said that they stopped teaching and that 'no work gets done', meaning that they stopped teaching the National Curriculum. The children begin to take responsibility for Christmas arrangements, indicating that the content and process of Christmas are actively being conveyed. We conspire in teaching children how to 'keep Christmas', to use Dickens' words, and this learning has priority over all other learning, even the National Curriculum. The children are learning to be memory-bearing people themselves, to create the ritual dramas, to retell the story and to maintain the traditions of Christmas.

Conclusion: Christmas as an opportunity for the development of collaborative learning

I have argued that some of the experiences of new teachers can be understood partly through an exploration of how their school staffs dealt with the pressure of Christmas, and how these experiences were interpreted by new teachers. The school staffs organized themselves in different ways in order to cope with the pressures, the resource problems, and the expectations of pupils, parents and communities. Plans did not always go as smoothly as the teachers wished. The processes of collaboration were complex, and determining factors included the amount of pressure, the ways negotiations were carried out, teachers' feelings of confidence, or lack of it, and their perceptions of the value of their experience and of how their contributions were being received by colleagues. New teachers learned about staff membership, and about schools' Christmas traditions, from observations, talk and discovery. Existing staff – the memory bearers – told and showed the new staff what to do. It was important to feel that everyone could belong, participate and contribute, and that no one was excluded from the proceedings. To put it briefly, Christmas, like learning, is shared, and problems arise when the processes of sharing are not understood.

Teachers spoke of sharing in relation to Christmas activities like carol services and parties rather than in relation to Christianity, Jesus or spirituality. Three of the schools involved in the study were church schools. The teachers who worked there did not appear to have significantly different experiences of Christmas from teachers in other schools. One teacher in a Roman Catholic school said:

> We're encouraged to push the religious aspect...so we actually did an assembly on the types of things that meant a lot to people at Christmas. I deliberately exploited the very commercialized side, Fenwicks windows, parties, etc., [and contrasted it with our school's] religious aspect. It was beautiful. It was a superb assembly.... [My class] invited the reception children up to make a big Circle of Light. You could see the tears in people's eyes.... When we came back, I said...you've got to write about what Christmas means to you: presents, presents, presents, presents. So what had I done wrong? I hadn't done anything wrong...I am battling against unseen forces.

Commercial interests have very cleverly orchestrated present-giving, which is a custom much older than capitalism.

In celebrating a midwinter festival, we are, in fact, joining with people from many religions, past and present, who have celebrated at this time. Sikhs, Hindus and Jews all have their midwinter celebrations, and many of these celebrations have features in common – exchanging gifts, sharing food (quoting from Delia Smith is not so trivial), decorating our homes with plant life and lights, celebrating the rebirth of life and the return of the sun to its life-bringing strength – all feature in more than one of the festivals. Midwinter is the harshest time of the year, a time when our dependencies on nature, climate and a fertile earth are most evident. In ancient times, it may have been comforting to recall that some animals and plants survive the coldest of conditions, and for people to come together in order to bring back the sun through the sympathetic magic of the creation of heat and light in yule logs and candles. Midwinter is a timely reminder of our need to collaborate with nature, and with each other.

I think that at Christmas, although the National Curriculum may be abandoned, children are learning a lot from the memory bearers. They, and the newly qualified teachers, are learning about how schools and communities organize themselves to mark and celebrate important events, and they are learning how to plan and carry out these celebrations collectively. The, are learning about collaborative processes. Unfortunately, the conception of collectivity can be narrow and only incorporate *our* family, *our* class, *our* school, *our* country, *our* religion. Christmas is also an opportunity for adults and children to begin to consider the processes by which collectivity may be extended to include people and life forms which are excluded from our present constructions of the concept, and to include them *on their terms*. If we can collaborate in learning how to take this opportunity, we may indeed have Peace on Earth.

Chapter 5

Experienced Teachers Planning Together: Belonging or Contractual Membership?

In the previous chapter we discussed how newly qualified teachers felt that they belonged, contributed and learned with other teachers as they created their 'school Christmas'. In this chapter, we look critically at the assumption that collaborative planning necessarily offers opportunities for experienced teachers to achieve a strong sense of belonging to a 'whole-school' and of contributing to 'whole-schoolness' as staff members. So far in this book, we have argued that a sense of belonging comes from working and learning together in ways which emphasize choice, commitment and contribution. However, being a member of a school staff may also involve working with others merely to fulfil a sense of duty. We might refer to this as 'contractual membership'.

In the first part of the chapter we concentrate on formal, written school development planning, drawing mainly on a study of 57 schools in northern England conducted during 1991. In each school the interviewees included the headteacher and a 'main professional grade' teacher. In the second part, we draw on another, smaller scale study of teacher planning in two schools carried out during 1993. In the latter study both interviews and classroom observations were used to examine the teachers' planning and its relationship to classroom teaching. Both studies draw attention to the importance of the contexts within which teachers either are expected to collaborate or do, in fact, work together. We begin with those events that are applicable to and might involve the whole staff.

Christmas and school development planning differ as contexts for collaboration in four main ways. First, Christmas is pervasive. Schools create displays, carol services and plays which are visible and public to the whole school and the local community. Its impact pervades the building. In many cases, teachers give it high priority and they put themselves out to do their best, even, as we saw from the previous chapter, to the extent of modifying their teaching and spending their own money to buy resources. So far, school development planning has had less impact. Whilst the requirement to produce written plans has been seen as worthwhile by most headteachers, many of them have limited the demands upon staff, or even shielded them completely and written the plans themselves. Some teachers we interviewed knew nothing of the plans, and of those who had helped to write them, few saw the job as significant. In many cases, the processes of producing the plan have been partly or fully hidden. The product itself belongs in the world of filing cabinets rather than in the living experiences of teachers and children.

The second difference between Christmas and school development planning as contexts for collaboration, relates to the role of the headteacher. The influence, confidence and strength of the whole staff group at Christmas meant that the headteacher was not the main referral point, whereas the headteachers did orchestrate and conduct the writing of the school development plans.

Third, there was a difference in the nature of staff involvement. It was not possible, in most cases, for teachers to stand back and be detached or semi-detached during the Christmas events in primary schools, whereas that is how most teachers saw their minimal contributions to school development planning.

Fourth, there is a difference in the extent to which formal development planning and 'making the school Christmas' relate to everyday processes in school and life outside schools. The making of 'school Christmas' mirrors how many people cope collectively with the hectic preparations for family Christmas. However, the writing of school development plans does not reflect how teachers work and learn together to develop their schools. Real development is slow moving, spasmodic, non-linear and often unpredictable. In contrast, the writing of a school development plan felt more like a bounded task with a specified date for handing over the document to the Local Education Authority. Even so, this did not match the immediacy of 'school Christmas' with its shared high points, its collective entertainment and celebrations and the clear sense of relief at the end of term.

For these reasons, school development planning was less likely to generate a sense of belonging and contributing than was taking part in preparing and celebrating Christmas. In the first part of this chapter, we question the extent to which development planning might be an empowering and meaningful focus for teachers to learn collaboratively. At the same time, we argue that teachers do work and learn together in informal ways to develop their schools.

The second part of the chapter explores teachers' activities during preparation for and engaging in classroom teaching. The original study covered all those things that teachers seemed to do when they prepared their teaching: written plans and mental plans, formal planning as part of the school's requirements and informal, more personal planning as a means of keeping on top of the job. Here we examine the changing nature of concerns as a teacher moves through long-term, mid-term, short-term and daily planning, comparing the formal and the informal aspects of planning and that which is done alone and that which is done with others. Many of the differences between Christmas and school development planning are mirrored in the differences between the planning that teachers do in order to cope with the demands of running complex classrooms and the planning that they do to meet the demands of school managers. In short, the immediacy and perceived importance of the former gives it a greater meaning for the class teacher than the latter.

Teachers' participation in school development planning

Case Study: School development planning

Attempts to improve the effectiveness of schools in recent years have tended to focus on identifying and defining 'quality' management processes, one of which has been considered to be the use of strategic planning for the school's development. Hopkins (1991), for example, sees school development planning as a means to 'deliver significant curriculum and teaching innovations, whilst at the same time adjusting the school's organisational characteristics or management arrangements' (p. 63). Furthermore, the active involvement of teaching staff in plan construction has been proposed as an important part of the process. This argument relates to other studies which suggest how valuable collaboration can be between teachers as a means of supporting professional learning and, therefore, enhancing the development of practice (Little, 1982; Nias *et al.*, 1989). Not surprisingly, then, schools have been required to produce written School Development Plans and advocates of strategic planning see these as the key to the successful management of the complexities inherent in multiple innovation and change (Hargreaves and Hopkins, 1991; HMI, 1991). One popular metaphor for the plan used by devotees is the 'tray' that enables the numerous and diverse plates, which teachers claim to be spinning, to be carried with ease. Taken up with enthusiasm by many managerialists, school development plans may tell us much about various aspects of school life.

Of particular interest to us was one finding that emerged from our 1991 study of school development planning, for it emphasized the limitations of simplistic notions of participation. In primary schools the pattern of staff participation in the construction of school development plans was very clear: most of the plans were either constructed by the headteacher on his or her own or by the whole of the teaching staff. Where all of the staff had been involved in discussion about the School Development Plan, the headteacher regarded this in itself as beneficial; indeed this participative process was seen as probably more important than the finished document and self-evidently a 'good thing'.

> There is no point in me sitting somewhere and developing a list of areas of concern and strategies to address them and then presenting them to staff...it is not what I understand or believe a school to be about.
> I used a whole school approach with active participation..I wanted to involve everybody... [so that] ...all staff know where the school stands... If your priorities are agreed the staff become used to it and the resource implications.

Here we can see that, for the headteachers quoted above, school development planning is regarded as a way for those involved to learn about the whole school. The findings on levels of participation do not, however, convey the subtlety of what was actually happening in the schools. The extent of staff participation in strategic planning may not necessarily be a reflection of the overall management style or of the professional culture of the schools. For example, most of the primary headteachers who wrote the plans themselves spoke in the interviews about how they were 'shielding colleagues' at a time of excessive external demands upon their time, but this did not mean that the staff were not working together on other aspects of school life.

> We are always fighting a backlog of things to talk about. There are lots of working parties anyway in the school going on already...(so)...some of the Plan I've written myself without any help and not discussed much.
> I can knock off policies dead easy – in a morning – sometimes the staff don't know we've got a policy...Everyone has so much on their plate that it's only me spends time on it [the plan]
> ...partly it was the time-scale [within which the plan had to be produced] and partly other things seemed more relevant.

Even in those schools where more staff participation was reported, it did not follow that the classroom teachers necessarily valued this or shared the headteacher's view of the worthwhileness of the plans. Some of those who had participated regarded their involvement as unimportant:

> ...it was like something that had to be done – something else –
> ...At the time I thought it was unnecessary.

Crude attempts to quantify participation, or indeed simplistic notions of the concept itself may not, therefore, reflect the nature of the school culture and particularly of staff working relationships. More importantly, it may not develop our knowledge about the ways in which teachers in schools learn through working together.

Attempting to understand the diversity of school development planning

The study itself generated a considerable amount of data about both school development plans and the practices adopted in schools for their construction. It became very clear that the concept of school development planning meant very different things to the various people engaged in the activity. In an attempt to convey the diversity, complexity and the subtlety of what was happening, we created a set of six dimensions to clarify variations between schools. Of these, three in particular relate to collective decision making and refer to the nature of teachers' participation in and membership of the organization. These particular dimensions were:-

1. *The construction relationship dimension*, concerned with how those involved in the construction of a school's plan interacted during the process.

2. *The managing planning dimension*, concerned with the extent to which the production of a School Development Plan was integrated into the normal processes of management of the school or was an isolated event.

3. *The participation and control dimension*, concerned with the extent to which control of the agend a, discussions and decisions related to the plan was retained by the head or exercised as a partnership with other staff.

Each dimension has a number of points against which a school might be located; see, for example, Figure 5.1 which shows the points on the 'construction relationship' dimension. In most, but not all, cases these positions seemed to represent an order. Although neither the continua nor the positions should be regarded as definitive, their contribution is as an analytical tool for examining patterns and relationships which are neither immediately obvious nor visible. They have been used subsequently to stimulate discussion, both within and across schools, about current practices and future aspirations.

The implications of this form of analysis may be seen through a detailed consideration of the 'construction relationship' dimension. Any School Development Plan represents the knowledge and understanding that its author(s) has of the school itself, of the planning process and of the way in which the latter may contribute to the development of the former. How that knowledge and understanding is created, therefore, and the extent to which it is shared by those involved in the plan's construction, may be a useful indicator of the nature of professional social interaction within a school. In other words, it may offer pointers to a school's professional culture and its potential for development and change if it is accepted that, in essence, these depend upon teachers learning together about what the whole school is, and might be. Although two primary schools may have involved all teaching staff in the construction of a plan, they may have used very different processes in order to do so. In one school, formal planning may have been a whole-staff activity with teachers meeting together to share, discuss and analyse views about school life. Through this everyone began to develop a shared set of meanings about the school.

Figure 5.1: The construction relationship dimension
Integrated Construction

Position 1	**'enmeshed construction'** was characterized by those involved thinking and acting as a unit. The generation, refinement and development of ideas tended to be through face-to-face interaction of all those involved and utlized collection decision making.
Position 2	**'communicative construction'** was characterized by building on the strengths of individual contributions. A series of bilateral face-to-face interactions tended to be used to discuss and build upon ideas in relation to specific areas where an individual was recognized as having expertise and/or responsibility. For example, the coordinator for a particular curriculum area of a primary school might undertake an audit of that curriculum area in the school and them meet with the headteacher to discuss what the implications were for the School Development Plan.
Position 3	**'connected construction'** was characterized by taking individual contributions as starting points for the thinking of the plan's author. Individuals would be asked to provide information related to a specific area where (s)he was recognized as having responsibility. Often information would be in written form and used by the author without further negotiation. The individuals may have contributed to the thinking represented in the plan but there was an absence of dialogue which might have enabled a more active shaping of the final form used in the plan.
Position 4	**'separated construction'** was characterized by taking individual contributions as the finalized form for part of the plan. No further processing of a contribution was undertaken and the plan, constructed on a simple principle of sharing out the tasks, represented no more than the sum of individual contributions.

> We had a training day set aside when we looked at the curriculum audit...the coordinators looked at their own role and resources and we all looked at our own professional needs and strengths.

In another school, drawing up the plan may have been merely an administrative exercise undertaken by a set of individuals and organized by the plan's author (usually the head).

> I identified priorities and set the time-scale...The class teachers provided information for their own particular children and curriculum area...Every member of staff got a draft and comments could be added.

In terms of the learning of those involved in producing the plan, these two procedures are qualitatively different types of experience. This suggests, then, that knowing who is involved in the construction of a plan is insufficient without some consideration of this dimension. How the involvement happens, the nature and quality of interaction, its contribution to the thinking encapsulated in the plan, and the extent to which the thinking is shared by those involved, are all features which need to be taken into account. We felt that the use of these dimensions not only added a further level of explanation about development planning in the schools but also helped pinpoint further questions about staff membership of the schools as organizations.

The subtlety of staff membership of schools

This study cast doubts upon some common assumptions about the relationship between school improvement and teacher participation in school management. The interviews indicated that whilst formal School Development Planning was meaningful for most headteachers of primary schools, this was not so for the main professional grade teachers. One of the headteachers remarked,

> I think it [the Plan] is a bit like Gibbon to them.

Even where there had been an attempt to involve the whole staff in democratic decision making, the teachers we interviewed had not felt that the activity was a significant aspect of their work. Its processes had not excited them nor had its values been internalized like cherished teaching beliefs and practices. This questions the extent to which teachers' involvement in formal whole-school planning and democratic decision making might be 'empowering' for them.

One clue to this heretical suggestion is provided by Louden (1991) who found that Australian teachers tended to contest the legitimacy of school management reform whilst accepting curriculum reform. The recent Australian management reform, known as the 'Better Schools Project', aimed for a system of 'self-determining schools' which would provide more democratic workplaces for teachers. As a result of their involvement, teachers certainly had their workloads increased but they found the outcomes to be unconvincing because these had more to do with school management than with the curriculum. In contrast, a parallel curriculum reform project, 'First Steps', was accepted by the teachers. Its values and aspirations to improve teaching and learning were considered to be legitimate.

As we noted earlier, many of the headteachers we interviewed were, in fact, reluctant to impose school development planning on all teachers at this time and Louden (1991, p.366) reports similar views from a group of Australian secondary school principals:

> teachers have to do so much committee work now that they do not have enough time to teach. School development planning often takes teachers away from teaching. (Western Australian Secondary Principals' Association, 1991, p.7)

This is not so much a rejection of the value of participation but more a recognition of the importance of context and of the meanings which the teachers make of working together. Louden, for instance, argues that a collegial culture in schools is still a powerful force in supporting educational improvement when it has a curriculum focus. What is essential is 'establishing the legitimacy, clarity and practicability of the changes' (Louden, 1991, p.370). On the other hand a management focus for working together seems to be deplored by some teachers as an inappropriate intensification of their labour. As one class teacher in our study expressed it:

> If too much time is spent on the School Development Plan it will be teaching time that is lost.

Acker (1991) has also raised a similar question of whether 'attempts to impose collegiality contain control features not necessarily in teachers' best interests' (p.302). The imposition she refers to is the 1988 Education Reform Act (ERA) in the UK with its drive towards national curriculum and assessment frameworks, formal planning and the production of written policies. She too considers how these imposed demands might affect the ways that teachers talk and work together. In the context of collegial primary schools she found that teachers' sense of membership and belonging was sustained by a range of shared social events, work routines and rituals which also sustained school values. The headteachers were pivotal in building and maintaining a culture of collaboration which was essentially about personal relationships. Significantly, at that time the schools had 'oral cultures with little reference to written documentation' (p.305).

It is too early to draw any firm conclusions about the lasting effects of the ERA on teachers' working relationships, but we can already begin to see the significance of some issues emerging from Acker's study. She does not mention school development planning specifically, but she does refer to the great deal of time which was spent, prior to the legislation, in meetings and conversations. The meetings were mainly about 'domestic' and 'curriculum' matters. Since the Act, she reports that staff meetings have become more serious and academic with more concern about having to write policies and keep records. She has observed that the schools had become no less collaborative but 'the preoccupations were shifting, with the division of labour becoming more pronounced' (p.310). She recognizes the potentially manipulative function of the recent encouragement to be collegial in order to implement the ideas of others. However, concluding from her own work and from two other recent studies (Ball and Bone, 1991; Osborn and Broadfoot, 1991) she suggests that teachers are striving to interpret the demands of the ERA collectively to help each other to cope creatively and to develop sensible ways of doing what is now expected of them.

Turning specifically to school development planning, then, it is perhaps to be expected that because it is congruent with what they do, we should find that it was meaningful to headteachers. In many cases headteachers told us that they were arranging their own informal self-help groups as well as using the telephone 'grapevine' to talk over the task of writing the School Development Plan. It was also the headteachers themselves who were most keen on training opportunities to refine their planning skills mainly for writing policies, establishing success criteria and involving staff. Most of the headteachers thought that school development planning should eventually generate high staff involvement, but in many cases they were biding their time and holding back from making extra demands upon their staff. The reasons given were that the imposed timescale was unrealistic, that there were too many unknown factors at this stage (especially about finance and staffing), that they needed to learn more about development planning themselves before involving others, and that teachers needed protecting from yet another chore.

Some headteachers, then, were aware of the lack of congruence between formalized whole-school planning and what teachers currently do. This was substantiated by the teachers themselves. Many had been involved minimally in the formal planning and were content with this detachment. Some knew little, or even nothing, about the existence of the plan and few saw it as a key part of their work. This should not be taken to mean that teachers do not want to be part of the whole school or that they do not want to plan. Perhaps the problem is that the ideology of the school management reform movement, which is translated into the requirement to produce annual written School Development Plans, does not match the way that teachers currently conceptualize 'whole school' or 'planning' or the way that schools function as organizations. Recent research in UK primary schools (Nias *et al.*, 1992) has suggested that there is much development but it is seldom sequential, rational and systematic. The authors' description of the nature of primary schools as organizations catches the active membership of the staff in ways which a study of the formal processes of school development planning would probably miss. Like Acker, they convey the strength of teachers' existing approaches to collaboration and development. This is not so much to do with written policies but is essentially about action which is rooted in beliefs and values. Real development is slow moving and involves teachers' learning to be likeminded. They learn key beliefs collectively in processes which are embedded in the everyday life of schools, such as in assemblies, through displays and in various interconnected and simultaneous events and occasions for working together, observing, talking and sharing.

Perhaps, then, the term 'participation' may serve to fudge rather than clarify the nature of the ways staff work together in developing schools. In some schools, participation may merely hold connotations of routinized and ritual involvement with opinions being solicited and 'inputs' being made in response. Even when headteachers assume that the best management style means involving others in the construction of an School Development Plan, in practice many maintained a strong, if subtle, control over both the planning and the plan.

> We have opposition – but if they have chosen not to speak, well....

Their strategies of control may have presented problems for the growth of collegiality and collaboration. Leithwood and Jantzi (1990), for instance, suggest that a more equitable distribution of power for decision making among staff is a *sine qua non* of a truly collaborative professional culture in a school.

However, participation, control and school development can take many forms. Nias *et al.* (1992) have taken a new look at the role of headteachers in 'whole schools' in which teachers do work and learn together for development and change. They found that headteachers were central, powerful figures who exercised a controlling influence upon school developments in ways which they formerly assumed to be incompatible with collegiality and democratic decision making. For this reason they distinguish between 'whole schools' and collegial ones. In 'whole schools' it is acceptable to both heads and teachers that the head has a powerful and pivotal role. Nias *et al.* conclude that 'whole schools' are characterized by a high degree of complex professional and personal interaction which is not to be mistaken for straightforward notions of collegiality or teacher democracy.

Like Acker and Louden, Nias *et al.* take a positive view of teachers' capacity to work together for change when the focus is directly on what they believe to be important, when it involves their own learning and when it is based mainly upon their own informal patterns of interaction. In different ways, all three studies have cast serious doubts on school development reforms which propose that teachers will necessarily find it empowering to produce formal, written school development plans on a pre-arranged timescale and, in some LEAs, to a standard proforma.

One of the main observations arising from our study also confirms the centrality of the headteachers' role. Many said they were judging how to incorporate the imposed requirement to produce a School Development Plan into the range of legitimate and competing demands upon their own time and that of their staffs. Most of the headteachers we interviewed were, at least for the time being, purposely restricting the scope and scale of the task. As well as protecting staff from additional burdens, most were not attending to the full set of development headings which had been provided: curriculum, staff development, fabric, community, and finance. There was a tendency for what Cyert and March (1963) have called 'uncertainty avoidance' and the 'quasi-resolution of conflict', where strain is reduced by limiting decisions to the familiar and more certain aspects about which 'local rationality' has already been established. We found that many schools avoided uncertainty by concentrating mainly upon curriculum planning with some links to staff development and, less commonly, to finance. Even then, in many primary schools, the subjects were being dealt with sequentially for the purposes of formal planning.

School development planning and whole-school development

Evidence from the study suggests that school development planning is regarded favourably by primary headteachers but that they also felt that the task should be accomplished in a realistic way. In many schools the mandate to produce written plans was not being translated readily into an urgent whole-school priority. In the main, the headteachers were taking a central role in limiting the scope and scale of the involvement of staff and of the content of the plan. In this sense, the heads were acting as a 'critical screen' (Fullan, 1988) for their staff in response to what they perceived as a constant bombardment of external change.

For this reason, the planning practices of these schools reflected the judgement of the heads about the place of formal written plans in the overall development of the school, and about the relative priority of different demands upon staff time and energies. Looking forward, most of the head-teachers anticipated that, in the longer term, they may pay more attention to formal written planning and in those circumstances might create more opportunities for staff involvement in the construction of the plans.

We found that the requirement to produce written School Development Plans was not immediately meaningful to teachers. In some cases they had been protected from the task, and most of those who had been involved had felt it to be neither significant nor a burden. In the few cases where the process had been seen as worthwhile, the focus was seen as most practicable when it was on the curriculum and domestic matters such as procedures for dealing with 'wet playtimes'. Most were, in any case, pre-occupied with the immediate and pressing demands of teaching the National Curriculum and working with new assessment requirements. Nevertheless, recent studies in primary schools (Acker, 1991; Nias *et al.*, 1992) have suggested that teachers are highly involved in real school development. They are working and learning together as active leaders and members to create 'whole schools' which are driven by shared values and beliefs.

The central issue, of course, is what impact school development planning may have on what is at the heart of school effectiveness and improvement, namely pupil learning. After all, Tomlinson (1981) suggested that effective schools are merely schools organized to pursue learning consistently. Such consistency derives from coherence in the individual and collective practices of teachers. The question is whether this is best done through strategic planning or the more embedded interaction, dialogue and communication built up through working together over time.

At the time of our study, formal school development planning was a new and under-researched concept. We still await further studies which investigate the relationship between the externally imposed mandate to produce written development plans and the processes of actual whole-school development. At the moment the effects of the attempt to introduce systematic and written whole-school development planning into what have previously been oral and action-orientated cultures remain unknown.

The importance of 'teacher planning'

Case Study: Teacher planning

Unlike school development planning, planning what to teach in the classroom and how it might be done is a familiar activity for most primary teachers. What has changed, of course, is the legal requirement to teach certain things. 'Teacher planning' now has to be carried out in the context of an assessed National Curriculum. Not only are these changes stemming from the ERA creating different demands on teachers, these are based on a number of assumptions about teacher planning and the development of classroom practice.

The discussion paper by Alexander *et al.* (1992), for example, claims that 'successful teaching depends upon thorough planning' (p.35) and proposes a number of criteria for planning (pp.37–38). Despite considerable belief in the value of teacher planning itself, there has been little research on it. This is, perhaps, rather surprising given the ubiquitous and historical practice of primary teachers planning their classroom teaching.

It is easy to understand why there has been so much store set by teacher planning: the main justification being that it may help a teacher to visualize his or her teaching activities in the context of his or her own classroom. In that sense it is an opportunity to mentally rehearse what is to be taught, how that will be done and the probable responses of the children. In this way it may contribute to a teacher being able to organize and structure his or her teaching for maximum effectiveness. The weakness of teacher planning, however, lies in its strength in that any attempt to reduce feelings of uncertainty on the part of the teacher by seeking to regulate the complexities of classroom life brings with it a form of 'control'. Too much anxiety about losing control in the classroom – either intellectually or physically – may result in an over-dependence by the teacher on planning and, as a consequence, insensitivity to the actual experiences and responses of the children.

Perhaps, then, our ideas about 'teacher planning' need refinement. Given the nature of primary classrooms, the experiencing of uncertainty can never be eliminated. On the other hand, the 'work of worrying' has to be dealt with in some form or other. There may, therefore, be some forms of teacher planning that are more sensitive to the development of childrens' learning and more effective in terms of supporting classroom teaching than others. This was the starting point for the study of teacher planning. Of particular interest to our themes was the strong emphasis on a rhetoric of collaborative planning that was found in the schools. This kind of collaboration was essentially a professional requirement, with structures imposed in the sense that 'directed time' was used for this purpose and that there was an expectation of active contribution on the part of all teachers. This is why we refer to it as 'contractual membership'. Inevitably we were drawn to consider what working with others in the planning of classroom teaching actually meant for those involved and what impact this might have had on the classroom experiences of the children.

Primary teachers planning their teaching

Every teacher involved in the study engaged in several different types of planning, each of which interrelated with the others. Consequently, the most useful way of understanding their planning processes was as a 'nested model'. By this we mean that the decisions they took at various stages in their thinking fitted within a framework that, through a process of increasing elaboration, sought to structure, organize and manage classroom teaching time. In most cases that framework or 'nested model' could be represented diagrammatically as in Figure 5.2. Each of these different types of planning had its own demands and, as a consequence, had its own distinguishing features.

One of the ways in which the types of planning varied was in terms of who was identified by the teacher as being involved at that stage. Of particular interest was the finding that the closer the planning got to the point of classroom implementation, the less collaboration was reported. Both schools in the study used an overarching curriculum framework which formed the basis of all teacher planning. This framework established an agreed 'long-term' perspective on appropriate curriculum provision at various stages,

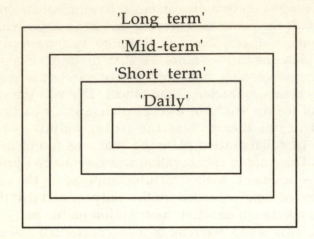

Figure 5.2 The 'nested model' of planning used

being organized in terms of 'key stages' and of the requirements of the National Curriculum. The whole staff was
involved at this level of planning. The school's framework
then provided the starting point for the 'mid-term' planning that normally covered half of a school term and began
collaboratively with teachers meeting in their appropriate
'stage team' eg, 'Early years' or 'Key stage 1'. Up to this
point collaboration with others was formalized by being
both expected by the headteacher and enabled through the
use of 'directed time'. Many of the teachers appreciated the
opportunities this provided to swap ideas in a supportive
way.

> I think it [planning with other teachers in the Key Stage] is
> quite important. It gives some balance and level. It also gives
> some progression. When there are three there isn't a lot of lee-
> way for individuality, but we can get suggestions from each
> other which are very cohesive. Together we plan activities
> which are going to provide evidence of attainment
> targets....We are all very experienced and full of ideas. We can
> bounce ideas off each other and the activities escalate from
> there.

Some of the teachers continued this process in their own
time and on their own initiative.

> I try to get together with the nursery team – the nursery nurses
> – and this is where time at lunch time or after school is invalu-
> able. We all look through the plans – actually we all brainstorm
> at the beginning – I involve the nursery nurses from the begin-
> ning – we look at the plans together and then I break it down
> into a fortnightly plan.

As the planning became more focused, however, teachers tended not to work with their colleagues. Most, but not all, teachers, mentioned 'short-term' planning. Usually this meant weekly plans constructed by the teachers on their own. 'Daily' planning was mentioned by all teachers and invariably was done in isolation.

This trend towards thinking about teaching on one's own as the planning moved closer to what would be happening was accompanied by other discernable changes. As the planning became more personal and less public, the real teaching concerns of the individual teacher became more evident and the written word less important. 'Daily planning', for example, may have involved considerable mental activity but, if transformed into anything written, such paper plans tended to be skeletal. Despite this, it was daily planning that tended to bring to life concepts such as 'differentiation' and 'diagnostic teaching'.

> ...its like a jotter for me for the next day...I tend to jot down things...like I have down here [numbers over 10 ropey for Charlotte and Stacey] I would pick them out individually and do some work with them.
>
> Those children who were doing the clock pictures...needed a bit of reinforcement in that they were managing reasonably well when we were looking at a clock and playing about with times on the little clocks I've got in the classroom, but they weren't really relating it to the normal day. They could read half past ten on their clock, but when I said 'Oh, it's playtime I think – what time is it?' (because it was 10.30 on the clock) they didn't seem able - they seemed to manage in the context of a maths activity but not in the context of real life, so I wondered whether the time pattern might help things along, but Leanne needs extra input there, so does Helen, so the actual activity hasn't benefited the children but it's benefited me because it's been diagnostic. I think it's benefited Lee because he was having the same problem, and he has related the times of his day to that piece of paper - he has just about got the link - he'll need something else, but he has just about got the link.

Teachers developing classroom practice through planning together

Given that there is considerable emphasis in many schools on 'mid-term' planning – indeed it might be regarded as the key feature of the current dominant model of teacher planning – it is interesting that the study found this part of the planning process being interpreted in subtly different ways by individual teachers even though they participated in team meetings about their plans. This suggested that teachers are engaging in different thinking processes as they approach the translation of general verbal agreements with their colleagues into the 'fleshing out' of their 'mid-term' planning. Although these differences exist, what is less clear is their importance for subsequent classroom practice. Nevertheless, planning together at this level, whilst it may help 'whole schoolness' in the sense of knowing in general terms what some colleagues may be doing, may be insufficient for developing 'whole schoolness' in the sense of a coherence of classroom practice throughout the school.

It is also interesting that the formalized collaboration, in many cases, seems to have less effect than might be expected on the subsequent detailed development of the 'mid-term' plan and even less on the actual classroom activities of individual teachers. At least as highly valued by some teachers were the informal discussions that sometimes took place.

> Well, I think it helps enormously...[to talk with other people] ...especially people who are in the same position as you, with the same age children. I discuss things with the Reception teacher. I find the nursery nurses invaluable. It's nice to have someone to bounce your ideas off.
> ...Mrs U. [the Head] usually brings it [the 'mid-term' plan] back across and she has a chat [about the ideas in it]...

Such discussions were often about the details of teaching and classrooms run on details. Classroom teaching requires an interweaving of particular activities requiring particular resources for particular children. Even though teachers tended to interpret 'planning' as the frequently copious 'mid-term' planning notes produced for the headteacher, the most powerful frameworks for their classroom action were the cryptic 'shopping lists' of their own daily plans. An important function of 'daily planning' seemed to be to help the teacher visualize in a detailed way the probable activities of herself and her children in the hectic round of tomorrow's classroom, and then to prepare for it. Particular children would be identified by name as requiring further help, some activities would be specified in detail to ensure that nothing might go wrong for lack of forethought, and time would be scheduled so that adult help was carefully deployed. Upon such pegs were hung a whole view of the teaching and learning processes of primary classrooms.

Nevertheless, this was the area of teacher planning where there was the least working together. Where this did happen it did seem to generate shared understandings and practices.

> ...the fortnightly plan is done day by day and it's discussed daily ...usually after school or at lunch times...we [the nursery teacher and nursery nurses] report back to each other to see how it's actually going. We keep notes on the activities and on the children and their response to them so that we can compare notes and see, well, have they learnt anything from that or has it fallen on deaf ears.

Conclusion

The messages coming from our studies of planning in primary schools, whether it be school development planning or teacher planning, seem to have a remarkable consistency. Although all of the types and levels of planning studied were concerned, in one way or another, with the professional problems of those involved, it was the planning that was perceived as being directly related to the problems of tomorrow that really mattered to many classroom teachers. It was not so much that other planning was not valued, but more a question of who would derive direct benefit from any investment of time and energy in that planning. The immediate problems of teaching particular children have a reality that even organizing a half-term's span of teaching time does not.

Working with others in order to plan how to tackle the immediate problems of teaching, however, was rare. If it did occur it tended to be informal, initiated to deal with the particular (not even the whole 'daily plan'), usually one-to-one and functioning to service the teacher's autonomy in the classroom. This was in stark contrast to the working together generated by the school's organizational devices for encouraging collaboration. Here whole staffs or teams talked in more general terms, negotiated agreements that were often perceived by participants as having little tangible effect on the substance of their daily working lives and, in many cases, where they reassured themselves that they had fulfilled the demands of their accountability. There is a difference between belonging to a group in order to achieve a goal that is perceived as meaningful to oneself, and having a sense of contractual membership of a group in order to achieve the goals of others.

PART TWO

Developing Collaboration through Enquiry

Chapter 6

Becoming a Good Response Partner

(with Jo Fawcett)

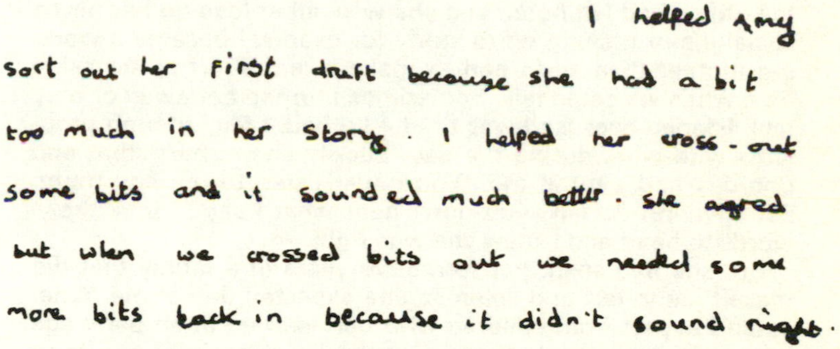

> I helped Amy sort out her first draft because she had a bit too much in her story. I helped her cross-out some bits and it sounded much better. she agreed but when we crossed bits out we needed some more bits back in because it didn't sound right.

Figure 6.1 Sally – aged 9 years

This chapter develops one of the key themes of the book: that teachers' and children's improving capacities to learn collaboratively are closely related and often interdependent. In this case study, Jo Fawcett, a teacher of 6- to 9-year old children in a small village school, traces connections between her own learning and her children's learning. Whilst she was learning with other teachers through a series of enquiries as part of action-research groups in Wiltshire LEA and at the University of Bath, she was also striving to create similar conditions for children to help each other to learn within a supportive classroom community. Two central developments emerged and helped to form common ground between herself and the children. First, both were writing about, and reflecting upon, their own progress and second, both were trying to become good listeners and readers of other people's ideas and thoughts. The latter was called being a good 'response partner' for other learners. After three years she described her own progress in this way:

I have spent three years now trying to become a good response partner and still catch myself failing although less frequently than before. I know that children have to learn how to listen and respond effectively, just as I did. It is harder today. Life is more high speed, families rarely spend time together and the dreaded TV is here to stay.

When I look back even 15 to 20 years to when my family was young, I can see changes. We spent time together over our meals. When the children were young, I was not a full-time working mother so lunch was not a grabbed snack whenever you were in. We sat down together with no rushing and ate in a civilized way and talked to each other. Yes, really, this is not some romantic ideal I've dreamed up! The same in the evenings, although by the time my daughter was a teenager the others had left home and she was either leading her hectic social life or rushing off to study for exams. I became a working mother then and I had to make a real effort to set aside time when we could talk. Sometimes I turned her away or only half listened because I was tired – I'd had, I felt, enough problems with work during the day. Luckily she is persistent and one day had a go at me. 'You never listen to me any more. Even when I do talk, you don't hear what I say'. I took those words to heart and I knew she was right.

But she had spent her formative years in a family that did make time to talk and listen so she expected this of me. What could I expect from children who had learned at an early age that nobody really listens to anybody, especially adults to children?

I went into school with my daughter's comments still ringing in my ears and looked at myself through her eyes. A child brought her writing up to me and began reading. I heard myself calling across the room 'Give it back to him Mark!'. I turned back to the child. She was still reading. I checked a child's maths. Lizzie read on. When she finished, she looked up at me. Had she realized my attention was not on her words? Why had she not stopped reading when I had so rudely interrupted her?

Throughout the next few days I caught myself frequently treating my children in this way. Whether they were reading or talking to me, half my attention was on the rest of the class. How could I expect children to respond to each other when they had such a poor example from their teacher? I resolved to change, little realizing how incredibly difficult it was going to be. At first it took an enormous effort of will to focus in on one child but I discovered that it was possible and that they began to respond to me too. This was because:

1. I had listened in a way that made them realize they had my attention and I valued what they said.
2. Because I HAD listened, I did value what they said and could comment constructively.

3. Their pride in their work was reflected in the way they read it.

4. They, in turn, listened to me and others and valued what we said.

Now, three years on, if I do let my attention be diverted, I apologize to the child concerned, resolve the problem elsewhere, and then return my attention to the child. When I do forget myself, which still happens, the child will stop reading and wait for me. I regard this as a very important sign that the children are beginning to accept that I really care about what they have to say.

When I felt I had become a better response partner, I began to model this for the children. We often start writing on a particular topic as a class. After an initial starting point, followed by brainstorming and sharing ideas, I would gather the class together to share the start of their writing. Again I had to make a real effort to give my undivided attention to the child who was reading or talking. It was hard to ignore Billy poking Peter with his pencil or Stacey staring out of the window, but I did. I found that the children began to realize that I took sharing seriously. I always began by saying something positive about what I liked and invited the children to do the same. I would then ask if anyone had any suggestions for improvement. By modelling a positive response and accepting all their comments, I showed the children that responding to someone else carries certain responsibilities and we learned principles, such as :

- Always start by saying something good.
- If you say you don't like something, you are expected to suggest an alternative or a strategy that might help.
- Whatever you say the final decision belongs to the writer. I found that hard at first, especially when I felt I knew better!

We had many sessions like this together at first but gradually the children became more willing and able to share in twos or small groups. By making collections of their developing writing in the form of 'writing journeys' they could see the value of response partners too.

I still do not regard myself as a very good listener but I am much better. I think my school report would read, 'Has tried hard but there is still room for improvement'.

The following extracts, drawn from her growing pile of writing, show how Jo developed her practices and clarified her guiding principles during a series of linked action-research projects. Part of the case study illustrates how Sally, one of the children in her class, learned to share ideas and get some feedback from other children and her teacher. Her comments emphasize how personal thinking and reflection can be enhanced when it is undertaken collaboratively with interested and supportive friends. Sally became increasingly reflective in her own head too. She was able to be her own response partner at times as she learned to rethink and redraft her writing.

Jo used a number of techniques like brainstorming and burst-writing to help children to list their ideas through combinations of talking together and writing privately. These techniques were used as means to help children to write and not as ends in themselves. She used the term 'writing journey' for a sequence of pieces of writing, and she kept these to display and to talk with children and their parents about progression in learning to write. What was particularly interesting for this book was the emphasis she placed on encouraging children to listen to each other and ask questions to help each other with the next steps in drafting their work. Jo had already experienced the benefit of this kind of support in her own teacher groups, and she continued to learn with the children.

Starting to share learning experiences with other teachers

Jo's participation in two different teacher groups taught her to value the challenge of writing as a way of both clarifying her own thinking and generating new ideas:

The sharing of learning experiences as part of a caring, supportive group of teachers gave me confidence to engender this atmosphere within my classroom. I found that *I could* change my approach to teaching and then I began to examine my actions and to encourage the children to look more closely at their own processes of learning. My involvement in the 'Write to Learn' group and a Further Professional Studies course on topic work led to my writing a booklet concerned with writing in topic work. This was the first time I had written anything apart from essays and reports for school or courses.

As a result of writing this booklet, I developed the habit of keeping examples of the children's work which I thought might illustrate the development of their writing. I had made the first 'writing journeys' in the Autumn term of 1987. These were for a parents' evening. I kept the first ones I made and added to them during the year. The children were happy to let me keep this work as I had explained that other teachers were interested in seeing it.

There were significant developments in the children's and my own abilities to reflect upon our own work. I was beginning to realize that some of the teaching strategies I used were of interest to other people. I gave a presentation to the teacher group to show how I was able to trace my learning through writing. We called our collections of notes our 'writing journey'. During this time I began to appreciate the value of these journeys. Pat D'Arcy, my Local Education Authority adviser, said 'One of the good things about teaching is that sometimes something that looks a very simple idea turns out to be something very powerful'. Having the opportunity to write up what I had been doing helped me to realize its significance.

The first action research cycle: writing journeys

The initial question Jo asked at this stage was, 'How can I explain to parents the ways I use various writing strategies with children in my class?'.

I introduced the children to strategies such as brainstorming, burst-writing, clustering and visualizing and I removed restraints such as correct spelling and neat handwriting during planning and drafting. Some parents came to me to express concerns they had about this way of working. These included:

Paper with scribbled, untidy writing.
No spelling corrections.
Why can't they write neatly and correctly
right from the start?

When I was able to spend time talking to parents who came to me, I could explain my aims and show them the whole writing process their children were going through. However, I wanted all the parents to understand the strategies I was using. We had a parents' evening due, and I would have the opportunity to spend about 10–15 minutes with each set of parents. I realized that I would need to find a way of displaying the children's work, partly to save time and also because I felt that the children's work would illustrate better their whole journeys of writing than a verbal explanation from me.

I decided against any kind of wall display. I wanted something that was easy to read and that I could sit down with parents and discuss. Any display had to be straightforward and to contain little comment from me. The strategy I decided upon was a simple book to show the stages of development of one piece of writing. I made one book for each child, all following the same basic pattern.

The children's books showed various kinds of writing. One example was developed from examining some crystals and then writing lists to catch all observations and ideas as they were expressed. Jo and her children called this activity 'brainstorming':

I use brainstorming for an unstructured capturing of ideas. It is an open-ended activity which can be used for recollecting, observing, questioning or speculating. The children then shared their favourite words or phrases with each other and with me.

I then asked them to burst-write for three minutes after having closed their eyes and visualized part, or the whole, of their crystal. I asked them to think about where their crystal was and to allow it to change size or form in their minds. I used burst-writing straight after this as we had to break for dinner and would not be able to return to our writing until the next day. Like brainstorming, 'burst-writing' is also an unstructured outpouring. Children know they have a limited amount of time for this. They were not used to this, at first, and found, as I did, that the pressure to write acted either as a spur, to encourage thoughts, or as a block to them! On this occasion they all wrote something and most of them found it useful. The following day the children re-read and shared their burst-writing. It helped them to go straight into a draft of a poem or story, whichever they chose. None of us was very experienced in editing then, so many of the drafts were edited just for spelling and not for meaning. We had begun to look at poetry and some children cut up their writing to rearrange the words. Only one child redrafted his story for content, and that was as a result of comments from his peers – not relevant comments from his teacher!

I collected all the papers they had used after they had made 'neat' copies from their final drafts. They were already accustomed to underlining words they thought were incorrectly spelt and to putting in basic punctuation after reading their writing aloud to me. We were all pleased with the final results, although the children could not see why I wanted to keep their lists and drafts. At this time, they only valued their final neat copies – as did their parents. I aimed to change this view with the parents, but did not appreciate, at this stage, how I could also use writing journeys to change the children's thinking.

To show progression, I mounted everything, not just the final copy. Each stage of the journey assumed equal importance in the books I made.

Each book was entitled '[name]'s ... Writing Journey '.

On the first page I mounted the child's first list. Underneath I just wrote 'Brainstorming, first impressions'.

The next page contained their burst-writing. Underneath I wrote 'Burst-writing further thoughts'.

Subsequent pages showed the drafts and, in two cases, pictures children had drawn to help extend their ideas.

I included a short explanation with each page. The final drafts showed how the children had edited for spelling or rearranged words in their poems. The final page contained the neat copies of the writing. The crystals were displayed for the parents to see with the children's names beside the one they had chosen to write about.

I was pleased at the response of all parents to their children's writing journeys, and also from the other members of staff. I was, at the time, alone in my enthusiasm for 'Write to Learn' in the school.

The writing journeys showed the parents how their child's thoughts developed through using the strategies shown. Some of the parents comments I recorded at the time showed me what impact these journeys made on them:

> Now I know what she means when she keeps on about brainstorms.
> Did my James really do all this work? I never did this at this age...never cared so much...just wrote to keep the teacher quiet.

Amazing vocabulary...yes, I see what you mean about spelling stopping you trying hard words.

I wish I'd been encouraged like this – Sally loves writing at home now too.

I see what you mean – she is picking out the words she spells wrongly – it's a good idea to make them find their mistakes – makes them think and not leave it to you.

I didn't think about all the work you need to do a poem – he's really been thinking hard, hasn't he?

The writing journeys I collected had done more than I hoped. They had introduced the parents to strategies I used used in my teaching, helped to show the staff what I was doing, enhanced children's growing awareness of processes of writing and posed more questions for me.

The second action research cycle: introducing Sally and Amy

My initial reason for keeping all writing was to show parents how I worked with their children. The collections had done far more than I had anticipated – and had led me to ask more questions about their use in my future teaching. Problems had arisen from having too many children all working on their listing and drafting at the same time! It resulted in:

long queues of children needing help;

the end product becoming all-important;

the children wrote all they had done using

my words from previous journeys – not their own;

only a few children actually finished as their

interest waned;

a very deflated teacher.

After a sharing session with them all, I decided to try a different strategy. I told them that it would be better if I worked with just two children to start with as I would be able to help them more easily.

The following story of how Sally and Amy learned and supported each other, also illustrates how Jo, their teacher, was creating clearer expectations about how they could collaborate.

Helping Sally and Amy

Sally and Amy were two enthusiastic Year 3 children – they often chose to work together and so I knew they would be happy to be response partners for each other. Both girls always gave of their best in everything. We decided to focus on writing they were already doing – Amy had started a story but Sally wanted to write a poem. Amy decided to do her writing about the same subject as Sally so they could share ideas. The weather had become very icy and cold so I had used this as a starting point for a group of children who brainstormed and shared ideas about 'cold'. I asked Sally and Amy to write about the brainstorming activity. Sally wrote straight away 'First we did a brainstorm on "cold" on our own. We shared with one person, got more words down and then we shared with another person. I thought the brainstorm was going to be hard but it wasn't because once we got started I found I knew lots of words'. Amy wrote 'I did a brainstorm'. I asked Amy what she thought of using brainstorming and she was able to tell me in great detail but found it difficult to put these thoughts down on paper. So now I had another question: how could I help Amy to express thoughts on paper? Asking her and talking with her didn't seem to help so I suggested that I wrote down what she said. We went ahead with this idea, and Amy later copied what I had taken down for her.

She said, 'This is my brainstorm about cold. I just put down all I could think of. You don't have to bother about spelling and you can share with someone to get more ideas. I think it is a good way to start.'

Sally then drew a picture and put words on it as well. She wrote, 'Then I drew a picture. It made you think you could make your words up together. It helped me choose what words I wanted to use'. Amy underlined the words in her brainstorm that she liked and wrote (after my writing first) 'I looked at my brainstorm and chose the words I liked as there were too many to think about'. At this point we were joined by Emma — a very enthusiastic writer. She had seen what Sally and Amy had done and brought me her brainstorm list with her written comments. 'First we had to do the brainstorm. We got everything down we could think of about cold. Then we shared with a partner, it was easier because we got more words down. It didn't matter about spelling because we can check them at the end'. I now had a group of three to work with. Emma said she wanted to write a poem too, but the picture she drew changed her mind, as her comments show. 'When we drew the picture, it helped because we could get an idea what our poem or story was going to be like. I was going to do a poem about a rabbit, but then I thought of doing a story of when I met a fox cub'.

I was beginning to realize that young children were capable of evaluating the strategies they used. I asked all the children who had been working on 'cold' to do a short burst-write exercise. It was Friday and I was interested to see if this would help when they continued the following week.

I asked the group to write about their burst-writing on the following Monday. They re-read their burst-writing and Sally wrote, 'burst-writing helped me start my poem because there were rhyming bits in it. Burst-writing was very helpful but for then I didn't think I could do it without stopping but I did do it'. Previously, Sally had tended to lack of confidence when faced with anything new but, in both her bits of writing, I sensed that her apprehension had been replaced with pride. Emma wrote, 'when we did our burst-writing we wrote a sort of writing about what our poem or story would be like. It gave me a good idea of a fox story. When you do burst-write you have to try not to stop'.

Both of their comments showed that they were beginning to look at the strategies they were using and to see that the burst-writing was a part of a whole process. By re-reading their burst-writing, the children found it easy to recapture their thoughts and feelings about the writing, so started in without any input from me. Both Sally's and Emma's comments reflected the effort that had gone into redrafting and their satisfaction with the final result. Emma wrote 'When I did my draft I didn't like writing it because I had to add bits in. Until I got to the fox bit. I had a bit about chestnuts that was in the wrong place. And I had to keep changing things around. But in the end I liked it'. These changes were made as a result of comments from myself and others in the class — Emma also made some changes after I had read her writing aloud to her.

After Sally had finished her poem, she wrote 'Then I got my spellings checked. Then I started my neat copy. After that I read it to myself and I thought it sounded very good. I felt very proud of myself, I liked it very much. The best bit I liked was when it said "Footsteps crunch through the snow." She had spent far more time on this writing than on any previous pieces and her final comments showed her pride.

Emma's final comments were much longer but she also wrote at some length about poems and stories...'poems have short lines and they don't always carry on'. Sally had to take words out when she wrote her poem and Amy had to put some in.

One thing which was particularly pleasing for Jo was the way in which some of the children were seeing the usefulness of getting responses to their writing from each other. The following section illustrates how Sally worked with response partners.

Sally and her response partners

Sally turned up on Monday morning with a writing journey she had made at home (this was definitely a high spot in my teaching life!). The comments were totally her own and the fact that she brought them showed that she knew that I valued all her comments – I had always emphasized this to them when I was their 'response partner'. Sally's first comments were 'brainstorming is easy at school but not at home because you can share with other people at school, but you can't at home. If you know how to do it at school, you can do it at home like I can'.

Sally's comments after each stage reflected the value of sharing to give initial confidence and to stimulate ideas. Sharing also sustained her interest in the writing and drew out more of her own thoughts. Her comments also indicated how both her confidence and her ideas grew. Once she had put her first marks on the empty page in front of her, she stopped feel-

140

ing threatened. There was no discussion about the form her writing was going to take at this stage, which also removed any constraints on the words she could write.

The writing journey record she made at home during the weekend, after having made her first one for me at school, reflected the lack of response partner with whom to share but showed that she already appreciated the value of this strategy and was quite able to use the other strategies which did not depend upon having a partner with whom to work.

Her first brainstorm at school (about the Easter holidays) lacked many ideas.

After being asked to select one particular event and tell a friend about it, her second brainstorm gave a lot more information.

Figure 6.2

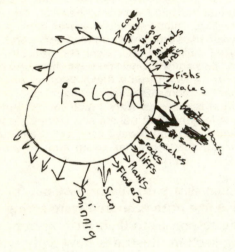

brain Storm

brain Storming in easy at School but not at home because you can Share with other people at School but you cant at home if you know how to do it if you can do it at School you can do it at home like I can.

The questions written by a friend helped Sally, but this was not the case with all the children. It seemed that children needed help and practice in formulating useful questions for each other. By having other children writing questions for her, I hoped Sally was being helped to develop an awareness of how questioning can help. She only answered the ones she thought would be useful to herself although she wrote that she found them all helpful. Sometimes when children were being 'response partners' for each other they tended to ask for more information rather than ask questions such as:

What is the most important bit?

What were your feelings?

Which part can you picture the most clearly?

The last two writing journeys Sally made for me were during the Christmas holidays after she had left my class. By this time her individual brainstorms and subsequent writing reflected her confidence to write down her ideas on her own without needing to share, although still appreciating the value of sharing at other times.

When I first started being a ' response partner' for the children, we would all gather together and I would ask them if they wanted to share their writing. Most of them did at first and others gained confidence later. I was modelling for them so I always asked them what they liked about the piece that had been read first. Then I asked for suggestions, comments or questions. At the stage when Sally was writing her 'cold' poem I was still taking an active part in responding but this grew less as she and the others grew more confident and began to realize what sorts of responses were helpful. They were nearly always very positive and supportive of each other. Two of Sally's comments (Figures 6.7 and 6.1) show her experiences as a response partner first with myself and then with a friend.

Figure 6.3

First we brain stormed about the Easter holidays. Then mrs Fawcett told us to under line two of the best things that happend to us. Then we shared with a friend

Figure 6.4

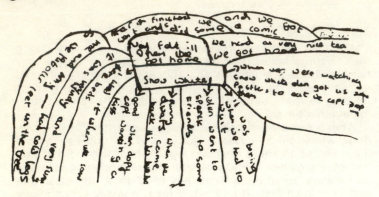

Sally was able to develop her own thinking and, eventually, to become her own response partner. This was evident, for instance, in her use of the computer to print a poem in a variety of ways. She learned that how you arrange words can affect their meaning. She could write comments for herself as well as for an audience. Her personal writing had become truly reflective.

Then we had to choose one of the things
We under lined. We brain stormed about that than
We shared with a friend that wrote us some
questions.

1 Want to know whos Boots ✓
2 Were did she get the comic
3 When what finished.
4 Were was it cold. ✓
5 What did you have to wait for ✓
6 Doppy wanted a kiss from who.
7 What did you have for tea.

I thought it helped a lot having questions because
it reminded me to put little bits in. They were all
good questions.

Figure 6.5

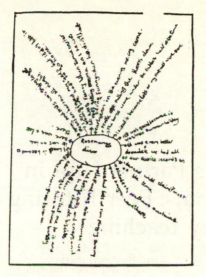

Brain storm

This is a brain storm. I do a
brain storm so it will help me.
to write a first draft, I find it is
easyer at school because when
we have done it we can all
share are ideas and they can
give us some more idea.

Figure 6.6

First draft

first I read the poem out to everybody them mrs
fawsett told me to read it out without the then
and I thought it was much better. Then she said
to try and re-arange the words to take
some of the ings away and I thought it was much
as well you have to take a lot of
words out when you write a poem.

Figure 6.7

Chapter 7

Learning Partnerships in Classrooms: Peer Tutoring and Advisory Teaching

(with Julia and Jo Ann Buczynskyj)

Like Chapter 6, this chapter explores the theme of creating and developing learning partnerships in classrooms. Using two more case studies of teachers' attempts to improve their work through action research, it emphasizes that arranging or forming pairs or groups is only the beginning of the job of encouraging and teaching people to learn collaboratively. The two action-research projects that we will describe continue to show the benefits of the mutuality involved when teaching and learning at the same time with the same people. We also reiterate our argument that it is important to collect evidence of what is happening. Like other teachers who have contributed case materials and accounts for this volume, both Julia Smith and Jo Ann Buczynskyj worked systematically to gain better understanding of what they were trying to do and then to try to do it better.

In the first case study we see how Julia introduced peer tutoring between Year 5 and Year 2 children in her primary school. As with Jo Fawcett, she set out to teach children some strategies and techniques of support. In the second case study, Jo Ann reviews her own attempt to create two learning partnerships with different teachers, another form of peer tutoring. She was an advisory teacher at the time, and she chose to focus on working with other teachers in their classrooms – the most demanding and difficult place to develop partnerships between teachers. It was comparatively easy to make plans at a distance from the classroom, and yet Jo Ann found that the ways that one of the partnerships evolved had more to do with the context and the teacher's sense of risk to self than with their original plans.

Case Study: Peer tutoring in reading

'Peer tutoring' is generally taken to mean some form of interaction between pupils on a one-to-one basis to support learning. Although we are familiar with the term 'tutoring' as a way of describing situations in which a learner receives individualised attention from a teacher, peer tutoring has some distinctive features. An important – and perhaps the most obvious – difference with peer tutoring is that the 'teacher' is a person of similar status and power as the 'learner'; a teacher-learner relationship that is unusual in the formal, imposed structures of our classrooms. Another important difference, however, is that there is an expectation that both parties will learn from the experience rather than merely one of them; again, a rather unusual expectation when we consider the more normal forms of teacher-learner relationship. Fitz-Gibbon (1988), a leading researcher in this field, describes it thus:

> In Peer Tutoring *all* pupils in a class, not just the most able, are trained to tutor on a *one-to-one* basis. Peer Tutoring offers all pupils the chance to be tutors.... Furthermore, the pupils who are expected to benefit from Peer Tutoring...are often those acting as the *tutors*, as much if not more than those receiving the individual tuition. Indeed, tutors are usually expected to benefit as much, if not more, than tutees, and not only in terms of academic achievement (p.218, emphasis in the original)

Peer tutoring has been used in a number of curriculum areas but here we focus on Julia's experience of applying it to Topping's (1985) model of paired reading.

> Paired Reading is a straightforward and enjoyable way for non-professionals to help children develop better reading skills. (Topping, 1985, p.109)

Getting started

> My first contact with peer tutoring was through a joint project with the local comprehensive school when Year 9 pupils tutored Year 6 pupils in science. As a result of the small suc-

cess of this project, I felt encouraged to try paired reading, using Year 6 and Year 2 children. The response from the children was encouraging. As far as I could see, the time the pupils were together seemed to be both supportive and beneficial on both sides. My intuition suggested that this might be a way in which to improve my pupils' learning experiences in reading. I decided, therefore, that I would establish a paired reading programme in the following term with my new class of Year 2 pupils. I also decided that this time I would carry out a more systematic study of the effectiveness of the programme. I thought that this would help the staff to make an informed decision about its use as a strategy to support learning.

Julia works in an inner-city primary school in an area which had experienced serious riots in the early 1990s. It serves a community suffering a number of problems arising from lack of jobs, training and opportunity as well as from poor-quality housing and a neglected physical environment. The city council has been successful in bidding for money made available by the government under the 'City Challenge' scheme and has established a 'Raising Standards in Inner City Schools' project. The background papers for this present a stark outline of the problems faced.

The areas...[in which the school is located]... are characteristic of an inner city culture which manifests itself in a lack of cash flow, a distrust and fear of larger society, social structures enhanced by a physically self-contained community, matriarchal and authoritarian families and early maturation of children. This in turn promotes a culture of poverty where feelings of helplessness and fatalism among individuals are endemic. More specifically, the area has high levels of overcrowded households, crime and vandalism, child abuse, single parent families, 17 year olds leaving education, 16-24 year olds unemployed and people from the New Commonwealth or Pakistan for whom English is not the first language.

The schools in the area, from nursery to secondary, contain a high proportion of pupils with low literacy levels..., early cognitive skills deprivation, high EBD population, under developed and ineffective learning strategies, and therefore then find it difficult to sustain the concept of an 'entitlement curriculum'. High truancy rates have been recorded in some young children, many of whom exhibit behavioural difficulties, with low expectations of education and low self-esteem. (Newcastle upon Tyne LEA, 1991, p.2)

The school is involved in the 'Raising Standards' project, receiving support for in-service education and reading resources. This encouraged Julia to embark on her own action-research which was launched during the Autumn term, beginning once the term had settled down, and continued into the Spring term. Julia taught the Year 2 class and she found a colleague willing to participate with her Year 5 class. Amongst other things, it required the coordination of 64 children and two teachers, using two classrooms, twice a week. In itself this proved difficult, but the problem was magnified over the Christmas period, when rehearsals for Christmas productions began to intrude. This was intensified by the fact that Julia played the piano and was required to attend most practices. Although the sessions were altered to accomodate these demands, Julia still managed to sustain the paired reading over this period.

Preparing to investigate peer tutoring

Having decided to undertake some small-scale action-research, Julia chose to use several methods to collect information about her project . This seemed important to her because she wanted to find out about more than reading improvement. She wanted to understand what the experience of peer tutoring itself was like for the children. Reading progress could be gauged from tests already used in the school. As part of the LEA's 'Raising Standards' project, the Macmillan Individual Reading Analysis test was already being used with Year 1 pupils. However, Julia also decided to interview tutors, tutees and the Year 5 teacher; to keep field notes in diary form based on observations during the paired reading sessions; and to collect comments from the tutors' reading diaries. She had too little time to test, observe and interview all of the children participating in the paired reading programme, so Julia chose a sample of six children who reflected the range of reading scores in her class. The six children included one boy and one girl from each of the top, middle and bottom of that range.

My field notes were kept in the form of a diary in which I recorded my observations of the sample of tutors and tutees as they took part in the paired reading session. I listed headings for my observations to enable me to compare what tutees and their partners said had happened. The headings I used were based on three questions:

- How quickly did the pair settle to their task?
- How long were they engaged in reading activities?
- How did the tutor and tutee work together?

In my diary, I noted also any events which took place during the paired reading sessions themselves, my feelings and my general impressions. The diary enabled me to build up a detailed picture of the sessions as they progressed, thus enabling me to reflect upon and review the project as it went on. One disadvantage of gathering data in this way was that I could only make limited observations; it was impossible to write down all the dialogue between tutee and tutor. However, it did help me to keep a sharp focus upon what was happening. For example, through my observations I noted that, although I had taught the tutors how to work with their partners, they were 'slipping' in their use of the agreed paired reading technique, not allowing the children time to correct themselves and also the frequency of praise was diminishing. This led to the children and me having a review of our paired reading technique.

I wanted to know what the children thought about paired reading. To do this, I decided to interview six pairs of children. The interviews, carried out after 12 weeks of the 'paired reading' programme, were informal and based loosely on the following set of questions:

1 Do you look forward to paired reading?
2 What do you think of paired reading?
   Can you tell me what you like about it?
   Can you tell me what you dislike about it?
3 Do you look forward to working with your
   reading partner?
4 Has reading become more enjoyable since you
   started paired reading?
5 Do you like having the same partner?
   Would you like to change your partner?
6 If you could change something about paired
   reading, can you tell me what it would be?

The children were interviewed individually and the responses were tape recorded for later analysis. Listening to the tapes helped me realize that the questions themselves did not really give the children the opportunity to open up the discussion about the programme in ways that may not have occurred to me. Fortunately, my field notes were another source as I had included casual comments made by children. Nevertheless, the interview with the Year 5 teacher was more non-directive, I had no fixed schedule of questions, wishing only to gain insights into her perception of the project.

Preparing for the classroom project

Before the project started, Julia held three meetings with the children: one a classroom discussion with her own class of 32 Year 2 pupils, aged 6 to 7, and the other two with the Year 5 class. During the meeting with her own class, she talked about the idea of a reading partner who would be the same person coming to help them each week in the classroom. At this meeting, one of the children expressed concerns about the possibility of a personality clash. Julia talked this through, making it clear that no one would be made to work with a partner with whom they were not comfortable. At the end of this session she felt that the attitudes of her children were very positive.

The first of the two meetings with the children in Year 5 was to let the children know what Julia was intending to do, asking the children what they thought of the plan and whether they would take part as tutors. After this meeting, two Year 5 girls approached her, saying they did not think they would be any good as tutors because they were 'no good at reading'. Julia explained to the girls that tutors and tutees would be paired and that they would be allocated to work with someone who needed their help.

The second meeting with the Year 5 class was an introduction to the technique of paired reading. Following the model described by Topping (1985), Julia demonstrated the overall approach to be used. For the purposes of the session, the Year 5 teacher acted as the tutee and Julia as the tutor. Together they modelled 'simultaneous' reading, when tutor and tutee read aloud, the tutor correcting 'mistakes' and carrying on at the tutee's pace. They then progressed to Topping's second phase, 'independent' reading, the tutee reading alone until an error was made, then signalling with a tap that she was confident enough to carry on alone, with the tutor giving praise. Both teachers felt that this meeting provided a clear introduction to the paired reading approach to be used.

As the issue of partner compatibility had already been raised by one of the prospective tutees, this factor, along with reading ability, had to be taken into consideration when making the pairings. The Year 5 teacher and Julia drew up a list together. They looked at personality, gender and reading ability. The latter was their first priority, as Topping (1985) recommended that tutors should be at least two years ahead of their tutees in reading age. After ranking their pupils by reading age, the teachers turned their attention to other factors. They looked closely at the pairings they were intending to make. They considered things such as which tutees needed a steadying influence, who needed a particularly sensitive tutor, which tutor needed a calm and steady tutee. Although they spent a great deal of time on these pairings, they were aware that probably there would be some mismatches. With this in mind, they decided that any changes would have to be made in the first two weeks of the study, as changes later than this might have a negative effect on the project. The initial pairings were presented to the classes separately, so that disagreements could be aired without constraint. As a result there were two changes at this stage, and one more after the first two paired reading sessions. The changes were all requested by tutees.

The paired reading sessions

Each session followed the same routine. They were fixed at the same time twice weekly and they lasted for 30 minutes. The tutors come to the classroom to collect their tutees, one half of the tutors and tutees went to the Year 5 classroom, the other pairs stayed in the Year 2 room. During the session the children worked at their own pace, changing books when necessary with the tutors being responsible for helping their tutees in their choice of reading material. The model described by Topping (1985) allowed a completely free choice of reading material, but Julia decided that the children could choose from the extensive range of books within their colour band which had been supplemented by the 'Raising Standards' project mentioned earlier. This decision was made to minimize the risk of a tutor encountering material with which he or she could not cope.

At the end of every session the tutors would make an entry in their reading diaries. Both the quantity and the quality of the entries varied, ranging from sad or smiling faces, to more detailed comments on their tutee's attitude and ability. Many recorded how quickly their partners settled to read, how well their attention seemed to stay on the book and whether they showed enjoyment of what they were reading. For example, Anne's reading tutor commented that 'she wants to read all the time, she doesn't like the reading games' and '... takes her time picking a new book, she likes chapter books best'. Commenting on reading ability, Anne's tutor reported 'her reading is very good, she works hard every week'. Similarly the tutor diary for Frank was very informative. The entry made after the first session was as follows:

Tuesday 20th October
Frank would not sit still for long. He didn't know many words I
think the book was too hard. He kept wanting to talk instead of
reading his book.

Midway through the project the comments of Frank's tutor
were:

Tuesday 5th January
Frank did the last of his sounds today. When we changed his
book he wanted to read it. Finished by playing a word game.

Entries from Julia's own field notes for Anne and Frank are
equally interesting.

October 20th
2.00 pm
Children from Year 5 arrive for first time. All gather on carpet
to wait for partner.
2.05 pm
Tutors and tutees go to their allotted classrooms 50/50 split
between my classroom and Y5 classroom.
2.15 pm
Observation of Anne and her tutor. Both quickly found a place
to sit. Anne led the way to a bay for two children. They talked
about what they had to do.
2.20 pm
Finished reading through sound and word walls, turned to the
reading book. Anne already had a book, they settled quickly.
2.25 pm
Book put away, Anne coloured in the sounds and words
checked off. Tutor commented on how many she knew.
2.30 pm
Session ended, tutors returned to their classroom tutees went
out to play.
November 3rd
2.00 pm
Tutors from Y5 arrive, both tutors and tutees go to respective
classrooms.
2.10 pm
Observation of Frank and tutor. Tutor led the way to a seat,
took out reading book from folder. Draws Frank's attention to
word/sound walls. He glances at page, tries a few sounds.
Asks tutor if it's playtime.
2.15 pm
Frank colours in two sounds, asks to go to toilet. Tutor looking
about, frustrated.
2.17 pm
Reading book. Frank looks at book, 'I've had this one'.
2.20 pm
Tutor and tutee go to change book.
2.25 pm
Return with new book, tutor writes title down. Frank flicks
book back and forward, makes no attempt to look at it. Tutor
takes book, 'Stop it, let's look at the pictures'.

2.30 pm
End of session. Y5 children return to classroom, Y2 children go out to play.
January 5th
2.00 pm
Tutors arrive, split into pairs and go to respective classrooms.
2.05 pm
Several pupils off today, had to mix up some pairs.
2.15 pm
Observation of tutor and Anne.
Both tutor and tutee engrossed in book. Their whole body language demonstrates a close relationship, heads close together, leaning towards each other.
2.20 pm
Still reading, tutor occasionally helping out, when needed. The tutor is very sensitive, waiting and quietly supporting.
2.23 pm
Stopped reading, having a quiet chat, very relaxed manner. Ask to go and choose a new book, leave room walking side by side.
2.30 pm
End of session, Y5 children return, Y2 children out to play.
January 12th
2.00 pm
Tutors arrive, pairs to usual rooms.
2.10 pm
Observation of tutor and Frank.
Pair playing a word game, lotto based on six basic words. Frank quite animated, shouting out the words he recognises, grabs a smiley face card to cover his word. Frank throws a word on the dice, can't read it, tutor tells him. Play on.
2.18 pm
They've put the game away, now looking at word wall in tutee's book. Frank indicates a word he knows, reads it, colours it in. Frank takes reading book out, turns to first page.
2.23 pm
Tutor and tutee still on task, coming to end of book. Frank comes and asks to change book, both go off together, tutor holding tutee's hand.
2.27 pm
Return with new book, sit and look at it. Frank's attention starting to wander, looking out of window. Tutor tries to draw him back, fails, puts book away.
2.30 pm
End of session.

Learning from the project

From the data that Julia gathered, she decided that the peer tutoring project had been worthwhile. Of the six children studied in depth, five made considerable gains in both reading accuracy and comprehension. However, one made no noticeable improvement at all. This child, Elizabeth, had other, more complex, language problems. Julia concluded that, for those children who are moving towards becoming readers, the support of another child during reading would seem to be invaluable. Nevertheless, the scheme was not an unbridled success and, as a consequence, although she felt peer tutoring had much to offer as help with reading, the approach, on its own, would not resolve all learning difficulties in this area of learning.

Julia considered that the pupil learning arising from the peer tutoring, however, was wider than reading itself. There were also social gains from the project. For example,

> While Elizabeth made no improvement in reading ability or in her attitude to reading, she did appear to enjoy having a partner and, for this reason alone, her peer tutoring might be deemed a worthwhile social experience.

Almost all the children involved in the project seemed to establish a supportive but not overbearing relationship with their reading partners. They did not appear to perceive an authoritarian attitude from their tutors, such as that which so concerned some writers on the subject.

Julia concluded that, in one way or another, the children in her class had benefited from the work. However, the time spent upon this project, and its future implications for the school, made the effect of peer tutoring upon the tutors a major issue. Through Julia's interviews with the tutors themselves and with their class teacher, she identified three reported benefits:

- the raising of self-esteem, especially in the case of the tutors with lower ability;
- a heightened awareness of and tolerance towards the younger children; and
- an increased skill and pleasure in reading.

> During an interview one tutor stated, 'I didn't like reading to my teacher, but I do much more reading now, I feel less embarrassed if I get something wrong'. The Year 5 teacher commented on the amount of time and patience her children used making games for their partners to play. After having to revise a game, one Year 5 child declared, 'I forgot she wouldn't be able to read capital letters, I'll make it easier next time'. It is this kind of considerate attitude that the school wishes to foster to help create a sensitive and caring environment for all pupils. Regardless of the educational benefits, the potential social advantages would justify the time spent on any peer tutoring.
>
> As a result of the action research carried out in my classroom, the issues raised by the findings have become points of

discussion for the whole staff. We had not previously considered the possibilities of children supporting other children's learning in this way in our classrooms. This work suggested that there is an untapped resource that the school could utilise in the areas other than teaching of reading alone – the implications of this are now being explored.

Case Study: Advisory teacher support in the humanities

Working together in a classroom also offers considerable scope for the teachers to learn about and develop their practice. At the same time, collaboration between teachers in classrooms presents enormous logistical difficulties to primary schools and a great challenge to the teachers themselves. It involves not just working together to help children learn but, inevitably, observation and interpretation of each others' teaching. Most of us are sensitive to being watched as we teach, probably because we are concerned about how our performance might be interpreted by someone who may not know all the nuances of the thinking that lies behind our actions. In this part of the chapter we describe how Jo Ann examined critically her role as an advisory teacher, but her experience has implications for anyone interested in supporting practice development.

As an advisory teacher I was sometimes in the unique position of actually working in a classroom alongside a teacher. I had time to talk with teachers. I was able to experience many different schools and classroom cultures. I had an overview of classrooms that few other teachers have an opportunity to see. I wanted to make the most of this by developing my understanding of how best to operate in the classroom so I decided to study more closely my classroom work with teachers.

At the time of my action research project the history and geography Standard Assessment Tasks (SATs) were not yet published. We had found that the teachers needed much help and support in understanding, interpreting and implementing the Attainment Targets (ATs) in the history and geography documents. Reporting in these subjects by levels was to come into operation in July 1993 and Key Stage 1 SATs (optional) were coming for Spring 1993 – requests from the coordinators for support and guidance were acquiring a sense of urgency.

The team of humanities advisory teachers with whom I worked felt very strongly that assessment should be meaningful and relevant, that activities assessing children's levels of understanding should be worth doing in their own right and that they should be part of the teaching process rather than bolted on the end as a separate entity. This is not always easy, bearing in mind the complexities of the documents and the volume of ATs to be assessed. As a consequence, when members of our team were invited into a school to help, our roles were various. Some coordinators invited us in to help them, as class teachers, to come to grips with some of the issues for themselves so that they would feel more able and confident to support the staff. Some invited us in to help at the planning stage, identifying opportunities where assessment could be integrated into existing curriculum plans. Some schools wanted whole staff meetings where assessment issues were thrashed out, and some wanted us to go in just to tell them what to do.

I decided to do some follow-up work with two humanities coordinators after they had been to an in-service half-day on assessment. They had both attended all our other in-service work for the previous two years, so they were familiar with the philosophy and thinking of the team. I chose one coordinator from each of the Key Stages so that we could compare the issues arising both from the different age groups and from the different levels of the National Curriculum documents. Another major decision at this stage was to choose teachers with whom I had worked before. I felt this was crucial as it would be difficult to reach a deeper understanding of the issues involved without having established a rapport which enabled these to be tackled. Both teachers saw the support as an opportunity to deepen their understanding of assessment issues for themselves as class teachers as well as for their coordinator roles in their schools.

Working with the teachers

Jo Ann planned to work with two teachers who were both experienced teachers and experienced coordinators. One was a Year 5 teacher who was also the deputy head of a junior school, the other was a Year 1 teacher who was also on the senior management team of her primary school. In order to widen her professional experience, the latter teacher had decided to work with children younger than those she had previously taught. In consultation with each teacher, Jo Ann drew up a programme for the first half of the Autumn term and arranged an initial interview to discuss any issues of concern with each of them. Despite the thorough nature of her planning, reality was to prove rather different.

Within minutes of the first interview it became confirmed for Jo Ann that the Key Stage 2 teacher's support programme would centre on the assessment issues as planned and that it would be a joint learning experience for both class teacher and advisory teacher. It was as quickly apparent to Jo Ann that the Key Stage 1 teacher's programme would not go as anticipated. As Jo Ann mentioned in her diary after the first interview:

> Her [the Year 1 teacher] main problem seems to be a lack of confidence in herself, in her judgement, in her handling of the little ones. (15.9.92)

Jo Ann had worked previously with this teacher when the latter had taught 9–10-year olds. At that time, Jo Ann had been impressed by her competence. In the new situation of teaching Year 1 pupils, however, this teacher seemed almost to be a different person. It was as if she had been deskilled and drained of all confidence by the changed circumstances. This was acknowledged, at two levels, in the final interview that Jo Ann conducted. Firstly, as a class teacher, secondly, as coordinator in the school:

> If you hadn't been coming in we wouldn't be doing what we are doing by now – I can't really have seen me do much group work with them. I wouldn't have tried it so quickly. (21.10.92)

This teacher acknowledged the value of group work and group interaction but did not have the confidence to try it in any curriculum area until she had Jo Ann's support. She had found detailed planning for the term impossible to do and was going from week to week without any sense of achievement.

> If you hadn't been there and made me focus my ideas and think about things...[the term might have]...vanished without planning, I might have found myself, quite merrily working till Christmas...if you hadn't come in.

Jo Ann wrote:

> At first I could not understand this attitude, knowing from the past how well organised she was. I now realise she was feeling overwhelmed by what was facing her, felt vulnerable and could not see her way out of it. She admitted 'I don't like working like that'. This lack of detailed planning in the humanities was a clear indication of her state of mind. On reflection, afterwards, I understand why she even refused my offer to do it for her. I think this would have exposed, even further, her uncertainties about her situation. I made the decision at that time not to press her and just to go from week to week carefully feeling my way.

So the purpose of the support with the Key Stage 1 teacher changed. This emphasized to Jo Ann the difficulty of analysing the processes and outcomes of learning relationships in advance. The needs expressed by both teachers after the initial interview were very similar. The Key Stage 2 teacher's support followed that initial analysis but the Key Stage 1 teacher's support changed.

Learning about working together in the classroom

In-service work is usually conceived as being of a cyclic nature and beginning with 'needs analysis'. This is what Jo Ann attempted with the two coordinators. Although Bolam (1982) points out how challenging and difficult this can be, few in-service providers seem to have recognized this. As Jo Ann came to realize, 'needs analysis' may sometimes not be the starting point for professional development but 'needs'can become clearer during the course of professional development. Systems that set out to identify needs before action may be too mechanistic for real development to take place. This also reminded us of the organic nature of teachers' professional development. Until a learning programme develops it is difficult to know which direction it will take and, subsequently, how best to help it progress.

> If I had continued a similar programme with the Key Stage 1 teacher as that carried out with the Key Stage 2 teacher, and tried to implement the original plans, then there is no doubt in my mind that it would have failed. Furthermore, it may have had a more damaging effect on the teacher by further emphasising her perceived lack of skills and competence in this age group. It was not until the support programme had started that I realised that the same strategies would not work with the Key Stage 1 teacher as with the Key Stage 2 teacher. I had not anticipated this. Her needs had to be analysed in a wider context than humanities assessment and I had to change direction very early on. I felt quite strongly about this. For me it created a considerable dilemma.
>
> I was going into her classroom, hoping to suggest group activities, discussion opportunities and assessment differentiation and instead I was talking and reassuring her about her role as a class teacher and co-ordinator, about coping with the very young class and above all listening to her anxieties about the impression formed by the new Head and the effect of her difficulties on the school and staff. This latter point was furthest from my thinking but obviously uppermost in hers, and until that was talked through there was no point in pursuing any humanities discussion. She was concerned at appearing incompetent in front of the other Infant teachers and the new Head.
>
> My focus then became a major confidence boosting programme for her. I suggested small steps to try, I identified overlaps with other subject areas such as English, and tried to point out simple things that were in fact geography but had not been apparent to her – such as vocabulary to do with place and writing their addresses.
>
> Until this teacher regained confidence and felt more in control, it was pointless to pursue the original programme of support. She says in her final interview:
>
>> I've sort of talked myself into the fact – Oh you're

158

> going to be absolutely useless at this. You're not going
> to be able to do it. That it's something entirely new. You
> coming along helped with that. And I'm thinking, of
> course I can do it. That I've actually blown it out of all
> proportion. (21.10.92)

Another vital ingredient that helped our support was her confidence and trust in me. The fact that she could talk safely to me about the situation in the school and get it 'off her chest'. She says of my role as a learning partner:

> ... somebody who you can be honest with. Somebody
> who you can say to – this is what's worrying me without
> ... going round everybody else and blab about it. You
> can be totally honest with and talk things through
> because I think everybody needs it. (21.10.92)

At the point when the aims of the two support programmes were the same, Jo Ann naturally assumed that the nature of the support to be produced and the learning involved would be similar. Those assumptions were challenged from the start, especially with the Key Stage 1 teacher. On the basis of her previous work with both teachers, Jo Ann had anticipated that the work would be to create two learning partnerships about assessing the humanities.

The Key Stage 2 teacher's support programme turned out to be just that. The programme and nature of the support with this teacher were carefully negotiated, and step-by-step procedures initiated. These were based on joint discussion and analysis of what had happened and where to go next. The whole process was planned together; sometimes Jo Ann took the initiative, sometimes the teacher led the way. The key to the whole support relationship rested on the reflective discussions at the end of the sessions.

> Certainly the Key Stage 2 teacher and I had no difficulties in
> our learning partnership. There were times when we were
> both challenged but never threatened. There seemed to be an
> 'intuitive' response to each other and my response to her
> needs was difficult to spotlight and analyse. *Because* I was so
> involved, *because* responses were automatic, almost without
> conscious thought or effort and *because* it did not seem out of
> the ordinary or unusual, the learning processes were difficult
> to identify.

Several key issues arose from this teacher's final interview about the nature of the support programme. In particular, she mentioned how important the discussion afterwards of particular classroom incidents had been for her. The dialogue had enabled her to clarify her thinking in several areas of practice.

Jo Ann found it difficult to place the Key Stage 1 teacher's support programme in the same way.

> It was still very much an evolving process but this was not an equal partnership in the way that I had expected. With the Key Stage 1 teacher, I became the expert and she the novice in *this context*. The fact that this was completely different from my previous support work with this teacher and with the way I prefer to work, caused me some misgivings. It made new demands on me and I had to develop different skills as a support teacher. I didn't learn what I had expected about assessment of the Humanities, but I learned a lot about working with another teacher.

The skills and strategies used with the Key Stage 2 teacher were completely different from those used with the Key Stage 1 teacher. The latter was still struggling with the teaching of humanities and was not ready to explore deeper issues of assessment. So the purpose of that partnership changed and with it the process of support was modified. Jo Ann became a counsellor, a role model, a positive supporter guiding and prompting the teacher to try different teaching strategies in the classroom.

> At this stage, I just wanted to encourage her to do assessment for diagnostic purposes, to identify starting points. Also to set up opportunities in the classroom where this could take place. She was more reliant on me to suggest activities, provide resources and emphasise the focus that the other teacher had been. I found this support much more demanding and threatening for me. With the Key Stage 2 teacher, we were learning together, with mutual responsibility, about assessing the Humanities. With the Key Stage 1 teacher, the heavier dependence on me meant that success or failure was mine. Also failure could have much more serious effects on the teacher's already battered self-esteem than on that of the Key Stage 2 teacher. I was very conscious of not over pressurising her during the support. Several times in my diary I have written things like:

> > I must be careful.
> > Maybe back off more than go on.

> My work became a careful balancing act between support and positive pressure.

> In her final interview the Key Stage 1 teacher mentions this pressure.

> > It's been worthwhile and I'm pleased that it had to happen. It made me get my finger out (21.10.92)

> Working with this teacher was like taking tiny steps, providing comfort and support along the way. Working with the Key Stage 2 teacher was like planning an activity, trying it, dis-

cussing, trying something else, discussing it, each step negotiated and reviewed. Such a contrast but equally valuable and
interesting in their own ways.

Many of the issues about both assessment of the humanities
and working with teachers in classrooms were reported
back to the humanities team by Jo Ann.

Some [of the issues] concerning assessment re-affirmed what
we had already anticipated in the in-service work which was
very reassuring. Others only emphasised what an impossible
task it was especially with the documents as they stood at that
time.

Perhaps the most important learning, however, was about
what a 'learning partnership' means in practice. From the
differing nature of the two support programmes, Jo Ann
identified the different styles demanded of an advisory
teacher when working in classrooms with teachers. The
skills of the advisory teacher are complex. Often they are
intuitive and not easily articulated. Jo Ann realized that the
different styles of working together may affect the nature of
what is learnt by the partners. A clearer understanding of
this would seem to be helpful to an advisory teacher when
working with a teacher in the classroom, otherwise little
learning – and possibly much damage – might ensue.

I learnt more about the assessment of humanities working
with the Key Stage 2 teacher. I learnt much more about different styles of teacher support working with the Key Stage 1
teacher. This support was the first in a long term context with
the opportunity to reflect, reassess and try again. Together
with the positive culture of the humanities advisory team this
encouraged deeper insights into our roles than any other
experience. Advisory teachers are *always* learners, they are
not always experts and it does not help to be always seen in
the role of an expert.

Conclusion

In this chapter we have sought to portray how both children and teachers can, through working together, develop
'learning partnerships'. We see these as having a mutuality
of emotional commitment, power and responsibility which
enables a process of development to take place for both parties. Such 'learning partnerships' are not necessarily easy to
forge but, in essence might be described as:

- a working relationship that is characterized by a shared

sense of purpose, mutual respect and a willingness to cooperate; and

- a framework within which each party's experience is seen as complementary and equally important.

This gives them a very human quality as each person in the 'learning partnership' seeks to understand and respond to the other in ways which enable both to learn.

Chapter 8

Children Working in Groups to Solve Real Problems

(with Karen Haggis)

In Chapter 5 we discussed the ways in which teachers seemed to collaborate when faced with different types of planning activities. In particular, we suggested that the teachers valued those activities which they saw as having real and tangible benefits for their classroom work. This seemed to have two effects. First, there was a greater sense of involvement in and joint contribution to working together. Second, there seemed to be more signs of teachers learning from each other. We return now to this theme of the meaningfulness of collaborative activities for participants and consider what happened when a teacher attempted to encourage groups of children to work collaboratively on 'real problem solving' activities. Although the nature of the activity does seem to be important, the next story suggests that, in the classroom at least, more would appear to be involved than simply setting apparently appropriate activities.

'Real problem solving' is claimed by its advocates to be one of the few approaches to teaching and learning that can prepare pupils for their lives in a rapidly changing society. Based on the assumption that survival in such a society depends on the ability to adapt to change and to solve new problems, real problem solving is said to develop the skills and attitudes needed for effective problem solving in adult life. In addition to meeting the immediate and future needs of pupils, a 'real problem solving' approach is claimed to 'empower' children both by developing their autonomy as learners and by raising their consciousness to the point where, ultimately, they are able to take control of their lives.

It is perhaps this 'political' aspect of 'real problem solving' which, more than anything else, sets it apart from the kinds of contrived 'problem solving' which are more commonly encountered in schools.

In this chapter we describe the experience of a primary teacher who set out to investigate 'real problem solving' in her classroom. The study was carried out over a period of five school terms with Year 3 and Year 4 children. One major issue that arose, and which had to be addressed in some detail, was that the children's effectiveness in solving real problems seemed to depend, to some extent, on the ways that they collaborated. It is this aspect of the teacher's work that is our focus. During her action-research project the teacher, Karen, had used a number of techniques to collect information about what was happening in real problem solving sessions. In particular, throughout the action phase of the study, her main means of data gathering was in the form of diary notes. However, she decided that as far as possible, it would be advisable to separate descriptions from 'observations, feelings, reactions, interpretations, reflections, hunches, hypotheses, and explanations' which Elliott (1991, p.77) suggests should also be recorded. Consequently, two diaries were used, one which aimed to provide a detailed account of the progress of each project and another in which reflections and 'analytic memos' were recorded. In general these diaries were completed at the end of the teaching day although often with reference to notes made in the classroom. The systematic manner in which she became a researcher into her own classroom practice enabled her to learn much about the nature of pupil collaboration through structures which she imposed. Fortunately, it also enabled us to share in her learning.

Real problem solving

We will begin by attempting to define the term 'real problem solving' in the context of Karen's study. The origins of the work may be found in the American 'Unified Science and Mathematics for Elementary Schools' (USMES) project (1973); later, the concept was elaborated by the British Open University 'Mathematics Across the Curriculum' course team (1980). It was from these sources that the initial inspiration sprang for the work to be described.

According to the Open University team, one of the distinctions that can be made between problems that occur in real life and those presented in textbooks is that a 'real' problem generally consists of 'a practical, immediate impediment to what is considered to be safe or satisfying living' (Open University, 1980, Unit 5, p.10). A 'real' problem is, therefore, one which the problem solver has 'come up against' and, in the classroom context, is either 'directly chosen by the children involved or firmly rooted in their concerns' (ibid, p.31). On this basis it could be argued that few, if any, of the problem-solving activities more commonly encountered in schools are 'real'.

This distinction is further emphasized by other features of 'real' problems. They are 'ill-defined, complex and many faceted' (ibid, p.10) requiring the problem-solver to consider the entire situation with all its accompanying factors. While the complex nature of real problems is cited by some as an argument against using this approach with younger children, both the USMES project and the Open University team maintained that it is only by grappling with the apparent 'messiness' of real problems that children will develop the skills and strategies needed for problem solving in the real world. Implicit in this is a criticism of alternative approaches which attempt to simplify the problem-solving process by presenting 'ready made' problems often contrived by others for the problem-solver.

The Open University team suggests five specific criteria for judging a problem to be 'real and suitable for the classroom'. The first of these is that '[the problem] should have an immediate, practical effect on the children's lives' (ibid, p. 13). Second, the problem should be such that 'it can lead to some improvement in the situation by children' (ibid, p.13). As this statement implies, a 'real' problem is one that has the potential to be resolved to the satisfaction of the children using their own efforts alone as opposed to one which may be of genuine concern but which has either no solution or can only be resolved with the help of adult intervention. Encompassed in this statement is the fourth criterion: that a 'real' problem should 'require the children to use their own ideas for solving the problem' (ibid, p.13).

The third criterion suggested by both the USMES project and the Open University team is that a 'real' problem 'should have neither known "right solutions" nor clear boundaries' (ibid, p.13). Although this criterion is not fully explained, the suggestion would seem to be that if the problem has only one solution then the task of resolving it may be more a game of 'guess what the teacher is thinking' than a genuine problem-solving activity. Clearly by this criterion, any 'problem' or 'puzzle' posed for pupils which has only one correct solution cannot be defined as 'real'; nor, indeed, can a 'problem' which is so clearly defined that it has an explicit or obvious formulation, since part of tackling real problems is to find a way of making sense of the problematic situation.

The fifth and final criterion is that a 'real' problem should be 'big enough to require many phases of class activity for any effective solution. In other words, the process of working upon the problem is long-term, requiring a considerable amount of different activities and stages of partial solution' (ibid, p.13). Again, it could be argued that the majority of 'problem solving' activities more commonly encountered in schools seldom meet this criterion.

The context of the work

The action-research described below was conducted in a small, inner-city Church of England primary school with 125 pupils on the roll (including 34 nursery places). Although denominational, the school is also the most accessible to the local community; the majority of the pupils, therefore, are not sent there specifically to receive a church education but because the school is convenient. Over half of the pupils are eligible for free school dinners partly as a result of the high proportion of unemployed and single parents with children at the school. Indeed, the school had been designated as being in an 'educational priority area' when such terms were still in use.

In spite of the school having many of the typical features of an older building including high windows and ceilings, the staff have created a school environment which visitors consider to be attractive, stimulating and welcoming. Displays of children's work line the corridors and rooms are comfortable and well-equipped. Directly adjacent to the school is the church, which can be reached through the school hall. Its main doors open out onto a busy road running parallel to the urban motorway that cuts through the centre of the town. The school and church are bordered on three sides by a hard-surface area. This is divided into small and large playing yards at the front of the school and a car park and nursery play area at the back. The nursery area has been landscaped and various play facilities provided for the children. Unfortunately, the older pupils' area has no play facilities apart from a wall which divides the two yards. This serves as a perimeter fence for football and something against which to bounce a ball.

The children involved in the real problem solving

The first year of the study was conducted in a mixed Years 4 and 5 class of 29 8–10-year old children. It included children who had come from two previous classes with very different histories. The 16 younger children had previously been in a small, single-age-group class with a permanent teacher of whom they were very fond. These children had some experience of both problem solving and group work. For example, in their final term they had all been involved in a project to redesign the school yard. In some superficial ways this had been similar to a real problem solving project although it appeared to be very much more directed and did not conclude with the children implementing their solutions. However, the project did seem to have provided opportunities for the children to work with others, identifying the causes of existing problems and proposing solutions to these. In this class the children had also been encouraged to take some responsibility for their learning in other areas of the curriculum. On regular occasions they had been given daily and weekly assignments to be completed at their own pace and in their chosen order. These assignments were sometimes done with others, particularly in 'topic work'.

In contrast, the 13 older children had had a very different experience. Previously they had been the younger part of a mixed-age class with several different teachers during the course of the year. Many of these children claimed that they had been 'put upon' by the older children and, in some instances, by one of the teachers. Although the curriculum and methods used by the various supply teachers is not known, it appeared from evidence in note books and discussions with pupils that they had been told what to do and how to do it. Certainly the teacher who had taken them for the last weeks of the year appeared to provide few, if any, opportunities for the children to develop their problem-solving and group-work skills.

The different histories of the two previous classes seem likely to have contributed to the difficulties that some of the children had in settling in to Karen's class. At the start of the study, the younger and less self-confident children were easily intimidated by those that were older and physically larger. These difficulties seemed to be compounded by the fact that the spread of achievement in the class was wide, with some of the younger children being more able than a few of their older class-mates. Similarly, the gap between the less able younger children and the most able of the older children was marked.

At the end of the first year of the study, all of the Year 5 children and eight of the oldest children in the Year 4 group moved on to a new teacher. The remaining seven children were joined by 15 others who were a year younger, to create a new Years 4 and 5 class. It was this class that took part in the second year of the study. From the beginning of the school year the second class seemed more homogeneous than the previous one had been at the same time in the year. The older children were familiar with the management and organization of the class as they had already spent a year in the same room with Karen. The spread of ages and ability in the new class was less marked, with the older children in the minority and enjoying their changed status from youngest to 'top dogs'. It was also a smaller class of only 22 children, making classroom organization and management significantly easier.

In the first year of the study, then, there was not a strong history of problem solving and collaborative groupwork to build upon. In the second year of the study the older part of the class consisted of a group of children who been involved in the first year of the study. They, therefore, had at least one year's experience of real problem solving.

The 'Real Problem Solving' projects undertaken in the classroom

In the first year of the study, the class began by tackling the planning and presenting of a class assembly on their chosen theme of Guy Fawkes Night. Prior to starting the class assembly project, the plan had been to present the children with the challenge of planning and organizing a Hallowe'en party. This had been greeted with great enthusiasm by the children who immediately 'got a handle' on what might be involved and started their discussions. It was shortly after this that an unanticipated difficulty arose when the mother of one of the children objected on religious grounds to her child being involved in either the preparations or the party itself. The headteacher supported her in this and, although having no personal objections to the party himself, instructed that the project be changed to something less controversial. Not surprisingly, the children's response to the change of plan was one of disappointment. The idea of organizing a party was clearly more motivating than planning a class assembly. However, with some effort, a degree of enthusiasm was generated by discussion of the possibilities of a Guy Fawkes theme.

After the assembly project, the children went on to resolve many of the problems they were having in their own classroom under the heading of the 'Classroom Project'. Some flavour of this project is conveyed by the list of problems (shown in Figure 8.1) generated by the class at an initial 'brainstorming' session.

As it was clearly impossible to resolve all 36 problems on the list at once, it was decided that they should be prioritized and that groups would then tackle the five most urgent or important. Using a form of 'nominal group technique' those items from the list of most concern to the class were identified as follows:

1 There's nowhere to get a drink;
2 The library carpet is too hard;
3 The walls are a horrible colour;
4 The room is too hot when the sun shines;
5 The trays are too small and squashed together.

In the third term, the class took up the challenges of starting a school football team, organizing an 'Open Day' for their parents and planning an end-of-year party for themselves and another class. Whilst rather different problems, each of these contributed to the growing facility of the children to cope with the demands both of real problem solving and of collaborative groupwork.

Figure 8.1 The list of problems from the 'Classroom Project' brainstorming session

Problems we have in our classroom

the walls are a horrible colour
the furniture is too squashed
the room is too bright
there are not enough rubbers
pencils get chewed and go missing
the felt pens and glue get dried out
the cloakroom is too far away
sharing books with other classes
the taps splash all over you
some cupboards are hard to get into
the trays are too small
the carpet is too hard
the blackboard is too shiny
glue and other things get wasted
we're not allowed to go
to the toilet
some cupboards wobble
people push at the door
some work is too hard

the desks are too small
the ceiling is too plain
everyone can't see the blackboard
the window blinds stick
some people's behaviour
the lights are dull
the door always swings open
we have to share the computer
there's nowhere to get a drink
there are not enough rulers
the trays are too close together
there are not enough pinboards
it's difficult to get the glue
out of the pot
the bins are too small
the windows are stuck closed
things lie around on the floor
the windows and blinds are dirty
the painting area is untidy

In the second year of the study, the oldest children from the class moved on to another teacher. As the two groups of children in the new class did not know each other very well, one of the teacher's aims for their first real problem solving project was to develop personal relationships within the class. Karen hoped that if an atmosphere of trust and cooperation could be established at an early stage, the children would feel more able to discuss their real problems and to collaborate on future real problem solving projects. As this seemed more likely to be achieved by spending some informal time in an out-of-school context, it was decided that the class would go away on a residential trip. At this time of the year the class were working on a topic about 'Islands' as part of a whole-school theme. A visit to Holy Island on the Northumbrian coast, therefore, seemed likely to be both an enjoyable and relevant climax to the project. It also seemed an ideal opportunity to develop some of the pupils' real problem solving skills by posing them the problem of planning and organizing the trip. Again the complexity of real problem-solving is clearly coveyed by Karen's account of the start of that project.

Many of the children had never spent a night away from home without their family and none had been on a residential trip with the school. Having explained that the problem of organizing the trip was to be their responsibility the children were then asked to contribute their initial ideas about what might be involved. These ideas were then categorized into six 'areas for investigation' and the following challenges agreed.

The 'Hostel' group	To book the hostel and organise to stay there for one night on 10th November
The 'Getting There and Back' group	To get the class to the hostel, to Holy Island and back again
The 'Things To Do' group	To organise how we will spend the evening at the hostel
The 'Food' group	To provide tea, breakfast and lunch for the class and helpers
The 'Adults' group	To organise helpers for the trip and get parents permission for people to come
The 'Rules' group	To decide on some rules for the bus trip, on the island and at the hostel

Each of these challenges was to be tackled by a different group which was expected to report back to and take note of the comments of the rest of the class from time to time.

Following the 'Holy Island' project, the children in this class tackled the problem of improving school dinners. This was a relatively long-term project involving the whole class and lasting for a term. At the end of the term the class made a large book of the project in which there were reports from each group, copies of observation schedules, graphs and tables showing results of investigations, photographs and other items of interest. A copy of this was given to the dining staff and shown to their supervisor who came in to talk to the class about their project. She was impressed with the children's work and the cooks were asked to put on the 'ideal menu' that the class had designed for one week. This was the official climax to the project and was a great success as far as the children were concerned. However, it had not escaped their notice that long-term changes to the organization of the dinners and the choice of food were limited to say the least!

Learning to collaborate in groups when tackling 'real problems'

The success of the children's efforts to tackle the 'real problems' described above was, to a large extent, dependent upon their being able to work together in organized, task-orientated groups. At the start of the study Karen had taken for granted that the children would do so as a matter of course.

> In the initial stages of my investigation the decision to implement a 'collaborative groupwork' approach to real problem-solving was made on the basis that those who were more experienced at this approach than me recommended this as the predominant model of child interaction for the work. Having been trained at a time when the advantages of 'groupwork' were espoused by most tutors, I did not question the values implicit in an approach which aimed to develop pupils' collaborative skills. Given that I was already organizing the pupils into groups for much of the curriculum, I was confident that this aspect of real problem-solving would present me with few difficulties.

As the study progressed however, it became increasingly clear that this was an area about which Karen felt she knew little and yet which was apparently crucial to effective real problem-solving when groups of pupils were involved. Referring to the 'real problem-solving' literature provided her with little help since this was an issue which was not addressed by either the USMES project or the Open University course team. Hence it became necessary for her to raise questions and attempt to find answers to these, both in the literature and in the classroom, in order to try to understand the causes of some of the difficulties which arose in the course of the projects. Over a period of several months she identified a number of issues which seemed to contribute to the success or otherwise of the pupils' attempts at collaboration.

One issue which was identified at an early stage in the study was whether pupils should be allowed to form groups for real problem-solving or whether, as the teacher, she should make this decision. Having found during the 'Class Assembly' and 'Classroom' projects that there seemed to be certain difficulties inherent in pupils self-chosen groups, during the remainder of the investigation she tried to identify criteria and methods which could be used by both the pupils and herself when forming groups.

As my experience and understanding developed it became apparent that successful groupwork was dependent on a variety of factors including the balance of personalities, gender, experience and ability within groups. The pupils' commitment to the task also seemed to be important as did the structure and cognitive level of this task. However, it was also clear that it would be impossible to form groups using all of these criteria and so the focus shifted from identifying criteria to trying to decide which of these should be of priority when forming groups for real problem-solving.

Criteria for group formation

For both the 'Class Assembly' and 'Classroom' projects, the class was divided into small groups using the criterion of pupil choice. This followed the Open University's (1980, Unit 6, p.11) advice that the resulting 'friendship' groups would be more likely to be cohesive than those formed by other possible criteria. Karen also hoped that if pupils were allowed to be responsible for forming their own groups this might help them to feel a sense of responsibility and ownership for the problem that she considered so important to successful real problem-solving.

For the 'Class Assembly' project the children identified five 'areas for investigation' and therefore they were grouped into this number of task-oriented groups. As there were 30 children in the class, the pupils were asked to form five groups of not more than six members, the assumption being that groups should be of roughly similar size.

One of the first difficulties to arise was that having got themselves into 'friendship' clusters of two, three or four most pupils did not want to extend their group to accommodate more members. There seemed to be only two possible solutions to this problem, either the pupils could be directed to form groups of the required size or the five 'areas for investigation' could be allocated to only some of the existing groups leaving others without a task. As both the pupils and I wanted everyone to be involved in the project there seemed to be no option but to ask the pupils again to form the required number of groups. Whilst the majority complied with this request it is debatable whether the resulting groups could be defined as 'self-chosen'.

Another difficulty with this strategy was that a small number of individuals were not invited to join any of the groups. These children tended to be those who had had to suffer the experience of being excluded by their classmates on other occasions both in and out of school. To have to cope with such feelings of rejection in public and in front of the teacher seemed unacceptably insensitive. To compound the situation, it was then necessary to persuade the 'friendship' groups to include those who had been left out, often against the will of some or all group members.

In addition, friendships seemed to be only between members of the same sex. In fact, so strong was the pupils' apparent aversion to members of the opposite sex that it was very difficult to match the number of groups with the number of 'areas for investigation'. This was only resolved by my intervention which resulted in one group being formed by joining together sub-groups of boys and girls. Of the remaining four, single sex groups, two contained individuals who had been allocated to the group against the wishes of some members.

As a result of these early attempts at forming 'friendship' groups, Karen decided that a more sensitive strategy had to be devised for the sake of the less popular children. A solution also had to be found to the problem of groups matching the number of areas of the problem under investigation whilst at the same time allowing pupils a genuine choice about with whom they would work. This latter problem was overcome to some extent when groups were formed for the next two projects. On these occasions the pupils were asked to form groups to match the number of 'areas for investigation' but were not directed as to the size of these. This resulted in groups of varying sizes which, although problematic in some ways, were more genuinely chosen by the pupils.

In the course of subsequent work on the 'Class Assembly' and 'Classroom' projects, several further difficulties arose which seemed to stem from the way in which groups had been formed originally. Although some groups were supposedly 'friendship'-based, they could not always be described as the most cohesive. For example, the group of boys who were trying to solve the problem of the lack of drinks in the classroom seemed to have particular difficulty working together. Conversely, amongst the groups which had been formed as a result of some teacher intervention were some, such as the 'Library' group, who worked together surprisingly well. Even at an early stage of the project, as they tried to get to grips with their particular part of the problem, they were also exploring what it means to work together and maintain a common focus. In doing so, they were learning what was really involved in belonging to a group and contributing to its endeavours.

Karen's observations of what was happening in the different groups raised the following questions for her:

(1) Could the groups formed in the ways described [above] really be defined as 'friendship' groups i.e. composed of members who were equally friendly with each other?
(2) Were 'friendship' groups necessarily the most 'cohesive'?
(3) Were there factors other than group composition which might account for the difficulties that some groups were having?

This helped Karen to focus on how the investigation might develop next.

> I decided to investigate the first of these questions by administering a simple sociometric test. The aim of this was to compare the structure of social relationships within the class as represented by the resulting sociogram with the existing 'Classroom' project groups. In addition to this it was hoped that the data gathered might prove useful when forming groups for subsequent projects.

Whilst Karen recognized the limitations of sociometry, the results of this exercise suggested that the pupils' self-chosen groups did indeed contain a 'mixed bag' of relationships. Comparing the patterns of relationships shown on the sociogram with the 'Classroom' project groups raised some interesting questions. Whilst several well-established friendship pairs and triads were contained within the problem-solving groups, there were also individuals who were in groups with those whom they had not identified as friends on the sociometric test. Also, several friendship clusters on the sociogram appeared to have been separated in the process of forming groups. This may have been a result of children choosing to be with one friend rather than another. However, as the strength of attraction that children hold for each other is not shown on a sociogram, this question could not be resolved without further investigation.

Following this activity, a further attempt was made to explore the extent to which pupils' self-chosen groups were really 'friendship'-based. Karen had video-recorded the pupils at the appropriate stage of the 'Classroom' project and, by analysing this section of the video-tape, she was able to look more closely at how groups were formed. She saw that some pupils were being denied their choice of group as they were rejected by some or all existing members. Others had to make a choice between joining good friends who were in different groups. There were also a few, more dominant, children who took on the responsibility for choosing group members on behalf of others either with or without their consent.

Whilst the results of this activity were in no way conclusive, a sufficient number of issues were raised for me to question the assumption that pupils' 'self-chosen' groups would be 'friendship' based. This seemed to be one possible explanation for why certain groups formed for both the 'Class Assembly' and 'Classroom' projects were less cohesive than might have been hoped.

Karen started to think, as a result of undertaking these two investigations, that it is probably impossible to divide a class into groups of five or six, all of whom would be close friends. Inevitably there will be less popular children as well as those who are so popular that they have to choose between friends. Furthermore, as children's friendships often change, groups that are based on friendship one day may not reflect friendships on the next. She was also beginning to question whether pupils would always want to be grouped with close friends. It seemed quite likely that children might sometimes prefer to work with those outside of their normal circle of friends, possibly because they had particular qualities or skills which were relevant to the task.

By this stage in the study the question of whether pupils' 'self-chosen' groups could really be defined as 'friendship' groups was receding in importance for Karen. Group cohesion, however, was still a concern. It now seemed clear that there were several other factors which might account for the fact that some groups were less cohesive than she had expected regardless of the closeness or otherwise of relationships between group members.

Amongst the other factors which seemed to be affecting group interaction were the ability levels of the pupils. As might be expected, asking pupils to form their own groups for the 'Class Assembly' and 'Classroom' projects had resulted in groups of very mixed ability with some being composed entirely of low-achieving children. The pupils in groups such as the 'Heat and Brightness' group which contained five low-achieving boys therefore had limited opportunities to learn from the more able, a factor which seemed to contribute to their relatively slow progress and waning motivation. This in turn required a disproportionate amount of my time to be spent both stimulating the pupils' interest and conducting the necessary 'skills sessions'.

However, aside from the very few groups that could be described as 'low ability', the fact that groups generally contained a good mix of ability levels seemed to be an advantage for most children. The exceptions to this were two particularly able pupils who at times seemed frustrated and bored by their group's apparent lack of progress.

Such interactional difficulties were not confined to this latter group, nor were they solely based on differences in abilities. They also arose sometimes in single-sex groups. Whilst this did not constitute a difficulty for all of these groups, some of which worked together very successfully, there were some groups of boys whose competitiveness often seemed to prevent them from focusing on the task. The 'Drinks' group from the 'Classroom' project was one such example. Sometimes these boys became increasingly outrageous in their suggestions in order, it seemed, to 'score points' over each other. Whilst a certain amount of this behaviour was no doubt a result of the particular combination of dispositions rather than their sex, more competitiveness was observed amongst this group than amongst any of the girls' or mixed sex groups.

> Although many of the other project groups were composed entirely of girls this generally seemed to be more of an advantage in that the girls seemed more mature in their social relationships than the boys. Many of the most able children were also girls which also seemed to contribute to the relative success of some of these groups.

Karen was unhappy about the majority of project groups being of single sex. Whilst the interaction within the groups did not seem to be adversely affected, she felt that the children being segregated by sex in this way seemed to reinforce and legitimize the gender-stereotyped views that most of them already held. This was particularly the case when tasks arose which the children perceived as suitable for either boys or girls. For example, sewing cushions for the library corner and preparing food were seen by many of the children as 'girls' work', whereas arranging the transport to Holy Island and organizing a new football team was seen as the boys' prerogative. Karen encouraged them to question such assumptions but many children still tended to opt for tasks which they felt were appropriate to their sex.

> It was for this reason that I decided that when tasks arose that the pupils perceived as gender specific, groups should be of mixed sex if at all possible. However, a balance had to be struck between my desire to challenge some of the children's gende-stereotyped views and the need for groups to be committed to and interested in their task. The interpersonal relationships between individuals also had to be taken into account as did the balance of abilities.

A further factor which seemed to contribute to the success or otherwise of the project groups was the amount of experience that members had both of working in collaborative groups and of real problem-solving. This became particularly apparent in the second year of the study when the new half of the class who had had no experience of real problem solving joined those who had had a year of working in this way.

> Regardless of ability levels the majority of the more experienced children, who it must be said were also a year older, were noticeably more successful both at collaborating with others and at contributing to the process of solving the problem.

By this stage in the investigation it had become clear to Karen that the development of the pupils' collaborative skills was crucial to the real problem-solving process. It was, however, some time before she felt that her understanding of this issue was such that she could begin making systematic attempts to improve the pupils' collaborative skills both in the context of real problem-solving sessions and on other occasions.

> As a result of all of these observations over a fairly lengthy period I came to the conclusion that to hope that pupils' self-chosen groups would be cohesive simply by virtue of the fact that they were friendship based was both over simplistic and optimistic. For the children to have the best possible chance of being successful in their real problem solving it seemed essential that we share the task of forming groups in order to try to achieve the best possible balance of abilities, personalities and previous experience of the children. On specific occasions there also seemed to be good arguments for mixing the sexes, something which seemed very unlikely to happen if the children alone were responsible for forming groups.

Group size

As the first class consisted of 30 children, organizing them into 'as many groups as there are areas for immediate investigation' (Open University, 1980, Unit 6, p.39) resulted in relatively large groups of between five and six members for both the 'Class Assembly' and 'Classroom' projects. At this stage in her action-research project, Karen thought that all groups should be of roughly the same size and that everyone in the class should be involved in the project.

> With hindsight it might have been more prudent to begin the pupils' and my first attempts at a very different approach with a more manageable size and number of groups. However, at the time I felt that by involving everyone both the pupils and I

would be more likely to feel a sense of commitment and enthusiasm for the project. A further advantage was that it avoided the problem of trying to integrate real problem-solving sessions with other classroom activities. Involving the whole class was also the model advocated by the Open University (1980), presumably for the above reasons.

Amongst the difficulties that arose as a result of trying to involve everyone and allocate an equal number of pupils to each 'area for investigation' was that some of the 'Class Assembly' and 'Classroom' project groups were too large for the amount of work involved in tackling their task. For example, the challenge of reducing the 'heat and brightness' in the classroom did not really require the efforts of five children. This meant that one or two boys were more or less uninvolved for unacceptably large amounts of time at various points in the project, no doubt contributing to the waning motivation of this group.

The large size of these project groups also seemed to add to the interactional difficulties which all groups experienced on occasion. This was particularly noticeable when group decisions had to be made. It was often at these times that quiet pupils took an increasingly passive role, others dominated the discussion, sub-groups formed, and so on.

One possible solution to the difficulties of the relatively large 'Class Assembly' and 'Classroom' project groups would have been to divide these problems into a larger number of 'areas for investigation'.

Assuming this would have been possible, creating groups of the optimum size suggested by some authors would have resulted in between eight and ten groups. However, as this would have created major organisational problems for me, particularly at this early stage in the study, I did not give it serious consideration either at this or a later stage. A further reason why I did not always attempt to keep project groups to less than six members during subsequent projects was that I had observed how well some of the relatively large 'Classroom' project groups had worked together.

Clearly there were factors other than the size which were affecting group performance. At least as important seemed to be the nature of the group task and the extent to which individuals and groups were interested in and committed to this.

The nature of the group challenge

From an early stage in the 'Class Assembly' project it was

evident that certain groups and individuals were more committed to the challenges facing their group than others. This seemed unsurprising given that some groups were spending the majority of their time writing while others were making papier mâché fireballs and experimenting with indoor fireworks. Furthermore, Karen had doubts about the 'realness' of the project.

> On reflection it seemed likely that the children's lack of commitment to the problem was at least partly due to the fact that it was not 'real' to them by either my own or the Open University team's criteria.

However, Karen was more concerned when some children appeared to be lacking in commitment to the challenges they had been allocated during the 'Classroom' project. This was a problem that had been carefully identified and which she was confident met the Open University's criteria for judging it 'real and suitable for the classroom'. Why then did some of the children appear to be 'off task' more often than she had expected?

> In the course of this project I tried to disentangle the variables which might account for the pupils' behaviour. In addition to questioning the criteria by which groups had been formed, I began to focus on the possible influence of the challenges facing and activities undertaken by the group.

Analysis of the progress of the 'Classroom' project groups raised the following questions in relation to this issue:

1 Did all the pupils perceive the relevance of what they had to do to their own concerns, i.e. was it 'real to everyone'?

2 Were some activities simply more stimulating and enjoyable than others?

3 Were some challenges too difficult or too easy for some children?

4 Was the structure of the activity such that everyone in the group could be actively involved?

One possible explanation for the difficulties experienced was that, in spite of having identified a problem which appeared to satisfy all of the Open University team's criteria, there was no guarantee that it was of genuine concern to every child. Karen, therefore, had to accept that some children's apparent lack of motivation might be due to the problem never having been 'real' to them. A second possibility was that whilst the overall problem was perhaps 'real' to everyone, the particular 'areas for investigation' might not be of sufficient concern to some group members to motivate them.

> In order to try to avoid this problem in the future I decided that any subsequent problems had to be of genuine concern to everyone who would be involved in the project. Furthermore, the pupils interest in the various specific activities had to be another criterion by which groups were formed at the stage of 'refining into areas for investigation'. For all subsequent projects I therefore asked the pupils to indicate in writing which of the 'areas of investigation' they would most like to work on giving their first, second and third choices.
>
> At the same time they were asked to identify the four people they would like to work with on each particular project. Together we then decided how many people were likely to be needed for each 'area for investigation'. Taking this information into account I then tried to form groups of the appropriate size for the challenge involved and composed of children who were both friendly with each other, or at least not hostile towards each other, and were interested in that part of the problem. In addition to this I tried to achieve a balance of personality and ability within each group, and, on occasion, a balance of boys and girls.

A further difficulty which arose was that some activities were more enjoyable than others. For example, distributing drinks of 'Coke' to the class seemed likely to be more motivating to most children than writing a group report. However, although every group had their share of less enjoyable things to do, this did not seem to present the same difficulties in all groups. What seemed to make the difference was how these had been delegated within each group.

> In those where this process had apparently been managed democratically there was noticeably less resentment on the part of those responsible for undertaking the less attractive activities. Hence I decided that rather than focusing on how enjoyable or otherwise the groups' activities were likely to be, I should concentrate on developing the pupils' group work skills, and in particular their decision making and delegation skills.

Another factor which seemed likely to influence the childrens' involvement and commitment to their part of the problem was the learning demands it made on them. When, despite considerable effort, a child seemed to be making little or no headway for too much of the time, it seemed likely that he or she would lose interest in the activity, particularly if help were not readily available from either the teacher or another child.

In my experience this difficulty was more likely to arise in groups which were composed of lower achieving children as they often had no one to turn to other than me when they got 'stuck'. For example the group of girls who were responsible for planning the evening meal on the 'Holy Island' trip had the demanding job of trying to find a menu with which everyone would be satisfied. Whilst they were very motivated by this at the start of the project it proved to be too challenging for them without some considerable help. However, with six groups to manage, I found it was not always possible to spend the time required to help this group over some of their difficulties.

Having said this, one of the most striking aspects of this work was how well the majority of children seemed to cope with activities that required a higher level of skill and understanding than Karen might have expected on the basis of their previous work. Once again this raised the issue of the criteria used for group formation.

It seemed that in order to help avoid children reaching 'frustration' level so frequently that they lost interest in the problem, I had to ensure that groups contained a mix of ability.

One final aspect was the extent to which the challenge drew on the children's existing knowledge and previous experience. Those groups which seemed to able to get started on their part of the problem most quickly tended to be those which could relate to it because they had done something similar in the past.

By the end of the study Karen concluded that the challenges and activities which seemed to be most successful in encouraging collaboration in groups during 'real problem solving' were those which were:

- relevant to the pupils' interests and concerns;
- relevant to the pupils' previous experience;
- enjoyable;
- demanding for the collective talents of group members- but not frustratingly so; and
- 'big' enough to involve all group members.

In short, challenges that are seen as both worth undertaking and exciting are likely to produce collaborative working in groups. That is, of course, providing participants feel that they can actively contribute to that working. Even so, children, in common with the rest of the human race, experience the highs and lows of enthusiasm. There may be times when the seemingly sure-fire winner of a challenge fails to excite some children or perhaps the underlying excitement is quenched by the burdens of the moment. That is part of the unpredictability of primary teaching.

Conclusion

Karen's study gives us a good insight into the complexity of organizing collaborative group-work in the classroom. As she discovered, there are no easy rules to follow nor does success come overnight. As with all primary teaching it requires flexibility and a willingness to be responsive to the multitude of messages embedded in the responses of the children. Children like to feel that they belong, that they can contribute and that what they do really matters. It is neither easy to create the conditions through which those feelings develop nor is it necessarily easy to live with the consequences when they do. If you belong you expect to have a say. If you contribute you expect to have that contribution recognized and valued. If what you do really matters to you then you may be prepared to assert your views and establish your rights. We have noted in this chapter how the development in children of those feelings, actions and expectations is affected by such things as the context of the learning activities, the nature of those activities and the children's perceptions of how influence and control operate within their group.

It is an important sub-text for the whole of this book that this type of classroom work and classroom research makes great demands upon the teacher. Why do we find it so difficult to cope with children arguing or not appearing to get along in groups? Is cohesiveness in groups the same as harmoniousness? Is the latter achievable or even desirable? What is it that impels us to want a 'smooth-running' classroom even when we know in our heads that a conflict of ideas can be stimulating and productive? These questions are uncomfortable ones, the more so when they arise from a study of our own practice because they are less easy to avoid. Perhaps what we have described in this chapter is what learning is often really like – untidy, uncomfortable and uncontrollable, especially when it develops through interaction with others. In the next chapter we focus on what it means to learn in a social context and try to pull the various themes of the book together.

PART THREE

Collaborating and Learning

Chapter 9

Collaborating to Learn and Learning to Collaborate

Wayne [indicating Daniel]: He'll stick the first one, I'll stick the second.

Amanda [to Johan]: You do the third and I'll do the last.

The strategy of sharing out the jobs in order to undertake a group activity is a common one. Indeed, you may remember that the management team of 9-year-olds mentioned in Chapter 2 used it as a fundamental principle for running their company. The use of sharing, with its implied norms of equality and fairness, however, is more than an expedient way for a group to get things done: it is a powerful reminder that children live (and therefore learn) in a social context. The children were using strategies they had learned as members of their own friendship groups. Even when the children are given work to do separately in the classroom, they may still have opportunities for learning from each other. This is one of the reasons why we felt that, in any discussion of collaborative learning, it was important to consider what we have called the 'emergent' structures of classrooms as well as the 'imposed' structures represented by teacher-determined group-work. Throughout this book we have described a variety of examples of both children and teachers working together within different structures and discussed the possibilities that collaboration seemed to offer for learning.

In this chapter, we look more closely at the processes involved in collaborative learning. Researchers have identified two main explanations for how learning may take place through collaboration. These are known as processes of 'socio-cognitive conflict' and of 'social marking'. Often classrooms and schools run in ways which draw on a mixture of these structures and processes, without those involved being fully aware of the implications of participating in different forms of collaboration. We have found it helpful to categorize our case studies using an explicit framework of these structures and processes (see Figure 9.1) as a way of analysing some of the implications for collaborative learning. Clearly these are gross oversimplifications as they focus only upon the main purpose for collaborating rather than the rich detail of what actually happens.

		TYPES OF STRUCTURE	
		Imposed	Emergent
TYPES OF PROCESS RELATED TO	Socio-cognitive conflict	Formal group work (Chapters 2 and 8)	Self-initiated peer review and critical feedback (Chapter 6)
MAIN PURPOSE	Social marking	Organized peer-tutoring (Chapter 7)	Acquiring membership of a pupil or staff culture (Chapters 1, 3, and 5)

Figure 9.1 Some possibilities for collaborative learning in classrooms and staffrooms

What this figure highlights is the diversity of collaborative learning in both theory and practice, and the rather different demands that it may make upon those involved. It also suggests that collaborative learning requires and develops a wide range of skills. This becomes even clearer when we look more closely at claims about these two processes of learning.

Looking more closely at children learning

Snatches of overheard conversations and snippets of observed activities can lead to doubts about whether anything worthwhile is being learned through collaboration.

We will begin with an example to illustrate how such doubts may arise, even though learning is taking place. This is taken from one of Karen's 'real problem solving' projects described in the last chapter. You may remember how, during the 'Classroom Project', groups were allocated to work on particular problems. In the following transcript we have part of the initial discussion of the 'Library' group. Its challenge was to do something about the library corner carpet being too hard. The group had been formed specifically to work on this part of the problem. The extract below is fairly typical of the sort of snippets that are often heard by a teacher as he or she moves around a classroom at the start of new group-work. A first glance would seem to endorse the old joke about camels being horses designed by a committee. Notice, for example, how frequently a statement is made which seems unrelated to the previous one, how unstructured the discussion appears to be when judged against formal models of problem-solving, and the circuitous nature of the path towards a shared understanding of what the group has to do. If this is what actually happens when children are working together then how is it helping their learning? A closer examination of their discussion, however, allows us to see that it does have a number of important features. First, the children are learning what is and what is not relevant to resolving their particular problem. This shaping of a problem-situation into a form with which they can work is one of the most difficult things to do when faced with a real problem. Second, they identify some possible strategies for dealing with relevant factors of their problem. This enables them to find a 'way in' to their problem. Third, they begin to realize how their own way of improving the library corner may have repercussions for other aspects of the classroom. This understanding that a real problem does not stand alone but has numerous interconnections to other related problems helps emphasize the relative nature of possible resolutions.

Chris	What we need is sort of them leather comfy chairs.
Garry	We need a desk what opens. We need higher desks and higher chairs.
Tom	Chrissy you try your grandma's. I'll try my relatives and see if they're hoying any furniture out.

Garry	Yeah! Get a settee if your mum and dad are getting a new one.
Tom	We need new desks. Look at the state o' these ones.
Garry	We need a new blackboard.
Chris	Garry, the blackboard's not furniture man! I mean these chairs. Whenever you swing back on them you're bound to lose something because they haven't got the rubber bits on the bottom.
David	I think we should start in the library corner first.
Garry	Yeah.
Tom	Yeah
David	We need a comfier carpet, a new carpet.
Chris	And bean bags and a half-let-down inflatable.
Garry	The carpet's too overcrowded, and the book shelves, the shelves are too little and the door keeps flying open and that.
Chris	The door is boring. We need something better than just a door!
Tom	Another flaming door handle I should think.
Garry	We need new rulers cause them are all, some people chew them.
Chris	And everybody dives at the plastic ones and if they get a wooden one they break it.
David	This isn't furniture man!
Chris	We need bigger tables for all the groups because all of the maths groups take up a canny lot of space doesn't it?
David	We should take the maths tables out the library corner 'cos they take up too much space.

A pause for thought, then, suggests that this group was learning both how to work together and some of the skills involved in real problem solving – a valuable combination of social and cognitive learning. Pauses for thought, however, are hard to come by in a primary classroom and most of us are only too aware of current pressures on teachers to identify learning. It takes a considerable leap of faith to move beyond the immediately obvious types of learning to collaborative work where the learning is more subtle and more difficult to identify. It is difficult to value a practice if it neither presents easily visible and tangible evidence of learning nor is seen as central to learning. This may, at least to some extent, explain the apparent paradox of classroom research findings which suggest that there is little 'imposed' but considerable 'emergent' collaborative learning. Perhaps children value implicitly the part that collaboration plays in their learning and find their own ways to engage in it; many teachers, on the other hand, conscious of their accountability for pupil learning, are more anxious about promoting collaboration as a means of achieving measurable goals.

Doubts about the contribution of collaboration to learning – and in particular to cognitive development – are understandable, given the traditions in which most of us were educated. For a long time, the dominant view of cognitive development theories was that learning was essentially an individual process. In other words, individuals were motived to undertake activities which produced individual results. Social factors such as language and social experience were relegated to a secondary role, or omitted from the account entirely. As Bruner (1985, p.26) puts it:

> In the Piagetian model a lone child struggles single-handed to strike some equilibrium between assimilating the world to himself (sic) or himself to the world.

Although there was an alternative tradition developed by Vygotsky, that saw cognitive development as essentially a social and cultural product, it is only in recent years that there has been a revival of interest in it from educators. Psychologists who support this explanation take account of the fact that virtually everything we attend to and everything we do involves other people. More than that, they argue that individual cognitive processes cannot be divorced from the social processes of which they are part. Not surprisingly, then, there are different explanations of how collaboration enhances learning, and this accounts for the processes of socio-cognitive conflict and of social marking, mentioned earlier. One of the most crucial distinctions between these explanations concerns the place of conflict in cognitive development.

Socio-cognitive conflict and collaborative learning

The 'Library' group, as we saw, began working on its problem from a number of different angles as each boy talked about what he thought was needed. Within a matter of minutes, chairs, desks, blackboards, rulers and tables were all suggested as aspects to be considered. As the group discussion moved to and fro, links between individual ideas began to be made and, from this, a better understanding of the challenge facing the group emerged. Piaget stressed that interaction between children could overcome what he termed the 'ego-centrism' of their thinking; by that Piaget meant the tendency of a child to centre his or her attention on just one aspect of the problem, ignoring other equally relevant aspects. Thus, working together, he claimed, helped children by emphasizing to each of those involved that they were ignoring dimensions of the problem. We can begin to see this happening in the 'Library' group. Disagreement between those working together, according to Piaget, could only be resolved by the children 'decentering' their attention, by thinking about alternatives and by reassessing possible solutions. Collaboration, therefore, might be seen as a 'deconstructive' learning process in the sense that it is likely to demand a challenging of existing ideas and a questioning of taken-for-granted assumptions. This process, whereby a learner is confronted with other conflicting views, is called 'socio-cognitive conflict'.

The word 'conflict' tends to conjure up rather negative images but, in this context at least, it is not meant in that way. Here it is seen as a positive force helping to move thinking on in a way that is more difficult for a person working on his or her own. Nor, indeed, does 'socio-cognitive conflict' need to be engineered by a teacher. In the following extract from Meg's account of mathematical learning in the Reception classroom, two children had offered to tidy up a box of empty wooden spindles. This collaboration 'emerged' with increasing challenge and debate. It was rich in learning.

> Some [of the spindles] were cone shaped and others mushroom shaped, made from blue and white plastic. They asked if they could play with them and 'build something'. First, they decided to share them. I thought they may have divided them on a 'one for you, one for me'basis. However, they decided to stack them into 'towers' of four, counting them as they took them from the heap of 48 spools. At first they were satisfied, but because the blue and white spools were different heights, they began trying to even up the appearance of their towers by adding extra spools. Eventually they had six spools in each tower and it was more difficult to tell at a glance how many each had. They watched each other like hawks to make sure neither had more than the other. Eventually, Paul suggested:

	Count them all together–
	1,2,3,4,5,6...7,8,9,10,11...have I counted
	that?...no...11,12,13,14,15...
John	No, you didn't count that one.
Paul	I'll count them again.
	1,2,3,4...15,16.
	I've got one more than you – I'd better count
	them again... I've took one of them in the

middle

John	OK I'll give you two of mine.
Paul	One of each [colour]

They continued counting, checking, giving each other extra spools, arguing, bartering and so on, for nearly twenty minutes. Checking on the transcript, the boys re-counted the spools on more than 25 occasions. They corrected each other if one mis-counted and never showed impatience or boredom.

Having ended a count yet again with un-equal numbers, it was Paul who spotted the problem.

John	1,2,3,4,5...23,24,25.
Paul	How's that?...I know, 'cos we keep forgetting...we're always counting.

They realised that between 'towers' they sometimes forgot the last number and therefore acknowledged that their technique was faulty, even though they were happy with their method of sharing the spools. My help was enlisted in keeping a check on the number of spools already counted as they moved from tower to tower so that they were able to 'count on' more accurately. Considering this entailed counting up to 24 they were remarkably efficient. Eventually they triumphed with each child having the magic total of 24 spools each. Their initial request to 'build something' had long ago been forgotten.

There seems little doubt that working together was very beneficial to the learning of both of these boys. Light (1991), in his discussion of experimental research on collaboration, suggests that pairs of children can do a task significantly better than individuals. Although the capacities of children to work in pairs improves as they grow older, a key factor in all paired work is the nature and extent of differences which give rise to a conflict of ideas. For example, conflict involved in collaborative activity may arise from differences in the understandings, information or viewpoints they bring to the particular task in hand. As Light (1991, p.4) comments: 'provided that the differences ... are not too massive as to defy resolution, this kind of conflict can be intellectually productive'.

Learning, it would seem, can take place through the very process of intellectual conflict. Swan (1992, p.92), for example, claims that: 'Conflict between ideas can lead to progress whether or not either solution is correct; and in many tasks there is in any case no 'correct' solution at all'.

This view of cognitive development emphasizes the role of conflict between individuals rather than internal cognitive conflict within an individual learner. Even so, learning is still seen primarily as a private matter, serviced from time to time by social interaction. In the next section we describe a rather different explanation of how learning takes place during collaboration.

Social marking and collaborative learning: creating 'common knowledge'

Edwards and Mercer (1987) write about 'common knowledge' as the understandings created and shared by people through their interaction. They claim that the basis of understanding and learning is 'inherently social, cultural and communicative' (p.168). Consequently, in their view, learning is essentially collaborative and it develops through people doing things and talking about those things together. In this next extract, Lisa and Paul (both 5-year olds), who have been looking at *The Three Bears* story book, are discussing some of the characters. In this interaction, both children help each other to clarify some of the different meanings and uses of 'big'. They do this by drawing on their wider social and cultural experience.

Lisa	She [Goldilocks] was big 'cos she's a human being – but she was not big beside Daddy Bear – she was big beside the baby (bear). I'm a big girl – the Nursery children are little.
Paul	I'm a big boy – my mammy is bigger than me. I'm a little bit big, but mummy is tall.
Lisa	She's a girl as well but a big one. Tall is big, isn't it? Bigger than me though.

Collaboration of this nature becomes particularly important when the framework necessary for understanding a problem draws on the implicit ground rules or norms of the culture. Sometimes in classrooms, activities may not make sense to 'outsiders' who lack knowledge of the particular meanings and ways of doing things that schools use. Furthermore, these educational ground-rules are usually left implicit. In the next example, Tom and Kevin (both 5-year olds) are tackling a mathematics work book with a page entitled 'Make 6'. The page has a row of five flowers, then a row of four pencils, then three cups and lastly two apples.

Kevin	There isn't room to draw six flowers.
Tom	You don't do six.
Kevin	What then?
Tom	When you count them there has to be six.

Kevin	So just one more.
Tom	Yes – sometimes I do too many and I have to cross them out.

Without Tom's explanation of what the instruction 'Make 6' really meant in this context, Kevin may have continued to have difficulties because he was relying upon the ordinary everyday meaning of 'make'. His drawings of six flowers, six pencils, six cups and six apples may have been interpreted as incompetence at following instructions or ignorance of what constituted 'six'.

Cullingford (1988, p.30) describes how much primary school children value collaboration in circumstances when they need to make sense of the task presented:

> Every child in the survey stressed the importance of working with a friend or a partner so that they could help each other over difficult bits, and explain more clearly than the teacher. For children the partner was a crucial factor in their learning.

Light and Perret-Clermont (1990, p.145) refer to the process involved in this type of learning interaction as 'social marking' by which they mean:

> …the way in which the ease or difficulty of a cognitive task can be affected by the extent to which it can be mapped on to social norms or rules with which the child is familiar.

In effect, from this view the child is an apprentice to his or her culture. There are many different things that he or she needs to learn in order to be able to belong to and contribute to that culture as a full and active member. Those things, however, are not necessarily obvious to an outsider and need to be interpreted and explained by someone on the inside. This learning can only take place, therefore, with the help of another person. Consequently, the process of interaction both builds and provides access to that culture.

Collaboration between children to create 'common knowledge' is both wide-spread and serving many purposes. Jan Mark (1978, pp.35-6) so vividly reminds us of this, when she describes Andrew's induction process into his new school.

> 'Miss Beale said you would show me round to look at the projects' said Andrew.
> 'Why, do you want to copy one?' asked Victor, lifting a strand of hair and exposing one eye. 'You could copy mine, only someone might recognize it. I've done that three times already.'
> 'Whatever for?' said Andrew. 'Don't you get tired of it?'

Victor shook his head and his hair. 'That's only once a year. I did that two times at the junior school and now I'm doing it again' he said. 'I do fish every time. Fish are easy. They're all the same shape.'

'No they're not' said Andrew.

'They are when I do them' said Victor. He spun his book round with one finger to show Andrew the drawings. His fish were not only all the same shape, they were all the same shape as slugs. Underneath each drawing was a printed heading: BRAEM: TENSH: CARP: STIKLBAK: SHARK. It was the only way of telling them apart. The shark and the bream were identical, except that the shark had a row of teeth like tank traps.

'Isn't there a 'c' in stickleback?' said Andrew. Victor looked at his work.

'You're right.' He crossed out both 'k's, substituted 'c's and pushed the book away, the better to study it. 'I got that wrong last year'.

Andrew flipped over a few more pages. There were more slugs: PLACE: COD: SAWFISH: and a stringy thing with a frill round its neck: EEL.

'Don't you have to write anything?' asked Andrew.

'Yes, look. I wrote a bit back here. About every four pages will do,' said Victor. 'Miss Beale, she keeps saying I ought to write more but she's glad when I don't. She's got to read it...'.

From a 'social marking' explanation, learning (in this case, learning both to be a pupil in Miss Beale's class and how to do a project) is fundamentally a social process. Vygotsky, for example, proposed that children develop through and as a result of social interaction. Central to this argument is his concept of the 'zone of proximal development'. By this he meant

> ...the distance between the actual development level as determined by independent problem solving and the level of potential development as determined through problem solving under adult guidance or in collaboration with more able peers. (Vygotsky, 1979, p.86)

If, as he suggests, children do learn new knowledge and skills through social support, then how does it take place? Bruner uses the term 'scaffolding' to describe the type of support for learning envisaged in this perspective. Essentially this allows someone to build up his or her fragile and partial understanding alongside someone else who has greater awareness and knowledge and who takes over large parts of the management of the task. The gradual removal of 'scaffolding' enables the construction of autonomous competence. In other words:

> ... the aiding peer serves the learner as a vicarious form of con-
> sciousness until such time as the learner is able to master his (sic)
> action through his own consciousness and control (Bruner, 1985,
> p.24)

What happens in collaborative learning, according to this explanation, is that meanings are constructed collectively which enables sense to be made of the subtle, culturally grounded definitions of the situation. Although there is a sense of apprenticeship involved in collaborating, it is more than a one-way learning experience, as in the case of peer tutoring where both parties benefit. As Edwards and Mercer (1987, p.3) suggest, the discussion and negotiation constitute much more than a mere passing on of information:

> When two people communicate, there is a real possibility that by
> pooling their experiences they achieve a new level of understand-
> ing beyond that which either had before.

Consequently, although conflict of ideas *may* be involved in collaborative learning, from this perspective it is not essential. Nevertheless, an understanding of the place of conflict in collaboration may help teachers to see how to support children so that more worthwhile learning will take place when they work together.

Understanding conflict in collaboration

Throughout the previous chapters one of the recurrent threads has been the emergence of conflict during collaborative processes. In Chapter 1 we noted, for example, the part that it played in the interactions of the 4- and 5-year olds in Debbie's classroom; whilst in this chapter we discussed how collaboration involving conflict of ideas might contribute to learning itself. The word 'conflict', however, tends to be more emotive than many of the others that we might use to discuss how people work and learn together. Although few people seem to write about conflict in schools it is, nevertheless, part of the experience of schooling for many children and teachers – even when it seems that everyone is trying to achieve similar goals.

The most obvious forms of conflict are those that we witness when individuals or groups express their differences. However, it is worth remembering that conflict may also be an individual, internal experience as well as a social, external experience. Indeed, often the two are linked. This may be particularly so when children are unsure of what to do in a specific situation where there is no clear-cut course of action. It is not just a matter of their being in conflict with each other, for individual children may also experience inner conflict about how to handle what confronts them. Confusion, no matter what its source, can be difficult to handle and may also create anxiety. It is not surprising, then, that there are times when children vent their anxieties on others in order to maintain personal equilibrium. In effect, inner, personal conflict becomes transformed into and magnifies external, interpersonal conflict. Often it is at that point that misunderstandings and miscommunications assume greater importance than usual. This is more than intellectual conflict: it is a conflict that is both expressive and charged with emotion. In the same way, a conflict of ideas between people can easily become an inner, emotional conflict for the individuals involved. This may be why open-ended and problem-solving activities sometimes break down in classrooms. Children may negotiate, through their responses, for a clearer, more closed specification of what to do, and teachers, feeling anxious and stressed, may comply even though by doing so they alter the nature of the learning experience.

Pondy (1972) makes a distinction between what he calls 'perceived conflict' and 'felt conflict', the latter having, in effect, a greater involvement of the person's sense of self. For Pondy this is important as it accounts for 'the personalization of conflict' (p.362) with its negative connotations and personal and social costs. One explanation for this, he suggests is the closeness often associated with commitment and which, for example, is found in the 'intimate relations that characterise total institutions' (p.363). Pondy's observations serve as a useful reminder that Nias *et al.'s* (1989) 'culture of collaboration' implies not just the potential for conflict but, possibly, an emotive form of it. Perhaps this also serves to emphasize a paradox of collaboration: involvement in and emotional commitment to the activity may bring with it intensive personal conflict. Part of an individual's response to collaborative experiences, then, are very personal in the sense that they are to do with how that person perceives the impact of involvement on his or her concept of self and with his or her capacity to cope with that.

At the same time, a person's response to collaborative experiences will be influenced by contextual features such as how power is considered to be allocated and the nature and extent of any control. For example, if power is perceived to be distributed unequally, or misused, the likelihood of this emerging in some form of conflict behaviour seems high. Jackson and Devlin (1992, p.19) describe the performance of a group of Year 6 children during a diamond-ranking activity based on the topic 'Our Town':

> Natasha's contributions were overpowering and the emphasis was often strong with commands...
>
> N. Give uz it here.
> N. Shops ARE second...
> N. PUT the Hospital first.
> N. Wait...(She lists the rank order)
> N. Oh. Shut up!...
> N. I know BUT...!
>
> Natasha discouraged the others and when they made suggestions, especially Karen, they were continually ignored and interrupted...

Apart from anything else, the group didn't complete the activity and failed to reach any rank order.

Yet again, we are reminded that learning through collaboration is complex and it can certainly present primary teachers with a conundrum. Although teacher-imposed formal collaboration may be, to some extent, an organizational necessity in today's classrooms, this may not, of itself, engender learning in the ways that teachers might desire. For example, tightly organized and controlled forms of interaction which offer limited opportunities for participants to define and shape the activity and how it is handled, tend to reproduce '... the asymmetrical relationship... (and define) ... the nature of interaction between peers in a particular way' (Swan, 1992, p.86).

A similar point is made by Hayes who, in reporting a study of collaborative problem solving by pupils, commented:

> Once the hierarchy (or dominance) is established, there is set in position an unwritten, yet sophisticated procedure for interaction. Despite the growth of mutual tolerance and striving towards a solution which became increasingly apparent, the performance of an individual was constrained by this social ordering.(Hayes, 1991, p.26).

Indeed an asymmetry of power may prevent learning because of its tendency to evoke attitudes of dominance and compliance, especially in relation to any conflict of ideas. Light and Glachan (1985, p.227), reflecting upon the lack of progress by children expected to collaborate, describe how:

> disagreements generally resulted in attempts by one or both of the children to defend or assert their 'status'. In such cases children would raise their voices, claim simply to *know* what was right or just attempt to press ahead despite their partner's protests. In the longer term either the partner established dominance over the other or rules such as turn-taking were invoked by the children to defuse the situation.

Problems of power were noted in the example of Natasha's group, as well as in Brian's detachment in response to Gillian's dominance in one of our case studies in Chapter 2. It is comparable with one of the pathological courses, identified by Deutsch (1987), that conflict may take. He refers to is as 'rigidification' and sees it as characterized by participants starting '... to have a kind of tunnel vision with regard to the issues in conflict' (p.40). Without strategies to challenge dominance, disruption or withdrawal may be the only alternatives left to cope with the pain.

Collaboration would seem to support learning best if it makes thinking explicit. Having to put ideas into words when talking, rather like writing, can enable reflection on one's mental processes. Unlike writing, however, talking to oneself tends to be regarded as a rather peculiar habit. Working with others provides a ready-made audience and, potentially, introduces the need to articulate ideas and explain one's thinking. Even so, whether this will happen or not may depend upon another condition – participants' perceptions of the distribution of power and its use within the collaboration.

In the context of adults, anyone seeking to establish and maintain control of the outcome by visibly (or invisibly) pre-empting group decisions would be regarded as using 'power politics'. This suggests that collaborating with others is less about the surface features of agendas and the chairing of discussions and more about participants knowing how to handle two types of conflict;

1 *intellectual conflict* between people in the sense that participants need to develop strategies of asking questions and analysing possi-

bilities rather tha using tactics of assertion and counter-assertion; and

2 *emotional conflict* experienced by people in the sense that participants need to develop the type of strategies often associated with counselling, such as acknowledgement, according personal respect and providing active listening, rather than engaging in tactics that block and reject other participants.

This sort of understanding about conflict during collaboration helps to explain the significance of the seven helping strategies identified by Burden *et al.* (1988). In their study of collaborative group work with pupils of primary school age, more successful groups used the strategies shown in Figure 9.2. Of these, 'challenging', 'suggesting alternatives' and 'explaining' might be considered to be crucial to collaboration involving conflict of ideas, whilst by 'supporting' and 'commenting', children may help one another to cope with emotional conflict.

These helping strategies, although derived from a study of primary children, may also be useful when thinking about how teachers might collaborate in classrooms. Alexander *et al.* (1989), in their evaluation of the Leeds Primary Needs Project, reported considerable difficulties with classroom collaboration between teachers. They used the term 'Teachers Teaching Together' (abbreviated to TTT) to refer to the varied nature of the collaborative practices that they found.

> Those professional development collaborations which are seen by the participants to operate with most success have some or all of the following four characteristics. First there is a clear recognition of the professional development function and an accompanying status differential...there is evidence of problems in an advisory collaboration between staff who are supposed to be of equal status. Second, the consultant teacher has the acknowledged backing of the headteacher's authority.... Third the consultant teacher needs to have negotiating skill, tact and sensitivity.... Fourth, the client teacher has to be amenable and to accept TTT as a strategy for her own professional development ...(p.231).

Our own work suggests that it may be possible, in some circumstances, for collaborative relationships between teachers to be different from that which is implied here. The Leeds study seems to emphasize the use of power differentials, so that an amenable or compliant teacher learns from a tactful consultant of higher status, who has the backing of the headteacher. Harland (1990) has provided a useful

Figure 9.2 Helping strategies used by successful groups
(Burden *et al.*, 1988, p.53)

HELPING STRATEGY	EXAMPLES FROM CLASSROOM TRANSCRIPTS
Organising	'Only one more thing' 'Now it's my go' 'You go first. Then I'm next'
Supporting	'I bet she tried hard' 'Go on, try' 'Yes, that's right'
Challenging	'I think that should be up there' 'No, wrong size, don't put it on there' 'No, you've done it the wrong way'
Suggesting alternatives	'What about these?' 'Why don't you do the back piece?' 'Why don't you put the big thin one there?'
Explaining	'Cos look, the thick one at the front and the thin one at the back' 'That goes in there because it's little' 'It's part of large and part of blue you see'
Commenting	'We've done it the wrong way' 'Looks like we're doing it that way again' 'It's double' (referring to a logic block with all three attributes)
Finishing	'Have we finished?' 'We've done it' 'I think we've built it'

typology of strategies that have been used by advisory teachers when working with other teachers: giving, telling, demonstrating and enquiring. He referred to some constraints which caused shifts of modes. These constraints included lack of time, unclear expectations, misrepresentations of the advisory teachers function, and the dominance of headteachers' priorities. Harland found that enquiry was the least used and highest risk strategy which, when it works, can be an inspiring and productive experience for all; when it fails, it can precipitate an aggressive response which leaves the advisory teacher little option but to withdraw from the input altogether (p.47) .

Somekh (1991) has also recognized that contextual and personal factors make enquiry difficult, but she goes on to offer practical advice about how pairs of teachers might establish collaborative action research,

grounded in the expectation that there will be free and open discussion of problematic issues between professionals ... [emphasizing]... equal rights for all participants in a non-judgemental, problem-solving environment (p.80).

Elsewhere, Easen (1991) has also compared different arrangements for allocating control when teachers work together in classrooms. There is a high degree of risk involved in teachers trying to achieve collaborative control, as in our second case study in Chapter 1, but he also argues that where it is achieved, the potential for teachers' learning is high. Relative judgements about the worthwhileness of such learning will depend upon whether the teachers are aiming for an 'implementation' or a ' development partnership' (Biott, 1992). The former is appropriate when one partner has to learn what the other already knows, whilst the latter can lead to both partners gaining new insights into their own work as well as new ways of looking at the job in hand.

This brings us to consider the place of diversity and common ground between partners. In Chapter 3 we referred to the idea that a school staff which is socially cohesive and professionally diverse can offer a fertile training context for student teachers. Campbell (1992) has also concluded that 'difference may be as important to the process of collaboration as similarity' (p.61). She reviewed the relationship between herself, as deputy headteacher, and the headteacher of her primary school during a year of school development, and described how their partnership was characterized by both similarity and difference. She suggests that having common beliefs and agreeing about how to translate them into action are necessary for effective collaboration, but that difference can be challenging. In their case, it led to their being adventurous enough to try new things and to take risks. She quotes from the headteacher's reflection that 'we could argue and talk things out...and you were going to make me justify what I was doing rather than just accepting it' (p.60). They learned collaboratively from a mixture of accord and challenge.

Learning from difference and diversity

So far, in this chapter, we have tended to concentrate on the cognitive effects of interaction between children or between teachers. There are, however, wider dimensions of learning of concern to most of us. For example, why do some people dislike other people? This is an important question whether we think about it in terms of playground disputes, the 'micro-politics' of some staffrooms or, indeed, the conflagrations that have given us, according to some estimates, 4,600,000 children in Europe who are living temporarily outside their home countries because of lack of tolerance of cultural diversity. The obvious answer, we might think, is that we dislike those who have caused or might cause us harm. Perhaps surprisingly, there is some evidence to suggest that there may be rather different explanations. Humphrey (1987), for example, claims that we dislike others not because of anything they have done to us but because of what we have done to them. In other words, hostility and hatred grow out of our own rationalizing rather than out of the actions of others; we develop our hostile attitudes as a result of – and in order to explain – our own behaviour. The extent to which self-justification is as conscious as he implies must be open to question, but, for what ever reason, there does appear to be a tendency for people to gravitate towards the people they *think* they will like and away from those that they *think* they will dislike. This means that rather than react directly to people themselves, we begin to react to our stereotyped thinking about them.

If all this sounds depressing, there is a positive side to explanations of this nature. Just as cycles of hostility can be created, so, too, can cycles of friendship through the use of interaction to break down stereotypical thinking. Much research has been conducted since the 1950s into the 'contact hypothesis' (see, for example, Pettigrew, 1986) which, briefly, states that bringing people into contact with each other is one of the best ways of reducing tension and hostility. Naturally, it is not as simple as that and, therefore, will not necessarily happen by chance. It seems important, for example, that the contact is prolonged so that interaction between people is sustained and that those involved have to see it as purposeful and successful. In short, if the collaboration is meaningful then there is potential for mutual understanding.

Although few people have heard of it, for over 40 years the organization 'Children's International Summer Villages' (CISV) has been working with the principles described in the previous paragraph. An independent, non-political volunteer organisation, CISV operates with the simple maxim that 'If I have a friend in another country I won't want to go to war with them'. People are involved in various activities at different ages, but central to its work are the 'villages' held for 11-year olds. A village usually contains 60 to 70 people representing between 10 and 12 countries. Each country sends a delegation of five people: two boys, two girls and an adult leader. Also present are six 'Junior Counsellors' (16-year olds) and a small 'camp staff' (adults) who help to organize and run the village. The children live together for a month in a very relaxed atmosphere, away from the public eye except on a few special days. Together they plan and do activities, tell each other about what life is like in their own country, swap gifts and generally learn to live with different cultures. Simple strategies are used to considerable effect. For example, on arrival each person chooses, but does not disclose, a name of another 'villager' out of a hat. The person named, without knowing it, then has to be treated to small acts of kindness by their 'secret friend' throughout the period of the village. The 'secret friend', whilst being kind to that person, comes to value him or her. Few who have been involved in the month-long experience of a CISV 'village' have not been profoundly touched by what they have learned during this time. For many it is one of the defining events of their lives.

Conclusion

When the two terms, 'collaboration' and 'learning' are linked together, as in the term 'collaborative learning', it seems to express a general optimism that the interaction will be fruitful whilst glossing over difficulties that are often to be found in practice. We think that one of the reasons for these difficulties is because the place of conflict is often misunderstood. In this chapter we have sought to show, through discussion of different explanations of learning, that conflict needs to be recognized as a positive and integral component of collaborative relationships. We have also indicated some of the strategies that have made this possible. At the same time, conflict can also become a negative factor if it is not successfully managed and, as a consequence, the possibilities for learning can be more limited.

Chapter 10

Understanding and Promoting Collaborative Learning

In this book we have tried to convey a breadth and depth of collaborative experiences and, in doing so, we have attempted to account for different ways in which collaborative learning has been defined and conceptualized. One of the points that we have emphasized is the complexity of working and learning together; another is the need to avoid narrow and restricting definitions. As we commented in the Introduction, we believe that there can be no blueprint for collaborative learning. Instead, we suggest that it can best be understood through particular instances and that this may be done through considering a number of its main dimensions.

In discussing these dimensions, we want to stress that collaborative learning is essentially about the development of the self in a social context. This implies that collaborative learning has both personal and contextual features which are closely interwoven.

Personal features of collaboration

Through working and learning together, both children and teachers develop a sense of who they are and what they can or cannot do. They learn about their own and each others' strengths and weaknesses as these are revealed in particular circumstances and contexts. For this reason, acts of collaboration may be perceived as involving various degrees of anxiety and risk for those involved. In particular, two key personal features of collaboration are:

- *Perceptions of the goals of the specific collaborative activity*. These may be concerned either with *performance* or with *learning* itself. The former stresses the need to establish evidence of adequacy, whilst the latter stresses the opportunity to wrestle with and understand something new.
- *Perceptions of the nature of the specific collaborative activity*. This may be seen as either *challenging* or *easy*. The former promises something difficult that may only be accomplished with effort and learning, whilst the latter promises something that may be tackled simply by drawing on existing knowledge and skills.

A growing body of research on 'helplessness', which seeks to explain differing feelings (or 'affect') and behaviours of learners in response to school tasks, seems to support our analysis that these are important personal features of collaborative learning. For example, Sylva and Wiltshire (1993), in their review of research on children's responses to different goals and tasks, comment that,

> ...Children who were encouraged towards performance orientation showed the same 'helpless' attributions, negative affect and strategy deterioration that characterised the helpless children in the original studies. (p.33)

'Helpless' children, like Phillip and David in the second case study in Chapter 1, tend to avoid challenge or give up easily.

The meaning of the collaborative activity for those involved, then, is crucial. We have seen in the case studies how important it has been for participants in a collaborative activity to retain a feeling of control of what was happening to them. Activities perceived as having 'performance goals' and as being 'challenging', therefore, may be seen as presenting a high degree of risk to the self. The same activities, of course, may be perceived quite differently by another participant. The differing responses of Jo Ann and the Key Stage 1 teacher (Chapter 7) at the start of their 'learning partnership' is a good illustration of this.

Contextual features of collaboration

As we noted in Chapter 1, children and teachers spend their working days in contexts with a number of features. Particular collaborative activities will involve various aspects of the context and may present various characteristics to which a person may respond. The two dimensions that we see as very influential on contextual aspects of collaboration are:

- *The structure through which the collaboration is constructed.* The main characteristic of concern with structure, for our purposes, has been the source of its initiation – in other words, whether it is related to the official, formal definitions of events and activities or to the actual events and activities that happen, including the definitions of those involved. In this book we have referred to two types of structure – the 'imposed' and the 'emergent'.
- *The cultural response to the collaborative activity.* The term 'culture' tends to be used to refer to the implicit and often invisible ways that members of a community shape their activities through the shared norms, values and traditions. It embodies the underlying deep structures of meaning, belief, assumptions and expectations on which interactions depend and which provide members of the culture with a shared way of making sense of their world. In particular, we are interested in the way that culture provides a shared set of beliefs about the subject matter for collaboration and of commitment to its worthwhileness.

Not only is it possible to be highly collaborative and highly autonomous, such qualities together are arguably the essence of being contributive members of social worlds. Collaboration, we would argue, is concerned with developing a contextual understanding of one's own experiences. Increased interaction with others, more than anything else, is how this learning develops.

If 'meaning' is socially constructed through interaction, then the process will inevitably be influenced by 'power' which is socially realized. A useful explanatory concept for this process is that of 'hegemony'. This concept was developed by Gramsci to explain social control. He asserted that control was achieved, not through direct coercion, but through more subtle processes which reach into and structure the experiences of others. Hegemony is not a fixed condition but a process which is constantly being enacted. The importance of the concept is the way it helps us to analyse how certain beliefs and assumptions become a taken-for-granted part of people's lives: 'These systems, sedimented over time, form the deep structure of our interpretation of reality which Gramsci has called 'common sense' (Grundy, 1989, p.90).

The key to hegemony is how power in relationships enables interactions to be moulded to support certain ways of doing things and thinking about things. It can serve to cement social organization in classrooms and schools by establishing common ways of seing things. This gives rise to what Gollop (1992), writing from a feminist perspective, refers to as the 'clipped wing syndrome'. Derived from de Beauvoir's statement 'Her wings are clipped and it is found deplorable she cannot fly', this syndrome is a more powerful image for what others, for example, Diener and Dweek, 1978, have termed 'learned helplessness'. Thus,...the wing-clipping process disempowers slowly, but not necessarily painfully' (Gollop, 1992, p.136).

The concepts of 'power' and 'meaning', then, are inseparable in collaborative learning. There are times when having the strategies and skills to create new meanings through collaboration are insufficient without the strategies and skills to handle any power issues that may arise during it. Hence our emphasis on trying to understand the place of conflict in collaborative relationships.

In summary, then, we have listed a number of guiding principles which have been identified and explored in previous chapters. They seem to fall into two main ways in which a teacher may use the messages embodied in this book. These are concerned with: creating favourable conditions for collaborative learning; and teaching, encouraging and fostering skills for collaborative learning.

Creating favourable conditions for collaborative learning

It is important that teachers create conditions for children to belong and contribute in classrooms, both for their own benefit and so that they learn how to support one anothers' learning. We argued, in Chapter 1, that the social organization of classrooms influences children's opportunities to learn informally from one another at various times during the day, and, in Chapter 3, we outlined students' views of staffrooms as informal learning contexts for themselves. We went on to show how arrangements for students' school placements tend to emphasize individual support from designated teachers and neglect to take account of the whole school as a learning environment. Yet, what students learned from watching, listening and taking part in school life far outweighed, and sometimes contradicted, what they were told or what was written in official documents. Like children, teachers have also learned informally and incidentally from each other in unplanned ways.

It follows, then, that there is more to improving collaborative learning than organizing children into groups and setting certain tasks. In addition, it is necessary to create favourable classroom conditions, so that children value working together and have opportunities to give and experience help, support and challenge in their relationships with each other. We have tried to show, throughout this book, that enabling conditions are often shaped by a number of key, guiding principles. Teachers who create these conditions:

- Offer opportunities for children to learn social competences in situations where they can make, and act upon, shared understandings of how to be both cooperative with others and assertive for themselves. The children learn how to show concern for others as well as how to argue their case and stop others interfering without having to hit them. The teachers convey, to the children, that collaboration may be unstable and unpredictable, that it is not based simply upon obedience and compliance and that conflict and disagreements can be constructive. The children learn that working with others can be both enabling and constraining.
- Provide a wide range of paired and group activities and also encourage children to consider working with a partner on some occasions when they are completing the same individual tasks, so that they can compare and talk about what they are doing.
- Expect that all children will be able to contribute, in different ways, to the quality of activities, and they do not stress leadership in ways which give status to superior knowledge or bossiness.
- Spend time listening to children when they are working collaboratively and give children time both to find ways to work together and to develop ideas. They are not be tempted to react instantly every time problems arise, because it is educative for children to overcome their own difficulties in collaborating and in handling ideas on some occasions.
- Model a collaborative approach in their interactions with children. They listen and discuss disagreements, interpret some conflicts and difficulties in children's relationships in positive ways, and do not expect everyone to be able to get everything right first time. They spend some time wondering about things with children, seeking alternatives and showing themselves to be uncertain, rather than always being concerned about knowing answers and being correct.
- Organize space, time and resources to allow some flexibility for some parts of each day. They provide a variety of possibilities for different kinds of purposeful activities in specific parts of the room, such as writing areas with all the equipment needed for individual and joint work; a listening area in which children could listen to

tapes alone or with others and where they could hear each other read aloud; and a comfortable, quiet corner.

- Do not rely solely on impressions of surface behaviour and snatches of overheard conversations when judging whether, or how well, children are learning collaboratively.
- Work, through systematic enquiry, towards understanding the most favourable ways to group children, when setting formal group assignments, taking into account sex, gender, racial and ability differences. They study the effects of different kinds of activities, such as practical or abstract tasks, on conversations and patterns of collaboration. They experiment to find helpful ways to prepare their children for collaboration; they think about different ways to start a group activity and how to participate once a group has started its work. Most importantly, they review how their approach affects children's sense of control over what they are doing and how leaning ensues. They do not simply rely on habitual custom or fashionable slogans.

Teaching, encouraging and fostering skills of collaborative learning.

How children learn to work together, and what they learn about doing it, can be haphazard, fragmented, inconsistent, ambiguous and sometimes contradictory. We have found that little help is given to children who seem to lack the necessary skills or are poorly disposed towards working collaboratively, unless their problems of participating in school life are so dramatic that they are disruptive or play truant. All children benefit from being taught to collaborate. Children's capacity to work well with other children may not necessarily match their attainment in other fields. We have seen evidence of poor collaborative skills and strategies from children who are adept at private, individual work, and been surprised by the exceptional capabilities of some who have been much less accomplished in written work.

As well as creating favourable conditions for children to learn collaboratively, helpful teachers also:

- Make their expectations about working together clear to the children and teach them how to collaborate.
- Give consistent feedback which embraces emergent as well as imposed collaboration. Feedback of this nature is concrete and focused, seeking also to explore children's perceptions of what is going on, rather than being judgemental. This helps children to understand processes of collaborative work so that they are not put off by challenge and disagreements and learn to develop strategies and skills to handle conflict constructively. Feedback, then, helps to maintain and enhance the collective as well as individual self-esteem of children.

- Take action if they notice that a child is vulnerable to domination or rejection by other children, intervening in a way which has positive effects upon the child's social identity and enhances future relationships.
- Encourage children to make contributions to collaborative activities by showing them how to listen, question and respond. They teach helping skills and techniques such as peer tutoring, including how to record what their partners like to do and how they learn best. They model, through their own actions, and teach, that some questions will be more helpful than others when children are responding to other children's ideas.

Although it would be inappropriate to list a set of principles which may guide the approaches of school management teams to promoting collaboration between teachers, many of the ideas embodied above may have as much relevance to the staffroom as they do to the classroom. Collaboration is multi-layered and pervasive, and learning may be carried over from one area of a teacher's professional life to another.

Throughout this book we have sought to expand the meaning of collaborative learning beyond formal group-work in classrooms and organized teamwork in staffrooms. We have tried to do this through examining a rich variety of actual experiences of working together. We hope that these accounts from classrooms and staffrooms may help to reduce the doubts, indifference or even inertia which may limit the use of collaborative learning. Perhaps the book may also help to overcome the tendency for collaboration to be used as a means of control rather than as a support for learning.

References

Alexander, R., Willcocks, J. and Kinder, K. (1989) *Changing Primary Practice*, London: Falmer Press.

Alexander, R., Rose, J. and Woodhead, C. (1992) *Curriculum Organisation and Classroom Practice in Primary Schools: A discussion paper*, London: DES.

Acker, S. (1991) 'Teacher relationships and educational reform in England and Wales', *The Curriculum Journal*, 2, 3, 301–16.

Alcott, LM (1977 edition) *Little Women*, London: Hamlyn.

Ball, S. J. and Bone, R. (1991) 'Subject to change? Subject departments and the implementation of National Curriculum policy: An overview of the issues', unpublished paper, King's College London.

Barrow, R. (1984) 'Problems in research into groupwork', *Durham and Newcastle Research Review*, X, 52, 122–25.

Biott, C. (1992) 'Imposed support for teachers' learning: Implementation or development partnerships', in Biott, C. and Nias, J. (eds) *Working and Learning Together for Change*, Buckingham: Open University Press.

Bolam, R. (1982) 'Inset for professional development and school improvement', *British Journal of Inservice Education*, 9, 1, 14–17.

Borba, M. and Borba, C. (1982) *Self Esteem: A classroom affair*, San Fransisco, CA: Harper and Row.

Bossert, S. (1987) 'Classroom task organisation and children's friendships', in Pollard, A. (ed.) *Children and their Primary Schools*, London: Falmer Press.

Bruner, J.S. (1985) 'Vygotsky: a historical and conceptual perspective', in Wertsch, J.v. (ed.) *Culture, Communication and Cognition: Vygotskian perspectives*, Cambridge: Cambridge University Press.

Burden, M, Emsley, M.and Constable , H. (1988) 'Encouraging progress in collaborative group-work', *Education 3-13*, 16, 1, pp.51-6.

Campbell, C. (1992)' Reflections on a head and deputy partnership', in Biott, C. and Nias, J. (eds) *Working and Learning Together for Change*, Buckingham: Open University Press.

Canfield, J. and Wells, H. (1976) *100 Ways to Enhance Self Concept in the Classroom*, New Jersey: Prentice Hall.

Cowie, H. and Rudduck, J. (1988) *Co-operative Groupwork - an overview*, London: BP Educational Service.

Cullingford, C. (1988)'Children's views about working together', *Education 3-13*, March, 29-34.

Cyert, R. M. and March, J. G. (1963) *The Behavioural Theory of the Firm*, New Jersey: Prentice Hall.

Daly, M. (1993) *Outercourse: The bedazzling voyage*, London: Women's Press.

Davies, B. (1982) *Life in Classroom and Playground*, London: Routledge and Kegan Paul.

Deutsch, M. (1987) 'A theoretical perspective on conflict and conflict resolution', in Sandole, D. and Sandole-Staroste, I. (eds) *Conflict Management and Problem solving: Interpersonal to International Application*, London: Francis Pinter, pp.38-49.

Diener, C. and Dweck, C. (1978) 'An analysis of learned helplessness: continuous change and performance, strategy and achievement cognition following failure', *Journal of Personality and Social Psychology*, 36, 5.

Dowrick, N. (1993) 'Side by side: A more appropriate form of deep interaction for infant pupils', *British Education Research Journal*, 19, 5, 499-515.

Drummond, M. J. (1993) *Assessing Children's Learning*, London: David Fulton Publishers.

Du Bois, B. (1983) 'Passionate scholarship : notes on values, knowing and method in feminist social science', in Bowles, G. and Klein, R. D. *Theories of Women's Studies*, London: Routledge and Kegan Paul.

Easen, P. (1991) 'The visible supporter with no invisible means of support', in Biott C. (ed.) *Semi-Detached Teachers: Building Advisory and Support Relationships in Classrooms*, London: Falmer Press.

Edwards, D. and Mercer, N. (1987) *Common Knowledge*, London: Methuen.

Elliot, J. (1991) *Action Research for Educational Change*, Buckingham: Open University Press.

Fitz-Gibbon, C.T. (1988) 'Peer tutoring as a teaching strategy', *Educational Management and Administration*, 16, 217–229.

Fullan, M. (1988) *What's Worth Fighting for in the Principalship?*, Toronto: Ontario Public School Teachers' Federation.

Galton, M. (1981) 'Teaching groups in the junior school: a neglected art?', *School Organisation*, 1, 2, 175–181.

Galton, M. and Patrick, H. (eds) (1990) *Curriculum Provision in Small Primary Schools*, London: Routledge.

Galton, M. and Williamson, J. (1992) *Groupwork in the Primary Classroom*, London: Routledge.

Galton, M., Simon, B. and Croll, P. (1980) *Inside the Primary Classroom*, London: Routledge and Kegan Paul.

Gollop, S. (1992) 'Emancipating Rita: the limits of change', in Biott, C. and Nias, J. (eds) *op. cit.*

Grundy, S. (1989) 'Beyond professionalism', in Carr, W. (ed.) *Quality in Teaching: Arguments for a Reflective Profession*, London: Falmer Press.

Hall, V. and Oldroyd, D. (1992) 'Development activities for managers of collaboration', University of Bristol, NDCEMP (quoted in Hall and Wallace (1993).

Hall, V. and Wallace, M. (1993) 'Collaboration as subversive activity : a professional response to externally imposed competition between schools', *School Organisation*, 13, 2, 101-117.

Harland, J. (1990) *The Work and Impact of Advisory Teachers*, Slough: NFER.

Hargreaves, A. (1991) 'Curriculum reform and the teacher', *The Curriculum Journal*, 2, 3, 249–58.

Hargreaves. D. and Hopkins, D. (1991) *The Empowered School: The management and practice of development planning*, London: Cassell Educational.

Hart, S. (1989) 'Collaborative Learning, Group Work and the Spaces in Between', Thames Polytechnic, mimeo.

Hart, S. (1992) 'Collaborative classrooms', in Booth T (ed.) *Curricula for Diversity in Education*, London: Routledge.

Hayes, D. (1991) 'Collaborative problem solving: Issues of social interaction and assessment', *Education 3-13*, March, 23–8.

HMI (1991) *Management of Educational Resources: 5 The role of school development plans in managing school effectiveness*, Edinburgh: Scottish Office Education Department.

HMSO (1983) *Middle Schools: An illustrative survey*, London: HMSO.

HMSO (1991) *School-based Teacher Education in England and Wales: A Report by H.M. Inspectorate*, London: HMSO.

Hopkins, D. (1991) 'Changing school culture through development planning', in Riddell, S. and Brown, S. (eds) *School Effectiveness Research: Its messages for school improvement*, Edinburgh: The Scottish Office Education Department, HMSO pp. 249–80.

Hornby, N. (1992) *Fever Pitch*, London: Victor Gollancz.

Humphrey, N. (1987) 'The best of enemies', *The Guardian*, 29 July.

Jackson, M. and Devlin, D (1992) 'Diamond ranking in co-operative groups: children supporting each other's learning', in Gulson, J. (ed.) *Action Research in South Tyneside LEA: Humanities in the primary school*, South Tyneside LEA in collaboration with the University of Northumbria, Newcastle.

Lather, P. (1986) 'Issues of validity in openly ideological research: between a rock and a soft place', *Interchange*, 17 4 63–84.

Leithwood, K. and Jantzi, D. (1990) 'Transformational leadership: how principals can help reform school cultures', *School Effectiveness and School Improvement* 1, 4, 249–280.

Light, P. (1991) 'New understanding through collaboration', *Open University Course E817, Curriculum, learning and assessment*, Milton Keynes: Open University.

Light, P. and Glachan, M. (1985) 'Facilitation of individual problem solving through peer interaction', *Educational Psychology*, 5, 217–26.

Light, P. and Perret-Clermont, A. (1990) 'Social context effects in learning and testing', in Light, P., Sheldon, S. and Woodhead, M. (eds.) *Learning to think*, London: Routledge/Open University.

Little, J. W. (1982), 'Norms of collegiality and experimentation: workplace conditions for school success', *American Educational Research Journal*, 19, 3, 325-40.

Louden, W. (1991) 'Collegiality, curriculum and education change', *The Curriculum Journal*, 2, 3, 361–73.

McLaughlin, M. W. and Yee, S. M. (1988) 'School as a place to have a career', in Lieberman, A. (ed.) *Building a Professional Culture in Schools*, New York: Teachers College Press.

McNeil, L. (1988) 'Contradictions of control, part one: Administrators and teachers', *Phi Delta Kappa*, January, 333–9.

Mark, J. (1978) *Thunder and Lightnings*, Harmondsworth: Puffin.

Mortimer, P. *et al.* (1988) *School Matters*, London: Open Books.

NCC (1990) *Education for Citizenship*, Curriculum Guidance No 8, York: National Curriculum Council.

Newcastle upon Tyne LEA (1991) Activity 31A (92): Raising standards in Inner-city schools, Mimeograph.

Nias, J., (1989) *Primary Teachers Talking: A study of teaching as work*, London: Routledge.

Nias, J. (1992) 'Introduction', in Biott, C. and Nias, J. (eds) *Working and Learning Together for Change*, Buckingham: Open University Press.

Nias J., Southworth, G.W. and Yeomans, R. (1989) *Staff Relationships in the Primary School: A study of organisational cultures*, London: Cassell.

Nias, J., Southworth, G., Campbell, P. (1992) *Whole School Curriculum Development in the Primary School*, London: Falmer Press.

Ollerenshaw, C. and Ritchie, R. (1993) *Primary Science, Making it Work* , London: David Fulton Publishers.

Open University (1980) *Mathematics Across the Curriculum. Unit 5, Getting Started, Unit 6, Making Plans, Unit 7, Finding Answers, Unit 8, Finishing Off*, Milton Keynes: Open University.

Opie, I. and Opie, P. (1959) *The Lore and Language of School Children*, Oxford: Oxford University Press.

Osborn, M. and Broadfoot, P. (1991) 'The impact of current changes in English primary schools on teacher professionalism', paper presented at the annual meeting of the American Educational Research Association in Chicago, Ill., April.

Pettigrew, T. (1986) 'The intergroup contact hypothesis reconsidered', in Hewstone, M. and Brown, R. (eds) *Contact and Conflict in Intergroup Encounters*, Oxford: Basil Blackwell.

Pollard, A. (1985) *The Social World of the Primary School*, London: Holt, Rinehart and Winston

Pondy, L.R. (1972) 'Organisational conflict: Concepts and models', in Thomas, J.M. and Bennis, W. (eds.) *Management of Change and Conflict*, Harmondsworth: Penguin, pp.359–80.

Prisk, T. (1987) 'Letting them get on with it: a study of unsupervised group talk in an infants school', in Pollard, A. (ed.) *Children and their Primary Schools*, London: Falmer Press.

Richards, C. (1987) 'Primary education in England', in Delamont, S. (ed.) *The Primary School Teacher*, London: Falmer Press.

Rowland, S. (1984) *The Enquiring Classroom*, London: Falmer Press.

Rubin, Z. (1980) *Children's Friendship*, London: Fontana.

Salaman, G. (1980) 'Classification of organisations and organisation structure: the main elelments and interrelationships', in Salaman, G. and Thompson, K. (eds) *Control and Ideologies in Organisations*, Buckingham: Open University Press.

Sluckin, A. (1981) *Growing up in the Playground*, London: Routledge and Kegan Paul.

Smith, D. (1990) *Delia Smith's Christmas*, London: BBC Books.

Somekh, B. (1991) 'Collaborative action research: working together towards professional development', in Biott C. (ed.) *Semi-Detached Teachers*, London: Falmer Press.

Swan, W. (1992) *Classroom Diversity*, Milton Keynes: Open University.

Sylva, K. and Wiltshire, J. (1993) 'The impact of early learning on children's later development: A review prepared for the RSA inquiry "Start Right"', *European Early Childhood Education Research Journal*, 1, 1.

Tickle, L. (1989) 'On probation: Preparation for professionalism', *Cambridge Journal of Education*, 21, 3, 291–29.

Tickle, L. (1991) 'New teachers and the emotions of learning teaching', *Cambridge Journal of Education*, 21, 3, 319–29.

Tizard, B. *et al.* (1988) *Young Children at School in the Inner City*, London: Lawrence Erlbaum Associates.

Tomlinson, T. (1981) 'The troubled years: an interpretive analysis of public schooling since 1950', *Phi Delta Kappa*, 62, 373-76.

Topping, K. (1985) 'An introduction to paired reading', in Topping, K. and Wolfendale, S. (eds) *Parental Involvement in Children's Reading'*, Beckenham: Croom Helm.

USMES (1973) *The USMES Guide*, Massachusetts: The Education Development Center.

Vygotsky, L.S. (1978) *Mind in Society: The Development of higher psychological processes*, Cambridge MA: Harvard University Press.

Woods, P. (1983) *Sociology and the School*, London: Routledge and Kegan Paul.

Wooldridge, I. and Yeomans, R. (1992) 'School-based initial teacher education in primary schools: Modelling, induction, acculturation or education', paper presented at the British Educational Research Association Annual Conference, Stirling University.

Yeomans, A. (1983) 'Collaborative group-work in primary and secondary schools: Britain and the USA', *Durham and Newcastle Research Review*, x, 51, 99–105.

Yeomans, R. (1986) 'Hearing secret harmonies: becoming a primary staff member', paper presented at the British Educational Research Association Annual Conference, Bristol University.

Yeomans, R. (1992) 'Preparing for school staff membership: students in primary teacher education', in Biott, C. and Nias, J. (eds) *Working and Learning Together for Change*, Buckingham: Open University Press.